The Portable CHEKHOV

My holy of holies is the human body, health, intelligence, talent, inspiration, love, and absolute freedom—freedom from violence and falsehood, no matter how the last two manifest themselves.

—CHEKHOV

The Portable

CHEKHOV

Edited, and with an Introduction, by
AVRAHM YARMOLINSKY

New York
THE VIKING PRESS

Contents

Editor's Note

THE translations of "The Privy Councilor," "The Kiss," "An Attack of Nerves," "The Name-Day Party," and "In the Ravine" are by Constance Garnett and are reprinted by permission of The Macmillan Company, of David Garnett, and of Messrs. Chatto and Windus. They are taken from the following volumes: *The Wife and Other Stories, The Party and Other Stories, The Schoolmistress and Other Stories, The Witch and Other Stories.* Grateful acknowledgment is also due to Bernard G. Guerney, who translated the Chekhov letters of May 16, June 5, and December 9, 1890. All these renderings have been revised by the editor, who is responsible for the translation of the rest of the Russian text.

With few exceptions, the stories are arranged chronologically. The dates in the Editor's Introduction are Old Style. To make them conform to our calendar (New Style), which was adopted by Russia in 1918, add twelve days for the nineteenth century and thirteen for the twentieth. The dates of Chekhov's letters written in Russia are Old Style, those of the letters written outside of Russia are presumably New Style. In the chronological outline of Chekhov's life each exact date is given according to both styles.

The editor is deeply indebted to Babette Deutsch for her help in the preparation of this book.

A. Y.

Editor's Introduction

THOUGH generally reticent about his personal history, Chekhov never attempted to conceal the sordidness of his beginnings. On one occasion he gave a fairly clear hint at what his early environment had been. As a successful young writer he made this suggestion to a fellow author: "Write a story of how a young man, the son of a serf, a former grocery boy, chorister, high school lad and university student, who was brought up to respect rank, to kiss priests' hands, to revere other people's ideas, to give thanks for every morsel of bread, who was whipped many times, who without rubbers traipsed from pupil to pupil, who used his fists and tormented animals, who was fond of dining with rich relatives, who was hypocritical in his dealings with God and men gratuitously, out of the mere consciousness of his insignificance—write how this youth squeezes the slave out of himself drop by drop, and how, waking up one fine morning, he feels that in his veins flows no longer the blood of a slave but that of a real man. . . ." He was talking about himself.

Perhaps he did not quite squeeze the last drop of the slave out of himself. Certainly he never felt that he was in any sense a master of life or of art. But he was a freedman. He bought his freedom at the cost of persistent effort, by a process of self-education, so that morally as well as economically he was a self-made man.

1

In the end, this boy who had been born into the meanest and the most backward section of Russian society, the lower middle class, and who had not been immune to its vulgarities, managed to make his way into what E. M. Forster happily describes as "the aristocracy of the considerate, the sensitive, and the plucky."

Chekhov was indeed the son of a serf and would have been born one himself, had not his grandfather, an acquisitive peasant, managed to purchase the family's freedom. His father rose in the world, becoming the owner of a grocery, or rather of a general store, which also dispensed liquor. This was in the wretched little southern seaport of Taganrog, where Anton was born on January 17, 1860, the third child in a family that was to include five boys and a girl.

The grocer was a strict disciplinarian who administered beatings to his children as a parental duty and forced them to attend church services, of which he was himself passionately fond. He was the kind of person who uses religion to make those about him miserable. In addition to attending endless masses, little Anton, though he had neither ear nor voice, had to sing in the church choir organized by his father. As he stood in the chancel under the admiring eyes of the congregation, the high-spirited boy felt like a little convict, and he came to associate religious education with torture behind unctuous smiles. "It is sickening and dreadful to recall," he once wrote to his eldest brother, "the extent to which despotism and lying mutilated our childhood." He grew up to abhor every form of deceit and coercion.

The population of Taganrog included a great many Greeks, some of them wealthy importers. They maintained a one-room parish school of their own for the children of the poor, which was presided over by an ignorant and brutal master. Anton was sent there in the hope that he might eventually obtain the position of bookkeeper with one of the Greek merchants. After a year's attendance, during which he didn't learn as much as the Greek alphabet, he was transferred, at the age of nine, to the local *gimnaziya*, a combined grammar and high school. There he gave a poor account of himself, partly perhaps because he had little time for study. Among other things, he had to play watchdog for his father at the store, where he became familiar with all the tricks of short-weighting and short-changing.

Anton was sixteen when the store failed and his father escaped debtors' prison by absconding. He went to Moscow, where his two older sons were studying. The rest of the family soon followed, except Anton. Left to shift for himself, he continued at school, earning his way by tutoring and getting some help from relatives. His situation was not a happy one, but at least his natural gaiety was no longer restrained by an oppressive domestic atmosphere.

After graduating from high school, he joined the family and, having a small stipend from the Taganrog municipality, entered the university as a medical student. The Chekhovs were in a sad way. Anton became virtually the head of the house, and it was to him that the family looked for support, as it was to go on doing through the years. That winter, the story goes, in order to buy a pie for his mother's birthday, he wrote a piece for a comic weekly. That brought him his first literary earnings.

"Oh, with what trash I began," Chekhov once said, "my God, with what trash!" He supplied the humbler public prints with fillers of all sorts: jokes, legends for cartoons, advertisements, aphorisms, recipes, all in a comic vein. He wrote sketches, theatrical notices, and short short stories. He even produced, on a bet, a romantic tale purporting to be a translation, and a full-length thriller, in which a *femme fatale* is murdered under baffling circumstances. (Unlike so many of his early pieces, this novel was not allowed to lie decently buried in the files of the paper in which it first appeared, but sixty years later was seized upon by the ghouls of Hollywood.) He also tried his hand at journalism. This was not yet serious writing, but it meant being occupied with serious subject matter. He was turning out a great amount of copy, being able to scribble under any conditions, whenever and wherever he pleased, and sometimes dashing off a sketch—such as "The Siren"—without a single erasure. The stuff wrote itself. For the most part it was farce, innocent banter, calculated to raise a good-natured laugh. Occasionally, however, a note of bitterness, a suggestion of civic feeling, a hint of sympathy for the underdog crept in. And, though his work did not show it, the humorist had his moods of self-disgust. The hacks with whom he associated were an unsavory lot. He hated to think of himself in that galley. "A newspaper man is a crook at best . . ." he wrote to one of his brothers. "I am one of them, I work with them, shake hands with them, and people say that at a distance I have begun to look like a crook." At any rate, he told himself he wouldn't die a journalist. Although he could not quite see himself as a doctor, perhaps medicine would be his salvation.

On receiving his medical diploma, he was for a while in charge of a hospital in a small town. Even earlier he had begun accumulating the knowledge of the peasant patients and provincial doctors who figure in his stories. After a few months he returned to Moscow to hang out his shingle. He was a hard-working and conscientious physician, but medicine did not prove his salvation, certainly not in a financial sense. His patients were mostly poor people, and in any case he regarded healing the sick as a humane duty, scarcely a means of livelihood. He continued to rely chiefly on his pen for his earnings and although he went on writing at a great rate, only the worst of the worrying and pinching was over. In time he came to take a certain satisfaction in having two occupations. "Medicine is my lawful wife," he wrote to a friend when he had been a doctor for four years, "and literature is my mistress. When I get fed up with one, I spend the night with the other. Though it is irregular, it is less boring this way, and besides, neither of them loses anything through my infidelity." Eventually the mistress came to supplant the wife.

There were times when he felt that medicine somewhat hampered him as a writer. A doctor has few illusions and that, he said, "somehow desiccates life." But his better judgment was that medical training helped his writing, giving him a more perceptive and penetrating knowledge of men and women, guarding him against the pitfalls of subjectivity, one of his bugbears. There are few clinical studies among his stories. And even when he deals with a case of typhus or with a woman having a miscarriage, however precise the delineation of the symptoms, he observes the patient for the sake of the human being, never the other way about. Basically his concern is not with illness, but with health.

Meanwhile there began to turn up among his writings, and with increasing frequency, pieces that gave promise of the harvest to come: bits of pure comedy, sharp character sketches, little masterpieces of pathos, candid studies of the folly of the heart. He was maturing, slowly, unevenly, yet unmistakably. To his astonishment he was discovering that he had a public and that, indeed, he was the object of critical consideration, in spite of the fact that he had not yet made the dignified "stout" monthlies. When, early in 1886, he scraped together enough rubles to take him to Petersburg, the intellectual and publishing center of the country, he was received "like the Shah of Persia." And then came a marvelous letter from Grigorovich, one of the Olympians, telling him that he was the foremost of the younger writers and pleading with him to take his talent seriously. Toward the end of the year when he again visited the capital he found that he was "the most fashionable writer" there. In the interim he had brought out a second and successful book of stories (the first had passed unnoticed), and had begun to write for the great daily, *Novoye vremya* (New Time), which meant better rates and greater prestige.

He was developing a literary conscience. Formerly, he joked, writing had been like eating pancakes; now when he took up his pen he trembled. He was anxious to undertake something serious, something that would engage all his powers and that he could work at without haste. In the summer of 1887 he fulfilled at least the first of these wishes by writing a drama, which he called *Ivanov* after its unhappy hero. He had always loved the theater and had written plays even as a schoolboy. *Ivanov*, however, was a failure, which he was in haste to forget, and he was soon at work on his first serious long narrative, "The Steppe." For this leisurely, tender, evocative "history of a journey" he drew largely upon childhood memories of the great southern plain. But the vein of comedy was not to dry up all at once. In a few days he dashed off *The Boor*, which he described as "an empty Frenchified little vaudeville piece." It proved to be a box-office hit that was to entertain generations of Russians. He was to write several more such skits, most of them dramatizations of his own early stories, but henceforth the comic spirit was practically absent from his fiction.

To his surprise, as much as to his delight, in the autumn of 1888 he received the Academy's Pushkin Prize for distinguished literary achievement. He was tasting the full sweetness of recognition. But there were times when he felt that he did not deserve it. "The Steppe" he had worked at slowly, "the way a gourmet eats woodcock." And yet, although its publication centered all eyes on him, he suspected that there was something radically wrong with it: it was not an organic whole, but a sequence of tableaux. "The Name-Day Party," which he wrote the same year, he had killed with hurry. He had a father and mother, a sister and younger brothers on his hands, living together in a two-story house that had to be kept up, and to pay his bills he had to meet deadlines. Shortly after he had received the prize he was writing to a friend that his literary activity had not yet begun in earnest. He was a mere apprentice, worse, "a complete ignoramus." He must start from scratch, learn everything from the beginning. If he were to spend forty years reading and studying, then perhaps he might fire such a cannon at his public that the skies would tremble. "As it is, I am a lilliputian like everybody else," he concluded.

Novoye vremya, the daily to which Chekhov began contributing in 1886, was an organ of reactionary opinion. He had no scruples about appearing in its pages, and he contracted a close friendship with its owner and editor, the renegade liberal, Alexey Suvorin. During his school and university years he had remained untouched by the radicalism that flourished among the students. He moved largely in conservative circles and shared the prejudices current there against socialists, "trouble-makers," and even, to some extent, against Jews. A couple of years after the beginning of his association with Suvorin's paper, he was writing for the monthlies, which belonged to the opposite camp. He was commencing to abandon political conformity, as he had earlier rid himself of the coarseness, servility, and hypocrisy to which he had also been bred. And yet he was far from having achieved a consistent outlook. He was on the hither side of thirty when he observed that he changed his political, religious, and philosophical *Weltanschauung* every month. He seems to have been at this time under the spell of Tolstoy's ideas. Some traces of this influence, which lasted several years, are to be found in his works.

But Chekhov was not the stuff of which disciples are made. In reaction against the authoritarian spirit of his upbringing, he developed a skeptical independence of judgment. In the end he discovered that he couldn't share Tolstoy's faith. He put his trust in science; he loved culture, by which he meant, he wrote on one occasion, carpets, carriage with springs, wit. Between being whipped as a matter of course and not being whipped there was a gulf that compelled him to believe in progress. He came to feel that there was more love of one's fellow men in steam and electricity than in chastity and vegetarianism. Once the spell of Tolstoy's influence was broken, he was in the position of a man whose house, as he put it, was left empty. No new tenant came to occupy it. His mind was not doctrinal, much less dogmatic. The nearest he came to formulating a positive credo was in a letter to a friend in which he remarked casually: "My holy of holies is the human body, health, intelligence, talent, inspiration, love and absolute freedom—freedom from violence and falsehood, no matter how the last two manifest themselves."

He had come by freedom the hard way and he prized it all the more highly. It was one of the few certainties in a world of shifting values, a firm principle, a guide for the perplexed. And freedom seemed to him to be menaced not so much from the Right as from the Left. It was this camp, he felt, that harbored a spirit of partisanship and intolerance that he recognized as a threat to his liberty both as man and writer. In a mood of prophecy, rare with him, he remarked that a time would come in Russia when "toads and crocodiles," giving lip service to "science, art and free thought" would outdo the horrors of the Spanish Inquisition.

He might have added another article to his credo. He put no stock in classes or institutions, he had no faith in the intelligentsia or the proletariat, or for that matter in the peasantry, although he shared the populists' belief in the essential moral soundness, indeed superiority, of the masses. It was in the individual that he put his trust. For him a man's own conscience was the sole arbiter of right and wrong. Little of the rebel as there was in him, he learned not merely to hate coercion in private relations, but to look quizzically at government itself. He saw no reason why the State should be excused from the decencies required of its subjects. In any case, as a writer of fiction he was little concerned with social questions and less with political matters. It should be noted that the greater part of his work was produced in the period of discouragement with political action following upon the failure of the inchoate radical movement of the seventies which culminated in the assassination of Alexander II. A sensitive writer could not help taking on to some degree the color of this twilight age.

Without being political-minded, Chekhov was yet

fully aware of social evils and had a strong sense of civic responsibility. Here too he felt that what counted was individual initiative, personal effort. This attitude makes intelligible a somewhat puzzling episode in his life. In the spring of 1890 he abandoned his manuscripts and his practice, his family and his friends, and traveled six thousand miles by train, by boat, by sledge, by coach, under the most exhausting and sometimes dangerous conditions—this was before the construction of the Trans-Siberian Railroad—to reach the penal colony on the island of Sakhalin. He spent over three months there, visiting practically every settlement—in fact, he claimed that single-handed he took a census of the population—and returned home via the Indian Ocean with material for a book. This was published between boards five years later. It is a hodge-podge of statistics, anecdotes, detailed geographical and historical data, thumbnail portraits, hardly redeemed by some pages that rival Dostoevsky's *Memoirs from the Dead House* in the candor with which they depict the degradation to which man can be reduced. Chekhov was glad to have written the book and proud to think of "this coarse convict's garb" hanging in his literary wardrobe. But was it for this satisfaction that he had endured the hardships of the trip to and of the sojourn on Sakhalin? Before he left he had given his friends an assortment of reasons for his enterprise. His real reason seems to have been to arouse public interest in the tragic lot of the convicts, for which he felt himself, with all his compatriots, responsible. It was in vain that he had gone freely where others were driven. His gesture was a quixotic one: the book did not rouse the public and seems not to have helped the convicts. It can only be surmised that it helped Chekhov to feel that he had attempted to pay his debt to society.

He made other attempts in that direction. Early in 1892 he traveled into the famine-stricken provinces to organize relief, and was nearly lost in a blizzard. Later in the year, when central Russia was threatened with cholera, he acted as medical supervisor of the district in which he was living. With characteristic candor he confessed to a friend that he was in the vexing position of being able to read of nothing but cholera, to think of nothing but diarrhoea, while feeling indifferent to the people he was treating. It was equally characteristic that he should give up every other activity for an entire summer in order to help them. He took an active part in the building of village schools near his home and interested himself in a project of founding a settlement house in Moscow. In 1897 he was a volunteer census-taker, going from one log cabin to another, in spite of illness.

Two years after his return from Sakhalin Chekhov settled in the country. Since his student days he had summered there, for much as he loved the bustle and the human contacts of the city, he relished the solitude and serenity that the rural scene offered. Now he bought an estate of six hundred acres near the village of Melihovo, in the province of Moscow, and made a home there for his parents, his sister, and his younger brothers. One reason why he wished to leave town was that his health was poor. He said he was like an old cupboard coming apart. He had never been strong. For years his digestion had been poor, he had been suffering from piles, and since his early twenties he had had a persistent cough and from time to time had spat blood. Though he resolutely ignored these symptoms and would not let himself be examined by a physician—he was the opposite of a hypochondriac—he supposed that the country might benefit his health. Besides, living

might be cheaper there, and perhaps he would be able
to write less and in a more leisurely and painstaking
fashion. Again, there would be fewer visitors and other
distractions.

Some weeks after he was installed at Melihovo he
was telling a friend that what with the chores and the
fresh air, he was getting so husky that if the place were
brought under the hammer, he would hire himself out
as a circus athlete. But he was soon forced to realize
that the change was doing him little good. He may have
lacked a certain spontaneity of feeling and his relations
with people may have been pretty much on the surface,
but he was incorrigibly gregarious, so that there were as
many guests as there had been in Moscow and they
were harder to get rid of. Then, too, life in the bosom
of the family had its drawbacks. Again there were the
patients: in a year nearly a thousand peasants were
treated by him, free of charge. It was delightful not to
have to pay rent, but the expenses had nowise de-
creased. In order to buy the property he had gone into
debt, and he was driven to fresh exertions by the oppressive thought of the money he owed. Some of it he had
borrowed from Suvorin, who, though Chekhov no longer
contributed to *Novoye vremya,* continued to publish his
books. He had scarcely made himself at home at Melihovo when he was complaining that while his soul
wanted to expand and soar, he had to go on scribbling
for lucre, without respecting what he wrote, and that
his only solace was medicine, which he practiced without thought of money. He had grown up among people
with whom money played "an infinitely great role," and
that, he confessed on another occasion, had terribly
depraved him. He should take a sulphuric acid bath, he
said, so as to have his old skin eaten away and then
grow a new hide. But if his soul had few opportunities

to expand and soar, he knew moods of animal contentment here, when he neither regretted yesterday nor anticipated tomorrow. Spring in the country was so exquisite that he could not but hope there would be spring in paradise. On a walk across the snowy fields he felt as detached, as remote from the humdrum and the hurly-burly as if he were on the moon. At moments he was so happy that he superstitiously brought himself up short by recalling his creditors.

Even at its best, the place could not hold him. The master of Melihovo was a restless man, craving new impressions, eager for all that was strange and fresh. He made frequent trips to Moscow, where he was profusely fêted. He visited friends in the provinces, sailed up and down the Volga, traveled to the Crimea and the Caucasus, and in Suvorin's company saw France and Italy. European comforts, European culture made Russia seem more drab and dingy than ever. His return from Sakhalin by the Orient route had whetted his appetite for the exotic. He longed to go to South America. He wanted to see Chicago. Lack of funds and lack of courage, according to him, prevented him from realizing these dreams. Probably lack of health also had a good deal to do with it.

On one of his trips to Moscow he was dining in a restaurant with Suvorin when he had a severe hemorrhage of the lungs. With his usual nonchalance, he went about his business as soon as the bleeding stopped, only to suffer a relapse three days later. He was taken to a hospital. This was in March 1897. An examination—the first he had permitted—showed that he was far gone in consumption.

While he was in the hospital he was correcting the proofs of his story "The Peasants," one of his finest and most substantial pieces. It was the fruit of that intimate knowledge of the people that life in the country had helped to give him. The years at Melihovo had not been as productive as the Moscow period had been. Nevertheless, it was then that he wrote most of his long stories and some shorter ones that are among his best.

The doctors prescribed a strict regimen, country air, and residence in a southern climate, and they forbade him to practice medicine. He was not the man to take their orders seriously. But that autumn he did go abroad for his health. He settled in Nice, and in the spring went up to Paris. The Dreyfus case had recently been reopened, and he became interested in it. He took his stand with the Dreyfusards. He was full of admiration for Zola. *Novoye vremya* stank in his nostrils; anti-Semitism smelt to him of the slaughter-house. What particularly disgusted him was that the paper reviled Zola in its editorial columns while pirating one of his novels in its supplement. Chekhov stated his position frankly enough to Suvorin, and their former intimacy became impossible, but he did not break completely with the old reactionary. He continued to count Suvorin among his friends, who included Tolstoy, the Christian anarchist, and were soon to be joined by Maxim Gorky, the revolutionist.

He could not stay abroad indefinitely. Whatever interest the foreign scene had for him, and that interest paled since he was ill, the pull of home was a strong one. On his return he was forced to give up Melihovo and go to live in Yalta, in the mild air of the southern coast of the Crimea.

He had visited the resort once or twice before, and it had depressed him profoundly. Now he was condemned to live in the Godforsaken place, where, he said, even the bacilli were asleep. It was exile to a warm Siberia, a balmy Devil's Island. When he had

been there over a year he wrote that he still felt like
a transplanted tree hesitating whether to take root or
begin to wither. Eventually he resigned himself to Yalta,
but he never got to like it, in spite of the fact that he
had the companionship of several fellow writers there,
including Tolstoy, whom he revered.

The exile did not do for him what it should have.
He did not get the proper diet or nursing, and he kept
breaking away to take trips that cannot have benefited
his health. His condition grew steadily worse. Nevertheless he was able to write. Such memorable stories as
"The Man in a Shell," "Gooseberries," "The Darling,"
"On Official Business," "The Lady With the Pet Dog,"
were composed during those years. He also prepared his
collected works for the press—not an unmixed pleasure,
since he was dissatisfied with much that he had written
and disgusted with his early stuff. They were issued in
ten volumes in 1899-1901 under the imprint of A. F.
Marx. He had sold his works to that publisher for
75,000 rubles, becoming, as he said, "a Marxist for
life."

It was during these years that Chekhov composed
his better known plays. He had made a fiasco of his first
attempt at playwriting with *Ivanov,* which was written
and staged in Moscow in 1887. Two years later he re-
wrote the play for a revival in Petersburg and found the
work of revision excruciating. He decided that he was
no playwright. "Shoot me," he wrote to a friend, "if I
go mad and occupy myself with what is not my business." In its revised form *Ivanov* proved a success, but
his next piece, *The Wood Demon,* put on the same
year, fell flat, and he disliked it so much that he refused
to have it published. It was six years before he tried
his hand at playwriting again. *The Sea Gull* was produced in Petersburg in 1896. Its failure verged on a

scandal. The unhappy author swore that he would never attempt a play again. Yet in 1898 his *Uncle Vanya,* a revised version of *The Wood Demon,* was produced in the provinces and met with a favorable reception. At the close of the same year a newly formed company which went by the name of The Moscow Art Theatre performed *The Sea Gull* with great success. This was the beginning of the association between Chekhov and the Art Theatre, which persisted in spite of the fact that he was not wholly satisfied with the way in which his plays were interpreted. All of them, including the last two: *The Three Sisters* and *The Cherry Orchard,* became the very backbone of the repertory of the Art Theatre, which, in fact, adopted the gull as its emblem.

The role of Irina in *The Sea Gull* was played by Olga Knipper. Chekhov met the actress at a rehearsal. Within less than three years, on May 25, 1901, they were married. He was then forty-one and his bride thirty-one. They spent their honeymoon in a sanatorium.

Some years earlier when Suvorin had been urging him to marry, Chekhov had declared: "Very well, I'll get married, if you wish. But my conditions are: everything must remain just as before, that is, she must live in Moscow and I in the country, and I'll go to see her. Happiness continuing day after day, from morning to morning, I shan't be able to stand. . . . I promise to be a splendid husband, but give me a wife who, like the moon, will not appear in my sky every day." He found precisely such a wife. To keep her engagements, she had to winter in the two capitals. His illness tied him to his southern place of exile. He went to see her in Moscow, occasionally she visited him at Yalta, or they would have a few weeks together elsewhere. They exchanged letters almost daily. Writing to her, before their marriage, of the fate that kept them apart, he said that neither of them was to blame: "It's the devil who has put the bacillus in me and the love of art in you." After they were married, he assured her that she need feel no pricking of conscience if she could not be at his side, that he didn't feel cheated, that all was going well with them, and that they were indeed a model couple, since they didn't interfere with one another's work. The arrangement, however, had its drawbacks. He missed her more than he had imagined possible. Separation was not a matter of choice: it was enforced by his ill health. On that account he was not with her when she had a miscarriage; she promised him a son the following year, but they were never to have the child that both longed for. There was something pathetic about this union, for all the insistent gaiety that marked his resigned acceptance of the situation.

The year before his marriage Chekhov was elected honorary member of the newly created Section of Belles Lettres in the National Academy of Sciences. He was at this time the most outstanding literary figure in Russia, next to Tolstoy. He did not long wear the academic laurels, however. In 1902 Maxim Gorky was accorded the same honor, but as he was then under indictment for a political offense, the authorities succeeded in having the election annulled. Thereupon Chekhov resigned from the august body. Though his protest was not a public one, the gesture was significant for a man of his temper. He had long since abandoned any attachment to the ideas that Suvorin championed in his paper. For at least a decade Chekhov's public—and that meant all literate Russia—had been taking it for granted that he belonged in the liberal camp. He still had no patience with cut-and-dried ideologies, owed no allegiance to any political group, nor did he show any leanings toward socialism. On occasion he could bracket "sulky-faced Marxists" with police inspectors. But he was now definitely with those who looked forward to the speedy downfall of the autocratic regime. What cropped up in the writings of his last years was something above and beyond millennial hopes: a dissatisfaction with quietism, a welcoming of the violent change that he saw on the way. At twenty-eight he had asserted that there would never be a revolution in Russia. At forty he believed differently. The country, he felt, was emerging from its torpor and beginning, as he put it, "to hum like a bee-hive." He wanted to catch this new mood of wakening energies. Indeed, in his last story, "Betrothed," a girl breaks away from her confining home environment and goes out into the world, and it has been stated that in the first draft Nadya, the heroine, joins the revolution-ists. Chekhov also spoke of wanting to write "a buoyant play." He did not write it. His last play, *The Cherry Orchard,* first staged the year before the upheaval of 1905, tolled the knell of old Russia rather than rang in the new. Nor did he witness its aborted start.

What with his trips north and the excitement attend-ant upon the production of his plays, his mode of living was scarcely what the doctor ordered. After he was married, he grew rapidly worse. The first night of *The Cherry Orchard* was set for January 17, 1904, the play-wright's forty-fourth birthday. His friends turned the evening into a celebration of the twenty-fifth anniver-sary of his literary activity, although he had actually broken into print in 1880, twenty-four years previously. Shaken with coughing, Chekhov was hardly able to stand up to receive the ovation and listen to the ad-dresses. He was critically ill that spring and yet, with the war against Japan in progress, he talked of going to the front as an army doctor. In June he was rushed to a health resort in the Black Forest and there, on July 2, he died. His body was taken to Moscow in a refrigerating car for the transportation of oysters. The last trick that Fate played on him was of the sort that it would have amused him to jot down in his notebook.

Toward the end of his life Chekhov remarked to a friend that people would stop reading him a year after his death. As a matter of fact, his vogue kept growing steadily until the cataclysm of 1917 and his position as the major figure of the Silver Age of Russian literature was becoming increasingly secure. During the harsh, strenuous revolutionary years his reputation suffered a partial eclipse, but by now it has regained its former luster, and his work is valued not alone for its intrinsic quality but also for the light that it throws on a dead past. Just when his compatriots, coping with the tasks and hardships of the new order, were looking away from Chekhov, the western world, especially England and America, was enthusiastically exploring him as a remarkable discovery. Indeed, shortly after the First World War, the homage paid to him in certain literary circles verged on a cult. That first fine careless rapture has since died down, and something closer to a just estimate of his significance can be arrived at.

As a playwright Chekhov made a virtue of his limitations and so brought something new into the theater. He lacked the dramatic instinct. His plays want the sense of crisis, the heightened tension, the clear-cut clash of wills that one expects on the stage. There is something loose and amorphous about them. Of the five full-sized pieces that he wrote, *The Cherry Orchard* alone comes near to answering the demands of the theater. It is also the play which has had the greatest box-office success. The supersession of the landed gentry by the mercantile middle class, which is its theme, is obviously one with abundant dramatic possibilities. The auctioning off of Mme. Ranevskaya's ancestral estate affords a definite climax toward which the action rises and from which it declines. The more important characters are drawn in such a fashion as to offset one another, and there is a good deal of suspense, first as to the fate of the property, and second as to whether the new owner will propose to the daughter of the house.

Not that the other plays are wholly wanting in theatrical moments. In fact, they are punctuated by pistol shots, accounting for two suicides, one fatal duel, and one attempted murder. But these outbursts of violence are of little dramatic significance and merely serve to underscore the static condition into which they irrupt. They are like stones flung into a stream and soon covered by the waters. With the exception of a few indurate egotists, the characters in all the plays are unhappy, defeated, and mostly futile, though restive, individuals, caught in situations that are pathetic and that skirt tragedy by suggesting what is irremediable in life. Aware of their failings, these people reach out for the meaning of their sufferings and on occasion dream of a glorious and distant future which would compensate for their wasted lives. For the rest, they are ordinary men and women, typical of the strata of society to which they belong, chiefly the intelligentsia and the rural gentry. The characters engage in much anguished talk about the shortcomings of Russian life and hold up work as the salvation of the country, but the heart of the plays lies not in action or in programs, but rather in states of mind, in the ebb and flow of feeling, in the nuances of inner experience. The frustration, the self-probing, the emotionalism, the starry-eyed aspiration—all this, with the enveloping mood of wistful musing, relieved by a saving touch of the grotesque, bathes the plays in an atmosphere peculiarly their own, gives them a lyrical quality which to a large degree compensates for their lack of drama.

Russian audiences are still receptive to the spell of Chekhov's plays, though one imagines that it is difficult for them to identify themselves with his weary, lackadaisical heroes. The foreign spectator, too, is apt to surrender to the emotional tone of *The Three Sisters* and *The Cherry Orchard*. As for the reader, by an imaginative effort he should be able to establish rapport with this elegiac poet of the theater.

Chekhov's stories are by far the larger and the more rewarding, as well as the more influential portion of his work. He limited himself to the short narrative not without a struggle. When his writing first assumed a serious cast, he was harassed by the feeling that he was doing less than his best. Characters, situations, scenes were crowding his mind, begging to be realized: what weddings, what funerals, what splendid women! The unborn figments were jealous, as he put it, of those that had seen the light. But he was hoarding this wealth, he was not going to throw it away on trifles, he was going to save it for some substantial work, for a novel. And he did start the novel. He kept mentioning it in his letters. He called it: "Stories from the Lives of My Friends." In spite of the suspicious title, he insisted that it was not going to be a patchwork, but a composed whole. He even chose a dedicatee. And then, about 1891, all references to the work cease, and no trace of the manuscript has been found to this day. Now and again, in later years his desire to write a novel would reawaken, and indeed he did produce several long narratives, but not one of them quite achieves the stature of a novel.

Perhaps to account for his failure, Chekhov threw out

the rather dubious suggestion that the writing of novels required a degree of cultivation, a mastery, a consciousness of personal freedom possessed only by members of the privileged classes, and that the art was beyond the powers of plebeians like himself. Aggravating the sense of his inadequacy was the belief that he belonged to a generation of epigoni, unworthy descendants of giants like Turgenev, Dostoevsky, Tolstoy. In any case, the short story remained his vehicle to the end. It offered a form admirably suited to his genius.

With few exceptions, the locale of his tales is the native one, their time that in which Chekhov himself lived, their approach realistic. Within these limits, their variety is enormous, taking in, as they do, men and women, old and young, rich and poor, people in every station: peasants, landowners, priests, policemen, school teachers, prostitutes, doctors, merchants, government officials. The human comedy, at least a large part of it, is enacted in a series of short scenes, some of them farcical, many of them deeply tinged with pathos, a few verging on tragedy or having a touch of irony. The interest may attach to a simple situation, as in "Vanka," or it may lie in a complex of relations, as in "The Name-Day Party," or again it may center on a psychological type, as in "The Man in a Shell."

In his notebook Chekhov entered this quotation from Daudet: " 'Why are your songs so short?' a bird was asked. 'Is it because you are short of breath?' 'I have a great many songs and I should like to sing them all.' " He wrote seven or eight hundred stories. A large number of them, including much, though by no means all, of his best work and every one of his longer narratives, are available in English. He was an uneven writer, and many pieces were omitted from the present volume without regret. Where he attempts a story involving action and suspense, one with a plot, a sharp point, a neat solution, the result is apt to be wanting in distinction. Probably his lack of dramatic instinct was responsible for this. Where, however, he uses the method that he made peculiarly his own, though it had been employed before his time by Turgenev and other Russians, he is one of the masters, and he shows his gifts often enough to embarrass an editor with riches.

The most characteristic of Chekhov's stories lack purely narrative interest. They no more bear retelling than does a poem. Nothing thrilling happens in them, nor are the few reflective passages particularly compelling. Some of the tales, having neither beginning nor end, are, as Galsworthy put it, "all middle like a tortoise." Others have a static quality, with no more progression than there is in a dance. Instead of moving toward a definite conclusion, they are apt to trail off or drop to an anti-climax. And yet they manage to take hold of the imagination in an amazing fashion. Precisely because of the lack of invention and contrivance, the absence of cleverness, the fact that the loose ends are not tucked up nor the rough edges beveled, and that they remain unfinished in more senses than one, they have the impact of a direct experience.

It lay within Chekhov's gift to create characters who have come to be a by-word in Russia. And this although the creatures of his imagination are somewhat shadowy, since he is inclined to sketch a type rather than to paint the portrait of an individual. He had an intimate understanding of the complexities, the non-sequiturs of the mind and particularly of the heart. His was an observant eye for the telling detail of appearance or behavior, for whatever would contribute to placing his characters within the proper physical or social setting. His stories have an atmosphere as distinct as an odor.

Chekhov's preoccupation is with existences that are commonplace, drab, narrow. The life he pictures is one in which there is cruelty, want, boredom, misunderstanding, with only an occasional interval of happiness or serenity, a rare intimation that justice and goodness may ultimately prevail—in sum, an unintelligible and largely painful business. A man and woman are involved with one another and can live neither together nor apart. A cabman loses his son and can find no one to give ear to his grief but his horse. A woman wastes her youth in the provinces. Human beings are broken by the machinery of the State. Chekhov's characters may long for something that would lend meaning and beauty to their existence, yet they do not act to bring that consummation nearer. Their frustration is apt to be the result of their own helplessness. Often we encounter them in the midst of their feeble struggles, or, already defeated, facing an impasse. Chekhov preached the gospel of work as the panacea for his country's ills, and his heart went out to non-conformists and to enterprising, courageous men, such as the explorers of the Russian North, and yet he was incapable of projecting successfully a fighter, a rebel, a man of steadfast purpose. It is as though he were so suspicious of power, associating it with its abuse, that he looked upon weakness with a forgiving, almost an affectionate eye. The situations he usually presents are at the opposite pole from melodrama, as is his style from the melodramatic. His language is simple, rather slovenly, with rare strokes of bold imagery, sometimes very expressive, always free from the emphatic, the rhetorical, the florid.

A man of a sober and naturalistic temper, Chekhov was dogged by the thought that our condition in this uncomfortable world is a baffling one. He liked to say that there was no understanding it. And, indeed, his writings heighten that sense of the mystery of life which is one of the effects of all authentic literature. At the same time they tend to discourage the view that existence is a meaningless play of chance forces. In "A Tedious Story," a work of his early maturity and one of the most somber pieces to have come from his pen, an old professor discovers to his deep distress that there is nothing in his thoughts and feelings that could be called "a general idea, or the god of living man." Chekhov's writings pay covert homage to such a life-giving idea. In the semblance of the image of beauty, of the impulse toward justice, of the ideal of saintliness, it glimmers through the daily commonplace. His men and women sometimes reach out for something "holy, lofty and majestic as the heavens overhead." On a few occasions he allows his characters intuitions tinged with mysticism. Thus "The Black Monk" is concerned, however ambiguously, with madness as the gateway to transcendental reality, and the examining magistrate in "On Official Business" is haunted by the thought that nothing is accidental or fragmentary in our existence, that "everything has one soul, one aim," that individual lives are all parts of an organic whole.

Like the student in "A Nervous Breakdown," Chekhov had a "talent for humanity"—a generous compassion that went hand in hand with understanding and with a profound regard for the health of body and soul. Asked to give his opinion about a story dealing with a syphilitic, he wrote to the author that syphilis was not a vice but a disease, and that those who suffer from it needed not censure but friendly care. It was a bad thing, he went on to say, for the wife in the story to desert her husband on the ground that he had a contagious or loathsome illness. "However," he concluded, "she may take what attitude she likes toward the malady. But the author must be humane to the tips of his fingers." Chekhov lived up to this precept.

Next to his humanity, his supreme virtue is his candor. He is no teller of fairy-tales, no dispenser of illusory solaces or promises. He does not tailor his material to fit our sense of poetic justice or to satisfy our desire for a happy ending. In his mature years he clung to the conviction that a writer was not an entertainer, not a confectioner, not a beautician, but a man working under contract who was bound by his conscience to tell the whole truth with the objectivity and the indifference to bad smells of a chemist. At the same time he was plagued, as has been seen, by a feeling of his insufficiency. He lived, he protested, in "a flabby, sour, dull time," and he had, like the rest of his generation, no goals toward which to lead his readers, no enthusiasm with which to infect them. And so he assigned to himself the modest role of a reporter, a witness, a man who, without presuming to solve any problems, merely posed them or recorded, to the best of ability, the way others posed them.

He was indeed an incorruptible witness, but he did not remain in the witness box all the time. Implicit in his writings is a judgment against cruelty, greed, hypocrisy, stupidity, snobbery, sloth—all the slavish traits he had been at pains to squeeze out of himself, against whatever degrades man and prevents him from achieving his full stature. Notwithstanding his protestations of objectivity, and though his attitude toward evil was not so much active hatred as abhorrence, there is indignation and indictment in his pages, a thinly veiled criticism of life. He even succumbs to the Russian weakness for preachment. There is no doubt that eventually he came to expect a corrective influence from his plays and stories. By telling the truth, he said to himself, he would help men to live more decently. "Man will become better when you show him what he is like," runs an entry in his notebook. One need not have faith in human perfectibility to acknowledge that there is something liberating and exalting in a frank facing of man's estate.

Just before the recent war so competent an observer as Somerset Maugham remarked: "Today most young writers of ambition model themselves on Chekhov." Unquestionably the Russian's influence has helped to direct public taste in the English-speaking countries toward the acceptance of a rather shapeless kind of short narrative implying the forlornness of man, morally flabby creature that he is, in a world he never made. There is, of course, bound to be a reaction against this trend, and it is to be expected that the conventional story of a less quietist and more optimistic tenor, which has never lost popularity with the general, will again be prized by both craftsmen and critics. But whatever the vicissitudes of literary fashion, men are likely to keep returning to a writer who, in addition to his other virtues, came as close as any of his fellows to being humane to the tips of his fingers.

AVRAHM YARMOLINSKY

Notable Dates in the Life of
Anton Pavlovich Chekhov

1860   January 17/29: Anton is born in Taganrog.

1869   Admitted to the local *gimnaziya*.

1876   The family moves to Moscow, leaving him behind.

1879   Summer: Graduates from the Taganrog *gimnaziya*. Autumn: Joins the family in Moscow and enrolls in the medical department of the university.

1880   March: Breaks into print with a short humorous piece.

1880-81 Writes a full-length play, first published in 1923 and translated into English under the title, *That Worthless Fellow Platonov*.

1884   Completes his studies and takes up the practice of medicine, continuing to live in Moscow with the family. *The Tales of Melpomene,* first collection of short stories.

1886   January: *Motley Tales,* a book of stories. February: Starts contributing short stories to the daily, *Novoye vremya*. April: Shows alarming symptoms of lung trouble.

1887   April: Revisits Taganrog and neighboring towns Summer: *Twilight* and *Innocent Words,* collections of stories. November 19/December 1: First performance of *Ivanov* in Moscow.

1888   January: Visits his friend Suvorin in the Crimea and travels in the Caucasus.

1888   March: For the first time makes the pages of a monthly with his long tale, "The Steppe."
December: Awarded the Pushkin prize by the Academy of Sciences.

1889   January 31/February 12: A revised version of *Ivanov* opens at the Alexandrinsky Theater in Leningrad.

1890   Leaves Moscow for Sakhalin in April, reaches the island on July 11/23, spends three months there and is back in Moscow on December 9/21.
Gloomy People, a collection of stories.

1891   Travels in Western Europe, visiting Vienna, Venice, Florence, Rome, Paris. *The Duel,* a short novel, his last contribution to *Novoye vremya.*

1892   January: Active in organizing relief for famine victims.
February: Acquires an estate near the village of Melihovo in the province of Moscow and settles there with his parents.
Summer: Acts as medical supervisor of a rural district in a campaign against an impending epidemic of cholera.

1893   Becomes a contributor to *Russkaya mysl,* a populist monthly, and to a liberal daily.

1894   His health worsens. Travels in the Crimea and in Southern Europe. *Tales and stories.*

1894-97   Takes an active interest in and partly finances the construction of schools at Melihovo and in two neighboring villages.

1895   June: *The Island of Sakhalin; travel notes* (serialized in 1893-94).
August: Visits Tolstoy at Yasnaya Polyana.

1896   Autumn: Revisits the Crimea and the Caucasus.
October 17/29: Premiere of *The Sea Gull,* which is a fiasco.

1897-98   March: Has a severe pulmonary hemorrhage. Spends the autumn and the following winter and spring in Nice. *The Peasants. My Life. The Plays* (including *Uncle Vanya*).

1898   In Nice, follows the Dreyfus case, siding with Zola.
         September: On the advice of his doctors gives up
         the practice of medicine and settles in a villa of
         his own in a suburb of Yalta.
         November: Starts corresponding with Maxim
         Gorky.
         December 17/29: First performance of *The Sea
         Gull* by the Moscow Art Theatre company is an
         immense success.

1899   Sells the right to publish all his works to A. F.
         Marx for 75,000 rubles. Ten volumes of his col-
         lected works came out in 1899-1901.
         October 26/November 7: Premiere of *Uncle Vanya*
         in the Moscow Art Theatre.

1900   January: Elected, with Tolstoy, honorary member
         of the newly created Section of Belles Lettres of
         the Academy of Sciences. Spends part of the win-
         ter of 1900-01 on the Riviera.

1901   January 31/February 12: Premiere of *The Three
         Sisters* at the Moscow Art Theatre.
         May 25/June 7: Marries Olga Knipper.
         Autumn: Sees a good deal of Tolstoy, Gorky, Ku-
         prin, Bunin, who were then staying in or near
         Yalta.

1902   His health continues to deteriorate.
         September: Resigns his membership in the Acad-
         emy as a protest against Gorky's exclusion from it.

1903   Spends the spring and part of the summer in Mos-
         cow and in the country near Moscow.
         Autumn: Becomes an editor of *Russkaya mysl*.
         "Betrothed," his last story.

1904   January 17/30: First performance of *The Cherry
         Orchard* at the Moscow Art Theatre.
         June 3/16: Goes, with his wife, to Badenweiler, a
         German health resort.
         July 2/15: Dies there and a week later is buried in
         Moscow.

Selected Bibliography:
WORKS BY CHEKHOV

A few of the stories appeared in English and American magazines during the first decade of this century. But not until the publication of *The Tales of Chekhov,* translated by Constance Garnett (London, 1916–1922; New York, 1916–1923, 13 vols.) did Chekhov cease to be an obscure figure in the Anglo-American world. Not that all his fiction is contained in that edition. A few of the omitted pieces, notably the four in the present volume, are admirable. Many of the others, largely early work, are without distinction, but quite a number of them, translated by various hands, found their way into print. A. E. Chamot Englished *The Shooting Party* (London, 1926), a full-length thriller that was eventually made into a movie. *The Unknown Chekhov,* edited and translated by Avrahm Yarmolinsky (New York, 1954), contains, in addition to fiction not rendered by Mrs. Garnett, Chekhov's remarkable account of his journey to Sakhalin, not previously translated. His monograph on the penal colony there has been rendered by Luba and Michael Terpak and published as *The Island* (New York, 1967). Selections from the Garnett version of the stories have been reprinted in numerous collections and anthologies. *Selected Stories,* translated by Jessie Coulson (London, New York, 1963), and *Lady with Lapdog and Other Stories,* translated by David Magarshack (Baltimore, 1964), exemplify the effort made in recent years to retranslate the stories.

The plays, too, were translated by Constance Garnett (London, 1923, New York, 1924, 2 vols.). The same text was reprinted (New York, 1930) with a preface by Eva Le Gallienne. Later editions of the collected plays include *Best Plays,* translated and with an introduction by Stark Young (New York, 1956); the Penguin *Plays,* translated by Elisaveta Fen (Baltimore, 1959, reissued in 1964); *Six Plays of Chekhov,* new English version by Robert W. Corrigan (New York, 1962). Mention should also be made of *Brute and Other Farces,* new versions by Eric Bentley and Theodore Hoffman (New York, 1958).

The plays have attracted more translators than have the stories. There are even four renderings of Chekhov's first work for the stage, written at the age of twenty-one and known as *Platonov* (the hero's name), since the early draft discovered after the author's death—he had destroyed the clean copy—lacks a title page. The full text of this wretched melodrama has been translated by David Magarshak (New York, 1964). As for *The Cherry Orchard*, it exists in nearly a dozen translations. The latest ones are: "English version by John Gielgud, introduction by Michel Saint-Denis" (New York, 1963); "a new translation by Ronald Hingley"—together with *Uncle Vania* (London, New York, 1965); a translation by Tyrone Guthrie and Leonid Kipnis (Minneapolis, 1965); and a translation by Avrahm Yarmolinsky, with ample commentaries by various hands (New York, 1965). *The Wisteria Trees*, by Joshua Logan (New York, 1950), is an adaptation of *The Cherry Orchard*. John Gielgud is also the author of a version of *Ivanov*, based on a translation by Ariadne Nikolaeff (London, 1966).

A considerable proportion of Chekhov's correspondence is available in: *Selected Letters*, edited by Lillian Hellman, translated by Sidonie Lederer (New York, 1955); *Letters by Anton Tchekhov to His Family and Friends*, translated by Constance Garnett (New York, 1920); and *Letters of Anton Tchekhov to Olga L. Knipper*, also translated by Constance Garnett (New York, 1925; reprinted in 1966). Then, too, there is *Letters on the Short Story, the Drama and other Literary Topics*, selected and edited by Louis S. Friedland (New York, 1924). A welcome addition to Chekhov literature is *The Personal Papers of Anton Chekhov*, introduced by Matthew Josephson (New York, 1948). The volume contains Chekhov's notebook, 1892–1904, his diary, 1896–1903, and "Selected letters on writing, writers, and the theatre, 1882–1904."

The Oxford University Press of London has recently launched *The Oxford Chekhov*, edited and translated by Ronald Hingley. To judge by the two volumes issued so far and dated respectively 1964 and 1965, this bids fair to be a model edition of a classic. It is based on the twenty-volume edition of Chekhov's works and letters, as well as notebook and diary (Moscow, 1944–51), which is the definitive edition of his works in the original.

See page 632 for bibliography of works about Chekhov.

STORIES

Vanka

VANKA ZHUKOV, a nine-year-old boy, who had been apprenticed to Alyahin the shoemaker these three months, did not go to bed on Christmas Eve. After his master and mistress and the journeymen had gone to midnight Mass, he got an inkpot and a penholder with a rusty nib out of the master's cupboard and having spread out a crumpled sheet of paper, began writing. Before he formed the first letter he looked fearfully at the doors and windows several times, shot a glance at the dark icon, at either side of which stretched shelves filled with lasts, and heaved a broken sigh. He was kneeling before a bench on which his paper lay.

"Dear Granddaddy, Konstantin Makarych," he wrote. "And I am writing you a letter. I wish you a merry Christmas and everything good from the Lord God. I have neither father nor mother, you alone are left me."

Vanka shifted his glance to the dark window on which flickered the reflection of his candle and vividly pictured his grandfather to himself. Employed as a watchman by the Zhivaryovs, he was a short, thin, but extraordinarily lively and nimble old man of about sixty-five whose face was always crinkled with laughter and who had a toper's eyes. By day he slept in the servants' kitchen or cracked jokes with the cook; at night, wrapped in an ample sheepskin coat, he made the rounds of the estate, shaking his clapper. The old

bitch, Brownie, and the dog called Wriggles, who had
a black coat and a long body like a weasel's, followed
him with hanging heads. This Wriggles was extraordinarily deferential and demonstrative, looked with
equally friendly eyes both at his masters and at strangers, but did not enjoy a good reputation. His deference
and meekness concealed the most Jesuitical spite. No
one knew better than he how to creep up behind you
and suddenly snap at your leg, how to slip into the
icehouse, or how to steal a hen from a peasant. More
than once his hind legs had been all but broken, twice
he had been hanged, every week he was whipped till
he was half dead, but he always managed to revive.

At the moment Grandfather was sure to be standing
at the gates, screwing up his eyes at the bright-red windows of the church, stamping his felt boots, and cracking jokes with the servants. His clapper was tied to his
belt. He was clapping his hands, shrugging with the
cold, and, with a senile titter, pinching now the house-
maid, now the cook.

"Shall we have a pinch of snuff?" he was saying,
offering the women his snuffbox.

They each took a pinch and sneezed. Grandfather,
indescribably delighted, went off into merry peals of
laughter and shouted:

"Peel it off, it has frozen on!"

The dogs too are given a pinch of snuff. Brownie
sneezes, wags her head, and walks away offended. Wriggles is too polite to sneeze and only wags his tail. And
the weather is glorious. The air is still, clear, and fresh.
The night is dark, but one can see the whole village
with its white roofs and smoke streaming out of the
chimneys, the trees silvery with hoarfrost, the snowdrifts. The entire sky is studded with gaily twinkling
stars and the Milky Way is as distinctly visible as

though it had been washed and rubbed with snow for the holiday. . . .

Vanka sighed, dipped his pen into the ink and went on writing:

"And yesterday I got it hot. The master pulled me out into the courtyard by the hair and gave me a hiding with a knee-strap because I was rocking the baby in its cradle and happened to fall asleep. And last week the mistress ordered me to clean a herring and I began with the tail, and she took the herring and jabbed me in the mug with it. The helpers make fun of me, send me to the pothouse for vodka and tell me to steal pickles for them from the master, and the master hits me with anything that comes handy. And there is nothing to eat. In the morning they give me bread, for dinner porridge, and in the evening bread again. As for tea or cabbage soup, the master and mistress bolt it all themselves. And they tell me to sleep in the entry, and when the baby cries I don't sleep at all, but rock the cradle. Dear Granddaddy, for God's sake have pity on me, take me away from here, take me home to the village, it's more than I can bear. I bow down at your feet and I will pray to God for you forever, take me away from here or I'll die."

Vanka puckered his mouth, rubbed his eyes with his black fist, and gave a sob.

"I will grind your snuff for you," he continued, "I will pray to God for you, and if anything happens, you may thrash me all you like. And if you think there's no situation for me, I will beg the manager for Christ's sake to let me clean boots, or I will take Fedka's place as a shepherd boy. Dear Granddaddy, it's more than I can bear, it will simply be the death of me. I thought of running away to the village, but I have no boots and I am afraid of the frost. And in return for this when I grow big, I will feed you and won't let anybody do you any harm, and when you die I will pray for the repose of your soul, just as for my Mom's.

"Moscow is a big city. The houses are all the kind the gentry live in, and there are lots of horses, but no sheep, and the dogs are not fierce. The boys here don't go caroling, carrying the star at Christmas, and they don't let anyone sing in the choir, and once in a shop window I saw fishing-hooks for sale all fitted up with a line, for every kind of fish, very fine ones, there was even one hook that will hold a forty-pound sheatfish. And I saw shops where there are all sorts of guns, like the master's at home, so maybe each one of them is a hundred rubles. And in butchers' shops there are woodcocks and partridge and hares, but where they shoot them the clerks won't tell.

"Dear Granddaddy, when they have a Christmas tree with presents at the master's, do get a gilt walnut and put it away in the little green chest. Ask the young lady, Olga Ignatyevna, for it, say it's for Vanka."

Vanka heaved a broken sigh and again stared at the window. He recalled that it was his grandfather who always went to the forest to get the Christmas tree for the master's family and that he would take his grandson with him. It was a jolly time! Grandfather grunted, the frost crackled, and, not to be outdone, Vanka too made a cheerful noise in his throat. Before chopping down the Christmas tree, Grandfather would smoke a pipe, slowly take a pinch of snuff, and poke fun at Vanka who looked chilled to the bone. The young firs draped in hoarfrost stood still, waiting to see which of them was to die. Suddenly, coming out of nowhere, a hare would dart across the snowdrifts like an arrow. Grandfather could not keep from shouting: "Hold him, hold him, hold him! Ah, the bob-tailed devil!"

When he had cut down the fir tree, Grandfather would drag it to the master's house, and there they would set to work decorating it. The young lady, Olga Ignatyevna, Vanka's favorite, was the busiest of all. When Vanka's mother, Pelageya, was alive and a chambermaid in the master's house, the young lady used to give him goodies, and, having nothing with which to occupy herself, taught him to read and write, to count up to a hundred, and even to dance the quadrille. When Pelageya died, Vanka had been relegated to the servants' kitchen to stay with his grandfather, and from the kitchen to the shoemaker's.

"Do come, dear Granddaddy," Vanka went on. "For Christ's sake, I beg you, take me away from here. Have pity on me, an unhappy orphan, here everyone beats me, and I am terribly hungry, and I am so blue, I can't tell you how, I keep crying. And the other day the master hit me on the head with a last, so that I fell down and it was a long time before I came to. My life is miserable, worse than a dog's— I also send greetings to Alyona, one-eyed Yegorka and the coachman, and don't give my harmonica to anyone. I remain, your grandson, Ivan Zhukov, dear Granddaddy, do come."

Vanka twice folded the sheet covered with writing and put it into an envelope he had bought for a kopeck the previous day. He reflected a while, then dipped the pen into the ink and wrote the address:

To Grandfather in the village

Then he scratched himself, thought a little, and added: *Konstantin Makarych*. Glad that no one had interrupted him at his writing, he put on his cap and, without slipping on his coat, ran out into the street with nothing over his shirt.

The clerks at the butchers' whom he had questioned

the day before had told him that letters were dropped into letter boxes and from the boxes they were carried all over the world in troikas with ringing bells and drunken drivers. Vanka ran to the nearest letter box and thrust the precious letter into the slit.

An hour later, lulled by sweet hopes, he was fast asleep. In his dream he saw the stove. On the stove sat grandfather, his bare legs hanging down, and read the letter to the cooks. Near the stove was Wriggles, wagging his tail.

1886

The Privy Councilor

AT THE beginning of April in 1870 my mother, Klavdia Arhipovna, the widow of a lieutenant, received from her brother Ivan, a privy councilor who lived in Petersburg, a letter in which, among other things, this passage occurred: "My liver trouble forces me to spend every summer abroad, and as I have not at the moment the money in hand for a trip to Marienbad, it is very possible, dear sister, that I may spend this summer with you at Kochuevko. . . ."

On reading the letter my mother turned pale and began trembling all over; then an expression of mingled tears and laughter came into her face. She began crying and laughing. This conflict of tears and laughter always reminds me of the flickering and spluttering of a brightly burning candle when one sprinkles it with water. Having reread the letter, mother called together all the household, and in a voice broken with emotion began explain-

ing to us that there had been four Gundasov brothers:
one Gundasov had died as a baby; another had gone
into the army, and he, too, was dead; the third, without
offence to him be it said, was an actor; the fourth—

"The fourth has risen far above us," my mother
brought out tearfully. "My own brother, we grew up together; and I am all of a tremble, all of a tremble! . . .
A privy councilor, a General! How shall I meet him,
my angel brother? What can I, a foolish, uneducated
woman, talk to him about? It's fifteen years since I've
seen him! Andryushenka," my mother turned to me,
"you must rejoice, little stupid! It's a piece of luck for
you that God is sending him to us!"

After we had heard a detailed history of the Gun-
dasovs, there followed a fuss and bustle in the place
such as I had been accustomed to see only before Christmas. The sky above and the water in the river were all
that escaped; everything else was subjected to a merci-
less cleansing, scrubbing, painting. If the sky had been
lower and smaller and the river had not flowed so
swiftly, they would have scoured them, too, with brick
dust and rubbed them, too, with tow. Our walls were as
white as snow, but they were whitewashed; the floors
were bright and shining, but they were washed every
day. The cat Bobtail (as a small child I had cut off a
good quarter of his tail with the knife used for chopping
sugar, and that was why he was called Bobtail) was carried off to the kitchen and put in care of Anisya; Fedka
was told that if any of the dogs came near the front-door
"God would punish him." But no one was treated so
roughly as the poor sofas, easy-chairs, and rugs! They
had never before been so violently beaten as on this occasion in preparation for our visitor. My pigeons took
fright at the loud thud of the sticks, and were continually soaring into the sky.

The tailor Spiridon, the only tailor in the whole district who ventured to work for the gentry, came over from Novostroevka. He was a hard-working, capable man who did not drink and was not without a certain fancy and feeling for form, but was nevertheless an atrocious tailor. His work was ruined by hesitation. . . The idea that his cut was not fashionable enough made him alter everything half a dozen times, walk all the way to the town simply to study the dandies, and in the end dress us in suits that even a caricaturist would have called *outré* and grotesque. We cut a dash in impossibly tight trousers and in such short jackets that we always felt quite abashed in the presence of young ladies.

This Spiridon spent a long time taking my measure. He measured me all over lengthways and crossways, as though he meant to put hoops round me like a barrel; then he spent a long time noting down my measurements with a thick pencil on a bit of paper, and ticked off all the measurements with triangular signs. When he had finished with me he set to work on my tutor, Yegor Alexeyevich Pobedimsky. My unforgettable tutor was then at the stage when young men watch the growth of their mustache and are critical of their clothes, and so you can imagine the religious awe with which Spiridon approached him! Yegor Alexeyevich had to throw back his head, straddle his legs like an inverted V, lift up his arms, let them fall. Spiridon measured him several times, walking round him during the process like a lovesick dove round its mate, going down on one knee, bending double. . . . My mother, weary, exhausted by her exertions and headachey from ironing, watched these lengthy proceedings, and said:

"Mind now, Spiridon, you will have to answer for it to God if you spoil the cloth! And you will never have any luck if the clothes don't fit!"

Mother's words threw Spiridon first into a fever, then into a perspiration, for he was convinced that the clothes wouldn't fit. He received one ruble twenty kopecks for making my suit, and for Pobedimsky's two rubles, we providing the cloth, the lining, and the buttons. The price cannot be considered excessive, as Novostroevka was about six miles from us, and the tailor came to fit us four times. When he came to try the things on and we squeezed ourselves into the tight trousers and jackets full of basting threads, mother always frowned contemptuously and expressed her surprise:

"Goodness knows what the fashions are coming to nowadays! I am positively ashamed to look at them. If brother were not used to Petersburg I would not get you fashionable clothes!"

Spiridon, relieved that the blame was thrown on the fashions and not on him, shrugged his shoulders and sighed, as though to say:

"There's no help for it; it's the spirit of the age!"

The excitement with which we awaited the arrival of our guest can only be compared to the strained suspense with which spiritualists await from minute to minute the appearance of a ghost. Mother went about with a sick headache, and was continually melting into tears. I lost my appetite, slept badly, and did not do my lessons. Even in my dreams I was haunted by an impatient longing to see a General—that is, a man with shoulder-straps and an embroidered collar sticking up to his ears, and with a naked sword in his hands, exactly like the one who hung over the sofa in our drawing room and glared with terrible black eyes at everybody who dared to look at him. Pobedimsky was the only one who felt himself in his element. He was neither terrified nor delighted, and merely from time to time, when he heard the history of the Gundasov family, said:

"Yes, it will be pleasant to have someone fresh to talk to."

My tutor was looked upon among us as an exceptional nature. He was a young man of twenty, with a pimply face, shaggy locks, a low forehead, and an unusually long nose. His nose was so big that when he wanted to look close at anything he had to put his head to one side like a bird. To our thinking, in the whole province there was not a cleverer, more cultivated, or more fashionably dressed man. He had left high school a year before he was due to graduate, and had then entered a veterinary college, from which he was expelled before the end of the first semester. The reason of his expulsion he carefully concealed, which enabled any one who wished to do so to look upon my instructor as an injured and to some extent mysterious person. He spoke little, and only on intellectual subjects; ate meat on fast days, and looked with contempt and condescension on the life around him, which did not prevent him, however, from taking presents, such as suits of clothes, from my mother, and drawing funny faces with red teeth on my kites. Mother disliked him for his "pride," but stood in awe of his brains.

Our visitor did not keep us long waiting. At the beginning of May two cart-loads of big trunks arrived from the station. These trunks looked so majestic that the drivers instinctively took off their hats as they lifted them down.

"There must be uniforms and gunpowder in those trunks," I thought.

Why "gunpowder"? Probably the conception of a General was closely connected in my mind with cannon and gunpowder.

When I woke up on the morning of the tenth of May, nurse told me in a whisper that "Uncle had arrived." I dressed rapidly and, washing after a fashion, flew out of my bedroom without saying my prayers. In the vestibule I came upon a tall, thick-set gentleman with fashionable whiskers and a foppish-looking overcoat. Half dead with religious awe, I went up to him and, remembering the ceremonial mother had impressed upon me, I scraped my foot before him, made a very low bow, and craned forward to kiss his hand; but the gentleman did not allow me to kiss his hand: he informed me that he was not my uncle, but my uncle's footman, Pyotr. The appearance of this Pyotr, who was far better dressed than Pobedimsky or me, filled me with utter astonishment, which, to tell the truth, has lasted to this day. Can such dignified, respectable people with stern and intellectual faces really be footmen? And what for?

Pyotr told me that my uncle was in the garden with my mother. I rushed into the garden.

Nature, ignorant of the history of the Gundasov family and of my uncle's rank, felt far more at ease and unconstrained than I. There was a clamor going on in the garden such as one only hears at fairs. Masses of starlings flitting through the air and hopping about the walks were noisily chattering as they hunted for Maybugs. There were swarms of sparrows in the lilacbushes, which thrust their tender, fragrant blossoms straight in one's face. Wherever one turned, from every direction came the note of the oriole and the shrill cry of the hoopoe and the kestoel. At any other time I should have begun chasing dragon-flies or throwing stones at a crow which was sitting on a low rick under an aspen tree, with its blunt beak turned away; but at that moment I was in no mood for mischief. My heart was throbbing, and I felt a cold sinking at my stomach; I was preparing myself to confront a gentleman with shoulderstraps, a naked sword, and terrible eyes!

But imagine my disappointment! A thin, dapper little man in white silk trousers and with a white cap on his head was walking beside my mother in the garden. With his hands behind him and his head thrown back, every now and then running on ahead of mother, he looked quite young. There was so much life and movement in his whole figure that I could only detect the treachery of age when I came close up behind and saw beneath his cap a fringe of close-cropped silver hair. Instead of the staid dignity and stolidity of a General, I saw an almost school-boyish nimbleness; instead of a collar sticking up to his ears, an ordinary light blue necktie. Mother and Uncle were walking in the alley talking. I went softly up to them from behind, and waited for one of them to look round.

"What a delightful place you have here, Klavdia!" said my uncle. "How charming and lovely it is! Had I known before that you had such a charming place, nothing would have induced me to go abroad all these years."

Uncle stooped down rapidly and sniffed at a tulip. Everything he saw moved him to rapture and curiosity, as though he had never been in a garden on a sunny day before. The queer man moved about as though he were on springs, and chattered incessantly, without allowing mother to utter a single word. All of a sudden Pobedimsky came into sight from behind an elder-tree at the turn of the alley. His appearance was so unexpected that my uncle positively started and took a step backward. On this occasion my tutor was attired in his best cape with sleeves, in which, especially from the back, he looked remarkably like a windmill. He had a solemn and majestic air. Pressing his hat to his bosom in Spanish style, he took a step towards my uncle and made a bow such as a marquis makes in a melodrama, bending forward, a little to one side.

"I have the honor to introduce myself to your High Excellency," he said aloud: "pedagogue and tutor of your nephew, formerly a student of the veterinary institute, and a nobleman by birth, Pobedimsky!"

Such civility on the part of my tutor pleased my mother very much. She gave a smile, and waited in thrilled suspense to hear what clever thing he would say next; but my tutor, expecting his dignified address to be answered with equal dignity—that is, that my uncle would say "H'm!" like a general and hold out two fingers—was greatly embarrassed and abashed when the latter laughed genially and shook hands with him. He muttered something incoherent, cleared his throat, and walked away.

"Come! isn't that charming?" laughed my uncle. "Just look! he has put on his cape and thinks he's a very clever fellow! I do like that—I swear to God! What youthful aplomb, what life in that cape! And what boy is this?" he asked, suddenly turning and looking at me.

"That is my Andryushenka," my mother introduced me, flushing crimson. "My consolation. . . ."

I made a scrape with my foot on the sand and dropped a low bow.

"A fine fellow . . . a fine fellow . . ." muttered my uncle, taking his hand from my lips and stroking me on the head. "So your name is Andrusha? Yes, yes. . . . H'm! . . . I swear to God! . . . Do you do your lessons?"

My mother, exaggerating and embellishing as all mothers do, began to describe my achievements in the sciences and the excellence of my behavior, and I walked round my uncle and, following the ceremonial laid down for me, I continued making low bows. Then my mother began throwing out hints that with my remarkable abilities it would not be amiss for me to get a government scholarship in the Corps of Cadets; but at the point when I was to have burst into tears and begged for my uncle's patronage my uncle suddenly stopped and flung up his hands in amazement.

"My goo-oodness! What's that?" he asked.

Tatyana Ivanovna, the wife of our steward, Fyodor Petrovna, was coming straight toward us. She was carrying a starched white skirt and a long ironing-board. As she passed us she looked shyly at the visitor through her eyelashes and flushed crimson.

"Wonders will never cease . . ." my uncle filtered through his teeth, looking after her with friendly interest. "You have a fresh surprise at every step, sister . . . I swear to God!"

"She's a beauty . . ." said mother. "They chose her as a bride for Fyodor, though she lived over seventy miles from here. . . ."

Not everyone would have called Tatyana a beauty. She was a plump little woman of twenty, with black eyebrows and a graceful figure, always rosy and attractive-looking, but in her face and in her whole person there was not one striking feature, not one bold line to catch the eye, as though nature had lacked inspiration and confidence when it created her. Tatyana Ivanovna was shy, bashful, and modest in her behavior; she moved softly and smoothly, said little, seldom laughed, and her whole life was as regular as her face and as flat as her sleek hair. My uncle screwed up his eyes looking after her, and smiled. Mother looked intently at his smiling face and grew serious.

"And so, brother, you've never married!" she sighed.

"No; I've not married."

"Why not?" asked mother softly.

"How can I tell you? It just happened so. In my youth I was too hard at work, I had no time to live, and when I longed to live—I looked round—and there I had fifty years on my back already. It was too late! However, talking about it . . . is depressing."

Mother and Uncle both sighed at once and walked on, and I left them and flew off to find my tutor, that I might share my impressions with him. Pobedimsky was standing in the middle of the yard, looking majestically at the heavens.

"One can see he is a man of culture!" he said, twisting his head round. "I hope we shall get on together."

An hour later mother came to us.

"I am in trouble, my dears!" she began, sighing. "You see, brother has brought a valet with him, and the valet, God bless him, is not one you can put in the kitchen or in the passage; he must have a room to himself. I can't think what I am to do! I tell you what, children, couldn't you move out somewhere—to Fyodor's lodge, for instance—and give your room to the valet? What do you say?"

We gave our ready consent, for living in the lodge we would be a great deal freer than in the house, under mother's eye.

"It's a nuisance, and that's a fact!" said mother. "Brother says he won't have dinner in the middle of the day, but between six and seven, as they do in Petersburg. I am simply distracted with worry! By seven o'clock the dinner will be ruined. Really, men don't understand anything about housekeeping, though they have so much intellect. Oh, dear! we shall have to cook two dinners every day! You will have dinner at midday as before, children, while your poor old mother has to wait till seven, for the sake of her brother."

Then my mother heaved a deep sigh, bade me try

and please my uncle, whose coming was a piece of luck for me for which we must thank God, and hurried off to the kitchen. Pobedimsky and I moved into the wing the same day. We were installed in a room between the entry to the steward's bedroom.

Contrary to my expectations, life went on just as before, drearily and monotonously, in spite of my uncle's arrival and our removal to new quarters. We were excused from lessons "on account of the visitor." Pobedimsky, who never read anything or occupied himself in any way, spent most of his time sitting on his bed, with his long nose thrust into the air, thinking. Sometimes he would get up, try on his new suit, and sit down again to relapse into contemplation and silence. Only one thing worried him, the flies, which he mercilessly swatted with his hands. After dinner he usually "rested," and his snores were a cause of annoyance to the whole household. I ran about the garden from morning to night, or sat in the room making kites.

For the first two or three weeks we did not see Uncle often. For days together he sat in his own room working, in spite of the flies and the heat. His extraordinary capacity for sitting as though glued to his table produced upon us the effect of an inexplicable conjuring trick. To us idlers, knowing nothing of systematic work, his industry seemed simply miraculous. Getting up at nine, he sat down at his desk, and did not leave it till dinnertime; after dinner he set to work again, and went on till late at night. Whenever I peeped through the keyhole I invariably saw the same thing: my uncle sitting at the desk working. The work consisted in his writing with one hand while he turned over the leaves of a book with the other, and, strange to say, all of him was in constant movement—his leg swinging as though it were a pendulum, his head nodding in time to his whistling. He had an extremely careless and frivolous expression all the while, as though he were not working, but playing tick-tack-toe. I always saw him wearing a smart short jacket and a jauntily tied cravat, and he always smelt, even through the keyhole, of delicate feminine perfume. He only left his room for dinner, but he ate little.

"I can't make brother out!" mother complained of him. "Every day we kill a turkey and squabs on purpose for him, I make a *compote* with my own hands, and he eats a plateful of broth and a bit of meat the size of a finger and gets up from the table. I begin begging him to eat; he comes back and drinks a glass of milk. And what is there in that, in a glass of milk? It's no better than dishwater! You may die of a diet like that. . . . If I try to persuade him, he laughs and makes a joke of it. . . . No; he does not care for our fare, poor dear!"

We spent the evenings far more gaily than the days. As a rule, by the time the sun was setting and long shadows were lying across the yard, we—that is, Tatyana Ivanovna, Pobedimsky, and I—were sitting on the steps of the lodge. We did not talk till it grew quite dark. And, indeed, what is one to talk of when every subject has been talked over already? There was only one piece of news, my uncle's arrival, and even that subject was soon exhausted. My tutor never took his eyes off Tatyana Ivanovna's face, and frequently heaved deep sighs. . . . At the time I did not understand those sighs, and did not try to fathom their significance; now they explain a great deal to me.

When the shadows merged into one thick mass, the steward Fyodor would come in from shooting or from the fields. This Fyodor gave me the impression of being a fierce and even terrible man. The son of a Russianized gypsy from Izyum, swarthy-faced and curly-headed, with big black eyes and a matted beard, he was never called among our Kochuevko peasants by any name but "The Devil." And, indeed, there was a great deal of the gypsy about him apart from his appearance. He could not, for instance, stay at home, and went off for days together into the country or into the woods to shoot. He was gloomy, ill-humored, taciturn, was afraid of no one, and recognized no authority. He was rude to mother, addressed me familiarly, and was contemptuous of Pobedimsky's learning. All this we forgave him, looking upon him as a hot-tempered and nervous man; mother liked him because, in spite of his gypsy nature, he was ideally honest and industrious. He loved his Tatyana Ivanovna passionately, like a gypsy, but this love took in him a gloomy form, as though it cost him suffering. He was never affectionate to his wife in our presence, but simply rolled his eyes angrily at her and twisted his mouth.

When he came in from the fields he would noisily and angrily put down his gun, would come out to us on the steps, and sit down beside his wife. After resting a little, he would ask his wife a few questions about household matters, and then sink into silence.

"Let's sing," I would suggest.

My tutor would tune his guitar, and in a deep deacon's bass strike up "Down in the Level Valley." The singing began. My tutor took the bass, Fyodor sang in a hardly audible tenor, while I sang soprano in unison with Tatyana Ivanovna.

When the whole sky was covered with stars and the frogs had left off croaking, they would bring in our supper from the kitchen. We went into the lodge and sat down to the meal. My tutor and the gypsy ate greedily, with such a noise that it was hard to tell whether it was the bones crunching or their jaws, while

Tatyana Ivanovna and I scarcely managed to eat our share. After supper the lodge was plunged in deep sleep.

One evening, it was at the end of May, we were sitting on the steps, waiting for supper. A shadow suddenly fell across us, and Uncle stood before us as though he had sprung out of the ground. He looked at us for a long time, then struck his hands together and laughed gaily.

"An idyll!" he said. "They sing and dream in the moonlight! It's charming, I swear to God! May I sit down and dream with you?"

We looked at one another and said nothing. My uncle sat down on the bottom step, yawned, and looked at the sky. A silence fell. Pobedimsky, who had for a long time now been wanting to talk to some person, was delighted at the opportunity, and was the first to break the silence. He had only one subject for intellectual conversation: epizootic diseases. It sometimes happens that after one has been in an immense crowd, only some one countenance of the thousands remains long imprinted on the memory; in the same way, of all that Pobedimsky had heard during his six months at the veterinary institute he remembered only one passage:

"Epizootics do immense damage to national economy. It is the duty of society to work hand in hand with the government in waging war upon them."

Before saying this to Uncle, my tutor cleared his throat three times, and several times, in his excitement, wrapped himself up in his cape. On hearing about the epizootics, my uncle looked intently at my tutor and made a sound between a snort and a laugh.

"Upon my soul, that's charming!" he said, scrutinizing us as though we were lay figures. "This is actually life. . . . This is what reality is bound to be. Why are you silent, Pelageya Ivanovna?" he said, addressing Tatyana Ivanovna.

She coughed, overcome with embarrassment.

"Talk, my friends, sing . . . play! . . . Don't lose time. You know, time, the rascal, runs away and waits for no man! I swear to God, before you have time to look round, old age is upon you. . . . Then it is too late to live! That's how it is, Pelageya Ivanovna. . . . We mustn't sit still and be silent. . . ."

At that point supper was brought in from the kitchen. Uncle went into the wing with us, and to keep us company ate five curd fritters and the wing of a duck. He ate and looked at us. He was touched and delighted by us all. Whatever silly nonsense my precious tutor talked, and whatever Tatyana Ivanovna did, he thought charming and delightful. When after supper Tatyana Ivanovna sat quietly down and took up her knitting, he kept his eyes fixed on her fingers and chatted away without ceasing.

"Make all the haste you can to live, my friends . . ." he said. "God forbid you should sacrifice the present for the future! There is youth, health, fire in the present; the future is smoke and deception! As soon as you are twenty begin to live."

Tatyana Ivanovna dropped a knitting-needle. Uncle jumped up, picked up the needle, and handed it to Tatyana Ivanovna with a bow, and for the first time in my life I learned that there were people in the world more refined than Pobedimsky.

"Yes . . ." my uncle went on, "love, marry . . . do silly things. Foolishness is a great deal more vital and healthy than our straining and striving after a meaningful life."

Uncle talked a great deal, so much that he bored us;

I sat on a chest listening to him and dropping to sleep. It distressed me that he did not once all the evening pay attention to me. He left the lodge at two o'clock, when, overcome with drowsiness, I was sound asleep.

From that time forth my uncle took to coming to the lodge every evening. He sang with us, had supper with us, and always stayed on till two o'clock in the morning, chatting incessantly, always about the same subject. His evening and night work was given up, and by the end of June, when the privy councilor had learned to eat mother's turkey and *compote,* his work by day was abandoned too. My uncle tore himself away from his desk and was drawn into "life." In the daytime he walked up and down the garden, whistled and interfered with the men's work, making them tell him various stories. When his eye fell on Tatyana Ivanovna he ran up to her and, if she was carrying anything, offered his assistance, which embarrassed her dreadfully.

As the summer advanced, Uncle grew more and more frivolous, volatile, and abstracted. Pobedimsky was completely disappointed in him.

"He is too one-sided," he said. "There is nothing to show that he is in the very foremost ranks of the service. And he doesn't even know how to talk. At every word it's 'I swear to God!' No, I don't like him!"

From the time that my uncle began visiting the lodge there was a noticeable change both in Fyodor and my tutor. Fyodor gave up going out shooting, came home early, sat more taciturn than ever, and stared with particular ill-humor at his wife. In my uncle's presence my tutor gave up talking about epizootics, frowned, and even laughed sarcastically.

"Here comes our little bantam cock!" he growled on one occasion when Uncle was coming into the wing.

I put down this change in them both to their being

offended with my uncle. My absent-minded uncle mixed up their names, and to the very day of his departure had not learned to tell my tutor from Tatyana Ivanovna's husband. Tatyana Ivanovna herself he sometimes called Nastasya, sometimes Pelageya, and sometimes Yevdokia. Touched and delighted by us, he laughed and behaved exactly as though he was in the company of small children. . . . All this, of course, might well offend young men. It was not a case of offended pride, however, but, as I realize now, of subtler feelings.

I remember one evening I was sitting on the chest struggling with sleep. My eyelids felt glued together and my body, tired out by running about all day, drooped sideways. But I struggled against sleep and tried to look on. It was about midnight. Tatyana Ivanovna, rosy and meek as always, was sitting at a little table sewing a shirt for her husband. Fyodor, sullen and gloomy, was staring at her from one corner, and in the other sat Pobedimsky, snorting angrily and retreating into the high collar of his shirt. Uncle was walking up and down the room, thinking. Silence reigned; nothing was to be heard but the rustling of the linen in Tatyana Ivanovna's hands. Suddenly my uncle stood still before Tatyana Ivanovna, and said:

"You are all so young, so fresh, so nice, you live so peacefully in this quiet place that I envy you. I have become attached to your way of life here; my heart aches when I remember I have to go away. . . . You may believe in my sincerity!"

Sleep closed my eyes and I dropped off. When some noise waked me, my uncle was standing before Tatyana Ivanovna, looking at her with a softened expression. His cheeks were flushed.

"My life has been wasted," he said. "I have not lived! Your young face makes me think of my own lost youth, and I should be ready to sit here watching you to my dying day. It would be a pleasure to me to take you with me to Petersburg."

"What for?" Fyodor asked in a husky voice.

"I should put her under a glass case on my desk. I should admire her and show her to other people. You know, Pelageya Ivanovna, we have no women like you there. We have wealth, distinction, sometimes beauty, but we have not this true sort of life, this healthy serenity. . . ."

My uncle sat down facing Tatyana Ivanovna and took her by the hand.

"So you won't come with me to Petersburg?" he laughed. "In that case give me your little hand. . . . A charming little hand! . . . You won't give it? Come, you miser! let me kiss it, anyway. . . ."

At that moment there was the scrape of a chair. Fyodor jumped up and with heavy, measured steps went up to his wife. His face was pale gray and quivering. He brought his fist down on the table with a bang, and said in a hollow voice: "I won't allow it!"

At the same moment Pobedimsky too jumped up from his chair. Pale and angry, he went up to Tatyana Ivanovna, and he, too, struck the table with his fist.

"I . . . I won't allow it!" he said.

"What? What's the matter?" asked my uncle in surprise.

"I won't allow it!" repeated Fyodor, banging on the table.

Uncle jumped up and blinked faint-heartedly. He tried to speak, but in his amazement and alarm could not utter a word; with an embarrassed smile, he shuffled out of the lodge with the mincing step of an old man, leaving his hat behind. When, a little later, my mother ran into the lodge, Fyodor and Pobedimsky were still hammering on the table like blacksmiths and repeating, "I won't allow it!"

"What has happened here?" asked mother. "Why has my brother been taken ill? What's the matter?"

Looking at Tatyana's pale, frightened face and at her infuriated husband, mother probably guessed what was the matter. She sighed and shook her head.

"Come! Quit banging on the table!" she said. "Leave off, Fyodor! And why are you thumping, Yegor Alexeyevich? What have you got to do with it?"

Pobedimsky was startled and confused. Fyodor looked intently at him, then at his wife, and began walking about the room. When mother had gone out of the lodge, I saw what for long afterwards I looked upon as a dream. I saw Fyodor seize my tutor, lift him up in the air, and thrust him out of the door.

When I woke up in the morning my tutor's bed was empty. To my question where he was nurse told me in a whisper that he had been taken off early in the morning to the hospital, as his arm was broken. Saddened by this news and remembering the scene of the previous evening, I went out of doors. It was a gray day. The sky was overcast and there was a wind blowing dust, bits of paper, and feathers along the ground. . . . It felt as though rain were coming. People and animals looked bored. When I went into the house I was told not to make such a noise with my feet, as mother was in bed with a migraine. What was I to do? I went outside the gate, sat down on the little bench there, and fell to trying to discover the meaning of what I had seen and heard the day before. From our gate there was a road which, passing the forge and the pool that never dried up, led to the highway. I looked at the telegraph-posts, about which clouds of dust were whirling, and at the sleepy birds sitting on the wires, and I suddenly felt so dreary that I began to cry.

A dusty bus crammed full of townspeople, probably going to visit the shrine, drove by along the highway. The bus was hardly out of sight when a light carriage drawn by a pair of horses came into view. In it was Akim Nikitich, the district police officer, standing up and holding on to the coachman's belt. To my great surprise, the carriage turned into our road and flew by me into the gate. While I was puzzling why the police inspector had come to see us, I heard a noise, and a troika came into sight on the road. In the carriage stood the chief of police, directing his coachman towards our gate.

"And why is he coming?" I thought, looking at the dusty chief of police. "Most probably Pobedimsky has complained of Fyodor to him, and they have come to take him to prison."

But the mystery was not so easily solved. The police officer and the chief of police were only forerunners, for five minutes had scarcely passed when another coach drove in at our gate. It dashed by me so swiftly that I could only get a glimpse of a red beard at the window.

Lost in conjecture and full of apprehension, I ran to the house. In the vestibule first of all I saw mother; she was pale and looking with horror towards the door, from which came the sounds of men's voices. The visitors had taken her by surprise at the height of her migraine.

"Who has come, mother?" I asked.

"Sister," I heard my uncle's voice, "will you send in something to eat for the Governor and me?"

"It is easy to say 'something to eat,'" whispered my

mother, numb with horror. "What have I time to get ready now? I am put to shame in my old age!"

Mother clutched at her head and ran into the kitchen. The Governor's sudden visit stirred and overwhelmed the whole household. A ferocious slaughter followed. A dozen hens, five turkeys, eight ducks were killed, and in the confusion the old gander, the progenitor of our whole flock of geese and a great favorite of mother's, was beheaded. The coachmen and the cook seemed frenzied, and slaughtered birds at random, without distinction of age or breed. For the sake of some wretched sauce a pair of valuable pigeons, as dear to me as the gander was to mother, were sacrificed. It was a long while before I could forgive the Governor their death.

In the evening, when the Governor and his suite, after a sumptuous dinner, had got into their carriages and driven away, I went into the house to look at the remains of the feast. Glancing into the drawing-room from the vestibule, I saw my uncle and my mother. My uncle, with his hands behind his back, was walking nervously up and down close to the wall, shrugging his shoulders. Mother, exhausted and looking much thinner, was sitting on the sofa and watching his movements with heavy eyes.

"Excuse me, sister, but this won't do at all," my uncle grumbled, wrinkling up his face. "I introduced the Governor to you, and you didn't offer to shake hands. You covered him with embarrassment, poor fellow! No, that won't do. . . . Simplicity is a very good thing, but there must be limits to it, too . . . I swear to God! And then that dinner! How can one give people such food? What was that mess, for instance, that they served for the fourth course?"

"That was duck with sweet sauce . . ." mother answered softly.

"Duck! Forgive me, sister, but . . . but here I've got heartburn! I am ill!"

Uncle made a sour, tearful face, and went on:

"It was the devil sent that Governor! As though I wanted his visit! Pff! . . . heartburn! I can't work or sleep . . . I am going to pieces. . . . And I can't understand how you can live here without anything to do . . . in this boredom! Here I've got a pain in the pit of my stomach! . . ."

My uncle frowned and strode more rapidly than ever.

"Brother," my mother inquired softly, "what does it cost to go abroad?"

"At least three thousand . . ." my uncle answered in a tearful voice. "I would go, but where am I to get the money? I haven't a kopeck. Pff! . . . heartburn!"

Uncle stopped, looked dejectedly at the gray, overcast prospect from the window, and began pacing to and fro again.

A silence followed. . . . Mother looked a long while at the icon, pondering something, then began crying, and said:

"I'll give you the three thousand, brother. . . ."

Three days later the majestic trunks went off to the station and the privy councilor drove off after them. As he said good-by to mother he dropped a tear, and it was a long time before he took his lips from her hands, but when he got into his carriage his face beamed with childlike pleasure. . . . Radiant and happy, he settled himself comfortably, blew a kiss to my mother, who was crying, and all at once I caught his eye. A look of the utmost astonishment came into his face.

"What boy is this?" he asked.

My mother, who had assured me that my uncle's coming was a piece of luck for which I must thank God, was bitterly mortified at this question. I was in no mood for questions. I looked at my uncle's happy face, and for some reason felt fearfully sorry for him. I could not control myself, jumped into the carriage and hugged that frivolous man, weak as all men are. Looking into his face and wanting to say something pleasant, I asked:

"Uncle, have you ever been in a battle?"

"Ah, the dear boy . . ." Uncle laughed, kissing me. "A charming boy, I swear to God! How natural, how true to life it all is, I swear to God! . . ."

The carriage set off. . . . I looked after him, and long afterwards that farewell "I swear to God" was ringing in my ears.

1886

A Calamity

SOFYA PETROVNA, the wife of Lubyantzev, the notary public, a beautiful young woman of twenty-five, was walking slowly along a lane that had been cleared through the woods, with Ilyin, a lawyer who occupied a summer cottage near hers. It was past four o'clock in the afternoon. Fluffy white clouds were massed just above; here and there patches of bright blue sky peeped out from under them. The clouds hung motionless, as though caught in the tops of the tall old pine-trees. It was still and sultry.

In the distance the lane was cut off by a low railway embankment on which just then a sentry with a gun was pacing to and fro for some reason. Right beyond the embankment there was a large white church with a rusty roof and six domes.

"I did not expect to meet you here," said Sofya Petrovna, looking at the ground and stirring last year's leaves with the tip of her parasol, "and now I am glad we have met. I must have a serious and final talk with you. I beg you, Ivan Mihailovich, if you really love and respect me, please stop pursuing me! You follow me about like a shadow, you constantly look at me in a way which isn't nice, you declare yourself repeatedly, you write me strange letters, and . . . and I don't know when it's all going to end! Lord, what can come of it?"

Ilyin was silent. Sofya Petrovna took a few steps and continued:

"And this abrupt change in you took place in the course of two or three weeks, after an acquaintance of five years. I don't recognize you, Ivan Mihailovich!"

Sofya Petrovna cast a sidelong glance at her companion. With narrowed eyes, he was staring intently at the fluffy clouds. His expression was harsh, capricious, and abstracted, like that of a man who suffers pain and at the same time is forced to listen to twaddle.

"It is surprising that you don't understand it yourself," she continued with a shrug of her shoulders. "You ought to realize that it is not a very nice game you've started. I am married, I love and respect my husband. . . . I have a daughter. . . . Does all that mean nothing to you? Besides, as an old friend you know what I think of marriage . . . and of the institution of the family—"

Ilyin grunted with disgust and sighed.

"The institution of the family—" he muttered. "Oh, Lord!"

"Yes, yes. . . . I love my husband, I respect him; and in any event I value the peace of my family life. I would rather die than cause Andrey and his daughter any unhappiness. And I beg you, Ivan Mihailovich, for

God's sake, leave me alone! Let us be good, kind friends, as before, and give up these sighs and groans, which don't become you. It's settled and done with! Not another word about it. Let us talk of something else."

Sofya Petrovna again cast a sidelong glance at Ilyin. Pale and angrily biting his trembling lips, he was looking upwards. She could not understand what made him angry and indignant, but his pallor touched her.

"So don't be angry, let's be friends," she said affectionately. "Agreed? Here is my hand."

Ilyin took her plump little hand into both of his, pressed it and slowly raised it to his lips.

"I am not a schoolboy," he muttered. "Friendship with the woman I love doesn't tempt me in the least."

"Enough, enough! It's settled and done with. We have reached the bench; let's sit down."

Sofya Petrovna was filled with a sweet sense of relief: the most difficult and ticklish things have been said, the painful question has been settled and disposed of. Now she could breathe freely and look him straight in the face. She looked at him, and the woman's selfish sense of superiority over the man who is in love with her flattered her agreeably. It gratified her to see this strong, huge man, clever, educated and, people said, gifted, with his sullen, masculine face and big black beard, sit down obediently beside her and drop his head dejectedly. For two or three minutes they sat in silence.

"Nothing is settled and done with," began Ilyin. "You recite copybook maxims to me: 'I love and respect my husband . . . the institution of the family . . .' I know all that without your saying anything, and I could tell you more about it, too. I admit frankly and honestly that I consider my behavior criminal and immoral. What more can one say? But what is the good of saying what is clear to anybody? Instead of feeding the nightingale heart-rending words, you'd much better tell me what I am to do."

"I've told you already: go away."

"As you know perfectly well, I went away five times, and every time I returned before I had gone half way. I can show you my through tickets—I have kept them all. I haven't the will power to run away from you! I am struggling, I am struggling hard, but what the devil am I good for if I have no character, if I am weak, faint-hearted! D'you understand? I can't, I can't fight Nature! I run away from here, and she holds on to my coattails and pulls me back. Vulgar, hideous weakness!"

Ilyin turned red, rose, and walked up and down in front of the bench.

"I feel as cross as a bear," he growled, clenching his fists. "I hate and despise myself! My God, like some dissolute schoolboy I run after another man's wife, write idiotic letters, degrade myself . . . ugh!

Ilyin clutched his head, grunted, and sat down.

"And then this insincerity of yours!" he continued bitterly. "If you really object to my ugly game, why have you come here? What drew you here? In my letters I only ask for a straight, unequivocal answer: yes or no, but instead of giving me a straight answer, every day you manage these 'chance' meetings with me and regale me with copybook maxims!"

She was frightened and flared up. She suddenly felt the embarrassment which a decent woman experiences when she is accidentally discovered undressed.

"You seem to suspect me of playing with you," she muttered. "I have always given you a straight answer, and . . . just now I begged you—"

"Oh, as though one begged in such matters! If you were to say right out: 'Go away,' I should have cleared out long ago; but you have never said that. You've never once given me a straight answer. Strange hesitancy! By God, either you're playing with me, or else—"

Ilyin broke off short and propped his head on his fists. Sofya Petrovna started going over her behavior from beginning to end in her own mind. She recalled that not only in her actions but even in her inmost thoughts she had never encouraged Ilyin's advances; at the same time she felt that there was some truth in the lawyer's words. But not knowing exactly to what extent he was right, she could find nothing to say in reply to his complaint, no matter how she racked her brain. It was awkward to be silent, and with a shrug of her shoulders she said:

"So it is I who am at fault!"

"I don't blame you for your insincerity," sighed Ilyin. "I just blurted out those words without meaning them. Your insincerity is natural and in the order of things. If people agreed suddenly to become sincere, everything would go to the devil, would fall to pieces."

Sofya Petrovna was in no mood for philosophizing, but she was glad of a chance to change the subject and asked: "But why?"

"Because only savages and animals are sincere. Once civilization has ushered in the need for such comforts as, for instance, feminine virtue, sincerity is out of place."

Ilyin drove his cane angrily into the sand. Madam Lubyantzeva listened to him and failed to understand a great deal, but relished his conversation. What gratified her in the first place was that a gifted man talked to her, an ordinary woman, on an "intellectual" subject; it afforded her great pleasure, too, to watch the working of his mobile, young, white face, which was still cross. Much of what he said she did not grasp, but what she found attractive about his talk was the temerity with which modern man, casting all hesitation and doubt to the winds, settles great questions once for all and reaches final conclusions.

She suddenly realized that she was admiring him, and took fright.

"Forgive me, but I don't understand," she made haste to say. "Why do you speak of insincerity? I repeat my request: be my good, kind friend; leave me alone! I earnestly beg you!"

"Very well; I'll try again," sighed Ilyin. "I am at your service. But I doubt if anything will come of my efforts. Either I shall put a bullet through my brain or take to drink in the silliest way. I shall bark my shins badly! There's a limit to everything, even to fighting against Nature. Tell me, how can one fight against madness? If you drink wine, how are you to fight against intoxication? What am I to do if your image has struck root in my soul, and day and night stands persistently before my eyes, the way that pine over there stands at this moment? Come, tell me, what feat must I perform to rid myself of this abominable, wretched condition, in which all my thoughts, desires, dreams are no longer my own, but belong to some demon who has gained possession of me? I love you, love you so much that I am completely thrown off balance; I have given up my work and turned my back on those dear to me; I have forgotten my God! I've never been in love like this in all my life."

Sofya Petrovna, who had not expected that the conversation would take such a turn, drew away from Ilyin and looked into his face, frightened. Tears came into his eyes, his lips trembled, and his face assumed an imploring, hungry expression.

"I love you," he muttered, bringing his eyes close to

her big, frightened eyes. "You are so beautiful! I am suffering now, but I'd be willing to sit here all my life agonizing, if I could only look into your eyes. But . . . do not speak, I implore you!"

Caught unawares, Sofya Petrovna tried to think quickly, quickly of something to say to stop him. "I'll go away," she decided, but no sooner did she make a movement to rise, than he was kneeling before her. He clasped her knees, looking into her face and speaking, passionately, ardently, eloquently. Terrified and dazed, she did not hear his words. For some reason now, at this dangerous moment while her knees were being agreeably pressed, as though she were in a warm bath, she was trying, with a sort of exasperated malice, to find the meaning of her own sensations. She was vexed that instead of brimming over with protesting virtue, she felt weak, indolent, and empty, like one who is half-seas over; only deep down within her a remote fragment of her consciousness was maliciously taunting her: "Then why don't you leave? So this is as it should be, eh?"

Seeking to understand herself, she could not grasp how it was that she did not pull away her hand to which Ilyin was clinging like a leech, and why she, like Ilyin, hastily glanced right and left to see if anyone was looking. The clouds and the pines were motionless, gazing at them severely like monitors seeing mischief but bribed not to report to the authorities. The sentry stood like a post on the embankment and seemed to have his eye on the bench.

"Let him look," thought Sofya Petrovna.

"But . . . but listen," she said at last with a note of despair in her voice. "What will this lead to? What will happen next?"

"I don't know, I don't know," he whispered, waving the disagreeable questions away with his hand.

The hoarse, tremulous whistle of the train was heard. This chilly, alien sound of humdrum prosiness roused Sofya Petrovna.

"I can't stay. . . . It's time for me to leave," she said, getting up quickly. "The train is coming in . . . Andrey is on it! He has to have his dinner."

Sofya Petrovna, her face burning, turned toward the embankment. At first the engine slowly crawled by, then came the cars. It was not the local passenger train, as she had supposed, but a freight train. The boxcars filed past in a long string against the background of the white church, one after another, like the days of a man's life, and it seemed as though there was no end to them.

But at last the train passed, and the caboose with its lanterns and the conductor had disappeared behind the foliage. Sofya Petrovna turned round abruptly and without looking at Ilyin walked rapidly back along the lane. She had regained her self-possession. Blushing with shame, humiliated, not by Ilyin, no, but by her own faint-heartedness, by the shamelessness with which she, a chaste and blameless woman, had allowed a strange man to hug her knees—she had only one thought now: to get back as quickly as possible to her summer cottage, to her family. The lawyer could hardly keep pace with her. Turning from the lane into a narrow path, she glanced at him so rapidly that she saw nothing but the sand on his knees, and signaled to him not to follow her.

Back home, Sofya Petrovna stood motionless in the middle of her room for some five minutes and looked now at the window and now at her desk.

"You vile creature!" she scolded herself. "You vile creature!"

To spite herself, she recalled in every detail, concealing nothing, how although all these days she had been averse to Ilyin's advances, something had *driven* her to have an explanation with him; and what was more, when he lay at her feet she had enjoyed it immensely. She remembered it all without sparing herself, and now, choking with shame, she would have liked to slap her own face again and again.

"Poor Andrey!" she said to herself, trying to assume the tenderest possible expression, as she thought of her husband. "Varya, my poor little girl, doesn't know what a mother she has! Forgive me, my dears! I love you very, very much!"

And wishing to prove to herself that she was still a good wife and mother, and that corruption had not yet touched "the institution of the family" of which she had spoken to Ilyin, Sofya Petrovna ran to the kitchen and raged at the cook for not yet having laid the table for Andrey Ilyich. She tried to picture to herself her husband's hungry and exhausted appearance, spoke of how hard he worked, and laid the table for him with her own hands, which she had never done before. Then she found her daughter Varya, picked her up in her arms and hugged her ardently. The child seemed to her rather heavy and irresponsive, but she was loath to admit this to herself, and she began explaining to the child what a nice, kind, and honorable man her papa was.

Yet when Andrey Ilyich arrived soon afterwards she hardly greeted him. The rush of sham feeling had already subsided, without proving anything to her, but only vexing and exasperating her by its lack of genuineness. She was sitting by the window, feeling unhappy and cross. It is only when they are in trouble that people can understand how difficult it is to control their thoughts and emotions. Sofya Petrovna said afterwards that there was "a confusion of feeling within her which it was as difficult to disentangle as to count sparrows rapidly flying in a flock." From the fact, for instance, that she was not overjoyed to see her husband, that she did not like the way he behaved at dinner, she suddenly concluded that she was beginning to hate him.

Andrey Ilyich, languid with hunger and fatigue, attacked the sausage while waiting for the soup to be served, and ate it chewing noisily and moving his temples.

"My God!" thought Sofya Petrovna. "I love and respect him, but . . . why does he chew his food so disgustingly?"

The disorder in her thoughts was no less than the disorder in her emotions. Like all persons inexperienced in warding off unpleasant thoughts, Madam Lubyantzeva did her utmost not to think of her predicament, and the harder she tried the more sharply did Ilyin, the sand on his knees, the fluffy clouds, the train stand out in her imagination.

"And why did I go there today, fool that I am?" she tormented herself. "And am I really so weak that I cannot trust myself?"

Fear has big eyes. By the time Andrey Ilyich was finishing his last course, she had firmly decided to tell her husband everything and to flee from danger!

"I must have a serious talk with you, Andrey," she began after dinner while her husband who was about to lie down for a nap was removing his coat and boots.

"Well?"

"Let's go away!"

"H'm! . . . Where shall we go? It is too early in the season to go back to town."

"No, let's take a trip or something—"

"A trip . . ." muttered the notary, stretching. "I

dream of that myself, but where are we to get the
money? And who is to take care of the office?"

And reflecting a little, he added, "Of course, it is
dull for you here. Go alone if you like."

Sofya Petrovna agreed, then it occurred to her that
Ilyin would welcome such an opportunity, and would
travel with her on the same train, in the same car . . .
As she reflected, she looked at her husband, now full of
food but still languid. For some reason, her glance
rested on his feet, very small, almost feminine, in striped
socks; there was a thread sticking up at the tip of each
sock.

Behind the lowered blind a bumblebee was bump-
ing against the window-pane and buzzing. Sofya Petrovna looked at the threads on the socks, listened to the
bee and pictured herself traveling . . . Ilyin sits opposite day and night, never taking his eyes off her,
angered by his own weakness and pale with mental
agony. He calls himself a dissolute schoolboy, abuses
her, tears his hair, but when darkness comes and the
passengers are asleep or get out at the station, he seizes
the opportunity to kneel before her and press her knees
as he had done at the bench. . . .

She stopped short, suddenly aware that she was daydreaming.

"Listen. I won't go alone," she said to her husband.
"You must come with me."

"Ridiculous, Sofochka!" said Lubyantzev. "One must
be sensible and only wish for what is possible."

"You will come when you find out," thought Sofya
Petrovna.

Having decided to leave at all costs, she felt herself
out of danger. Little by little, order came into her
thoughts, she grew more cheerful and she even allowed
herself to dwell upon it all, since no matter what she

thought about, no matter what she dreamed of, she would leave anyway.

While her husband was sleeping, evening gradually advanced. She sat in the drawing-room playing the piano. The stir out-of-doors that comes at dusk, the strains of music, and above all, the thought that she had used her head, that she had solved her problem, completely restored her spirits. Other women in her position, her now serene conscience told her, would probably have been carried away and lost their balance, while she had almost died of shame, had been unhappy and was now fleeing from a danger which, indeed, might be non-existent! She was soon so impressed by her own virtuous and resolute conduct that she even looked at herself in the mirror two or three times.

When it got dark, company arrived. The men sat down in the dining room to play cards; the ladies occupied the drawing-room and the porch. The last to arrive was Ilyin. He was gloomy, morose, and looked ill. He sat down in the corner of the couch and did not budge all evening. Usually high-spirited and talkative, this time he was silent and kept frowning and rubbing his eyes. When someone asked him a question, he gave a forced smile with his upper lip only and answered curtly and with irritation. He cracked several jokes, but his witticisms were harsh and impertinent. It seemed to Sofya Petrovna that he was on the verge of hysteria. Only now, sitting at the piano, she realized fully for the first time that this unhappy man was in no mood for jokes, that his soul was sick and that he was in torment. It was on her account that he was wasting the best days of his youth, ruining his career, spending the last of his money on a summer cottage; it was because of her that he had left his mother and sisters to the mercy of Fate, and, worst of all, was enduring a martyrdom in a struggle with himself that was undoing him. Out of mere common humanity, he ought to be taken seriously. . . .

She was so keenly aware of all this that it made her heart ache, and if at that moment she had gone up to him and said, "No," there would have been a force in her voice that would have commanded obedience. But she did not go up to him and did not speak, indeed, she did not consider doing so. She had never, perhaps, exhibited more clearly the pettiness and selfishness of youth than that evening. She realized that Ilyin was miserable and that he was sitting on the couch as on hot coals; she was sorry for him but, at the same time, the presence of a man who loved her so passionately filled her with triumph, with a sense of her own power. She was conscious of her youth, her beauty, and her inviolable virtue, and since she had decided to leave she gave herself full liberty for that evening. She flirted, laughed incessantly, sang with peculiar animation and feeling. Everything entertained and amused her. She was amused by the recollection of what had happened at the bench in the woods, by the memory of the sentry who had looked on. She was amused by her guests, by Ilyin's impertinent witticisms, by the pin in his cravat which she had never noticed before. The pin was in the shape of a red snake with diamond eyes. This snake struck her as so amusing that she could have covered it with kisses.

Sofya Petrovna sang nervously with a kind of half-intoxicated bravado, and as though in mockery of another's sorrow she chose sad, melancholy songs about blasted hopes, the past, old age. "Old age comes closer and closer . . ." she sang. But what was old age to her?

"I am behaving oddly," flashed through her mind as she laughed and sang.

The party broke up at midnight. Ilyin was the last to leave. Sofya Petrovna was still giddy enough to see him off to the bottom step of the porch. She wanted to tell him that she was going away with her husband, and to watch the effect this news would have on him.

The moon was hidden behind the clouds, but it was light enough for Sofya Petrovna to see how the wind flipped the skirts of Ilyin's overcoat and the blinds of the porch. She could also see how pale he was and how he twisted his upper lip in an effort to smile.

"Sonya, Sonichka, dearest!" he muttered, not letting her speak. "My dear, my darling!"

In a fit of tenderness, with tears in his voice, he showered her with caressing words, one more tender than the other, and even addressed her in the intimate second person singular, as though she were his wife or mistress. He surprised her by suddenly putting one arm around her waist and grasping her elbow with the other.

"My precious, my darling," he whispered, kissing the nape of her neck; "be sincere, come to me at once!"

She slipped out of his embrace and raised her head to vent her indignation and resentment, but the indignation did not come off, and all her vaunted virtue and purity was only sufficient to enable her to say the phrase which all ordinary women use under such circumstances:

"You're mad."

"Really, let's go," Ilyin continued. "I realized just now, as I did at the bench in the woods, that you are as helpless as I am, Sonya. You, too, will bark your shins! You love me and are bargaining with your conscience to no purpose."

Seeing that she was moving away, he caught her by

her lace cuff and rapidly finished what he had started to say:

"If not today, then tomorrow, but you will have to give in! Why this delay then? My precious, my darling, Sonya, the sentence has been passed, why put off the execution? Why deceive ourselves?"

Sofya Petrovna tore herself away and darted through the door. Returning to the drawing-room, she shut the piano automatically, stared for a long time at the vignette on a sheet of music, and sat down. She could not stand up, nor could she think. All that was left of her excitement and bravado was a fearful exhaustion, apathy, and ennui. Her conscience whispered to her that she had behaved badly, foolishly that evening, like a giddy girl, that she had just been making love on the porch and still had an odd feeling about her waist and her elbow.

The drawing-room was deserted; there was only one candle burning. Madam Lubyantzeva sat on the round stool before the piano motionless, waiting for something. And as though taking advantage of the darkness and of her extreme lassitude, desire, oppressive, irresistible, began to take possession of her. Like a boa constrictor, it tightened about her limbs and her soul, grew stronger every moment and no longer menaced her, as it had before, but stood plainly before her in all its nakedness.

She sat without stirring for half an hour, permitting herself to think freely of Ilyin. Then she got up languidly and dragged herself to her bedroom. Andrey Ilyich was already in bed. She sat down by the open window and gave herself up to desire. There was now no confusion in her mind. All her thoughts and feelings were directed with one accord toward a single object. She tried to struggle against it, but at once gave up the effort. It was clear to her that she was dealing with a strange and implacable enemy. To fight it she needed strength and courage, yet her family background, her education, and her experience in life had given her nothing to lean upon.

"Shameless thing! Vile creature!" she scored herself for her weakness. "So that's what you're like!"

Her sense of propriety, outraged by this weakness moved her to such indignation that she heaped upon herself every term of abuse she knew and told herself many biting and humiliating truths. Thus, for instance, she told herself that she had never been virtuous, that she had not fallen before simply because she had had no opportunity, that her inner conflict that day had all been a comedy and a pastime.

"And even if I did put up a fight," she reflected, "what sort of fight was it? Even the women who sell themselves struggle before they bring themselves to do it, and yet they do sell themselves. A fine struggle! Like milk, I've turned in one day! In one day!"

What drew her from home, she now knew, was not emotion, not Ilyin's person, but the sensations that awaited her . . . She was a lady, one of many, who was making the most of the summer season!

"And when the fledgling's mother had been slain," someone sang in a husky tenor outside the window.

"If I am to go, it's time," thought Sofya Petrovna. Her heart suddenly began beating with terrible violence.

"Andrey!" she almost shrieked. "Listen! We . . . we are going, aren't we?"

"Yes . . . I've told you already: you go alone."

"But listen," she began. "If you don't go with me, you risk losing me. I believe I am . . . in love already."

"With whom?" asked Andrey Ilyich.

"It's all one to you who it is!" cried Sofya Petrovna.

Andrey Ilyich sat up, put his legs over the edge of the bed and looked in wonder at his wife's dark figure.

"Ridiculous!" he yawned.

He did not believe her, and yet he was frightened. After thinking awhile and asking his wife several trivial questions, he delivered himself of his opinions on the family, on infidelity . . . He spoke dully for about ten minutes and lay down again. His sententious pronouncements had no effect. There are a great many opinions in this world, and a good half of them are professed by people who have never been in trouble!

In spite of the late hour, summer folk were still promenading outside. Sofya Petrovna threw on a light cape, stood about awhile, thought a little . . . She still had enough determination to say to her sleepy husband:

"Are you asleep? I am going for a walk. Do you want to come along?"

That was her last hope. Receiving no answer, she went out . . . It was fresh and blowy. She was conscious neither of the wind nor the darkness, but walked on and on. An irresistible force was driving her forward, and it seemed as though, if she had stopped, it would have pushed her in the back.

"Shameless thing!" she muttered mechanically. "Vile creature!"

She was choking, burning with shame, she did not feel her legs under her, but what pushed her forward was stronger than shame, reason, or fear.

1886

At the Mill

THE miller, Alexey Birukov, a big, powerful, thick-set middle-aged man who resembled in face and figure the uncouth, heavy-footed, rough seamen of whom boys dream after reading Jules Verne, sat at the threshold of his hut, sucking lazily at his pipe that had gone out. He wore gray breeches made of coarse army cloth, and large clumsy boots, but no jacket or cap, although it was late autumn and the weather was chilly and damp. The mist seeped freely through his unbuttoned shirt, but the miller's huge body that was as tough as a bunion seemed to be insensitive to cold. His red, beefy face was, as usual, apathetic and flabby, as if he had just been sleeping, and his small eyes drowned in fat stared grimly from under his eyebrows, surveying the dam, the two sheds, and the ancient, awkward willows.

Two monks from the neighboring monastery, who had just arrived, Kleopa, a tall, white-haired old man in a cassock bespattered with mud and a patched skullcap, and Diodor, black-haired and swarthy, apparently a Georgian, in an ordinary peasant sheepskin coat, were bustling near the sheds. They were unloading from carts sacks of rye brought to be ground. At some distance, on the brown, muddy grass sat the miller's helper, Yevsey, a beardless young fellow in a tattered coat that was too short for him. He was dead drunk. He crumpled a fishing net in his hands, making believe that he was mending it.

For a long time the miller looked about and held his peace, then he stared at the monks who were hauling the sacks and said in a thick voice:

"You monks, why have you been fishing in the river? Who said you could?"

The monks made no reply and did not even glance at the miller.

He kept quiet for a while, then lit his pipe and went on:

"You fish yourselves, and you let the townsmen do it, too. I leased the river from you and from the town, too. I pay you money, so the fish is mine and nobody's got the right to catch it. You pray all right, but you don't think it's a sin to steal."

The miller yawned, fell silent again, and then went on grumbling:

"Look at the habit they've got into! They think because they're monks and they're signed up to be saints, there's no law against them. I'll lodge a complaint with the justice of the peace. He won't pay no mind to your cassock and you'll have plenty of time to find out what the clink's like. Or maybe I'll settle your hash for you without troubling His Honor. If I just catch you fishing I'll give it you in the neck so you'll lose your appetite for fish till Judgment Day."

"Don't use such language, Alexey Dorofeich," said Kleopa in a gentle tenor. "Decent, God-fearing people wouldn't talk that way to a dog, and we are monks!"

"Monks!" the miller sneered. "You want fish? Yes? Then buy it from me, don't steal!"

"Good Lord, are we stealing?" Kleopa frowned. "Why use such words? True, our lay brothers did catch fish, but they had had Father Superior's permission to do so. Father Superior reasons that you paid out the money not for the whole river, but only so you'd have the right to set out nets near our bank. You didn't get the rights to the whole river. It isn't yours, or ours, it is God's. . . ."

"Father Superior is no better'n you," the miller grumbled, knocking his pipe against his boot. "He likes cheating, too. I don't make no distinctions. Father Superior is the same to me as you or Yevsey there. If I catch him fishing, he'll get it from me too. . . ."

"As for your getting ready to beat up the monks, do as you please. It will be all the better for us in the world to come. You have already beaten up Vissarion and Antipy, so beat up the others."

"Keep still, don't start anything with him!" said Diodor, pulling the other by the sleeve.

Kleopa quieted down, stopped talking and started hauling sacks again, while the miller went on scolding. He was speaking lazily, sucking at his pipe after each phrase and spitting. When he had exhausted the subject of fish, he recalled two sacks of his that the monks had allegedly made off with, and he began to abuse them on account of the sacks. Then, noticing that Yevsey was drunk and idling, he left the monks alone and began bawling out his hired men, filling the air with foul curses.

At first the monks restrained themselves and only uttered loud sighs, but soon Kleopa could stand it no longer. He clapped his hands together and said in a tearful voice: "Holy Saints, there is no worse penance for me than to go to the mill! It's hell! Veritable hell!"

"Don't come then!" the miller snapped.

"Queen of Heaven, we'd gladly keep away from here, but where shall we find another mill? Judge for yourself. Except for yours, there isn't a mill in this district! It's a choice between starving and eating unmilled grain!"

The miller wouldn't give in but kept on cursing. It was plain that grumbling and swearing were as much a habit with him as sucking on his pipe.

"If only you didn't mention the Evil One, at least!" Kleopa implored, blinking unhappily. "Keep still a while, I beg you!"

The miller soon desisted, but not because of Kleopa's request. A tiny stooped old woman, with a kindly face, wearing a queer striped jacket, that looked like the back of a bug, appeared on the dam. She carried a small bundle and leaned on a little stick.

"A good day to you, my dears!" she lisped, making a low bow to the monks. "The Lord be good to you! A good day, my little Alyosha! A good day to you, Yevsey darling. . . ."

"Good day, Maminka," the miller mumbled, with a frown, not looking at the old woman.

"And here I've come to see you, my dear," she said, smiling and peering tenderly into the miller's face. "I haven't seen you in a long time. Why, I haven't seen you since the Feast of the Assumption. Whether it pleases you or not, receive me! I believe you have gotten a bit thin."

The old woman seated herself beside the miller, and near this huge man her little jacket looked even more strikingly like the back of a bug.

"Yes, since the Feast of the Assumption!" she continued. "I've been missing you sorely, sonny, my heart has been aching for you, but whenever I got ready to come to you, it would either start raining or I would fall sick."

"You are coming from town now?" asked the miller morosely.

"Yes, from town, straight from home—"

"With all your ailments and in your condition you

should stay home, and not traipse about visiting. What did you come here for? Just wearing out shoe-leather!"

"I've come to have a look at you. I have two of them, sons, I mean," she said, turning to the monks, "this one and Vasily, who lives in town. Just the two of them. It's all the same to them if I am alive or dead, but they are my own, my joy. They can do without me, but without them I don't think I could live a day. Only, fathers, I'm getting old and it is hard for me now to come to him all the way from town."

A silence fell. The monks had carried the last sack to the shed and were sitting down in the cart resting. The drunken Yevsey kept crumpling the net in his hands and nodding sleepily.

"You've come at the wrong time, Maminka," said the miller. "I have to drive out to Karyazhino now."

"Do drive out. God speed you!" sighed the old woman. "Naturally, you can't drop business on my ac- count. I will rest here a while and then go back. . . . Vasya and his children send you greetings, Alyosha darling. . . ."

"He still swills vodka?"

"Not so much, but he does take a drop. No use hiding the sin, he does drink. You know yourself he hasn't the money to drink a lot. Except perhaps when good people stand him a treat. It's a wretched life he leads, Alyosha! It hurts me to see it. Nothing to eat, the children in tat- ters, he ashamed to show himself in the street, what with holes in his pants and no boots. All the six of us sleep in one room. Such poverty, such bitter poverty. You can't imagine anything worse. Indeed, I've come to beg you to help us out. For the old woman's sake, Alyosha, do help Vasily. After all, he is your brother!"

The miller was silent and kept looking in the other direction.

"He is poor, but you—the Lord be praised!—you have a mill of your own, and orchards, and you trade in fish. The Lord has given you wisdom, He has raised you above all and given you bounty—and you are all alone. But Vasya has four children, and I, the accursed one, am a burden to him, and all he earns is seven rubles. How can he feed us all that way? You help us. . . ." In silence the miller carefully filled his pipe.

"Won't you help?" asked the old woman.

The miller was as silent as a clam. Receiving no answer, the old woman sighed, looked round at the monks and at Yevsey, then got up and said:

"Well, God bless you, don't help us—I knew you wouldn't—I've come to you more on account of Nazar Andreich—He cried so, Alyosha darling! He kissed my hands and kept asking me to go to you and beg you."

"What does he want?"

"He begs you to give him what's coming to him. He brought you his rye to be ground, he says, and you never gave him the flour."

"It isn't your business to meddle in other people's affairs, Maminka," the miller growled. "Your business is to say your prayers."

"I do pray, but it looks as though God doesn't heed my prayers. Vasily is a pauper, and as for me, I beg my bread and wear a cast-off jacket, while you are well-off, but the Lord knows what kind of a soul you have. Oh, Alyosha darling, the envious have put the evil eye on you! You've been blessed in everything. You're clever and handsome and you are a prince among merchants, but you're not human. You're unfriendly, you never smile or say a kind word, you're as pitiless as a beast. Look at your face! And what people say about you, my grief! Ask the fathers here! They lie about you, they say that you suck people's blood, that there are evil deeds upon your soul, that with your helpers you rob pass-ers-by at night and that you are a horse-thief. Your mill is like an accursed place. Boys and girls are afraid to come near it, all creatures keep clear of you. They have no other name for you but Cain and Herod—"

"You are a fool, Maminka!"

"Where your foot steps, the grass does not grow, where you breathe, not a fly buzzes. All I hear is 'Ah, if only someone did him in or if he were put away!' What does it do to a mother when she has to hear that? How does she feel? You are my own child, my flesh and blood—"

"It's time for me to go," muttered the miller, rising. "Good-by, Maminka!"

He wheeled a carriage out of the shed, led out a horse and, shoving it between the shafts as if it were a small dog, started hitching it up. The old woman hovered about him, looked into his face, and blinked tear-fully.

"Well, good-by!" she said, as her son started hur-riedly shouldering into a coat. "Stay here with God's blessing and do not forget us. Wait, I have a present for you." She mumbled, lowering her voice and untying her bundle, "Yesterday I was at the deaconess's, and they passed something round. So I put one away for you."

And the old woman held out to her son a small spice-cake.

"Leave off!" snarled the miller and pushed her hand away.

Embarrassed, the old woman dropped the cake and quietly waddled off towards the dam. It was a painful scene. Not to mention the monks, who exclaimed and held out their arms in horror, even the drunken Yevsey was petrified and stared at his master in dismay.

Whether because the miller was impressed by the re-action of the monks and his helper or because an emotion long dormant stirred in his breast, something like an expression of fear flashed across his face.

"Maminka!" he called.

The old woman started and looked back. The miller hurriedly plunged his hand into his pocket and drew out a large leather purse.

"There," he mumbled, pulling out of the purse a wad of paper money in which some silver coins were stuck, "take it!"

He rolled the wad in his hand, crushed it, for some reason looked at the monks, then fingered it again. The bills and the silver coins, slipping between his fingers, dropped back into the purse one after another, and only a twenty-kopeck piece remained in his hand. The miller examined it, rubbed it between his fingers and, groaning and getting purple, handed it to his mother.

1886

The Chameleon

POLICE INSPECTOR Ochumelov[1], wearing a new uniform and carrying a bundle in his hand, is crossing the market place. Behind him strides a red-headed policeman with a sieve that is filled to the brim with confiscated gooseberries. Silence reigns. Not a soul on the square. . . . The open doors of shops and taverns look out on God's world dejectedly, like hungry jaws. Not even a beggar is to be seen about them.

---

[1] The name may be rendered as Daft or Whacky.

"So you bite, do you, you devil!" Ochumelov hears suddenly. "Don't let her get away, fellows! It's against the law to bite nowadays. Hold her! A-ahh!"

A canine squeal is heard. Ochumelov looks about and sees a dog dash out of merchant Pichugin's lumberyard, limping on three legs and looking behind it as it runs. It is being chased by a man in a starched cotton shirt, with his vest unbuttoned. He dashes after it, throwing himself forward, drops to the ground, and seizes the dog by its hind legs. The canine squeal sounds again, and the cry: "Don't let her get away!" Sleepy faces appear in the doorways of the shops, and soon, as though it had sprung out of the ground, a crowd gathers near the lumberyard.

"Looks like trouble, Your Honor," says the policeman.

Ochumelov makes a half turn to the left and strides toward the crowd. At the very gates of the lumberyard he sees the man with the unbuttoned vest, described above, holding up his right hand and showing the crowd a bleeding finger. On his rather groggy-looking face is written, as it were: "I'll let you have it, you brute!" and his very finger looks like the banner of victory. Ochumelov recognizes Hrukin,[1] the goldsmith. In the center of the crowd crouches the culprit responsible for the scandal, a white borzoi puppy with a pointed muzzle and a yellow spot on its back, its forepaws spread out, and trembling all over. There is an expression of anguish and terror in its moist eyes.

"What's going on here?" demands Ochumelov, shouldering his way through the crowd. "What's it about? What's that finger? Who was hollering?"

"Here I'm on my way, Your Honor," begins Hrukin, coughing into his fist, "to talk to Mitry Mitrich about firewood, not harming a soul, and all at once this nasty

[1] The name suggests the grunting of a pig.

creature for no reason at all snaps at my finger. Excuse me, but I'm a man what works . . . and mine's delicate work. They've got to pay me damages. Maybe it'll be a week before I can move this finger again. It don't say in the law that you must put up with injury from a beast. If they're all going to bite, there'll be no living. . . ."

"Mm. . . . Right!" says Ochumelov severely, clearing his throat and knitting his eyebrows. "Right. . . . Whose dog is it? I won't stand for this! I'll teach you to let your dogs run wild. It's time we took notice of these people who won't obey regulations. When he's fined, the scamp, he'll know, thanks to me, what a dog is, and other stray cattle. I'll show him what's what. Yeldyrin," he turns to the policeman, "find out whose dog it is and draw up a report. As for the dog, she must be done away with. At once! She's sure to be mad. Whose dog is it, I ask you?"

"Could be General Zhigalov's," says someone in the crowd.

"General Zhigalov's? H'mm! Yeldyrin, help me off with my coat. It's terribly hot! Guess it's going to rain. There's just one thing I can't make out: how could she possibly bite you?" Ochumelov turns to Hrukin. "How could she reach your finger? She's a little bit of a thing and you're a big husky. You must have scratched your finger on a nail and you got it into your head to blame it on the dog. I know your sort. I know you devils!"

"He poked a cigarette into its snout, Your Honor, for fun, and the dog's no fool—she snapped at him. He's an ugly customer, Your Honor."

"You're lying, you with the one eye! You didn't see it, so why tell lies about it? His Honor is an intelligent gentleman, His Honor knows the difference between a liar and an honest man who speaks God's truth. And if it's me that's lying, let the justice of the peace decide.

He knows what the law says. We're all equal nowadays. My own brother's a gendarme, if you want to know."

"None of your lip!" says the police inspector.

"No, it's not the General's," observes the policeman thoughtfully. "The General ain't got none like this. He's got mostly setters."

"Are you sure about that?"

"Sure, Your Honor."

"Of course, I know. The General's dogs are all thoroughbreds, and worth a lot of money, and this is some kind of mutt! No points, no looks, just a mean tyke. The idea of keeping a dog like that! Where's your brains? If a dog like that turned up in Petersburg or Moscow, do you know what would happen? They wouldn't think twice about the law—to the pound with it! Hrukin, you're the injured party, and don't you drop the case. They've got to be taught a lesson! High time!"

"But maybe she is the General's," the policeman thinks out loud. "It ain't written on her snout. The other day I saw one just like her in the General's courtyard."

"Sure she's the General's," says a voice from the crowd.

"H'mm. . . . Help me on with my coat, brother Yeldyrin. It's blowing up, getting chilly. You take the dog to the General, and make inquiries. Tell him I was the one that found her and saw he got her back. . . . And tell them there to keep her off the street. . . . It may be a valuable dog, and if every swine pokes his cigarette into her snout she may get damaged. A dog is a delicate creature. . . . And you, you blockhead, put your hand down. What's the sense of sticking up your silly finger? It's your own fault!"

"There's the General's cook! Let's ask him. Hey, Prohor! Come here, brother. Look at this dog. Is that yours?"

"Nonsense! We never had no such dogs."

"No need to ask questions," says Ochumelov. "She's a stray. No use talking about it. I said she was a stray, and she is a stray. To the pound with her and that's all!"

"She's not one of ours," Prohor continues. "She belongs to the General's brother, he came a few days ago. Our General don't fancy borzois, but His Excellency's brother, he likes 'em."

"You don't mean to say His Excellency's brother is here! Vladimir Ivanych?" asks Ochumelov, and a smile of exaltation suffuses his face. "Good Lord! and I didn't know! Has the dear man come on a visit?"

"Yes, on a visit."

"Good Lord! So the dear man got lonesome for his brother. And to think I didn't know! So the little dog belongs to His Excellency's brother! I'm mighty glad! Take her. She's not a bad little dog! So smart! Chkk! Snapped at that fellow's finger! Ha-ha-ha! What are you shaking about, puppy? Grr-grr . . . The rascal's cross, the little pet!"

Prohor calls the dog and leaves the lumberyard with it . . . The crowd howls at Hrukin.

"I'll get you yet!" Ochumelov threatens him, and wrapping his coat about him, continues his way across the market place.

1884

The Siren

AFTER one of the sessions of the assizes of the peace, the Justices withdrew to the chamber where they usually deliberated. They wanted to get into their street clothes, and after resting a while, go off to dine. The Presiding Judge, a very presentable man with fluffy side-whiskers, had failed to concur with his associates in a case that had just been tried and was sitting at a desk hastening to set down his dissenting opinion. An Acting Justice of the Peace, Milkin, a young man with a languid, melancholy face, who had a reputation as a philosopher at odds with the world and distressed by the emptiness of existence, stood at a window and gazed sadly out into the courtyard. Two judges had already left. An Honorary Justice, a fat man with a bloated look who breathed heavily, and the Assistant Prosecuting Attorney, a young man of German extraction with a catarrhal complexion, sat on a couch and waited for their colleague to finish writing his opinion so that they could all go to dinner together. Standing before them was the secretary, a short man with side-whiskers growing close to his ears and a sugary expression on his face. He was looking at the fat man with a honeyed smile and speaking in a low voice:

"We are all hungry now, it's true, but that's because we're tired and it's after three: it's not, my dear Grigory Savvich, what you would call real appetite. I mean real appetite, the wolfish sort, when you're ready to make a meal of your own father. That comes only after physical exertion, for instance, when you've ridden to hounds, or say after you've been jolted over a hundred versts[1] without a stop in a wretched conveyance. Of course, I won't deny, sir, that imagination has something to do with it, too. Suppose you are coming home after a day's shooting and you want to bring an appetite to your dinner. Then you mustn't let your mind dwell on anything intellectual. Intellectual things, learned things, ruin the appetite. You know yourself that thinkers and scholars are just nowhere when it comes to eating. Even pigs, pardon the expression, pay more regard to their food than such people do. As I was saying, you are on your way home, and you must make sure that your mind dwells on nothing but the wineglass and the appetizer. Once as I was traveling I closed my eyes and pictured to myself a sucking-pig with horseradish. Well, sir, I became virtually hysterical with sheer appetite! Now this is important: when you drive into your own courtyard, you should be aware of a smell from the kitchen, a smell of something, you know. . . ."

"Roast goose is a prime smeller," observed the Honorary Justice, breathing heavily.

"Don't say that, my dear Grigory Savvich. Duck or woodcock, those are the trumps! The bouquet of a goose lacks refinement, lacks delicacy. The richest odor is that of young onions when they just begin to get golden-brown, you know, and when the rascals fill the house with their sizzling. Another thing: when you come in, the table must be set, and when you sit down you tuck the napkin into your collar and you take your time about reaching for the vodka decanter. And mind you, you don't pour it into an ordinary wineglass, you don't treat the sweetheart that way! No. You pour it into something

---

[1] A verst is two thirds of a mile.

antique, made of silver, an heirloom, or into a quaint pot-bellied little glass with an inscription on it, something like this: 'As you clink, you may think, monks also thus do drink.' And you don't gulp it down, straight off, but first you sigh, you rub your hands together, you gaze nonchalantly at the ceiling, and only then, slowly, you raise it to your lips, and at once sparks from your stomach flash through your whole body."

An expression of beatitude spread over the secretary's sugary face.

"Sparks," he repeated, screwing up his eyes. "And as soon as you have had your snifter, you turn to the appetizers."

"See here," put in the Presiding Judge, raising his eyes to the secretary, "be quiet! You've made me spoil two sheets!"

"Oh, I am so sorry, Pyotr Nikolaich! I will speak more quietly," murmured the secretary, and continued in a half whisper. "Well, my dear Grigory Savvich, as I was about to say, when it comes to appetizers, one must know one's way about. The best appetizer is herring. You eat a bit of herring with onion and mustard sauce, and without waiting, my friend, while the sparks are still flying in the stomach, you help yourself to caviar, with lemon juice, if you prefer it that way, then you have a radish with salt, and another piece of herring. But I'll tell you what's better still, my friend: salted pink mushrooms, minced as fine as caviar and served with onion and olive oil . . . exquisite! But eel-pout liver— that's beyond anything!"

"Mm—yes . . ." agreed the Honorary Justice, screwing up his eyes in turn. "Another good appetizer is stewed white mushrooms."

"Yes, yes, with onion, you know, and bay leaf and other spices. You lift the lid off the dish, and the steam

rises, a smell of mushrooms . . . sometimes it really
brings tears to my eyes! Well, sir, the meat pie is
brought in from the kitchen and at once, without delay,
another glass of vodka is in order."

"Ivan Guryich!" exclaimed the Presiding Judge in a
tearful voice. "You made me ruin the third sheet!"

"Deuce take him, he can't think of anything but
food!" grumbled Milkin, the philosopher, with a look
of contempt. "Is there nothing to live for but mushrooms
and meat pie?"

"Well, sir, before the meat pie you down another
one," the secretary repeated in a low tone. He was so
carried away that, like a nightingale singing, he heard
only his own voice. "The meat pie must make your
mouth water, it must lie there before you, naked, shameless, a temptation! You wink at it, you cut off a sizable
slice, and you let your fingers just play over it, this way,
out of excess of feeling. You eat, the butter drips from
it like tears, and the filling is fat, juicy, rich, with eggs,
giblets, onions. . . ."

The secretary rolled up his eyes and his mouth
stretched to his ears. The Honorary Justice groaned and
twiddled his fingers, apparently seeing the meat pie before him.

"What the devil!" grumbled the Acting Justice, walking over to the farther window.

"You eat only two slices, the third you keep for the
shchi," the secretary went on like a man inspired. "And
as soon as you've finished with the meat pie, have the
shchi served, to keep the appetite at pitch. The *shchi*
must be piping hot. But even better than *shchi*, with all
that cabbage, is a *borshch*, prepared with sugar beets,
Ukrainian style, you know the way, my friend, with ham
and country sausages. It should be served with sour
cream, of course, and a sprinkling of fresh parsley and

dill. Another excellent thing is a *rassolnik*,[1] with tripe in it and giblets and young kidneys, and then if you want a soup, the best thing is a vegetable soup, with carrots, fresh asparagus, a bit of cauliflower and whatever else is legitimate."

"Yes, it's an excellent thing," sighed the Presiding Judge, lifting his eyes from his papers, but at once he caught himself up and moaned, "For heaven's sake! If you go on like that, it'll be evening by the time I get through with my opinion! I've spoiled the fourth sheet!"

"Not a word more, not a word! I am very sorry!" the secretary apologized, and went on in a whisper, "After you have had your *borshch* or your soup, as you prefer, have the fish course served, and immediately, my friend. Of all the mute race, the finest is crucian carp, fried in sour cream. But so that it shouldn't have any odor of silt, and to give it true delicacy, it must be kept alive in milk for twenty-four hours."

"A fish ring made of sterlet is good, too," put in the Honorary Justice, closing his eyes, and then suddenly, astonishingly, with a ferocious air he rushed from his seat, and roared at the Presiding Judge, "Pyotr Nikolaich, will you be done soon? I can't wait any longer, I just can't!"

"Just let me finish!"

"The deuce! I'll eat alone!"

The fat man waved his hand in despair, seized his hat and without a good-by ran out of the chamber. The secretary sighed, and bending over the ear of the Assistant Prosecuting Attorney, proceeded in a low voice:

"Pike perch or carp with tomato and mushroom sauce isn't to be sneezed at, either. But fish doesn't really satisfy one, you'll admit, Stepan Frantzych: there's no sub-

---

[1] A meat or fish soup; *shchi* is a vegetable soup of which cabbage is the main ingredient.

stance to it. The main thing in a dinner isn't the fish, no matter with what sauce, but the roast. Which are you fondest of?"

The Assistant Prosecuting Attorney made a sour face and said, sighing:

"Unfortunately, I can't share your transports: I have catarrh of the stomach."

"Tut, tut, my dear sir! Catarrh of the stomach is an invention of the doctors! It's a complaint that comes mostly from pride and free-thinking. Don't give it a thought. Suppose you don't feel like eating or you're even nauseated, just pay no attention, but go right ahead and eat. Say the roast is a snipe or two, and perhaps a partridge with it, or a brace of fat quail, then you'll forget all about your catarrh, I give you my word of honor. And what about roast turkey? The bird should be a hen, with fat, juicy, white meat—the breast of a nymph. . . ."

"That should be tasty," murmured the Prosecuting Attorney, with a wistful smile. "Perhaps I would enjoy a slice of turkey."

"Good Lord! and what about duck? If you take a duckling, one that has had a taste of the ice during the first frost, and roast it, and be sure to put the potatoes, cut small, of course, in the dripping-pan too, so that they get browned to a turn and soaked with duck fat and—"

Milkin, the philosopher, made a ferocious face and was apparently about to say something but instead suddenly smacked his lips, probably dreaming of roast duck, and without a word, as though pulled by some mysterious force, seized his hat and ran out.

"Yes, perhaps I would enjoy a bit of duck, too," breathed the Assistant Prosecuting Attorney.

The Presiding Judge got up, walked about the chamber, and sat down again.

"After the roast, sir, a man is full, and he goes off into

a sweet eclipse," continued the secretary. "The body is basking, the soul is transported. And then for the crowning touch, two or three glasses of spiced brandy."

The Presiding Judge grunted and struck out what he had written.

"I have ruined the sixth sheet!" he exclaimed angrily. "This is monstrous!"

"Go on, go on writing, my friend," murmured the secretary. "I shan't say another word. You won't hear a thing. Believe me, Stepan Frantzych," he went on in a scarcely audible whisper, "spiced brandy, if it's home-made, is better than the finest champagne. After the very first glass your whole being is suffused with a kind of fragrance, enveloped in a mirage, as it were, and it seems to you as if you aren't at home, in your own arm-chair, but somewhere in Australia, that you are astride a downy ostrich—"

"Oh, let's be off, Pyotr Nikolaich!" cried the Prosecuting Attorney, with an impatient jerk of his leg.

"Yes, my friend," the secretary continued. "And while you are sipping your brandy, it's not a bad thing to smoke a cigar, and you blow rings, and you begin to fancy that you are a generalissimo, or better still, you are married to the most beautiful woman in the world, and all day long she is floating under your windows in a kind of pool with goldfish in it. She floats there, and you call to her: 'Darling, come and give me a kiss.'"

"Pyotr Nikolaich!" moaned the Prosecuting Attorney.

"Yes, my friend," the secretary proceeded. "And when you have had your smoke, you lift the skirts of your dressing-gown and climb into bed! You lie on your back, and you pick up a newspaper. When you can hardly keep your eyes open, and your whole body is ready for sleep, politics makes agreeable reading: Austria made a misstep, France got somebody's back up, the Pope put a spoke in someone's wheel—it's a pleasure, sir, to read of such things."

The Presiding Judge threw down his pen, jumped up and seized his hat in both hands. The Assistant Prosecuting Attorney, who had quite forgotten his catarrh and was nearly fainting with impatience, jumped up, too.

"Let's be off!" he cried.

"Pyotr Nikolaich, and what about your dissenting opinion?" asked the secretary in dismay. "My dear friend, when will you write it? You have to be in town at six o'clock!"

The Presiding Judge waved his hand in despair and made a dash for the door. The Assistant Prosecuting Attorney made the same gesture and, seizing his brief case, vanished together with the judge. The secretary looked after them reproachfully and began to gather up the papers.

1887

Sergeant Prishibeyev

SERGEANT PRISHIBEYEV,[1] the charge against you is that on the third of September you committed assault and battery on Constable Zhigin, Elder Alyapov, Policeman Yefimov, special deputies Ivanov and Gavrilov, and on six other peasants, the three first-named having been attacked by you while they were performing their official duties. Do you plead guilty?"

---

[1] An English equivalent of the name would be Squelch.

Prishibeyev, a wrinkled non-com with a face that seemed to bristle, comes to attention and replies in a hoarse, choked voice, emphasizing each word, as though he were issuing a command:

"Your Honor, Mr. justice of the peace! It follows, according to all the articles of the law, there is cause to attest every circumstance mutually. It's not me that's guilty, but all them others. This whole trouble started on account of this dead corpse, the Kingdom of Heaven be his! On the third instant my wife, Anfisa, and I was walking quiet and proper. Suddenly I look and what do I see but a crowd of all sorts of people standing on the river bank. By what rights, I ask, have people assembled there? What for? Is there a law that says people should go about in droves? Break it up, I holler. And I start shoving people, telling them to go on home, and I order the policeman to chase 'em and give it 'em in the neck. . . ."

"Allow me, but you are not a constable, not an elder —is it your business to break up crowds?"

"It ain't! It ain't!" voices are heard from various parts of the courtroom. "There's no standing him, Your Honor! It's fifteen years he's been plaguing us! Since the day he came back from the army, there's no living in the village. He's done nothing but badger us."

"Just so, Your Honor," says the elder. "The whole village is complaining. There's no standing him! No matter whether we carry the icons in a church procession, or have a wedding, or some accident happens, there he is, shouting, making a racket, setting things straight. He pulls the children's ears, he spies on the women folk, afraid something might go amiss, like he were their father-in-law. The other day he made the round of the cabins, ordering everybody not to sing songs, not to burn lights. 'There ain't no law,' he tells 'em, 'as says people should sing songs.' "

"Hold on, you'll have a chance to testify," says the justice of the peace; "and now let Prishibeyev continue. Go on, Prishibeyev!"

"Yes, sir!" crows the sergeant. "Your Honor, you're pleased to say that it ain't my business to break up crowds. . . . Very well, sir. . . . But what if there's breach of the peace? You can't allow folks to carry on disgracefully. Where is the law that says people should do as they please? I won't have it, sir! If I don't chase 'em and call 'em to account, who will? Nobody here knows the rights of things; I'm the only one, Your Honor, I'm the only one in the whole village, you might say, who knows how to deal with the common people. And I know what's what, Your Honor. I'm no hick, I'm a non-commissioned officer, a retired quartermaster-sergeant. I served in Warsaw, I was attached to head-quarters, sir, and after, when I got my honorable dis-charge, I was on duty as a fireman, and then on account of ill health I retired from the fire department, and for two years I held the post of doorman in a junior high school for boys of good family. I know all the rules and regulations, sir. But the peasant, he's ignorant, he don't understand the first thing, and he's got to do as I say, seeing as how it's for his own good. Take this affair, for instance. Here I was, breaking up the crowd, and right there on the shore, on the sand, lies the drowned corpse of a dead man. What right has he got to lie there, I asks. Is that proper? What's the constable thinking of? How come, constable, says I, that you didn't notify the authorities? Maybe this drowned corpse drowned him-self or maybe this smells of Siberia? Maybe it's a case of criminal homicide. But Zhigin, the constable, he don't take no notice, but just puffs away at a cigarette. 'Who is this,' says he, 'as is laying down the law to you fellows? Where does he come from?' says he. 'Don't we know what's what without him putting in his oar?' says he. 'It looks as if you don't know what's what, you fool, you,' says I, 'if you stand there and don't take no notice.' 'I notified the district police officer yesterday,' says he. 'Why the district police officer?' says I. 'According to what article of the Code of Laws? In cases like drowning and hanging and matters of a similar kind, is there anything the district police officer can do about them? Here's a corpse,' says I, 'this is a criminal case, plainly a civil suit. The thing to do,' says I, sir, 'is to send a dispatch right away to His Honor the examining magistrate and Their Honors the judges. And first off,' says I, 'you ought to draw up a report and send it to His Honor the justice of the peace.' But the constable, he just listens to it all, and laughs. And the peasants, too. They all laughed, Your Honor. I can testify to it under oath. This one here laughed, and that one there, and Zhigin, he laughed too. 'What's the joke?' says I. And the constable, he says: 'Such cases ain't within the jurisdiction of the justice of the peace.' I got hot under the collar when I heard them words. 'You did say them words, didn't you, constable?'" The sergeant turned to Zhigin.

"I did."

"Everybody heard you say them very words in front of the common people: 'Such cases ain't within the jurisdiction of the justice of the peace.' Everybody heard you say them words. I got hot under the collar, Your Honor. Honest, it took away my breath. 'Repeat,' says I, 'repeat, you blankety blank, what you just said.' And he did. 'How can you say them words,' says I, 'about His Honor the justice of the peace? You, a police officer,

and you're against the government! What! Do you
know, says I, 'that if he takes it into his head, His
Honor the justice of the peace can ship you off to the
provincial office of the gendarmerie on account of your
unreliable conduct? Do you know,' says I, 'where His
Honor the justice of the peace can send you for such
political words?' And the elder, he says: 'The justice of
the peace can't do nothing,' he says, 'beyond his limits.
Only minor cases comes within his jurisdiction.' Them's
his exact words, everybody heard him. 'How dare you
belittle the authorities?' says I. 'Don't you get gay with
me,' says I, 'or you'll come to grief, brother.' When I
was serving in Warsaw and when I was doorman at the
junior high school for boys of good family, if I heard
something as shouldn't be said, I'd look up and down
the street for a gendarme. 'Come here, officer,' I'd say,
and I'd make a report of the whole affair to him. But
here in the village, to whom can you report? This made
me sore. It got under my skin to see folks indulge in
license and insubordination, and I gave the elder a
crack. Of course, not much of a one, just easy like, so
he'd know better than to say such words about Your
Honor. The constable stuck up for the elder. So, naturally, I went for the constable, too. And then there was
a rumpus. I forgot myself, Your Honor. But how'll you
get along if you don't punch 'em sometimes? If you
don't thrash a fool, you take a sin on your soul. And
all the more if he deserves it, if there's a breach of the
peace."

"Allow me, but there are proper authorities to keep
order. There is the constable, the elder, the policeman."

"The constable can't keep an eye on everything, and
besides he don't understand things like I do. . . ."

"But get it into your head: this is none of your business!"

"How's that, sir? What do you mean—none of my business? That's queer, sir. People carry on disgracefully, and it's none of my business! Should I pat 'em on the back for it? Here they kick because I don't let 'em sing. What's the good of singing? Instead of doing something useful, they sing. And now they've got into the way of sitting up evenings and burning lights. They should go to bed, and instead they gab and cackle. I've got it all wrote down!"

"What have you written down?"

"About them as sit up and burns lights."

Prishibeyev takes a greasy sheet of paper out of his pocket, puts on his spectacles, and reads:

"Peasants what burn lights: Ivan Prokhorov, Savva Mikiforov, Pyotr Petrov, Shustrova, soldier's widow, lives in sin with Semyon Kislov. Ignat Sverchok practices witchcraft and his wife Mavra is a witch: she milks other folks' cows at night."

"That will do," says the judge, and starts to question the witnesses.

Sergeant Prishibeyev shoves his spectacles up on his forehead and stares in astonishment at the judge, who appears not to side with him. His protruding eyes glitter, his nose turns bright red. He gazes at the justice of the peace, and at the witnesses, and cannot grasp why the judge is so agitated or why now a murmur, now subdued laughter is heard from all the corners of the courtroom. The sentence, too, is incomprehensible to him: a month in jail!

"What for?" says he, throwing up his hands in bewilderment. "By what law?"

And it is clear to him that the world has changed and that it is utterly impossible to go on living. He falls prey to gloomy, despondent thoughts. But when he leaves the courtroom and catches sight of a crowd of peasants milling about and talking, a habit that he can no longer control makes him come to attention and shout in a hoarse, angry voice:

"Break it up, folks! Move along! Go on home!"

1885

The Culprit

A PUNY little peasant, exceedingly skinny, wearing patched trousers and a shirt made of ticking, stands before the investigating magistrate. His hairy, pockmarked face, and his eyes, scarcely visible under thick, overhanging brows, have an expression of grim sullenness. The mop of tangled hair that has not known the touch of a comb for a long time gives him a spiderish air that makes him look even grimmer. He is barefoot.

"Denis Grigoryev!" the magistrate begins. "Step nearer and answer my questions. On the morning of the seventh of this present month of July, the railway watchman, Ivan Semyonovich Akinfov, making his rounds, found you, near the hundred-and-forty-first milepost, unscrewing the nut of one of the bolts by which the rails are fastened to the sleepers. Here is the nut! . . . With the said nut he detained you. Is this true?"

"Wot?"

"Did all this happen as stated by Akinfov?"

"It did, sure."

"Very well; now, for what purpose were you unscrewing the nut?"

"Wot?"

"Stop saying 'wot' and answer the question: for **what** purpose were you unscrewing the nut?"

"If I didn't need it, I wouldn't've unscrewed it," croaks Denis, with a sidelong glance at the ceiling.

"What did you want that nut for?"

"The nut? We make sinkers of these nuts."

"Who are 'we'?"

"We, folks. . . . The Klimovo peasants, that is."

"Listen, brother; don't play the fool with me, but talk sense. There's no use lying to me about sinkers."

"I never lied in my life, and here I'm lying . . ." mutters Denis, blinking. "But can you do without a sinker, Your Honor? If you put live bait or worms on a hook, would it go to the bottom without a sinker? . . . So I'm lying," sneers Denis. "What the devil is the good of live bait if it floats on the surface? The perch and the pike and the eel-pout will bite only if your line touches bottom, and if your bait floats on the surface, it's only a bullhead will take it, and that only sometimes, and there ain't no bullhead in our river . . . That fish likes plenty of room."

"What are you telling me about bullhead for?"

"Wot? Why, you asked me yourself! Up our way the gentry catch fish that way, too. Even a little kid wouldn't try to catch fish without a sinker. Of course, somebody with no sense might go fishing without a sinker. No rules for fools."

"So you say you unscrewed this nut to make a sinker of it?"

"What else for? Not to play knucklebones with!"

"But you might have taken a bit of lead or a bullet for a sinker . . . a nail . . ."

"You don't pick up lead on the road, you have to pay for it, and a nail's no good. You can't find nothing better than a nut . . . It's heavy, and it's got a hole."

"He keeps playing the fool! As though he'd been born yesterday or dropped out of the sky! Don't you understand, you blockhead, what this unscrewing leads to? If the watchman hadn't been on the lookout, the train might have been derailed, people would have been killed—*you* would have killed people."

"God forbid, Your Honor! Kill people? Are we unbaptized, or criminals? Glory be to God, sir, we've lived our lives without dreaming of such a thing, much less killing anybody . . . Save us, Queen of Heaven, have mercy on us! What are you saying, sir?"

"And how do you suppose train wrecks happen? Unscrew two or three nuts, and you have a wreck!"

Denis sneers and screws up his eyes at the magistrate incredulously.

"Well! How many years have all of us here in the village been unscrewing nuts, and the Lord's protected us; and here you talk about wrecks, killing people. If I'd carried off a rail or put a log in the way, then maybe the train might've gone off the track, but . . . ppfff! a nut!"

"But try to get it into your head that the nut holds the rail fast to the sleepers!"

"We understand that . . . We don't unscrew all of 'em . . . We leave some . . . We don't do things without using our heads . . . We understand."

Denis yawns and makes the sign of the cross over his mouth.

"Last year a train was derailed here," says the magistrate. "Now it's plain why!"

"Beg pardon?"

"I say that it's plain why the train was derailed last year . . . Now I understand!"

"That's what you're educated for, our protectors, to understand. The Lord knew to whom to give understanding . . . Here you've figured out how and what, but the watchman, a peasant like us, with no brains at all, he gets you by the collar and pulls you in. You should figure it out first and then pull people in. But it's known, a peasant has the brains of a peasant. . . . Write down, too, Your Honor, that he hit me twice on the jaw, and on the chest, too."

"When your house was searched they found another nut. . . . At what spot did you unscrew that, and when?"

"You mean the nut under the little red chest?"

"I don't know where you kept it, but it was found. When did you unscrew it?"

"I didn't unscrew it; Ignashka, one-eyed Semyon's son, he gave it to me. I mean the one that was under the chest, but the one that was in the sledge in the yard, that one Mitrofan and I unscrewed together."

"Which Mitrofan?"

"Mitrofan Petrov . . . Didn't you hear of him? He makes nets and sells them to the gentry. He needs a lot of those nuts. Reckon a matter of ten for every net."

"Listen. According to Article 1081 of the Penal Code, deliberate damage to a railroad, calculated to jeopardize the trains, provided the perpetrator of the damage knew that it might cause an accident—you understand? Knew! And you couldn't help knowing what this unscrewing might lead to—is punishable by hard labor."

"Of course, you know best . . . We're ignorant folk . . . What do we understand?"

"You understand all about it! You are lying, faking!"

"Why should I lie? Ask in the village if you don't believe me. Only bleak is caught without a sinker. And a gudgeon's no kind of fish, but even gudgeon won't bite without a sinker."

"Tell me about bullhead, now," says the magistrate with a smile.

"There ain't no bullhead in our parts. . . . If we cast our lines without a sinker, with a butterfly for bait, we can maybe catch a chub that way, but even that not often."

"Now, be quiet."

There is silence. Denis shifts from one foot to the other, stares at the table covered with green cloth, and blinks violently as though he were looking not at cloth but at the sun. The magistrate writes rapidly.

"Can I go?" asks Denis, after a silence.

"No. I must put you in custody and send you to prison."

Denis stops blinking and, raising his thick eyebrows, looks inquiringly at the official.

"What do you mean, prison? Your Honor! I haven't the time; I must go to the fair; I must get three rubles from Yegor for lard!"

"Be quiet; don't disturb me."

"Prison . . . If I'd done something, I'd go; but to go just for nothing! What for? I didn't steal anything, so far as I know, I wasn't fighting . . . If there's any question about the arrears, Your Honor, don't believe the elder . . . Ask the permanent member of the Board . . . the elder, he's no Christian."

"Be quiet."

"I'm quiet as it is," mutters Denis; "as for the elder, he's lied about the assessment, I'll take my oath on it . . . We're three brothers: Kuzma Grigoryev, then Yegor Grigoryev, and me, Denis Grigoryev."

"You're disturbing me . . . Hey, Semyon," cries the magistrate, "take him out."

"We're three brothers," mutters Denis, as two husky soldiers seize him and lead him out of the chamber. "A brother don't have to answer for a brother. Kuzma don't pay, so you, Denis, have to answer for it . . . Judges!

Our late master the general is dead—the Kingdom of Heaven be his!—or he'd have shown you judges what's what . . . You must have the know-how when you judge, not do it any which way . . . All right, flog a man, but justly, when it's coming to him."

1885

Daydreams

TWO rural constables—one a black-bearded stocky fellow with such extraordinarily short legs that if you look at him from the rear it seems as though they begin much lower down than other people's; the other, tall, lean, and straight as a stick, with a skimpy reddish beard—are taking to the county seat a tramp who has refused to give his name. The first waddles along, glances about, chews now a straw, now his own sleeve, slaps himself on the thighs, hums, and generally has a carefree, lighthearted air about him; the other, in spite of his gaunt face and narrow shoulders, looks solid, serious, and substantial; his whole appearance and the way he carries himself suggest a priest of the Old Believers' sect or a warrior in an ancient icon. "Forasmuch as he is wise, God hath added unto his brow"—in other words, he is bald—which increases the resemblance just mentioned. The name of the first is Andrey Ptaha, that of the second Nikandr Sapozhnikov.

The man they are escorting does not at all fit the usual conception of a tramp. He is a puny little man, feeble and sickly with small, colorless, extremely blurred features. His eyebrows are scanty, his expression gentle and submissive; he has hardly a trace of a mustache, although he is over thirty. He moves timidly, a hunched figure, his hands thrust into his sleeves. The collar of his threadbare cloth overcoat, which is not a peasant's, is turned up to the very edge of his cap, so that only his little red nose ventures to peep out into God's world. He speaks in a small, wheedling tenor and coughs continually. It is very, very hard to accept him as a tramp who is concealing his identity. He looks more like a priest's son, a poor devil of a fellow, reduced to beggary; a clerk sacked for drunkenness; a merchant's son or nephew who has tested his feeble powers on the stage and is now going home to play the last act in the parable of the prodigal son. Perhaps, to judge from the dull patience with which he is struggling against the impassable autumn mud, he is a fanatic, a novice, wandering from one Russian monastery to another, continually seeking "a life of peace that knoweth no sin" and not finding it. . . .

The men have been walking for a long time but they seem to be unable to leave one small patch of land. Before them stretch some thirty feet of road, black-brown and muddy, behind them is an identical stretch of road, and beyond, wherever one looks, there is an impenetrable wall of white fog. They walk on and on, but the ground remains the same, the wall is no nearer, and the patch is the same. Sometimes there floats past them a white, angular boulder, a gulley, or an armful of hay fallen from a passing cart; or a large, muddy puddle will gleam briefly, or, suddenly, a shadow with vague outlines will come into view ahead of them, growing smaller and darker as they approach, and finally there will loom before the wayfarers a slanting milestone with a half-effaced number on it, or a pitiful birch tree, drenched and bare as a wayside beggar. The little birch whispers something with what remains of its yellow leaves, one leaf breaks off and floats lazily to the ground. . . . And then once more, fog, mud, brown grass at the edges of the road. Dull, unkind tears hang on the grass. They are not the tears of quiet joy that the earth sheds on greeting the summer sun and on parting from it, not the tears that she gives the quails, corncrakes, and graceful, long-beaked curlews to drink at dawn. The wayfarers' feet stick in the heavy, clinging mud. Every step costs an effort.

Andrey Ptaha is somewhat agitated. He keeps staring at the tramp and trying to understand how a living, sober human being can fail to recall his own name.

"You are an Orthodox Christian, no?" he asks.

"I am that," the tramp answers meekly.

"Hm—then you were christened?"

"Why, sure! I'm no Turk. I go to church and take the sacrament and don't eat forbidden food on fast days. I don't neglect my religious duties none—"

"Well, what name do they call you by, then?"

"Call me what you please, mate."

Ptaha shrugs his shoulders and slaps himself on the thighs in extreme perplexity. The other constable, Nikandr Sapozhnikov, maintains a dignified silence. He is not so naive as Ptaha, and knows very well the reasons why an Orthodox Christian may wish to conceal his name from people. His expressive face is cold and stern. He walks apart and does not condescend to chatter idly with his companions, but tries to show everyone, as it were, even the fog, that he is staid and sensible.

"God knows what to make of you," Ptaha persists in pestering the tramp. "Peasant you ain't and gentleman you ain't, but something betwixt and between. The other day I was washing the sieves in the pond and I caught a viper—see, as long as a finger, with gills and a tail. At first I thought it was a fish, and then I looked—and damn the creature, if it hadn't paws! Maybe it was a fish, maybe it was a viper, the devil only knows what it was. Same with you. What are your folks?"

"I am a peasant, of peasant stock," the tramp sighs. "My dear mother was a house serf. True, I don't look like a peasant, but that was the way of it, my friend. My dear mother was a nurse to the master's children, and she had it very well, and I was her flesh and blood, so I lived with her in the big house. She took care of me and spoiled me and did all she could to raise me above my class and make something of me. I slept in a bed, I ate a regular dinner every day, I wore breeches and shoes like any gentleman's child. My dear mother fed me just what she ate; if they gave her material for a present, she made clothes for me out of it. What a life we had of it! I ate so much candy and cake when I was a child that if it could be sold now it would bring the price of a good horse. My dear mother taught me how to read and write, she put the fear of God in me when I was little, and she brought me up so that now I can't get myself to say an indelicate peasant word. And I don't drink vodka, mate, and I'm neat about my person, and I know how to behave properly in good society. If my dear mother is still living, God give her health; and if she has departed this life, then God rest her soul, and may she know peace in Thy kingdom, Lord, where the righteous are at rest."

The tramp bares his head with its scanty bristles, turns his eyes upward, and crosses himself twice.

"Grant her, O Lord, a green and peaceful resting-place," he says in a drawling voice, rather like an old woman's than a man's. "Instruct Thy servant, Xenia, in Thy ways, O Lord! If it had not been for my dear, darling mother I should have been a plain peasant with no understanding of anything! Now, mate, ask me what you like and I understand it all: the Holy Scriptures and profane writings, and every prayer and catechism. And I live according to the Scriptures, too. I don't harm anybody, I keep my body pure and chaste, I observe the fasts, I eat when it is proper. Another man takes no pleasure in anything but vodka and beastliness, but I, when I have time, I sit in a corner and read a book. I read and I cry and cry—"

"What do you cry about?"

"They write so pitifully! For some little book you pay no more than a five-kopeck piece, but how you weep and groan over it!"

"Is your father dead?" asks Ptaha.

"I don't know, mate. I don't know my father; it's no use hiding the sin. I judge that I was my dear mother's illegitimate child. My dear mother lived with the gentry all her life and she didn't want to marry a plain peasant—"

"And so she lit upon a master," Ptaha grins.

"She did not preserve her honor, that's true. She was pious and God-fearing, but she did not keep her maiden purity. Of course, it is a sin, a great sin, there's no doubt about it, but then, maybe there is noble blood in my veins. Maybe I am only a peasant by rank, but by nature I am a noble gentleman."

The "noble gentleman" says all this in a low, mawkish tenor voice, wrinkling up his narrow forehead and making creaking sounds with his red, frozen little nose. Ptaha listens and looks askance at him in wonder, and does not stop shrugging his shoulders.

After walking nearly four miles the constables and the tramp sit down on a hillock to rest.

"Even a dog knows his own name," mutters Ptaha.

"My name is Andryushka, his is Nikandr; every man has his holy name, and it can't be forgotten. Nohow!"

"Who has any need to know my name?" sighs the tramp, resting his cheek on his fist. "And what good would it do me if they did know it? If they let me go where I liked—but this way, it would be worse for me than it is now. I know the law, friends. Now I am one of those tramps who don't tell who they are, and the most they can do is exile me to Eastern Siberia and give me thirty or forty lashes; but if I told them my real name and rank they would send me back to hard labor, I know!"

"Why, were you a convict?"

"I was, dear friend. For four years I went about with my head shaved and irons on my legs."

"What for?"

"For murder, my good friend! When I was still a lad of about eighteen, my dear mother accidentally poured arsenic instead of soda and acid into the master's glass. There were powders of all sorts in the storeroom; it was easy to make a mistake."

The tramp sighs, shakes his head, and says:

"My mother was a pious woman, but who knows? The soul of another is a dark forest! Maybe it was an accident, and maybe she couldn't bear the humiliation of seeing the master make a favorite of another servant. Maybe she put it in on purpose, God alone knows! I was young then, and didn't understand everything. Now I remember that as a matter of fact our master did take another paramour and my dear mother was greatly distressed. Our trial lasted nearly two years. My dear mother was sentenced to twenty years of hard labor, and I, because of my youth, only to seven."

"And where did you come in?"

"As an accomplice. It was me handed the glass to the master. That was how it always was. My dear mother prepared the soda and I handed it to him. Only I'm telling you this, brothers, as Christian to Christian, as I would say it before God. And don't you go telling anybody—"

"Oh, nobody's going to ask us," says Ptaha. "So you've run away from hard labor, have you?"

"Yes, dear friend. Some fourteen of us ran away. They ran away, God bless them, and took me with them. Now answer me, on your conscience, mate, what reason have I to tell who I am? They'll send me back to hard labor, you know! And what sort of a convict am I! I'm a refined man, and not in the best of health. I like it clean where I sleep and eat. When I pray to God I like to light a little lamp or a candle, and not have a racket around me. When I bow down and touch the ground with my forehead, I don't like the floor to be dirty or covered with spittle. And for my dear mother's sake I bow down forty times morning and evening."

The tramp takes off his cap and crosses himself.

"Let them exile me to Eastern Siberia," he says. "I'm not afraid of that."

"Is that any better?"

"It's a different thing altogether. Doing hard labor you're like a lobster in a basket: there's crowding, crushing, jostling, no room to breathe; it's plain hell—may the Queen of Heaven deliver us from such hell! You're a criminal and treated like a criminal—worse than any dog. You can't eat, you can't sleep, or even say your prayers. But it's not like that in a colony of exiles. In such a settlement, first thing I do is join the community like the others. The authorities are bound by law to give me my allotment. Ye-es! They say the land is free there, like snow; take as much as you please! They'll give me

plow land, and land for a kitchen garden, and a building lot. . . . I'll plow my fields like other people, I'll
sow. I'll have cattle and all sorts of things, bees, sheep,
dogs—a Siberian cat, so that rats and mice don't eat up
my stores. I'll build a house, brothers, I'll buy icons—
Please God, I'll get married, and have children. . . ."

The tramp mumbles and looks away from his listeners.
Naive as his daydreams are, they are uttered in such a
sincere, heartfelt manner that it is hard not to credit
them. The tramp's little mouth is distorted by a smile.
His eyes, his little nose, his whole face, are set and
dazed with blissful anticipation of distant happiness.
The constables listen and look at him gravely, not without sympathy. They share his faith.

"I am not afraid of Siberia," the tramp goes on mumbling. "Siberia is Russia too, and has the same God and
Czar as here. They talk the language of Orthodox Christians, just like you and me. Only there's more free space
there and people are better off. Everything's better
there. The rivers there, for instance, are way better than
those we have here. And there's fish, and game, no end
of it all. And there's nothing in the world, brothers, that
I'd rather do than fish. Don't give me bread, just let me
sit with a hook and line, by God! I use a line and I set
creels and when the ice breaks then I take a casting-net.
If I'm not strong enough to handle the net, I hire a man
for five kopecks. And, Lord, what a pleasure it is! You
catch an eel-pout or a chub of some sort and are as
pleased as if you'd found your own brother. And let me
tell you, there's a special trick with every fish: you catch
one with a minnow, you catch another with a worm,
the third with a frog or a grasshopper. You have to understand all that, of course! Take the eel-pout, for instance. An eel-pout is a coarse fish—it will grab even
a perch; a pike loves a gudgeon, the bullhead likes a

butterfly. There's no greater pleasure than to fish for chub where the current is strong. You cast a seventy-foot line without a sinker, using a butterfly or a beetle, so that the bait floats on the surface; you stand in the water with your pants off and let it go with the current, and smack! the chub jerks it! Only you've got to be on the lookout that it doesn't snatch your bait away, the damned creature. As soon as it tugs at your line, you must give it a pull: don't wait. What a lot of fish I've caught in my time! When we ran away, the other convicts used to sleep in the forest; but I couldn't sleep, I made for the river. The rivers there are wide and rapid, the banks are steep—fearfully! And all along the banks there are dense forests. The trees are so tall that you get dizzy looking up to the top of them. At the prices timber brings here, every pine would fetch ten rubles."

Overwhelmed by the disorderly onrush of reveries, idealized images of the past, and sweet anticipations of happiness, the wretched fellow sinks into silence, merely moving his lips as though whispering to himself. A dazed, blissful smile never leaves his face. The constables are silent. They are sunk in thought, their heads bowed. In the autumn stillness, when the chill, sullen mist that hangs over the earth weighs upon the heart, when it looms like a prison wall before the eyes, and bears witness to the limited scope of man's will, it is sweet to think of broad, swift rivers, with steep banks open to the sky, of impenetrable forests, of boundless plains. Slowly and tranquilly imagination conjures up the picture of a man, early in the morning, before the flush of dawn has left the sky, making his way along the steep, lonely bank, looking like a tiny speck: age-old pines, fit for ships' masts, rise up in terraces on both sides of the torrent, gaze sternly at the free man and murmur menacingly; roots, huge boulders, and thorny bushes bar his way, but he is strong in body and bold in spirit, and fears neither the pine trees nor the boulders, nor his solitude, nor the reverberant echo that repeats the sound of his every footstep.

The constables picture to themselves a free life such as they have never lived; whether they vaguely remember scenes from stories heard long ago or whether they have inherited notions of a free life from remote free ancestors with their flesh and blood, God alone knows!

The first to break the silence is Nikandr Sapozhnikov, who until now has not uttered a single word. Whether he envies the tramp's illusory happiness, or whether he feels in his heart that dreams of happiness are out of keeping with the gray fog and the dirty brown mud—at all events, he looks grimly at the tramp and says:

"That's all right, to be sure, but you won't never get to them free lands, brother. How can you? You'd walk two hundred miles and you'd give up the ghost. Look, you're half dead already! You've hardly gone five miles and you can't get your breath."

The tramp turns slowly toward Nikandr, and his blissful smile vanishes. He looks with a scared and guilty air at the constable's sedate face, apparently remembers something, and lets his head drop. Silence falls again. All three are pensive. The constables are struggling to grasp with their imagination what can perhaps be grasped by none but God—that is, the vast expanse which separates them from the land of freedom. But the tramp's mind is filled with clear, distinct images more terrible than that expanse. He envisages vividly legal red tape and procrastinations, jails used as distributing centers and regular penal institutions, prison barracks, exhausting delays en route, cold winters, illnesses, deaths of comrades. . . .

The tramp blinks guiltily, passes his sleeve across his forehead that is beaded with tiny drops of sweat, and puffs hard as though he had just emerged from a steaming bathhouse, then wipes his forehead with his other sleeve and looks round timorously.

"That's a fact; you won't get there!" Ptaha agrees. "What kind of a walker are you, anyway? Look at you —nothing but skin and bone! You'll die, brother!"

"Sure he'll die. How can he help it?" says Nikandr. "They'll put him in the hospital straight off. Sure!"

The man who will not reveal his identity looks with horror at the stern, dispassionate faces of his sinister companions, and without removing his cap, hurriedly crosses himself, his eyes bulging. He trembles all over, shakes his head, and begins writhing, like a caterpillar that has been stepped on.

"Well, it's time to go," says Nikandr, getting to his feet; "we've had a rest."

A minute later the wayfarers are stepping along the muddy road. The tramp is more hunched than before, and his hands are thrust deeper into his sleeves. Ptaha is silent.

1886

Heartache

"To whom shall I tell my sorrow?" [1]

EVENING twilight. Large flakes of wet snow are circling lazily about the street lamps which have just been lighted, settling in a thin soft layer on roofs,

---

[1] From an old Russian song comparable to a Negro Spiritual.

horses' backs, peoples' shoulders, caps. Iona Potapov, the cabby, is all white like a ghost. As hunched as a living body can be, he sits on the box without stirring. If a whole snowdrift were to fall on him, even then, perhaps, he would not find it necessary to shake it off. His nag, too, is white and motionless. Her immobility, the angularity of her shape, and the sticklike straightness of her legs make her look like a penny gingerbread horse. She is probably lost in thought. Anyone who has been torn away from the plow, from the familiar gray scenes, and cast into this whirlpool full of monstrous lights, of ceaseless uproar and hurrying people, cannot help thinking.

Iona and his nag have not budged for a long time. They had driven out of the yard before dinnertime and haven't had a single fare yet. But now evening dusk is descending upon the city. The pale light of the street lamps changes to a vivid color and the bustle of the street grows louder.

"Sleigh to the Vyborg District!" Iona hears. "Sleigh!"

Iona starts, and through his snow-plastered eyelashes sees an officer in a military overcoat with a hood.

"To the Vyborg District!" repeats the officer. "Are you asleep, eh? To the Vyborg District!"

As a sign of assent Iona gives a tug at the reins, which sends layers of snow flying from the horse's back and from his own shoulders. The officer gets into the sleigh. The driver clucks to the horse, cranes his neck like a swan, rises in his seat and, more from habit than necessity, flourishes his whip. The nag, too, stretches her neck, crooks her sticklike legs and irresolutely sets off.

"Where are you barging in, damn you?" Iona is promptly assailed by shouts from the massive dark wavering to and fro before him. "Where the devil are you going? Keep to the right!"

"Don't you know how to drive? Keep to the right," says the officer with vexation.

A coachman driving a private carriage swears at him; a pedestrian who was crossing the street and brushed against the nag's nose with his shoulder, looks at him angrily and shakes the snow off his sleeve. Iona fidgets on the box as if sitting on needles and pins, thrusts out his elbows and rolls his eyes like a madman, as though he did not know where he was or why he was there.

"What rascals they all are," the officer jokes. "They are doing their best to knock into you or be trampled by the horse. It's a conspiracy."

Iona looks at his fare and moves his lips. He wants to say something, but the only sound that comes out is a wheeze.

"What is it?" asks the officer.

Iona twists his mouth into a smile, strains his throat and croaks hoarsely: "My son, sir . . . er, my son died this week."

"H'm, what did he die of?"

Iona turns his whole body around to his fare and says, "Who can tell? It must have been a fever. He lay in the hospital only three days and then he died. . . . It is God's will."

"Get over, you devil!" comes out of the dark. "Have you gone blind, you old dog? Keep your eyes peeled!"

"Go on, go on," says the officer. "We shan't get there until tomorrow at this rate. Give her the whip!"

The driver cranes his neck again, rises in his seat, and with heavy grace swings his whip. Then he looks around at the officer several times, but the latter keeps his eyes closed and is apparently indisposed to listen. Letting his fare off in the Vyborg District, Iona stops by a teahouse and again sits motionless and hunched on the box. Again the wet snow paints him and his nag white. One hour passes, another . . .

Three young men, two tall and lanky, one short and hunchbacked, come along swearing at each other and loudly pound the pavement with their galoshes.

"Cabby, to the Police Bridge!" the hunchback shouts in a cracked voice. "The three of us . . . twenty kopecks!"

Iona tugs at the reins and clucks to his horse. Twenty kopecks is not fair, but his mind is not on that. Whether it is a ruble or five kopecks, it is all one to him now, so long as he has a fare. . . . The three young men, jostling each other and using foul language, go up to the sleigh and all three try to sit down at once. They start arguing about which two are to sit and who shall be the one to stand. After a long ill-tempered and abusive altercation, they decide that the hunchback must stand up because he is the shortest.

"Well, get going," says the hunchback in his cracked voice, taking up his station and breathing down Iona's neck. "On your way! What a cap you've got, brother! You won't find a worse one in all Petersburg—"

"Hee, hee . . . hee, hee . . ." Iona giggles, "as you say—"

"Well, then, 'as you say,' drive on. Are you going to crawl like this all the way, eh? D'you want to get it in the neck?"

"My head is splitting," says one of the tall ones. "At the Dukmasovs' yesterday, Vaska and I killed four bottles of cognac between us."

"I don't get it, why lie?" says the other tall one angrily. "He is lying like a trouper."

"Strike me dead, it's the truth!"

"It is about as true as that a louse sneezes."

"Hee, hee," giggles Iona. "The gentlemen are feeling good!"

"Faugh, the devil take you!" cries the hunchback indignantly. "Will you get a move on, you old pest, or won't you? Is that the way to drive? Give her a crack of the whip! Giddap, devil! Giddap! Let her feel it!"

Iona feels the hunchback's wriggling body and quivering voice behind his back. He hears abuse addressed to him, sees people, and the feeling of loneliness begins little by little to lift from his heart. The hunchback swears till he chokes on an elaborate three-decker oath and is overcome by cough. The tall youths begin discussing a certain Nadezhda Petrovna. Iona looks round at them. When at last there is a lull in the conversation for which he has been waiting, he turns around and says: "This week . . . er . . . my son died."

"We shall all die," says the hunchback, with a sigh wiping his lips after his coughing fit. "Come, drive on, drive on. Gentlemen, I simply cannot stand this pace! When will he get us there?"

"Well, you give him a little encouragement. Biff him in the neck!"

"Do you hear, you old pest? I'll give it to you in the neck. If one stands on ceremony with fellows like you, one may as well walk. Do you hear, you old serpent? Or don't you give a damn what we say?"

And Iona hears rather than feels the thud of a blow on his neck.

"Hee, hee," he laughs. "The gentlemen are feeling good. God give you health!"

"Cabby, are you married?" asks one of the tall ones.

"Me? Hee, hee! The gentlemen are feeling good. The only wife for me now is the damp earth . . . Hee, haw, haw! The grave, that is! . . . Here my son is dead and me alive . . . It is a queer thing, death comes in at the wrong door . . . It don't come for me, it comes for my son. . . ."

And Iona turns round to tell them how his son died, but at that point the hunchback gives a sigh of relief and announces that, thank God, they have arrived at last. Having received his twenty kopecks, for a long while Iona stares after the revelers, who disappear into a dark entrance. Again he is alone and once more silence envelops him. The grief which has been allayed for a brief space comes back again and wrenches his heart more cruelly than ever. There is a look of anxiety and torment in Iona's eyes as they wander restlessly over the crowds moving to and fro on both sides of the street. Isn't there someone among those thousands who will listen to him? But the crowds hurry past, heedless of him and his grief. His grief is immense, boundless. If his heart were to burst and his grief to pour out, it seems that it would flood the whole world, and yet no one sees it. It has found a place for itself in such an insignificant shell that no one can see it in broad daylight.

Iona notices a doorkeeper with a bag and makes up his mind to speak to him.

"What time will it be, friend?" he asks.

"Past nine. What have you stopped here for? On your way!"

Iona drives a few steps away, hunches up and surrenders himself to his grief. He feels it is useless to turn to people. But before five minutes are over, he draws himself up, shakes his head as though stabbed by a sharp pain and tugs at the reins . . . He can bear it no longer.

"Back to the yard!" he thinks. "To the yard!"

And his nag, as though she knew his thoughts, starts out at a trot. An hour and a half later, Iona is sitting beside a large dirty stove. On the stove, on the floor, on benches are men snoring. The air is stuffy and foul. Iona looks at the sleeping figures, scratches himself and regrets that he has come home so early.

"I haven't earned enough to pay for the oats," he reflects. "That's what's wrong with me. A man that knows his job . . . who has enough to eat and has enough for his horse don't need to fret."

In one of the corners a young driver gets up, hawks sleepily and reaches for the water bucket.

"Thirsty?" Iona asks him.

"Guess so."

"H'm, may it do you good, but my son is dead, brother . . . did you hear? This week in the hospital. . . . What a business!"

Iona looks to see the effect of his words, but he notices none. The young man has drawn his cover over his head and is already asleep. The old man sighs and scratches himself. Just as the young man was thirsty for water so he thirsts for talk. It will soon be a week since his son died and he hasn't talked to anybody about him properly. He ought to be able to talk about it, taking his time, sensibly. He ought to tell how his son was taken ill, how he suffered, what he said before he died, how he died. . . . He ought to describe the funeral, and how he went to the hospital to fetch his son's clothes. His daughter Anisya is still in the country. . . . And he would like to talk about her, too. Yes, he has plenty to talk about now. And his listener should gasp and moan and keen. . . . It would be even better to talk to women. Though they are foolish, two words will make them blubber.

"I must go out and have a look at the horse," Iona thinks. "There will be time enough for sleep. You will have enough sleep, no fear. . . ."

He gets dressed and goes into the stable where his

horse is standing. He thinks about oats, hay, the weather. When he is alone, he dares not think of his son. It is possible to talk about him with someone, but to think of him when one is alone, to evoke his image is unbearably painful.

"You chewing?" Iona asks his mare seeing her shining eyes. "There, chew away, chew away. . . . If we haven't earned enough for oats, we'll eat hay. . . . Yes. . . . I've grown too old to drive. My son had ought to be driving, not me. . . . He was a real cabby. . . . He had ought to have lived. . . ."

Iona is silent for a space and then goes on: "That's how it is, old girl. . . . Kuzma Ionych is gone. . . . Departed this life. . . . He went and died to no purpose. . . . Now let's say you had a little colt, and you were that little colt's own mother. And suddenly, let's say, that same little colt departed this life. . . . You'd be sorry, wouldn't you?"

The nag chews, listens and breathes on her master's hands. Iona is carried away and tells her everything.

1886

An Encounter

YEFREM DENISOV anxiously looked round. He was tormented by thirst and he ached all over. His horse, who had not eaten for a long time and was miserable with the heat, drooped his head sadly. The road went downhill and disappeared in a vast forest of evergreens. The treetops in the distance merged with the blue of the sky, and above the deserted fields one could see nothing but birds lazily winging their way and a shimmering haze in the air. The forest, a green monster, climbed up a terraced hill, and seemed endless.

Yefrem was traveling about to collect money for the building of a church to replace the one that had burned down in his native village in the province of Kursk. In his cart was set up an icon of the Virgin of Kazan, its paint faded and peeling; before the image stood a capacious tin box with bent sides and a slit in the top large enough to admit a good-sized rye cake. A board nailed to the back of the cart bore an inscription stating that on such and such a date "by an act of God the flames of a conflagration had destroyed a church" in the village of Malinovtzy, and that the village meeting, with the sanction and blessing of the proper authorities, had resolved to dispatch volunteers to collect contributions for the building of a new church. At one side of the cart hung a twenty-pound bell.

Yefrem did not know where he was, and the forest, which swallowed the road, held out no promise of a settlement near by. He stood still for a while, adjusted the breeching, and then began to lead the horse cautiously downhill. The cart creaked and the bell rang out, breaking the silence of the sultry day.

In the woods the air was close and thick with the smell of resin, moss, and rotting needles. Nothing was to be heard except the twanging of gnats and Yefrem's muffled footsteps. The sunlight lay in patches on the tree trunks, the lower branches, and the dark earth strewn with needles. The ground was bare, except for the ferns and stone brambles showing here and there at the base of the trees.

"Hello, Daddy!" Yefrem suddenly heard a sharp, rasping voice. "Good luck to the traveler!"

Close to the road, his head propped on an ant-hill, lay a lanky peasant of about thirty wearing a cotton shirt and tight citified trousers tucked into reddish boots. Near his head was a cap that went with some uniform, now so faded that its original color could only be guessed from the spot that had once flaunted a cockade. The man did not lie still: all the while that Yefrem was looking at him, he kept jerking his arms and legs, as if attacked by gnats or suffering from the itch. But neither his garb nor his movements were as odd as his face. Yefrem had never seen such a face before. Pale, with a scanty beard, a jutting chin and a forelock, in profile it looked like the new moon; the nose and ears were strikingly small, the eyes had a fixed look that might have been one of imbecility or astonishment, and, to add to its oddity, the skull was flattened on the sides, so that the back of the head projected in a regular semicircle.

"Fellow Christian," Yefrem addressed him, "how far is it to the next village?"

"Not so far. Maloye ain't no more'n three or four miles from here."

"Am I dry!"

"Sure!" said the queer peasant, grinning. "It's a scorcher! Must be a hundred and twenty degrees or more. What's your name?"

"Yefrem, brother."

"Mine's Kuzma. As they say: Kuzma's my name, and great's my fame!"

Kuzma stepped on a wheel, thrust out his lips, and kissed the icon.

"Have you far to go?" he asked.

"Yes, fellow Christian. I was to Kursk and even to Moscow, and now I'm on my way to the fair at Nizhny."

"You're collecting for a church?"

"Just so, brother . . . for the Virgin of Kazan . . . Our church burned down!"

"How did that happen?"

Yefrem, articulating lazily, started telling how lightning struck the church at Malinovtzy on St. Elijah's day, while both the priest and the sexton and the peasants were in the fields.

"The boys who stayed in the village saw the smoke and wanted to ring the church bells, but Elijah the Prophet must have been wroth, the church was locked, and the whole belfry was in flames, so there was no getting at the bells. We came from the fields and, good Lord, the church was ablaze—it was terrible to go near it."

Kuzma strode alongside and listened. He was sober, but he walked as though he were drunk, waving his arms and tramping now beside the cart, now in front of it . . .

"And what do *you* get out of it? They pay you wages?" he asked.

"What wages? I am traveling for the salvation of my soul, the community sent me . . ."

"So you're traveling for nothing?"

"Who's to pay me wages? The community sent me, you know—they'll harvest my crops, sow the rye, pay the taxes for me . . . So it's not for nothing!"

"And how do you eat?"

"I beg my bread."

"And your gelding, does it belong to the community?"

"Why, yes."

"So, brother . . . You don't happen to have some tobacco on you?"

"I don't smoke, brother."

"And if your horse croaks, what will you do then? How will you travel?"

"Why should he croak? He don't need to do that."

"And if robbers go for you?"

And Kuzma inquired further, what would happen to the horse and the money if Yefrem himself died, where would people put their contributions if the box were suddenly filled, and what if the bottom of the box fell out, and so on. Yefrem, getting no chance to answer all these queries, merely panted and stared at his fellow traveler in wonder.

"What a pot-bellied box," Kuzma chattered on, prodding it with his fist. "Oho, it's heavy! Must be a mint of silver in it! Maybe there's nothing but silver in it. Listen, did you collect a lot?"

"I didn't count, I don't know. People put in coppers and silver, but how much—I don't look."

"And do they put in paper money too?"

"The better people, gentlefolk or merchants, they put in paper money."

"Well, do you keep that in the box too?"

"No, what for? Paper's soft, it may tear . . . I keep it in my bosom."

"And did you collect much paper?"

"About twenty-six rubles."

"Twenty-six rubles!" exclaimed Kuzma with a shrug of his shoulders. "At Kachabrov, ask anyone, they were building a church, and for the plans alone they paid three thousand rubles! Your money won't pay for the nails. Twenty-six rubles nowadays—why, that's chicken-feed! Nowadays you pay a ruble and a half for a pound of tea, and you can't even drink it . . . And look at the tobacco I smoke. It's all right for me, because I'm a peasant, a plain fellow, but an officer or a student . . ."

Kuzma suddenly struck his hands together and continued, smiling:

"A German from the railway was with us in the

lockup, and, would you believe it? he smoked cigars ten kopecks apiece! Ah-h! Ten kopecks apiece! Why, that way, grandfather, you can burn up a hundred rubles a month!"

Kuzma fairly choked at this agreeable recollection, and started blinking.

"They kept you in the lockup?" asked Yefrem.

"Sure enough," Kuzma answered and glanced at the sky. "They let me out two days ago. I was there a whole month."

Evening was coming on, the sun was setting, but it was still sultry. Yefrem was dead tired and scarcely listened to Kuzma. Finally they came upon a peasant who told them that they were within less than a mile of Maloye. And now the travelers were out of the woods and had emerged into an open meadow, where an animated scene opened up before them. The cart drove straight into a herd of cows, sheep, and tethered horses. Back of the pasture stretched green fields of rye and barley and a white patch of blossoming buckwheat, and farther on lay Maloye with a dark church that appeared flattened against the ground. Beyond the village loomed the forest, which now looked black.

"Here is Maloye!" said Kuzma. "The peasants are well-to-do, but they're robbers."

Yefrem took off his cap and rang the bell. Immediately two peasants came walking towards him from the well which was at the entrance to the village. Then began the usual queries: Where do you come from? Where are you bound for?

"Well, cousins, give the man of God a drink of water!" Kuzma started chattering, slapping now one, now the other on the shoulder. "Look lively!"

"How do we get to be cousins? How d'you make that out?"

"Haw-haw-haw! Your granny pulled my granddad by the hair, or so I'm told, because I wasn't there. That's how!"

While the cart was rolling through the village, Kuzma kept up his ceaseless chatter and rough-housed with everyone they met. He snatched one man's cap, rammed his fist into another's stomach, pulled a third by the beard. He called the women darling, dearie, mamasha, and addressed the men, according to their peculiarities, as Carrots, Tawny, Nosey, One-Eye, and the like. All this aroused lively, hearty laughter. Soon Kuzma found acquaintances. Greetings were heard: "Ah, Kuzma Rivet," "Hello, gallows bird!" "How long since you've been out of jail?"

"Hey, folks, give something to the man of God!" Kuzma cried, waving his arms. "Shake a leg! Look lively!"

He held himself with dignity and shouted as if he had taken the man of God under his wing or was his guide and mentor.

It was decided that Yefrem would spend the night at Grandmother Avdotya's, where those passing through the village usually stopped. Unhurriedly Yefrem took the horse out of the shafts and watered him at the well, where he spent half an hour talking to the peasants, then went indoors. Kuzma was waiting for him.

"Here you are!" the queer peasant rejoiced. "You're coming to the teahouse?"

"Tea would be fine," said Yefrem scratching himself, "fine, but I haven't any money, brother. Will you stand treat?"

"Me—treat? What with?"

Kuzma stood there a moment, disappointed, then sat down. Moving clumsily, sighing, and scratching himself, Yefrem placed the icon and the collection box under the holy images, undressed, took off his boots, sat about awhile, then got up and removed the box to a bench, sat down again and started eating. He chewed slowly, as a cow chews her cud, and sipped water noisily.

"The poverty!" Kuzma sighed. "Some vodka would be fine now, and tea . . ."

The evening light came feebly through the two windows. The village was already in deep shade, the cottages were somber; the church, merging into the darkness, seemed to grow wider and flatten itself more against the ground. A faint red gleam, apparently the reflection of the sunset, twinkled gently on the church cross. Having eaten, Yefrem sat motionless for a long time, his hands clenched on his knees, and stared at the windows. What was he thinking of? In the evening hush, when you see before you one dull window behind which the natural scene softly fades away, when the hoarse barking of strange dogs and the muffled squeaking of a strange accordion reaches your ear, it is difficult not to think of home. He who has been a wanderer, whom necessity or Fate or whim has separated from his kin, knows how long and wearisome an evening in the country among strangers can be.

Then Yefrem stood for a long time before his icon, praying. As he finally settled himself down on the bench to sleep, he sighed deeply and observed, as though reluctantly:

"You're a queer one . . . The Lord knows what sort you are . . ."

"What d'you mean?"

"Why, you don't look like a regular peasant . . . you clown, you wisecrack, and you've just come from the lockup."

"That don't matter! You'll even find fine gentlemen in the lockup sometimes . . . The lockup, brother, that's nothing, it don't matter, I can put in a whole year there, but if it's prison, that's bad! Tell you the truth, I've been in prison three times, and there ain't a week that I don't get a flogging at village headquarters . . . They're sore at me, damn 'em. The community's ready to deport me to Siberia. They've already passed a resolution."

"You're a fine one!"

"What do I care? In Siberia people live too."

"Your mother and father living?"

"Yes, they're living, they haven't croaked yet . . ."

"And what about honoring your father and mother?"

"Don't matter . . . If you ask me, they're my worst enemies. Who egged the community on against me? It's them and Uncle Stepan. Nobody else."

"Much you understand, you fool . . . The community don't need your uncle to see what sort you are. And why do the folks here call you gallows bird?"

"When I was little, our peasants nearly killed me. They hanged me by the neck on a tree, the damned brutes, but men from the next village were passing by and they saved me . . ."

"A dangerous member of society!" observed Yefrem and sighed.

Then he turned to the wall and was soon snoring.

When he woke up in the middle of the night to have a look at his horse, Kuzma was not in the house. A white cow stood at the wide-open door looking into the entry and knocking her horn against the jamb. The dogs were asleep. Somewhere in the distance, beyond the shadows a corn crake was calling in the stillness of the night, and the long-drawn-out sobbing hoot of an owl broke upon the quiet air.

And when he woke up for the second time at dawn,

Kuzma was sitting on a bench at the table, looking thoughtful. A drunken, blissful smile was frozen on his pale face. Rosy thoughts were roaming through his flattened skull and agitating him; he breathed fast, as though panting from a walk uphill.

"Ah, man of God!" he exclaimed, seeing that Yefrem was awake, and he grinned. "How would you like a white roll?"

"Where were you?" asked Yefrem.

"Hee, hee, hee!" Kuzma laughed foolishly. A dozen times he uttered this silly sound with his queer fixed grin, and then shook with convulsive laughter.

"I was drinking tea . . . tea," he brought out, still laughing, "I drank vo . . . vodka!"

And he started telling a long story about how he had been drinking tea and vodka with passing carters at the tavern, and as he talked, he kept pulling matches, tobacco, pretzels out of his pocket.

"Shwedish matches—no less! Psh!" he was saying, striking matches one after another and lighting a cigarette. "Shwedish matches, real ones! Look!"

Yefrem was yawning and scratching himself, but suddenly he jumped to his feet as though something bit him, lifted up his shirt and began feeling his bare chest, then, stomping about the bench like a bear, he went through his rags, looked under the platform, felt his chest again.

"The money is gone!" he exclaimed.

Yefrem stood awhile motionless and stared at the platform, then began searching again.

"Heavenly Mother, the money is gone! D'you hear?" he turned to Kuzma. "The money is gone!"

Kuzma was carefully examining the picture on the box of matches and held his peace.

"Where's the money?" asked Yefrem, taking a step toward him.

"What money?" drawled Kuzma in an offhand manner, scarcely opening his mouth and not taking his eyes off the box.

"The money . . . the money I kept in my bosom! . . ."

"Why pester me? If you've lost it, look for it!"

"Where can I look? Where is it?"

Kuzma glanced at Yefrem's purple face and grew purple himself.

"What money?" he shouted, jumping up.

"The money! The twenty-six rubles!"

"Have I taken it? He plagues me, the dirty dog!"

"Don't call me dirty dog! You tell me where the money is!"

"Did I take your money? Did I take it? You tell me: did I? When I get through with you, damn you and your money, you won't know your own father and mother!"

"If you didn't take it, why do you turn away your mug? It was you took it! Besides, where did you get the money to buy tobacco, and booze all night at the tavern? You're a foolish fellow, you're cracked. Is it me you done wrong? You done God wrong!"

"Did I . . . take it? When did I take it?" Kuzma shouted in a high squeaky voice, then he swung his arm and hit Yefrem on the face. "There you are! You want some more? I don't give a damn that you're a man of God!"

Yefrem merely shook his head and, without saying a word, began to pull on his boots.

"What a crook!" Kuzma went on shouting, getting more and more excited. "You drank up the money, and now you're blaming it on others, you dirty dog! I'll have the law on you! I'll see that you cool your heels in the lockup for trying to frame me!"

"You didn't take it, so keep quiet," Yefrem said mildly.

"Here, search me!"

"If you didn't take it . . . why should I search you? You didn't take it, well and good . . . No use shouting, you cannot shout down God . . ."

Yefrem put on his boots and went outdoors. When he returned, Kuzma, still flushed, was sitting at the window, lighting a cigarette with trembling hands.

"The old devil," he grumbled. "There's plenty of your sort riding about, plaguing people. You've come to the wrong man, brother! You won't pull the wool over my eyes! I know all these tricks myself. Send for the Elder!"

"What for?"

"To draw up charges! We'll go to the courthouse. Let them judge between us!"

"Why should they judge between us! It's not my money, it's God's . . . God will do the judging."

Yefrem said his prayers and, taking the box and the icon, left the cottage.

An hour later the cart was entering the forest. The village with its flattened church, the meadow, and patches of rye were already left behind, wrapped in light morning mist. The sun had risen, but it was still hidden by the forest and only gilded the edges of the clouds facing eastward. Kuzma followed the cart at some distance. He looked like an innocent man who had been terribly wronged. He wanted very much to talk, but kept quiet, waiting for Yefrem to begin.

"I don't want to have a row with you, or you'd get it from me," he dropped, as though talking to himself. "I'd show you what comes of trying to frame people, you bald devil . . ."

Another half-hour passed in silence. The man of God, who was saying his prayers as he walked, started crossing himself rapidly, drew a deep sigh and climbed into the cart to fetch some bread.

"When we get to Telibeyevo," began Kuzma, "our justice of the peace lives there. Hand your complaint to him!"

"You're talking rot. What's the justice of the peace to do with it? Is it his money? It's God's money. You're answerable to God."

"You keep on saying God's! God's! Like a crow. If I stole it, let them try me; if I didn't steal it, you should get it in the neck for false charges."

"I got no time to hang around courts!"

"So you don't care about the money?"

"Why should I care? It ain't my money, it's God's."

Yefrem spoke reluctantly, calmly, and his face wore a dispassionate, unconcerned expression, as if he really did not care about this money or had forgotten the theft. Such indifference toward the loss and the crime seemed to nonplus and irritate Kuzma. It was incomprehensible to him. It is natural when an offense is countered by cunning or force, when it leads to a struggle which turns the offender into one offended. If Yefrem had acted like an ordinary human being, that is, if he had taken umbrage, started a fight, lodged a complaint, if the justice of the peace had sentenced the accused to prison or dismissed the charge against him for lack of evidence, Kuzma would have quieted down. But now, as he walked behind the cart, he had the look of a man who missed something.

"I didn't take your money!" he said.

"You didn't take it, so well and good."

"When we get to Telibeyevo, I'll call the Elder. Let him . . . look into the matter . . ."

"There's nothing to look into. It ain't his money. And you'd better take yourself off, brother. Go your ways! I've had enough of you!"

For a long time Kuzma kept casting sidelong glances at Yefrem, trying to guess what he was thinking about, what terrible plot he was hatching, and finally he decided to tack about.

"Hey, you peacock, there's no having any fun with you, you get sore so easy. Here, here, take your money! It was a joke."

Kuzma drew several ruble bills from his pocket and handed them to Yefrem. The latter was neither surprised nor gladdened. It was as though he expected it. He took the money and, without a word, stuck it in his pocket.

"I just wanted to have some fun with you," Kuzma continued, looking searchingly into Yefrem's dispassionate face. "I reckoned it would scare you. I thought I'd give you a scare and return the money in the morning . . . Altogether there was twenty-six rubles, and I just gave you ten, or nine. The carters took the rest . . . Don't be sore, grandfather . . . It wasn't me drank it up, but them . . . I swear to God!"

"Why should I be sore? It's God's money . . . It wasn't me you wronged, but the Queen of Heaven."

"Maybe I drunk up a ruble, no more."

"What's that to me? Take it and drink it all up . . . A ruble, a kopeck—it's all the same to God. You'll have to answer for it just the same."

"But don't get sore, grandfather. Please don't get sore! Don't!"

Yefrem said nothing. Kuzma began blinking and his face assumed a childishly tearful expression.

"Forgive me, for Christ's sake!" he said, looking im-

ploringly at the back of Yefrem's neck. "Don't take offense, uncle. I was joking."

"Oh, you're plaguing me!" said Yefrem with irritation. "I'm telling you: it's not my money! Pray to God he
should forgive you, it's none of my business!"

Kuzma gazed at the icon, at the sky, at the trees,
looking for God, as it were, and an expression of terror
distorted his face. Under the influence of the forest silence, the icon with its austere colors, and Yefrem's dispassionate attitude, which was so unusual and inhuman,
he felt alone, helpless, abandoned to the mercies of a
terrible, wrathful Deity. He ran in front of Yefrem and
looked into his eyes, as though to assure himself that
he was not alone.

"Forgive me, for Christ's sake!" he said, beginning
to tremble all over. "Forgive me, grandfather!"

"Go away!"

Once more Kuzma cast a rapid glance at the sky, the
trees, the cart with the icon, and then sank at Yefrem's
feet. In his terror he mumbled incoherently, struck the
ground with his forehead, clasped the old man's feet,
and wept aloud like a child.

"Granddaddy! Kinsman! Uncle! Man of God!"

At first Yefrem recoiled from him perplexed, and
pushed him away, but then he himself started glancing
fearfully at the sky. He was frightened, and he felt pity
for the thief.

"Stop, brother, listen!" he said persuasively to Kuzma.
"Listen to what I tell you, you fool! Eh, he blubbers
like a woman! Listen, if you want God to forgive you:
as soon as you get home, go to the priest right away
. . . D'you hear me?"

Yefrem began to explain to Kuzma what to do to
atone for his sin: he must confess to the priest, lay a

penance on his soul, then get together the money he
had stolen and drunk up and send it to Malinovtzy, and
in future he must lead a quiet, honest, sober, Christian
life. Kuzma heard him out, calmed down little by little,
and appeared to have forgotten his trouble completely.
He teased Yefrem, and began chattering again. Without
stopping for a moment, he went on talking about people who lived at ease, about the lockup and the German
there, about prison, in a word, about all the things of
which he had talked the previous day. He guffawed,
struck his hands together, recoiled reverently, and altogether behaved as though he were recounting something new. He spoke smoothly, like a man who had
been around, peppering his talk with saws and sayings,
but it was painful to listen to him, because he repeated
himself and often stopped to recall a suddenly forgotten
thought, and then he would knit his brow, spin about
like a top and wave his arms. And how he bragged,
how he lied!

At noon, when the cart stopped at Telibeyevo,
Kuzma disappeared in the pot-house. Yefrem rested for
about two hours and all that time Kuzma stayed in the
pot-house. One could hear him swearing in there and
bragging, pounding the bar with his fist, and the drunken
peasants jeering at him. And when Yefrem was leaving
Telibeyevo, a brawl had started in the pot-house, and
Kuzma was shrilly threatening someone and shouting
that he would send for the police.

1887

The Letter

ARCHDEACON Fyodor Orlov, a presentable, well-nourished man of fifty, with an expression of self-importance, severity, and dignity that never left his face, but now looking exceedingly weary, was pacing his small living room from one end to the other and thinking hard about the same thing: "When would his visitor finally leave?" This thought fretted him and stayed with him all the time. The visitor, Father Anastasy, whose parish was a village not far from the city, had come to call on him some three hours before on a very unpleasant and tedious business of his own, had stayed on and was now seated at a small round table in the corner with his elbow on a thick account book, apparently with no thought of leaving, although it was already past eight in the evening.

Not everyone knows how to stop talking in good time and how to leave in good time. Not seldom it happens that even tactful, well-bred people who have had a secular education fail to notice that their presence is arousing a feeling resembling hatred in a tired or busy host and that this feeling is being laboriously concealed and covered up with a lie. Yet Father Anastasy perceived plainly that his presence was burdensome and out of place, that the archdeacon, who had officiated at a night service and at a long noonday Mass, was now tired and longing for rest; every moment he meant to get up and go, but he didn't get up, he sat on, as though waiting for something. He was an old man of sixty-five, prematurely decrepit, stooped and bony, with a senile, dark-skinned, emaciated face, red eyelids, and a long, narrow back like that of a fish. He wore a fashionable cassock, pale lilac in color, but too large for him (it had been presented to him by the widow of a recently deceased young priest), a cloth jacket with a broad leather belt, and clumsy boots the size and color of which showed plainly that Father Anastasy got along without galoshes. In spite of his rank and advanced years, there was a suggestion of something pitiful, humbled, and crushed about his red, clouded eyes, the thin greenish-gray plaits of hair on his nape, the prominent shoulder blades of his lean back . . . He held his peace, did not move, and coughed with caution, as if afraid that the noise of his coughing would render his presence more noticeable.

The old man had come to the archdeacon several times on business. Some two months previously he had been forbidden to officiate till further notice and been subjected to judicial investigation. His transgressions were numerous. He was addicted to drink, was on bad terms with the clergy and the laity, was negligent in recording vital statistics and keeping the church accounts —these were the formal charges against him. In addition, it had long been rumored that he performed illegal marriages for a consideration and sold certificates of the performance of religious duties to officials and army officers who came to him from the city. These rumors persisted all the more stubbornly since he was poor and had nine children who depended on him and were failures like himself. His sons were spoiled, uneducated, and without occupation, and his homely daughters could find no husbands.

Lacking the force to be frank, the archdeacon paced

the room from one end to the other, was silent, or else threw out hints:

"So you are not driving home tonight?" he asked, stopping at the dark window and poking his little finger into the cage where a canary was asleep with its feathers fluffed up.

Father Anastasy gave a start, coughed cautiously and spoke hurriedly:

"Home? No, I'm not going there, Fyodor Ilyich. You know yourself, I cannot officiate, so what am I to do there? I went away on purpose, so as not to have to look people in the face. You know yourself, it is a disgrace not to be allowed to officiate. Besides, I have business here, Fyodor Ilyich. Tomorrow after breaking fast I want to have a long talk with the Father who is investigating my case."

"So . . ." the archdeacon yawned. "And where are you stopping?"

"At Zyavkin's."

Father Anastasy suddenly recalled that in about two hours the archdeacon was to officiate at the Easter midnight service and he felt so keenly ashamed of his disagreeable, embarrassing presence that he decided to leave at once and give the tired man a rest. And the old man got up to leave, but before starting to say his farewells, he stood a while clearing his throat and looking inquiringly at the archdeacon's back with the same air of indefinite expectation in his entire frame; his face was contorted with shame, timidity, and the pathetic forced smile of people who do not respect themselves. With a resolute wave of his hand and a husky, jarring laugh he brought out:

"Father Fyodor, let your graciousness go a little further: have them give me at parting . . . just a little wee glass of vodka!"

"This isn't the time to drink vodka," said the arch-deacon sternly. "One must have a sense of propriety."

Father Anastasy was greatly embarrassed. He gave a laugh and, forgetting his decision to leave, sat down again. The archdeacon glanced at his abashed, embarrassed face and his stooped body and felt sorry for the old man.

"Please God, we will drink tomorrow," he said, wishing to soften his harsh refusal. "Everything in good time."

The archdeacon believed that people could reform, but now, as a feeling of pity rose within him, it seemed to him that this disreputable, hollow-cheeked old man, caught in a network of sins and infirmities, was lost beyond all hope, that there was no power on earth that could straighten his back, give serenity to his look, check the disagreeable timid laugh that he laughed on purpose, in order to counteract at least a little the repulsive impression he made on people. Already the old man seemed to Father Fyodor not guilty and vicious, but humiliated, insulted, unfortunate; he recalled the man's wife, his nine children, the dirty beggarly bed at Zyavkin's; for some reason he also recalled the people who take pleasure in seeing priests drunk and officials convicted of crimes, and it occurred to him that the best thing Father Anastasy could do now was to die as soon as possible and to depart this life forever.

Steps were heard.

"Father Fyodor, you are not resting?" a bass voice came from the anteroom.

"No, deacon, come in."

Into the room walked Father Orlov's colleague, deacon Lubimov, an old man with a bald patch extending over the entire top of his head, but still vigorous, with a fringe of black hair and with bushy black eyebrows like a Georgian's. He bowed to Father Anastasy and sat down.

"What good news have you brought us?"

"What good news?" replied the deacon, and after a pause continued with a smile: "Small children—small troubles; big children—big troubles. Here's such a kettle of fish, Father Fyodor, that I don't know where I'm at. A regular farce, that's what it is."

He paused again, smiled even more broadly and said:

"Nikolay Matveich has just come back from Kharkov. He was telling me about my Pyotr. He went to see him once or twice, he said."

"What has he been telling you, then?"

"He has upset me, God forgive him. He meant to give me joy, but when I thought it over, I found there wasn't much to rejoice over. There is more cause for grief than for joy. 'Your Petrushka,' says he, 'lives in style, he's way beyond our reach,' says he. 'Well, thank God for that,' says I. 'I had dinner with him,' says he, 'and saw the way he lives. He lives like the gentry. You couldn't want anything better.' Of course, I'm curious and I ask him: 'And what did they serve for dinner?' 'First of all, there was a fish course, something like a chowder, then tongue with peas, and then,' says he, 'roast turkey.' 'Roast turkey in Lent? That's something to rejoice me!' says I. Turkey in Lent, eh?"

"There's little surprising about that," said the arch-deacon, narrowing his eyes sarcastically.

And inserting both thumbs in his belt, he drew himself up and declaimed in the tone in which he preached sermons or gave lessons in religion at the high school:

"People who do not keep the fasts fall into two different categories: some fail to keep them out of laxity, others through unbelief. Your Pyotr fails to keep them through unbelief. Yes."

The deacon looked timidly at Father Fyodor's stern face and said:

"That isn't the worst of it . . . We talked about this and that and it turned out that my infidel of a son is living with some sort of a lady, another man's wife. There she is in his lodgings, taking the place of a wife and a hostess, she pours out the tea, receives guests and all that sort of thing, like a wedded wife. It is the third year now that he has been making merry with this viper. A regular farce, that's what it is. Three years together and no children."

"So they must be living in chastity!" giggled Father Anastasy, coughing hoarsely. "There are children, Father Deacon, there are, but they are not kept at home! They're packed off to the Foundling Hospital! Hee-hee-hee . . ." (Here Father Anastasy had a coughing fit.)

"Don't meddle, Father Anastasy," the archdeacon said sternly.

"Nikolay Matveich asks him: 'Who's this lady who dishes out the soup at your table?'" the deacon continued, gloomily examining Father Anastasy's stooped body. " 'She is my wife,' says he. 'And how long ago were you married?' Nikolay Matveich inquires. 'We were married in Kulikov's pastry shop,' Pyotr answers."

The archdeacon's eyes flashed angrily and there were red spots on his temples. He disliked Pyotr not only because of his sins but because he found him personally repellent. In fact, Father Fyodor had a grudge against him. He remembered him as a schoolboy, remembered him distinctly, because even then the boy had seemed to him abnormal. He had been ashamed to help at the altar, had taken offense at being addressed familiarly, had not crossed himself on entering the house, and what was most memorable, had liked to talk a great deal and heatedly, and in Father Fyodor's opinion loquacity was unseemly in and harmful to children. Furthermore, Petrushka had assumed a critical and contemptuous attitude toward fishing, to which both the archdeacon and the deacon were much addicted. As a student Pyotr had not gone to church at all, had slept until noon, had looked down on people, and had taken pleasure in raising ticklish and insoluble questions with an air of bravado.

"What do you want?" the archdeacon said, going up to the deacon and looking at him angrily. "What do you want? This was to be expected! I always knew that nothing good would come of your Pyotr, was certain of it! I told you so and I am telling you so again. What you sowed, now you must reap! Reap!"

"But what have I sown, Father Fyodor?" the deacon asked quietly, looking up at the archdeacon.

"Who but you is to blame? You are the parent, he is your offspring! You should have instructed him, instilled the fear of God in him. You must teach them! You bring them into the world, but you don't instruct them. It's a sin! It is wrong! It's a disgrace!"

The archdeacon forgot his fatigue, paced the room and continued to talk. Fine drops of sweat came out on the deacon's forehead and bare pate. He looked guiltily at the archdeacon and said:

"But didn't I instruct him, Father Fyodor? Lord have mercy, haven't I been a father to my child? You know yourself I refused him nothing, and all my life I prayed to God and I did my best to give him a good education. He went to high school and had tutors and graduated from the university. As for my failing to direct his mind the right way, Father Fyodor, why, that is because I haven't the ability, as you well know! When he used to come home as a student, I would begin to instruct him in my own way, but he wouldn't listen. I would say to

him: 'Go to church,' and he would snap back: 'Why?'
I would start explaining, and he'd say: 'Why? What
for?' Or he would clap me on the shoulder and say:
'Everything in this world is relative, approximate, and
conditional. Neither I nor you know anything, papasha.' "

Father Anastasy laughed huskily, had another coughing spell and wagged his fingers in the air as though
getting ready to say something. The archdeacon glanced
at him and said severely:

"Don't meddle, Father Anastasy."

The old man laughed, beamed, and listened to the
deacon with apparent pleasure, as though glad that there
were other sinners in this world besides himself. The
deacon spoke sincerely, out of a contrite heart, and tears
even came into his eyes. Father Fyodor felt sorry for
him.

"You're to blame, deacon, you're to blame," he said,
but not so sternly and vehemently. "You knew how to
bring him into the world, you should know how to instruct him. You should have taught him in his childhood; who's to reform a student?"

Silence fell. The deacon struck his hands together and
said with a sigh:

"But I shall have to answer for him, you know."

"True enough."

After a short pause the archdeacon gave a yawn that
turned into a sigh and asked:

"Who reads The Acts?"

"Yevstrat. Yevstrat always reads that."

The deacon got up and, looking imploringly at the
archdeacon, asked:

"So, Father Fyodor, what am I to do now?"

"Do as you please. You are the father, not I. You
ought to know best."

"I don't know anything, Father Fyodor! Tell me what

I am to do, for pity's sake! Would you believe me, I am heartsick! I am in a state now where I can neither sleep nor sit quietly, and the holiday is no holiday for me. Tell me what to do, Father Fyodor!"

"Write him a letter."

"What shall I write to him?"

"Write him that this must come to an end. Write briefly, but severely, and take due note of everything, without minimizing or extenuating his guilt. It is your parental duty. Once you've written, you will have done your duty and you will be at peace."

"That's true, but what shall I write to him? In what terms? I will write to him, and he will come back at me: 'Why? What for? Why is it a sin?'"

Father Anastasy again laughed huskily and wagged his fingers.

"Why? What for? Why is it a sin?" he wheezed. "I was once confessing a gentleman and I told him that excessive reliance on Divine mercy is a sin, and he asked: 'Why?' I wanted to answer him, but—" Father Anastasy slapped himself on the forehead, "there was nothing here! Hee-hee-hee—"

Father Anastasy's words, his husky, quivering laughter at something that was not laughable, made a disagreeable impression on the archdeacon and the deacon. The archdeacon was on the point of cutting the old man short with a "don't meddle," but did not do so, and merely frowned.

"I cannot write to him!" sighed the deacon.

"If you can't, who can?"

"Father Fyodor!" said the deacon, putting his head to one side and pressing his hand to his heart. "I am an uneducated man, with a poor mind, but you the Lord has endowed with intelligence and wisdom. You know and understand everything, you have a mind that can fathom anything, while I'm not able to put two words together. Be charitable, instruct me as to how I am to go about writing. Tell me how to phrase it and just what to say . . ."

"What is there to instruct you in? There is no question of instruction. You simply sit down and write."

"No, do me the favor, Father! I implore you. I know, your letter will put the fear of God in him and command his obedience, because you, too, are an educated man. Be so kind! I'll sit down and you dictate to me. Tomorrow it will be a sin to write, but now is just the time, and then my mind would be at peace?"

The archdeacon looked at the deacon's beseeching face, recalled the refractory Pyotr and agreed to dictate. He seated the deacon at his desk and began:

"Well, write . . . 'Christ is risen, my dear son . . .' exclamation mark. 'Rumors have reached your father's ear . . .' then in parentheses: 'from what source they came to me does not concern you . . .' close parentheses . . . Have you written? '. . . that you are leading a life incompatible with the laws of both God and man. Neither the creature comforts, nor the worldly magnificence, nor again the show of culture with which you cover yourself outwardly can conceal your heathenishness. You call yourself a Christian, but in essence you are a heathen, as wretched and miserable as all other heathens, nay, more wretched, for those other heathens, not knowing Christ, go to perdition out of ignorance, whereas you go to perdition because, possessing a treasure, you neglect it. I shall not enumerate your vices here, these being well known to you; I shall only say that I see the cause of your perdition in your unbelief. You consider yourself to be wise, you boast of your knowledge of the sciences, but you do not wish to understand that science without faith not only fails to elevate man, but in fact degrades him to the level of a low animal, forasmuch . . .'"

The whole letter was couched in these terms. Having finished writing, the deacon read it aloud, beamed, and jumped to his feet.

"A gift, verily a gift!" he exclaimed, looking rapturously at the archdeacon and striking his hands together. "To think that the Lord bestows such a talent on man! Eh? Holy Mother and Queen of Heaven! I believe that I could not have written a letter like that in a hundred years! May the Lord preserve you!"

Father Anastasy, too, was enraptured.

"It's a gift to be able to write like that!" he said, getting up and wagging his fingers.

"To write like that! There is such rhetoric here as would stump any philosopher, and would make him see stars! A mind! A brilliant mind! If you hadn't married, Father Fyodor, you would have been a bishop long ago, verily you would!"

Having poured out his wrath in the letter, the archdeacon felt relieved. Fatigue, the feeling of being fagged out came back. The deacon was an intimate and so Father Fyodor did not scruple to say to him:

"Well, deacon, go now, and God be with you. I'll nap for half an hour, I must have a rest."

The deacon went away and took Anastasy with him. As always happens on Easter eve, the street was dark, but the entire sky was sparkling with bright, shining stars. The soundless, motionless air was redolent of spring and holiday.

"How long did he dictate?" the deacon continued to voice his admiration. "Some ten minutes, no more! Another person wouldn't have composed a letter like that in a month. Eh? What an intellect! I have no words for such an intellect! A marvel! Verily, a marvel!"

"Education!" sighed Anastasy as he crossed the muddy street, lifting his cassock up to his belt. "We are not to be compared with him. We come of the lowest order of the clergy, while he is a man of learning. Yes. He's a real man, there's no gainsaying it."

"And you ought to hear how he reads the Gospel in Latin at Mass! He knows Latin and he knows Greek. . . . Ah, Petruha, Petruha!" the deacon exclaimed, suddenly brought back to his problem. "Well, now he'll scratch his head! He'll shut his mouth! He'll find out what's what! Now he won't ask: 'Why?' He has met his match, he has indeed! Ha-ha-ha!"

The deacon burst out into gay, loud laughter. As soon as the letter was written his spirits had risen and he had grown serene. The consciousness of having done his parental duty and his faith in the efficacy of the letter had restored his gaiety and good-nature.

"Pyotr in translation means 'a stone,'" he said, as they were approaching his house. "But my Pyotr is not a stone, he is a rag. The viper has laid hold of him, and he pets her and hasn't the strength to cast her off. Fie! To think that there should be such women, God forgive me for mentioning them! Eh? Has she no shame? She has got hold of the boy, she won't let go of him and keeps him trailing after her. . . . To the dickens with her!"

"Maybe, though, it isn't she who holds on to him, but he to her?"

"Still, it means she's a Jezebel! I am not defending Pyotr. He'll get what's coming to him. He'll read the letter, and he'll scratch the back of his neck! He'll burn up with shame!"

"It's a fine letter, only . . . maybe you shouldn't send it off, Father Deacon. Let Pyotr be!"

"What's that?" asked the deacon, scared.

"Just so! Don't send it, deacon! What's the good of it? You'll send it, he'll read it, and then what? You'll only upset him. Forgive him, let him be!"

The deacon looked in surprise at Anastasy's dark face, at his open cassock which looked like wings in the night, and shrugged his shoulders.

"How can I forgive him just like that?" he asked. "I shall have to answer for him to God, you know."

"Even so, you forgive him, all the same. Really! And because of your loving kindness God will forgive you, too."

"But isn't he my son? Is it my duty to teach him, or not?"

"Teach him? Why not? You may teach him; but why call him a heathen? That will hurt his feelings, deacon, you know—"

The deacon was a widower and lived in a small house with three windows. His housekeeping was done by his sister, a spinster who had lost the use of her legs three years previously and was bedridden. He was afraid of her, complied wholly with her wishes, and did nothing without her advice. Father Anastasy went into the house with the deacon. Seeing the table already set with the tall Easter cakes and Easter eggs, and perhaps remembering his own home, he began to weep and, to cover his tears, at once started laughing huskily.

"Yes, it will soon be time to break fast," he said. "Yes . . . It would not come amiss . . . to take a wee glass even now. May I? I'll down it," he whispered, stealing a glance at the door, "so that the old one in there . . . won't hear a thing . . . no, no . . ."

The deacon silently shoved the decanter and the glass toward Father Anastasy, unfolded the letter, and began to read it aloud. The letter pleased him just as much as it had when the archdeacon was dictating it. He beamed with satisfaction and wagged his head as though he had just savored something very sweet.

"Well, what a letter!" he said. "Petruha never can have dreamt of such a letter. Just what he needs, something to throw him into a fever . . . the very thing!"

"You know what, deacon? Don't send it!" said Anastasy, pouring out another glass with seeming absent-mindedness. "Forgive him, let him be! I am speaking to you . . . from the heart. If his own father will not forgive him, who will? And is he to live so, unforgiven? Figure it out for yourself, deacon: there will be enough to mete out punishment without you, but you'd better seek out those who will show mercy to your own son! I'll . . . I'll . . . just have another little one, brother . . . the last . . . Now you just sit down and write to him: 'I forgive you, Pyotr!' He'll understa-and! He'll fee-eel it! I know it from my own experience, brother . . . deacon, I mean. When I lived like other people there was little to fret me, but now that I have betrayed the image and likeness of God, all I crave is that good people should forgive me. Judge for yourself, it isn't the righteous that should be forgiven, but the sinners. Why should you forgive the old one in there, if she is no sinner? No, you should forgive a man who is a pitiful sight . . . that's it."

Anastasy propped his head on his fist and grew thoughtful.

"It is dreadful, deacon," he sighed, obviously struggling with the desire to have another drink. "Dreadful! In sin my mother brought me into the world, in sin I lived, in sin I shall die . . . Lord forgive me, sinner that I am. I have strayed from the path, deacon! I am beyond salvation! And it isn't as though I had strayed from the path in the prime of life, but in my old age, on the brink of the grave . . . I . . ."

With a hopeless wave of the hand the old man drank one more glass, then went and sat down in another chair. The deacon, still clutching the letter, started pacing the room. He was thinking of his son. Dissatisfaction, sorrow, and anxiety no longer fretted him: all that had vented itself in the letter. Now he was simply calling up the image of Pyotr, picturing his face, remembering the years when his son would come home for the holidays. His mind dwelt only on what was good, heartwarming, touched with melancholy, on what one could contemplate for a lifetime without getting tired. Missing his son, he read the letter through once more and looked questioningly at Anastasy.

"Don't send it!" said the latter, with a wave of the hand.

"No, all the same . . . I must. All the same, it will . . . I mean . . . have a good effect on him . . . It can't hurt . . ."

The deacon got an envelope from a drawer, but before placing the letter in it, he sat down at the table, smiled, and added these words of his own at the bottom of the letter: "They have sent us a new school supervisor. He is spryer than the old one. He is a dancer, a talker, and a jack-of-all-trades, so that the Govorov girls are wild about him. The army chief Kostyrev, too, will soon be sent packing, they say. High time!" Well pleased with himself, and not realizing that his postscript had completely spoiled the stern missive, he addressed the envelope and laid the letter in the most conspicuous place on the table.

1887

The Kiss

AT EIGHT o'clock on the evening of the twentieth of May all the six batteries of the N—— Reserve Artillery Brigade halted for the night in the village of Mestechki on their way to camp. At the height of the general commotion, while some officers were busily occupied around the guns, and others, gathered together in the square near the church enclosure, were receiving the reports of the quartermasters, a man in civilian dress, riding a queer horse, came into sight round the church. The little dun-colored horse with a fine neck and a short tail came, moving not straight forward, but as it were sideways, with a sort of dance step, as though it were being lashed about the legs. When he reached the officers the man on the horse took off his hat and said:

"His Excellency Lieutenant-General von Rabbeck, a local landowner, invites the officers to have tea with him this minute. . . ."

The horse bowed, danced, and retired sideways; the rider raised his hat once more and in an instant disappeared with his strange horse behind the church.

"What the devil does it mean?" grumbled some of the officers, dispersing to their quarters. "One is sleepy, and here this von Rabbeck with his tea! We know what tea means."

The officers of all the six batteries remembered vividly an incident of the previous year, when during maneuvers they, together with the officers of a Cossack regi-

ment, were in the same way invited to tea by a count
who had an estate in the neighborhood and was a retired army officer; the hospitable and genial count made
much of them, dined and wined them, refused to let
them go to their quarters in the village, and made them
stay the night. All that, of course, was very nice—nothing better could be desired, but the worst of it was, the
old army officer was so carried away by the pleasure of
the young men's company that till sunrise he was telling
the officers anecdotes of his glorious past, taking them
over the house, showing them expensive pictures, old
engravings, rare guns, reading them autograph letters
from great people, while the weary and exhausted officers looked and listened, longing for their beds and
yawning in their sleeves; when at last their host let
them go, it was too late for sleep.

Might not this von Rabbeck be just such another?
Whether he were or not, there was no help for it. The
officers changed their uniforms, brushed themselves,
and went all together in search of the gentleman's
house. In the square by the church they were told they
could get to his Excellency's by the lower road—going
down behind the church to the river, walking along the
bank to the garden, and there the alleys would take
them to the house; or by the upper way—straight from
the church by the road which, half a mile from the village, led right up to his Excellency's barns. The officers
decided to go by the upper road.

"Which von Rabbeck is it?" they wondered on the
way. "Surely not the one who was in command of the
N—— cavalry division at Plevna?"

"No, that was not von Rabbeck, but simply Rabbe
and no 'von.'"

"What lovely weather!"

At the first of the barns the road divided in two: one

branch went straight on and vanished in the evening darkness, the other led to the owner's house on the right. The officers turned to the right and began to speak more softly. . . . On both sides of the road stretched stone barns with red roofs, heavy and sullen-looking, very much like barracks in a district town. Ahead of them gleamed the windows of the manor house.

"A good omen, gentlemen," said one of the officers. "Our setter leads the way; no doubt he scents game ahead of us! . . ."

Lieutenant Lobytko, who was walking in front, a tall and stalwart fellow, though entirely without mustache (he was over twenty-five, yet for some reason there was no sign of hair on his round, well-fed face), renowned in the brigade for his peculiar ability to divine the presence of women at a distance, turned round and said:

"Yes, there must be women here; I feel that by instinct."

On the threshold the officers were met by von Rabbeck himself, a comely looking man of sixty in civilian dress. Shaking hands with his guests, he said that he was very glad and happy to see them, but begged them earnestly for God's sake to excuse him for not asking them to stay the night; two sisters with their children, his brothers, and some neighbors, had come on a visit to him, so that he had not one spare room left.

The General shook hands with everyone, made his apologies, and smiled, but it was evident by his face that he was by no means so delighted as last year's count, and that he had invited the officers simply because, in his opinion, it was a social obligation. And the officers themselves, as they walked up the softly carpeted stairs, as they listened to him, felt that they had been invited to this house simply because it would have been awkward not to invite them; and at the sight of the footmen, who hastened to light the lamps at the entrance below and in the anteroom above, they began to feel as though they had brought uneasiness and discomfort into the house with them. In a house in which two sisters and their children, brothers, and neighbors were gathered together, probably on account of some family festivity or event, how could the presence of nineteen unknown officers possibly be welcome?

Upstairs at the entrance to the drawing room the officers were met by a tall, graceful old lady with black eyebrows and a long face, very much like the Empress Eugénie. Smiling graciously and majestically, she said she was glad and happy to see her guests, and apologized that her husband and she were on this occasion unable to invite *messieurs les officiers* to stay the night. From her beautiful majestic smile, which instantly vanished from her face every time she turned away from her guests, it was evident that she had seen numbers of officers in her day, that she was in no humor for them now, and if she invited them to her house and apologized for not doing more, it was only because her breeding and position in society required it of her.

When the officers went into the big dining-room, there were about a dozen people, men and ladies, young and old, sitting at tea at the end of a long table. A group of men wrapped in a haze of cigar smoke was dimly visible behind their chairs; in the midst of them stood a lanky young man with red whiskers, talking loudly in English, with a burr. Through a door beyond the group could be seen a light room with pale blue furniture.

"Gentlemen, there are so many of you that it is impossible to introduce you all!" said the General in a loud voice, trying to sound very gay. "Make each other's acquaintance, gentlemen, without any ceremony!"

The officers—some with very serious and even stern faces, others with forced smiles, and all feeling extremely awkward—somehow made their bows and sat down to tea.

The most ill at ease of them all was Ryabovich—a short, somewhat stooped officer in spectacles, with whiskers like a lynx's. While some of his comrades assumed a serious expression, while others wore forced smiles, his face, his lynx-like whiskers, and spectacles seemed to say, "I am the shyest, most modest, and most undistinguished officer in the whole brigade!" At first, on going into the room and later, sitting down at table, he could not fix his attention on any one face or object. The faces, the dresses, the cut-glass decanters of brandy, the steam from the glasses, the molded cornices—all blended in one general impression that inspired in Ryabovich alarm and a desire to hide his head. Like a lecturer making his first appearance before the public, he saw everything that was before his eyes, but apparently only had a dim understanding of it (among physiologists this condition, when the subject sees but does not understand, is called "mental blindness"). After a little while, growing accustomed to his surroundings, Ryabovich regained his sight and began to observe. As a shy man, unused to society, what struck him first was that in which he had always been deficient—namely, the extraordinary boldness of his new acquaintances. Von Rabbeck, his wife, two elderly ladies, a young lady in a lilac dress, and the young man with the red whiskers, who was, it appeared, a younger son of von Rabbeck, very cleverly, as though they had rehearsed it beforehand, took seats among the officers, and at once got up a heated discussion in which the visitors could not help taking part. The lilac young lady hotly asserted that the artillery had a much better time than the cavalry and the infantry, while von Rabbeck and the elderly ladies maintained the opposite. A brisk interchange followed. Ryabovich looked at the lilac young lady who argued so hotly about what was unfamiliar and utterly uninteresting to her, and watched artificial smiles come and go on her face.

Von Rabbeck and his family skillfully drew the officers into the discussion, and meanwhile kept a sharp eye on their glasses and mouths, to see whether all of them were drinking, whether all had enough sugar, why someone was not eating cakes or not drinking brandy. And the longer Ryabovich watched and listened, the more he was attracted by this insincere but splendidly disciplined family.

After tea the officers went into the drawing-room. Lieutenant Lobytko's instinct had not deceived him. There were a great many girls and young married ladies. The "setter" lieutenant was soon standing by a very young blonde in a black dress, and, bending over her jauntily, as though leaning on an unseen sword, smiled and twitched his shoulders coquettishly. He probably talked very interesting nonsense, for the blonde looked at his well-fed face condescendingly and asked indifferently, "Really?" And from that indifferent "Really?" the "setter," had he been intelligent, might have concluded that she would never call him to heel.

The piano struck up; the melancholy strains of a waltz floated out of the wide open windows, and everyone, for some reason, remembered that it was spring, a May evening. Everyone was conscious of the fragrance of roses, of lilac, and of the young leaves of the poplar. Ryabovich, who felt the brandy he had drunk, under the influence of the music stole a glance towards the window, smiled, and began watching the movements of the women, and it seemed to him that the smell of roses, of poplars, and lilac came not from the garden, but from the ladies' faces and dresses.

Von Rabbeck's son invited a scraggy-looking young lady to dance and waltzed round the room twice with her. Lobytko, gliding over the parquet floor, flew up to the lilac young lady and whirled her away. Dancing began. . . . Ryabovich stood near the door among those who were not dancing and looked on. He had never once danced in his whole life, and he had never once in his life put his arm round the waist of a respectable woman. He was highly delighted that a man should in the sight of all take a girl he did not know round the waist and offer her his shoulder to put her hand on, but he could not imagine himself in the position of such a man. There were times when he envied the boldness and swagger of his companions and was inwardly wretched; the knowledge that he was timid, round-shouldered, and uninteresting, that he had a long waist and lynx-like whiskers deeply mortified him, but with years he had grown used to this feeling, and now, looking at his comrades dancing or loudly talking, he no longer envied them, but only felt touched and mournful.

When the quadrille began, young von Rabbeck came up to those who were not dancing and invited two officers to have a game at billiards. The officers accepted and went with him out of the drawing room. Ryabovich, having nothing to do and wishing to take at least some part in the general movement, slouched after them. From the big drawing room they went into the little drawing room, then into a narrow corridor with a glass roof, and thence into a room in which on their entrance three sleepy-looking footmen jumped up quickly from couches. At last, after passing through a long succession of rooms, young von Rabbeck and the officers came into a small room where there was a billiard table. They began to play.

Ryabovich, who had never played any game but cards, stood near the billiard table and looked indifferently at the players, while they in unbuttoned coats, with cues in their hands, stepped about, made puns, and kept shouting out unintelligible words.

The players took no notice of him, and only now and then one of them, shoving him with his elbow or accidentally touching him with his cue, would turn round and say *"Pardon!"* Before the first game was over he was weary of it, and began to feel that he was not wanted and in the way. . . . He felt disposed to return to the drawing-room and he went out.

On his way back he met with a little adventure. When he had gone half-way he noticed that he had taken a wrong turning. He distinctly remembered that he ought to meet three sleepy footmen on his way, but he had passed five or six rooms, and those sleepy figures seemed to have been swallowed up by the earth. Noticing his mistake, he walked back a little way and turned to the right; he found himself in a little room which was in semidarkness and which he had not seen on his way to the billiard room. After standing there a little while, he resolutely opened the first door that met his eyes and walked into an absolutely dark room. Straight ahead could be seen the crack in the doorway through which came a gleam of vivid light; from the other side of the door came the muffled sound of a melancholy mazurka. Here, too, as in the drawing-room, the windows were wide open and there was a smell of poplars, lilac, and roses. . . .

Ryabovich stood still in hesitation. . . . At that moment, to his surprise, he heard hurried footsteps and the rustling of a dress, a breathless feminine voice

whispered "At last!" and two soft, fragrant, unmistakably feminine arms were clasped about his neck; a
warm cheek was pressed against his, and simultaneously
there was the sound of a kiss. But at once the bestower
of the kiss uttered a faint shriek and sprang away from
him, as it seemed to Ryabovich, with disgust. He, too,
almost shrieked and rushed towards the gleam of light
at the door. . . .

When he returned to the drawing-room his heart was
palpitating and his hands were trembling so noticeably
that he made haste to hide them behind his back. At
first he was tormented by shame and dread that the
whole drawing-room knew that he had just been kissed
and embraced by a woman. He shrank into himself and
looked uneasily about him, but as he became convinced
that people were dancing and talking as calmly as ever,
he gave himself up entirely to the new sensation which
he had never experienced before in his life. Something
strange was happening to him. . . . His neck, round
which soft, fragrant arms had so lately been clasped,
seemed to him to be anointed with oil; on his left cheek
near his mustache where the unknown had kissed him
there was a faint chilly tingling sensation as from peppermint drops, and the more he rubbed the place the
more distinct was the chilly sensation; all of him, from
head to foot, was full of a strange new feeling which
grew stronger and stronger. . . . He wanted to dance,
to talk, to run into the garden, to laugh aloud. . . . He
quite forgot that he was round-shouldered and uninteresting, that he had lynx-like whiskers and an "undistinguished appearance" (that was how his appearance had
been described by some ladies whose conversation he
had accidentally overheard). When von Rabbeck's wife
happened to pass by him, he gave her such a broad and

friendly smile that she stood still and looked at him inquiringly.

"I like your house immensely!" he said, setting his
spectacles straight.

The General's wife smiled and said that the house
had belonged to her father; then she asked whether his
parents were living, whether he had long been in the
army, why he was so thin, and so on. . . . After receiving answers to her questions, she went on, and after his
conversation with her his smiles were more friendly than
ever, and he thought he was surrounded by splendid
people. . . .

At supper Ryabovich ate mechanically everything offered him, drank, and without listening to anything,
tried to understand what had just happened to him. . . .
The adventure was of a mysterious and romantic character, but it was not difficult to explain it. No doubt
some girl or young married lady had arranged a tryst
with some man in the dark room; had waited a long
time, and being nervous and excited had taken Ryabovich for her hero; this was the more probable as Ryabovich had stood still hesitating in the dark room, so that
he, too, had looked like a person waiting for something.
. . . This was how Ryabovich explained to himself the
kiss he had received.

"And who is she?" he wondered, looking round at the
women's faces. "She must be young, for elderly ladies
don't arrange rendezvous. That she was a lady, one
could tell by the rustle of her dress, her perfume, her
voice. . . ."

His eyes rested on the lilac young lady, and he
thought her very attractive; she had beautiful shoulders
and arms, a clever face, and a delightful voice. Ryabovich, looking at her, hoped that she and no one else was

his unknown. . . . But she laughed somehow artificially and wrinkled up her long nose, which seemed to him to make her look old. Then he turned his eyes upon the blonde in a black dress. She was younger, simpler, and more genuine, had a charming brow, and drank very daintily out of her wineglass. Ryabovich now hoped that it was she. But soon he began to think her face flat, and fixed his eyes upon the one next her.

"It's difficult to guess," he thought, musing. "If one were to take only the shoulders and arms of the lilac girl, add the brow of the blonde and the eyes of the one on the left of Lobytko, then . . ."

He made a combination of these things in his mind and so formed the image of the girl who had kissed him, the image that he desired but could not find at the table. . . .

After supper, replete and exhilarated, the officers began to take leave and say thank you. Von Rabbeck and his wife began again apologizing that they could not ask them to stay the night.

"Very, very glad to have met you, gentlemen," said von Rabbeck, and this time sincerely (probably because people are far more sincere and good-humored at speeding their parting guests than on meeting them). "Delighted. Come again on your way back! Don't stand on ceremony! Where are you going? Do you want to go by the upper way? No, go across the garden; it's nearer by the lower road."

The officers went out into the garden. After the bright light and the noise the garden seemed very dark and quiet. They walked in silence all the way to the gate. They were a little drunk, in good spirits, and contented, but the darkness and silence made them thoughtful for a minute. Probably the same idea occurred to each one of them as to Ryabovich: would there ever come a time for them when, like von Rabbeck, they would have a large house, a family, a garden—when they, too, would be able to welcome people, even though insincerely, feed them, make them drunk and contented?

Going out of the garden gate, they all began talking at once and laughing loudly about nothing. They were walking now along the little path that led down to the river and then ran along the water's edge, winding round the bushes on the bank, the gulleys, and the willows that overhung the water. The bank and the path were scarcely visible, and the other bank was entirely plunged in darkness. Stars were reflected here and there in the dark water; they quivered and were broken up —and from that alone it could be seen that the river was flowing rapidly. It was still. Drowsy sandpipers cried plaintively on the farther bank, and in one of the bushes on the hither side a nightingale was trilling loudly, taking no notice of the crowd of officers. The officers stood round the bush, touched it, but the nightingale went on singing.

"What a fellow!" they exclaimed approvingly. "We stand beside him and he takes not a bit of notice! What a rascal!"

At the end of the way the path went uphill, and, skirting the church enclosure, led into the road. Here the officers, tired with walking uphill, sat down and lighted their cigarettes. On the farther bank of the river a murky red fire came into sight, and having nothing better to do, they spent a long time in discussing whether it was a camp fire or a light in a window, or something else. . . . Ryabovich, too, looked at the light, and he fancied that the light looked and winked at him, as though it knew about the kiss.

On reaching his quarters, Ryabovich undressed as

quickly as possible and got into bed. Lobytko and Lieutenant Merzlyakov—a peaceable, silent fellow, who was considered in his own circle a highly educated officer, and was always, whenever it was possible, reading *The Messenger of Europe,* which he carried about with him everywhere—were quartered in the same cottage with Ryabovich. Lobytko undressed, walked up and down the room for a long while with the air of a man who has not been satisfied, and sent his orderly for beer. Merzlyakov got into bed, put a candle by his pillow and plunged into *The Messenger of Europe.*

"Who was she?" Ryabovich wondered, looking at the sooty ceiling.

His neck still felt as though he had been anointed with oil, and there was still the chilly sensation near his mouth as though from peppermint drops. The shoulders and arms of the young lady in lilac, the brow and the candid eyes of the blonde in black, waists, dresses, and brooches, floated through his imagination. He tried to fix his attention on these images, but they danced about, broke up and flickered. When these images vanished altogether from the broad dark background which everyone sees when he closes his eyes, he began to hear hurried footsteps, the rustle of skirts, the sound of a kiss—and an intense baseless joy took possession of him. . . . Abandoning himself to this joy, he heard the orderly return and announce that there was no beer. Lobytko was terribly indignant, and began pacing up and down the room again.

"Well, isn't he an idiot?" he kept saying, stopping first before Ryabovich and then before Merzlyakov. "What a fool and a blockhead a man must be not to get hold of any beer! Eh? Isn't he a blackguard?"

"Of course you can't get beer here," said Merzlyakov, not removing his eyes from *The Messenger of Europe.*

"Oh! Is that your opinion?" Lobytko persisted. "Lord have mercy upon us, if you dropped me on the moon I'd find you beer and women directly! I'll go and find some at once. . . . You may call me a rascal if I don't!"

He spent a long time in dressing and pulling on his high boots, then finished smoking his cigarette in silence and went out.

"Rabbeck, Grabbeck, Labbeck," he muttered, stopping in the outer room. "I don't care to go alone, damn it all! Ryabovich, wouldn't you like to go for a walk? Eh?"

Receiving no answer, he returned, slowly undressed, and got into bed. Merzlyakov sighed, put *The Messenger of Europe* away, and extinguished the light.

"H'm! . . ." muttered Lobytko, lighting a cigarette in the dark.

Ryabovich pulled the bedclothes over his head, curled himself up in bed, and tried to gather together the flashing images in his mind and to combine them into a whole. But nothing came of it. He soon fell asleep, and his last thought was that someone had caressed him and made him happy—that something extraordinary, foolish, but joyful and delightful, had come into his life. The thought did not leave him even in his sleep.

When he woke up the sensations of oil on his neck and the chill of peppermint about his lips had gone, but joy flooded his heart just as the day before. He looked enthusiastically at the window-frames, gilded by the light of the rising sun, and listened to the movement of the passers-by in the street. People were talking loudly close to the window. Lebedetzky, the commander of Ryabovich's battery, who had only just overtaken the brigade, was talking to his sergeant at the top of his voice, having lost the habit of speaking in ordinary tones.

"What else?" shouted the commander.

"When they were shoeing the horses yesterday, your Honor, they injured Pigeon's hoof with a nail. The vet put on clay and vinegar; they are leading him apart now. Also, your Honor, Artemyev got drunk yesterday, and the lieutenant ordered him to be put in the limber of a spare gun-carriage."

The sergeant reported that Karpov had forgotten the new cords for the trumpets and the pegs for the tents, and that their Honors the officers had spent the previous evening visiting General von Rabbeck. In the middle of this conversation the red-bearded face of Lebedetzky appeared in the window. He screwed up his short-sighted eyes, looking at the sleepy faces of the officers, and greeted them.

"Is everything all right?" he asked.

"One of the horses has a sore neck from the new collar," answered Lobytko, yawning.

The commander sighed, thought a moment, and sai' in a loud voice:

"I am thinking of going to see Alexandra Yevgrafovna. I must call on her. Well, good-by. I shall catch up with you in the evening."

A quarter of an hour later the brigade set off on its way. When it was moving along the road past the barns, Ryabovich looked at the house on the right. The blinds were down in all the windows. Evidently the household was still asleep. The one who had kissed Ryabovich the day before was asleep too. He tried to imagine her asleep. The wide-open window of the bedroom, the green branches peeping in, the morning freshness, the scent of the poplars, lilac, and roses, the bed, a chair, and on it the skirts that had rustled the day before, the little slippers, the little watch on the table—all this he pictured to himself clearly and distinctly, but the features of the face, the sweet sleepy smile, just what was characteristic and important, slipped through his imagination like quicksilver through the fingers. When he had ridden a third of a mile, he looked back: the yellow church, the house, and the river, were all bathed in light; the river with its bright green banks, with the blue sky reflected in it and glints of silver in the sunshine here and there, was very beautiful. Ryabovich gazed for the last time at Mestechki, and he felt as sad as though he were parting with something very near and dear to him.

And before him on the road were none but long familiar, uninteresting scenes. . . . To right and to left, fields of young rye and buckwheat with rooks hopping about in them; if one looked ahead, one saw dust and the backs of men's heads; if one looked back, one saw the same dust and faces. . . . Foremost of all marched four men with sabers—this was the vanguard. Next came the singers, and behind them the trumpeters on horseback. The vanguard and the singers, like torch-bearers in a funeral procession, often forgot to keep the regulation distance and pushed a long way ahead. . . . Ryabovich was with the first cannon of the fifth battery. He could see all the four batteries moving in front of him. To a civilian the long tedious procession which is a brigade on the move seems an intricate and unintelligible muddle; one cannot understand why there are so many people round one cannon, and why it is drawn by so many horses in such a strange network of harness, as though it really were so terrible and heavy. To Ryabovich it was all perfectly comprehensible and therefore uninteresting. He had known for ever so long why at the head of each battery beside the officer there rode a stalwart noncom, called bombardier; immediately behind him could be seen the horsemen of the first and then of the middle units. Ryabovich knew that of the horses on which they rode, those on the left were called one name, while those on the right were called another —it was all extremely uninteresting. Behind the horsemen came two shaft-horses. On one of them sat a rider still covered with the dust of yesterday and with a clumsy and funny-looking wooden guard on his right leg. Ryabovich knew the object of this guard, and did not think it funny. All the riders waved their whips mechanically and shouted from time to time. The cannon itself was not presentable. On the limber lay sacks of oats covered with a tarpaulin, and the cannon itself was hung all over with kettles, soldiers' knapsacks, bags, and looked like some small harmless animal surrounded for some unknown reason by men and horses. To the leeward of it marched six men, the gunners, swinging their arms. After the cannon there came again more bombardiers, riders, shaft-horses, and behind them another cannon, as unpresentable and unimpressive as the first. After the second came a third, a fourth; near the fourth there was an officer, and so on. There were six batteries in all in the brigade, and four cannon in each battery. The procession covered a third of a mile; it ended in a string of wagons near which an extremely appealing creature—the ass, Magar, brought by a battery commander from Turkey—paced pensively, his long-eared head drooping.

Ryabovich looked indifferently ahead and behind him, at the backs of heads and at faces; at any other time he would have been half asleep, but now he was entirely absorbed in his new agreeable thoughts. At first when the brigade was setting off on the march he tried to persuade himself that the incident of the kiss could only be interesting as a mysterious little adventure, that it was in reality trivial, and to think of it seriously, to say the least, was stupid; but now he bade

farewell to logic and gave himself up to dreams. . . .
At one moment he imagined himself in von Rabbeck's
drawing-room beside a girl who was like the young
lady in lilac and the blonde in black; then he would
close his eyes and see himself with another, entirely unknown girl, whose features were very vague. In his
imagination he talked, caressed her, leaned over her
shoulder, pictured war, separation, then meeting again,
supper with his wife, children. . . .

"Brakes on!" The word of command rang out every
time they went downhill.

He, too, shouted "Brakes on!" and was afraid this
shout would disturb his reverie and bring him back to
reality. . . .

As they passed by some landowner's estate Ryabovich looked over the fence into the garden. A long
avenue, straight as a ruler, strewn with yellow sand
and bordered with young birch-trees, met his eyes. . . .
With the eagerness of a man who indulges in daydreaming, he pictured to himself little feminine feet tripping
along yellow sand, and quite unexpectedly had a clear
vision in his imagination of her who had kissed him and
whom he had succeeded in picturing to himself the
evening before at supper. This image remained in his
brain and did not desert him again.

At midday there was a shout in the rear near the
string of wagons:

"Attention! Eyes to the left! Officers!"

The general of the brigade drove by in a carriage
drawn by a pair of white horses. He stopped near the
second battery, and shouted something which no one
understood. Several officers, among them Ryabovich,
galloped up to him.

"Well? How goes it?" asked the general, blinking his
red eyes. "Are there any sick?"

Receiving an answer, the general, a little skinny man, chewed, thought for a moment and said, addressing one of the officers:

"One of your drivers of the third cannon has taken off his leg-guard and hung it on the fore part of the cannon, the rascal. Reprimand him."

He raised his eyes to Ryabovich and went on:

"It seems to me your breeching is too long."

Making a few other tedious remarks, the general looked at Lobytko and grinned.

"You look very melancholy today, Lieutenant Lobytko," he said. "Are you pining for Madame Lopuhova? Eh? Gentlemen, he is pining for Madame Lopuhova."

Madame Lopuhova was a very stout and very tall lady long past forty. The general, who had a predilection for large women, whatever their ages, suspected a similar taste in his officers. The officers smiled respectfully. The general, delighted at having said something very amusing and biting, laughed loudly, touched his coachman's back, and saluted. The carriage rolled on. . . .

"All I am dreaming about now which seems to me so impossible and unearthly is really quite an ordinary thing," thought Ryabovich, looking at the clouds of dust racing after the general's carriage. "It's all very ordinary, and everyone goes through it. . . . That general, for instance, was in love at one time; now he is married and has children. Captain Wachter, too, is married and loved, though the nape of his neck is very red and ugly and he has no waist. . . . Salmanov is coarse and too much of a Tartar, but he had a love affair that has ended in marriage. . . . I am the same as everyone else, and I, too, shall have the same experience as everyone else, sooner or later. . . ."

And the thought that he was an ordinary person and

that his life was ordinary delighted him and gave him courage. He pictured *her* and his happiness boldly, just as he liked. . . .

When the brigade reached their halting-place in the evening, and the officers were resting in their tents, Ryabovich, Merzlyakov, and Lobytko were sitting round a chest having supper. Merzlyakov ate without haste and, as he munched deliberately, read *The Messenger of Europe,* which he held on his knees. Lobytko talked incessantly and kept filling up his glass with beer, and Ryabovich, whose head was confused from dreaming all day long, drank and said nothing. After three glasses he got a little drunk, felt weak, and had an irresistible desire to relate his new sensations to his comrades.

"A strange thing happened to me at those von Rabbecks'," he began, trying to impart an indifferent and ironical tone to his voice. "You know I went into the billiard-room. . . ."

He began describing very minutely the incident of the kiss, and a moment later relapsed into silence. . . . In the course of that moment he had told everything, and it surprised him dreadfully to find how short a time it took him to tell it. He had imagined that he could have been telling the story of the kiss till next morning. Listening to him, Lobytko, who was a great liar and consequently believed no one, looked at him skeptically and laughed. Merzlyakov twitched his eyebrows and, without removing his eyes from *The Messenger of Europe,* said:

"That's an odd thing! How strange! . . . throws herself on a man's neck, without addressing him by name. . . . She must have been some sort of lunatic."

"Yes, she must," Ryabovich agreed.

"A similar thing once happened to me," said Lobytko, assuming a scared expression. "I was going last year to

Kovno. . . . I took a second-class ticket. The train was crammed, and it was impossible to sleep. I gave the guard half a ruble; he took my luggage and led me to another compartment. . . . I lay down and covered myself with a blanket. . . . It was dark, you understand. Suddenly I felt someone touch me on the shoulder and breathe in my face. I made a movement with my hand and felt somebody's elbow. . . . I opened my eyes and only imagine—a woman. Black eyes, lips red as a prime salmon, nostrils breathing passionately—a bosom like a buffer. . . ."

"Excuse me," Merzlyakov interrupted calmly, "I understand about the bosom, but how could you see the lips if it was dark?"

Lobytko began trying to put himself right and laughing at Merzlyakov's being so dull-witted. It made Ryabovich wince. He walked away from the chest, got into bed, and vowed never to confide again.

Camp life began. . . . The days flowed by, one very much like another. All those days Ryabovich felt, thought, and behaved as though he were in love. Every morning when his orderly handed him what he needed for washing, and he sluiced his head with cold water, he recalled that there was something warm and delightful in his life.

In the evenings when his comrades began talking of love and women, he would listen, and draw up closer; and he wore the expression of a soldier listening to the description of a battle in which he has taken part. And on the evenings when the officers, out on a spree with the setter Lobytko at their head, made Don-Juanesque raids on the neighboring "suburb," and Ryabovich took part in such excursions, he always was sad, felt profoundly guilty, and inwardly begged *her* forgiveness. . . . In hours of leisure or on sleepless nights when he felt moved to recall his childhood, his father and mother—everything near and dear, in fact, he invariably thought of Mestechki, the queer horse, von Rabbeck, his wife who resembled Empress Eugénie, the dark room, the light in the crack of the door. . . .

On the thirty-first of August he was returning from the camp, not with the whole brigade, but with only two batteries. He was dreamy and excited all the way, as though he were going home. He had an intense longing to see again the queer horse, the church, the insincere family of the von Rabbecks, the dark room. The "inner voice," which so often deceives lovers, whispered to him for some reason that he would surely see her . . . And he was tortured by the questions: How would he meet her? What would he talk to her about? Had she forgotten the kiss? If the worst came to the worst, he thought, even if he did not meet her, it would be a pleasure to him merely to go through the dark room and recall the past. . . .

Towards evening there appeared on the horizon the familiar church and white barns. Ryabovich's heart raced. . . . He did not hear the officer who was riding beside him and saying something to him, he forgot everything, and looked eagerly at the river shining in the distance, at the roof of the house, at the dovecote round which the pigeons were circling in the light of the setting sun.

When they reached the church and were listening to the quartermaster, he expected every second that a man on horseback would come round the church enclosure and invite the officers to tea, but . . . the quartermaster ended his report, the officers dismounted and strolled off to the village, and the man on horseback did not appear.

"Von Rabbeck will hear at once from the peasants

that we have come and will send for us," thought Ryabovich, as he went into the peasant cottage, unable to understand why a comrade was lighting a candle and why the orderlies were hastening to get the samovars going.

A crushing uneasiness took possession of him. He lay down, then got up and looked out of the window to see whether the messenger were coming. But there was no sign of him.

He lay down again, but half an hour later he got up and, unable to restrain his uneasiness, went into the street and strode towards the church. It was dark and deserted in the square near the church enclosure. Three soldiers were standing silent in a row where the road began to go down-hill. Seeing Ryabovich, they roused themselves and saluted. He returned the salute and began to go down the familiar path.

On the farther bank of the river the whole sky was flooded with crimson: the moon was rising; two peasant women, talking loudly, were pulling cabbage leaves in the kitchen garden; beyond the kitchen garden there were some cottages that formed a dark mass. . . . Everything on the near side of the river was just as it had been in May: the path, the bushes, the willows over-hanging the water . . . but there was no sound of the brave nightingale and no scent of poplar and young grass.

Reaching the garden, Ryabovich looked in at the gate. The garden was dark and still. . . . He could see nothing but the white stems of the nearest birch-trees and a little bit of the avenue; all the rest melted to-gether into a dark mass. Ryabovich looked and listened eagerly, but after waiting for a quarter of an hour without hearing a sound or catching a glimpse of a light, he trudged back. . . .

He went down to the river. The General's bathing cabin and the bath-sheets on the rail of the little bridge showed white before him. . . . He walked up on the bridge, stood a little, and quite unnecessarily touched a sheet. It felt rough and cold. He looked down at the water. . . . The river ran rapidly and with a faintly audible gurgle round the piles of the bathing cabin. The red moon was reflected near the left bank; little ripples ran over the reflection, stretching it out, breaking it into bits, and seemed trying to carry it away. . . .

"How stupid, how stupid!" thought Ryabovich, looking at the running water. "How unintelligent it all is!"

Now that he expected nothing, the incident of the kiss, his impatience, his vague hopes and disappointment, presented themselves to him in a clear light. It no longer seemed to him strange that the General's messenger never came and that he would never see the girl who had accidentally kissed him instead of someone else; on the contrary, it would have been strange if he had seen her. . . .

The water was running, he knew not where or why, just as it did in May. At that time it had flowed into a great river, from the great river into the sea; then it had risen in vapor, turned into rain, and perhaps the very same water was running now before Ryabovich's eyes again. . . . What for? Why?

And the whole world, the whole of life, seemed to Ryabovich an unintelligible, aimless jest. . . . And turning his eyes from the water and looking at the sky, he remembered again how Fate in the person of an unknown woman had by chance caressed him, he recalled his summer dreams and fancies, and his life struck him as extraordinarily meager, poverty-stricken, and drab. . . .

When he had returned to the cottage he did not find

a single comrade. The orderly informed him that they had all gone to "General Fontryabkin, who had sent a messenger on horseback to invite them. . . ."

For an instant there was a flash of joy in Ryabovich's heart, but he quenched it at once, got into bed, and in his wrath with his fate, as though to spite it, did not go to the General's.

1887

The Name-Day Party

AFTER the festive dinner with its eight courses and its endless conversation, Olga Mihailovna, whose husband's name-day was being celebrated, went out into the garden. The duty of smiling and talking incessantly, the clatter of the crockery, the stupidity of the servants, the long intervals between the courses, and the stays she had put on to conceal her pregnancy from the visitors, wearied her to exhaustion. She longed to get away from the house, to sit in the shade and rest her mind with thoughts of the baby which was to be born to her in another two months. She was used to these thoughts coming to her as she turned to the left out of the big avenue into the narrow path. Here in the thick shade of the plums and cherry-trees the dry branches would scratch her neck and shoulders; a spider's web would settle on her face, and there would rise up in her mind the image of a little creature of undetermined sex and undefined features, and it began to seem as though it were not the spider's web that tickled her face and neck caressingly, but that little creature. When, at the end of the path, a thin wicker fence came into sight, and behind it podgy beehives with tiled roofs; when into the motionless, stagnant air there came a smell of hay and honey, and a soft buzzing of bees was audible, then the little creature would take complete possession of Olga Mihailovna. She used to sit down on a bench near the shanty of woven branches, and fall to thinking.

This time, too, she went on as far as the seat, sat down, and began thinking; but instead of the little creature there rose up in her imagination the figures of the grown-up people whom she had just left. She felt dreadfully uneasy that she, the hostess, had deserted her guests, and she remembered how her husband, Pyotr Dmitrich, and her uncle, Nikolay Nikolaich, had argued at dinner about trial by jury, about the press, and about the higher education of women. Her husband, as usual, argued in order to show off his Conservative ideas before his visitors—but chiefly in order to disagree with her uncle, whom he disliked. Her uncle contradicted him and wrangled over every word he uttered, so as to show the company that he, Uncle Nikolay Nikolaich, still retained his youthful freshness of spirit and free-thinking in spite of his fifty-nine years. And towards the end of dinner even Olga Mihailovna herself could not resist taking part and unskillfully attempting to defend university education for women—not that it stood in need of her defense, but simply because she wanted to annoy her husband, who to her mind was unfair. The guests were wearied by this discussion, but they all thought it necessary to take part in it, and talked a great deal, although none of them took any interest in trial by jury or the higher education of women. . . .

Olga Mihailovna was sitting on the hither side of the fence near the shanty. The sun was hidden behind the clouds. The trees and the air were frowning as before rain, but in spite of that it was hot and stifling. The hay cut under the trees on the previous day was lying ungathered, looking melancholy, with here and there a patch of color from the faded flowers, and from it came a heavy, sickly scent. It was still. On the other side of the fence there was a monotonous hum of bees. . . .

Suddenly she heard footsteps and voices; someone was coming along the path towards the apiary.

"How stifling it is!" said a feminine voice. "What do you think—is it going to rain, or not?"

"It is going to rain, my charmer, but not before night," a very familiar male voice answered languidly. "There will be a good rain."

Olga Mihailovna figured that if she made haste to hide in the shanty they would pass by without seeing her, and she would not have to talk and to force herself to smile. She picked up her skirts, bent down, and crept into the shanty. At once she felt upon her face, her neck, her arms, the hot air as heavy as steam. If it had not been for the stuffiness and the close smell of rye bread, fennel, and brushwood, which prevented her from breathing freely, it would have been delightful to hide from her visitors here under the thatched roof in the dusk, and to think about the little creature. It was cozy and quiet.

"What a pretty spot!" said a feminine voice. "Let us sit here, Pyotr Dmitrich."

Olga Mihailovna began peeping through a crack between two branches. She saw her husband, Pyotr Dmitrich, and Lubochka Scheller, a girl of seventeen who had recently left boarding-school. Pyotr Dmitrich, with his hat on the back of his head, languid and indolent from having drunk so much at dinner, slouched past the fence and raked the hay into a heap with his foot;

Lubochka, pink with the heat and pretty as ever, stood with her hands behind her, watching the lazy movements of his big handsome body.

Olga Mihailovna knew that her husband was attractive to women, and did not like to see him with them. There was nothing out of the way in Pyotr Dmitrich's lazily raking together the hay in order to sit down on it with Lubochka and chatter to her of trivialities; there was nothing out of the way, either, in pretty Lubochka's looking at him meekly; but yet Olga Mihailovna felt vexed with her husband and frightened and pleased that she could eavesdrop.

"Sit down, enchantress," said Pyotr Dmitrich, sinking down on the hay and stretching. "That's right. Come, tell me something."

"What next! If I begin telling you anything you will go to sleep."

"Me go to sleep? Allah forbid! Can I go to sleep while eyes like yours are watching me?"

In her husband's words, and in the fact that he was lolling with his hat on the back of his head in the presence of a lady, there was nothing out of the way either. He was spoiled by women, knew that they found him attractive, and had adopted with them a special tone which everyone said suited him. With Lubochka he behaved as with all women. But, all the same, Olga Mihailovna was jealous.

"Tell me, please," said Lubochka, after a brief silence, "is it true that you are to be tried for something?"

"I? Yes, I am numbered among the transgressors, my charmer."

"But what for?"

"For nothing, just so . . . it's chiefly a question of politics," yawned Pyotr Dmitrich, "the antagonisms of Left and Right. I, an obscurantist and reactionary, ventured in an official paper to make use of an expression offensive to such immaculate Gladstones as Vladimir Pavlovich Vladimirov and our local justice of the peace, Kuzma Grigorich Vostryakov."

Pyotr Dmitrich yawned again and went on:

"And it is the way with us that you may express disapproval of the sun or the moon, or anything you like, but God preserve you from touching the Liberals! Heaven forbid! A Liberal is like the horrid dry fungus which covers you with a cloud of dust if you accidentally touch it with your finger."

"What happened to you?"

"Nothing particular. The whole flare-up started from the merest trifle. A teacher, a detestable person of clerical associations, hands to Vostryakov a petition against a tavern-keeper, charging him with insulting language and behavior in a public place. Everything suggests that both the teacher and the tavern-keeper were drunk as cobblers and that they behaved equally badly. If there had been insulting behavior, the insult had anyway been mutual. Vostryakov ought to have fined them both for a breach of the peace and have turned them out of the court—that is all. But that's not our way of doing things. With us what stands first is not the person—not the fact itself, but the trademark and label. However great a rascal a teacher may be, he is always in the right because he is a teacher; a tavern-keeper is always in the wrong because he is a tavern-keeper and a moneygrubber. Vostryakov placed the tavern-keeper under arrest. The man appealed to the Circuit Court; the Circuit Court triumphantly upheld Vostryakov's decision. Well, I stuck to my own opinion. . . . Got a little hot. . . . That was all."

Pyotr Dmitrich spoke calmly with careless irony. In reality the trial that was hanging over him worried him

extremely. Olga Mihailovna remembered how on his return from the unfortunate session he had tried to conceal from his household how troubled he was and how
dissatisfied with himself. As an intelligent man he could
not help feeling that he had gone too far in expressing
his disagreement; and how much lying had been need-
ful to conceal that feeling from himself and from others!
How many unnecessary conversations there had been!
How much grumbling and insincere laughter at what
was not laughable! When he learned that he was to be
brought up before the Court, he suddenly felt very tired
and depressed; he began to sleep badly, stood oftener
than ever at the windows, drumming on the panes with
his fingers. And he was ashamed to let his wife see that
he was worried, and it vexed her.

"Is it true, as they say, that you've been to the province of Poltava?" Lubochka asked him.

"Yes," answered Pyotr Dmitrich. "I came back the
day before yesterday."

"I expect it is very nice there."

"Yes, it is very nice, very nice indeed; in fact, I arrived just in time for the haymaking, I must tell you,
and in the Ukraine the haymaking is the most poetical
moment of the year. Here we have a big house, a big
garden, a lot of servants, and a lot going on, so that you
don't see the haymaking; here it all passes unnoticed.
There, at the farm, I have a meadow of forty acres as
flat as my hand. You can see the men mowing from any
window you stand at. They are mowing in the meadow,
they are mowing in the garden. There are no visitors,
no fuss nor hurry either, so that you can't help seeing,
feeling, hearing nothing but the haymaking. There is a
smell of hay indoors and outdoors. There's the sound
of the scythes from sunrise to sunset. Altogether Little
Russia is a charming country. Would you believe it,

when I was drinking water from the rustic wells and filthy vodka in some Jew's tavern, when on quiet evenings the strains of the Little Russian fiddle and the tambourines reached me, I was tempted by a fascinating idea—to settle down on my place and live there as long as I chose, far away from Circuit Courts, intellectual conversations, philosophizing women, long dinners. . . ."

Pyotr Dmitrich was not lying. He was unhappy and really longed for a rest. And he had visited his Poltava property simply to avoid seeing his study, his servants, his acquaintances, and everything that could remind him of his wounded vanity and his mistakes.

Lubochka suddenly jumped up and waved her hands about in horror. "Oh! A bee, a bee!" she shrieked. "It will sting!"

"Nonsense; it won't sting," said Pyotr Dmitrich. "What a coward you are!"

"No, no, no," cried Lubochka; and looking round at the bees, she walked rapidly back.

Pyotr Dmitrich walked away after her, looking at her with a softened and melancholy face. He was probably thinking, as he looked at her, of his farm, of solitude, and—who knows?—perhaps he was even thinking how snug and cozy life would be at the farm if his wife had been this girl—young, pure, fresh, not corrupted by higher education, not with child. . . .

When the sound of their footsteps had died away, Olga Mihailovna came out of the shanty and turned towards the house. She wanted to cry. She was by now acutely jealous. She could understand that her husband was worried, dissatisfied with himself and ashamed, and when people are ashamed they hold aloof, above all from those nearest to them, and are unreserved with strangers; she could understand, also, that she had nothing to fear from Lubochka or from those women who were now drinking coffee indoors. But everything in general was terrible, incomprehensible, and it already seemed to Olga Mihailovna that Pyotr Dmitrich only half belonged to her. . . .

"He has no right!" she muttered, trying to find reasons for her jealousy and her vexation with her husband. "He has no right at all. I will tell him so plainly!"

She made up her mind to find her husband at once and tell him all about it: it was disgusting, absolutely disgusting, that he was attractive to other women and sought their admiration as though it were heavenly manna; it was unjust and dishonorable that he should give to others what belonged by right to his wife, that he should hide his soul and his conscience from his wife to reveal them to the first pretty face he came across. What harm had his wife done him? How was she to blame? She had grown sick of his lying long ago; he was forever posing, flirting, saying what he did not think, and trying to seem different from what he was and what he ought to be. Why this falsity? Was it seemly in a decent man? If he lied he was demeaning himself and those to whom he lied, and slighting what he lied about. Could he not understand that if he swaggered and posed at the judicial table, or held forth at dinner on the prerogatives of Government, simply to provoke her uncle, he was showing thereby that he had not a groat's worth of respect for the Court, or himself, or any of the people who were listening and looking at him?

Coming out into the big avenue, Olga Mihailovna assumed an expression of face as though she had just gone away to look after some domestic matter. On the veranda the gentlemen were drinking liqueur and eating strawberries: one of them, the Examining Magistrate—a stout elderly man, a chatter-box and wit—must have been telling some rather broad anecdote, for, seeing their hostess, he suddenly clapped his hands over his fat lips, rolled his eyes, and sat down. Olga Mihailovna did not like the local officials. She did not care for their clumsy, ceremonious wives, their scandalmongering, their frequent visits, their flattery of her husband, whom they all hated. Now, when they were drinking, were replete with food and showed no signs of going away, she felt their presence an agonizing weariness; but not to appear impolite, she smiled cordially to the magistrate and shook her finger at him. She walked across the dining-room and drawing-room smiling and looking as though she had gone to give some order and make some arrangement. "God grant no one stops me," she thought, but she forced herself to stop in the drawing-room to listen from politeness to a young man who was sitting at the piano playing; after standing for a minute, she cried, "Bravo, bravo, M. Georges!" and clapping her hands twice, went on.

She found her husband in his study. He was sitting at the table, thinking of something. His face looked stern, thoughtful, and guilty. This was not the same Pyotr Dmitrich who had been arguing at dinner and whom his guests knew, but a different man—tired, feeling guilty and dissatisfied with himself, whom nobody knew but his wife. He must have come to the study to get cigarettes. Before him lay an open cigarette-case full of cigarettes, and one of his hands was in the table drawer; he had paused and sunk into thought as he was taking the cigarettes.

Olga Mihailovna felt sorry for him. It was as clear as day that this man was harassed, could find no rest, and was perhaps struggling with himself. Olga Mihailovna went up to the table in silence: wanting to show that she had forgotten the argument at dinner and was not cross, she shut the cigarette-case and put it in her husband's coat pocket.

"What should I say to him?" she wondered. "I shall say that lying is like a forest—the further one goes into it the more difficult it is to get out of it. I shall tell him, 'You have been carried away by the false part you are playing; you have insulted people who were attached to you and have done you no harm. Go and apologize to them, laugh at yourself, and you will feel better. And if you want peace and solitude, let us go away together.'"

Meeting his wife's gaze, Pyotr Dmitrich's face immediately assumed the expression it had worn at dinner and in the garden—indifferent and slightly ironical. He yawned and got up.

"It's past five," he said, looking at his watch. "If our guests are merciful and leave us at eleven, even then we have another six hours of it. It's a cheerful prospect, there's no denying!"

And whistling something, he walked slowly out of the study with his usual dignified gait. She could hear his dignified tread as he crossed the ballroom and the drawing-room, and hear him laugh with pompous assurance, as he said to the young man who was playing, "Bravo! bravo!" Soon his footsteps died away: he must have gone out into the garden. And now not jealousy, not vexation, but real hatred of his footsteps, his insincere laugh and voice, took possession of Olga Mihailovna. She went to the window and looked out into the garden. Pyotr Dmitrich was already walking along the avenue. Putting one hand in his pocket and snapping the fingers of the other, he walked with confident swinging steps, throwing his head back a little and

looking as though he were very well satisfied with himself, with his dinner, with his digestion, and with Nature. . . .

Two little schoolboys, the children of Madame Chiz-
hevskaya, who had only just arrived, made their appearance in the avenue, accompanied by their tutor, a student wearing a white tunic and very tight trousers.
When they reached Pyotr Dmitrich, the boys and the
student stopped, and probably congratulated him on his
name-day. With a graceful swing of his shoulders, he
patted the children on their cheeks and carelessly offered the student his hand without looking at him. The
student must have praised the weather and compared it
with the climate of Petersburg, for Pyotr Dmitrich said
in a loud voice, in a tone as though he were speaking
not to a guest, but to a sergeant-at-arms or a witness at
court:

"What? It's cold in Petersburg? And here, my good
sir, we have the finest weather and the fruits of the earth
in abundance. Eh? What?"

And thrusting one hand in his pocket and snapping
the fingers of the other, he walked on. Till he had disappeared behind the hazel bushes, Olga Mihailovna
watched the back of his head in perplexity. How had
this man of thirty-four come by this staid gait of a
general? How had he come by that impressive, elegant
manner? Where had he got that vibration of authority
in his voice? Where had he got these "what's," "to be
sure's," and "my good sir's"?

Olga Mihailovna remembered how in the first months
of her marriage she had felt dreary at home alone and
had driven into town to the Circuit Court, at which
Pyotr Dmitrich had sometimes presided in lieu of her
godfather, Count Alexey Petrovich. In the presidential
chair, wearing his uniform and the chain of office on his

breast, he was completely transformed. Stately gestures, a voice of thunder, "what?" "to be sure," a careless tone. . . . Everything, all that was ordinary and human, all that was individual and personal to himself that Olga Mihailovna was accustomed to seeing in him at home, vanished in grandeur, and in the presidential chair there sat not Pyotr Dmitrich but another man whom everyone called Mr. President. This consciousness of power prevented him from sitting still in his place, and he seized every opportunity to ring his bell, to glance sternly at the public, to shout. . . . Where had he got his short-sight and his deafness when he suddenly began to see and hear with difficulty, and, frowning majestically, insisted on people speaking louder and coming closer to the table? From the height of his grandeur he could hardly distinguish faces or sounds, so that it seemed that if Olga Mihailovna herself had gone up to him he would have shouted even to her, "Your name?" Peasant witnesses he addressed familiarly, he shouted at the public so that his voice could be heard even in the street, and behaved incredibly with the lawyers. If an attorney had to speak to him, Pyotr Dmitrich, turning a little away from him, looked with half-closed eyes at the ceiling, meaning to signify thereby that the lawyer was utterly superfluous and that he was neither recognizing him nor listening to him; if a badly dressed private solicitor spoke, Pyotr Dmitrich pricked up his ears and looked the man up and down with a sarcastic, annihilating stare as though to say: "Queer sort of lawyers nowadays!" "What do you mean by that?" he would interrupt the man. If a lawyer with pretensions to eloquence mispronounced a foreign word, saying, for instance, "factitious" instead of "fictitious," Pyotr Dmitrich brightened up at once and asked, "What? How? Factitious? What does that mean?" and then observed impressively: "Don't make use of words you do not understand." And the lawyer, finishing his speech, would walk away from the table, red and perspiring, while Pyotr Dmitrich, with a self-satisfied smile, would lean back in his chair triumphant. In his manner with the lawyers he imitated Count Alexey Petrovich a little, but when the latter said, for instance, "Counsel for the defense, you keep quiet for a little!" it sounded paternally good-natured and natural, while the same words in Pyotr Dmitrich's mouth were rude and strained.

II

There were sounds of applause. The young man had finished playing. Olga Mihailovna remembered her guests and hurried into the drawing-room.

"I have so enjoyed your playing," she said, going up to the piano. "I have so enjoyed it. You have a wonderful talent! But don't you think our piano's out of tune?"

At that moment the two schoolboys walked into the room, accompanied by the student.

"My goodness! Mitya and Kolya," Olga Mihailovna drawled joyfully, going to meet them: "How big you have grown! One would not know you! But where is your mamma?"

"I congratulate you on the name-day," the student began in a free-and-easy tone, "and I wish you all happiness. Yekaterina Andreyevna sends her congratulations and begs you to excuse her. She is not very well."

"How unkind of her! I have been expecting her all day. Is it long since you left Petersburg?" Olga Mihailovna asked the student. "What kind of weather have you there now?" And without waiting for an answer, she looked cordially at the schoolboys and repeated:

"How tall they have grown! It is not long since they

used to come with their nurse, and they are at school already! The old grow older while the young grow up. . . . Have you had dinner?"

"Oh, please don't trouble!" said the student.

"Why, you have not had dinner?"

"For goodness' sake, don't trouble!"

"But I suppose you are hungry?" Olga Mihailovna said it in a harsh, rude voice, with impatience and vexation—it escaped her unawares, but at once she coughed, smiled, and flushed crimson. "How tall they have grown!" she said softly.

"Please don't trouble!" the student said once more.

The student begged her not to trouble; the boys said nothing; obviously all three of them were hungry. Olga Mihailovna took them into the dining-room and told Vasily to lay the table.

"How unkind of your mamma!" she said as she made them sit down. "She has quite forgotten me. Unkind, unkind, unkind . . . you must tell her so. What are you studying?" she asked the student.

"Medicine."

"Well, I have a weakness for doctors, only fancy. I am very sorry my husband is not a doctor. What courage anyone must have to perform an operation or dissect a corpse, for instance! Horrible! Aren't you frightened? I believe I should die of terror! Of course, you will have some vodka?"

"Please don't trouble."

"After your journey you must, you must have a drink. Though I am a woman, even I drink sometimes. And Mitya and Kolya will have some Malaga. It's not a strong wine; you needn't be afraid of it. What fine fellows they are, really! They'll be thinking of getting married next."

Olga Mihailovna talked without ceasing; she knew by

experience that when she had guests to entertain it was far easier and more comfortable to talk than to listen. When you talk there is no need to strain your attention, to think of answers to questions, and to change your expression of face. But unawares she asked the student a serious question; the student began a lengthy speech and she was forced to listen. The student knew that she had once been at the university, and so tried to seem a serious person as he talked to her.

"What subject are you studying?" she asked, forgetting that she had already put that question to him.

"Medicine."

Olga Mihailovna now remembered that she had been away from the ladies for a long while.

"Yes? Then I suppose you are going to be a doctor?" she said, getting up. "That's splendid. I am sorry I did not go in for medicine myself. So you will finish your dinner here, gentlemen, and then come into the garden. I will introduce you to the young ladies."

She went out and glanced at her watch: it was five minutes to six. And she wondered that the time had gone so slowly, and thought with horror that there were six more hours before midnight, when the party would break up. How could she get through those six hours? What phrases could she find? How should she behave to her husband?

There was not a soul in the drawing-room or on the veranda. All the guests were scattered about the garden.

"I shall have to suggest a walk in the birchwood before tea, or that we take out the rowboats," thought Olga Mihailovna, hurrying to the croquet lawn, from which came the sounds of voices and laughter. "And sit the old people down to vint. . . ." She met Grigory the footman coming from the croquet lawn with empty bottles.

"Where are the ladies?" she asked.

"In the raspberry patch. The master's there, too."

"Oh, good heavens!" someone on the croquet lawn shouted with exasperation. "I have told you a thousand times over! To know the Bulgarians you must see them! You can't judge from the papers!"

Either because of this outburst or for some other reason, Olga Mihailovna was suddenly aware of a terrible weakness all over, especially in her legs and in her shoulders. She felt she could not bear to speak, to listen, or to move.

"Grigory," she said languidly and with an effort, "when you have to serve tea or anything, please don't appeal to me, don't ask me anything, don't speak of anything. . . . Do it all yourself, and . . . and don't make a noise with your feet, I entreat you. . . . I can't, because . . ."

Without finishing, she walked on towards the croquet lawn, but on the way she thought of the ladies and turned towards the raspberry-bushes. The sky, the air, and the trees looked gloomy again and threatened rain; it was hot and stifling. An immense flock of crows, foreseeing a storm, flew cawing over the garden. The paths were more overgrown, darker, and narrower as they got nearer the kitchen garden. On one of them, buried in a thick tangle of wild pear, crabapple, sorrel, young oaks, and hop-bine, clouds of tiny black flies swarmed round Olga Mihailovna. She covered her face with her hands and began forcing herself to think of the little creature. . . . There floated through her imagination the figures of Grigory, Mitya, Kolya, the faces of the peasants who had come in the morning to present their congratulations. . . .

She heard footsteps, and opened her eyes. Uncle Nikolay Nikolaich was coming rapidly towards her.

"It's you, dear? I am very glad—" he began, breath-less. "Just a word—" He mopped with his handkerchief his red shaven chin, then suddenly stepped back a pace, clapped his hands together, and opened his eyes wide. "My dear girl, how long will this go on?" he said rapidly, spluttering. "I ask you: is there no limit to it? I say noth-ing of the demoralizing effect of his martinet views on all around him, of the way he insults all that is sacred and best in me and in every honest thinking man—I will say nothing about that, but he might at least behave de-cently! Why, he shouts, he bellows, gives himself airs, poses as a sort of Bonaparte, does not let one say a word. . . . I don't know what the devil's the matter with him! These lordly gestures, this condescending tone; and laughing like a general! Who is he, allow me to ask you? I ask you, who is he? The husband of his wife, with a few paltry acres and the rank of a titular councilor who has had the luck to marry an heiress! An upstart and a Junker, of whom there are many! A type out of Shche-drin! Upon my word, it's either that he's suffering from megalomania, or that old rat in his dotage, Count Alexey Petrovich, is right when he says that children and young people are a long time growing up nowadays, and go on playing they are cabmen and generals till they are forty!"

"That's true, that's true," Olga Mihailovna assented. "Let me pass."

"Now just consider: what is it leading to?" her uncle went on, barring her way. "How will this playing at being a general and a Conservative end? Already he has got himself into trouble! Yes, he'll have to stand trial! I am very glad of it! That's what his noise and shouting has brought him to—the prisoner's dock. And it's not as though it were the Circuit Court or something: it's the

Central Court! Nothing worse could be imagined, I think! And then he has quarreled with everyone! He is celebrating his name-day, and look, Vostryakov's not here, nor Yahontov, nor Vladimirov, nor Shevud, nor the Count. . . . There is no one, I imagine, more conservative than Count Alexey Petrovich, yet even he has not come. And he never will come again. He won't come, you will see!"

"My God! but what has it to do with me?" asked Olga Mihailovna.

"What has it to do with you? Why, you are his wife! You are clever, you have had a university education, and it was in your power to make him an honest worker!"

"At the lectures I went to they did not teach us how to influence difficult people. It seems as though I should have to apologize to all of you for having been at the university," said Olga Mihailovna sharply. "Listen, uncle. If people played the same scales over and over again all day long in your hearing, you wouldn't be able to sit still and listen, but would run away. I hear the same thing over again for days together all the year round. You must have pity on me at last."

Her uncle pulled a very long face, then looked at her searchingly and twisted his lips into a mocking smile.

"So that's how it is," he piped in a voice like an old woman's. "I beg your pardon, ma'am!" he said, and made a ceremonious bow. "If you have fallen under his influence yourself, and have abandoned your convictions, you should have said so before. I beg your pardon!"

"Yes, I have abandoned my convictions," she cried. "There; make the most of it!"

"I beg your pardon, ma'am!"

Her uncle for the last time made her a ceremonious bow, a little on one side, and, shrinking into himself, made a scrape with his foot and walked back.

"Idiot!" thought Olga Mihailovna. "I hope he will go home."

She found the ladies and the young people near the raspberry patch in the kitchen garden. Some were eating raspberries; others, tired of eating raspberries, were strolling about the strawberry beds or foraging among the sugar-peas. A little to one side of the raspberry patch, near a branching apple-tree propped up by posts which had been pulled out of an old fence, Pvotr Dmitrich was mowing the grass. His hair was falling over his forehead, his cravat was untied. His watch-chain was hanging loose. Every step and every swing of the scythe showed skill and the possession of immense physical strength. Near him were standing Lubochka and the daughters of a neighbor, Colonel Bukreyev—two anemic and unhealthily stout blondes, Natalya and Valentina, or, as they were always called, Nata and Vata, both wearing white frocks and strikingly like each other. Pyotr Dmitrich was teaching them how to mow.

"It's very simple," he said. "You have only to know how to hold the scythe and not to get too hot over it— that is, not to use more force than is necessary! Like this. . . . Wouldn't you like to try?" he said, offering the scythe to Lubochka. "Come!"

Lubochka took the scythe clumsily, blushed crimson, and laughed.

"Don't be afraid, Lubov Alexandrovna!" cried Olga Mihailovna, loud enough for all the ladies to hear that she was with them. "Don't be afraid! You must learn! If you marry a Tolstoyan he will make you mow."

Lubochka raised the scythe, but began laughing again, and, helpless with laughter, let go of it at once.

She was ashamed and pleased at being talked to as though she were a grown-up. Nata, with a cold, serious face, with no trace of smiling or shyness, took the scythe, swung it and caught it in the grass; Vata, also without a smile, as cold and serious as her sister, took the scythe, and silently thrust it into the earth. Having done this, the two sisters linked arms and walked in silence to the raspberry patch.

Pyotr Dmitrich laughed and played about like a boy, and this childish, frolicsome mood in which he became exceedingly good-natured suited him far better than any other. Olga Mihailovna loved him when he was like that. But his boyishness did not usually last long. It didn't this time; after playing with the scythe, he for some reason thought it necessary to take a serious tone about it.

"When I am mowing, I feel, do you know, healthier and more normal," he said. "If I were forced to confine myself to an intellectual life I believe I should go out of my mind. I feel that I was not born to be a man of culture! I ought to mow, plow, sow, break in horses."

And Pyotr Dmitrich began a conversation with the ladies about the advantages of physical labor, about culture, and then about the pernicious effects of money, of property. Listening to her husband Olga Mihailovna, for some reason, thought of her dowry.

"And the time will come, I suppose," she thought, "when he will not forgive me for being richer than he. He is proud and vain. Maybe he will hate me because he owes so much to me."

She stopped near Colonel Bukreyev, who was eating raspberries and also taking part in the conversation.

"Come," he said, making room for Olga Mihailovna and Pyotr Dmitrich. "The ripest are here. . . . And so, according to Proudhon," he went on, raising his voice, "property is theft. But I must confess I don't believe in Proudhon, and don't consider him a philosopher. To my thinking the French are no authorities—God bless them!"

"Well, as for Proudhons and Buckles and the rest of them, I am weak in that department," said Pyotr Dmitrich. "For philosophy you must apply to my wife. She has been to the university, and knows all your Schopenhauers and Proudhons by heart. . . ."

Olga Mihailovna felt bored again. She walked again along a little path, past apple-and pear-trees, and again looked as though she was on some very important errand. She reached the gardener's cottage. In the doorway the gardener's wife, Varvara, was sitting with her four little children who had big close-cropped heads. Varvara, too, was with child and expecting to be confined by Elijah's Day. After greeting her, Olga Mihailovna looked at her and the children in silence and asked:

"Well, how do you feel?"

"Oh, all right. . . ."

A silence followed. The two women seemed to understand each other without words.

"It's dreadful having one's first baby," said Olga Mihailovna after a moment's thought. "I keep feeling as though I shall not get through it, as though I shall die."

"I fancied that, too, but here I am alive. . . . One has all sorts of fancies."

Varvara, who was just going to have her fifth, looked down a little on her mistress from the height of her experience and spoke in a rather didactic tone, and Olga Mihailovna could not help feeling her authority; she would have liked to have talked of her fears, of the child, of her sensations, but she was afraid it might

strike Varvara as naive and trivial. And she waited in
silence for Varvara to say something herself.

"Olga, we are going indoors," Pyotr Dmitrich called
from the raspberries.

Olga Mihailovna liked being silent, waiting and
watching Varvara. She would have been ready to stay
like that till night without speaking or having any duty
to perform. But she had to go. She had hardly left the
cottage when Lubochka, Nata, and Vata came running
to meet her. The sisters stopped short abruptly a couple
of yards away; Lubochka ran right up to her and flung
herself on her neck.

"You dear, darling, precious," she said, kissing her
face and her neck. "Let us go and have tea on the
island!"

"On the island, on the island!" said the precisely
similar Nata and Vata, both at once, without a smile.

"But it's going to rain, my dears."

"It's not, it's not," cried Lubochka with a woebegone
face. "They've all agreed to go. Dear! darling!"

"They are all getting ready to have tea on the island,"
said Pyotr Dmitrich, coming up. "See to the arrangements . . . We will all go in the boats, and the samovars and all the rest of it must be sent in the carriage
with the servants."

He walked beside his wife and gave her his arm. Olga
Mihailovna had a desire to say something disagreeable
to her husband, something biting, even about her dowry
perhaps—the crueler the better, she felt. She thought a
little, and said:

"Why is it Count Alexey Petrovich hasn't come?
What a pity!"

"I am very glad he hasn't come," said Pyotr Dmitrich,
lying. "I'm sick to death of that old lunatic."

"But yet before dinner you were expecting him so eagerly!"

III

Half an hour later all the guests were crowding on the bank near the piles to which the boats were fastened. They were all talking and laughing, and were in such excitement and commotion that they could hardly get into the boats. Three boats were crammed with passengers, while two stood empty. The keys to the padlocks on these two boats had been somehow mislaid, and messengers were continually running from the river to the house to look for them. Some said Grigory had the keys, others that the steward had them, while others again suggested sending for a blacksmith and breaking the padlocks. And all talked at once, interrupting and shouting one another down. Pyotr Dmitrich paced impatiently to and fro on the bank, saying:

"What the devil's the meaning of it! The keys ought always to be lying on the hall window sill! Who has dared to take them away? The steward can get a boat of his own if he wants one!"

At last the keys were found. Then it appeared that two oars were missing. Again there was a great hullabaloo. Pyotr Dmitrich, who was weary of pacing about the bank, jumped into a long, narrow skiff hollowed out of the trunk of a poplar, and, lurching from side to side and almost falling into the water, pushed off from the bank. The other boats followed him one after another, amid loud laughter and the shrieks of the young ladies.

The white cloudy sky, the trees on the banks, the boats with the people in them, and the oars, were reflected in the water as in a mirror; under the boats, far away below in the bottomless depths, was a second sky with birds flying across it. The bank on which the house stood was high, steep, and covered with trees; on the other, which was sloping, stretched broad green water-meadows with sheets of water glistening in them. The boats had floated a hundred yards when, behind the mournfully drooping willows on the sloping banks, huts and a herd of cows came into sight; they began to hear songs, drunken shouts, and the strains of an accordion.

Here and there on the river darted the boats of fishermen who were going out to set their nets for the night. In one of these boats was a festive party, playing on homemade violins and a cello.

Olga Mihailovna was sitting at the rudder; she was smiling affably and talking a great deal to entertain her visitors, while stealing a glance at her husband from time to time. He was ahead of them all, standing up and punting with one oar. The light sharp-nosed canoe, which all the guests called the "deathtrap"—while Pyotr Dmitrich, for some reason, called it *Penderaklia*—moved along quickly; it had a brisk, crafty expression, as though it hated its heavy occupant and was waiting for a favorable moment to glide away from under his feet. Olga Mihailovna kept glancing at her husband, and she loathed his good looks which attracted everyone, the back of his head, his attitude, his familiar manner with women; she hated all the women sitting in the boat with her, was jealous, and at the same time was trembling every minute in terror that her husband's frail craft would upset and cause an accident.

"Take care, Pyotr!" she cried, while her heart fluttered with terror. "Sit down! We believe in your courage without all that!"

She was worried, too, by the people who were in the boat with her. They were all ordinary, good people like thousands of others, but now each one of them struck her as exceptional and evil. In each one of them she saw nothing but falsity. "That young man," she thought, "rowing, in gold-rimmed spectacles, with chestnut hair and a nice-looking beard; he is a mamma's darling, rich, and well-fed, and always fortunate, and everyone considers him an honorable, free-thinking, progressive person. It's not a year since he left the university and came to live in the district, but he already talks of himself as 'we active members of the Zemstvo.' But in another year he will be bored like so many others and go off to Petersburg, and to justify his running away, will tell everyone that the Zemstvo is good for nothing, and that it has disappointed him. And from the other boat his young wife keeps her eyes fixed on him, and believes that he is 'an active member of the Zemstvo,' just as in a year she will believe that the Zemstvo is good for nothing. And that stout, carefully shaven gentleman in the straw hat with the broad ribbon, with an expensive cigar in his mouth: he is fond of saying, 'It is time to put away dreams and set to work!' He has Yorkshire pigs, Butler's hives, rape, pineapples, a dairy, a cheese factory, Italian bookkeeping by double entry; but every summer he sells his timber and mortgages part of his land to spend the autumn with his mistress in the Crimea. And there's Uncle Nikolay Nikolaich, who has quarreled with Pyotr Dmitrich, and yet for some reason does not go home."

Olga Mihailovna looked at the other boats, and there, too, she saw only uninteresting, queer creatures, affected or stupid people. She thought of all the people she knew in the district, and could not remember one person of whom one could say or think anything good. They all seemed to her mediocre, insipid, unintelligent, narrow, false, heartless; they all said what they did not think, and did what they did not want to. Dreariness and despair were stifling her; she longed to stop smiling, to leap up

and cry out, "I am sick of you," and then jump out and
swim to the bank.

"I say, let's take Pyotr Dmitrich in tow!" someone
shouted.

"In tow, in tow!" the others chimed in. "Olga Mihailovna, take your husband in tow."

To take him in tow, Olga Mihailovna, who was steer-
ing, had to seize the right moment and to catch hold of
his boat by the chain at the prow. When she bent over
to grasp the chain Pyotr Dmitrich frowned and looked
at her in alarm.

"I hope you won't catch cold," he said.

"If you are uneasy about me and the child, why do
you torment me?" thought Olga Mihailovna.

Pyotr Dmitrich acknowledged himself vanquished,
and, not caring to be towed, jumped from the *Penderaklia* into the boat which was overfull already, and
jumped so carelessly that the boat lurched violently, and
everyone cried out in terror.

"He did that to please the ladies," thought Olga Mihailovna; "he knows it's charming." Her hands and feet
began trembling, as she supposed, from boredom, vexation, the strain of smiling, and the discomfort she felt
all over her body. And to conceal this trembling from
her guests, she tried to talk more loudly, to laugh, to
move.

"If I suddenly begin to cry," she thought, "I shall say
I have toothache. . . ."

But at last the boats reached the "Island of Good
Hope," as they called the peninsula formed by a bend
in the river at an acute angle and covered with a copse
of birch-trees, oaks, willows, and poplars. The tables
were already laid under the trees; the samovars were
smoking, and Vasily and Grigory, in their swallowtails

and white knitted gloves, were already busy with the tea-things. On the other bank, opposite the Island of Good Hope, there stood the carriages which had come with the provisions. The baskets and parcels of provisions were carried across to the island in a canoe like the *Penderaklia*. The footmen, the coachmen, and even the peasant who rowed the skiff, had the solemn expression befitting a name-day such as one only sees in children and servants.

While Olga Mihailovna was making the tea and pouring out the first glasses, the visitors were busy with the liqueurs and sweets. Then there was the general commotion usual at picnics over drinking tea, very wearisome and exhausting for the hostess. Grigory and Vasily had hardly had time to take the glasses round before hands were being stretched out to Olga Mihailovna with empty glasses. One wanted tea with no sugar, another wanted it stronger, another weak, a fourth declined another glass. And all this Olga Mihailovna had to remember, and then to call, "Ivan Petrovich, is it without sugar for you?" or, "Gentlemen, which of you wanted it weak?" But the guest who had asked for weak tea, or no sugar, had by now forgotten it, and, absorbed in agreeable conversation, took the first glass that came. Depressed-looking figures wandered like shadows at a little distance from the table, pretending to look for mushrooms in the grass, or reading the labels on the boxes— these were those for whom there were no glasses. "Have you had tea?" Olga Mihailovna kept asking, and the guest so addressed begged her not to trouble and said, "I will wait," though it would have suited the hostess better if the visitors did not wait but made haste.

Some, absorbed in conversation, drank their tea slowly, keeping their glasses for half an hour; others, especially some who had drunk a good deal at dinner,

would not leave the table and kept on drinking glass
after glass, so that Olga Mihailovna scarcely had time
to fill them. One young wag sipped his tea through a
lump of sugar and kept saying, "Sinful man that I am,
I love to indulge myself with the Chinese herb." He
kept asking with a heavy sigh: "Another rotsherd of tea
more, if you please." He drank a great deal, nibbled at
his sugar, and thought it all very amusing and original,
and imagined that he was doing a clever imitation of a
Russian merchant. None of them understood that these
trifles were agonizing to their hostess, and, indeed, it
was hard to understand it, as Olga Mihailovna went on
all the time smiling affably and talking nonsense.

But she felt ill. . . . She was irritated by the crowd
of people, the laughter, the questions, the young wag,
the footmen harassed and run off their legs, the children
who hung round the table; she was irritated at Vata's
being like Nata, at Kolya's being like Mitya, so that one
could not tell which of them had had tea and which of
them had not. She felt that her smile of forced affability
was passing into an expression of anger, and she felt
every minute as though she would burst into tears.

"Rain, gentlemen," cried someone.

Everyone looked at the sky.

"Yes, it really is rain . . ." Pyotr Dmitrich assented,
and wiped his cheek.

Only a few drops were falling from the sky—the real
rain had not begun yet; but the company abandoned
their tea and made haste to leave. At first they all
wanted to drive home in the carriages, but changed
their minds and made for the boats. On the pretext that
she had to hasten home to give directions about the supper, Olga Mihailovna asked to be excused for leaving
the others, and went home in a carriage.

When she got into the carriage, she first of all gave

her face a rest from smiling. With an angry face she drove through the village and with an angry face acknowledged the bows of the peasants she met. When she got home, she went to the bedroom by the back way and lay down on her husband's bed.

"Merciful God!" she whispered. "What is all this hard labor for? Why do all these people jostle each other here and pretend that they are enjoying themselves? Why do I smile and lie? I don't understand it."

She heard steps and voices. The visitors had come back.

"Let them come," thought Olga Mihailovna; "I shall lie a little longer."

But a maidservant came and said:

"Marya Grigoryevna is going, Madam."

Olga Mihailovna jumped up, tidied her hair and hurried out of the room.

"Marya Grigoryevna, what is the meaning of this?" she began in an injured voice, going to meet Marya Grigoryevna. "Why are you in such a hurry?"

"I can't help it, darling! I've stayed too long as it is; my children are expecting me home."

"It's too bad of you! Why didn't you bring your children with you?"

"If you will let me, dear, I will bring them on some ordinary day, but today—"

"Oh, please do," Olga Mihailovna interrupted. "I shall be delighted! Your children are so sweet! Kiss them all for me. . . . But, really, you've hurt my feelings! I don't understand why you are in such a hurry!"

"I really must, I really must. . . . Good-by, dear. Take care of yourself. In your condition, you know . . ."

And the ladies kissed each other. After seeing the departing guest to her carriage, Olga Mihailovna went in to the ladies in the drawing-room. There the lamps were

already lighted and the gentlemen were sitting down to
cards.

IV

The party broke up after supper about a quarter past
twelve. Seeing her visitors off, Olga Mihailovna stood
at the door and said:

"You really ought to take a shawl! It's turning a little
chilly. You may catch cold, God forbid!"

"Don't trouble, Olga Mihailovna," the ladies answered as they got into the carriage. "Well, good-by.
Mind now, we are expecting you; don't disappoint
us!"

"Whoa!" the coachman checked the horses.

"Let's go, Denis! Good-by, Olga Mihailovna!"

"Kiss the children for me!"

The carriage started and immediately disappeared
into the darkness. In the red circle of light cast by the
lamp on the road a fresh pair or a team of three impatient horses and the silhouette of a coachman with
his arms held out stiffly before him would come into
view. Again there began kisses, reproaches, and en-
treaties to come again or to take a shawl. Pyotr Dmitrich
kept running out and helping the ladies into their carriages.

"You go now by Yefremovshchina," he directed the
coachman. "It's nearer through Mankino, but the road
is worse that way. You might take a tumble. . . .
Good-by, my charmer. *Mille compliments* to your artist!"

"Good-by, Olga Mihailovna, darling! Go indoors, or
you will catch cold! It's damp!"

"Whoa! you rascal!"

"What horses have you got here?" Pyotr Dmitrich
asked.

"They were bought from Haydarov, in Lent," answered the coachman.

"Capital horses. . . ."

And Pyotr Dmitrich patted the trace horse on the haunch.

"Well, you can start! God give you good luck!"

The last visitor was gone at last; the red circle on the road quivered, moved aside, contracted and went out, as Vasily carried away the lamp from the porch. On previous occasions when they had seen off their visitors, Pyotr Dmitrich and Olga Mihailovna had begun dancing about the drawing-room, facing each other, clapping their hands and singing: "They're gone! They're gone!" But now Olga Mihailovna was not equal to that. She went to her bedroom, undressed, and got into bed.

She fancied she would fall asleep at once and sleep soundly. Her legs and her shoulders ached painfully, her head was heavy from the strain of talking, and she was conscious, as before, of discomfort all over her body. Having drawn the cover over her head, she lay still for three or four minutes, then peeped out from under the bedclothes at the icon lamp, listened to the silence, and smiled.

"It's nice, it's nice," she whispered, curling up her legs, which felt as if they had grown longer from so much walking. "Sleep, sleep. . . ."

Her legs would not get into a comfortable position; she felt uneasy all over, and she turned on the other side. A big fly was buzzing about the bedroom and thumped against the ceiling in distress. She could hear, too, Grigory and Vasily stepping cautiously about the drawing-room, putting the chairs back in their places; it seemed to Olga Mihailovna that she could not go to sleep, nor be comfortable till those sounds were hushed.

And again she turned over on the other side impatiently.

She heard her husband's voice in the drawing-room. Someone must be staying the night, as Pyotr Dmitrich was addressing someone and speaking loudly:

"I don't say that Count Alexey Petrovich is a fraud. But he can't help seeming to be one, because all of you gentlemen attempt to see in him something different from what he really is. His craziness is looked upon as originality, his familiar manners as good-nature, and his complete absence of opinions as conservatism. Even granted that he is a Conservative 84 proof, what after all is conservatism?"

Pyotr Dmitrich, angry with Count Alexey Petrovich, his visitors, and himself, was relieving his heart. He abused both the Count and his visitors, and in his vexation with himself was ready to say and champion anything. After seeing his guest to his quarters, he paced up and down the drawing-room, walked through the dining-room, down the corridor, then into his study, then again went into the drawing-room, and came into the bedroom. Olga Mihailovna was lying on her back, with the bedclothes only to her waist (by now she felt hot), and with an angry face watched the fly that was thumping against the ceiling.

"Is someone staying the night?" she asked.

"Yegorov."

Pyotr Dmitrich undressed and got into his bed. Without speaking, he lighted a cigarette, and he, too, fell to watching the fly. There was an uneasy and forbidding look in his eyes. Olga Mihailovna looked at his handsome profile for five minutes in silence. It seemed to her for some reason that if her husband were suddenly to turn facing her and to say, "Olga, I am unhappy," she would cry or laugh, and she would be at ease. She fancied that her legs were aching and her body was uncomfortable all over because of her mental strain.

"Pyotr, what are you thinking of?" she said.

"Oh, nothing . . ." her husband answered.

"You have taken to having secrets from me of late: that's not right."

"Why is it not right?" answered Pyotr Dmitrich dryly and not at once. "We all have our personal life, every one of us, and we are bound to have our secrets."

"Personal life, our secrets . . . that's all words! Just realize that you are insulting me!" said Olga Mihailovna, sitting up in bed. "If you have a load on your heart, why do you hide it from me? And why do you find it more suitable to open your heart to women who are nothing to you, instead of to your wife? I overheard your outpourings to Lubochka by the hives today."

"Well, I congratulate you. I am glad you did overhear it."

This meant "Leave me alone and let me think." Olga Mihailovna was indignant. Vexation, hatred, and wrath, which had been accumulating within her during the whole day, suddenly boiled over; she wanted at once to speak out, to hurt her husband without putting it off till tomorrow, to wound him, to punish him. . . . Making an effort to control herself and not to scream, she said:

"Let me tell you, then, that it's all vile, vile, vile! I've been hating you all day; you see what you've done."

Pyotr Dmitrich, too, sat up in bed.

"It's vile, vile, vile," Olga Mihailovna went on, beginning to tremble all over. "There's no need to congratulate me; you had better congratulate yourself! It's a shame, a disgrace. You're so full of lies that you are ashamed to be alone in the room with your wife! You are a deceitful man! I see through you and understand every step you take!"

"Olya, I wish you would please warn me when you are out of humor. Then I will sleep in the study."

Saying this, Pyotr Dmitrich picked up his pillow and walked out of the bedroom. Olga Mihailovna had not foreseen this. For some minutes she remained silent, her mouth open, trembling all over and looking at the door by which her husband had gone out, and trying to understand what it meant. Was this one of the devices to which deceitful people have recourse when they are in the wrong, or was it a deliberate insult aimed at her pride? How was she to take it? Olga Mihailovna remembered her cousin, a lively young officer, who often used to tell her, laughing, that when "his spouse started nagging at him" at night, he usually picked up his pillow and went whistling to spend the night in his study, leaving his wife in a foolish and ridiculous position. This officer was married to a rich, capricious, and foolish woman whom he did not respect but simply put up with.

Olga Mihailovna jumped out of bed. To her mind there was only one thing left for her to do now; to dress with all possible haste and to leave the house forever. The house was her own, but so much the worse for Pyotr Dmitrich. Without pausing to consider whether this was necessary or not, she went quickly to the study to inform her husband of her intention ("Feminine logic!" flashed through her mind), and to say something wounding and sarcastic at parting. . . .

Pyotr Dmitrich was lying on the sofa and pretending to read a newspaper. There was a candle burning on a chair near him. His face could not be seen behind the newspaper.

"Be so kind as to tell me what this means? I am asking you."

"Be so kind . . ." Pyotr Dmitrich mimicked her, not

showing his face. "It's sickening, Olga! Upon my honor, I am exhausted and not up to it. . . . Let us do our quarreling tomorrow."

"No, I understand you perfectly!" Olga Mihailovna went on. "You hate me! Yes, yes! You hate me because I am richer than you! You will never forgive me that, and will always be lying to me!" ("Feminine logic!" flashed through her mind again.) "You are laughing at me now. . . . I am convinced, in fact, that you only married me in order to have property qualifications and those vile horses. . . . Oh, I am miserable!"

Pyotr Dmitrich dropped the newspaper and got up. The unexpected insult overwhelmed him. With a child-ishly helpless smile he looked desperately at his wife, and holding out his hands to her as though to ward off blows, he said imploringly:

"Olya!"

And expecting her to say something else that was aw-ful, he thrust his shoulders against the back of the sofa, and his huge figure seemed as helplessly childish as his smile.

"Olya, how could you say it?" he whispered.

Olga Mihailovna came to herself. She was suddenly aware of her passionate love for this man, remembered that he was her husband, Pyotr Dmitrich, without whom she could not live for a day, and who loved her passionately, too. She burst into loud sobs that sounded strange and unlike her, and ran back to her bedroom.

She fell on the bed, and short hysterical sobs, choking her and making her arms and legs twitch, resounded in the bedroom. Remembering that there was a visitor sleeping three or four rooms away, she buried her head under her pillow to stifle her sobs, but the pillow dropped to the floor, and she almost fell on the floor her-self when she stooped to pick it up. She pulled the quilt up to her face, but her hands would not obey her and tore convulsively at everything she clutched.

She thought that everything was lost, that the lie she had told to wound her husband had shattered her life into fragments. Her husband would not forgive her. The insult she had hurled at him was not one that could be effaced by any caresses, by any vows. . . . How could she convince her husband that she did not believe what she had said?

"It's finished, it's finished!" she cried, not noticing that the pillow had slipped onto the floor again. "For God's sake, for God's sake!"

Probably roused by her cries, the guest and the servants were now awake; next day all the neighborhood would know that she had been in hysterics and would blame Pyotr Dmitrich. She made an effort to restrain herself, but her sobs grew louder and louder every minute.

"For God's sake," she cried in a voice not like her own, and not knowing why she cried it. "For God's sake!"

She felt as though the bed were heaving under her and her feet were entangled in the bedclothes. Pyotr Dmitrich, in his dressing-gown, with a candle in his hand, came into the bedroom.

"Olya, hush!" he said.

She raised herself, and kneeling in bed, screwing up her eyes at the light, articulated through her sobs:

"Understand . . . understand! . . ."

She wanted to tell him that she was worn out by the guests, by his lying, by her own lying, and that it had all come to a head, but she could only articulate:

"Understand . . . understand!"

"Come, drink!" he said, handing her some water.

She took the glass obediently and began drinking, but

the water splashed over and was spilt on her arms, her throat and knees.

"I must look a sight," she thought.

Pyotr Dmitrich put her back into bed without a word, and covered her with the quilt, then he took the candle and went out.

"For God's sake!" Olga Mihailovna cried again. "Pyotr, understand, understand!"

Suddenly something gripped her in the lower part of her abdomen and her back with such violence that her wailing was cut short, and she bit the pillow from the pain. But the pain let her go at once, and she began sobbing again.

The maid came in, and arranging the quilt over her, asked in alarm:

"Mistress, darling, what is the matter?"

"Get out of here," said Pyotr Dmitrich sternly, going up to the bed.

"Understand . . . understand! . . ." Olga Mihailovna began.

"Olya, I entreat you, calm yourself," he said. "I did not mean to hurt you. I would not have gone out of the room if I had known it would have hurt you so much; I simply felt depressed. I tell you, on my honor—"

"Understand! . . . You were lying, I was lying. . . ."

"I understand. . . . Come, come, that's enough! I understand," said Pyotr Dmitrich tenderly, sitting down on her bed. "You said that in anger; I quite understand. I swear to God I love you beyond anything on earth, and when I married you I never once thought of your being rich. I loved you immensely, and that's all . . . I assure you. I have never been in want of money or felt the value of it, and so I cannot feel the difference between your fortune and mine. It always seemed to me we were equally well off. And that I have been deceitful in little things, that . . . of course, is true. My life has hitherto been arranged so frivolously that it has some-how been impossible to get on without paltry lying. It weighs on me, too, now. . . . Let us leave off talking about it, for goodness' sake!"

Olga Mihailovna again felt an acute pain, and clutched her husband by the sleeve.

"I am in pain, in pain, in pain . . ." she said rapidly. "Oh, what pain!"

"Damnation take those visitors!" muttered Pyotr Dmi-trich, getting up. "You ought not to have gone to the island today!" he cried. "What an idiot I was not to prevent you! Oh, my God!"

He scratched his head in vexation, and, with a wave of his hand, walked out of the room.

Then he came into the room several times, sat down on the bed beside her, and talked a great deal, some-times tenderly, sometimes angrily, but she hardly heard him. Her sobs were continually interrupted by fearful attacks of pain, and each time the pain was more acute and prolonged. At first she held her breath and bit the pillow during the pain, but then she began screaming in an unseemly piercing voice. Once, seeing her husband near her, she remembered that she had insulted him, and without pausing to think whether it were really Pyotr Dmitrich or whether she were in delirium, clutched his hand in both of hers and began kissing it.

"You were lying, I was lying . . .' she began justify-ing herself. "Understand, understand. . . . They have exhausted me, driven me out of all patience."

"Olya, we are not alone," said Pyotr Dmitrich.

Olga Mihailovna raised her head and saw Varvara, who was kneeling by the chest of drawers and pulling out the bottom drawer. The top drawers were already open. Then Varvara got up, red from the strain, and with a cold, solemn face began trying to unlock a box.

"Marya, I can't unlock it!" she said in a whisper. "You unlock it, won't you?"

Marya, the maid, was digging a candle end out of the candlestick with a pair of scissors, so as to put in a new candle; she went up to Varvara and helped her to unlock the box.

"There should be nothing locked . . ." whispered Varvara. "Unlock this casket, too, my good girl. Master," she said, "you should send word to Father Mihail to unlock the holy gates! You must!"

"Do what you like," said Pyotr Dmitrich, breathing hard, "only, for God's sake, make haste and fetch the doctor or the midwife! Has Vasily gone? Send someone else. Send your husband!"

"I'm in labor," Olga Mihailovna thought. "Varvara," she moaned, "but he won't be born alive!"

"It's all right, it's all right, mistress," whispered Varvara. "Please God, he will be alive! He will be alive!"

When Olga Mihailovna came to herself again after a pain she was no longer sobbing nor tossing from side to side, but moaning. She could not refrain from moaning even in the intervals between the pains. The candles were still burning, but the morning light was coming through the blinds. It was probably about five o'clock in the morning. At the round table there was sitting some unknown woman with a very discreet air, wearing a white apron. From her whole appearance it was evident she had been sitting there a long time. Olga Mihailovna guessed that she was the midwife.

"Will it soon be over?" she asked, and in her voice she heard a peculiar and unfamiliar note which had never been there before. "I must be dying in childbirth," she thought.

Pyotr Dmitrich came cautiously into the bedroom,

dressed for the day, and stood at the window with his back to his wife. He lifted the blind and looked out the window.

"What rain!" he said.

"What time is it?" asked Olga Mihailovna, in order to hear the unfamiliar note in her voice again.

"A quarter to six," answered the midwife.

"And what if I really am dying?" thought Olga Mihailovna, looking at her husband's head and the windowpanes on which the rain was beating. "How will he live without me? With whom will he have tea and dinner, talk in the evening, sleep?"

He looked little to her and orphaned; she felt sorry for him and wanted to say something nice, caressing and consolatory. She remembered how in the spring he had meant to buy himself some hounds, and she, thinking it a cruel and dangerous sport, had prevented him from doing it.

"Pyotr, buy yourself hounds," she moaned.

He lowered the blind and went up to the bed, and would have said something; but at that moment the pain came back, and Olga Mihailovna uttered an unseemly, piercing scream.

The pain and the constant screaming and moaning stupefied her. She heard, saw, and sometimes spoke, but hardly understood anything, and was only conscious that she was in pain or was just going to be in pain. It seemed to her that the name-day party had been long, long ago—not yesterday, but a year ago perhaps; and that her new life of agony had lasted longer than her childhood, her schooldays, her time at the university, and her marriage, and would go on for a long, long time, endlessly. She saw them bring tea to the midwife and summon her at midday to lunch and afterwards to dinner; she saw Pyotr Dmitrich grow used to coming in.

standing for long intervals by the window, and going out again; saw strange men, the maid, Varvara, come in as though they were at home. . . . Varvara said nothing but, 'He will, he will," and was angry when anyone closed the drawers of the bureau. Olga Mihailovna saw the light change in the room and in the windows: at one time it was pale as at dusk, then thick like fog, then bright as it had been at dinnertime the day before, then pale again . . . and each of these changes lasted as long as her childhood, her schooldays, her years at the university. . . .

In the evening two doctors—one bony, bald, with a big red beard, the other swarthy with a Jewish face and cheap spectacles—performed some sort of operation on Olga Mihailovna. To these unknown men touching her body she felt utterly indifferent. By now she had no feeling of shame, no will, and anyone might do what he would with her. If anyone had rushed at her with a knife, or had insulted Pyotr Dmitrich, or had robbed her of her right to the little creature, she would not have said a word.

They gave her chloroform during the operation. When she came to again, the pain was still there and insufferable. It was night. And Olga Mihailovna remembered that there had been just such a night with the stillness, the lamp, with the midwife sitting motionless by the bed, with the drawers of the chest pulled out, with Pyotr Dmitrich standing by the window, but some time very, very long ago. . . .

v

"I am not dead . . ." thought Olga Mihailovna when she began to understand her surroundings again, and when the pain was over.

A bright summer day looked in at the widely open windows; in the garden below the windows, sparrows and magpies never ceased chattering for one instant.

The drawers were shut now, her husband's bed had been made. There was no sign of the midwife or of the maid or of Varvara in the room, only Pyotr Dmitrich was standing, as before, motionless by the window looking into the garden. There was no sound of a child's crying, no one was congratulating her or rejoicing, it was evident that the little creature had not been born alive.

"Pyotr!" Olga Mihailovna called to her husband.

Pyotr Dmitrich looked round. It seemed as though a long time must have passed since the last guest had departed and Olga Mihailovna had insulted her husband, for Pyotr Dmitrich was perceptibly thinner and hollow-eyed.

"What is it?" he asked, coming up to the bed.

He looked away, moved his lips and smiled with childlike helplessness.

"Is it all over?" asked Olga Mihailovna.

Pyotr Dmitrich tried to make some answer, but his lips quivered and his mouth worked like a toothless old man's, like Uncle Nikolay Nikolaich's.

"Olya," he said, wringing his hands; big tears suddenly dropping from his eyes. "Olya, I don't care about your property qualification, nor the Circuit Courts" (he gave a sob) "nor dissenting opinions, nor those visitors, nor your dowry. . . . I don't care about anything! Why didn't we take thought for our child? Oh, it's no good talking!"

With a despairing wave of the hand he went out of the bedroom.

But nothing mattered to Olga Mihailovna now. There was a mistiness in her brain from the chloroform, an emptiness in her soul. . . . The dull indifference to life which possessed her when the two doctors were performing the operation was still with her.

1888

An Attack of Nerves

A MEDICAL student called Meier, and a pupil of the Moscow School of Painting, Sculpture, and Architecture called Rybnikov, went one evening to see their friend Vasilyev, a law student, and suggested that he should go with them to S—— Street. For a long time Vasilyev would not consent to go, but in the end he put on his overcoat and went with them.

He knew nothing of fallen women except by hearsay and from books, and he had never in his life been to the houses in which they live. He knew that there are immoral women who, under the pressure of fatal circumstances—environment, bad education, poverty, and so on—are forced to sell their honor for money. They know nothing of pure love, have no children, have no civil rights; their mothers and sisters weep over them as though they were dead, science treats of them as an evil, men address them with contemptuous familiarity. But in spite of all that, they do not lose the image and likeness of God. They all acknowledge their sin and hope for salvation. Of the means that lead to salvation they can avail themselves to the fullest extent. Society, it is true, will not forgive people their past, but in the sight of God St. Mary of Egypt is no lower than the other saints. When it had happened to Vasilyev in the street to recognize a fallen woman by her dress or her manners, or to see a picture of one in a comic paper, he always remembered a story he had once read: a young man, pure and self-sacrificing, loves a fallen woman and asks her to become his wife; she, considering herself unworthy of such happiness, takes poison.

Vasilyev lived in one of the side streets leading into Tverskoy Boulevard. When he came out of the house with his two friends it was about eleven o'clock. The first snow had recently fallen, and all nature was under its spell. There was the smell of snow in the air, the snow crunched softly under the feet; the earth, the roofs, the trees, the seats in the boulevards, everything was soft, white, young, and this made the houses look quite different from the way they did the day before; the street lamps burned more brightly, the air was more transparent, the carriages rumbled with a deeper note, and with the fresh, light, frosty air a feeling stirred in the soul akin to the white, youthful, fluffy snow.

"Against my will an unknown force," hummed the medical student in his agreeable tenor, "has led me to these mournful shores."

"Behold the mill . . ." the artist seconded him, "in ruins now. . . ."

"Behold the mill . . . in ruins now," the medical student repeated, raising his eyebrows and shaking his head mournfully.

He paused, rubbed his forehead, trying to remember the words, and then sang aloud, so well that passers-by looked round:

> Here in old days when I was free,
> Love, free, unfettered, greeted me.

The three of them went into a restaurant and, without taking off their overcoats, drank a couple of glasses of vodka each. Before drinking the second glass, Vasilyev noticed a bit of cork in his vodka, raised the glass to his eyes, and gazed into it for a long time, frowning, screwing up his shortsighted eyes. The medical student misunderstood his expression, and said:

"Come, why look at it? No philosophizing, please. Vodka is given us to be drunk, sturgeon to be eaten, women to be visited, snow to be walked upon. For one evening anyway live like a human being!"

"But I haven't said anything . . ." Vasilyev protested, laughing. "Am I refusing to?"

There was a warmth inside him from the vodka. He looked with emotion at his friends, admired and envied them. In these strong, healthy, cheerful people how wonderfully balanced everything is, how finished and smooth is everything in their minds and souls! They sing, and have a passion for the theater, and draw, and talk a great deal, and drink, and they don't have headaches the day after; they are both poetical and debauched, both soft and hard; they can work, too, and be indignant, and laugh without reason, and talk nonsense; they are warm, honest, self-sacrificing, and as human beings are in no way inferior to himself, who watches over every step he takes and every word he utters, who is fastidious and cautious, and ready to raise every trifle to the level of a problem. And he longed for one evening to live as his friends did, to open out, to free himself from his own control. If vodka had to be drunk, he would drink it, though his head would be splitting next morning. If he were taken to the women he would go. He would laugh, play the fool, gaily respond to the passing advances of strangers in the street. . . .

He went out of the restaurant laughing. He liked his friends—one in a crushed broad-brimmed hat, with an affectation of artistic disorder; the other in a sealskin

cap, a man not poor, though he affected to belong to the
Bohemia of learning. He liked the snow, the pale street
lamps, the sharp black tracks left in the first snow by the
feet of the passers-by. He liked the air, and especially
that limpid, tender, naive, as it were virginal tone, which
can be observed in nature only twice in the year—when
everything is covered with snow, and in spring on
bright days and moonlight evenings when the ice breaks
on the river.

> Against my will an unknown force,
> Has led me to these mournful shores,

he hummed in an undertone.

And the lines for some reason haunted him and his
friends all the way, and all three of them hummed it
mechanically, not in time with one another.

Vasilyev's imagination was picturing how, in another
ten minutes, he and his friends would knock at a door;
how by little dark passages and dark rooms they would
steal in to the women; how, taking advantage of the
darkness, he would strike a match, would light up and
see a martyred face and a guilty smile. The unknown,
fair or dark, would certainly have her hair down and be
wearing a white bed-jacket; she would be frightened
by the light, would be fearfully confused, and would
say: "For God's sake, what are you doing? Put it out!"
It would all be dreadful, but interesting and novel.

II

The friends proceeded from Trubnoy Square to Gra-
chevka, and soon reached the side street which Vasilyev
only knew by reputation. Seeing two rows of houses
with brightly lighted windows and wide-open doors,
and hearing gay strains of pianos and violins, sounds

which floated out from every door and formed a strange
medley, as though an unseen orchestra were tuning up
in the darkness above the roofs, Vasilyev was surprised
and said:

"What a lot of houses!"

"That's nothing," said the medical student. "In London there are ten times as many. There are about a
hundred thousand such women there."

The cabmen were sitting on their boxes as calmly and
indifferently as in any other side street; there were
passers-by on the sidewalks as in other streets. No one
was hurrying, no one was hiding his face in his coat-
collar, no one shook his head reproachfully. . . . And
in this indifference, in the mingled sounds of pianos and
violins, in the bright windows and wide-open doors,
there was something immodest, insolent, reckless, and
extravagant. Probably it was as gay and noisy at the
slave-markets in their day, and people's faces and gait
showed the same indifference.

"Let us begin from the beginning," said the artist.

The friends went into a narrow passage lighted by a
lamp with a reflector. When they opened the door
a man in a black coat, with an unshaven face like a
flunkey's, and sleepy-looking eyes, got up lazily from a
yellow sofa in the hall. The place smelled like a laundry
with an odor of vinegar in addition. A door from the
hall led into a brightly lighted room. The medical student and the artist stopped at this door and, craning
their necks, peeped into the room.

"Buona sera, signori, rigolleto—hugenotti—traviata!"
began the artist, with a theatrical bow.

"Havanna—tarakano—pistoleto!" said the medical
student, pressing his cap to his breast and bowing low.

Vasilyev was standing behind them. He would have
liked to make a theatrical bow and say something silly,

too, but he only smiled, felt an awkwardness that was like shame, and waited impatiently for what would happen next.

A little blond girl of seventeen or eighteen, with bobbed hair, in a short light-blue frock with a white bow on her bosom, appeared in the doorway.

"Why do you stand at the door?" she said. "Take off your coats and come into the drawing-room."

The medical student and the artist, still talking Italian, went into the drawing-room. Vasilyev followed them irresolutely.

"Gentlemen, take off your coats!" the flunkey said sternly; "you can't go in like that."

In the drawing-room there was, besides the girl, another woman, very stout and tall, with a foreign face and bare arms. She was sitting near the piano, laying out a game of patience on her lap. She took no notice whatever of the visitors.

"Where are the other young ladies?" asked the medical student.

"They are having their tea," said the blonde. "Stepan," she called, "go and tell the young ladies some students have come!"

A little later a third young lady came into the room. She was wearing a bright red dress with blue stripes. Her face was painted thickly and unskillfully, her brow was hidden under her hair, and there was an unblinking, frightened stare in her eyes. As she came in, she began at once singing some song in a coarse, powerful contralto. After her a fourth appeared, and a fifth. . . .

In all this Vasilyev saw nothing novel or interesting. It seemed to him that this room, the piano, the looking-glass in its cheap gilt frame, the bow, the dress with the blue stripes, and the blank indifferent faces, he had seen before and more than once. Of the darkness, the silence, the secrecy, the guilty smile, of all that he had expected to meet here and had dreaded, he saw no trace.

Everything was ordinary, prosaic, and uninteresting. Only one thing faintly stirred his curiosity—the terrible, as it were intentional, bad taste which was visible in the cornices, in the absurd pictures, in the dresses, in the sash. There was something characteristic and peculiar in this bad taste.

"How poor and stupid it all is!" thought Vasilyev. "What is there in all this trumpery I see now that can tempt a normal man and excite him to commit the horrible sin of buying a human being for a ruble? I understand any sin for the sake of splendor, beauty, grace, passion, taste; but what is there here? What is there here worth sinning for? But . . . I mustn't think!"

"Beardy, treat me to some porter!" said the blonde, addressing him.

Vasilyev was at once overcome with embarrassment.

"With pleasure," he said, bowing politely. "Only excuse me, madam, I . . . I won't drink with you. I don't drink."

Five minutes later the friends went off into another house.

"Why did you ask for porter?" said the medical student angrily. "What a millionaire! You have thrown away six rubles for no reason whatever—simply waste!"

"If she wants it, why not let her have the pleasure?" said Vasilyev, justifying himself.

"You did not give pleasure to her, but to the madam. They are told to ask the visitors to stand them treat because it is a profit to the house."

"Behold the mill . . ." hummed the artist, "in ruins now. . . ."

Entering the next house, the friends stopped in the hall and did not go into the drawing-room. Here, as in the first house, a figure in a black coat, with a sleepy face like a flunkey's, got up from a sofa in the hall. Looking at this flunkey, at his face and his shabby black coat, Vasilyev thought: "What must an ordinary simple Russian have gone through before Fate flung him down as a flunkey here? Where had he been before and what had he done? What was awaiting him? Was he married? Where was his mother, and did she know that he was employed here as a flunkey?" And Vasilyev took particular notice of the flunkey in each house. In one of the houses—he thought it was the fourth—there was a little spare, frail-looking flunkey with a watch-chain on his waistcoat. He was reading a newspaper, and took no notice of them when they came in. Looking at his face Vasilyev, for some reason, thought that a man with such a face might steal, might murder, might bear false witness. But the face was really interesting: a big forehead, gray eyes, a little flattened nose, thin compressed lips, and a blankly stupid and at the same time insolent expression like that of a young harrier overtaking a hare. Vasilyev thought it would be well to touch this man's hair, to see whether it was soft or coarse. It must be coarse like a dog's.

III

Having drunk two glasses of porter, the artist became suddenly tipsy and grew unnaturally lively.

"Let's go to another!" he said peremptorily, waving his arms. "I will take you to the best one."

When he had brought his friends to the house which in his opinion was the best, he declared his firm intention of dancing a quadrille. The medical student grumbled something about their having to pay the musicians a ruble, but agreed to be his vis-à-vis. They began dancing.

It was just as nasty in the best house as in the worst.

Here there were just the same looking-glasses and pictures, the same styles of coiffure and dress. Looking round at the furnishing of the rooms and the costumes, Vasilyev realized that this was not lack of taste, but something that might be called the taste, and even the style, of S—— Street, which could not be found elsewhere—something integral in its ugliness, not accidental, but elaborated in the course of years. After he had been in eight houses he was no longer surprised at the color of the dresses, at the long trains, the gaudy bows, the sailor dresses, and the thick purplish rouge on the cheeks; he saw that it all had to be like this, that if a single one of the women had been dressed like a human being, or if there had been one decent engraving on the wall, the general tone of the whole street would have suffered.

"How unskillfully they sell themselves!" he thought. "How can they fail to understand that vice is only alluring when it is beautiful and hidden, when it wears the mask of virtue? Modest black dresses, pale faces, mournful smiles, and darkness would be far more effective than this clumsy tinsel. Stupid things! If they don't understand it of themselves, their visitors might surely have taught them. . . ."

A young lady in a Polish dress edged with white fur came up to him and sat down beside him.

"You nice dark man, why aren't you dancing?" she asked. "Why are you so dull?"

"Because it is dull."

"Treat me to some Lafitte. Then it won't be dull."

Vasilyev made no answer. He was silent for a little, and then asked:

"What time do you get to sleep?"

"At six o'clock."

"And what time do you get up?"

"Sometimes at two and sometimes at three."

"And what do you do when you get up?"

"We have coffee, and at six o'clock we have dinner."

"And what do you have for dinner?"

"Usually soup, beefsteak, and dessert. Our madam keeps the girls well. But why do you ask all this?"

"Oh, just to talk. . . ."

Vasilyev longed to talk to the young lady about many things. He felt an intense desire to find out where she came from, whether her parents were living, and whether they knew that she was here; how she had come into this house; whether she was cheerful and satisfied, or sad and oppressed by gloomy thoughts; whether she hoped some day to get out of her present position. . . . But he could not think how to begin or in what shape to put his questions so as not to seem impertinent. He thought for a long time, and asked:

"How old are you?"

"Eighty," the young lady jested, looking with a laugh at the antics of the artist as he danced

All at once she burst out laughing at something, and uttered a long cynical sentence loud enough to be heard by everyone. Vasilyev was aghast, and not knowing what kind of a face to put on the matter, gave a constrained smile. He was the only one who smiled; all the others, his friends, the musicians, the women, did not even glance towards his neighbor, but seemed not to have heard her.

"Stand me some Lafitte," his neighbor said again.

Vasilyev felt a repulsion for her white fur and for her voice, and walked away from her. It seemed to him hot and stifling, and his heart began pounding slowly but violently, like a hammer—one! two! three!

"Let us go away!" he said, pulling the artist by his sleeve.

"Wait a little; let me finish."

While the artist and the medical student were finishing the quadrille, to avoid looking at the women, Vasilyev scrutinized the musicians. A respectable-looking old man in spectacles, rather like Marshal Bazaine, was playing the piano; a young man with a fair beard, dressed in the latest fashion, was playing the violin. The young man had a face that did not look stupid or hollow-cheeked, but intelligent, youthful, and fresh. He was dressed fancifully and with taste; he played with feeling. It was a mystery how he and the respectable-looking old man had got here. How was it they were not ashamed to sit here? What were they thinking about when they looked at the women?

If the violin and the piano had been played by men in rags, hungry, gloomy, drunken, with dissipated or stupid faces, then one could have understood their presence, perhaps. As it was, Vasilyev was at a loss to understand it. He recalled the story of the fallen woman he had once read, and he thought now that that human image with the guilty smile had nothing in common with what he was seeing now. It seemed to him that he was seeing not fallen women, but beings belonging to a different world quite apart, alien to him and incomprehensible; if he had seen this world before on the stage, or read of it in a book, he would not have believed it could exist.

The woman with the white fur burst out laughing again and uttered a loathsome phrase in a loud voice. A feeling of disgust took possession of him. He blushed and went out of the room.

"Wait a minute, we are coming too!" the artist shouted to him.

IV

"While we were dancing," said the medical student, as they all three went out into the street, "I had a conversation with my partner. We talked about her first romance. He, the hero, was an accountant at Smolensk with a wife and five children. She was seventeen, and she lived with her papa and mamma, who sold soap and candles."

"How did he win her heart?" asked Vasilyev.

"By spending fifty rubles on underwear for her. What the devil!"

"So he knew how to get his partner's story out of her," thought Vasilyev about the medical student. "But I don't know how."

"Gentlemen, I am going home!" he said.

"What for?"

"Because I don't know how to behave here. Besides, I am bored, disgusted. What is there amusing in it? If they were human beings—but they are savages and animals. I am going; do as you like."

"Come, Grisha, Grigory, darling . . ." said the artist in a tearful voice, hugging Vasilyev, "come along! Let's go to one more together and damnation take them! . . . Please do, Grisha!"

They persuaded Vasilyev and led him up a staircase. In the carpet and the gilt banisters, in the doorman who opened the door, and in the panels that decorated the hall, the same S—— Street style was apparent, but carried to a greater perfection, more imposing.

"I really will go home!" said Vasilyev as he was taking off his coat.

"Come, come, dear boy," said the artist, and he kissed him on the neck. "Don't be tiresome. - - - Gri-

gri, be a good comrade! We came together, we will go back together. What a beast you are, really!"

"I can wait for you in the street. I think it's loathsome here, really!"

"Come, come, Grisha. . . . If it is loathsome, observe it! Do you understand? Observe!"

"One must take an objective view of things," said the medical student gravely.

Vasilyev went into the drawing-room and sat down. There were a number of visitors in the room besides him and his friends: two infantry officers, a bald, gray-haired gentleman in spectacles, two beardless youths from the Institute of Surveying, and a very tipsy man who looked like an actor. All the young ladies were taken up with these visitors and paid no attention to Vasilyev.

Only one of them, dressed à la *Aïda,* glanced sideways at him, smiled, and said, yawning: "A dark one has come. . . ."

Vasilyev's heart was pounding and his face burned. He felt ashamed before these visitors of his presence here, and he felt disgusted and miserable. He was tormented by the thought that he, a decent and affectionate person (such as he had hitherto considered himself), hated these women and felt only repelled by them. He felt pity neither for the women nor the musicians nor the flunkeys.

"It is because I am not trying to understand them," he thought. "They are all more like animals than human beings, but of course they are human beings all the same, they have souls. One must understand them and then judge. . . ."

"Grisha, don't go, wait for us," the artist shouted to him and disappeared.

The medical student disappeared soon after.

"Yes, one must make an effort to understand, one mustn't be like this . . ." Vasilyev went on thinking.

And he began gazing at each of the women with strained attention, looking for a guilty smile. But either he did not know how to read their faces, or not one of these women felt guilty; he read on every face nothing but a blank expression of everyday vulgar boredom and complacency. Stupid faces, stupid smiles, harsh, stupid voices, insolent movements, and nothing else. Apparently each of them had in the past a romance with an accountant based on fifty rubles' worth of underwear, and looked for no other delights in the present but coffee, a dinner of three courses, wines, quadrilles, sleeping till two in the afternoon. . . .

Finding no guilty smile, Vasilyev began to look round to see if there were one intelligent face. And his attention was caught by one pale, rather sleepy, tired-looking face. . . . It was a brunette, not very young, wearing a dress covered with spangles; she sat in an easy-chair, looking at the floor and lost in thought. Vasilyev walked from one corner of the room to the other, and, as though casually, sat down beside her.

"I must begin with something trivial," he thought, "and pass to what is serious. . . ."

"What a pretty dress you have," and with his finger he touched the gold fringe of her fichu.

"Oh, is it? . . ." said the dark woman listlessly.

"What province do you come from?"

"I? From a distance. . . . From Chernigov."

"A fine province. It's nice there."

"Any place seems nice when one is not in it."

"It's a pity I cannot describe nature," thought Vasilyev. "I might touch her by a description of nature in Chernigov. No doubt she loves the place if she was born there."

"Are you dull here?" he asked.

"Of course I am dull."

"Why don't you go away from here if you are dull?"

"Where should I go to? Go begging or what?"

"Begging would be easier than living here."

"How do you know that? Have you begged?"

"Yes, when I hadn't the money to study. Even if I hadn't, anyone could understand that. A beggar is anyway a free man, and you are a slave."

The brunette stretched, and with sleepy eyes watched the footman who was carrying a trayful of glasses and soda water.

"Stand me a glass of porter," she said, and yawned again.

"Porter," thought Vasilyev. "And what if your brother or mother walked in at this moment? What would you say? And what would they say? There would be porter then, I imagine. . . ."

All at once there was the sound of weeping. From the adjoining room, to which the footman had taken the soda water, a fair-haired man with a red face and angry eyes ran rapidly. He was followed by the tall, stout madam, who was shouting in a shrill voice:

"Nobody has given you leave to slap girls on the cheeks! We have visitors better than you, and they don't fight! You fourflusher!"

A hubbub arose. Vasilyev was frightened and turned pale. In the next room there was the sound of bitter, genuine weeping, as though of someone insulted. And he realized that there were real people living here who, like people everywhere else, felt insulted, suffered, wept, and cried for help. The feeling of choking hate and disgust gave way to an acute feeling of pity and anger against the aggressor. He rushed into the room where there was weeping. Across rows of bottles on a marble-top table he distinguished a suffering face, wet with tears, stretched out his hands towards that face, took a step towards the table, but at once drew back in horror. The weeping woman was drunk.

As he made his way through the noisy crowd gathered about the fair-haired man, his heart sank and he felt frightened like a child; and it seemed to him that in this alien, incomprehensible world people wanted to pursue him, to beat him, to pelt him with filthy words. . . . He tore down his coat from the hanger and ran headlong downstairs.

v

Pressed against the fence, he stood near the house waiting for his friends to come out. The sounds of the pianos and violins, gay, reckless, insolent, and mournful, mingled in the air in a sort of chaos, and this tangle of sounds seemed again like an unseen orchestra tuning up on the roofs. If one looked upwards into the darkness, the black background was all spangled with white, moving specks: it was snow falling. As the snowflakes came into the light they floated round lazily in the air like down, and still more lazily fell to the ground. The snowflakes whirled thickly round Vasilyev and hung upon his beard, his eyelashes, his eyebrows. . . . The cabmen, the horses, and the passers-by were white.

"And how can the snow fall in this street!" thought Vasilyev. "Damnation take these houses!"

His legs seemed to be giving way from fatigue, simply from having run down the stairs; he gasped for breath as though he had been climbing uphill, his heart beat so loudly that he could hear it. He was consumed by a desire to get out of the street as quickly as possible and to go home, but even stronger was his desire to wait for his companions and vent upon them his oppressive feeling.

There was much he did not understand about these houses, the souls of ruined women were a mystery to him as before; but it was clear to him that the situation was far worse than could have been believed. If that sinful woman who had poisoned herself was called fallen, it was difficult to find a fitting name for all these who were dancing now to this tangle of sound and uttering long, loathsome sentences. They were not on the road to ruin, but ruined.

"There is vice," he thought, "but neither consciousness of sin nor hope of salvation. People sell and buy them, drown them in wine and steep them in abominations, while, like sheep, they are stupid, indifferent, and don't understand. My God! My God!"

It was clear to him, too, that everything that is called human dignity, personality, the divine image and likeness, was defiled to the uttermost and that not only the street and the stupid women were responsible for it.

A group of students, white with snow, passed him, laughing and talking gaily; one, a tall thin fellow, stopped, glanced at Vasilyev's face, and said in a drunken voice:

"One of us! A bit high, old man? Aha-ha! Never mind, have a good time! Don't be downhearted, old chap!"

He took Vasilyev by the shoulders and pressed his cold wet mustaches against his cheek, then he slipped, staggered, and, waving both hands, cried:

"Hold on! Don't tumble!"

And laughing, he ran to overtake his companions.

Through the noise came the sound of the artist's voice:

"Don't you dare to hit women! I won't let you, damnation take you! You scoundrels!"

The medical student appeared in the doorway. He looked from side to side, and seeing Vasilyev, said in an agitated voice:

"You here! I tell you it's really impossible to go anywhere with Yegor! What a fellow he is! I don't understand him! He has got up a scene! Do you hear? Yegor!" he shouted at the door. "Yegor!"

"I won't allow you to hit women!" the artist's piercing voice sounded from above. Something heavy and lumbering rolled down the stairs. It was the artist falling headlong. Evidently he had been pushed downstairs.

He picked himself up from the ground, shook his hat, and, with an angry and indignant face, brandished his fist towards the top of the stairs and shouted:

"Scoundrels! Torturers! Bloodsuckers! I won't allow you to hit them! To hit a weak, drunken woman! Oh, you . . ."

"Yegor! . . . Come, Yegor! . . ." the medical student began imploring him. "I give you my word of honor I'll never come with you again. On my word of honor I won't!"

Little by little the artist was pacified and the friends went homewards.

"Against my will an unknown force," hummed the medical student, "has led me to these mournful shores."

" 'Behold the mill,' " the artist chimed in a little later, " 'in ruins now.' What a lot of snow, Holy Mother! Grisha, why did you go? You are a coward, a regular old woman."

Vasilyev walked behind his companions, looked at their backs, and thought:

"One of two things: either we only fancy prostitution is an evil, and we exaggerate it; or, if prostitution really is as great an evil as is generally assumed, these dear friends of mine are as much slave-owners, ravishers, and murderers, as the inhabitants of Syria and Cairo, that are described in *Niva*. Now they are singing, laughing, talking sense, but haven't they just been exploiting hunger, ignorance, and stupidity? They have—I have been a witness of it. What is the use of their humanity, their medicine, their painting? The science, art, and lofty sentiments of these assassins remind me of the piece of bacon in the story. Two brigands murdered a beggar in a forest; they began sharing his clothes between them, and found in his wallet a piece of bacon. 'Well found,' said one of them; 'let us have a bit.' 'What do you mean? How can you?' cried the other in horror. 'Have you forgotten that today is Wednesday?' And they would not eat it. After murdering a man, they came out of the forest in the firm conviction that they were good Christians. In the same way these men, after buying women, go their way imagining that they are artists and men of science. . . ."

"Listen!" he said sharply and angrily. "Why do you come here? Is it possible—is it possible you don't understand how horrible it is? Your medical books tell you that every one of these women dies prematurely of consumption or something; art tells you that morally they are dead even earlier. Every one of them dies because she has in her time to entertain five hundred men on an average, let us say. Each one of them is killed by five hundred men. You are among those five hundred! If each of you in the course of your life visits this place or others like it two hundred and fifty times, it follows that one woman is killed by every two of you! Can't you understand that? Isn't it horrible for two of you, three of you, five of you, to murder a foolish, hungry woman! Ah! isn't it awful, my God!"

"I knew it would end like that," the artist said frowning. "We ought not to have gone with this fool and ass! You imagine you have grand notions in your head now, ideas, don't you? No, it's the devil knows what, but not ideas. You are looking at me now with hatred and repulsion, but I tell you it's better you should set up twenty more houses like those than look like that. There's more vice in your look than in the whole street! Come along, Volodya, let him go to the devil! He's a fool and an ass, and that's all. . . ."

"We human beings do murder each other," said the medical student. "It's immoral, of course, but philosophizing won't help it. Good-by!"

At Trubnoy Square the friends said good-by and parted. When he was left alone, Vasilyev strode rapidly along the boulevard. He felt frightened of the darkness, of the snow which was falling in heavy flakes on the ground and seemed as though it would cover up the whole world; he felt frightened of the street lamps glimmering feebly through the clouds of snow. His soul was possessed by an unaccountable, faint-hearted terror. Passers-by came towards him from time to time, but he timidly edged away; it seemed to him that women, none but women, were coming from all sides and staring at him. . . .

"It's beginning," he thought, "I am going to have an attack of nerves."

VI

At home he lay on his bed and said, shuddering all over: "They are alive! Alive! My God, those women are alive!"

He stimulated his imagination in all sorts of ways; he pictured himself the brother of a fallen woman, or her father, then a fallen woman herself, with her painted cheeks, and it all moved him to horror.

It seemed to him that he must settle the question at once at all costs, and that this question was not one that did not concern him, but was his own personal problem. He made an immense effort, repressed his despair, and, sitting on the bed, holding his head in his hands, began thinking how one could save all the women he had seen that day. The method for attacking problems of all kinds was, as he was an educated man, well known to him. And however excited he was, he strictly adhered to that method. He recalled the history of the problem and its literature, and for a quarter of an hour paced from one end of the room to the other trying to remember all the methods for saving women employed at the present time. He had very many good friends and acquaintances who lived in rooming-houses. Among them were a good many honest and self-sacrificing men. Some of them had attempted to save women. . . .

"All these not very numerous attempts," thought Vasilyev, "can be divided into three groups. Some, after buying the woman out of the brothel, took a room for her, bought her a sewing-machine, and she became a seamstress. And whether he wanted to or not, after having bought her out he made her his mistress; then when he had taken his degree, he went away and handed her into the keeping of some other decent man as though she were a thing. And the fallen woman remained a fallen woman. Others, after buying her out, took a lodging apart for her, bought the inevitable sewing-machine, and tried teaching her to read, preaching at her, and giving her books. The woman stayed and sewed as long as it was interesting and a novelty to her, then getting bored, began receiving men on the sly, or ran away and went back where she could sleep till three o'clock, drink coffee, and have good dinners. Finally, those who were most ardent and self-sacrificing took a bold, resolute step: they married the woman. And when the insolent and spoiled, or stupid and crushed animal became a wife, the head of a household, and afterwards a mother, it turned her whole existence and attitude to life upside down, so that it was hard to recognize the fallen woman afterwards in the wife and the mother. Yes, marriage was the best and perhaps the only means."

"But it is impossible!" Vasilyev said aloud, and he sank upon his bed. "I, to begin with, could not marry one! To do that one must be a saint and be unable to feel hatred or repulsion. But let us suppose that I, the medical student, and the artist mastered ourselves and did marry them—suppose they were all married. What would be the result? The result would be that while here in Moscow they were being married, some Smolensk accountant would be debauching another lot, and that lot would be streaming here to fill the vacant places, together with others from Saratov, Nizhni-Novgorod, Warsaw. . . . And what is one to do with the hundred thousand in London? What's one to do with those in Hamburg?"

The lamp in which the oil had burnt down began to smoke. Vasilyev did not notice it. He began pacing to and fro again, still thinking. Now he put the question differently: what must be done that fallen women should not be needed? For that, it was essential that the men who buy and kill them should feel all the immorality of their share in enslaving them and should be horrified. One must save the men.

"Art and science are of no use here, that is clear . . ." thought Vasilyev. "The only way out of it is missionary work."

And he began to dream how the next evening he would stand at the corner of the street and say to every passer-by: "Where are you going and what for? Have the fear of God!"

He would turn to the apathetic cabmen and say to them: "Why are you staying here? Why aren't you revolted? Why aren't you indignant? I suppose you believe in God and know that it is a sin, that people go to hell for it? Why don't you speak? True, they are strangers to you, but you know even they have fathers, brothers, who are just like yourselves. . . ."

One of Vasilyev's friends had once said of him that he was a talented man. There are all sorts of talents—talent for writing, talent for the stage, talent for art; but he had a peculiar talent—a talent for *humanity*. He possessed an extraordinarily fine delicate scent for pain in general. As a good actor reflects in himself the movements and voice of others, so Vasilyev could reflect in his soul the sufferings of others. When he saw tears, he wept; beside a sick man, he felt sick himself and moaned; if he saw an act of violence, he felt as though he himself were the victim of it, he was frightened as a child, and in his fright ran to help. The pain of others worked on his nerves, excited him, roused him to a state of frenzy, and so on.

Whether this friend were right I don't know, but what Vasilyev experienced when he thought this question was settled was something like inspiration. He cried and laughed, spoke aloud the words that he should say next day, felt a fervent love for those who would listen to him and would stand beside him at the corner of the street to preach; he sat down to write letters, made vows to himself. . . .

All this was like inspiration also in that it did not last long. Vasilyev soon grew tired. The mass of the cases in London, in Hamburg, in Warsaw, weighed upon him as a mountain weighs upon the earth; he felt dispirited, bewildered, in the face of this mass; he remembered that he was no speaker, that he was cowardly and timid, that indifferent people were unlikely to be willing to listen and understand him, a law student in his third year, a timid and insignificant person, that genuine missionary work meant not only preaching but deeds. . . .

When it was daylight and carriages were already beginning to rumble in the street, Vasilyev was lying motionless on the sofa, staring into space. He was no longer thinking of the women, nor of the men, nor of missionary work. His whole attention was turned upon the mental agony which was torturing him. It was a dull, vague, indefinite pain akin to anguish, to an extreme form of terror, and to despair. He could point to the place where the pain was: in his chest under his heart; but he could not compare it with anything. In the past he had had acute toothache, he had had pleurisy and neuralgia, but all that was insignificant compared with this mental anguish. In the presence of this pain life seemed loathsome. The dissertation, the excellent work he had written already, the people he loved, the salvation of fallen women—everything that only the day before he had cared about or been indifferent to, now when he thought of it irritated him in the same way as the noise of the carriages, the scurrying footsteps of the waiters in the passage, the daylight. . . . If at that moment someone had performed a great deed of mercy or had committed a revolting outrage, he would have felt the same repulsion for both actions. Of all the thoughts that strayed through his mind only two did not irritate him: one was that at every moment he had the power to kill himself, the other was that this agony would not last more than three days. This last he knew by experience.

After lying for a while he got up and, wringing his hands, paced the room, not as usual from corner to corner, but round the room along the walls. As he passed he glanced at himself in the looking-glass. His face looked pale and thin, his temples hollow, his eyes were bigger, darker, more staring, as though they belonged to someone else, and they had an expression of intolerable mental agony.

At midday the artist knocked at the door.

"Grigory, are you at home?" he asked.

Getting no answer, he stood for a minute, pondered, and answered himself in Ukrainian: "Not there. The confounded fellow has gone to the university."

And he went away. Vasilyev lay down on the bed and, thrusting his head under the pillow, began crying with agony, and the more freely his tears flowed the more terrible his mental anguish became. As it began to get dark, he thought of the agonizing night awaiting him, and was overcome by horrible despair. He dressed quickly, ran out of his room, and, leaving his door wide open, for no object or reason went out into the street. Without asking himself where he should go, he walked quickly along Sadovaya Street.

Snow was falling as heavily as the day before; it was thawing. Thrusting his hands into his sleeves, shuddering and frightened by the noises, the street car bells, and the passers-by, Vasilyev walked along Sadovaya Street as far as Suharev Tower; then to the Red Gate;

from there he turned off to Basmannaya Street. He went into a tavern and drank off a big glass of vodka, but that did not make him feel better. When he reached Razgulyay he turned to the right, and strode along side streets in which he had never been before in his life. He reached the old bridge under which the Yauza runs gurgling and from which one can see long rows of lights in the windows of the Red Barracks. To counteract his mental anguish by some new sensation or some other pain, Vasilyev, not knowing what to do, crying and shuddering, undid his overcoat and jacket and exposed his bare chest to the wet snow and the wind. But that did not lessen his suffering either. Then he bent down over the rail of the bridge and looked down into the black, yeasty Yauza, and he longed to plunge down head-foremost; not out of loathing for life, not for the sake of suicide, but in order to bruise himself at least, and by one pain ease the other. But the black water, the darkness, the deserted banks covered with snow were terrifying. He shivered and walked on. He walked up and down by the Red Barracks, then turned back and went down to a copse, from the copse back to the bridge again.

"No, home, home!" he thought. "At home I believe it's better. . . ."

And he went back. When he reached home he pulled off his wet overcoat and cap, began pacing round the room, and went on pacing round and round without stopping till morning.

VII

When next morning the artist and the medical student went in to him, he was tossing about the room with his shirt torn, biting his hands, and moaning with pain.

"For God's sake!" he sobbed when he saw his friends, "take me where you please, do what you can; but for God's sake, save me quickly! I shall kill myself!"

The artist turned pale and lost his head. The medical student, too, almost cried, but considering that doctors ought to be cool and composed in every emergency, said coldly:

"It's an attack of nerves. But it's nothing. Let us go at once to the doctor."

"Wherever you like, only for God's sake, make haste!"

"Don't excite yourself. You must try and control yourself."

The artist and the medical student with trembling hands dressed Vasilyev and led him out into the street.

"Mihail Sergeyich has been wanting to make your acquaintance for a long time," the medical student said on the way. "He is a very nice man and thoroughly good at his work. He took his degree in 1882, and he has an immense practice already. He treats students as though he were one himself."

"Make haste, make haste! . . ." Vasilyev urged.

Mihail Sergeyich, a stout, fair-haired doctor, received the friends with politeness and frigid dignity, and smiled only on one side of his face.

"Rybnikov and Meier have spoken to me of your illness already," he said. "Very glad to be of service to you. Well? Sit down, I beg you."

He made Vasilyev sit down in a big armchair near the desk, and moved a box of cigarettes towards him.

"Now then!" he began, stroking his knees. "Let us get to work. . . . How old are you?"

He asked questions and the medical student answered them. He asked whether Vasilyev's father had suffered from certain special diseases, whether he drank to excess, whether he was remarkable for cruelty or any

peculiarities. He made similar inquiries about his grandfather, mother, sisters, and brothers. On learning that
his mother had a beautiful voice and sometimes acted
on the stage, he suddenly grew more animated, and
asked:

"Excuse me, but do you perhaps remember if your
mother's interest in the stage was a passionate one?"

Twenty minutes passed. Vasilyev was annoyed by
the way the doctor kept stroking his knees and talking
of the same thing.

"So far as I understand your questions, doctor," he
said, "you want to know whether my illness is heredi-
tary or not. It is not."

The doctor proceeded to ask Vasilyev whether he had
had any secret vices as a boy, or had received injuries
to his head; whether he had had any aberrations, any
peculiarities, or exceptional propensities. Half the questions usually asked by doctors of their patients can be
left unanswered without the slightest ill effect on the
health, but Mihail Sergeyich, the medical student, and
the artist all looked as though if Vasilyev failed to answer one question all would be lost. As he received
answers, the doctor for some reason noted them down
on a slip of paper. On learning that Vasilyev had taken
his degree in the natural sciences and was now studying
law, the doctor grew thoughtful.

"He wrote an excellent thesis last year, . . ." said
the medical student.

"I beg your pardon, but don't interrupt me; you're
preventing me from concentrating," said the doctor,
and he smiled on one side of his face. "Though, of
course, that does enter into the case history. Intense
intellectual work, nervous exhaustion. . . . Yes, yes.
. . . And do you drink vodka?" he said, addressing
Vasilyev.

"Very rarely."

Another twenty minutes passed. The medical student began telling the doctor in a low voice his opinion as to the immediate cause of the attack, and related how the day before yesterday the artist, Vasilyev, and he had visited S—— Street.

The indifferent, reserved, and frigid tone in which his friends and the doctor spoke of the women and that miserable street struck Vasilyev as strange in the extreme. . . .

"Doctor, tell me one thing only," he said, controlling himself so as not to speak rudely. "Is prostitution an evil or not?"

"My dear fellow, who disputes it?" said the doctor, with an expression that suggested that he had settled all such questions for himself long ago. "Who disputes it?"

"You are a psychiatrist, aren't you?" Vasilyev asked curtly.

"Yes, a psychiatrist."

"Perhaps all of you are right!" said Vasilyev, getting up and beginning to walk from one end of the room to the other. "Perhaps! But it all seems amazing to me! That I should have taken my degree in two faculties you look upon as a great achievement; because I have written a thesis which in three years will be thrown aside and forgotten, I am praised up to the skies; but because I cannot speak of fallen women as unconcernedly as of these chairs, I am being examined by a doctor, I am called mad, I am pitied!"

Vasilyev for some reason suddenly felt unutterably sorry for himself, for his companions, for all the people he had seen two days before, and for the doctor; he burst into tears and sank into a chair.

His friends looked inquiringly at the doctor. The latter, with the air of completely comprehending the tears and the despair, of feeling himself a specialist in that line, went up to Vasilyev and, without a word, gave him some medicine to drink; and then, when he was calmer, undressed him and began to investigate the degree of sensibility of the skin, the reflex action of the knees, and so on.

And Vasilyev felt easier. When he came out from the doctor's office he was beginning to feel ashamed; the rattle of the carriages no longer irritated him, and the load under his heart grew lighter and lighter as though it were melting away. He had two prescriptions in his hand: one was for bromide, the other for morphine. . . . He had taken all these remedies before!

In the street he stood still for a while and, saying good-by to his friends, dragged himself languidly to the university.

1888

Gusev

IT IS already dark, it will soon be night.

Gusev, a discharged private, half rises in his bunk and says in a low voice:

"Do you hear me, Pavel Ivanych? A soldier in Suchan was telling me: while they were sailing, their ship bumped into a big fish and smashed a hole in its bottom."

The individual of uncertain social status whom he is addressing, and whom everyone in the ship infirmary calls Pavel Ivanych, is silent as though he hasn't heard.

And again all is still. The wind is flirting with the rigging, the screw is throbbing, the waves are lashing, the bunks creak, but the ear has long since become used to these sounds, and everything around seems to slumber in silence. It is dull. The three invalids—two soldiers and a sailor—who were playing cards all day are dozing and talking deliriously.

The ship is apparently beginning to roll. The bunk slowly rises and falls under Gusev as though it were breathing, and this occurs once, twice, three times . . . Something hits the floor with a clang: a jug must have dropped.

"The wind has broken loose from its chain," says Gusev, straining his ears.

This time Pavel Ivanych coughs and says irritably:

"One minute a vessel bumps into a fish, the next the wind breaks loose from its chain . . . Is the wind a beast that it breaks loose from its chain?"

"That's what Christian folks say."

"They are as ignorant as you . . . They say all sorts of things. One must have one's head on one's shoulders and reason it out. You have no sense."

Pavel Ivanych is subject to seasickness. When the sea is rough he is usually out of sorts, and the merest trifle irritates him. In Gusev's opinion there is absolutely nothing to be irritated about. What is there that is strange or out of the way about that fish, for instance, or about the wind breaking loose from its chain? Suppose the fish were as big as the mountain and its back as hard as a sturgeon's, and supposing, too, that over yonder at the end of the world stood great stone walls and the fierce winds were chained up to the walls. If they haven't broken loose, why then do they rush all over the sea like madmen and strain like hounds tugging at their leash? If they are not chained up what becomes of them when it is calm?

Gusev ponders for a long time about fishes as big as a mountain and about stout, rusty chains. Then he begins to feel bored and falls to thinking about his home, to which he is returning after five years' service in the Far East. He pictures an immense pond covered with drifts. On one side of the pond is the brick-colored building of the pottery with a tall chimney and clouds of black smoke; on the other side is a village. His brother Alexey drives out of the fifth yard from the end in a sleigh; behind him sits his little son Vanka in big felt boots, and his little girl Akulka also wearing felt boots. Alexey has had a drop, Vanka is laughing, Akulka's face cannot be seen, she is muffled up.

"If he doesn't look out, he will have the children frostbitten," Gusev reflects. "Lord send them sense that they may honor their parents and not be any wiser than their father and mother."

"They need new soles," a delirious sailor says in a bass voice. "Yes, yes!"

Gusev's thoughts abruptly break off and suddenly without rhyme or reason the pond is replaced by a huge bull's head without eyes, and the horse and sleigh are no longer going straight ahead but are whirling round and round, wrapped in black smoke. But still he is glad he has had a glimpse of his people. In fact, he is breathless with joy, and his whole body, down to his fingertips, tingles with it. "Thanks be to God we have seen each other again," he mutters deliriously, but at once opens his eyes and looks for water in the dark.

He drinks and lies down, and again the sleigh is gliding along, then again there is the bull's head without eyes, smoke, clouds . . . And so it goes till daybreak.

II

A blue circle is the first thing to become visible in the darkness—it is the porthole; then, little by little, Gusev makes out the man in the next bunk, Pavel Ivanych. The man sleeps sitting up, as he cannot breathe lying down. His face is gray, his nose long and sharp, his eyes look huge because he is terribly emaciated, his temples are sunken, his beard skimpy, his hair long. His face does not reveal his social status: you cannot tell whether he is a gentleman, a merchant, or a peasant. Judging from his expression and his long hair, he may be an assiduous churchgoer or a lay brother, but his manner of speaking does not seem to be that of a monk. He is utterly worn out by his cough, by the stifling heat, his illness, and he breathes with difficulty, moving his parched lips. Noticing that Gusev is looking at him he turns his face toward him and says:

"I begin to guess . . . Yes, I understand it all perfectly now."

"What do you understand, Pavel Ivanych?"

"Here's how it is . . . It has always seemed strange to me that terribly ill as you fellows are, you should be on a steamer where the stifling air, the heavy seas, in fact everything, threatens you with death; but now it is all clear to me . . . Yes . . . The doctors put you on the steamer to get rid of you. They got tired of bothering with you, cattle . . . You don't pay them any money, you are a nuisance, and you spoil their statistics with your deaths . . . So, of course, you are just cattle. And it's not hard to get rid of you . . . All that's necessary is, in the first place, to have no conscience or humanity, and, secondly, to deceive the ship

authorities. The first requirement need hardly be given
a thought—in that respect we are virtuosos, and as for
the second condition, it can always be fulfilled with a
little practice. In a crowd of four hundred healthy soldiers and sailors, five sick ones are not conspicuous;
well, they got you all onto the steamer, mixed you with
the healthy ones, hurriedly counted you over, and in
the confusion nothing untoward was noticed, and when
the steamer was on the way, people discovered that
there were paralytics and consumptives on their last
legs lying about the deck . . ."

Gusev does not understand Pavel Ivanych; thinking
that he is being reprimanded, he says in self-justifica-
tion:

"I lay on the deck because I was so sick; when we
were being unloaded from the barge onto the steamer,
I caught a bad chill."

"It's revolting," Pavel Ivanych continues. "The main
thing is, they know perfectly well that you can't stand
the long journey and yet they put you here. Suppose
you last as far as the Indian Ocean, and then what? It's
horrible to think of . . . And that's the gratitude for
your faithful, irreproachable service!"

Pavel Ivanych's eyes flash with anger. He frowns
fastidiously and says, gasping for breath, "Those are the
people who ought to be given a drubbing in the newspapers till the feathers fly in all directions."

The two sick soldiers and the sailor have waked up
and are already playing cards. The sailor is half reclin-
ing in his bunk, the soldiers are sitting near by on the
floor in most uncomfortable positions. One of the soldiers has his right arm bandaged and his wrist is heavily
swathed in wrappings that look like a cap, so that he
holds his cards under his right arm or in the crook of his

elbow while he plays with his left. The ship is rolling heavily. It is impossible to stand up, or have tea, or take medicine.

"Were you an orderly?" Pavel Ivanych asks Gusev.

"Yes, sir, an orderly."

"My God, my God!" says Pavel Ivanych and shakes his head sadly. "To tear a man from his home, drag him a distance of ten thousand miles, then wear him out till he gets consumption and . . . and what is it all for, one asks? To turn him into an orderly for some Captain Kopeykin or Midshipman Dyrka! How reasonable!"

"It's not hard work, Pavel Ivanych. You get up in the morning and polish the boots, start the samovars going, tidy the rooms, and then you have nothing more to do. The lieutenant drafts plans all day, and if you like, you can say your prayers, or read a book or go out on the street. God grant everyone such a life."

"Yes, very good! The lieutenant drafts plans all day long, and you sit in the kitchen and long for home . . . Plans, indeed! . . . It's not plans that matter but human life. You have only one life to live and it mustn't be wronged."

"Of course, Pavel Ivanych, a bad man gets no break anywhere, either at home or in the service, but if you live as you ought and obey orders, who will want to wrong you? The officers are educated gentlemen, they understand . . . In five years I have never once been in the guard house, and I was struck, if I remember right, only once."

"What for?"

"For fighting. I have a heavy hand, Pavel Ivanych. Four Chinks came into our yard; they were bringing firewood or something, I forget. Well, I was bored and I knocked them about a bit, the nose of one of them, damn him, began bleeding . . . The lieutenant saw it all through the window, got angry, and boxed me on the ear."

"You are a poor, foolish fellow . . ." whispers Pavel Ivanych. "You don't understand anything."

He is utterly exhausted by the rolling of the ship and shuts his eyes; now his head drops back, now it sinks forward on his chest. Several times he tries to lie down but nothing comes of it: he finds it difficult to breathe.

"And what did you beat up the four Chinks for?" he asks after a while.

"Oh, just like that. They came into the yard and I hit them."

There is silence . . . The card-players play for two hours, eagerly, swearing sometimes, but the rolling and pitching of the ship overcomes them, too; they throw aside the cards and lie down. Again Gusev has a vision: the big pond, the pottery, the village . . . Once more the sleigh is gliding along, once more Vanka is laughing and Akulka, the silly thing, throws open her fur coat and thrusts out her feet, as much as to say: "Look, good people, my felt boots are not like Vanka's, they're new ones."

"Going on six, and she has no sense yet," Gusev mutters in his delirium. "Instead of showing off your boots you had better come and get your soldier uncle a drink. I'll give you a present."

And here is Andron with a flintlock on his shoulder, carrying a hare he has killed, and behind him is the decrepit old Jew Isaychik, who offers him a piece of soap in exchange for the hare; and here is the black calf in the entry, and Domna sewing a shirt and crying about something, and then again the bull's head without eyes, black smoke . . .

Someone shouts overhead, several sailors run by; it seems that something bulky is being dragged over the deck, something falls with a crash. Again some people run by. . . . Has there been an accident? Gusev raises his head, listens, and sees that the two soldiers and the sailor are playing cards again; Pavel Ivanych is sitting up and moving his lips. It is stifling, you haven't the strength to breathe, you are thirsty, the water is warm, disgusting. The ship is still rolling and pitching.

Suddenly something strange happens to one of the soldiers playing cards. He calls hearts diamonds, gets muddled over his score, and drops his cards, then with a frightened, foolish smile looks round at all of them.

"I shan't be a minute, fellows . . ." he says, and lies down on the floor.

Everybody is nonplussed. They call to him, he does not answer.

"Stepan, maybe you are feeling bad, eh?" the soldier with the bandaged arm asks him. "Perhaps we had better call the priest, eh?"

"Have a drink of water, Stepan . . ." says the sailor. "Here, brother, drink."

"Why are you knocking the jug against his teeth?" says Gusev angrily. "Don't you see, you cabbage-head?"

"What?"

"What?" Gusev mimics him. "There is no breath in him, he's dead! That's what! Such stupid people, Lord God!"

III

The ship has stopped rolling and Pavel Ivanych is cheerful. He is no longer cross. His face wears a boastful, challenging, mocking expression. It is as though he wants to say: "Yes, right away I'll tell you something that will make you burst with laughter." The round porthole is open and a soft breeze is blowing on Pavel Ivanych. There is a sound of voices, the splash of oars in the water . . . Just under the porthole someone is droning in a thin, disgusting voice; must be a Chinaman singing.

"Here we are in the harbor," says Pavel Ivanych with a mocking smile. "Only another month or so and we shall be in Russia. M'yes, messieurs of the armed forces! I'll arrive in Odessa and from there go straight to Kharkov. In Kharkov I have a friend, a man of letters. I'll go to him and say, 'Come, brother, put aside your vile subjects, women's amours and the beauties of Nature, and show up the two-legged vermin . . . There's a subject for you."

For a while he reflects, then says:

"Gusev, do you know how I tricked them?"

"Tricked who, Pavel Ivanych?"

"Why, these people . . . You understand, on this steamer there is only a first class and a third class, and they only allow peasants, that is, the common herd, to go in the third. If you have got a jacket on and even at a distance look like a gentleman or a bourgeois, you have to go first class, if you please. You must fork out five hundred rubles if it kills you. 'Why do you have such a regulation?' I ask them. 'Do you mean to raise the prestige of the Russian intelligentsia thereby?' 'Not a bit of it. We don't let you simply because a decent person can't go third class; it is too horrible and disgusting there.' 'Yes, sir? Thank you for being so solicitous about decent people's welfare. But in any case, whether it's nasty there or nice, I haven't got five hundred rubles. I didn't loot the Treasury, I didn't exploit the natives, I didn't traffic in contraband, I flogged nobody to death, so judge for yourselves if I have the right to occupy a first class cabin and even to reckon myself among the Russian intelligentsia.' But logic means nothing to them. So I had to resort to fraud. I put on a peasant coat and high boots, I pulled a face so that I looked like a common drunk, and went to the agents: 'Give us a little ticket, your Excellency,' said I—"

"You're not of the gentry, are you?" asked the sailor.

"I come of a clerical family. My father was a priest, and an honest one; he always told the high and mighty the truth to their faces and, as a result, he suffered a great deal."

Pavel Ivanych is exhausted from talking and gasps for breath, but still continues:

"Yes, I always tell people the truth to their faces. I'm not afraid of anyone or anything. In this respect, there is a great difference between me and all of you, men. You are dark people, blind, crushed; you see nothing and what you do see, you don't understand . . . You are told that the wind breaks loose from its chain, that you are beasts, savages, and you believe it; someone gives it to you in the neck—you kiss his hand; some animal in a racoon coat robs you and then tosses you a fifteen-kopeck tip and you say: 'Let me kiss your hand, sir.' You are outcasts, pitiful wretches. I am different, my mind is clear. I see it all plainly like a hawk or an eagle when it hovers over the earth, and I understand everything. I am protest personified. I see tyranny—I protest. I see a hypocrite—I protest, I see a triumphant swine—I protest. And I cannot be put down, no Spanish Inquisition can silence me. No. Cut out my tongue and I will protest with gestures. Wall me up in a cellar—I will shout so that you will hear me half a mile away, or will starve myself to death, so that they may have another weight on their black consciences. Kill me and I will haunt them. All my acquaintances say to me: 'You are a most insufferable person, Pavel Ivanych.' I am proud of such a reputation. I served three years in the Far East and I shall be remembered there a hundred years. I had rows there with everybody. My friends wrote to me from Russia: 'Don't come back,' but here I am going back to spite them . . . Yes . . . That's life as I understand it. That's what one can call life."

Gusev is not listening; he is looking at the porthole. A junk, flooded with dazzling hot sunshine, is swaying on the transparent turquoise water. In it stand naked Chinamen, holding up cages with canaries in them and calling out: "It sings, it sings!"

Another boat knocks against it; a steam cutter glides past. Then there is another boat: a fat Chinaman sits in it, eating rice with chopsticks. The water sways lazily, white sea gulls languidly hover over it.

"Would be fine to give that fat fellow one in the neck," reflects Gusev, looking at the stout Chinaman and yawning.

He dozes off and it seems to him that all nature is dozing too. Time flies swiftly by. Imperceptibly the day passes. Imperceptibly darkness descends . . . The steamer is no longer standing still but is on the move again.

IV

Two days pass. Pavel Ivanych no longer sits up but is lying down. His eyes are closed, his nose seems to have grown sharper.

"Pavel Ivanych," Gusev calls to him. "Hey, Pavel Ivanych."

Pavel Ivanych opens his eyes and moves his lips.

"Are you feeling bad?"

"No . . . It's nothing . . ." answers Pavel Ivanych gasping for breath. "Nothing, on the contrary . . . I am better . . . You see, I can lie down now . . . I have improved . . ."

"Well, thank God for that, Pavel Ivanych."

"When I compare myself to you, I am sorry for you, poor fellows. My lungs are healthy, mine is a stomach cough . . . I can stand hell, let alone the Red Sea. Besides, I take a critical attitude toward my illness and the medicines. While you— Your minds are dark . . . It's hard on you, very, very hard!"

The ship is not rolling, it is quiet, but as hot and stifling as a Turkish bath; it is hard, not only to speak, but even to listen. Gusev hugs his knees, lays his head on them and thinks of his home. God, in this stifling heat, what a relief it is to think of snow and cold! You're driving in a sleigh; all of a sudden, the horses take fright at something and bolt. Careless of the road, the ditches, the gullies, they tear like mad things right through the village, across the pond, past the pottery, across the open fields. "Hold them!" the pottery hands and the peasants they meet shout at the top of their voices. "Hold them!" But why hold them? Let the keen cold wind beat in your face and bite your hands; let the lumps of snow, kicked up by the horses, slide down your collar, your neck, your chest; let the runners sing, and the traces and the whippletrees break, the devil take them. And what delight when the sleigh upsets and you go flying full tilt into a drift, face right in the snow, and then you get up, white all over with icicles on your mustache, no cap, no gloves, your belt undone . . . People laugh, dogs bark . . .

Pavel Ivanych half opens one eye, fixes Gusev with it and asks softly:

"Gusev, did your commanding officer steal?"

"Who can tell, Pavel Ivanych? We can't say, we didn't hear about it."

And after that, a long time passes in silence. Gusev broods, his mind wanders, and he keeps drinking water: it is hard for him to talk and hard for him to listen, and he is afraid of being talked to. An hour passes, a second, a third; evening comes, then night, but he doesn't notice it; he sits up and keeps dreaming of the frost.

There is a sound as though someone were coming into the infirmary, voices are heard, but five minutes pass and all is quiet again.

"The kingdom of Heaven be his and eternal peace," says the soldier with a bandaged arm. "He was an uneasy chap."

"What?" asks Gusev. "Who?"

"He died, they have just carried him up."

"Oh, well," mutters Gusev, yawning, "the kingdom of Heaven be his."

"What do you think, Gusev?" the soldier with the bandaged arm says after a while. "Will he be in the kingdom of Heaven or not?"

"Who do you mean?"

"Pavel Ivanych."

"He will . . . He suffered so long. Then again, he belonged to the clergy and priests have a lot of relatives. Their prayers will get him there."

The soldier with the bandage sits down on Gusev's bunk and says in an undertone:

"You too, Gusev, aren't long for this world. You will never get to Russia."

"Did the doctor or the nurse say so?" asks Gusev.

"It isn't that they said so, but one can see it. It's plain when a man will die soon. You don't eat, you don't drink, you've got so thin it's dreadful to look at you. It's consumption, in a word. I say it not to worry you, but because maybe you would like to receive the sacrament and extreme unction. And if you have any money, you had better turn it over to the senior officer."

"I haven't written home," Gusev sighs. "I shall die and they won't know."

"They will," the sick sailor says in a bass voice. "When you die, they will put it down in the ship's log, in Odessa they will send a copy of the entry to the army authorities, and they will notify your district board or somebody like that."

Such a conversation makes Gusev uneasy and a vague craving begins to torment him. He takes a drink —it isn't that; he drags himself to the porthole and breathes the hot, moist air—it isn't that; he tries to think of home, of the frost—it isn't that . . . At last it seems to him that if he stays in the infirmary another minute, he will certainly choke to death.

"It's stifling, brother," he says. "I'll go on deck. Take me there, for Christ's sake."

"All right," the soldier with the bandage agrees. "You can't walk, I'll carry you. Hold on to my neck."

Gusev puts his arm around the soldier's neck, the latter places his uninjured arm round him and carries him up. On the deck, discharged soldiers and sailors are lying asleep side by side; there are so many of them it is difficult to pass.

"Get down on the floor," the soldier with the bandage says softly. "Follow me quietly, hold on to my shirt."

It is dark, there are no lights on deck or on the masts or anywhere on the sea around. On the prow the seaman on watch stands perfectly still like a statue, and it looks as though he, too, were asleep. The steamer seems to be left to its own devices and to be going where it pleases.

"Now they'll throw Pavel Ivanych into the sea," says the soldier with the bandage, "in a sack and then into the water."

"Yes, that's the regulation."

"At home, it's better to lie in the earth. Anyway, your mother will come to the grave and shed a tear."

"Sure."

There is a smell of dung and hay. With drooping heads, steers stand at the ship's rail. One, two, three—eight of them! And there's a pony. Gusev puts out his hand to stroke it, but it shakes its head, shows its teeth, and tries to bite his sleeve.

"Damn brute!" says Gusev crossly.

The two of them thread their way to the prow, then stand at the rail, peering. Overhead there is deep sky, bright stars, peace and quiet, exactly as at home in the village. But below there is darkness and disorder. Tall waves are making an uproar for no reason. Each one of them as you look at it is trying to rise higher than all the rest and to chase and crush its neighbor; it is thunderously attacked by a third wave that has a gleaming white mane and is just as ferocious and ugly.

The sea has neither sense nor pity. If the steamer had been smaller, not made of thick iron plates, the waves would have crushed it without the slightest remorse, and would have devoured all the people in it without distinguishing between saints and sinners. The steamer's expression was equally senseless and cruel. This beaked monster presses forward, cutting millions of waves in its path; it fears neither darkness nor the wind, nor space, nor solitude—it's all child's play for it, and if the ocean had its population, this monster would crush it, too, without distinguishing between saints and sinners.

"Where are we now?" asks Gusev.

"I don't know. Must be the ocean."

"You can't see land . . ."

"No chance of it! They say we'll see it only in seven days."

The two men stare silently at the white phosphorescent foam and brood. Gusev is first to break the silence.

"There is nothing frightening here," he says. "Only

you feel queer as if you were in a dark forest; but if, let's say, they lowered the boat this minute and an officer ordered me to go fifty miles across the sea to catch fish, I'll go. Or, let's say, if a Christian were to fall into the water right now, I'd jump in after him. A German or a Chink I wouldn't try to save, but I'd go in after a Christian."

"And are you afraid to die?"

"I am. I am sorry about the farm. My brother at home, you know, isn't steady; he drinks, he beats his wife for no reason, he doesn't honor his father and mother. Without me everything will go to rack and ruin, and before long it's my fear that my father and old mother will be begging their bread. But my legs won't hold me up, brother, and it's stifling here. Let's go to sleep."

v

Gusev goes back to the infirmary and gets into his bunk. He is again tormented by a vague desire and he can't make out what it is that he wants. There is a weight on his chest, a throbbing in his head, his mouth is so dry that it is difficult for him to move his tongue. He dozes and talks in his sleep and, worn out with nightmares, with coughing and the stifling heat, towards morning he falls into a heavy sleep. He dreams that they have just taken the bread out of the oven in the barracks and that he has climbed into the oven and is having a steam bath there, lashing himself with a besom of birch twigs. He sleeps for two days and on the third at noon two sailors come down and carry him out of the infirmary. He is sewn up in sailcloth and to make him heavier, they put two gridirons in with him. Sewn up in sailcloth, he looks like a carrot or a radish: broad at the head and narrow at the feet. Before sunset, they

carry him on deck and put him on a plank. One end of
the plank lies on the ship's rail, the other on a box placed
on a stool. Round him stand the discharged soldiers and
the crew with heads bared.

"Blessed is our God," the priest begins, "now, and
ever, and unto ages of ages."

"Amen," three sailors chant.

The discharged men and the crew cross themselves
and look off at the waves. It is strange that a man should
be sewn up in sailcloth and should soon be flying into
the sea. Is it possible that such a thing can happen to
anyone?

The priest strews earth upon Gusev and makes obei-
sance to him. The men sing "Memory Eternal."

The seaman on watch duty raises the end of the plank,
Gusev slides off it slowly and then flying, head foremost,
turns over in the air and—plop! Foam covers him, and
for a moment, he seems to be wrapped in lace, but the
instant passes and he disappears in the waves.

He plunges rapidly downward. Will he reach the bottom? At this spot the ocean is said to be three miles
deep. After sinking sixty or seventy feet, he begins to
descend more and more slowly, swaying rhythmically as
though in hesitation, and, carried along by the current,
moves faster laterally than vertically.

And now he runs into a school of fish called pilot fish.
Seeing the dark body, the little fish stop as though petrified and suddenly all turn round together and disappear.
In less than a minute they rush back at Gusev, swift as
arrows and begin zigzagging round him in the water.
Then another dark body appears. It is a shark. With
dignity and reluctance, seeming not to notice Gusev, as
it were, it swims under him; then while he, moving
downward, sinks upon its back, the shark turns, belly
upward, basks in the warm transparent water and lan-

guidly opens its jaws with two rows of teeth. The pilot fish are in ecstasy; they stop to see what will happen next. After playing a little with the body, the shark nonchalantly puts his jaws under it, cautiously touches it with his teeth and the sailcloth is ripped the full length of the body, from head to foot; one of the gridirons falls out, frightens the pilot fish and striking the shark on the flank, sinks rapidly to the bottom.

Meanwhile, up above, in that part of the sky where the sun is about to set, clouds are massing, one resembling a triumphal arch, another a lion, a third a pair of scissors. A broad shaft of green light issues from the clouds and reaches to the middle of the sky; a while later, a violet beam appears alongside of it and then a golden one and a pink one . . . The heavens turn a soft lilac tint. Looking at this magnificent enchanting sky, the ocean frowns at first, but soon it, too, takes on tender, joyous, passionate colors for which it is hard to find a name in the language of man.

1890

Anna on the Neck

AFTER the ceremony not even light refreshments were served; the bride and groom each drank a glass of wine, changed their clothes, and drove to the station. Instead of having a gay ball and supper, instead of music and dancing, they traveled a hundred and fifty miles to perform their devotions at a shrine. Many people commended this, saying that Modest Alexeich had already reached a high rank in the service and was no longer young, and that a noisy wedding might not have seemed quite proper; and besides, music is likely to sound dreary when a fifty-two-year-old official marries a girl who has just turned eighteen. It was also said that Modest Alexeich, being a man of principle, had really arranged this visit to the monastery in order to make it clear to his young bride that in marriage, too, he gave the first place to religion and morality.

The couple were seen off by relatives and the groom's colleagues. The crowd stood, with the glasses in their hands, waiting to shout "hurrah" as soon as the train should start, and the bride's father, Pyotr Leontyich, in a top hat and the dress coat of a schoolmaster, already drunk and very pale, kept craning toward the window, glass in hand, and saying imploringly, "Anyuta! Anya, Anya! Just one word!"

Anya leaned out of the window toward him and he whispered something to her, enveloping her in a smell of alcohol and blowing into her ear—she could understand nothing—and made the sign of the cross over her face, her bosom, and her hands. His breathing came in gasps and tears shone in his eyes. And Anya's brothers, Petya and Andrusha, schoolboys, pulled at his coattails from behind, whispering embarrassedly: "Papa dear, enough . . . Papa dear, don't—"

When the train started, Anya saw her father run a little way after the coach, staggering and spilling his wine, and what a pitiful, kindly, guilty face he had! "Hurrah!" he shouted.

The couple were left alone. Modest Alexeich looked about the compartment, arranged their things on the shelves, and sat down opposite his young wife, smiling. He was an official of medium height, rather stout, who looked bloated and very well fed and wore Dundreary whiskers. His clean-shaven, round, sharply outlined chin looked like a heel. The most characteristic thing about his face was the absence of a mustache, this bare, freshly shaven spot which gradually passed into fat cheeks that quivered like jelly. His demeanor was digni-fied, his movements unhurried, his manners suave.

"At the moment I cannot help recalling one circum-stance," he said smiling. "When, five years ago, Kosoro-tov received the order of St. Anna of the second class, and came to thank His Excellency for the honor, His Excellency expressed himself thus: 'So now you have three Annas: one in your buttonhole and two on your neck.' I must tell you that at that time Kosorotov's wife, a quarrelsome person of a giddy disposition, had just returned to him and that her name was Anna. I trust that when I receive the Anna of the second class, His Excellency will have no cause to say the same thing to me."

He smiled with his small eyes. And she, too, smiled, troubled by the thought that at any moment this man might kiss her with his full, moist lips and that she no longer had the right to prevent him from doing so. The soft movements of his bloated body frightened her; she felt both terrified and disgusted. He got up without haste, took the order off his neck, took off his dress coat and waistcoat and put on his dressing-gown. "That's better," he said, sitting down beside Anya.

She remembered what agony the marriage ceremony had been, when it had seemed to her that the priest, the guests, and everyone in the church had looked at her sadly: why was she, such a sweet, nice girl, marrying an elderly uninteresting man? Only that morning she had been in raptures over the fact that everything had been satisfactorily arranged, but during the ceremony and now in the railway carriage, she felt guilty, cheated, and ridiculous. Here she had married a rich man and yet she had no money. Her wedding dress had been bought on credit, and just now when her father and brothers had been saying good-by, she could see from their faces that they had not a kopeck to their name. Would they have any supper tonight? And tomorrow? And for some reason it seemed to her that her father and the boys without her were suffering from hunger and feeling as miserable as they did the day after their mother's funeral. "Oh, how unhappy I am," she thought. "Why am I so unhappy?"

With the awkwardness of a man of dignified habits who is unaccustomed to dealing with women, Modest Alexeich touched her on the waist and patted her on the shoulder while she thought of money, of her mother, and her mother's death. When her mother died, her father, a high school teacher of calligraphy and drawing, had taken to drink and they had begun to feel the pinch of poverty; the boys had no shoes or galoshes. Time and again her father was hauled before the justice of the peace, the process-server came and made an inventory of the furniture . . . What a disgrace! Anya had to look after her drunken father, darn her brothers' socks, do the marketing, and when she was complimented on her beauty, her youth, and her elegant manner, it seemed to her that the whole world was looking at her cheap hat and the holes in her shoes that were inked over. And at night there were tears and the disturbing persistent thought that soon, very soon, her father would be dismissed from the school for his failing and that he would not be able to endure it and would die like their mother. But then some ladies they knew had bestirred themselves and started looking about for a good match for Anya. This Modest Alexeich, who was neither young nor good-looking but had money, was soon found. He had 100,000 in the bank and a family estate which he rented to a tenant. He was a man of principle and was in favor with His Excellency; it would be very easy for him, Anya was told, to get a note from His Excellency to the high school principal or even to the trustee, and Pyotr Leontyich would not be dismissed . . .

While she was recalling these details, strains of music together with a sound of voices suddenly burst in at the window. The train had stopped at a small station. On the other side of the platform in the crowd an accordion and a cheap squeaky fiddle were being played briskly, and from beyond the tall birches and poplars and the small cottages that were flooded with moonlight came the sound of a military band: there must have been a dance in the place. Summer visitors and townspeople who came here by train in fine weather for a breath of fresh air were promenading on the platform. Among them was the owner of all the summer cottages, Arty-nov, a man of wealth. Tall, stout, black-haired, with prominent eyes, he looked like an Armenian. He wore a strange costume: an unbuttoned shirt that left his chest bare, high boots with spurs, and a black cloak which hung from his shoulders and trailed on the ground. Two borzois followed him with their sharp muzzles to the ground.

Tears were still glistening in Anya's eyes, but she was now no longer thinking of her mother or money or her marriage. She was shaking hands with high school boys and officers of her acquaintance, laughing gaily and saying quickly, "How do you do? How are you?"

She went out into the moonlight and stood so that they could all see her in her new splendid costume and hat.

"Why are we stopping here?" she asked.

"This is a siding. They are waiting for the mail train to pass."

Noticing that Artynov was looking at her, she
screwed up her face coquettishly and began talking
aloud in French; and because her voice sounded so well
and because music was heard and the moon was reflected in the pond, and because Artynov, the notorious
Don Juan and rake, was looking at her greedily and in-
quisitively, and because everyone was gay, she suddenly
felt happy, and when the train started, and her friends
the officers saluted her, she was humming a polka, the
strains of which reached her from the military band
which was blaring somewhere beyond the trees; and she
returned to her compartment feeling as if she had been
persuaded at the station that she would certainly be
happy in spite of everything.

The couple spent two days at the monastery, then returned to town. They lived in an apartment supplied by
the government. When Modest Alexeich left for the
office, Anya would play the piano or cry out of sheer
boredom or lie down on a couch and read novels or look
through fashion journals. At dinner Modest Alexeich ate
a great deal, talked about politics, new appointments,
transfers and bonuses, and declared that one should
work hard, that family life was not a pleasure but a
duty, that if you took care of the kopecks, the rubles
would take care of themselves, and that he put religion
and morality above everything else in the world. And
holding the knife in his fist like a sword, he would say:

"Everyone must have his duties!"

And Anya listened to him, was frightened, and could
not eat, so that she usually rose from the table hungry.
After dinner her husband took a nap and snored loudly
while she went to see her own people. Her father and
the boys looked at her in a peculiar way, as if just before
she came they had been blaming her for having married
for money a tedious, tiresome man whom she did not

love. Her rustling skirts, her bracelets, and her general ladylike air made them uncomfortable, offended them. In her presence they felt a little embarrassed and did not know what to talk to her about; but they still loved her as before and were not used to having dinner without her. She sat down with them to cabbage soup, thick porridge, and potatoes fried in mutton fat that smelled of tallow candles. With a trembling hand Pyotr Leontyich filled his glass from a decanter and drank it off quickly, greedily, with disgust, then drank a second glass, then a third. Petya and Andrusha, thin, pale boys with big eyes, would take the decanter and say with embarrassment:

"You mustn't, Papa dear . . . Enough, Papa dear."

Anya, too, was troubled and would beg him to drink no more; and he would suddenly fly into a rage and strike the table with his fist. "I will not be dictated to!" he would shout. "Wretched boys! Wretched girl! I will turn you all out!"

But there was a note of weakness, of kindness in his voice, and no one was afraid of him. After dinner he usually spruced himself up. Pale, with cuts on his chin from shaving, he would stand for half an hour before the mirror, craning his thin neck, preening himself, combing his hair, twisting his black mustache, sprinkling himself with scent, tying his cravat in a bow; then he would put on his gloves and his top hat and would go off to give private lessons. If there was a holiday, he would stay at home and paint or play the harmonium, which hissed and growled; he would try to wrest melodious tones from it and would storm at the boys: "Scamps! Wretches! They have spoiled the instrument!"

Evenings Anya's husband played cards with his colleagues who lived under the same roof in the government quarters. During these parties the wives of the functionaries would also assemble—homely, tastelessly dressed women, as coarse as cooks, and gossip, as ugly and insipid as the women themselves, would start in the apartment. Sometimes Modest Alexeich would take Anya to the theater. During the intermissions he would not let her go a step from his side but walked about arm in arm with her through the corridors and the foyer. When he bowed to anyone, he immediately whispered to Anya: "A councilor of state . . . received by His Excellency," or "A man of means . . . has a house of his own." When they passed the buffet Anya had a great longing for sweets; she was fond of chocolate and apple tarts, but she had no money and she did not like to ask her husband. He would take a pear, feel it with his fingers, and ask uncertainly, "How much?"

"Twenty-five kopecks."

"I say!" he would exclaim and put the pear back, but as it was awkward to leave the buffet without buying anything, he would order a bottle of soda water and drink it all himself, and tears would come into his eyes. At such times Anya hated him.

Or suddenly turning quite red, he would say to her hurriedly: "Bow to that old lady!"

"But I am not acquainted with her—"

"No matter. That is the wife of the director of the local treasury office! Bow to her, I mean you," he said grumbling insistently. "Your head won't fall off."

Anya bowed and her head really didn't fall off, but it was very painful. She did everything her husband told her to do, and was very angry with herself that she had let herself be deceived like the silliest little fool. She had married him only for his money, and yet she had less money now than before her marriage. Formerly her father would sometimes give her a twenty-kopeck piece, but now she never had a groat. To take money on the quiet or to ask for it, she couldn't; she was afraid of her husband. She trembled before him. It seemed to her as though she had been afraid of him for a long time. In her childhood the high school principal had always seemed to her the most imposing and terrible power in the world, moving along like a thundercloud or a steam locomotive ready to crush everything in its way. Another such power of which they often talked at home, and which for some reason they feared, was His Excellency. Then, there were a dozen other, less formidable powers, and among them were the high school teachers, strict and impeccable, with shaven upper lip. And now finally, it was Modest Alexeich, a man of principle, who resembled the head of the school in every particular, including his face. And in Anya's imagination, all these powers combined into one, and, in the shape of a terrible, huge white bear, bore down upon the weak and guilty, such as her father. And she was afraid to contradict her husband, and with a forced smile and a show of pleasure, submitted to his coarse caresses and defiling embraces which terrified her.

Only once did Pyotr Leontyich make bold to ask his son-in-law for a loan of fifty rubles in order to pay a very unpleasant debt, but what agony it was!

"Very well, I'll give you the money," said Modest Alexeich after a moment's thought, "but I warn you, I won't help you again until you stop drinking. Such a weakness is disgraceful in a man holding a government post! I cannot refrain from calling your attention to the well-known fact that many able people have been ruined by that passion, though temperance might perhaps have permitted them to attain a very high rank."

Followed long-winded sentences with such phrases as, "in proportion to," "whereas," "in view of the aforesaid," while poor Pyotr Leontyich was in an agony of humiliation and felt an intense craving for alcohol.

And when the boys came to visit Anya, generally in worn shoes and threadbare trousers, they too had to listen to lectures.

"Everyone must have his duties!" Modest Alexeich would say to them. But he would not give them money. To Anya, he would give rings, bracelets, brooches, saying that these things would come in handy on a rainy day. And he often unlocked her chest of drawers to see if they were all safe.

II

Meanwhile the cold season arrived. Before Christmas it was announced in the local newspaper that the usual winter ball would take place on December 29 in the Hall of the Nobility. Every evening after the card-playing, Modest Alexeich was excitedly conferring in whispers with his colleagues' wives and glancing anxiously at Anya, and afterwards he paced the room from corner to corner for a long time, thinking. At last, late one evening he stood still before Anya and said, "You must have a ball dress made for yourself. Do you understand? Only, please consult Marya Grigoryevna and Natalya Kuzminishna."

And he gave her one hundred rubles. She took the money but didn't consult anyone when she ordered the gown. She spoke to no one but her father and tried to imagine how her mother would have dressed for the ball. Her mother had always dressed in the latest fashion and had always taken great pains with Anya, fitting her out elegantly like a doll, and had taught her to speak French and dance the mazurka magnificently (she had been a governess for five years prior to her marriage).

Like her mother, Anya could make a new dress out of an old one, clean gloves with benzine, hire jewelry and, like her mother, she knew how to screw up her eyes, speak with a burr, strike pretty poses, fly into ecstasies when necessary and assume a sad and enigmatic air. And from her father she inherited dark hair and eyes, sensitive nerves, and the habit of always trying to look her best.

When, half an hour before they had to start for the ball, Modest Alexeich went into her room coatless to put his order round his neck in front of her mirror, he was so struck by her beauty and the splendor of her crisp gauzy attire, that he combed his side-whiskers complacently and said, "So that's how my wife can look . . . So that's how you can look!" And he went on, suddenly assuming a tone of solemnity, "Anyuta, I have made you happy, and tonight you can make me happy. I beg you to get yourself introduced to His Excellency's spouse. Do it for me, for God's sake! Through her I may get the post of senior reporting secretary."

They drove to the ball. There it was, the Hall of the Nobility, the lobby and the stately doorman. The vestibule was full of hangers, fur coats, footmen scurrying about and décolleté ladies putting up their fans to protect themselves from the draft; the place smelled of illuminating gas and soldiers.

When Anya, walking up the stairs on her husband's arm, heard the music and saw herself full-length in the huge pier glass glowing with numberless lights, her heart leapt with joy and with that presentiment of happiness which she had experienced in the moonlight at the station. She walked in proudly, confidently, for the first time feeling herself not a little girl but a lady, and unwittingly imitating her late mother's gait and manners. And for the first time in her life, she felt rich and free. Even her husband's presence did not embarrass her, for as she crossed the threshold of the hall she had guessed instinctively that the proximity of her elderly husband did not humiliate her in the least, but on the contrary, gave her that touch of piquant mystery that is so attractive to men.

In the ballroom the orchestra was already thundering, and dancing had already begun. After their apartment, Anya, overwhelmed by the lights, the bright colors, the music, the din, looked round the hall and thought: "Oh, how lovely!" and instantly spotted in the crowd all her acquaintances, everyone she had met before at parties or at picnics, all these officers, teachers, lawyers, officials, landowners. His Excellency, too, was there, and Arty-nov, and society ladies in low-neck dresses, the pretty ones and the ugly. These were already taking up positions in the booths and pavilions of the charity bazaar, ready to begin selling things for the benefit of the poor. A huge officer with shoulder-straps—she had been introduced to him when she was a schoolgirl and now could not remember his name—loomed up before her, as though he had sprung out of the ground and asked her for a waltz, and she flew away from her husband. She felt as though she were sailing in a boat during a violent storm, while her husband remained far away on the shore . . . She danced passionately, eagerly—waltzes, polkas, quadrilles—passing from one pair of arms to another, dizzy with the music and the hubbub, mixing Russian and French, speaking with a burr, laughing, and not giving a thought to her husband or anybody or anything. She scored a success with the men—that was clear and it couldn't have been otherwise. She was breathless with excitement, she squeezed her fan in her hand convulsively and felt thirsty. Her father in a crumpled coat that smelled of benzine came up to her offering her a saucer of pink ice cream.

"You are ravishing tonight," he said, looking at her enraptured, "and I have never so regretted that you were in such a hurry to get married . . . Why? I know you did it for our sake, but . . ." With a shaking hand, he drew out a roll of notes and said: "I got the money for lessons today, and can pay my debt to your husband."

She thrust the saucer back into his hand and, snatched by someone, was carried off far away. Over her partner's shoulder she caught a glimpse of her father gliding across the parquet putting his arm round a lady and whirling her down the hall.

"How charming he is when he is sober," she thought.

She danced the mazurka with the same huge officer. He moved gravely and heavily, like a lifeless carcass in uniform, twitching his shoulders and his chest, stamping his feet almost imperceptibly—he was loath to dance— while she fluttered round him, teasing him with her beauty, her bare neck. Her eyes glowed provokingly, her movements were passionate, while he grew more and more indifferent, and held out his hands to her graciously like a king.

"Bravo! Bravo!" people were exclaiming in the crowd.

But little by little the huge officer, too, lost his composure; he came to life, grew excited, and yielding to her fascination, was carried away and danced lightly, youthfully, while she merely moved her shoulders and looked slyly at him as though she were now the queen and he were her slave. At that moment it seemed to her that the whole ballroom was looking at them, and that everyone was thrilled and envious of them.

The huge officer had hardly had time to thank her for

the dance when the crowd suddenly parted and the men drew themselves up queerly and let their arms drop. It was His Excellency, with two stars on his dress coat, walking toward her. Yes, His Excellency was really walking toward her, for he was looking directly at her with a sugary smile and was chewing his lips as he always did when he saw pretty women.

"Delighted, delighted," he began, "I shall have your husband put under arrest for keeping such a treasure hidden from us till now. I have come to you with a commission from my wife," he went on, offering her his arm. "You must help us. M-m-yes . . . We ought to award you a prize for beauty as they do in America. . . . M-m-yes . . . The Americans . . . My wife is waiting for you impatiently." He led her to a booth and presented her to an elderly lady, the lower part of whose face was disproportionately large, so that she looked as though she had a big stone in her mouth.

"You must help us," she said through her nose in a singsong voice. "All the pretty women are working for our charity bazaar, and for some reason, you alone are doing nothing. Why won't you help us?"

She went away and Anya took her place beside the silver samovar and the cups. She was soon doing a rushing business. Anya charged no less than a ruble for a cup of tea, and forced the huge officer to empty three cups. Artynov, the rich man with the bulging eyes, who suffered from asthma, came up too; he no longer wore the strange costume in which Anya had seen him in the summer at the station, but was in evening clothes like everyone else. Without taking his eyes off Anya, he drank a glass of champagne and paid one hundred rubles for it, then had a cup of tea and gave another hundred, all this without saying a word and wheezing with asthma. Anya solicited customers and got money out of them, firmly convinced by now that her smiles and glances could afford these people nothing but great pleasure. It had dawned upon her that she was made exclusively for this noisy, brilliant life, with laughter, music, dances, admirers, and her old dread of a power that was bearing down upon her and threatened to crush her now seemed ridiculous to her. She was afraid of no one and only regretted that her mother was not there to rejoice with her at her success. Her father, pale by this time, but still steady on his legs, came up to the booth and asked for a glass of cognac. Anya turned crimson, expecting him to say something inappropriate (she was already ashamed of having such a poor, ordinary father), but he emptied his glass, took a ten-ruble note from his roll, threw it down, and walked away with silent dignity. A little later she saw him dancing in the *grand rond* and by now he was staggering and kept calling out something, to his partner's great embarrassment. And Anya remembered how, at a ball three years before, he had staggered and called out in the same way, and it had ended by a police officer taking him home to bed, and the next day, the principal had threatened to dismiss him from his post. What an inappropriate recollection it was!

When the samovars in the booths were no longer alight and the weary charity workers had handed over their takings to the middle-aged lady with the stone in her mouth, Artynov led Anya on his arm to the hall where supper was being served for all who had helped at the bazaar. There were some twenty people at supper, not more, but it was very noisy. His Excellency proposed this toast: "This luxurious dining room is the appropriate place in which to drink to the success of the soup kitchens for which the bazaar was held."

The Brigadier General proposed a toast "to the power to which even the artillery must bow," and all the men proceeded to clink glasses with the ladies. It was very, very jolly!

When Anya was escorted home, it was daylight and the cooks were going to market. Elated, intoxicated, full of new sensations, exhausted, she undressed, sank into bed and instantly fell asleep.

It was past one in the afternoon when the maid waked her and announced Mr. Artynov who had come to call on her. She dressed quickly and went into the drawing-room. Soon after Artynov left, His Excellency called to thank her for her part in the bazaar. Eyeing her with a sugary smile and chewing his lips, he kissed her hand, asked her permission to come again and took his leave, while she remained standing in the middle of the drawing room, amazed, entranced, unable to believe that a change in her life, a marvelous change, had occurred so quickly. And just then her husband walked in. He stood before her now with that ingratiating, sugary, cringingly respectful expression that she was accustomed to see on his face in the presence of the illustrious and the powerful, and with rapture, with indignation, with contempt, confident now that she could do it with impunity, she said, articulating each word distinctly:

"Get out, you blockhead!"

After that, Anya never had a single free day, as she was constantly taking part in picnics, excursions, private theatricals. Each day she returned home in the early hours of the morning and lay down on the floor in the drawing-room, and afterwards told everyone touchingly that she slept under flowers. She needed a great deal of money, but she was no longer afraid of Modest Alexeich, and spent his money as though it were her own; and she did not ask or demand it, but simply sent him the bills or brief notes like these: "Give the bearer 200 rubles," or "Pay 100 rubles at once."

At Easter Modest Alexeich received the order of St. Anna of the second class. When he went to offer his thanks, His Excellency put aside the newspaper he was reading and sank deeper into his armchair: "So now you have three Annas," he said, examining his white hands with their pink nails, "one in your buttonhole and two on your neck."

Modest Alexeich put two fingers to his lips as a precaution against laughing out loud and said: "Now I have only to look forward to the arrival of a little Vladimir. May I make bold to beg Your Excellency to stand godfather?"

He was alluding to the Vladimir of the fourth class and was already imagining how he would repeat everywhere this joke of his, so felicitous in its aptness and audacity, and he was making ready to say something equally good, but His Excellency was again absorbed in his newspaper and merely nodded to him.

And Anya went on driving about in troikas, hunting with Artynov, playing in one-acters, going out to supper parties, and she saw less and less of her own people. They dined alone now. Her father was drinking more heavily than ever; there was no money, and the harmonium had long since been sold for debt. The boys did not let him go out alone in the street now, but followed him for fear he might fall; and whenever they met Anya driving down Old Kiev Street in a smart carriage drawn by a team of two horses abreast and an outrunner, with Artynov on the box instead of a coachman, Pyotr Leontyich would take off his top hat, and would be about to shout something at her, but Petya and Andrusha would take him by the arms and say imploringly: "Don't, Papa dear . . . enough, Papa dear . . ."

1895

In the Cart

THEY drove out of the town at half past eight in the morning.

The paved road was dry, a splendid April sun was shedding warmth, but there was still snow in the ditches and in the woods. Winter, evil, dark, long, had ended so recently; spring had arrived suddenly; but neither the warmth nor the languid, transparent woods, warmed by the breath of spring, nor the black flocks flying in the fields over huge puddles that were like lakes, nor this marvelous, immeasurably deep sky, into which it seemed that one would plunge with such joy, offered anything new and interesting to Marya Vasilyevna, who was sitting in the cart. She had been teaching school for thirteen years, and in the course of all those years she had gone to the town for her salary countless times; and whether it was spring, as now, or a rainy autumn evening, or winter, it was all the same to her, and what she always, invariably, longed for was to reach her destination as soon as possible.

She felt as though she had been living in these parts for a long, long time, for a hundred years, and it seemed to her that she knew every stone, every tree on the road from the town to her school. Here was her past and her present, and she could imagine no other future than

the school, the road to the town and back, and again
the school and again the road.

She had lost the habit of thinking of the time before
she became a schoolmistress and had almost forgotten
all about it. She had once had a father and mother;
they had lived in Moscow in a big apartment near the
Red Gate, but all that remained in her memory of that
part of her life was something vague and formless like
a dream. Her father had died when she was ten years
old, and her mother had died soon after. She had a
brother, an officer; at first they used to write to each
other, then her brother had stopped answering her letters, he had lost the habit. Of her former belongings, all
that remained was a photograph of her mother, but the
dampness in the school had faded it, and now nothing
could be seen on it but the hair and the eyebrows.

When they had gone a couple of miles, old Semyon,
who was driving, turned round and said:

"They have nabbed an official in the town. They have
sent him away. They say that he and some Germans
killed Alexeyev, the mayor, in Moscow."

"Who told you that?"

"They read it in the papers, in Ivan Ionov's teahouse."

And again there was a long silence. Marya Vasilyevna
thought of her school, of the examinations that were
coming soon, and of the girl and the four boys whom
she was sending up for them. And just as she was thinking about the examinations she was overtaken by a
landowner named Hanov in a carriage with four horses,
the very man who had acted as examiner in her school
the previous year. As he drew alongside he recognized
her and bowed.

"Good morning," he said. "Are you driving home,
madam?"

This Hanov, a man of about forty, with a worn face and a lifeless expression, was beginning to age noticeably, but was still handsome and attractive to women. He lived alone on his large estate, was not in the service, and it was said of him that he did nothing at home but pace from one end of the room to the other, whistling, or play chess with his old footman. It was said, too, that he drank heavily. And indeed, at the examination the previous year the very papers he had brought with him smelt of scent and wine. On that occasion everything he wore was brand-new, and Marya Vasilyevna had found him very attractive and, sitting next to him, had felt embarrassed. She was used to seeing cold, hardheaded examiners at the school, but this one did not remember a single prayer, did not know what questions to ask, was exceedingly polite and considerate, and gave only the highest marks.

"I am on my way to visit Bakvist," he continued, addressing Marya Vasilyevna, "but I wonder if he is at home."

They turned off the highway onto a dirt road, Hanov leading the way and Semyon following. The team of four horses kept to the road, slowly pulling the heavy carriage through the mud. Semyon changed his course continually, leaving the road now to drive over a hillock, now to skirt a meadow, often jumping down from the cart and helping the horse. Marya Vasilyevna kept thinking about the school, and wondering whether the arithmetic problem at the examination would be hard or easy. And she was annoyed with the Zemstvo office, where she had found no one the previous day. What negligence! For the past two years she had been asking them to discharge the janitor, who did nothing, was rude to her, and cuffed the boys, but no one paid any attention to her. It was hard to find the chairman at the office and when you did find him, he would say with tears in his eyes that he had no time; the inspector visited the school once in three years and had no understanding of anything connected with it, since he had formerly been employed in the Finance Department and had obtained the post of school inspector through pull; the School Board met very rarely and no one knew where; the Trustee was a half literate peasant, the owner of a tannery, stupid, coarse, and a bosom friend of the janitor's—and heaven knows to whom she could turn with complaints and inquiries.

"He is really handsome," she thought, glancing at Hanov.

Meanwhile the road was growing worse and worse. They drove into the woods. Here there was no turning off the road, the ruts were deep, and water flowed and gurgled in them. Twigs struck them stingingly in the face.

"How's the road?" asked Hanov, and laughed.

The schoolmistress looked at him and could not understand why this odd fellow lived here. What could his money, his interesting appearance, his refinement get him in this Godforsaken place, with its mud, its boredom? Life granted him no privileges, and here, like Semyon, he was jogging slowly along over an abominable road and suffering the same discomforts. Why live here, when one had a chance to live in Petersburg or abroad? And it seemed as though it would be a simple matter for a rich man like him to turn this bad road into a good one so as to avoid having to endure this misery and seeing the despair written on the faces of his coachman and Semyon? But he merely laughed, and apparently it was all the same to him, and he asked nothing better of life. He was kind, gentle, naive; he had no grasp of this coarse life, he did not know it, any more than he had known the prayers at the examination. He presented nothing to the schools but globes, and sincerely regarded himself as a useful person and a prominent worker in the field of popular education. And who had need of his globes here?

"Hold on, Vasilyevna!" said Semyon.

The cart lurched violently and was about to turn over; something heavy fell on Marya Vasilyevna's feet —it was her purchases. There was a steep climb uphill over a clayey road; noisy rivulets were flowing in winding ditches; the water had gullied the road; and how could one drive here! The horses breathed heavily. Hanov got out of the carriage and walked at the edge of the road in his long coat. He was hot.

"How's the road?" he repeated, and laughed. "This is the way to smash your carriage."

"But who tells you to go driving in such weather?" asked Semyon in a surly voice. "You ought to stay home."

"I'm bored at home, grandfather. I don't like staying home."

Next to old Semyon he seemed well-built and vigorous, but there was something barely perceptible in his gait which betrayed him as a weak creature, already blighted, approaching its end. And suddenly it seemed as though there were a whiff of liquor in the woods. Marya Vasilyevna felt frightened and was filled with pity for this man who was going to pieces without rhyme or reason, and it occurred to her that if she were his wife or his sister she would devote her whole life to his rescue. His wife! Life was so ordered that here he was living in his great house alone, while she was living in a Godforsaken village alone, and yet for some reason the mere thought that he and she might meet on an equal footing and become intimate seemed impossible, absurd. Fundamentally, life was so arranged and human relations were complicated so utterly beyond all understanding that when you thought about it you were terrified and your heart sank.

"And you can't understand," she thought, "why God gives good looks, friendliness, charming, melancholy eyes to weak, unhappy, useless people—why they are so attractive."

"Here we must turn off to the right," said Hanov, getting into his carriage. "Good-by! All good wishes!"

And again she thought of her pupils, of the examination, of the janitor, of the School Board; and when the wind brought her the sound of the receding carriage these thoughts mingled with others. She wanted to think of beautiful eyes, of love, of the happiness that would never be. . . .

His wife? It is cold in the morning, there is no one to light the stove, the janitor has gone off somewhere; the children come in as soon as it is light, bringing in snow and mud and making a noise; it is all so uncomfortable, so unpleasant. Her quarters consist of one little room and a kitchen close by. Every day when school is over she has a headache and after dinner she has heartburn. She has to collect money from the children for firewood and to pay the janitor, and to turn it over to the Trustee, and then to implore him—that overfed, insolent peasant —for God's sake to send her firewood. And at night she dreams of examinations, peasants, snowdrifts. And this life has aged and coarsened her, making her homely, angular, and clumsy, as though they had poured lead into her. She is afraid of everything, and in the presence of a member of the Zemstvo Board or of the Trustee, she gets up and does not dare sit down again. And she uses obsequious expressions when she mentions any one of them. And no one likes her, and life is passing drearily, without warmth, without friendly sympathy, without interesting acquaintances. In her position how terrible it would be if she were to fall in love!

"Hold on, Vasilyevna!"

Another steep climb.

She had begun to teach school from necessity, without feeling called to it; and she had never thought of a call, of the need for enlightenment; and it always seemed to her that what was most important in her work was not the children, not enlightenment, but the examinations. And when did she have time to think of a call, of enlightenment? Teachers, impecunious physicians, doctors' assistants, for all their terribly hard work, do not even have the comfort of thinking that they are serving an ideal or the people, because their heads are always filled with thoughts of their daily bread, of firewood, of bad roads, of sickness. It is a hard, humdrum existence, and only stolid cart horses like Marya Vasilyevna can bear it a long time; lively, alert, impressionable people who talk about their calling and about serving the ideal are soon weary of it and give up the work.

Semyon kept on picking out the driest and shortest way, traveling now across a meadow, now behind the cottages, but in one place the peasants would not let them pass and in another the land belonged to the priest and so they could not cross it, in yet another Ivan Ionov had bought a plot from the landowner and had dug a ditch round it. They kept turning back.

They reached Nizhneye Gorodishche. Near the teahouse, on the dung-strewn, snowy ground, there stood wagons loaded with great bottles of oil of vitriol. There were a great many people in the teahouse, all drivers, and it smelled of vodka, tobacco, and sheepskins. The place was noisy with loud talk and the banging of the door which was provided with a pulley. In the shop next door someone was playing an accordion steadily. Marya Vasilyevna was sitting down, having tea, while at the next table some peasants were drinking vodka and beer, sweaty with the tea they had had and the bad air.

"Hey, Kuzma!" people kept shouting confusedly. "What's doing?" "The Lord bless us!" "Ivan Dementy-ich, that I can do for you!" "See here, friend!"

A little pockmarked peasant with a black beard, who was quite drunk, was suddenly taken aback by some-thing and began using foul language.

"What are you cursing about, you there?" Semyon, who was sitting some way off, remarked angrily. "Don't you see the young lady?"

"The young lady!" someone jeered in another corner.

"The swine!"

"I didn't mean nothing—" The little peasant was embarrassed. "Excuse me. I pays my money and the young lady pays hers. How-de-do, ma'am?"

"How do you do?" answered the schoolmistress.

"And I thank you kindly."

Marya Vasilyevna drank her tea with pleasure, and she, too, began turning red like the peasants, and again she fell to thinking about firewood, about the janitor. . . .

"Wait, brother," came from the next table. "It's the school-ma'am from Vyazovye. I know; she's a good sort."

"She's all right!"

The door was banging continually, some coming in, others going out. Marya Vasilyevna went on sitting there, thinking of the same things all the time, while the accordion went on playing and playing behind the wall. There had been patches of sunlight on the floor, they shifted to the counter, then to the wall, and finally disappeared altogether; this meant that it was past midday. The peasants at the next table were getting ready to leave. The little peasant went up to Marya Vasilyevna somewhat unsteadily and shook hands with her; following his example, the others shook hands with her at parting, and filed out singly, and the door squeaked and slammed nine times.

"Vasilyevna, get ready," Semyon called to her.

They drove off. And again they went at a walking pace.

"A little while back they were building a school here at this Nizhneye Gorodishche," said Semyon, turning round. "There were wicked doings then!"

"Why, what?"

"They say the chairman pocketed a cool thousand, and the Trustee another thousand, and the teacher five hundred."

"The whole school only cost a thousand. It's wrong to slander people, grandfather. That's all nonsense."

"I don't know. I only repeat what folks say."

But it was clear that Semyon did not believe the schoolmistress. The peasants did not believe her. They always thought she received too large a salary, twenty-one rubles a month (five would have been enough), and that she kept for herself the greater part of the money that she received for firewood and for the janitor's wages. The Trustee thought as the peasants did, and he himself made something on the firewood and received a salary from the peasants for acting as Trustee —without the knowledge of the authorities.

The woods, thank God, were behind them, and now it would be clear, level ground all the way to Vyazovye, and they had not far to go now. All they had to do was to cross the river and then the railway line, and then they would be at Vyazovye.

"Where are you going?" Marya Vasilyevna asked Semyon. "Take the road to the right across the bridge."

"Why, we can go this way just as well, it's not so deep."

"Mind you don't drown the horse."

"What?"

"Look, Hanov is driving to the bridge, too," said Marya Vasilyevna, seeing the four-horse team far away to the right. "I think it's he."

"It's him all right. So he didn't find Bakvist in. What a blockhead he is. Lord have mercy on us! He's driving over there, and what for? It's all of two miles nearer this way."

They reached the river. In summer it was a shallow stream, easily forded and usually dried up by August, but now, after the spring floods, it was a river forty feet wide, rapid, muddy, and cold; on the bank, and right up to the water, there were fresh wheel tracks, so it had been crossed there.

"Giddap!" shouted Semyon angrily and anxiously, tugging violently at the reins and flapping his elbows as a bird does its wings. "Giddap!"

The horse went into the water up to its belly and stopped, but at once went on again, straining its muscles, and Marya Vasilyevna felt a sharp chill in her feet.

"Giddap!" she shouted, too, standing up. "Giddap!"

They got to the bank.

"Nice mess, Lord have mercy on us!" muttered Semyon, setting the harness straight. "It's an affliction, this Zemstvo."

Her shoes and rubbers were full of water, the lower edge of her dress and of her coat and one sleeve were wet and dripping; the sugar and flour had got wet, and that was the worst of it, and Marya Vasilyevna only struck her hands together in despair and said:

"Oh, Semyon, Semyon! What a fellow you are, really!"

The barrier was down at the railway crossing. An express was coming from the station. Marya Vasilyevna stood at the crossing waiting for the train to pass, and shivering all over with cold. Vyazovye was in sight now, and the school with the green roof, and the church with its blazing crosses that reflected the setting sun; and the station windows were aflame, too, and a pink smoke rose from the engine. . . . And it seemed to her that everything was shivering with cold.

Here was the train; the windows, like the crosses on the church, reflected the blazing light; it hurt her eyes to look at them. On the platform of one of the first-class carriages a lady was standing, and Marya Vasilyevna glanced at her as she flashed by. Her mother! What a resemblance! Her mother had had just such luxuriant hair, just such a forehead and that way of holding her head. And with amazing distinctness, for the first time in those thirteen years, she imagined vividly her mother, her father, her brother, their apartment in Moscow, the aquarium with the little fishes, everything down to the smallest detail; she suddenly heard the piano playing, her father's voice; she felt as then, young, good-looking, well-dressed, in a bright warm room among her own people. A feeling of joy and happiness suddenly overwhelmed her, she pressed her hands to her temples in ecstasy, and called softly, imploringly:

"Mama!"

And she began to cry, she did not know why. Just at that moment Hanov drove up with his team of four horses, and seeing him she imagined such happiness as had never been, and smiled and nodded to him as an equal and an intimate, and it seemed to her that the sky, the windows, the trees, were glowing with her happiness, her triumph. No, her father and mother had never died, she had never been a schoolmistress, that had been a long, strange, oppressive dream, and now she had awakened. . . .

"Vasilyevna, get in!"

And suddenly it all vanished. The barrier was slowly rising. Marya Vasilyevna, shivering and numb with cold, got into the cart. The carriage with the four horses crossed the railway track, Semyon followed. The guard at the crossing took off his cap.

"And this is Vyazovye. Here we are."

1897

At Home

THE Donetz Railroad. A cheerless station, quiet and lonely, gleaming white on the steppe, with walls hot from the sun, with not a speck of shade and, it appears, with not a single human being. The train which brought you here has left; the sound of it is scarcely audible and at last dies away. The neighborhood of the station is deserted, and there are no carriages but your own. You get into it—this is so pleasant after the train —and you roll along the road through the steppe, and by degrees, a landscape unfolds such as one does not see near Moscow—immense, endless, fascinating in its monotony. The steppe, the steppe, and nothing else; in the distance an ancient grave-mound or a windmill; oxcarts laden with coal file by. Birds fly singly low over the plain and the monotonous beat of their wings induces a drowsiness. It is hot. An hour or two passes, and still the steppe, the steppe, and still in the distance the grave-mound. The driver rambles on telling you some long-drawn-out, irrelevant tale, frequently pointing at something with his whip, and tranquillity takes possession of your soul, you are loath to think of the past. . . .

A troika had been sent to fetch Vera Ivanovna Kardina. The driver put in her bags and started setting the harness to rights.

"Everything is just as it used to be," said Vera, looking about her. "I was a little girl when I was here last, some ten years ago. I remember old Boris came to fetch me then. Is he still living?"

The driver made no reply, but gave her a sour, peculiarly Ukrainian look and climbed onto the box.

It was a drive of twenty miles from the station, and Vera too yielded to the fascination of the steppe, forgot the past and thought only of how spacious and unconfined this region was. Healthy, clever, beautiful, and young—she was only twenty-three—she had hitherto lacked nothing but just this space and freedom.

The steppe, the steppe . . . The horses trotted along, the sun rose higher and higher, and it seemed to Vera that never in her childhood had the steppe been so rich, so luxuriant in June; the field flowers were in bloom, yellow, green, lilac, white, and a fragrance rose from them and from the warmed earth, and there were strange blue birds along the road. Vera had long since lost the habit of praying, but now, struggling with drowsiness, she murmured, "Lord, grant that I may be happy here."

There was a sweet feeling of serenity in her heart, and she felt as though she would have been glad to go on driving like that all her life, looking at the steppe.

Suddenly they reached a deep ravine overgrown with oak saplings and alders. One felt a breath of moisture in the air—there must have been a stream at the bottom. On the near side, at the very edge of the ravine, a flock of partridge rose noisily. Vera remembered that in former days they used to go to this ravine for evening walks; so the house must be near. And now she could actually see the poplars, the barn; black smoke was rising a little way off—they were burning old straw. And there was Aunt Dasha coming to meet her and waving her handkerchief. Grandfather was on the terrace. Oh, dear, what a joy!

"My darling, my darling!" shrieked her aunt as though she were in hysterics. "Our real mistress has come! You understand, you are our mistress, our queen! Here everything is yours! My darling, my beauty, I am not your aunt but your obedient slave!"

Vera had no relatives but her aunt and her grandfather; her mother had long been dead; her father, an engineer, had died three months before in Kazan on his way to Siberia. Her grandfather had a big gray beard, was stout, red-faced and asthmatic, and he thrust out his stomach as he walked leaning on a cane. Her aunt, a lady of forty-two or so, who wore a fashionable dress with sleeves puffed at the shoulders and was tightly laced at the waist, evidently tried to look young and was still anxious to attract men; she walked mincingly, her back twitching as she went.

"Will you love us?" she asked, embracing Vera. "You are not proud?"

In accordance with her grandfather's wish a thanksgiving service was held, then they spent a long while over dinner, and Vera's new life began. She was given the best room, all the rugs in the house were put in it, and a great many flowers; and when at night she lay down in her cozy, wide, very soft bed and covered herself with a silk quilt that smelled of old clothes long stored away, she laughed out loud with pleasure. Aunt Dasha came in for a minute to wish her good night.

"Here you are home, thank God," she said, sitting down on the bed. "As you see, we are very well off, couldn't be better. There is only one thing: your grandfather is in a bad way! A bad way, indeed. He is short of breath and he is getting senile. And remember how robust, how vigorous he used to be! What a man he was! In former days, if a servant displeased him or anything else went wrong, he would jump up at once and shout, 'Twenty-five strokes! Flog him! Hard!' But now he has drawn in his horns and never opens his mouth. And besides, times have changed, darling; one mayn't strike servants nowadays. Of course, why should one? But, on the other hand, they have to be held in."

"And are they beaten now, Auntie?" asked Vera.

"The steward hits them sometimes, but I never do, bless their hearts! And your grandfather sometimes lifts his stick from old habit, but he never strikes them." Aunt Dasha yawned and made the sign of the cross over her mouth and her right ear.

"It isn't dull here?" Vera inquired.

"What shall I say? There are no landowners hereabouts, they don't live here now, but iron works have been built all over the place, darling, and there are lots of engineers, doctors, and mine superintendents. Of course, we have private theatricals and concerts, but most of the time it's cards. They call on us, too. Dr. Neshchapov, from the iron works, comes to see us—such a handsome interesting man! He has fallen in love with your photograph. I made up my mind: he is meant for Verochka. He is young, handsome, well-to-do—a good match, in a word. But of course, you are a fine catch, too. You are of good family; the property is mortgaged, it is true, but it is in good order and not neglected; there is my share in it, but it will all come to you—I am your obedient slave. And my brother, your late father, has left you fifteen thousand rubles . . . But I see you can't keep your eyes open. Sleep, my child."

The next day Vera spent a long time walking round the house. The garden, which was old and inattractive, lying inconveniently on a slope, had no paths and was completely neglected: it was apparently regarded as superfluous. There were numbers of grass snakes in it. Hoopoes flew about under the trees calling "Oo-too-toot!" in a tone which suggested that they were trying to remind people of something. At the bottom of the hill there was a stream, overgrown with tall reeds, and half a mile beyond it was the village. From the garden Vera went out into the fields; looking into the distance, thinking of her new life on her native heath, she kept trying to grasp what was in store for her. The spaciousness, the lovely calm of the steppe, told her that happiness was near at hand and that, perhaps, it was here already. In fact, thousands of people would have said: "What happiness to be young, healthy, well-educated and to live on one's own estate!" At the same time, the endless plain, monotonous, without a single living soul, frightened her, and at moments it was clear to her that this quiet green monster would swallow up her life and reduce it to nothingness. She was young, elegant, fond of life; she had graduated from an aristocratic boarding-school, had learned to speak three languages, had read a great deal, had traveled with her father—and could it be that she had done all this only in the end to settle down on a remote farm lost in the steppe, and day after day wander from the garden into the fields and from the fields into the garden, having nothing to do, and then sit at home listening to her grandfather's heavy breathing? What could she do? Where could she go? She found no answer, and as she was returning home she doubted whether she would be happy here, and thought that riding from the station was far more interesting than living here.

Dr. Neshchapov came over from the iron works. He was a physician, but three years previously he had bought a share in the enterprise and had become one of the partners; and now he no longer looked upon medicine as his chief occupation, though he still practiced. Looking at him, one saw a pale, dark-haired man in a white waistcoat, with a good figure; but to guess what there was in his heart and in his mind was difficult. He kissed Aunt Dasha's hand on greeting her and was continually jumping up to move a chair or give his seat to someone; he was very grave and silent all the while and when he started speaking, it was for some reason impossible to hear and understand his first sentence, although he spoke clearly and not too low.

"You play the piano?" he asked Vera, and suddenly jumped up, as she had dropped her handkerchief.

He stayed from midday to midnight without saying anything, and Vera found him very unattractive. It seemed to her that a white waistcoat in the country was in bad taste, and his excessive politeness, his refined manners, and his pale, serious face with dark eyebrows struck her as mawkish; she fancied that he never opened his mouth probably because he was stupid. When he had gone, her aunt said enthusiastically, "Well? Isn't he charming?"

II

Aunt Dasha managed the property. Tightly laced, jingling bracelets on her wrist, she would walk mincingly into the kitchen, the barn, the cattle yard, her back twitching, and whenever she talked to the steward or to the peasants, for some reason, she would put on her pince-nez. Grandfather always sat in the same place, playing patience or dozing. He ate a very great deal at dinner and supper; he was served a freshly cooked dinner, as well as leftovers and the cold remnants of Sunday's pie and salt meat from the servants' dinner, and he ate it all greedily. The impression every dinner made on Vera was such that afterwards when she saw a flock of sheep driven by or flour being brought from the mill, she thought: "Grandfather will eat that." Most of the time he was silent, absorbed in eating or in patience; but it sometimes happened at dinner that, at the sight of Vera, he would get emotional and say tenderly, "My only grandchild! Verochka!"

And tears would glisten in his eyes. Or his face would turn suddenly crimson, his neck would swell, he would look with fury at the servants and, banging his stick, demand, "Why hasn't the horseradish been served?"

In winter he led a completely sedentary existence; in summer he sometimes drove out into the fields to have a look at the oats and the hay; and when he came back he would declare that everything was neglected now with him away, and he rapped his stick.

"Your grandfather is out of humor," Aunt Dasha would whisper. "Still, it is nothing now. But formerly it was terrible: 'Twenty-five strokes!' he would shout. 'Flog him! Hard!'"

Aunt Dasha complained that everyone had grown lazy, that no one did anything, and that the estate yielded no income. Indeed, there was no regular farming on the place; they plowed and sowed a little simply from habit and in reality did nothing and lived in idleness. And yet all day long there was running to and fro, figuring and worrying. The bustle in the house began

at five o'clock in the morning; one heard continually:
"Bring it," "Fetch it," "Run an errand," and as a rule
by evening the servants were utterly exhausted. Aunt
Dasha's cooks and housemaids changed every week;
sometimes she discharged them for immorality; sometimes they left of their own accord, saying that they
were worn out. None of the villagers would come to the
house as a servant; it was necessary to hire people from
a distance. There was only one girl from the village
living in the house, Alyona, and she stayed because her
whole family—old women and children—were living
on her wages. This Alyona, a pale, rather stupid little
thing, spent the whole day doing the rooms, waiting at
tables, lighting the stove, sewing, washing; it always
seemed as though she were only puttering about, making a noise with her boots and were nothing but a
nuisance in the house. Dreading that she might be dismissed and sent home, she often dropped and broke the
crockery, and they deducted the value of it from her
wages, and then her mother and grandmother would
come and fall down at Aunt Dasha's feet.

Once a week and sometimes oftener, guests would
arrive. Aunt Dasha would come to Vera and say, "You
should show yourself to the guests, or they'll think that
you are stuck-up."

Vera would go in to the guests and play vint with
them for hours together or play the piano while the
guests danced. Her aunt, in high spirits and breathless
from dancing, would come up and whisper to her, "Be
nice to Marya Nikiforovna."

On the 6th of December, St. Nicholas' Day, a lot of
guests, about thirty of them, arrived all at once; they
played vint until late and many of them stayed the
night. In the morning they sat down to cards again, then
had dinner, and when Vera went to her room after

dinner to rest from conversation and tobacco smoke, she found guests there, too, and she almost wept with despair. And when they began to get ready to leave in the evening, so great was her relief to see them go at last that she said, "Do stay a little longer!"

Company wearied and constrained her, yet nearly every day as soon as it began to grow dark something pulled her out of the house and she drove off to visit either the iron works or some landowner in the neighborhood, and then there were cards, dancing, forfeits, supper . . . The young people employed in the plants or the mines sometimes sang Little Russian songs and sang them rather well. It made one sad to hear them. Or they all gathered together in one room and talked in the dusk about the mines, the treasure troves, famous grave-mounds. Sometimes it happened that as they were talking in the late hours, a shout of "Help!" was heard. It was a drunken man going home or someone who was being robbed near the pits in the neighborhood. Or else the wind howled in the chimneys, shutters banged, then they would hear the uneasy peals of church bells announcing the beginning of a snowstorm.

At all the evening parties, picnics and dinners, Aunt Dasha was invariably the most interesting woman and Dr. Neshchapov the most interesting man. People living near the iron works or in the country houses did little reading; they played only marches and polkas, and the young people always argued hotly about things they did not understand, and the effect was crude. The arguments were loud and heated, but, strange to say, nowhere had Vera met people who were as unconcerned and lackadaisical as these. They seemed to have no fatherland, no religion, no public interests. When they talked of literature or discussed some abstract problem, it was obvious from Dr. Neshchapov's face that the matter was of no interest to him whatever, and that for a long, long time he had read nothing and cared to read nothing. Grave and expressionless like a badly painted portrait, forever in his white waistcoat, he was uncommunicative and incomprehensible as before; but the ladies, young and old, thought him interesting, were enthusiastic over his manners and envied Vera whom he apparently found very attractive. And Vera always came away from the visit with a feeling of vexation, vowing inwardly to stay home; but the day passed, evening came and again she hurried off to the iron works. And so it went on almost all winter.

She ordered books and magazines and used to read them in her room. She also read at night in bed. When the clock in the hall struck two or three and her temples were beginning to ache from reading, she sat up in bed and thought: "What shall I do? Where shall I go?" Accursed, galling questions to which there were a number of ready-made answers and in reality none at all.

Oh, how noble, how blessed, how beautiful it must be to serve the people, to alleviate their sufferings, to enlighten them! But she, Vera, did not know the people. And how could she approach them? They were alien and uninteresting to her; she could not endure the bad smell of the peasant cabins, the tavern oaths, the unwashed children, the women's talk of illness. To walk over snowdrifts, to freeze, then to sit in the stifling air of the cabin to teach children she did not love, no, she would rather die! And to teach the peasants' children while Aunt Dasha took in rent for the taverns and fined the peasants—what a farce it would have been! What a lot of talk there was of schools, of village libraries, of universal education; but if all these engineers, industrialists, and ladies of her acquaintance had not been hypocrites and had really believed that schooling was necessary, they would not have paid the teachers fifteen rubles a month as they did now and would not have starved them. And all the talk about schools and ignorance—that was only to stifle the voice of conscience, since people were ashamed to own fifteen or thirty thousand acres and to be indifferent to the lot of the people. Here the ladies were saying about Dr. Neshchapov that he was a kind man and that he had built a school at the iron works. Yes, he had built a school out of used bricks at a cost of some eight hundred rubles, and they chanted "Long life," to him when the building was consecrated, but there was no chance of his giving up his shares and it certainly never entered his head that the peasants were human beings like himself, and that they too should be taught in universities, not in these wretched factory schools.

And Vera was angry at herself and at everyone else. She took up a book again and tried to read it, but soon afterwards sat down, plunged into thought again. To become a doctor? But to do that you must pass an examination in Latin, besides she had an invincible aversion to corpses and illnesses. It would be fine to become a mechanic, a judge, a captain of a ship, a savant, to do something into which she could put all her powers, physical and spiritual, and to be tired out and sleep soundly at night; it would be fine to devote her life to something that would make her an interesting person, able to attract interesting people, to love, to have a real family of her own. But what was she to do? How was she to begin?

One Sunday in Lent her aunt came into her room early in the morning to get her umbrella. Vera was sitting up in bed clasping her head in her hands, thinking.

"You ought to drive to church, darling," said her aunt, "or people will think you are an unbeliever."

Vera made no answer.

"I see you are bored, child," said Aunt Dasha, sinking on her knees by the bedside; she adored Vera. "Tell me the truth, are you bored?"

"Dreadfully."

"My beauty, my queen, I am your obedient slave, I wish you nothing but good and all happiness. Tell me, why don't you want to marry Neshchapov? Whom else do you want, my child? Forgive me, darling, but you can't be so finicky, we are not princes. . . . Time is passing, you are not seventeen. . . . And I don't understand it! He loves you, idolizes you!"

"Oh, heavens," said Vera with vexation, "how can I tell? He sits there and never opens his mouth."

"He is shy, darling. . . . He is afraid you will refuse him."

And when afterwards her aunt had left, Vera stood still in the middle of her room uncertain whether to dress or to go back to bed. The bed was hateful and if one looked out of the window, one saw bare trees, gray snow, hateful jackdaws, pigs that her grandfather would eat . . .

"Yes, really," she thought, "perhaps, I'd better get married!"

III

For two days Aunt Dasha went about with a tear-stained and heavily powdered face, and at dinner she kept sighing and looking at the icon. And it was impossible to discover what was the trouble. At last she made up her mind, went in to Vera and said in an offhand way, "The fact is, child, we have to pay interest on the bank loan, and the tenant has defaulted on his rent. Allow me to pay it out of the fifteen thousand your papa left you."

Afterwards Aunt Dasha did nothing all day but make cherry jam in the garden. Alyona, her cheeks flushed with the heat, kept running to the garden, to the house, to the cellar. When Aunt Dasha was making jam, her face very serious as though she were performing a religious rite, her sleeves displaying her small, strong, despotic arms, and the servants running about incessantly, bustling about the jam which others would eat, there was always a feeling of torment in the air.

The garden smelled of hot cherries. The sun had set. The brazier had been carried away, but the pleasant sweetish smell still lingered in the air. Vera sat on a bench in the garden and watched a new hired man, a young soldier on leave who had been passing through the neighborhood and who was, by her orders, making paths. He was cutting the sod with a spade and throwing it onto a wheelbarrow.

"Where were you stationed when you were in service?" Vera asked him.

"At Berdyansk."

"And where are you going now, home?"

"No, ma'am," answered the man, "I have no home."

"But where were you born and raised?"

"In the Province of Orel. Till I went into the army I lived with my mother and stepfather. My mother was a good housewife, and people looked up to her, and I was well-off. But while I was in the army I got a letter saying my mother died . . . and now I don't seem to care to go home. It's not my own father, so it's not my home."

"Is your father dead?"

"I don't know, ma'am. I was born out of wedlock."

At that moment Aunt Dasha appeared at the window and said: *"Il ne faut pas parler aux gens. . . .* Go into the kitchen, my good man," she said to the soldier; "you can tell your story there."

And then came supper, as it had the previous day and did every day, reading, a sleepless night and endless thoughts about the same thing. At three o'clock it began to grow light; Alyona was already busy in the corridor, and Vera was not asleep yet and was trying to read. She heard the creaking of the wheelbarrow: it was the new hired man at work in the garden. She seated herself at the open window with a book and, half-dozing, watched the soldier make paths for her, and that entertained her. The paths were even as a leather strap and level, and it was pleasant to imagine what they would be like when they were strewn with yellow sand.

Soon after five o'clock she saw her aunt come out of the house in a pink dressing-gown and curl-papers. She stood silently on the steps for about three minutes and then said to the soldier:

"Take your passport and go in peace. I can't have anyone in my house who is illegitimate."

Pain and anger wrenched Vera's heart. She was indignant with her aunt, she hated her; she was sick of her, she loathed her. But what was she to do? Cut her short? Be rude to her? But what would be the use? Suppose she were to stand up to her, get her out of the way, make her harmless; suppose she were to prevent her grandfather from raising his stick to strike—what would be the use? It would be like killing one mouse or one snake in the boundless steppe. The vast expanse, the long winters, the monotony and dreariness of life generated a sense of helplessness; the situation seems hopeless, and one wants to do nothing—all is useless.

Alyona came in and, bowing low to Vera, began

carrying out the armchairs to beat the dust out of them.

"A fine time you have chosen to do the room," said Vera, annoyed. "Go away!"

Alyona lost her head and in her terror could not grasp what was wanted of her. She began hurriedly tidying up the top of the chest of drawers.

"Go away, I tell you!" Vera shouted, turning cold; she had never felt so exasperated. "Go away!"

Alyona uttered a sort of birdlike moan and dropped Vera's gold watch on the carpet.

"Get out of here!" shrieked Vera in a voice not her own, jumping up and trembling all over. "Chase her off, she has worn me out!" she continued, walking rapidly after Alyona down the passage and stamping her feet. "Get out! The rods! Flog her!"

Then suddenly she came to herself and just as she was, unwashed, uncombed, in her dressing-gown and bedroom slippers, she rushed out of the house. She ran to the familiar ravine and hid herself there among the bramble bushes so as to see no one and be unseen. Lying there motionless on the grass, she did not weep, she was not horror-stricken, but staring at the sky open-eyed, she reflected coldly and clearly that something had happened which she could never forget and for which she could never forgive herself as long as she lived.

"No, enough, enough!" she thought. "It's time to take myself in hand or there'll be no end to it . . . Enough!"

At midday Dr. Neshchapov drove by the ravine on his way to the manor house. She saw him and quickly decided that she would begin a new life, that she would force herself to begin it, and this decision calmed her. And following the doctor's well-built figure with her eyes, she said as though trying to soften the harshness of her decision, "He is nice. . . . We shall manage a life somehow."

She returned home. While she was dressing, Aunt Dasha came into the room and said, "Alyona upset you, darling; I have sent her home to the village. Her mother thrashed her within an inch of her life and came here crying."

"Auntie," said Vera quickly, "I am going to marry Dr. Neshchapov. Only talk to him yourself . . . I can't."

And again she went out into the fields. And wandering aimlessly about, she made up her mind that when she was married she would keep house, doctor the peasants, teach school, do all the things that other women of her circle did. And this constant dissatisfaction with herself and everyone else, this succession of bad mistakes that loom up like a mountain before you whenever you look back on your past, she would accept as her real life, her destiny, and she would expect nothing better. . . . And indeed, there is nothing better! Glorious nature, dreams, music, tell one story, but reality another. Evidently goodness and happiness exist somewhere outside of life. . . . It is necessary not to live your separate life, but become at one with this luxurious steppe, boundless and indifferent as eternity, with its flowers, its ancient grave-mounds, and its spaciousness, and then all will be well.

A month later Vera was living at the iron works.

1897

Peasants

NIKOLAY CHIKILDEYEV, a waiter in the Moscow hotel, Slavyansky Bazar, had been taken ill. His legs went numb and his gait became unsteady, so that one day as he was going along the corridor, carrying an order of ham and peas on a tray, he stumbled and fell. He had to give up his job. Whatever money he and his wife had was spent on doctors and medicines; they had nothing left to live on; idleness weighed heavily upon him and he decided to go back to the village from which he had come. It was easier to be ill at home, and it was cheaper living there; and not for nothing is it said that there is help in the walls of home.

He arrived in his native Zhukovo toward evening. In his childhood the house in which he was born figured as a bright, cosy, comfortable place. But now, going into the log cabin, he was positively frightened: it was so dark and crowded and squalid. His wife Olga and his daughter Sasha, who had come with him, stared in bewilderment at the big dirty stove, which occupied almost half the room and was black with soot and flies. What a lot of flies! The stove was lopsided, the logs in the walls sloped, and it looked as though the cabin were about to collapse. In the corner, near the icons, bottle labels and scraps of newspaper were pasted on the walls instead of pictures. The poverty, the poverty! None of the grown-ups were at home; all were at work, reaping. On the stove sat a flaxen-haired girl of eight, unwashed, apathetic; she did not even look up at the newcomers. Below, a white cat was rubbing itself against the oven fork.

"Pussy, pussy!" Sasha called to it coaxingly. "Pussy!"

"It can't hear," said the little girl; "it's gone deaf."

"Why?"

"Oh, it was hit."

Nikolay and Olga realized at first glance what life was like here, but said nothing to each other; silently they put down their bundles, and silently went out into the village street. Their cabin was the third from the end and seemed the poorest and oldest-looking; the second was not much better; but the last one had an iron roof and curtains at the windows. That cottage stood apart, and was not enclosed; it was a tavern. The cabins were all in a single row, and the entire little village—quiet and pensive, with willows, elders, and mountain ash peeping out from the courtyards—had a pleasant look.

Behind the peasant homesteads the ground sloped down to the river steeply and precipitously, so that huge boulders jutted out here and there through the clay. On the steep slope paths wound among the stones and pits dug by the potters; pieces of broken pottery, brown and red, lay about in heaps, and below there stretched a broad, level, bright-green meadow, already mown, over which the peasants' cattle were now wandering. The river, two thirds of a mile from the village, ran, twisting and turning, between beautiful wooded banks. Beyond it was another broad meadow, a herd of cattle, long files of white geese; then, just as on the hither side, there was a steep rise, and at the top of it, on a ridge, a village with a church that had five domes, and, at a little distance, a manor house.

"It's nice here!" said Olga, crossing herself at the sight of the church. "Lord, what space!"

Just at that moment the bells began ringing for vespers (it was Saturday evening). Two little girls, down below, who were carrying a pail of water, looked round at the church to listen to the chimes.

"About this time they are serving the dinners at the Slavyansky Bazar," said Nikolay dreamily.

Sitting on the edge of the ravine, Nikolay and Olga watched the sunset, and saw how the gold and crimson sky was reflected in the river, in the church windows, and in the very air, which was soft and still and inexpressibly pure, as it never was in Moscow. And when the sun had set, the herds went past, bleating and bellowing; geese flew across from the other side of the river, and then all was hushed; the soft light faded from the air, and dusk began its rapid descent.

Meanwhile Nikolay's father and mother, two gaunt, bent, toothless old people, of the same height, had returned. The daughters-in-law, Marya and Fyokla, who had been working on the estate across the river, came home, too. Marya, the wife of Nikolay's brother Kiryak, had six children, and Fyokla, the wife of his brother Denis, who was in the army, had two; and when Nikolay, stepping into the cabin, saw the whole family, all those bodies big and little stirring on the sleeping platforms, in the cradles and in all the corners, and when he saw the greed with which his old father and the women ate the black bread, dipping it in water, it was borne in upon him that he had made a mistake in coming here, sick, penniless, and with a family, too—a mistake!

"And where is brother Kiryak?" he asked, when they had greeted each other.

"He works as a watchman for a merchant," answered his father; "he stays there in the woods. He ain't a bad worker, but he's too fond of the drink."

"He's no breadwinner," said the old woman tearfully. "Our men are a poor lot; they bring nothing into the house, but take plenty out. Kiryak drinks, and the old man too knows his way to the tavern—it's no use hiding the sin. The wrath of the Queen of Heaven is on us."

On account of the guests they heated the samovar. The tea smelt of fish; the sugar was gray and had been nibbled; cockroaches ran about over the bread and the crockery. It was disgusting to drink the tea, and the conversation was disgusting, too—about nothing but poverty and sickness. And before they had emptied their first cups there came a loud, long-drawn-out, drunken shout from the courtyard:

"Ma-arya!"

"Looks like Kiryak's coming," said the old man. "Talk of the devil—"

Silence fell. And after a little while, the shout sounded again, coarse and long-drawn-out, as though it came from under the ground:

"Ma-arya!"

Marya, the elder daughter-in-law, turned pale and huddled against the stove, and it was odd to see the look of terror on the face of this strong, broad-shouldered, homely woman. Her daughter, the apathetic-looking little girl who had been sitting on the stove, suddenly broke into loud weeping.

"What are you bawling for, you pest?" Fyokla, a handsome woman, also strong and broad-shouldered, shouted at her. "He won't kill her, no fear!"

From the old man Nikolay learned that Marya was

afraid to live in the woods with Kiryak, and that whenever he was drunk he came for her, raised Cain, and beat her mercilessly.

"Ma-arya!" the shout sounded at the very door.

"Help me, for Christ's sake, good people," stammered Marya, breathing as though she were being plunged into icy water. "Help me, good people—"

All the children in the cabin began crying, and affected by their example, Sasha, too, began to cry. A drunken cough was heard, and a tall, black-bearded peasant wearing a winter cap came into the cabin, and because his face could not be seen in the dim light of the little lamp, he looked terrifying. It was Kiryak. Going up to his wife, he swung his arm and punched her in the face; stunned by the blow, she did not utter a sound, but sank down, and her nose instantly began bleeding.

"What a shame! What a shame!" muttered the old man, clambering up onto the stove. "Before guests, too! What a sin!"

The old woman sat silent, hunched, lost in thought; Fyokla rocked the cradle.

Evidently aware of inspiring terror, and pleased by it, Kiryak seized Marya by the arm, dragged her toward the door, and growled like a beast in order to seem still more terrible; but at that moment he suddenly caught sight of the guests and halted.

"Oh, they have come . . ." he said, letting go of his wife; "my own brother with his family . . ."

Staggering and opening his blood-shot, drunken eyes wide, he muttered a prayer before the icon and went on:

"My dear brother and his family, come to the parental house—from Moscow, I mean. The ancient capital city of Moscow, I mean, mother of cities— Excuse me."

He sank down on the bench near the samovar and began drinking tea, sipping it loudly from the saucer amid general silence. He drank a dozen cups, then lay down on the bench and began to snore.

They started going to bed. Nikolay, being ill, was to sleep on the stove with the old man; Sasha lay down on the floor, while Olga went into the shed with the other women.

"Now, now, dearie," she said, lying down on the hay beside Marya; "tears won't help. Bear your cross, that's all. It says in Scripture: 'Whosoever shall smite thee on thy right cheek, turn to him the other also.' . . . Now, now, dearie."

Then, speaking under her breath in a singsong, she told them about Moscow, about her life, how she had been a chambermaid in furnished rooms.

"And in Moscow the houses are big, made of stone," she said; "and there are many, many churches, forty times forty, dearie; and in the houses they're all gentry, so goodlooking and so proper!"

Marya said that not only had she never been to Moscow, but had not even been in their own district town; she could neither read nor write, and knew no prayers, not even "Our Father." Both she and Fyokla, her sister-in-law, who was sitting a little way off listening, were exceedingly backward and dull-witted. They both disliked their husbands; Marya was afraid of Kiryak, and whenever he stayed with her she shook with fear, and always got a headache from the fumes of vodka and tobacco of which he reeked. And in response to the question whether she did not miss her husband, Fyokla replied sourly:

"Deuce take him!"

They talked a while and then grew silent.

It was cool, and a cock was crowing at the top of his

voice near the shed, interfering with sleep. When the
bluish morning light was already showing through every
crack, Fyokla got up quietly and went out, and then
they heard her hurry off somewhere, her bare feet
thumping as she ran.

II

Olga went to church, and took Marya with her. As
they went down the path toward the meadow both
were cheerful. Olga liked the open country, and Marya
felt that in her sister-in-law she had found someone near
and dear to her. The sun was rising. Low over the
meadow hovered a drowsy hawk; the river looked dull;
wisps of mist were floating here and there, but on the
farther shore a streak of light already lay across the
hill; the church was shining, and in the garden attached
to the manor the rooks were cawing frantically.

"The old man ain't bad," Marya told her, "but
Granny is strict, and is free with her hand. Our own
flour lasted till Carnival, and now we buy it at the
tavern; so she's cross; she says we eat too much."

"Now, now, dearie! Bear your cross, that's all. It's
written: 'Come unto me, all ye that labor and are heavy
laden.'"

Olga spoke sedately, in a singsong, and her gait was
that of a pilgrim woman, rapid and fidgety. Every day
she read the gospel, read it aloud like a deacon; a great
deal of it she did not understand, but the sacred phrases
moved her to tears, and such words as "behold" and
"whosoever" she pronounced with a sweet faintness at
her heart. She believed in God, in the Holy Virgin, in
the saints; she believed that it was wrong to harm anyone—whether simple folk, or Germans, or gypsies, or
Jews—and that misfortune awaited even those who did
not pity animals. She believed that this was written in

the Scriptures; and so when she pronounced words from
Holy Writ, even though she did not understand them,
her face softened with emotion, grew compassionate
and radiant.

"Where do you come from?" Marya asked her.

"I am from the province of Vladimir. But I was taken
to Moscow long ago, when I was eight years old."

They reached the river. On the other side a woman
stood at the water's edge, taking off her clothes.

"That's our Fyokla," said Marya, recognizing her.
"She's been across the river to the manor yard. She's
been with the squire's men. She's a hussy and foul-
mouthed—she is that!"

Black-browed Fyokla, her hair undone, still young
and with the firm flesh of a girl, jumped off the bank
and began thrashing the water with her feet, sending
waves in all directions.

"A hussy—she is that!" repeated Marya.

The river was spanned by a rickety little bridge of
logs, and below in the clean, clear water shoals of broad-
headed chub were swimming. The dew was glistening
on the green shrubs that were mirrored in the water.
Then the air grew warmer; it was pleasant. What a
glorious morning it was! And how glorious life would
probably be in this world, were it not for want, horrible,
inescapable want, from which you cannot hide anywhere! Only to look round at the village was to remember all that had happened the day before, and the spell
of the happiness that they thought they felt around
them vanished instantly.

They went into the church. Marya stood in the entrance and did not dare to go farther. Nor did she dare
to sit down either, though they only began ringing for
Mass after eight o'clock. She remained standing the
whole time.

While the gospel was being read the crowd suddenly
parted to make way for the squire's family. Two young
ladies in white frocks and wide-brimmed hats walked
in, and with them was a chubby, rosy boy in a sailor
suit. Their appearance moved Olga; she concluded at
first glance that they were decent, elegant, cultivated
people. But Marya glared at them from under her brows,
sullenly, dejectedly, as though they were not human
beings but monsters who might crush her if she did not
move aside.

And every time the deacon intoned in his bass voice,
she imagined that she heard the cry, "Ma-arya!" and she
shuddered.

III

The arrival of the guests became known in the village, and directly after Mass a great many people assembled in the cabin. The Leonychevs and the Matveichevs and the Ilyichovs came to make inquiries about
relatives of theirs who had situations in Moscow. All the
lads of Zhukovo who could read and write were packed
off to Moscow and hired out as bellboys or waiters (just
as the lads from the village on the other side of the
river all apprenticed to bakers), and this had been the
custom from the days of serfdom, long ago, when a certain Luka Ivanych, a peasant from Zhukovo, now a
legendary figure, who had been a bartender in one of
the Moscow clubs, would take none but his fellow villagers into his service, and these in turn, as they got up
in the world, sent for their kinsfolk and found jobs for
them in taverns and restaurants; and from that time on
the village of Zhukovo was known throughout the coun-
tryside round about as Flunkeyville or Toadytown. Nikolay had been taken to Moscow when he was eleven, and

gotten a situation by Ivan Makarych, a Matveichev,
who was then an attendant at the Hermitage garden
restaurant. And now, addressing the Matveichevs, Nikolay said unctuously:

"Ivan Makarych is my benefactor, and I am bound
to pray for him day and night, because it was he who
set me on the right path."

"God bless you!" a tall old woman, the sister of Ivan
Makarych, said tearfully, "and not a word have we
heard about him, the dear man."

"Last winter he was in service at Omon's, and there
was a rumor that this season he was somewhere out of
town, in a garden restaurant. He has aged! Why, it
used to be that he would bring home as much as ten
rubles a day in the summertime, but now things are very
quiet everywhere. It's hard on the old man."

The women and the old crones looked at Nikolay's
feet, shod in felt boots, and at his pale face, and said
mournfully:

"You're no breadwinner, Nikolay Osipych; you're no
breadwinner! No, indeed!"

And they all fondled Sasha. She was going on eleven,
but she was small and very thin, and she looked no more
than seven. Among the other little girls, with their sunburnt faces and roughly cropped hair, and their long,
faded shifts, she, with her pallor, her big dark eyes and
the red ribbon in her hair, looked droll, as though she
were some little wild thing that had been caught in the
fields and brought into the cabin.

"She can read, too," said Olga, looking tenderly at
her daughter and showing her off. "Read a little, child!"
she said, taking the Gospels from the corner. "You read,
and the good Christian folk will listen."

It was an old, heavy volume in a leather binding with

dog-eared edges, and it gave off a smell as though monks had come into the house. Sasha raised her eyebrows and began in a loud singsong:

"'And when they were departed, behold, the angel of the Lord . . . appeareth to Joseph in a dream, saying, Arise, and take the young child and his mother . . .'"

"'The young child and his mother,'" Olga repeated, and flushed all over with emotion.

"'And flee into Egypt, and be thou there until I bring thee word: for Herod will seek the young child, to destroy him . . .'"

At these words Olga could not contain herself and burst into tears. Affected by her example, Marya began to whimper, and then Ivan Makarych's sister followed suit. The old man coughed and bustled about looking for a present for his granddaughter, but finding nothing, gave it up with a wave of his hand. And when the reading was over the neighbors dispersed to their homes, deeply moved and very much pleased with Olga and Sasha.

Because of the holiday, the family stayed home all day. The old woman, whom her husband, her daughters-in-law, her grandchildren, all alike called Granny, always tried to do everything herself; she lit the stove and heated the samovar with her own hands, even carried the midday meal to the men in the fields, and then complained that she was worn out with work. And all the time she fretted for fear that someone should eat a bite too much or that her husband and daughters-in-law should sit idle. Now she would hear the tavernkeeper's geese making for her kitchen garden by the back way, and she would run out of the cabin with a long stick and spend half an hour screaming beside her cabbages which were as meager and flabby as herself; again she would imagine that a crow was after her chickens and would rush at it with loud words of abuse. She was cross and full of complaints from morning till night, and often raised such a hubbub that passers-by stopped in the street.

She treated the old man roughly, calling him a lazy-bones and a plague. He was a shiftless, undependable man, and perhaps if she had not been prodding him continually he would not have worked at all, but would just have sat on the stove and talked. He told his son at great length about certain enemies of his, complained of the injuries he suffered every day at the hands of the neighbors, and it was tedious to listen to him.

"Yes," he would hold forth, with his arms akimbo, "yes— A week after the Exaltation of the Cross I sold my hay at thirty kopecks a pood, of my own free will. Yes, well and good. So you see I was taking the hay in the morning of my own free will; I wasn't doing no one no harm. In an unlucky hour I see the village headman, Antip Sedelnikov, coming out of the tavern. 'Where are you taking it, you blank blank?' says he, and fetches me a box on the ear."

Kiryak had a terrible hangover and was ashamed to face his brother.

"What vodka will do! Oh, my God!" he muttered as he shook his throbbing head. "For Christ's sake, forgive me, dear brother and sister; I'm not happy about it myself."

Because it was a holiday, they bought a herring at the tavern and made a soup of the herring head. At midday they sat down to have tea and went on drinking it until they were all perspiring; they looked actually swollen with tea; and then they attacked the soup, all helping themselves out of one pot. The herring itself Granny hid away.

In the evening a potter was firing pots on the slope.

Down below in the meadow the girls got up a round dance and sang songs. Someone played an accordion. On the other side of the river, too, one kiln was going, and the girls sang songs, and in the distance the singing sounded soft and melodious. In and about the tavern the peasants were making a racket. They sang with drunken voices, discordantly, and swore at one another so filthily that Olga could only shudder and repeat:

"Oh, holy saints!"

What amazed her was that the swearing was incessant, and that the old men who were near their end were the loudest and most persistent in using this foul language. And the girls and children listened to the swearing without turning a hair; it was evident that they had been used to it from their cradles.

It got to be past midnight, the fire in the kilns on both sides of the river died down, but in the meadow below and in the tavern the merrymaking continued. The old man and Kiryak, both drunk, walking arm in arm, their shoulders jostling, went up to the shed where Olga and Marya were lying.

"Let her be," the old man pleaded; "let her be— She's a harmless woman— It's a sin—"

"Ma-arya!" shouted Kiryak.

"Let her be— It's a sin— She's not a bad woman."

Both stood there for a minute and then went on.

"I lo-ove the flowers of the fi-ield," the old man burst forth in a high, piercing tenor. "I lo-ove to pick them in the meadows!"

Then he spat, swore filthily, and went into the cabin.

IV

Granny stationed Sasha near her kitchen garden and ordered her to see to it that the geese did not get in. It was a hot August day. The tavernkeeper's geese could get into the kitchen garden by the back way, but at the moment they were seriously engaged: they were picking up oats near the tavern, peacefully chatting together, and only the gander craned his neck as though to see if the old woman were not coming with a stick. Other geese from down below might have trespassed, but they were now feeding far away on the other side of the river, stretching across the meadow in a long white garland. Sasha stood about a while, grew bored, and, seeing that the geese were not coming, went up to the brink of the slope.

There she saw Marya's eldest daughter Motka, who was standing motionless on a huge boulder, staring at the church. Marya had been brought to bed thirteen times, but she had only six living children, all girls, not one boy, and the eldest was eight. Motka, barefoot and wearing a long shift, was standing in the full sunshine; the sun was blazing down right on her head, but she did not notice it, and seemed as though turned to stone. Sasha stood beside her and said, looking at the church:

"God lives in the church. People have lamps and candles, but God has little green and red and blue icon-lamps like weeny eyes. At night God walks about the church, and with Him the Holy Mother of God and Saint Nicholas—clump, clump, clump they go! And the watchman is scared, so scared! Now, now, dearie," she added, imitating her mother. "And when the end of the world comes, all the churches will fly up to heaven."

"With the be-elfri-ies?" Motka asked in a deep voice, drawling the syllables.

"With the belfries. And when the end of the world comes, the good people will go to Paradise, but the wicked will burn in fire eternal and unquenchable, dearie. To my mama and to Marya, too, God will say:

'You never harmed anyone, and so you go to the right, to Paradise'; but to Kiryak and Granny He will say: 'You go to the left, into the fire.' And the ones who ate forbidden food on fast days will be sent into the fire, too."

She looked up at the sky, opening her eyes wide, and said:

"Look at the sky and don't blink and you will see angels."

Motka began looking at the sky, too, and a minute passed in silence.

"Do you see them?" asked Sasha.

"I don't," said Motka in her deep voice.

"But I do. Little angels are flying about the sky and go flap, flap with their little wings like midges."

Motka thought for a while, with her eyes on the ground, and asked:

"Will Granny burn?"

"She will, dearie."

From the boulder down to the very bottom there was a smooth, gentle slope, covered with soft green grass, which one longed to touch with one's hands or to lie upon.

Sasha lay down and rolled to the bottom. Motka, with a grave, stern face, and breathing heavily, followed suit, and as she did so, her shift rolled up to her shoulders.

"What fun!" said Sasha, delighted.

They walked up to the top to roll down again, but just then they heard the familiar, shrill voice. Oh, how awful it was! Granny, toothless, bony, hunched, her short gray hair flying in the wind, was driving the geese out of the kitchen garden with a long stick, screaming.

"They have trampled all the cabbages, the cursed creatures! May you croak, you thrice accursed plagues! Why don't the devil take you!"

She saw the little girls, threw down the stick, picked

up a switch, and, seizing Sasha by the neck with her
fingers, dry and hard as spikes, began whipping her.
Sasha cried with pain and fear, while the gander, wad-
dling and craning his neck, went up to the old woman
and hissed something, and when he went back to his
flock all the geese greeted him approvingly with a "Ga-
ga-ga!" Then Granny proceeded to whip Motka, and so
Motka's shift was rolled up again. In despair and crying loudly, Sasha went to the cabin to complain. Motka
followed her; she, too, was crying, but on a deeper note,
without wiping her tears, and her face as wet as though
it had been dipped in water.

"Holy Fathers!" cried Olga, dismayed, as the two
came into the cabin. "Queen of Heaven!"

Sasha began telling her story, when Granny walked
in with shrill cries and abuse; then Fyokla got angry,
and there was a hubbub in the house.

"Never mind, never mind!" Olga, pale and distressed,
tried to comfort the children, stroking Sasha's head.
"She's your grandmother; it's a sin to be cross with her.
Never mind, child."

Nikolay, who was already worn out by the continual
clamor, the hunger, the sickening fumes, the stench,
who already hated and despised the poverty, who was
ashamed of his father and mother before his wife and
daughter, swung his legs off the stove and said to his
mother in an irritable, tearful voice:

"You shouldn't beat her! You have no right to beat
her!"

"You're ready to croak there on the stove, you loafer!"
Fyokla snapped at him spitefully. "The devil has
brought you here, you spongers!"

Sasha and Motka and all the little girls in the household huddled into a corner on top of the stove behind
Nikolay's back, and from there listened to all this in

silence and terror, and one could hear the beating of their little hearts. When there is someone in a family who has long been ill, and hopelessly ill, there come terrible moments when all those close to him timidly, secretly, at the bottom of their hearts wish for his death, and only the children fear the death of someone close to them, and always feel horrified at the thought of it. And now the little girls, with bated breath and a mournful look on their faces, stared at Nikolay and thought that he would soon die; and they wanted to cry and to say something friendly and compassionate to him.

He was pressing close to Olga, as though seeking her protection, and saying to her softly in a shaking voice:

"Olya dear, I can't bear it here any longer. I haven't the strength. For Christ's sake, for the sake of God in heaven, write to your sister, Klavdia Abramovna. Let her sell and pawn everything she has; let her send us the money, and we'll go away from here. Oh, Lord," he went on with anguish, "to have one peep at Moscow! To see mother Moscow, if only in my dreams!"

And when evening came, and it was dark in the cabin, it got so dismal that it was hard to bring out a word. Granny, cross as ever, soaked some crusts of rye bread in a cup, and was a whole hour sucking at them. Marya, having milked the cow, brought in a pail of milk and set it on a bench; then Granny poured it from the pail into jugs slowly and deliberately, evidently pleased that it was now the Fast of Assumption, so that no one would drink milk and all of it would be left untouched. And she only poured out just a little into a saucer for Fyokla's baby. When she and Marya carried the jugs down to the cellar, Motka suddenly came to life, slipped down from the stove, and going to the bench where the wooden cup full of crusts was standing, splashed some milk from the saucer into it.

Granny, coming back into the cabin, attacked her soaked crusts again, while Sasha and Motka sat on the stove, staring at her, and were glad that she had taken forbidden food and now was sure to go to hell. They were comforted and lay down to sleep, and as she dozed off, Sasha pictured the Last Judgment to herself: a fire was burning in a stove something like a potter's kiln, and the Evil One, with horns like a cow's and black all over, was driving Granny into the fire with a long stick, just as Granny herself had driven the geese.

v

On the Feast of Assumption, after ten o'clock at night, the girls and boys who were making merry down in the meadow suddenly began to scream and shout, and ran in the direction of the village; and those who were sitting on the brink of the slope at first could not make out what was the matter.

"Fire! Fire!" desperate shouts sounded from below. "The place is on fire!"

Those who were sitting above looked back and a terrible and extraordinary spectacle presented itself to them. From the thatched roof of one of the last cabins in the village rose a pillar of flame, seven feet high, which coiled and scattered sparks in all directions as though it were a fountain playing. And all at once the whole roof burst into bright flame, and the crackling of the fire was heard.

The moonlight was dimmed, and now the whole village was enveloped in a quivering red glow: black shadows moved over the ground, there was a smell of burning, and those who ran up from below were all gasping and trembling so that they could not speak; they jostled each other, fell down, and, unaccustomed to the bright light, could hardly see and did not recognize each other. It was terrifying. What was particularly frightening was that pigeons were flying in the smoke above the flames, and that in the tavern, where they did not yet know of the fire, people were still singing and playing the accordion as though nothing was wrong.

"Uncle Semyon's place is on fire," someone shouted in a loud, coarse voice.

Marya was rushing about near her cabin, weeping and wringing her hands, her teeth chattering, though the fire was a long way off, at the other end of the village. Nikolay came out in felt boots, the children ran about in their little shifts. Near the village policeman's cabin an iron sheet was struck. Boom, boom, boom! floated through the air, and this rapid, incessant sound sent a pang to the heart and turned one cold. The old women stood about, holding the icons. Sheep, calves, cows were driven out of the courtyards into the street; chests, sheepskins, tubs were carried out. A black stallion, that was kept apart from the drove of horses because he kicked and injured them, was set free and ran back and forth through the village once or twice, neighing and pawing the ground, then suddenly stopped short near a cart and started kicking it with his hind legs.

The bells in the church on the other side of the river began ringing.

Near the burning cabin it was so hot and so bright that every blade of grass on the ground was distinctly visible. On one of the chests that they had managed to carry out sat Semyon, a carrot-haired peasant with a long nose, wearing a jacket and a cap pulled down over his ears; his wife was lying face down, unconscious and moaning. A little old man of eighty with a big beard,

who looked like a gnome, a stranger to the village, but
apparently connected in some way with the fire, walked
about near it, bareheaded, with a white bundle in his
arms. The flames were reflected on his bald spot. The
village headman, Antip Sedelnikov, as swarthy and
black-haired as a gypsy, went up to the cabin with an
ax, and hacked out the windows one after another—no
one knew why—and then began chopping up the porch.

"Women, water!" he shouted. "Bring the engine!
Shake a leg!"

The peasants who had just been carousing in the
tavern were dragging up the engine. They were all
drunk; they kept stumbling and falling down, and all
had a helpless expression and tears in their eyes.

"Girls, water!" shouted the headman, who was drunk,
too. "Shake a leg, girls!"

The women and the girls ran downhill to a spring,
and hauled pails and tubs of water up the hill, and, after
pouring it into the engine, ran down again. Olga and
Marya and Sasha and Motka, too, all carried water. The
women and the boys pumped the water; the hose hissed,
and the headman, directing it now at the door, now at
the windows, held back the stream with his finger,
which made it hiss yet more sharply.

"He's a top-notcher, Antip is!" voices shouted approvingly. "Keep it up!"

Antip dove into the burning cabin and shouted from
within.

"Pump! Lend a hand, good Orthodox folk, on the
occasion of such a terrible accident!"

The peasants stood round in a crowd, doing nothing
and staring at the fire. No one knew what to do, no one
knew how to do anything, and there were stacks of
grain and hay, piles of faggots, and sheds all about.

Kiryak and old Osip, his father, both tipsy, stood there, too. And, as though to justify his inaction, old Osip said to the woman lying on the ground:

"Why carry on so, friend? The cabin's insured—why worry?"

Semyon, addressing himself now to one person, now to another, kept telling how the fire had started.

"That same old man, the one with the bundle, a house-serf of General Zhukov's— He was cook at our general's, God rest his soul! He came over this evening: 'Let me stay the night,' says he. Well, we had a glass, to be sure. The wife got busy with the samovar—we were going to give the old man some tea, and in an unlucky hour she set the samovar in the entry. And the sparks from the chimney blew straight up to the thatch; well, that's how it was. We were nearly burnt up ourselves. And the old man's cap got burnt up; it's a shame!"

And the sheet of iron was struck tirelessly, and the bells of the church on the other side of the river kept ringing. Ruddy with the glow, and breathless, Olga, looking with horror at the red sheep and at the pink pigeons flying through the smoke, kept running down the slope and up again. It seemed to her that the ringing had entered her soul like a sharp thorn, that the fire would never be over, that Sasha was lost. . . . And when the ceiling of the cabin fell in with a crash, the thought that now the whole village was sure to burn down made her faint, and she could no longer go on carrying water, but sat down on the edge of the slope, setting the buckets near her; beside her and below her, the peasant women sat wailing as though at a wake.

Then, from the village across the river, came men in two carts, bringing a fire-engine with them. A very young student, his white tunic wide open, rode up on horseback. There was the sound of axes. A ladder was placed against the burning frame of the house, and five men ran up it at once, led by the student, who was red in the face and shouted in a harsh, hoarse voice, and in the tone of one who was used to putting out fires. They pulled the house to pieces, a log at a time; they took apart the stable and the wattled fence, and removed the near-by stack of hay.

"Don't let them smash things!" cried stern voices in the crowd. "Don't let them."

Kiryak made his way to the cabin with a resolute air, as though he meant to prevent the newcomers from smashing things, but one of the workmen turned him round and hit him on the neck. There was the sound of laughter, the workman struck him again, Kiryak fell and crawled back into the crowd on all fours.

Two pretty girls in hats, probably the student's sisters, came from the other side of the river. They stood at a distance, looking at the fire. The logs that had been pulled away were no longer burning, but were smoking badly; the student, who was working the hose, turned the stream first on the logs, then on the peasants, then on the women who were hauling the water.

"Georges!" the girls called to him reproachfully and anxiously, "Georges!"

The fire was over. And only when the crowd began to disperse they noticed that day was breaking, that all were pale and rather dark in the face, as people always appear in the early morning when the last stars are fading. As they separated, the peasants laughed and cracked jokes about General Zhukov's cook and his cap which had been burnt; they already wanted to turn the fire into a jest, and even seemed sorry that it had been put out so soon.

"You were good at putting out the fire, sir!" said Olga

to the student. "You ought to come to us in Moscow; there we have a fire 'most every day."

"Why, do you come from Moscow?" asked one of the young ladies.

"Yes, miss. My husband was employed at the Slavyansky Bazar. And this is my daughter," she said, pointing to Sasha, who was chilly and huddled up to her. "She is a Moscow girl, too."

The two young ladies said something in French to the student and he gave Sasha a twenty-kopeck piece.

Old Osip noticed this, and a gleam of hope came into his face.

"We must thank God, your honor, there was no wind," he said, addressing the student, "or else we should have been all burnt out in no time. Your honor, kind gentlefolk," he added, with embarrassment in a lower tone, "the dawn's chilly . . . something to warm a man . . . half a bottle to your honor's health."

He was given nothing, and clearing his throat, he shuffled off towards home. Afterwards Olga stood on the edge of the slope and watched the two carts fording the river and the gentlefolk walking across the meadow; a carriage was waiting for them on the other side of the river. Going into the cabin, she said to her husband with enthusiasm:

"Such kind people! And so good-looking! The young ladies were like cherubs!"

"May they burst!" Fyokla, who was sleepy, said spitefully.

VI

Marya thought herself unhappy, and often said that she longed to die; Fyokla, on the contrary, found everything in this life to her taste: the poverty, the filth, the incessant cursing. She ate whatever was given her indiscriminately, slept anywhere and on whatever came to hand. She would empty the slops just at the porch, would splash them out from the doorsill, and then walk barefoot through the puddle. And from the very first day she conceived a hatred for Olga and Nikolay just because they did not like this life.

"I'll see what you'll eat here, you Moscow gentry!" she would say maliciously. "I'll see!"

One morning at the beginning of September Fyokla, vigorous, good-looking, and rosy from the cold, brought up two pails of water from down below on a yoke; Marya and Olga were just then sitting at the table, having tea.

"Enjoy your tea!" said Fyokla sarcastically. "The fine ladies!" she added, setting down the pails. "They've gotten into the habit of tea every day. You'd better look out you don't swell up with your tea-drinking," she went on, looking at Olga with hatred. "She's come by her fat mug in Moscow, the tub of lard!"

She swung the yoke and hit Olga a blow on the shoulder so that the two sisters-in-law could only strike their hands together and say:

"Oh, holy saints!"

Then Fyokla went down to the river to wash the clothes, swearing all the time so loudly that she could be heard in the house.

The day passed and then came the long autumn evening. They wound silk in the cabin; everyone did it except Fyokla; she had gone across the river. They got the silk from a factory near by, and the whole family working together earned a mere trifle, some twenty kopecks a week.

"Under the masters things were better," said the old man as he wound silk. "You worked and ate and slept, everything in its turn. At dinner you had *shchi* and *kasha,* and at supper the same again. Cucumbers and cabbage galore: you could eat to your heart's content, as much as you liked. And there was more strictness. Everyone knew his place."

The cabin was lighted by a single little lamp, which burned dimly and smoked. When someone stood in front of the lamp and a large shadow fell across the window, one noticed the bright moonlight. Speaking unhurriedly, old Osip related how people used to live before the Emancipation; how in these very parts, where life was now so poverty-stricken and dreary, they used to hunt with harriers, greyhounds, and specially trained stalkers, and the peasants who were employed as beaters got vodka; how caravans loaded with slaughtered fowls were sent to Moscow for the young masters; how the serfs that were bad were beaten with rods or sent off to the Tver estate, while those who were good were rewarded. And Granny, too, had something to tell. She remembered everything, absolutely everything. She told about her mistress, a kind, God-fearing woman, whose husband was a boozer and a rake, and all of whose daughters made wretched marriages: one married a drunkard, another a commoner, a third eloped (Granny herself, a young girl at the time, had helped with the elopement), and they had all three soon died of grief, as did their mother. And remembering all this, Granny actually shed a tear.

Suddenly someone knocked at the door, and they all started.

"Uncle Osip, put me up for the night."

The little bald old man, General Zhukov's cook, the very one whose cap had been burnt, walked in. He sat down and listened. Then he, too, began to reminisce and tell stories. Nikolay, sitting on the stove with his legs hanging down, listened and asked questions about the dishes that were prepared for the gentry in the old days. They talked about chops, cutlets, various soups and sauces, and the cook, who remembered everything very well, mentioned dishes that are no longer prepared; there was one, for instance—a dish made of bulls' eyes, that was called "Waking up in the morning."

"And did you have cutlets *maréchal* then?" asked Nikolay.

"No."

Nikolay shook his head scornfully and said:

"Ah-h! Fine cooks you were!"

The little girls, who were sitting or lying on the stove, stared down without blinking; there seemed to be a lot of them, like cherubs in the clouds. They liked the stories; they sighed and shuddered and turned pale with rapture or terror, and to Granny, whose stories were the most interesting of all, they listened breathlessly, afraid to stir.

They lay down to sleep in silence; and the old people, stirred up and troubled by their reminiscences, thought what a fine thing it was to be young: youth, whatever it may have been like, left nothing in the memory but what was buoyant, joyful, touching; and death, they thought, how terribly cold was death, which was not far off—better not think of it! The little lamp went out. The darkness, and the two little windows brightly lit by the moon, and the stillness and the creak of the cradle, for some reason made them think of nothing but that life was over and that there was no way of bringing it back. You doze off, you sink into obliviousness, and suddenly someone touches your shoulder or breathes on your cheek—and sleep is gone; your body feels numb, as though circulation had stopped, and thoughts of death keep coming into your head. You turn on the other side: you forget about death, but old, dull, dismal thoughts of want, of fodder, of how dear flour is getting, stray through the mind, and a little later you remember again that life is over and there is no way of bringing it back. . . .

"Oh, Lord!" sighed the cook.

Someone rapped gently, ever so gently, at the window. It must have been Fyokla, come back. Olga got up, and yawning and whispering a prayer, unlocked the door, then pulled the bolt of the outer door. But no one came in; only there was a cold draft of air from the street and the entry suddenly grew bright with moonlight. Through the open door could be seen the silent, deserted street, and the moon itself floating across the sky.

"Who's there?" called Olga.

"Me," came the answer, "it's me."

Near the door, hugging the wall, stood Fyokla, stark naked. She was shivering with cold, her teeth were chattering, and in the bright moonlight she looked very pale, strange, and beautiful. The shadows and the bright spots of moonlight on her skin stood out sharply, and her dark eyebrows and firm, young breasts were defined with peculiar distinctness.

"The ruffians over there stripped me and turned me out like this," she muttered. "I had to go home without my clothes—mother-naked. Bring me something to put on."

"But come inside," Olga said softly, beginning to shiver, too.

"I don't want the old folks to see." Granny was, in fact, already stirring and grumbling, and the old man asked: "Who's there?" Olga brought out her own shift and skirt, dressed Fyokla, and then both went softly into the house, trying to close the door noiselessly.

"Is that you, you slick one?" Granny grumbled angrily, guessing who it was. "Curse you, you nightwalker! Why don't the devil take you!"

"It's all right, it's all right," whispered Olga, wrapping Fyokla up; "it's all right, dearie."

All was quiet again. They always slept badly; each one was kept awake by something nagging and persistent: the old man by the pain in his back, Granny by anxiety and malice, Marya by fear, the children by itch and hunger. Now, too, their sleep was restless; they kept turning from one side to the other, they talked in their sleep, they got up for a drink.

Fyokla suddenly burst out into a loud, coarse howl, but checked herself at once, and only sobbed from time to time, her sobs growing softer and more muffled until she was still. Occasionally from the other side of the river came the sound of the striking of the hours; but the clock struck oddly—first five and then three.

"Oh, Lord!" sighed the cook.

Looking at the windows, it was hard to tell whether the moon was still shining or whether it was already dawn. Marya got up and went out, and could be heard milking the cows and saying, "Stea-dy!" Granny went out, too. It was still dark in the cabin, but already one could distinguish all the objects in it.

Nikolay, who had not slept all night, got down from the stove. He took his dress-coat out of a green chest, put it on, and going to the window, stroked the sleeves, fingered the coat-tails—and smiled. Then he carefully removed the coat, put it away in the chest, and lay down again.

Marya came in again and started to light the stove. She was evidently half asleep and was waking up on her feet. She must have had some dream, or perhaps the stories of the previous night came into her mind, for she stretched luxuriously before the stove and said:

"No, freedom is better!"

"The master" arrived—that was what they called the district police inspector. When he would come and what he was coming for had been known for a week. There were only forty households in Zhukovo, but they had accumulated more than two thousand rubles of arrears in Zemstvo and other taxes.

The police inspector stopped at the tavern. There he drank two glasses of tea, and then went on foot to the headman's house, near which a crowd of tax defaulters stood waiting. The headman, Antip Sedelnikov, in spite of his youth—he was only a little over thirty—was strict and always sided with the authorities, though he himself was poor and remiss in paying his taxes. Apparently he enjoyed being headman, and liked the sense of power, which he could only display by harshness. At the village meetings he was feared and obeyed. Occasionally he would pounce on a drunken man in the street or near the tavern, tie his hands behind him, and put him in jail. Once he even put Granny under arrest and kept her in the lock-up for a whole day and a night because, coming to the village meeting instead of Osip, she started to curse. He had never lived in a city or read a book, but somewhere or other he had picked up various bookish expressions, and loved to employ them in conversation, and people respected him for this although they did not always understand him.

When Osip came into the headman's cabin with his tax book, the inspector, a lean old man with long gray side-whiskers, who wore a gray tunic, was sitting at a table in a corner writing something down. The cabin was clean; all the walls were bright with pictures clipped from magazines, and in the most conspicuous place near the icons there was a portrait of Prince Battenberg of Bulgaria. Beside the table stood Antip Sedelnikov with his arms folded.

"He owes one hundred and nineteen rubles, Your Honor," he said, when Osip's turn came. "Before Easter he paid a ruble, and he's not paid a kopeck since."

The inspector looked up at Osip and asked:

"Why is this, brother?"

"Show heavenly mercy, Your Honor," began Osip, growing agitated. "Allow me to say, last year the master from Lutoretzk said to me, 'Osip,' says he, 'sell me your hay . . . you sell it,' says he. Well, why not? I had a hundred *poods*[1] for sale; the women mowed it on the water-meadow. Well, we struck a bargain. It was all right and proper."

He complained of the headman, and kept turning round to the peasants as though inviting them to bear witness; his face got red and sweaty and his eyes grew sharp and angry.

"I don't know why you're saying all this," said the inspector. "I am asking you—I am asking you why you don't pay your arrears. You don't pay, any of you, and am I to answer for you?"

"I just can't."

"These words are of no consequence, Your Honor," said the headman. "The Chikildeyevs certainly are of the needy class, but please just inquire of the others, the root of it all is vodka, and they are a disorderly lot. With no understanding at all."

---

[1] *Pood* is a unit of weight, a little over 36 pounds.

The inspector wrote something down, and then said to Osip quietly, in an even tone, as though he were asking him for a drink of water:

"Get out."

Soon he drove off; and as he was climbing into his cheap buggy, coughing as he did so, it could be seen from the very look of his long lean back that he no longer remembered Osip or the village headman or the Zhukovo arrears, but was thinking of his own affairs. Before he had gone two thirds of a mile Antip was already carrying off the samovar from the Chikildeyevs' cabin, while Granny followed him, screaming shrilly, straining her lungs:

"I won't let you have it! I won't let you have it, goddamn you!"

He walked rapidly with long strides, and she ran after him, panting, almost falling down, a hunched infuriated creature; her kerchief slipped onto her shoulders, her gray hair with a greenish tint to it blew in the wind. She suddenly stood still, and like a real insurgent, fell to thumping her breast with her fists and shouting louder than ever in a singsong voice, seeming to sob:

"Christians, all you who believe in God! Dear friends, they have wronged me! Darlings, they're trampling on me! Oh, oh, darlings, come and help me!"

"Granny, Granny!" said the village headman sternly, "get some sense into your head!"

With no samovar it was hopelessly dismal in the Chikildeyevs' cabin. There was something humiliating in this deprivation, something insulting, as though the honor of the house were lost. It would have been better, had the headman carried off the table, all the benches, all the pots—the place would not have seemed so bare. Granny screamed, Marya cried, and the little girls, seeing her tears, cried too. The old man, feeling guilty, sat

in the corner, silent, with hanging head. Nikolay too was
silent. Granny loved him and was sorry for him, but
now, forgetting her pity, she fell upon him with abuse,
with reproaches, shaking her fist right in his face. She
screamed that it was all his fault; indeed, why had he
sent them so little when he bragged in his letters that
he was earning fifty rubles a month at the Slavyansky
Bazar? Why had he come, and with his family, too? If
he died, where would the money come from for his
funeral? And it was pitiful to look at Nikolay, Olga, and
Sasha.

The old man sighed hoarsely, took his cap, and went
off to the headman. It was getting dark. Antip was sol-
dering something by the stove, puffing out his cheeks;
the air was full of fumes. His children, thin and unwashed, no better than the Chikildeyev brood, were
scrambling about on the floor; his wife, an ugly, freckled,
big-bellied woman, was winding silk. They were a
wretched, unlucky family, and Antip was the only one
who looked sturdy and handsome. On a bench stood five
samovars in a row. The old man muttered a prayer to
Battenberg and then said:

"Antip, show heavenly mercy, give me back the samovar! For Christ's sake!"

"Bring three rubles, then you can have it."

"I just can't."

Antip puffed out his cheeks, the fire hummed and
hissed, and was reflected in the samovars. The old man
kneaded his cap and said after a moment's thought:

"You give it back to me."

The dark-skinned headman looked quite black and
resembled a magician; he turned round to Osip and
said sternly, speaking rapidly:

"It all depends on the district magistrate. On the
twenty-sixth instant you can state the grounds of your

dissatisfaction before the administrative session, verbally or in writing."

Osip did not understand a word, but he was satisfied with that and went home.

Some ten days later the police inspector came again, stayed for an hour and drove away. During those days it had been cold and windy; the river had been frozen for a long time, but still there was no snow, and people were worn to a frazzle because the roads were impassable. On the eve of a holiday some of the neighbors came in to Osip's to sit and have a chat. They talked in the dark, because it was a sin to work and so they did not light the lamp. There were some scraps of news, all rather unpleasant. In two or three households hens had been taken for the arrears and had been sent to the district office, and there they had died because no one had fed them; sheep had been taken, and while they were being carted away tied to one another, and shifted into another cart at each village, one of them had died. And now the question was being discussed: who was to blame?

"The Zemstvo," said Osip. "Who else?"

"Of course, the Zemstvo."

The Zemstvo was blamed for everything—for the arrears, the unjust exactions, the failure of the crops, though no one of them knew what was meant by the Zemstvo. And this dated from the time when well-to-do peasants who had factories, shops, and inns of their own served as members of the Zemstvo boards, were dissatisfied with them, and took to berating the Zemstvos in their factories and taverns.

They talked about how God was not sending the snow; wood had to be hauled for fuel, yet there was no driving or walking over the frozen ruts. In former days, fifteen to twenty years ago, talk had been much more interesting in Zhukovo. In those days every old man looked as though he were guarding some secret; as though he knew something and were waiting for something. They used to talk about a charter with a golden seal, about the division of acreage, about new lands, about treasure troves; they hinted at something. Now the folk of Zhukovo had no secrets at all; their whole life lay bare and clear to all, as though on the palm of your hand, and they could talk of nothing but want, food and fodder, the absence of snow.

There was a lull. Then they recalled the hens again, and the sheep, and began arguing once more as to who was at fault.

"The Zemstvo," said Osip dejectedly. "Who else?"

VIII

The parish church was nearly four miles away at Kosogorovo, and the peasants only attended it when they had to do so, for christenings, weddings, or funerals; for regular services they went to the church across the river. On holidays in fine weather the girls dressed up in their best and went to Mass in a crowd, and it was a cheering sight to see them walk across the meadow in their red, yellow, and green frocks; when the weather was bad they all stayed home. To confess and to take the communion, they went to the parish church. The priest, making the round of the cabins with the cross at Easter, took fifteen kopecks from each of those who had not managed to take the sacrament during Lent.

The old man did not believe in God, for he had hardly ever given Him a thought; he acknowledged the supernatural, but felt that it could be of concern to

women only, and when religion or miracles were discussed in his presence, and a question about these matters
was put to him, he would say reluctantly, scratching
himself:

"Who can tell!"

Granny did believe, but somehow her faith was hazy;
everything was mixed up in her memory, and no sooner
did she begin to think of sins, of death, of the salvation
of the soul, than want and cares took possession of her
mind, and she instantly forgot what she had started to
think about. She remembered no prayers at all, and
usually in the evenings, before lying down to sleep, she
would stand before the icons and whisper:

"Virgin Mother of Kazan, Virgin Mother of Smolensk,
Virgin Mother of the Three Arms. . . ."

Marya and Fyokla crossed themselves regularly,
fasted, and took communion every year, but quite igno-
rantly. The children were not taught any prayers, nothing was told them about God, and no moral precepts
were given them; they were merely forbidden to take
certain foods on fast days. In other families it was much
the same: there were few who believed, few who had
any understanding. At the same time all loved the Holy
Scripture, loved it tenderly, reverently; but they had no
books, there was no one to read the Bible and explain it,
and because Olga sometimes read them the Gospels,
they respected her, and they all addressed her and Sasha
in the deferential second-person plural.

For local holidays and special services Olga often
went to neighboring villages and to the county seat, in
which there were two monasteries and twenty-seven
churches. She was abstracted, and when she went on
these pilgrimages she quite forgot her family, and
only when she was on her way home would suddenly
make the joyful discovery that she had a husband and

daughter, and then she would say, smiling and radiant:
"God has blessed me!"

What went on in the village seemed to her revolting
and was a source of torment to her. On St. Elijah's Day
they drank, at the Assumption they drank, at the Exaltation of the Cross they drank. The Feast of the Intercession was the parish holiday for Zhukovo, and on that
occasion the peasants drank for three days on end; they
drank up fifty rubles belonging to the communal fund,
and on top of that collected money for vodka from each
household. On the first day the Chikildeyevs slaughtered
a sheep and ate mutton in the morning, at noon, and in
the evening; they ate large amounts of it, and the children got up at night to eat some more. Those three days
Kiryak was fearfully drunk; he drank up all his belongings, even his cap and boots, and beat Marya so terribly
that they had to pour water over her to revive her. Afterwards they were all ashamed and felt sick.

However, even in Zhukovo, in this "Flunkeyville,"
once a year there was a genuine religious event. It was
in August, when they carried the icon of the Life-Bear-
ing Mother of God from village to village throughout
the district. The day on which it was expected at Zhukovo was windless and the sky was overcast. The girls,
in their bright holiday frocks, set off in the morning to
meet the icon, and they brought it to the village towards
evening, in solemn procession, singing, while the bells
pealed in the church across the river. A huge crowd of
villagers and strangers blocked the street; there was
noise, dust, a crush of people. . . . The old man and
Granny and Kiryak all stretched out their hands to the
icon, gazed at it greedily and cried, weeping:

"Intercede for us! Mother! Intercede!"

All seemed suddenly to grasp that there was no void
between earth and heaven, that the rich and powerful

had not seized everything, that there was still protection from abuse, from bondage, from crushing, unbearable want, from the terrible vodka.

"Intercede for us! Mother!" sobbed Marya. "Mother!"

But the service ended, the icon was carried away, and
everything went on as before; and again the sound of
coarse, drunken voices came from the tavern.

Only the well-to-do peasants were afraid of death:
the richer they grew the less they believed in God and
in the salvation of the soul, and only through fear of
their earthly end did they light candles and have Masses
said, in order to be on the safe side. The poorer peasants
did not fear death. The old man and Granny were told
to their faces that they had lived too long, that it was
time they were dead, and they did not mind. They did
not scruple to tell Fyokla in Nikolay's presence that
when Nikolay died her husband Denis would be discharged from the army and return home. And Marya,
far from dreading death, regretted that it was so long in
coming, and was glad when her children died.

Death they did not fear, but they had an exaggerated
terror of every disease. The merest trifle—an upset
stomach, a slight chill, and Granny would lie down on
the stove, wrap herself up, and start moaning loudly
and incessantly: "I am dy-ing!" The old man would
hurry off for the priest, and Granny would receive the
sacrament and extreme unction. They often talked of
colds, of worms, of tumors that shifted about in the
stomach and moved up close to the heart. Most of all
they feared catching cold, and so dressed in heavy
clothes even in summer and warmed themselves on the
stove. Granny was fond of doctoring herself and often
drove to the dispensary, where she always said she was
fifty-eight instead of seventy; she supposed that if the
doctor knew her real age he would not treat her, but

would say it was time she died instead of doctoring herself. She usually went to the dispensary early in the morning, taking with her two or three of the little girls, and came back in the evening, hungry and cross, with drops for herself and salves for the little girls. Once she had Nikolay go along with her, too, and for a fortnight afterwards he took drops, and said he felt better.

Granny knew all the doctors, medical assistants, and quacks for twenty miles round, and not one of them she liked. At the Feast of the Intercession, when the priest made the round of the cabins with the cross, the deacon told her that in the town near the prison lived an old man who had been an army surgeon's assistant and who worked many cures, and advised her to turn to him. Granny took his advice. After the first snowfall she drove to the town and fetched a little bearded old man, in a long coat, a converted Jew, whose face was covered with a network of tiny blue veins. Just then there were people working in the house: an old tailor, in terrifying spectacles, was cutting a waistcoat out of some rags, and two young men were making felt boots out of wool; Kiryak, who had been sacked for drunkenness and now lived at home, was sitting beside the tailor mending a horse-collar. And the place was crowded, stuffy, and evil-smelling. The converted Jew examined Nikolay and said that it was necessary to cup the patient.

He put on the cups, and the old tailor, Kiryak, and the little girls stood round and looked on, and it seemed to them that they saw the disease coming out of Nikolay; and Nikolay, too, watched how the cups sucking at his breast gradually filled with dark blood, and felt as though there really were something coming out of him, and smiled with pleasure.

"That's fine," said the tailor. "Please God, it will do you good."

The convert put on twelve cups and then another twelve, had tea, and drove away. Nikolay began shivering; his face took on a drawn look, and, as the women put it, shrank up into a little fist; his fingers turned blue. He wrapped himself up in a quilt and a sheepskin coat, but felt colder and colder. Towards evening he began to feel very ill, asked to be laid on the floor, begged the tailor not to smoke; then he grew quiet under the coat, and towards morning he died.

IX

Oh, what a hard, what a long, winter it was!

Already by Christmas their own flour had given out and they started buying flour. Kiryak, who lived at home now, was disorderly in the evenings, terrifying everyone, and in the mornings he was tormented by headache and shame, and it was pitiful to look at him. Day and night the bellowing of the starved cow came from the barn—breaking the hearts of Granny and Marya. And as though out of spite, the frosts were bitter the whole time and the snowdrifts high; and the winter dragged on. At Annunciation there was a regular blizzard, and snow fell at Easter.

But after all, the winter did end. At the beginning of April there were warm days and frosty nights; winter would not yield, but one warm day overpowered it at last, and the streams began to flow and the birds to sing. The whole meadow and the shrubs that fringed the river were submerged by the spring floods, and the area between Zhukovo and the farther bank was one vast sheet of water, from which wild ducks rose up in flocks here and there. Every evening a fiery spring sunset, with superb clouds, offered new, extraordinary, incredible sights, just the sort of thing that one does not credit afterwards, when one sees those very colors and those very clouds in a painting.

The cranes flew swiftly, swiftly, uttering mournful sounds, and there seemed to be a summoning note in their cries. Standing on the edge of the slope, Olga stared for a long time at the flooded meadow, at the sunshine, at the church, which looked bright and rejuvenated, as it were; and her tears flowed and she gasped for breath: so passionate was her longing to go away, anywhere, to the end of the world. It was already decided that she should return to Moscow to go into service as a chambermaid, and that Kiryak should set off with her to get a job as a gatekeeper or something of the sort. Oh, to get away quickly!

As soon as the ground was dry and it was warm, they made ready to leave. Olga and Sasha, with bundles on their backs and sandals of plaited bast on their feet, left at daybreak: Marya came out, too, to see them off. Kiryak was not well and remained at home for another week. For the last time Olga, looking at the church, crossed herself and murmured a prayer; thought of her husband, and though she did not cry, her face puckered up and turned ugly, like an old woman's. During the winter she had grown thinner and plainer, her hair had gone a little gray, and instead of her former attractive appearance and pleasant smile, her face now had the sad, resigned expression left by the sorrows she had experienced, and there was something obtuse and wooden about her gaze, as though she were deaf.

She was sorry to leave the village and the peasants. She kept remembering how they had carried Nikolay down the street, and how a Mass for the repose of his soul had been said at every cabin, and how all had wept in sympathy with her grief. During the summer and the winter there had been hours and days when it seemed as though these people lived worse than cattle, and it was terrible to be with them; they were coarse, dishonest, dirty, and drunken; they did not live at peace with one another but quarreled continually, because they feared, suspected, and despised each other. Who keeps the tavern and encourages drunkenness? The peasant. Who embezzles and drinks up the funds that belong to the community, the schools, the church? The peasant. Who steals from his neighbors, sets fire to their property, bears false witness at court for a bottle of vodka? At meetings of the Zemstvo and other local bodies, who is the first to raise his voice against the peasants? The peasant. Yes, to live with them was terrible; but yet, they were human beings, they suffered and wept like human beings, and there was nothing in their lives for which one could not find justification. Crushing labor that made the whole body ache at night, cruel winters, scanty crops, overcrowding; and no help, and nowhere to look for help. Those who were stronger and better-off could give no assistance, as they were themselves coarse, dishonest, drunken, and swore just as foully. The most insignificant little clerk or official treated the peasants as though they were tramps, and addressed even the village elders and church wardens as inferiors, and as though they had a right to do so. And indeed, can any sort of help or good example be given by lazy, grasping, greedy, dissolute men who only visit the village in order to outrage, to despoil, to terrorize? Olga recalled the wretched, humiliated look of the old folks when in the winter Kiryak had been led off to be flogged. . . . And now she felt sorry for all these people, it hurt her, and as she walked on she kept looking back at the cabins.

After walking two miles with them Marya said

good-by, then she knelt, and pressing her face against the earth, began wailing:

"Again I am left alone. Poor me! poor unhappy soul that I am!"

And for a long time she went on wailing like this, and for a long time Olga and Sasha could see her still on her knees, as she kept bowing sideways, clutching her head in her hands, while the rooks flew over her.

The sun rose high; it turned hot. Zhukovo was left far behind. Walking was pleasant; Olga and Sasha soon forgot both the village and Marya; they were cheerful and everything entertained them: an ancient burial-mound; a row of telegraph posts marching one after another into the distance and disappearing on the horizon, the wires humming mysteriously; a farmhouse, half hidden by green foliage, and with a scent of dampness and hemp coming from it, a place that for some reason seemed inhabited by happy people; a horse's skeleton making a lonely white spot in the open fields. And the larks trilled tirelessly, quails called to one another, and the corncrake cawed as though someone were jerking an old cramp-iron.

At noon Olga and Sasha came to a large village. There on the broad street they encountered the little old man who had been General Zhukov's cook. He was hot, and his red, perspiring bald spot shone in the sun. At first he and Olga failed to recognize each other, then they looked round at the same moment, did recognize each other, and went their separate ways without saying a word. Stopping before the open windows of a cottage which looked newer and more prosperous than the rest, Olga bowed down and said in a loud, thin, singsong voice:

"Orthodox Christians, give alms, for Christ's sake, as

much as you can, and in the Kingdom of Heaven may your parents know peace eternal."

"Orthodox Christians," Sasha echoed her chant, "give alms, for Christ's sake, as much as you can, and in the Kingdom of Heaven. . . ."

1897

The Man in a Shell

ON THE outskirts of the village of Mironositzkoe two belated huntsmen had settled for the night in the barn belonging to the Elder, Prokofy. They were the veterinary, Ivan Ivanych, and the high school teacher, Burkin. Ivan Ivanych had a rather queer double surname—Chimsha-Himalaisky—which did not suit him at all, and he was known as Ivan Ivanych all over the province. He lived on a stud-farm near the town, and had gone out shooting to breathe some fresh air. As for Burkin, the high school teacher, he spent every summer at Count P——'s, and had long been thoroughly at home in the district.

They did not sleep. Ivan Ivanych, a tall, spare old man with long mustaches, was sitting outside the door, smoking a pipe in the moonlight. Burkin was lying inside on the hay, and could not be seen for the darkness.

They were telling each other stories. Among other things, they spoke of the Elder's wife, Mavra, a healthy and by no means stupid woman, observing that she had never been beyond her native village, had never seen a city or a railway in her life, and had spent the last

ten years hugging the stove and only going out into the
street at night.

"There's nothing remarkable about that!" said Burkin.
"There are not a few people in the world, temperamentally unsociable, who try to withdraw into a shell like
a hermit crab or a snail. Perhaps it is a manifestation of
atavism, a return to the time when man's ancestor was
not yet a gregarious animal and lived alone in his lair,
or perhaps it is only one of the varieties of human character—who knows? I am no naturalist, and it is not my
business to settle such questions; I only mean to say
that people like Mavra are by no means rare. Why, not
to go far afield, there was Belikov, a colleague of mine,
a teacher of Greek, who died in our town two months
ago. You have heard of him, no doubt. The curious
thing about him was that he wore rubbers, and a warm
coat with an interlining, and carried an umbrella even
in the finest weather. And he kept his umbrella in its
cover and his watch in a gray chamois case, and when
he took out his penknife to sharpen his pencil, his penknife, too, was in a little case; and his face seemed to be
in a case too, because it was always hidden in his
turned-up collar. He wore dark spectacles and a sweater,
stuffed his ears with cotton-wool, and when he got into
a cab always told the driver to put up the hood. In
short, the man showed a constant and irrepressible inclination to keep a covering about himself, to create for
himself a membrane, as it were, which would isolate
him and protect him from outside influences. Actuality
irritated him, frightened him, kept him in a state of
continual agitation, and, perhaps to justify his timidity,
his aversion for the present, he would always laud the
past and things that had never existed, and the dead
languages that he taught were in effect for him the

same rubbers and umbrella in which he sought conceal-
ment from real life.

" 'Oh, how sonorous, how beautiful the Greek language is!' he would say, with a saccharine expression;
and as though to prove his point, he would screw up
his eyes and, raising one finger, utter: 'Anthropos!'

"His thoughts, too, Belikov tried to tuck away in a
sheath. The only things that were clear to him were
Government regulations and newspaper notices in which
something was forbidden. When some ruling prohibited
high school students from appearing on the streets after
nine o'clock at night, or some article censured carnal
love, this he found clear and definite: it was forbidden,
and that was that. But there was always a doubtful
element for him, something vague and not fully expressed in any sanction or permission. When a dramatic
club or a reading-room or a teahouse was licensed in the
town, he would shake his head and say in a low voice:

" 'Of course, it's all very well, but you can't tell what
may come of it.'

"Any infringement of the rules, any deviation or departure from them, plunged him into gloom, though
one would have thought it was no concern of his. If
one of his colleagues was late for the thanksgiving service, or if rumors reached him of some prank of the high
school boys, or if one of the female members of the
staff had been seen late in the evening in the company
of an officer, he would become very much agitated and
keep saying that one couldn't tell what might come of
it. At faculty meetings he simply crushed us with his
cautiousness, his suspiciousness, and his typical remarks
to the effect that the young people in the girls' as well
as in the boys' high school were unruly, that there was
much noise in the classrooms, that it might reach the
ears of the authorities, that one couldn't tell what might

come of it, and that it would be a good thing if Petrov were expelled from the second form and Yegorov from the fourth. And what do you think, with his sighs, his moping, the dark spectacles on his pale little face, a little face like a polecat's, you know, he weighed us all down, and we submitted, reduced Petrov's and Yegorov's marks for conduct, detained them, and in the end expelled them both.

"He had a peculiar habit of visiting our lodgings. He would call on some teacher, would sit down, and remain silently staring, as though he were trying to detect something. He would sit like this in silence for an hour or two and then leave. This he called 'maintaining good relations with his colleagues'; and it was obvious that making these calls and sitting there like that was painful to him, and that he went to see us simply because he considered it his duty to his colleagues. We teachers were afraid of him. And even the principal was afraid of him. Would you believe it, our teachers were all thoughtful, decent people, brought up on Turgenev and Shchedrin, yet this little man, who always wore rubbers and carried an umbrella, had the whole high school under his thumb for fully fifteen years! The high school? The whole town! Our ladies did not get up private theatricals on Saturdays for fear he should find it out, and the clergy dared not eat meat in Lent or play cards in his presence. Under the influence of people like Belikov the whole town spent ten to fifteen frightened years. We were afraid to speak out loud, to write letters, to make acquaintances, to read books, to help the poor, to teach people how to read and write. . . ."

Ivan Ivanych coughed, as a preliminary to making some remark, but first lighted his pipe, gazed at the moon, and then said, between pauses:

"Yes, thoughtful, decent people, readers of Shchedrin and Turgenev, of Buckle and all the rest of them, yet they knuckled under and put up with it—that's just how it is."

"Belikov and I lived in the same house," Burkin went on, "on the same floor, his door facing mine; we often saw each other, and I was acquainted with his domestic arrangements. It was the same story: dressing-gown, nightcap, blinds, bolts, prohibitions and restrictions of all sorts, and, 'Oh, you can't tell what may come of it!' Lenten fare didn't agree with him, yet he could not eat meat, as people might say that Belikov did not keep the fasts, and he ate perch fried in butter—not a Lenten dish, yet one could not call it meat. He did not keep a female servant for fear people might think evil of him, but instead employed an old man of sixty, called Afanasy, half-witted and given to drinking, who had once been an orderly and could cook after a fashion. This Afanasy was usually standing at the door with folded arms; he would sigh deeply and always mutter the same thing:

" 'The likes of *them* is thick as hops hereabouts!'

"Belikov's bedroom was tiny and boxlike; his bed was curtained. When he went to bed he drew the bed-clothes over his head; it was hot and stuffy; the wind rattled the closed doors; a humming noise came from the stove and the sound of sighs from the kitchen, ominous sighs— And he lay under the quilt, terrified. He was afraid that something might happen, that Afanasy would murder him, that thieves would break in, and he had bad dreams all night long, and in the morning when we went to school together, he was downcast and pale, and it was plain that the place, swarming with people, towards which he was going, filled his whole being with dread and aversion, and that walking beside me

was disagreeable to a man of his unsociable tempera-
ment.

" 'How noisy the classrooms are,' he used to say, as
though trying to find an explanation for his distress.
'It's an outrage.'

"And imagine, this teacher of Greek—this man in a
shell—came near to getting married."

Ivan Ivanych glanced rapidly into the barn, and said,
"You are joking!"

"Yes, strange as it seems, he nearly got married. A
new teacher of geography and history, a certain Mihail
Savvich Kovalenko, a Ukrainian, was assigned to our
school. He did not come alone, but with his sister,
Varenka. He was a tall, dark young man with huge
hands, and one could see from his face that he spoke
in a deep voice, and, in fact, his voice seemed to come
out of a barrel: 'Boom, boom, boom!' She was not so
young, about thirty, but she too was tall, well built,
with black eyebrows and red cheeks—in a word, she
was not a girl but a peach, and so lively, so noisy; she
was always singing Little Russian songs and laughing.
At the least provocation, she would go off into ringing
laughter: 'Ha-ha-ha!' We first got well acquainted with
the Kovalenkos, I remember, at the principal's name-
day party. Among the morose, emphatically dull pedagogues who attend even a name-day party as a duty,
we suddenly saw a new Aphrodite risen from the foam;
she walked with her arms akimbo, laughed, sang,
danced. She sang with feeling 'The Winds Are Blowing' and then another Ukrainian song and another, and
she fascinated us all, all, even Belikov. He sat down
beside her and said with a saccharine smile:

" 'The Little Russian tongue reminds one of ancient
Greek in its softness and agreeable sonority.'

"That flattered her, and she began telling him with

feeling and persuasiveness that they had a farm in the Gadyach district, and that her Mummy lived there, and that they had such pears, such melons, such *kabaki!* The Little Russians call a pumpkin *kabak* [Russian for tavern], while their taverns they call *shinki,* and they make a *borshch* with tomatoes and eggplant in it, 'which is so delicious—ever so delicious!'

"We listened, and listened, and suddenly the same idea occurred to all of us:

" 'It would be a good thing to marry them off,' the principal's wife whispered to me.

"For some reason we all recalled that our friend Belikov was unmarried, and it seemed strange to us now that we had failed to notice it before, and in fact had completely lost sight of so important a detail in his life. What was his attitude towards women? How had he settled for himself this vital problem? Until then we had had no interest in the matter; perhaps we had not even admitted the idea that a man who wore rubbers in all weathers and slept behind curtains was capable of love.

" 'He is way past forty and she is thirty,' the principal's wife clarified her idea. 'I believe she would marry him.'

"What isn't done in the provinces out of boredom, how many useless and foolish things! And that is because what is necessary isn't done at all. What need was there, for instance, for us to make a match for this Belikov, whom one could not even imagine as a married man? The principal's wife, the inspector's wife, and all our high school ladies, grew livelier and even better looking, as though they had suddenly found an object in life. The principal's wife would take a box at the theater, and lo and behold! Varenka would be sitting in it, fanning herself, beaming and happy, and beside her would be Belikov, a twisted little man, looking as though he had been pulled out of his lodging by pincers. I would give an evening party and the ladies would insist on my inviting Belikov and Varenka. In short, the machine was set in motion. It turned out that Varenka was not averse to matrimony. Her life with her brother was not very cheerful: they did nothing but argue and quarrel with one another for days on end. Here is a typical scene: Kovalenko strides down the street, a tall, husky fellow, in an embroidered shirt, a lock of hair falling over his forehead from under his cap, in one hand a bundle of books, in the other a thick, knotted stick; he is followed by his sister, also carrying books.

" 'But you haven't read it, Mihailik!' she is arguing loudly. 'I tell you, I swear you haven't read it at all!'

" 'And I tell you I have read it,' bellows Kovalenko, banging his stick on the sidewalk.

" 'Oh, my goodness, Mihailik, why are you so cross? We are only discussing principles.'

" 'I tell you that I have read it!' Kovalenko shouts, more loudly than ever.

"And at home, if there was an outsider present, there was sure to be a fusillade. She must have been fed up with such a life and longed for a home of her own. Besides, there was her age; there was no time left to pick and choose; she was apt to marry anybody, even a teacher of Greek. Come to think of it, most of our young ladies don't care whom they marry so long as they do marry. Be that as it may, Varenka began to show an unmistakable inclination for Belikov.

"And Belikov? He used to call on Kovalenko just as he did on the rest of us. He would arrive, sit down, and go on sitting there in silence. He would sit quietly, and Varenka would sing to him 'The Winds Are Blowing' or would stare at him pensively with her dark eyes, or would suddenly go off into a peal of laughter—'Ha-ha-ha!'

"In amorous affairs and in marrying, suggestion plays a great part. Everybody—both his colleagues and the ladies—began assuring Belikov that he ought to get married, that there was nothing left for him in life but to get married; we all felicitated him, and with solemn faces delivered ourselves of various platitudes, such as 'Marriage is a serious step.' Besides, Varenka was good-looking and attractive; she was the daughter of a civil councilor, and she owned a farm; above all, she was the first woman who had treated him cordially and affectionately. His head was turned, and he decided that he really ought to get married."

"Well, at that point," said Ivan Ivanych, "you should have taken away his rubbers and umbrella."

"Just fancy, that proved to be impossible. He put Varenka's portrait on his table, kept calling on me and talking about Varenka, and about family life, saying that marriage was a serious step. He went frequently to the Kovalenkos, but he did not alter his habits in the least. On the contrary, his decision to get married seemed to have a deleterious effect on him. He grew thinner and paler and seemed to retreat further into his shell.

" 'I like Varvara Savvishna,' he would say to me, with a faint and crooked smile, 'and I know that everyone ought to get married, but—you know, all this has happened so suddenly— One must think it over a little.'

" 'What is there to think over?' I would say to him. 'Get married—that's all.'

" 'No; marriage is a serious step; one must first weigh the impending duties and responsibilities—so that nothing untoward may come of it. It worries me so much that I don't sleep nights. And I must confess I am afraid: she and her brother have such a peculiar way of thinking; they reason so strangely, you know, and she has a very impetuous disposition. You get married, and then, there is no telling, you may get into trouble.'

"And he did not propose; he kept putting it off, to the great vexation of the principal's wife and all our ladies; he kept weighing his future duties and responsibilities, and meanwhile he went for a walk with Varenka almost every day—possibly he thought that this was the proper thing under the circumstances—and came to see me to talk about family life. And in all probability he would have ended by proposing to her, and would have made one of those needless, stupid marriages thousands of which are made among us out of sheer boredom and idleness, if it had not been for a *kolossalischer Skandal*.

"I must tell you that Varenka's brother conceived a hatred of Belikov from the first day of their acquaintance and couldn't endure him.

" 'I don't understand,' he used to say to us, shrugging his shoulders, 'I don't understand how you can put up with that informer, that nasty mug. Ugh! how can you live here? The atmosphere you breathe is vile, stifling! Are you pedagogues, teachers? No, you are piddling functionaries; yours is not a temple of learning but a police station, and it has the same sour smell. No, brothers, I will stay with you for a while, and then I will go to my farm and catch crayfish there and teach Ukrainian brats. I will go, and you can stay here with your Judas—blast him!'

"Or he would laugh till tears came to his eyes, his laughter now deep, now shrill, and ask me, throwing up his hands, 'What does he come here for? What does he want? He sits and stares.'

"He even gave Belikov a nickname, 'The Spider.' Of course, we avoided talking to him about his sister's planning to marry 'The Spider.' And when, on one occasion, the principal's wife hinted to him what a good thing it would be if his sister settled down with such a substantial, universally respected man as Belikov, he frowned and grumbled:

" 'It's none of my business; let her marry a viper if she likes. I don't care to meddle in other people's affairs.'

"Now listen to what happened next. Some wag drew a caricature of Belikov walking along under his umbrella, wearing his rubbers, his trousers tucked up, with Varenka on his arm; below there was the legend 'Anthropos in love.' The artist got the expression admirably, you know. He must have worked more than one night, for the teachers of both the boys' and the girls' high schools, the teachers of the theological seminary, and the government officials all received copies. Belikov received one, too. The caricature made a very painful impression on him.

"We left the house together; it was the first of May, a Sunday, and all of us, the boys and the teachers, had agreed to meet at the high school and then to walk to a grove on the outskirts of the town. We set off, and he was green in the face and gloomier than a thundercloud.

" 'What wicked, malicious people there are!' he said, and his lips quivered.

"I couldn't help feeling sorry for him. We were walking along, and all of a sudden—imagine!—Kovalenko came rolling along on a bicycle, and after him, also on a bicycle, Varenka, flushed and exhausted, but gay and high-spirited.

" 'We are going on ahead,' she shouted. 'What lovely weather! Just too lovely!'

"And they both vanished. Belikov turned from green to white, and seemed petrified. He stopped short and stared at me.

" 'Good heavens, what is this?' he asked. 'Can my eyes be deceiving me? Is it proper for high school teachers and ladies to ride bicycles?'

" 'What's improper about it?' I asked. 'Let them ride and may it do them good.'

" 'But you can't mean it,' he cried, amazed at my calm. 'What are you saying?'

"And he was so shocked that he refused to go farther, and returned home.

"Next day he was continually twitching and rubbing his hands nervously, and it was obvious from the expression of his face that he was far from well. And he left before the school day was over, for the first time in his life. And he ate no dinner. Towards evening he wrapped himself up warmly, though it was practically summer weather, and made his way to the Kovalenkos'. Varenka was out; he found only her brother at home.

" 'Please sit down,' Kovalenko said coldly, frowning. He had a sleepy look; he had just taken an after-dinner nap and was in a very bad humor.

"Belikov sat in silence for about ten minutes, and then began, 'I have come to you to relieve my mind. I am very, very much troubled. Some malicious fellow has drawn a caricature of me and of another person who is close to both of us. I regard it as my duty to assure you that I had nothing to do with it. I have given no grounds for such an attack—on the contrary, I have always behaved as a respectable person would.'

"Kovalenko sat there sulking without a word. Belikov

waited a while, and then went on in a low, mournful voice; 'And I have something else to say to you. I have been in the service for years, while you have entered it only lately, and I consider it my duty as an older colleague to give you a warning. You ride a bicycle, and that pastime is utterly improper for an educator of youth.'

" 'Why so?' asked Kovalenko in his deep voice.

" 'Surely that needs no explanation, Mihail Savvich— surely it is self-evident! If the teacher rides a bicycle, what can one expect of the pupils? The only thing left them is to walk on their heads! And so long as it is not explicitly permitted, it should not be done. I was horrified yesterday! When I saw your sister, everything went black before my eyes. A lady or a young girl on a bicycle—it's terrible!'

" 'What is it you wish exactly?'

" 'All I wish to do is to warn you, Mihail Savvich. You are a young man, you have a future before you, you must be very, very careful of your behavior, and you are so neglectful, oh, so neglectful! You go about in an embroidered shirt, are constantly seen in the street carrying books, and now the bicycle, too. The principal will learn that you and your sister ride bicycles, and then it will reach the Trustee's ears. No good can come of that.'

" 'It's nobody's business if my sister and I do bicycle,' said Kovalenko, and he turned crimson. 'And whoever meddles in my private affairs can go to the devil!'

"Belikov turned pale and got up.

" 'If you speak to me in that tone, I cannot continue,' he said. 'And I beg you never to express yourself in that manner about our superiors in my presence; you should be respectful to the authorities.'

" 'Have I said anything offensive about the authorities?' asked Kovalenko, looking at him angrily. 'Please leave me in peace. I am an honorable man, and do not care to talk to gentlemen of your stripe. I hate informers!'

"Belikov fidgeted nervously and hurriedly began putting on his coat, with an expression of horror on his face. It was the first time in his life he had been spoken to so rudely.

" 'You can say what you please,' he declared, as he stepped out of the entry onto the staircase landing. 'Only I must warn you: someone may have overheard us, and lest our conversation be misinterpreted and harm come of it, I shall have to inform the principal of the contents of our conversation—in a general way. I am obliged to do so.'

" 'Inform him? Go, make your report and be damned to you!'

"Kovalenko seized him from behind by the collar and gave him a shove, and Belikov rolled noisily downstairs, rubbers and all. The staircase was high and steep, but he arrived at the bottom safely, got up, and felt his nose to see whether his spectacles were intact. But just as he was rolling down the stairs, Varenka came in, accompanied by two ladies; they stood below, staring, and this was more dreadful to Belikov than anything else. I believe he would rather have broken his neck or both legs than have been an object of ridicule. Why, now the whole town would hear of it; it would come to the principal's ears, it would reach the Trustee. Oh, there was no telling what might come of it! There would be another caricature, and it would all end in his being ordered to retire from his post.

"When he got up, Varenka recognized him and, looking at his ludicrous face, his crumpled overcoat, and his rubbers, not grasping the situation and supposing that he had fallen by accident, could not restrain herself and burst into laughter that resounded throughout the house:

" 'Ha-ha-ha!'

"And this reverberant, ringing 'Ha-ha-ha!' put an end to everything: to the expected match and to Belikov's earthly existence. He did not hear what Varenka was saying; he saw nothing. On reaching home, the first thing he did was to remove Varenka's portrait from the table; then he went to bed, and he never got up again.

"Two or three days later Afanasy came to me and asked whether the doctor should not be sent for, as there was something wrong with his master. I went in to see Belikov. He lay silent behind the curtains, covered with a quilt; when you questioned him, he answered 'yes' and 'no' and nothing more. He lay there while Afanasy, gloomy and scowling, hovered about him, sighing heavily and reeking of vodka like a tavern.

"A month later Belikov died. We all went to his funeral—that is, all connected with both high schools and with the theological seminary. Now when he was lying in his coffin his expression was mild, pleasant, even cheerful, as though he were glad that he had at last been put into a case that he would never leave again. Yes, he had attained his ideal! And as though in his honor, it was cloudy, rainy weather on the day of his funeral, and we all wore rubbers and carried umbrellas. Varenka, too, was at the funeral, and when the coffin was lowered into the grave, she dropped a tear. I have noticed that Ukrainian women always laugh or cry— there is no intermediate state for them.

"I confess, it is a great pleasure to bury people like Belikov. As we were returning from the cemetery we wore discreet Lenten faces; no one wanted to display this feeling of pleasure—a feeling like that we had experienced long, long ago as children when the grownups had gone out and we ran about the garden for an hour or two, enjoying complete freedom. Ah, freedom, freedom! A mere hint, the faintest hope of its possibility, gives wings to the soul, isn't that true?

"We returned from the cemetery in good humor. But not more than a week had passed before life dropped into its old rut, and was as gloomy, tiresome, and stupid as before, the sort of life that is not explicitly forbidden, but on the other hand is not fully permitted; things were no better. And, indeed, though we had buried Belikov, how many such men in shells were left, how many more of them there will be!"

"That's the way it is," said Ivan Ivanych, and lit his pipe.

"How many more of them there will be!" repeated Burkin.

The high school teacher came out of the barn. He was a short, stout man, completely bald, with a black beard that nearly reached his waist; two dogs came out with him.

"What a moon!" he said, looking up.

It was already midnight. On the right could be seen the whole village, a long street stretching far away for some three miles. Everything was sunk in deep, silent slumber; not a movement, not a sound; one could hardly believe that nature could be so still. When on a moonlight night you see a wide village street, with its cottages, its haystacks, and its willows that have dropped off to sleep, a feeling of serenity comes over the soul; as it rests thus, hidden from toil, care, and sorrow by the nocturnal shadows, the street is gentle, sad, beautiful, and it seems as though the stars look down upon it kindly and tenderly, and as if there were no more evil on earth, and all were well. On the left, where the village ended, the open country began; the fields could be seen stretching far away to the horizon, and there was no movement, no sound in that whole expanse drenched with moonlight.

"Yes, that's the way it is," repeated Ivan Ivanych; "and isn't our living in the airless, crowded town, our writing useless papers, our playing vint—isn't all that a sort of shell for us? And this spending our lives among pettifogging, idle men and silly, unoccupied women, our talking and our listening to all sorts of poppycock— isn't that a shell, too? If you like, I will tell you a very instructive story."

"No; it's time to turn in," said Burkin. "Tomorrow's another day."

They went into the barn and lay down on the hay. And they were both covered up and had dozed off when suddenly there was the sound of light footsteps— tap, tap. Someone was walking near the barn, walking a little and stopping, and a minute later, tap, tap again. The dogs began to growl.

"That's Mavra," said Burkin.

The footsteps died away.

"To see and hear them lie," said Ivan Ivanych, turning over on the other side, "and to be called a fool for putting up with their lies; to endure insult and humiliation, and not dare say openly that you are on the side of the honest and the free, and to lie and smile yourself, and all for the sake of a crust of bread, for the sake of a warm nook, for the sake of a mean, worthless rank in the service—no, one cannot go on living like that!"

"Come, now, that's a horse of another color, Ivan Ivanych," said the teacher. "Let's go to sleep."

And ten minutes later Burkin was asleep. But Ivan

Ivanych kept sighing and turning from one side to the other; then he got up, went outside again, and seating himself near the door, lighted his pipe.

1898

Gooseberries

THE sky had been overcast since early morning; it was a still day, not hot, but tedious, as it usually is when the weather is gray and dull, when clouds have been hanging over the fields for a long time, and you wait for the rain that does not come. Ivan Ivanych, a veterinary, and Burkin, a high school teacher, were already tired with walking, and the plain seemed endless to them. Far ahead were the scarcely visible windmills of the village of Mironositzkoe; to the right lay a range of hills that disappeared in the distance beyond the village, and both of them knew that over there were the river, and fields, green willows, homesteads, and if you stood on one of the hills, you could see from there another vast plain, telegraph poles, and a train that from afar looked like a caterpillar crawling, and in clear weather you could even see the town. Now, when it was still and when nature seemed mild and pensive, Ivan Ivanych and Burkin were filled with love for this plain, and both of them thought what a beautiful land it was.

"Last time when we were in Elder Prokofy's barn," said Burkin, "you were going to tell me a story."

"Yes; I wanted to tell you about my brother."

Ivan Ivanych heaved a slow sigh and lit his pipe before beginning his story, but just then it began to rain.

And five minutes later there was a downpour, and it was hard to tell when it would be over. The two men halted, at a loss; the dogs, already wet, stood with their tails between their legs and looked at them feelingly.

"We must find shelter somewhere," said Burkin. "Let's go to Alyohin's; it's quite near."

"Let's."

They turned aside and walked across a mown meadow, now going straight ahead, now bearing to the right, until they reached the road. Soon poplars came into view, a garden, then the red roofs of barns; the river gleamed, and the view opened on a broad expanse of water with a mill and a white bathing-cabin. That was Sofyino, Alyohin's place.

The mill was going, drowning out the sound of the rain; the dam was shaking. Wet horses stood near the carts, their heads drooping, and men were walking about, their heads covered with sacks. It was damp, muddy, dreary; and the water looked cold and unkind. Ivan Ivanych and Burkin felt cold and messy and uncomfortable through and through; their feet were heavy with mud and when, having crossed the dam, they climbed up to the barns, they were silent as though they were cross with each other.

The noise of a winnowing-machine came from one of the barns, the door was open, and clouds of dust were pouring from within. On the threshold stood Alyohin himself, a man of forty, tall and rotund, with long hair, looking more like a professor or an artist than a gentleman farmer. He was wearing a white blouse, badly in need of washing, that was belted with a rope, and drawers, and his high boots were plastered with mud and straw. His eyes and nose were black with dust. He recognized Ivan Ivanych and Burkin and was apparently very glad to see them.

"Please go up to the house, gentlemen," he said, smiling; "I'll be there directly, in a moment."

It was a large structure of two stories. Alyohin lived downstairs in what was formerly the stewards' quarters: two rooms that had arched ceilings and small windows; the furniture was plain, and the place smelled of rye bread, cheap vodka, and harness. He went into the showy rooms upstairs only rarely, when he had guests. Once in the house, the two visitors were met by a chambermaid, a young woman so beautiful that both of them stood still at the same moment and glanced at each other.

"You can't imagine how glad I am to see you, gentlemen," said Alyohin, joining them in the hall. "What a surprise! Pelageya," he said, turning to the chambermaid, "give the guests a change of clothes. And, come to think of it, I will change, too. But I must go and bathe first, I don't think I've had a wash since spring. Don't you want to go into the bathing-cabin? In the meanwhile things will be got ready here."

The beautiful Pelageya, with her soft, delicate air, brought them bath towels and soap, and Alyohin went to the bathing-cabin with his guests.

"Yes, it's a long time since I've bathed," he said, as he undressed. "I've an excellent bathing-cabin, as you see—it was put up by my father—but somehow I never find time to use it." He sat down on the steps and lathered his long hair and neck, and the water around him turned brown.

"I say—" observed Ivan Ivanych significantly, looking at his head.

"I haven't had a good wash for a long time," repeated Alyohin, embarrassed, and soaped himself once more; the water about him turned dark-blue, the color of ink.

Ivan Ivanych came out of the cabin, plunged into the

water with a splash and swam in the rain, thrusting his arms out wide; he raised waves on which white lilies swayed. He swam out to the middle of the river and dived and a minute later came up in another spot and swam on and kept diving, trying to touch bottom. "By God!" he kept repeating delightedly, "by God!" He swam to the mill, spoke to the peasants there, and turned back and in the middle of the river lay floating, exposing his face to the rain. Burkin and Alyohin were already dressed and ready to leave, but he kept on swimming and diving. "By God!" he kept exclaiming. "Lord, have mercy on me."

"You've had enough!" Burkin shouted to him.

They returned to the house. And only when the lamp was lit in the big drawing room upstairs, and the two guests, in silk dressing-gowns and warm slippers, were lounging in armchairs, and Alyohin himself, washed and combed, wearing a new jacket, was walking about the room, evidently savoring the warmth, the cleanliness, the dry clothes and light footwear, and when pretty Pelageya, stepping noiselessly across the carpet and smiling softly, brought in a tray with tea and jam, only then did Ivan Ivanych begin his story, and it was as though not only Burkin and Alyohin were listening, but also the ladies, old and young, and the military men who looked down upon them, calmly and severely, from their gold frames.

"We are two brothers," he began, "I, Ivan Ivanych, and my brother, Nikolay Ivanych, who is two years my junior. I went in for a learned profession and became a veterinary; Nikolay at nineteen began to clerk in a provincial branch of the Treasury. Our father was a *kantonist*,[1] but he rose to be an officer and so a nobleman,

---

[1] The son of a private, registered at birth in the army and trained in a military school.

a rank that he bequeathed to us together with a small estate. After his death there was a lawsuit and we lost the estate to creditors, but be that as it may, we spent our childhood in the country. Just like peasant children we passed days and nights in the fields and the woods, herded horses, stripped bast from the trees, fished, and so on. And, you know, whoever even once in his life has caught a perch or seen thrushes migrate in the autumn, when on clear, cool days they sweep in flocks over the village, will never really be a townsman and to the day of his death will have a longing for the open. My brother was unhappy in the government office. Years passed, but he went on warming the same seat, scratching away at the same papers, and thinking of one and the same thing: how to get away to the country. And little by little this vague longing turned into a definite desire, into a dream of buying a little property somewhere on the banks of a river or a lake.

"He was a kind and gentle soul and I loved him, but I never sympathized with his desire to shut himself up for the rest of his life on a little property of his own. It is a common saying that a man needs only six feet of earth. But six feet is what a corpse needs, not a man. It is also asserted that if our educated class is drawn to the land and seeks to settle on farms, that's a good thing. But these farms amount to the same six feet of earth. To retire from the city, from the struggle, from the hubbub, to go off and hide on one's own farm—that's not life, it is selfishness, sloth, it is a kind of monasticism, but monasticism without works. Man needs not six feet of earth, not a farm, but the whole globe, all of Nature, where unhindered he can display all the capacities and peculiarities of his free spirit.

"My brother Nikolay, sitting in his office, dreamed of eating his own *shchi,* which would fill the whole farmyard with a delicious aroma, of picnicking on the green grass, of sleeping in the sun, of sitting for hours on the seat by the gate gazing at field and forest. Books on agriculture and the farming items in almanacs were his joy, the delight of his soul. He liked newspapers too, but the only things he read in them were advertisements of land for sale, so many acres of tillable land and pasture, with house, garden, river, mill, and millpond. And he pictured to himself garden paths, flowers, fruit, birdhouses with starlings in them, crucians in the pond, and all that sort of thing, you know. These imaginary pictures varied with the advertisements he came upon, but somehow gooseberry bushes figured in every one of them. He could not picture to himself a single countryhouse, a single rustic nook, without gooseberries.

" 'Country life has its advantages,' he used to say. 'You sit on the veranda having tea, and your ducks swim in the pond, and everything smells delicious and—the gooseberries are ripening.'

"He would draw a plan of his estate and invariably it would contain the following features: a) the master's house; b) servants' quarters; c) kitchen-garden; d) a gooseberry patch. He lived meagerly: he deprived himself of food and drink; he dressed God knows how, like a beggar, but he kept on saving and salting money away in the bank. He was terribly stingy. It was painful for me to see it, and I used to give him small sums and send him something on holidays, but he would put that away too. Once a man is possessed by an idea, there is no doing anything with him.

"Years passed. He was transferred to another province, he was already past forty, yet he was still reading newspaper advertisements and saving up money. Then I heard that he was married. Still for the sake of buying a property with a gooseberry patch he married an elderly, homely widow, without a trace of affection for her, but simply because she had money. After marrying her, he went on living parsimoniously, keeping her half-starved, and he put her money in the bank in his own name. She had previously been the wife of a postmaster, who had got her used to pies and cordials. This second husband did not even give her enough black bread. She began to sicken, and some three years later gave up the ghost. And, of course, it never for a moment occurred to my brother that he was to blame for her death. Money, like vodka, can do queer things to a man. Once in our town a merchant lay on his deathbed; before he died, he ordered a plateful of honey and he ate up all his money and lottery tickets with the honey, so that no one should get it. One day when I was inspecting a drove of cattle at a railway station, a cattle dealer fell under a locomotive and it sliced off his leg. We carried him in to the infirmary, the blood was gushing from the wound —a terrible business, but he kept begging us to find his leg and was very anxious about it: he had twenty rubles in the boot that was on that leg, and he was afraid they would be lost."

"That's a tune from another opera," said Burkin.

Ivan Ivanych paused a moment and then continued:

"After his wife's death, my brother began to look around for a property. Of course, you may scout about for five years and in the end make a mistake, and buy something quite different from what you have been dreaming of. Through an agent my brother bought a mortgaged estate of three hundred acres with a house, servants' quarters, a park, but with no orchard, no gooseberry patch, no duck-pond. There was a stream, but the water in it was the color of coffee, for on one of its banks there was a brickyard and on the other a glue factory. But my brother was not at all disconcerted: he ordered a score of gooseberry bushes, planted them, and settled down to the life of a country gentleman.

"Last year I paid him a visit. I thought I would go and see how things were with him. In his letter to me my brother called his estate 'Chumbaroklov Waste, or Himalaiskoe' (our surname was Chimsha-Himalaisky). I reached the place in the afternoon. It was hot. Everywhere there were ditches, fences, hedges, rows of fir trees, and I was at a loss as to how to get to the yard and where to leave my horse. I made my way to the house and was met by a fat dog with reddish hair that looked like a pig. It wanted to bark, but was too lazy. The cook, a fat, barelegged woman, who also looked like a pig, came out of the kitchen and said that the master was resting after dinner. I went in to see my brother, and found him sitting up in bed, with a quilt over his knees. He had grown older, stouter, flabby; his cheeks, his nose, his lips jutted out: it looked as though he might grunt into the quilt at any moment.

"We embraced and dropped tears of joy and also of sadness at the thought that the two of us had once been young, but were now gray and nearing death. He got dressed and took me out to show me his estate.

" 'Well, how are you getting on here?' I asked.

" 'Oh, all right, thank God. I am doing very well.'

"He was no longer the poor, timid clerk he used to be but a real landowner, a gentleman. He had already grown used to his new manner of living and developed a taste for it. He ate a great deal, steamed himself in the bathhouse, was growing stout, was already having a lawsuit with the village commune and the two factories and was very much offended when the peasants failed to address him as 'Your Honor.' And he concerned himself with his soul's welfare too in a substantial, upperclass manner, and performed good deeds not simply, but pompously. And what good works! He dosed the peasants with bicarbonate and castor oil for all their ailments and on his name day he had a thanksgiving service celebrated in the center of the village, and then treated the villagers to a gallon of vodka, which he thought was the thing to do. Oh, those horrible gallons of vodka! One day a fat landowner hauls the peasants up before the rural police officer for trespassing, and the next, to mark a feast day, treats them to a gallon of vodka, and they drink and shout 'Hurrah' and when they are drunk bow down at his feet. A higher standard of living, overeating and idleness develop the most insolent self-conceit in a Russian. Nikolay Ivanych, who when he was a petty official was afraid to have opinions of his own even if he kept them to himself, now uttered nothing but incontrovertible truths and did so in the tone of a minister of state: 'Education is necessary, but the masses are not ready for it; corporal punishment is generally harmful, but in some cases it is useful and nothing else will serve.'

"'I know the common people, and I know how to deal with them,' he would say. 'They love me. I only have to raise my little finger, and they will do anything I want.'

"And all this, mark you, would be said with a smile that bespoke kindness and intelligence. Twenty times over he repeated: 'We, of the gentry,' 'I, as a member of the gentry.' Apparently he no longer remembered that our grandfather had been a peasant and our father just a private. Even our surname, 'Chimsha-Himalaisky,' which in reality is grotesque, seemed to him sonorous, distinguished, and delightful.

"But I am concerned now not with him, but with me. I want to tell you about the change that took place in me during the few hours that I spent on his estate. In the evening when we were having tea, the cook served a plateful of gooseberries. They were not bought, they were his own gooseberries, the first ones picked since the bushes were planted. My brother gave a laugh and for a minute looked at the gooseberries in silence, with tears in his eyes—he could not speak for excitement. Then he put one berry in his mouth, glanced at me with the triumph of a child who has at last been given a toy he was longing for and said: 'How tasty!' And he ate the gooseberries greedily, and kept repeating: 'Ah, how delicious! Do taste them!'

"They were hard and sour, but as Pushkin has it,

> The falsehood that exalts we cherish more
> Than meaner truths that are a thousand strong.

I saw a happy man, one whose cherished dream had so obviously come true, who had attained his goal in life, who had got what he wanted, who was satisfied with his lot and with himself. For some reason an element of sadness had always mingled with my thoughts of human happiness, and now at the sight of a happy man I was assailed by an oppressive feeling bordering on despair. It weighed on me particularly at night. A bed was made up for me in a room next to my brother's bedroom, and I could hear that he was wakeful, and that he would get up again and again, go to the plate of gooseberries and eat one after another. I said to myself: how many contented, happy people there really are! What an overwhelming force they are! Look at life: the insolence and idleness of the strong, the ignorance and brutishness of the weak, horrible poverty everywhere, overcrowding, degeneration, drunkenness, hypocrisy, lying— Yet in all the houses and on all the streets there is peace and quiet; of the fifty thousand people who live in our town there is not one who would cry out, who would vent his indignation aloud. We see the people who go to market, eat by day, sleep by night, who babble nonsense, marry, grow old, good-naturedly drag their dead to the cemetery, but we do not see or hear those who suffer, and what is terrible in life goes on somewhere behind the scenes. Everything is peaceful and quiet and only mute statistics protest: so many people gone out of their minds, so many gallons of vodka drunk, so many children dead from malnutrition— And such a state of things is evidently necessary; obviously the happy man is at ease only because the unhappy ones bear their burdens in silence, and if there were not this silence, happiness would be impossible. It is a general hypnosis. Behind the door of every contented, happy man there ought to be someone standing with a little hammer and continually reminding him with a knock that there are unhappy people, that however happy he may be, life will sooner or later show him its claws, and trouble will come to him—illness, poverty, losses, and then no one will see or hear him, just as now he neither sees nor hears others. But there is no man with a hammer. The happy man lives at his ease, faintly fluttered by small daily cares, like an aspen in the wind—and all is well."

"That night I came to understand that I too had been contented and happy," Ivan Ivanych continued, getting up. "I too over the dinner table or out hunting would hold forth on how to live, what to believe, the right way to govern the people. I too would say that learning was the enemy of darkness, that education was necessary but that for the common people the three R's were sufficient for the time being. Freedom is a boon, I used to say, it is as essential as air, but we must wait awhile. Yes, that's what I used to say, and now I ask: Why must we wait?" said Ivan Ivanych, looking wrathfully at Burkin. "Why must we wait, I ask you? For what reason?

I am told that nothing can be done all at once, that every idea is realized gradually, in its own time. But who is it that says so? Where is the proof that it is just? You cite the natural order of things, the law governing all phenomena, but is there law, is there order in the fact that I, a living, thinking man, stand beside a ditch and wait for it to close up of itself or fill up with silt, when I could jump over it or throw a bridge across it? And again, why must we wait? Wait, until we have no strength to live, and yet we have to live and are eager to live!

"I left my brother's place early in the morning, and ever since then it has become intolerable for me to stay in town. I am oppressed by the peace and the quiet, I am afraid to look at the windows, for there is nothing that pains me more than the spectacle of a happy family sitting at table having tea. I am an old man now and unfit for combat, I am not even capable of hating. I can only grieve inwardly, get irritated, worked up, and at night my head is ablaze with the rush of ideas and I cannot sleep. Oh, if I were young!"

Ivan Ivanych paced up and down the room excitedly and repeated, "If I were young!"

He suddenly walked up to Alyohin and began to press now one of his hands, now the other.

"Pavel Konstantinych," he said imploringly, "don't quiet down, don't let yourself be lulled to sleep! As long as you are young, strong, alert, do not cease to do good! There is no happiness and there should be none, and if life has a meaning and a purpose, that meaning and purpose is not our happiness but something greater and more rational. Do good!"

All this Ivan Ivanych said with a pitiful, imploring smile, as though he were asking a personal favor.

Afterwards all three of them sat in armchairs in different corners of the drawing room and were silent. Ivan Ivanych's story satisfied neither Burkin nor Alyohin. With the ladies and generals looking down from the golden frames, seeming alive in the dim light, it was tedious to listen to the story of the poor devil of a clerk who ate gooseberries. One felt like talking about elegant people, about women. And the fact that they were sitting in a drawing room where everything—the chandelier under its cover, the armchairs, the carpets underfoot—testified that the very people who were now looking down from the frames had once moved about here, sat and had tea, and the fact that lovely Pelageya was noiselessly moving about—that was better than any story.

Alyohin was very sleepy; he had gotten up early, before three o'clock in the morning, to get some work done, and now he could hardly keep his eyes open, but he was afraid his visitors might tell an interesting story in his absence, and he would not leave. He did not trouble to ask himself if what Ivan Ivanych had just said was intelligent or right. The guests were not talking about groats, or hay, or tar, but about something that had no direct bearing on his life, and he was glad of it and wanted them to go on.

"However, it's bedtime," said Burkin, rising. "Allow me to wish you good night."

Alyohin took leave of his guests and went downstairs to his own quarters, while they remained upstairs. They were installed for the night in a big room in which stood two old wooden beds decorated with carvings and in the corner was an ivory crucifix. The wide cool beds which had been made by the lovely Pelageya gave off a pleasant smell of clean linen.

Ivan Ivanych undressed silently and got into bed.

"Lord forgive us sinners!" he murmured, and drew the bedclothes over his head.

His pipe, which lay on the table, smelled strongly of burnt tobacco, and Burkin, who could not sleep for a long time, kept wondering where the unpleasant odor came from.

The rain beat against the window panes all night.

1898

About Love

FOR breakfast next day delicious little patties, cray-fish and mutton croquettes were served, and while we were eating Nikanor the cook came up to ask what the guests would like for dinner. He was a man of medium height, with a puffy face and small eyes; he was clean-shaven, and it looked as though his mustache had not been shaven off but plucked out.

According to Alyohin, the beautiful Pelageya was in love with this cook. As he drank and had a violent temper, she did not want to marry him, but was willing to live with him just so. But he was very devout, and his religious convictions did not allow him to live "just so"; he insisted that she marry him, and didn't want it otherwise, and when he was drunk he used to swear at her and even beat her. Whenever he was drunk she would hide upstairs and sob, and on such occasions Alyohin and the servants stayed in the house to defend her if necessary.

The conversation turned to love.

"How love is born," said Alyohin, "why Pelageya hasn't fallen in love with somebody more like herself both inwardly and outwardly, and why she fell in love with Nikanor, that mug—we all call him the Mug—to what extent personal happiness counts in love—all that is uncertain; and one can argue about it as one pleases. So far only one incontestable truth has been stated about love: 'This is a great mystery'; everything else that has been written or said about love is not a solution, but only a statement of questions that have remained unanswered. The explanation that would fit one case does not apply to a dozen others, and the very best thing, to my mind, would be to explain every case separately without attempting to generalize. Each case should be individualized, as the doctors say."

"Perfectly true," Burkin assented.

"We Russians who are cultivated have a weakness for these questions that remain unanswered. Love is usually poeticized, embellished with roses, nightingales; but we Russians embellish our loves with these fatal questions, and choose the least interesting of them, at that. In Moscow, when I was a student, there was a girl with whom I lived, a charming creature, and every time I held her in my arms she was thinking about what I would allow her a month for housekeeping and about the price of beef. Similarly, when we are in love, we never stop asking ourselves whether it is honorable or dishonorable, sensible or stupid, what this love will lead to, and so on. If that is a good thing or not I don't know, but that it is a hindrance and a source of dissatisfaction and irritation, of that I am certain."

It looked as though he wanted to tell a story. People who lead a lonely existence always have something on their minds that they are eager to talk about. In town bachelors visit baths and restaurants in order to have a chance to talk, and sometimes tell very interesting stories to bath attendants and waiters; in the country they usually unbosom themselves to their guests. At the moment we could see a gray sky from the windows and trees drenched with rain; in such weather we could go nowhere and there was nothing for us to do but to tell and listen to stories.

"I have been living at Sofyino and been farming for a long time," Alyohin began, "ever since I graduated from the University. My education did not fit me for rough work and temperamentally I am a bookish fellow, but when I came here the estate was heavily mortgaged, and as my father had gone into debt partly because he had spent a great deal on my education, I decided not to leave the place but to work till I had paid off the debt. I made up my mind to this and set to work, not, I must confess, without some repugnance. The land here does not yield much, and if you are not to farm at a loss you must employ serf labor or hired help, which comes to almost the same thing, or work it like a peasant—that is, you must work in the fields yourself with your family. There is no middle way. But in those days I did not go into such niceties. I did not leave an inch of earth unturned; I got together all the peasants, men and women, from the neighboring villages; the work hummed. I myself plowed and sowed and reaped, and found it awfully tedious, and frowned with disgust, like a village cat driven by hunger to eat cucumbers in the kitchen garden. My body ached, and I slept on my feet.

"At first it seemed to me that I could easily reconcile this life of toil with civilized living; to achieve that, I thought, all that was necessary was to secure a certain external order. I established myself upstairs here in the best rooms, and had them serve me coffee and liqueurs after lunch and dinner, and every night I read *The Mes-*

senger of Europe in bed. But one day our priest, Father Ivan, came and drank up all my liqueurs at one sitting, and the *The Messenger of Europe* went to the priest's daughters, because in summer, especially at haymaking time, I couldn't drag myself to bed at all, but fell asleep on a sledge in the shed or somewhere in a shack in the woods, and how could I think of reading? Little by little I moved downstairs, began to eat in the servants' kitchen, and nothing is left of my former luxury but the people who were in father's service and whom it would be painful to discharge.

"Before I had been here many years I was elected honorary justice of the peace. Now and then I had to go to town and take part in the assizes of the peace and the sessions of the circuit court, and this diverted me. When you live here for two or three months without seeing a soul, especially in winter, you begin at last to pine for a black coat. And at the circuit court there were black coats and uniforms and frock coats, too, all worn by lawyers, educated men; there were always people to talk to. After sleeping on the sledge and dining in the kitchen, to sit in an armchair wearing clean linen, in light boots, with the chain of office around one's neck—that was such luxury!

"I would be warmly received in the town. I made friends readily. And of all my friendships the most intimate and, to tell the truth, the most agreeable to me was my acquaintance with Luganovich, the assistant president of the circuit court. You both know him: an extremely charming man. This was just after the celebrated arson case; the preliminary investigation had lasted two days and we were worn out. Luganovich looked at me and said:

" 'You know what? Come and dine with me.'

"This was unexpected, as I knew Luganovich very

slightly, only officially, and I had never been to his house. I went to my hotel room for a minute to change and then went off to dinner. And here came my opportunity to meet Anna Alexeyevna, Luganovich's wife. She was then still a very young woman, not more than twenty-two, and her first baby had been born just six months before. It is all a thing of the past; and now I should find it hard to determine what was so exceptional about her, what it was about her that I liked so much; but at the time, at dinner, it was all perfectly clear to me. I saw a young woman, beautiful, kind, intelligent, fascinating, such a woman as I had never met before; and at once I sensed in her a being near to me and already familiar, as though I had seen that face, those friendly, intelligent eyes long ago, in my childhood, in the album which lay on my mother's chest of drawers.

"In the arson case the defendants were four Jews who were charged with collusion, and in my opinion they were quite innocent. At dinner I was very much agitated and out of sorts, and I don't recall what I said, but Anna Alexeyevna kept shaking her head, and saying to her husband,

" 'Dmitry, how can this be?'

"Luganovich is one of those good-natured, simple-minded people who firmly adhere to the belief that once a man is indicted in court he is guilty, and that one should not express doubt as to the correctness of a verdict except with all legal formalities on paper, but never at dinner and in private conversation.

" 'You and I didn't commit arson,' he said gently, 'and you see we are not on trial and not in prison.'

"Both husband and wife tried to make me eat and drink as much as possible. From some details, from the way they made the coffee together, for instance, and the way they understood each other without completing their phrases, I gathered that they lived in peace and harmony, and that they were glad of a guest. After dinner they played a duet on the piano; then it got dark, and I drove home.

"That was at the beginning of spring. I spent the whole summer at Sofyino without a break, and I had no time even to think of the town, but the memory of the willowy, fair-haired woman remained in my mind all those months; I did not think of her, but it was as though her shadow were lying lightly on my soul.

"In the late autumn a benefit performance was given in the town. I entered the governor's box (I had been invited there in the intermission); and there I saw Anna Alexeyevna sitting beside the governor's wife; and again there was the same irresistible, striking impression of beauty and lovely, caressing eyes, and again the same feeling of nearness. We sat side by side, then went out into the foyer.

" 'You've grown thinner,' she said; 'have you been ill?'

" 'Yes, I had rheumatism in my shoulder, and in rainy weather I sleep badly.'

" 'You look listless. In spring, when you came to dinner, you seemed younger, livelier. You were animated, and talked a great deal then; you were very interesting, and I must confess I was a little carried away. For some reason I often thought of you during the summer, and this evening when I was getting ready to go to the theater it occurred to me that I might see you.'

"And she laughed.

" 'But you look listless tonight,' she repeated; 'it makes you seem older.'

"The next day I lunched at the Luganoviches'. After lunch they drove out to their summer villa, to make arrangements to close it up for the winter, and I went along. I went back to the town with them, and at midnight we had tea together in quiet domesticity, while the fire glowed, and the young mother kept going to see if her little girl were asleep. And after that, every time I went to the town I never failed to visit the Luganoviches. They grew used to me and I grew used to them. As a rule I went in unannounced, as though I were one of the family.

" 'Who is there?' would be heard from a faraway room, in the drawling voice that seemed to me so lovely.

" 'It is Pavel Konstantinovich,' the maid or the nurse would answer.

"Anna Alexeyevna would come out to me with an anxious air and would invariably ask, 'Why haven't we seen you for so long? Is anything wrong?'

"Her gaze, the elegant, exquisite hand she gave me, her simple dress, the way she did her hair, her voice, her gait, always produced the same impression on me of something new and extraordinary, and very significant. We would talk together for hours, there would be long silences, while we were each thinking our own thoughts, or she would play to me for hours on the piano. If I found no one in, I stayed and waited, chatted with the nurse, played with the child, or lay on the couch in the study and read a newspaper; and when Anna Alexeyevna came back I met her in the hall, took all her parcels from her, and for some reason I carried those parcels every time with as much love, as much solemnity, as if I were a boy.

" 'The old woman had it easy,' the proverb runs, 'so she bought a pig.' The Luganoviches had it easy, so they made friends with me. If I was long in coming to the town, I must be ill, or something must have happened to me, and both of them would be very anxious. They were distressed that I, an educated man with a

knowledge of languages, instead of devoting myself to
scholarship or literary work, should live in the country,
rush around like a squirrel in a cage, work hard and yet
always be penniless. They imagined that I was unhappy, and that I only talked, laughed, and ate to conceal my sufferings, and even at cheerful moments when
I was quite at ease I was aware of their searching eyes
fixed upon me. They were particularly touching when
I was really in trouble, when I was being hard pressed
by some creditor and was unable to meet a payment on
time. The two of them, husband and wife, would whisper together at the window; then he would come over
to me and say with a grave face:

"'If you are in need of money at the moment, Pavel
Konstantinovich, my wife and I beg you not to stand on
ceremony, but borrow from us.'

"And in his agitation his ears would turn red. Or
again, after whispering in the same way at the window,
he would come up to me, his ears red, and say, 'My
wife and I earnestly beg you to accept this present from
us.'

"And he would hand me studs, a cigarette case, or a
lamp, and I would send them fowls, butter, and flowers
from the farm. Both of them, by the way, were very
well off. In the early days I often borrowed money, and
was not very choosy about it—borrowed wherever I
could—but nothing in the world would have induced
me to borrow from the Luganoviches. But why mention
the matter?

"I was unhappy. At home, in the fields, in the shed, I
kept thinking of her. I tried to understand the mystery
of a beautiful, intelligent young woman marrying someone so uninteresting, almost an old man (her husband
was over forty), and having children by him; I tried to
fathom the mystery of this dull, kindly, simple-hearted

man, who reasoned with such tiresome good sense, who at evening parties and balls kept near the more substantial people, looking listless and superfluous, with a submissive, apathetic expression, as though he had been brought there for sale, who yet believed in his right to be happy, to have children by her; and I kept trying to understand why she had met just him first and not me, and why such a terrible mistake need have happened in our lives.

"And every time I came to the town I saw from her eyes that she had been expecting me, and she would tell me herself that she had had a peculiar feeling all that day and had guessed that I would come. We would talk a long time, and then we would be silent, yet we did not confess our love to each other, but timidly and jealously concealed it. We were afraid of everything that would reveal our secret to ourselves. I loved her tenderly, deeply, but I reflected and kept asking myself what our love could lead to if we did not have the strength to fight against it. It seemed incredible to me that my gentle, sad love could all at once rudely break up the even course of the life of her husband, her children, and the whole household in which I was so loved and trusted. Would it be honorable? She would follow me, but where? Where could I take her? It would have been different if I had led a beautiful, interesting life—if I had been fighting for the liberation of my country, for instance, or had been a celebrated scholar, an actor, or a painter; but as things were it would mean taking her from one humdrum life to another as humdrum or perhaps more so. And how long would our happiness last? What would happen to her if I fell ill, if I died, or if we simply stopped loving each other?

"And she apparently reasoned the same way. She thought of her husband, her children, and of her mother, who loved her son-in-law like a son. If she yielded to her feeling she would have to lie, or else to tell the truth, and in her position either would have been equally inconvenient and terrible. And she was tormented by the question whether her love would bring me happiness— whether she would not complicate my life, which as it was she believed to be hard enough and full of all sorts of trouble. It seemed to her that she was not young enough for me, that she was not industrious or energetic enough to begin a new life, and she often said to her husband that I ought to marry a girl of intelligence and worth who would be a good housewife and a helpmate —and she would add at once that such a girl was not likely to be found in the whole town.

"Meanwhile the years were passing. Anna Alexeyevna already had two children. Whenever I arrived at the Luganoviches' the servants smiled cordially, the children shouted that Uncle Pavel Konstantinovich had come, and hung on my neck; everyone was happy. They did not understand what was going on within me, and thought that I too was happy. Everyone regarded me as a noble fellow. Both grown-ups and children felt that a noble fellow was walking about the room, and that gave a peculiar charm to their relations with me, as though in my presence their life, too, was purer and more beautiful. Anna Alexeyevna and I used to go to the theater together, always on foot. We used to sit side by side, our shoulders touching; I would take the opera glass from her hands without a word, and feel at that moment that she was close to me, that she was mine, that we could not live without each other. But by some strange misunderstanding, when we came out of the theater we always said good-by and parted like strangers. Goodness knows what people were saying about us in the town already, but there was not a word of truth in it all.

"Latterly Anna Alexeyevna took to going away frequently to stay with her mother or her sister; she began to be moody, she was coming to recognize that her life was without satisfaction, was ruined, and at such times she did not care to see her husband or her children. She was already being treated for nervous prostration.

"We continued to say nothing, and in the presence of strangers she displayed an odd irritation with me; no matter what I said she disagreed with me, and if I had an argument she sided with my opponent. If I dropped something, she would say coldly:

" 'I congratulate you.'

"If I forgot to take the opera glass when we were going to the theater she would say afterwards:

" 'I knew you would forget.'

"Luckily or not, there is nothing in our lives that does not come to an end sooner or later. The time came when we had to part, as Luganovich received an appointment in one of the western provinces. They had to sell their furniture, their horses, their summer villa. When we drove out to the villa and afterwards, as we were going away, looked back to see the garden and the green roof for the last time, everyone was sad, and I realized that the time had come to say good-by not only to the villa. It was arranged that at the end of August we should see Anna Alexeyevna off to the Crimea, where the doctors were sending her, and that a little later Luganovich and the children would set off for the western province.

"A great crowd had collected to see Anna Alexeyevna off. When she had said good-by to her husband and children and there was only a minute left before the third bell, I ran into her compartment to place on the rack a basket that she had almost forgotten, and then I

had to say good-by. When our eyes met right there in
the compartment our spiritual strength deserted us both,
I took her in my arms, she pressed her face to my breast,
and tears flowed from her eyes. Kissing her face, her
shoulders, her hands wet with tears—oh, how miserable
we were!—I confessed my love to her, and with a burning pain in my heart I realized how needless and petty
and deceptive was all that had hindered us from loving
each other. I realized that when you love you must
either, in your reasoning about that love, start from what
is higher, more important than happiness or unhappiness, sin or virtue in their usual meaning, or you must
not reason at all.

"I kissed her for the last time, pressed her hand, and
we parted forever. The train was already moving. I
walked into the next compartment—it was empty—and
until I reached the next station I sat there crying. Then
I walked home to Sofyino. . . ."

While Alyohin was telling his story, the rain stopped
and the sun came out. Burkin and Ivan Ivanych went
out on the balcony, from which there was a fine view
of the garden and the river, which was shining now in
the sunshine like a mirror. They admired it, and at the
same time they were sorry that this man with the kind,
intelligent eyes who had told them his story with such
candor should be rushing round and round on this huge
estate like a squirrel in a cage instead of devoting himself to some scholarly pursuit or something else which
would have made his life pleasanter; and they thought
what a sorrowful face Anna Alexeyevna must have had
when he said good-by to her in the compartment and
kissed her face and shoulders. Both of them had come
across her in the town, and Burkin was acquainted with
her and thought she was beautiful.

1898

The Darling

OLENKA PLEMYANNIKOVA, the daughter of a retired collegiate assessor, was sitting on her porch, which gave on the courtyard, deep in thought. It was hot, the flies were persistent and annoying, and it was pleasant to think that it would soon be evening. Dark rainclouds were gathering in the east and there was a breath of moisture in the wind that occasionally blew from that direction.

Kukin, a theater manager who ran a summer garden known as The Tivoli and lodged in the wing of the house, was standing in the middle of the courtyard, staring at the sky.

"Again!" he was saying in despair. "It's going to rain again! Rain every day, every day, as if to spite me! It will be the death of me! It's ruin! Such a frightful loss every day!"

He struck his hands together and continued, turning to Olenka:

"There, Olga Semyonovna, that's our life. It's enough to make you weep! You work, you try your utmost, you wear yourself out, you lie awake nights, you rack your brains trying to make a better thing of it, and what's the upshot? In the first place, the public is ignorant, barbarous. I give them the very best operetta, an elaborate spectacle, first-rate vaudeville artists. But do you think they want that? It's all above their heads. All they want is slapstick! Give them trash! And then look at the weather! Rain almost every evening. It started raining on the tenth of May, and it has kept it up all May and June. It's simply terrible! The public doesn't come, but don't I have to pay the rent? Don't I have to pay the artists?"

The next day toward evening the sky would again be overcast and Kukin would say, laughing hysterically:

"Well, go on, rain! Flood the garden, drown me! Bad luck to me in this world and the next! Let the artists sue me! Let them send me to prison—to Siberia—to the scaffold! Ha, ha, ha!"

The next day it was the same thing all over again.

Olenka listened to Kukin silently, gravely, and sometimes tears would come to her eyes. In the end his misfortunes moved her and she fell in love with him. He was a short, thin man with a sallow face, and wore his hair combed down over his temples. He had a thin tenor voice and when he spoke, his mouth twisted, and his face perpetually wore an expression of despair. Nevertheless he aroused a genuine, deep feeling in her. She was always enamored of someone and could not live otherwise. At first it had been her papa, who was now ill and sat in an armchair in a darkened room, breathing with difficulty. Then she had devoted her affections to her aunt, who used to come from Bryansk every other year. Still earlier, when she went to school, she had been in love with her French teacher. She was a quiet, kind, soft-hearted girl, with meek, gentle eyes, and she enjoyed very good health. At the sight of her full pink cheeks, her soft white neck with a dark birthmark on it, and the kind artless smile that came into her face when she listened to anything pleasant, men said to themselves, "Yes, not half bad," and smiled too, while the ladies present could not refrain from suddenly seizing her hand in the middle of the conversation and exclaiming delightedly, "You darling!"

The house in which she lived all her life and which was to be hers by her father's will, was situated on the outskirts of the city on what was known as Gypsy Road, not far from The Tivoli. In the evening and at night she could hear the band play and the skyrockets go off, and it seemed to her that it was Kukin fighting his fate and assaulting his chief enemy, the apathetic public. Her heart contracted sweetly, she had no desire to sleep, and when he returned home at dawn, she would tap softly at her bedroom window and, showing him only her face and one shoulder through the curtain, give him a friendly smile.

He proposed to her, and they were married. And when he had a good look at her neck and her plump firm shoulders, he struck his hands together, and exclaimed, "Darling!"

He was happy, but as it rained on their wedding day and the night that followed, the expression of despair did not leave his face.

As a married couple, they got on well together. She presided over the box office, looked after things in the summer garden, kept accounts and paid salaries; and her rosy cheeks, the radiance of her sweet artless smile showed now in the box office window, now in the wings of the theater, now at the buffet. And she was already telling her friends that the theater was the most remarkable, the most important, and the most essential thing in the world, and that it was only the theater that could give true pleasure and make you a cultivated and humane person.

"But do you suppose the public understands that?" she would ask. "What it wants is slapstick! Yesterday we gave 'Faust Inside Out,' and almost all the boxes were empty, and if Vanichka and I had put on something vulgar, I assure you the theater would have been packed. Tomorrow Vanichka and I are giving 'Orpheus in Hell.' Do come."

And what Kukin said about artists and the theater she would repeat. Like him she despised the public for its ignorance and indifference to art; she took a hand in the rehearsals, correcting the actors, kept an eye on the musicians, and when there was an unfavorable notice in the local paper, she wept and went to see the editor about it.

The actors were fond of her and called her "the darling," and "Vanichka-and-I." She was sorry for them and would lend them small sums, and if they cheated her, she cried in private but did not complain to her husband.

The pair got on just as well together when winter came. They leased the municipal theater for the season and sublet it for short periods to a Ukrainian troupe, a magician, or a local dramatic club. Olenka was gaining weight and beamed with happiness, but Kukin was getting thinner and more sallow and complained of terrible losses, although business was fairly good during the winter. He coughed at night, and she would make him drink an infusion of raspberries and linden blossoms, rub him with eau de Cologne and wrap him in her soft shawls.

"What a sweet thing you are!" she would say quite sincerely, smoothing his hair. "My handsome sweet!"

At Lent he left for Moscow to engage a company of actors for the summer season, and she could not sleep with him away. She sat at the window and watched the stars. It occurred to her that she had something in common with the hens: they too stayed awake all night and were disturbed when the cock was absent from the henhouse. Kukin was detained in Moscow, and wrote that he would return by Easter, and in his letters he sent instructions about The Tivoli. But on the Monday of Passion Week, late in the evening, there was a sudden ominous knock at the gate; someone was banging at the wicket as though it were a barrel—boom, boom, boom! The sleepy cook, her bare feet splashing through the puddles, ran to open the gate.

"Open, please!" someone on the other side of the gate was saying in a deep voice. "There's a telegram for you."

Olenka had received telegrams from her husband before, but this time for some reason she was numb with fright. With trembling hands she opened the telegram and read the following:

"Ivan Petrovich died suddenly today awaiting prot instructions tuneral Tuesday."

That is exactly how the telegram had it: "tuneral," and there was also the incomprehensible word "prot"; the signature was that of the director of the comic opera company.

"My precious!" Olenka sobbed. "Vanichka, my precious, my sweet! Why did we ever meet! Why did I get to know you and to love you! To whom can your poor unhappy Olenka turn?"

Kukin was buried on Tuesday in the Vagankovo Cemetery in Moscow. Olenka returned home on Wednesday, and no sooner did she enter her room than she sank onto the bed and sobbed so loudly that she could be heard in the street and in the neighboring courtyards.

"The darling!" said the neighbors, crossing themselves. "Darling Olga Semyonovna! How the poor soul takes on!"

Three months later Olenka was returning from Mass one day in deep mourning and very sad. It happened that one of her neighbors, Vasily Andreich Pustovalov, the manager of Babakayev's lumberyard, who was also returning from church, was walking beside her. He was wearing a straw hat and a white waistcoat, with a gold watch-chain, and he looked more like a landowner than a businessman.

"There is order in all things, Olga Semyonovna," he was saying sedately, with a note of sympathy in his voice; "and if one of our dear ones passes on, then it means that this was the will of God, and in that case we must keep ourselves in hand and bear it submissively."

Having seen Olenka to her gate, he took leave of her and went further. All the rest of the day she heard his sedate voice, and as soon as she closed her eyes she had a vision of his dark beard. She liked him very much. And apparently she too had made an impression on him, because a little later a certain elderly lady, whom she scarcely knew, called to have coffee with her, and no sooner was she seated at table than the visitor began to talk about Pustovalov, saying that he was a fine, substantial man, and that any marriageable woman would be glad to go to the altar with him. Three days later Pustovalov himself paid her a visit. He did not stay more than ten minutes and he said little, but Olenka fell in love with him, so deeply that she stayed awake all night burning as with fever, and in the morning she sent for the elderly lady. The match was soon arranged and then came the wedding.

As a married couple Pustovalov and Olenka got on very well together. As a rule he was in the lumberyard till dinnertime, then he went out on business and was replaced by Olenka, who stayed in the office till evening, making out bills and seeing that orders were shipped.

"We pay twenty per cent more for lumber every year," she would say to customers and acquaintances. "Why, we used to deal in local timber, and now Vasichka has to travel to the province of Mogilev for timber regularly. And the freight rates!" she would exclaim, putting her hands to her cheeks in horror. "The freight rates!"

It seemed to her that she had been in the lumber business for ages, that lumber was the most important, the most essential thing in the world, and she found something intimate and touching in the very sound of such words as beam, log, batten, plank, box board, lath, scantling, slab . . .

At night she would dream of whole mountains of boards and planks, of endless caravans of carts hauling lumber out of town to distant points. She would dream that a regiment of beams, 28 feet by 8 inches, standing on end, was marching in the lumberyard, that beams, logs, and slabs were crashing against each other with the hollow sound of dry wood, that they kept tumbling down and rising again, piling themselves on each other. Olenka would scream in her sleep and Pustovalov would say to her tenderly: "Olenka, what's the matter, darling? Cross yourself!"

Whatever ideas her husband had, she adopted as her own. If he thought that the room was hot or that business was slow, she thought so too. Her husband did not care for entertainments and on holidays stayed home— so did she.

"You are always at home or in the office," her friends would say. "You ought to go to the theater, darling, or to the circus."

"Vasichka and I have no time for the theater," she would answer sedately. "We are working people, we're not interested in such foolishness. What good are these theaters?"

On Saturdays the two of them would go to evening service, on holidays they attended early Mass, and returning from the church they walked side by side, their

faces wearing a softened expression. There was an agreeable aroma about them, and her silk dress rustled pleas-
antly. At home they had tea with shortbread, and various kinds of jam, and afterwards they ate pie. Every day
at noon, in the yard and on the street just outside the
gate, there was a delicious smell of *borshch* and roast
lamb or duck, and on fast days there was the odor of
fish, and one could not pass the Pustovalov gate without one's mouth watering.

In the office the samovar was always boiling and the
customers were treated to tea with doughnuts. Once a
week the pair went to the baths and returned side by
side, both with red faces.

"Yes, everything goes well with us, thank God,"
Olenka would say to her friends. "I wish everyone were
as happy as Vasichka and I."

When Pustovalov went off to the provinces of Mogilev
for timber, she missed him badly and lay awake nights,
crying. Sometimes, in the evening, a young army veterinary, by the name of Smirnin, who rented the wing
of their house, would call on her. He chatted or played
cards with her and that diverted her. What interested
her most was what he told her about his domestic life.
He had been married and had a son, but was separated
from his wife because she had been unfaithful to him,
and now he hated her; he sent her forty rubles a month
for the maintenance of the child. And listening to him,
Olenka would sigh and shake her head: she was sorry
for him.

"Well, God keep you," she would say to him as she
took leave of him, going to the stairs with him, candle
in hand. "Thank you for relieving my boredom, and may
the Queen of Heaven give you health!"

She always expressed herself in this sedate and reasonable manner, in imitation of her husband. Just as the

veterinary would be closing the door behind him, she would recall him and say:

"You know, Vladimir Platonych, you had better make up with your wife. You ought to forgive her, at least for your son's sake! I am sure the little boy understands everything."

And when Pustovalov came back, she would tell him in low tones about the veterinary and his unhappy domestic life, and both of them would sigh and shake their heads and speak of the boy, who was probably missing his father. Then by a strange association of ideas they would both turn to the icons, bow down to the ground before them and pray that the Lord would grant them children.

Thus the Pustovalovs lived in peace and quiet, in love and harmony for six years. But one winter day, right after having hot tea at the office, Vasily Andreich went out without his cap to see about shipping some lumber, caught a chill and was taken sick. He was treated by the best doctors, but the illness had its own way with him, and he died after four months. Olenka was a widow again.

"To whom can I turn now, my darling?" she sobbed when she had buried her husband. "How can I live without you, wretched and unhappy as I am? Pity me, good people, left all alone in the world—"

She wore a black dress with white cuffs and gave up wearing hat and gloves for good. She hardly ever left the house except to go to church or to visit her husband's grave, and at home she lived like a nun. Only at the end of six months did she take off her widow's weeds and open the shutters. Sometimes in the morning she was seen with her cook going to market for provisions, but how she lived now and what went on in her house could only be guessed. People based their guesses on such facts as that they saw her having tea with the veterinary in her little garden, he reading the newspaper aloud to her, and that, meeting an acquaintance at the post office, she would say:

"There is no proper veterinary inspection in our town, and that's why there is so much illness around. So often you hear of people getting ill from the milk or catching infections from horses and cows. When you come down to it, the health of domestic animals must be as well cared for as the health of human beings."

She now repeated the veterinary's words and held the same opinions about everything that he did. It was plain that she could not live even for one year without an attachment and that she had found new happiness in the wing of her house. Another woman would have been condemned for this, but of Olenka no one could think ill: everything about her was so unequivocal. Neither she nor the veterinary mentioned to anyone the change that had occurred in their relations; indeed, they tried to conceal it, but they didn't succeed, because Olenka could not keep a secret. When he had visitors, his regimental colleagues, she, pouring the tea or serving the supper, would begin to talk of the cattle plague, of the pearl disease, of the municipal slaughter-houses. He would be terribly embarrassed and when the guests had gone, he would grasp her by the arms and hiss angrily:

"I've asked you before not to talk about things that you don't understand! When veterinaries speak among themselves, please don't butt in! It's really annoying!"

She would look at him amazed and alarmed and ask, "But Volodichka, what shall I talk about?"

And with tears in her eyes she would hug him and beg him not to be angry, and both of them were happy.

Yet this happiness did not last long. The veterinary

left, left forever, with his regiment, which was moved to some remote place, it may have been Siberia. And Olenka remained alone.

Now she was quite alone. Her father had died long ago, and his armchair stood in the attic, covered with dust and minus one leg. She got thinner and lost her looks, and passers-by in the street did not glance at her and smile as they used to. Obviously, her best years were over, were behind her, and now a new kind of life was beginning for her, an unfamiliar kind that did not bear thinking of. In the evening Olenka sat on her porch, and heard the band play at The Tivoli and the rockets go off, but this no longer suggested anything to her mind. She looked apathetically at the empty courtyard, thought of nothing, and later, when night came, she would go to bed and dream of the empty courtyard. She ate and drank as though involuntarily.

Above all, and worst of all, she no longer had any opinions whatever. She saw objects about her and understood what was going on, but she could not form an opinion about anything and did not know what to talk about. And how terrible it is not to have any opinions! You see, for instance, a bottle, or the rain, or a peasant driving in a cart, but what is the bottle for, or the rain, or the peasant, what is the meaning of them, you can't tell, and you couldn't, even if they paid you a thousand rubles. When Kukin was about, or Pustovalov or, later, the veterinary, Olenka could explain it all and give her opinions about anything you like, but now there was the same emptiness in her head and in her heart as in her courtyard. It was weird, and she felt as bitter as if she had been eating wormwood.

Little by little the town was extending in all directions. Gypsy Road was now a regular street, and where

The Tivoli had been and the lumberyards, houses had sprung up and lanes had multiplied. How swiftly time passes! Olenka's house had taken on a shabby look, the roof was rusty, the shed sloped, and the whole yard was invaded by burdock and stinging nettles. Olenka herself had aged and grown homely. In the summer she sat on the porch, feeling empty and dreary and bitter, as before; in the winter she sat by the window and stared at the snow. Sometimes at the first breath of spring or when the wind brought her the chime of church bells, memories of the past would overwhelm her, her heart would contract sweetly and her eyes would brim over with tears. But this only lasted a moment, and then there was again emptiness and once more she was possessed by a sense of the futility of life; Trot, the black kitten, rubbed against her and purred softly, but Olenka was not affected by these feline caresses. Is that what she needed? She needed an affection that would take possession of her whole being, her soul, her mind, that would give her ideas, a purpose in life, that would warm her aging blood. And she would shake the kitten off her lap, and say irritably: "Scat! Scat! Don't stick to me!"

And so it went, day after day, year after year, and no joy, no opinion! Whatever Mavra the cook would say, was well enough.

One hot July day, toward evening, when the cattle were being driven home and the yard was filled with clouds of dust, suddenly someone knocked at the gate. Olenka herself went to open it and was dumfounded at what she saw: at the gate stood Smirnin, the veterinary, already gray, and wearing civilian clothes. She suddenly recalled everything and, unable to control herself, burst into tears, silently letting her head drop on his breast. She was so agitated that she scarcely noticed how the two of them entered the house and sat down to tea.

"My dear," she murmured, trembling with joy, "Vladimir Platonych, however did you get here?"

"I have come here for good," he explained. "I have retired from the army and want to see what it's like to be on my own and live a settled life. And besides, my son is ready for high school. I have made up with my wife, you know."

"Where is she?"

"She's at the hotel with the boy, and I'm out looking for lodgings."

"Goodness, Vladimir Platonych, take my house! You don't need to look further! Good Lord, and you can have it free," exclaimed Olenka, all in a flutter and beginning to cry again. "You live here in the house, and the wing will do for me. Heavens, I'm so glad!"

The next day they began painting the roof and whitewashing the walls, and Olenka, her arms akimbo, walked about the yard, giving orders. The old smile had come back to her face, and she was lively and spry, as though she had waked from a long sleep. Presently the veterinary's wife arrived, a thin, homely lady with bobbed hair who looked as if she were given to caprices. With her was the little boy, Sasha, small for his age (he was going on ten), chubby, with clear blue eyes and dimples in his cheeks.

No sooner did he walk into the yard than he began chasing the cat, and immediately his eager, joyous laughter rang out.

"Auntie, is that your cat?" he asked Olenka. "When she has little ones, please give us a kitten. Mama is terribly afraid of mice."

Olenka chatted with him, then gave him tea, and her heart suddenly grew warm and contracted sweetly, as if this little boy were her own son. And in the evening, as he sat in the dining-room doing his homework, she looked at him with pity and tenderness and whispered:

"My darling, my pretty one, my little one! How blond you are, and so clever!"

"An island," he was reciting from the book, "is a body of land entirely surrounded by water."

"An island is a body of land . . ." she repeated and this was the first opinion she expressed with conviction after so many years of silence and mental vacuity.

She now had opinions of her own, and at supper she had a conversation with Sasha's parents, saying that studying in high school was hard on the children, but that nevertheless the classical course was better than the scientific one because a classical education opened all careers to you: you could be either a doctor or an engineer.

Sasha started going to high school. His mother went off to Kharkov to visit her sister and did not come back; every day his father left town to inspect herds and sometimes he stayed away for three days together, and it seemed to Olenka that Sasha was wholly abandoned, that he was unwanted, that he was being starved, and she moved him into the wing with her and settled him in a little room there.

For six months now Sasha has been living in her wing. Every morning Olenka comes into his room; he is fast asleep, his hand under his cheek, breathing quietly. She is sorry to wake him.

"Sashenka," she says sadly, "get up, my sweet! It's time to go to school."

He gets up, dresses, says his prayers, and sits down

to his breakfast: he drinks three glasses of tea and eats two large doughnuts, and half a buttered French roll. He is hardly awake and consequently cross.

"You haven't learned the fable, Sashenka," says Olenka, looking at him as though she were seeing him off on a long journey. "You worry me. You must do your best, darling, study. And pay attention to your teachers."

"Please leave me alone!" says Sasha.

Then he walks down the street to school, a small boy in a big cap, with his books in a rucksack. Olenka follows him noiselessly.

"Sashenka!" she calls after him. He turns around and she thrusts a date or a caramel into his hand. When they turn into the school lane, he feels ashamed at being followed by a tall stout woman; he looks round and says: "You'd better go home, auntie; I can go alone now."

She stands still and stares after him until he disappears at the school entrance. How she loves him! Not one of her former attachments was so deep; never had her soul surrendered itself so unreservedly, so disinterestedly and with such joy as now when her maternal instinct was increasingly asserting itself. For this little boy who was not her own, for the dimples in his cheeks, for his very cap, she would have laid down her life, would have laid it down with joy, with tears of tenderness. Why? But who knows why?

Having seen Sasha off to school, she goes quietly home, contented, tranquil, brimming over with love; her face, grown younger in the last six months, beams with happiness; people meeting her look at her with pleasure and say:

"Good morning, Olga Semyonovna, darling! How are you, darling?"

"They make the children work so hard at high school nowadays," she says, as she does her marketing. "Think of it: yesterday in the first form they had a fable to learn by heart, a Latin translation and a problem for homework. That's entirely too much for a little fellow."

And she talks about the teachers, the lessons, the textbooks—saying just what Sasha says about them.

At three o'clock they have dinner together, in the evening they do the homework together, and cry. When she puts him to bed, she takes a long time making the sign of the cross over him and whispering prayers. Then she goes to bed and thinks of the future, distant and misty, when Sasha, having finished his studies, will become a doctor or an engineer, will have a large house of his own, horses, a carriage, will marry and become a father. She falls asleep and her dreams are of the same thing, and tears flow down her cheeks from her closed eyes. The black kitten lies beside her purring: Purr-purrr-purrr.

Suddenly there is a loud knock at the gate. Olenka wakes up, breathless with fear, her heart palpitating. Half a minute passes, and there is another knock.

"That's a telegram from Kharkov," she thinks, beginning to tremble from head to foot. "Sasha's mother is sending for him from Kharkov— O Lord!"

She is in despair. Her head, her hands, her feet grow chill and it seems to her that she is the most unhappy woman in the whole world. But another minute passes, voices are heard: it's the veterinary returning from the club.

"Well, thank God!" she thinks.

Little by little the load rolls off her heart and she is again at ease; she goes back to bed and thinks of Sasha who is fast asleep in the next room and sometimes shouts in his sleep:

"I'll give it to you! Scram! No fighting!"

1899

The Lady With the Pet Dog

A NEW person, it was said, had appeared on the esplanade: a lady with a pet dog. Dmitry Dmitrich Gurov, who had spent a fortnight at Yalta and had got used to the place, had also begun to take an interest in new arrivals. As he sat in Vernet's confectionery shop, he saw, walking on the esplanade, a fair-haired young woman of medium height, wearing a beret; a white Pomeranian was trotting behind her.

And afterwards he met her in the public garden and in the square several times a day. She walked alone, always wearing the same beret and always with the white dog; no one knew who she was and everyone called her simply "the lady with the pet dog."

"If she is here alone without husband or friends," Gurov reflected, "it wouldn't be a bad thing to make her acquaintance."

He was under forty, but he already had a daughter twelve years old, and two sons at school. They had found a wife for him when he was very young, a student in his second year, and by now she seemed half as old again as he. She was a tall, erect woman with dark eyebrows, stately and dignified and, as she said of herself, intellectual. She read a great deal, used simplified spelling in her letters, called her husband, not Dmitry, but Dimitry, while he privately considered her of limited intelligence, narrow-minded, dowdy, was afraid of her, and did not like to be at home. He had begun being unfaithful to her long ago—had been unfaithful to her often and, probably for that reason, almost always spoke ill of women, and when they were talked of in his presence used to call them "the inferior race."

It seemed to him that he had been sufficiently tutored by bitter experience to call them what he pleased, and yet he could not have lived without "the inferior race" for two days together. In the company of men he was bored and ill at ease, he was chilly and uncommunicative with them; but when he was among women he felt free, and knew what to speak to them about and how to comport himself; and even to be silent with them was no strain on him. In his appearance, in his character, in his whole make-up there was something attractive and elusive that disposed women in his favor and allured them. He knew that, and some force seemed to draw him to them, too.

Oft-repeated and really bitter experience had taught him long ago that with decent people—particularly Moscow people—who are irresolute and slow to move, every affair which at first seems a light and charming adventure inevitably grows into a whole problem of extreme complexity, and in the end a painful situation is created. But at every new meeting with an interesting woman this lesson of experience seemed to slip from his memory, and he was eager for life, and everything seemed so simple and diverting.

One evening while he was dining in the public garden the lady in the beret walked up without haste to take the next table. Her expression, her gait, her dress, and the way she did her hair told him that she belonged to the upper class, that she was married, that she was in Yalta for the first time and alone, and that she was bored there. The stories told of the immorality in Yalta are to a great extent untrue; he despised them, and knew that such stories were made up for the most part by persons who would have been glad to sin themselves if they had had the chance; but when the lady sat down at the next table three paces from him, he recalled these stories of easy conquests, of trips to the mountains, and the tempting thought of a swift, fleeting liaison, a romance with an unknown woman of whose very name he was ignorant suddenly took hold of him.

He beckoned invitingly to the Pomeranian, and when the dog approached him, shook his finger at it. The Pomeranian growled; Gurov threatened it again.

The lady glanced at him and at once dropped her eyes.

"He doesn't bite," she said and blushed.

"May I give him a bone?" he asked; and when she nodded he inquired affably, "Have you been in Yalta long?"

"About five days."

"And I am dragging out the second week here."

There was a short silence.

"Time passes quickly, and yet it is so dull here!" she said, not looking at him.

"It's only the fashion to say it's dull here. A provincial will live in Belyov or Zhizdra and not be bored, but when he comes here it's 'Oh, the dullness! Oh, the dust!' One would think he came from Granada."

She laughed. Then both continued eating in silence, like strangers, but after dinner they walked together and there sprang up between them the light banter of people who are free and contented, to whom it does not matter where they go or what they talk about. They walked and talked of the strange light on the sea: the water was a soft, warm, lilac color, and there was a golden band of moonlight upon it. They talked of how sultry it was after a hot day. Gurov told her that he was a native of Moscow, that he had studied languages and literature at the university, but had a post in a bank; that at one time he had trained to become an opera singer but had given it up, that he owned two houses in Moscow. And he learned from her that she had grown up in Petersburg, but had lived in S—— since her marriage two years previously, that she was going to stay in Yalta for about another month, and that her husband, who needed a rest, too, might perhaps come to fetch her. She was not certain whether her husband was a member of a Government Board or served on a Zemstvo Council, and this amused her. And Gurov learned too that her name was Anna Sergeyevna.

Afterwards in his room at the hotel he thought about her—and was certain that he would meet her the next day. It was bound to happen. Getting into bed he recalled that she had been a schoolgirl only recently, doing lessons like his own daughter; he thought how much timidity and angularity there was still in her laugh and her manner of talking with a stranger. It must have been the first time in her life that she was alone in a setting in which she was followed, looked at, and spoken to for one secret purpose alone, which she could hardly fail to guess. He thought of her slim, delicate throat, her lovely gray eyes.

"There's something pathetic about her, though," he thought, and dropped off.

II

A week had passed since they had struck up an acquaintance. It was a holiday. It was close indoors, while in the street the wind whirled the dust about and blew people's hats off. One was thirsty all day, and Gurov

often went into the restaurant and offered Anna Sergeyevna a soft drink or ice cream. One did not know what
to do with oneself.

In the evening when the wind had abated they went
out on the pier to watch the steamer come in. There
were a great many people walking about the dock;
they had come to welcome someone and they were
carrying bunches of flowers. And two peculiarities of a
festive Yalta crowd stood out: the elderly ladies were
dressed like young ones and there were many generals.

Owing to the choppy sea, the steamer arrived late,
after sunset, and it was a long time tacking about before it put in at the pier. Anna Sergeyevna peered at
the steamer and the passengers through her lorgnette
as though looking for acquaintances, and whenever she
turned to Gurov her eyes were shining. She talked a
great deal and asked questions jerkily, forgetting the
next moment what she had asked; then she lost her
lorgnette in the crush.

The festive crowd began to disperse; it was now too
dark to see people's faces; there was no wind any more,
but Gurov and Anna Sergeyevna still stood as though
waiting to see someone else come off the steamer. Anna
Sergeyevna was silent now, and sniffed her flowers without looking at Gurov.

"The weather has improved this evening," he said.
"Where shall we go now? Shall we drive somewhere?"

She did not reply.

Then he looked at her intently, and suddenly embraced her and kissed her on the lips, and the moist
fragrance of her flowers enveloped him; and at once he
looked round him anxiously, wondering if anyone had
seen them.

"Let us go to your place," he said softly. And they
walked off together rapidly.

The air in her room was close and there was the smell of the perfume she had bought at the Japanese shop. Looking at her, Gurov thought: "What encounters life offers!" From the past he preserved the memory of carefree, good-natured women whom love made gay and who were grateful to him for the happiness he gave them, however brief it might be; and of women like his wife who loved without sincerity, with too many words, affectedly, hysterically, with an expression that it was not love or passion that engaged them but something more significant; and of two or three others, very beautiful, frigid women, across whose faces would suddenly flit a rapacious expression—an obstinate desire to take from life more than it could give, and these were women no longer young, capricious, unreflecting, domineering, unintelligent, and when Gurov grew cold to them their beauty aroused his hatred, and the lace on their lingerie seemed to him to resemble scales.

But here there was the timidity, the angularity of inexperienced youth, a feeling of awkwardness; and there was a sense of embarrassment, as though someone had suddenly knocked at the door. Anna Sergeyevna, "the lady with the pet dog," treated what had happened in a peculiar way, very seriously, as though it were her fall—so it seemed, and this was odd and inappropriate. Her features drooped and faded, and her long hair hung down sadly on either side of her face; she grew pensive and her dejected pose was that of a Magdalene in a picture by an old master.

"It's not right," she said. "You don't respect me now, you first of all."

There was a watermelon on the table. Gurov cut himself a slice and began eating it without haste. They were silent for at least half an hour.

There was something touching about Anna Sergeyevna; she had the purity of a well-bred, naive woman who has seen little of life. The single candle burning on the table barely illumined her face, yet it was clear that she was unhappy.

"Why should I stop respecting you, darling?" asked Gurov. "You don't know what you're saying."

"God forgive me," she said, and her eyes filled with tears. "It's terrible."

"It's as though you were trying to exonerate yourself."

"How can I exonerate myself? No. I am a bad, low woman; I despise myself and I have no thought of exonerating myself. It's not my husband but myself I have deceived. And not only just now; I have been deceiving myself for a long time. My husband may be a good, honest man, but he is a flunkey! I don't know what he does, what his work is, but I know he is a flunkey! I was twenty when I married him. I was tormented by curiosity; I wanted something better. 'There must be a different sort of life,' I said to myself. I wanted to live! To live, to live! Curiosity kept eating at me—you don't understand it, but I swear to God I could no longer control myself; something was going on in me: I could not be held back. I told my husband I was ill, and came here. And here I have been walking about as though in a daze, as though I were mad; and now I have become a vulgar, vile woman whom anyone may despise."

Gurov was already bored with her; he was irritated by her naive tone, by her repentance, so unexpected and so out of place; but for the tears in her eyes he might have thought she was joking or play-acting.

"I don't understand, my dear," he said softly. "What do you want?"

She hid her face on his breast and pressed close to him.

"Believe me, believe me, I beg you," she said, "I love honesty and purity, and sin is loathsome to me; I don't know what I'm doing. Simple people say, 'The Evil One has led me astray.' And I may say of myself now that the Evil One has led me astray."

"Quiet, quiet," he murmured.

He looked into her fixed, frightened eyes, kissed her, spoke to her softly and affectionately, and by degrees she calmed down, and her gaiety returned; both began laughing.

Afterwards when they went out there was not a soul on the esplanade. The town with its cypresses looked quite dead, but the sea was still sounding as it broke upon the beach; a single launch was rocking on the waves and on it a lantern was blinking sleepily.

They found a cab and drove to Oreanda.

"I found out your surname in the hall just now: it was written on the board—von Dideritz," said Gurov. "Is your husband German?"

"No; I believe his grandfather was German, but he is Greek Orthodox himself."

At Oreanda they sat on a bench not far from the church, looked down at the sea, and were silent. Yalta was barely visible through the morning mist; white clouds rested motionlessly on the mountaintops. The leaves did not stir on the trees, cicadas twanged, and the monotonous muffled sound of the sea that rose from below spoke of the peace, the eternal sleep awaiting us. So it rumbled below when there was no Yalta, no Oreanda here; so it rumbles now, and it will rumble as indifferently and as hollowly when we are no more. And in this constancy, in this complete indifference to the life and death of each of us, there lies, perhaps, a pledge of our eternal salvation, of the unceasing advance of life upon earth, of unceasing movement towards perfection. Sitting beside a young woman who in the dawn seemed so lovely, Gurov, soothed and spellbound by these magical surroundings—the sea, the mountains, the clouds, the wide sky—thought how everything is really beautiful in this world when one reflects: everything except what we think or do ourselves when we forget the higher aims of life and our own human dignity.

A man strolled up to them—probably a guard—looked at them and walked away. And this detail, too, seemed so mysterious and beautiful. They saw a steamer arrive from Feodosia, its lights extinguished in the glow of dawn.

"There is dew on the grass," said Anna Sergeyevna, after a silence.

"Yes, it's time to go home."

They returned to the city.

Then they met every day at twelve o'clock on the esplanade, lunched and dined together, took walks, admired the sea. She complained that she slept badly, that she had palpitations, asked the same questions, troubled now by jealousy and now by the fear that he did not respect her sufficiently. And often in the square or the public garden, when there was no one near them, he suddenly drew her to him and kissed her passionately. Complete idleness, these kisses in broad daylight exchanged furtively in dread of someone's seeing them, the heat, the smell of the sea, and the continual flitting before his eyes of idle, well-dressed, well-fed people, worked a complete change in him; he kept telling Anna Sergeyevna how beautiful she was, how seductive, was urgently passionate; he would not move a step away from her, while she was often pensive and continually pressed him to confess that he did not respect her, did not love her in the least, and saw in her nothing but a common woman. Almost every evening rather late they drove somewhere out of town, to Oreanda or to the waterfall; and the excursion was always a success, the scenery invariably impressed them as beautiful and magnificent.

They were expecting her husband, but a letter came from him saying that he had eye-trouble, and begging his wife to return home as soon as possible. Anna Sergeyevna made haste to go.

"It's a good thing I am leaving," she said to Gurov. "It's the hand of Fate!"

She took a carriage to the railway station, and he went with her. They were driving the whole day. When she had taken her place in the express, and when the second bell had rung, she said, "Let me look at you once more—let me look at you again. Like this."

She was not crying but was so sad that she seemed ill, and her face was quivering.

"I shall be thinking of you—remembering you," she said. "God bless you; be happy. Don't remember evil against me. We are parting forever—it has to be, for we ought never to have met. Well, God bless you."

The train moved off rapidly, its lights soon vanished, and a minute later there was no sound of it, as though everything had conspired to end as quickly as possible that sweet trance, that madness. Left alone on the platform, and gazing into the dark distance, Gurov listened to the twang of the grasshoppers and the hum of the telegraph wires, feeling as though he had just waked up. And he reflected, musing, that there had now been another episode or adventure in his life, and it, too, was at an end, and nothing was left of it but a memory. He was moved, sad, and slightly remorseful: this young woman whom he would never meet again had not been happy with him; he had been warm and affectionate with her, but yet in his manner, his tone, and his caresses there had been a shade of light irony, the slightly coarse arrogance of a happy male who was, besides, almost twice her age. She had constantly called him kind, exceptional, high-minded; obviously he had seemed to her different from what he really was, so he had involuntarily deceived her.

Here at the station there was already a scent of autumn in the air; it was a chilly evening.

"It is time for me to go north, too," thought Gurov as he left the platform. "High time!"

III

At home in Moscow the winter routine was already established: the stoves were heated, and in the morning it was still dark when the children were having breakfast and getting ready for school, and the nurse would light the lamp for a short time. There were frosts already. When the first snow falls, on the first day the sleighs are out, it is pleasant to see the white earth, the white roofs; one draws easy, delicious breaths, and the season brings back the days of one's youth. The old limes and birches, white with hoar-frost, have a good-natured look; they are closer to one's heart than cypresses and palms, and near them one no longer wants to think of mountains and the sea.

Gurov, a native of Moscow, arrived there on a fine frosty day, and when he put on his fur coat and warm gloves and took a walk along Petrovka, and when on Saturday night he heard the bells ringing, his recent trip and the places he had visited lost all charm for him. Little by little he became immersed in Moscow life, greedily read three newspapers a day, and declared that he did not read the Moscow papers on principle. He already felt a longing for restaurants, clubs, formal dinners, anniversary celebrations, and it flattered him to entertain distinguished lawyers and actors, and to play cards with a professor at the physicians' club. He could eat a whole portion of meat stewed with pickled cabbage and served in a pan, Moscow style.

A month or so would pass and the image of Anna Sergeyevna, it seemed to him, would become misty in his memory, and only from time to time he would dream of her with her touching smile as he dreamed of others. But more than a month went by, winter came into its own, and everything was still clear in his memory as though he had parted from Anna Sergeyevna only yesterday. And his memories glowed more and more vividly. When in the evening stillness the voices of his children preparing their lessons reached his study, or when he listened to a song or to an organ playing in a restaurant, or when the storm howled in the chimney, suddenly everything would rise up in his memory: what had happened on the pier and the early morning with the mist on the mountains, and the steamer coming from Feodosia, and the kisses. He would pace about his room a long time, remembering and smiling; then his memories passed into reveries, and in his imagination the past would mingle with what was to come. He did not dream of Anna Sergeyevna, but she followed him about everywhere and watched him. When he shut his eyes he saw her before him as though she were there in the flesh, and she seemed to him lovelier, younger, tenderer than she had been, and he imagined himself a finer man than he had been in Yalta. Of evenings she peered out at him from the bookcase, from the fireplace, from the corner—he heard her breathing, the caressing rustle of her clothes. In the street he followed the women with his eyes, looking for someone who resembled her.

Already he was tormented by a strong desire to share his memories with someone. But in his home it was impossible to talk of his love, and he had no one to talk to outside; certainly he could not confide in his tenants or in anyone at the bank. And what was there to talk about? He hadn't loved her then, had he? Had there been anything beautiful, poetical, edifying, or simply interesting in his relations with Anna Sergeyevna? And he was forced to talk vaguely of love, of women, and no one guessed what he meant; only his wife would twitch her black eyebrows and say, "The part of a philanderer does not suit you at all, Dimitry."

One evening, coming out of the physicians' club with an official with whom he had been playing cards, he could not resist saying:

"If you only knew what a fascinating woman I became acquainted with at Yalta!"

The official got into his sledge and was driving away, but turned suddenly and shouted:

"Dmitry Dmitrich!"

"What is it?"

"You were right this evening: the sturgeon was a bit high."

These words, so commonplace, for some reason moved Gurov to indignation, and struck him as degrading and unclean. What savage manners, what mugs! What stupid nights, what dull, humdrum days! Frenzied gambling, gluttony, drunkenness, continual talk always about the same things! Futile pursuits and conversations always about the same topics take up the better part of one's time, the better part of one's strength, and in the end there is left a life clipped and wingless, an absurd mess, and there is no escaping or getting away from it—just as though one were in a madhouse or a prison.

Gurov, boiling with indignation, did not sleep all night. And he had a headache all the next day. And the following nights too he slept badly; he sat up in bed, thinking, or paced up and down his room. He was fed up with his children, fed up with the bank; he had no desire to go anywhere or to talk of anything.

In December during the holidays he prepared to take a trip and told his wife he was going to Petersburg to do what he could for a young friend—and he set off for S—— What for? He did not know, himself. He wanted to see Anna Sergeyevna and talk with her, to arrange a rendezvous if possible.

He arrived at S—— in the morning, and at the hotel took the best room, in which the floor was covered with gray army cloth, and on the table there was an inkstand, gray with dust and topped by a figure on horseback, its hat in its raised hand and its head broken off. The porter gave him the necessary information: von Dideritz lived in a house of his own on Staro-Goncharnaya Street, not far from the hotel: he was rich and lived well and kept his own horses; everyone in the town knew him. The porter pronounced the name: "Dridiritz."

Without haste Gurov made his way to Staro-Goncharnaya Street and found the house. Directly opposite the house stretched a long gray fence studded with nails.

"A fence like that would make one run away," thought Gurov, looking now at the fence, now at the windows of the house.

He reflected: this was a holiday, and the husband was apt to be at home. And in any case, it would be tactless to go into the house and disturb her. If he were to send her a note, it might fall into her husband's hands, and that might spoil everything. The best thing was to rely on chance. And he kept walking up and down the street and along the fence, waiting for the chance. He saw a beggar go in at the gate and heard the dogs attack him; then an hour later he heard a piano, and the sound came to him faintly and indistinctly. Probably it was Anna Sergeyevna playing. The front door opened suddenly, and an old woman came out, followed by the familiar white Pomeranian. Gurov was on the point of calling to the dog, but his heart began beating violently, and in his excitement he could not remember the Pomeranian's name.

He kept walking up and down, and hated the gray fence more and more, and by now he thought irritably that Anna Sergeyevna had forgotten him, and was perhaps already diverting herself with another man, and that that was very natural in a young woman who from morning till night had to look at that damn fence. He went back to his hotel room and sat on the couch for a long while, not knowing what to do, then he had dinner and a long nap.

"How stupid and annoying all this is!" he thought when he woke and looked at the dark windows: it was already evening. "Here I've had a good sleep for some reason. What am I going to do at night?"

He sat on the bed, which was covered with a cheap gray blanket of the kind seen in hospitals, and he twitted himself in his vexation:

"So there's your lady with the pet dog. There's your adventure. A nice place to cool your heels in."

That morning at the station a playbill in large letters had caught his eye. *The Geisha* was to be given for the first time. He thought of this and drove to the theater.

"It's quite possible that she goes to first nights," he thought.

The theater was full. As in all provincial theaters, there was a haze above the chandelier, the gallery was noisy and restless; in the front row, before the beginning of the performance the local dandies were standing with their hands clasped behind their backs; in the Governor's box the Governor's daughter, wearing a boa, occupied the front seat, while the Governor himself hid modestly behind the portiere and only his hands were visible; the curtain swayed; the orchestra was a long time tuning up. While the audience were coming in and taking their seats, Gurov scanned the faces eagerly.

Anna Sergeyevna, too, came in. She sat down in the third row, and when Gurov looked at her his heart contracted, and he understood clearly that in the whole world there was no human being so near, so precious, and so important to him; she, this little, undistinguished woman, lost in a provincial crowd, with a vulgar lorgnette in her hand, filled his whole life now, was his sorrow and his joy, the only happiness that he now desired for himself, and to the sounds of the bad orchestra, of the miserable local violins, he thought how lovely she was. He thought and dreamed.

A young man with small side-whiskers, very tall and stooped, came in with Anna Sergeyevna and sat down beside her; he nodded his head at every step and seemed to be bowing continually. Probably this was the husband whom at Yalta, in an access of bitter feeling, she had called a flunkey. And there really was in his lanky figure, his side-whiskers, his small bald patch, something of a flunkey's retiring manner; his smile was mawkish, and in his buttonhole there was an academic badge like a waiter's number.

During the first intermission the husband went out

to have a smoke; she remained in her seat. Gurov, who was also sitting in the orchestra, went up to her and said in a shaky voice, with a forced smile:

"Good evening!"

She glanced at him and turned pale, then looked at him again in horror, unable to believe her eyes, and gripped the fan and the lorgnette tightly together in her hands, evidently trying to keep herself from fainting. Both were silent. She was sitting, he was standing, frightened by her distress and not daring to take a seat beside her. The violins and the flute that were being tuned up sang out. He suddenly felt frightened: it seemed as if all the people in the boxes were looking at them. She got up and went hurriedly to the exit; he followed her, and both of them walked blindly along the corridors and up and down stairs, and figures in the uniforms prescribed for magistrates, teachers, and officials of the Department of Crown Lands, all wearing badges, flitted before their eyes, as did also ladies, and fur coats on hangers; they were conscious of drafts and the smell of stale tobacco. And Gurov, whose heart was beating violently, thought:

"Oh, Lord! Why are these people here and this orchestra!"

And at that instant he suddenly recalled how when he had seen Anna Sergeyevna off at the station he had said to himself that all was over between them and that they would never meet again. But how distant the end still was!

On the narrow, gloomy staircase over which it said "To the Amphitheatre," she stopped.

"How you frightened me!" she said, breathing hard, still pale and stunned. "Oh, how you frightened me! I am barely alive. Why did you come? Why?"

"But do understand, Anna, do understand—" he said

hurriedly, under his breath. "I implore you, do understand—"

She looked at him with fear, with entreaty, with love;
she looked at him intently, to keep his features more
distinctly in her memory.

"I suffer so," she went on, not listening to him. "All
this time I have been thinking of nothing but you; I
live only by the thought of you. And I wanted to forget,
to forget; but why, oh, why have you come?"

On the landing above them two high school boys
were looking down and smoking, but it was all the same
to Gurov; he drew Anna Sergeyevna to him and began
kissing her face and her hands.

"What are you doing, what are you doing!" she was
saying in horror, pushing him away. "We have lost our
senses. Go away today; go away at once— I conjure you
by all that is sacred, I implore you— People are coming
this way!"

Someone was walking up the stairs.

"You must leave," Anna Sergeyevna went on in a
whisper. "Do you hear, Dmitry Dmitrich? I will come
and see you in Moscow. I have never been happy; I
am unhappy now, and I never, never shall be happy,
never! So don't make me suffer still more! I swear I'll
come to Moscow. But now let us part. My dear, good,
precious one, let us part!"

She pressed his hand and walked rapidly downstairs,
turning to look round at him, and from her eyes he
could see that she really was unhappy. Gurov stood for
a while, listening, then when all grew quiet, he found
his coat and left the theater.

IV

And Anna Sergeyevna began coming to see him in Moscow. Once every two or three months she left S——, telling her husband that she was going to consult a doctor about a woman's ailment from which she was suffering—and her husband did and did not believe her. When she arrived in Moscow she would stop at the Slavyansky Bazar Hotel, and at once send a man in a red cap to Gurov. Gurov came to see her, and no one in Moscow knew of it.

Once he was going to see her in this way on a winter morning (the messenger had come the evening before and not found him in). With him walked his daughter, whom he wanted to take to school: it was on the way. Snow was coming down in big wet flakes.

"It's three degrees above zero, and yet it's snowing," Gurov was saying to his daughter. "But this temperature prevails only on the surface of the earth; in the upper layers of the atmosphere there is quite a different temperature."

"And why doesn't it thunder in winter, papa?"

He explained that, too. He talked, thinking all the while that he was on his way to a rendezvous, and no living soul knew of it, and probably no one would ever know. He had two lives: an open one, seen and known by all who needed to know it, full of conventional truth and conventional falsehood, exactly like the lives of his friends and acquaintances; and another life that went on in secret. And through some strange, perhaps accidental, combination of circumstances, everything that was of interest and importance to him, everything that was essential to him, everything about which he felt sincerely and did not deceive himself, everything that

constituted the core of his life, was going on concealed
from others; while all that was false, the shell in which
he hid to cover the truth—his work at the bank, for
instance, his discussions at the club, his references to
the "inferior race," his appearances at anniversary celebrations with his wife—all that went on in the open.
Judging others by himself, he did not believe what he
saw, and always fancied that every man led his real,
most interesting life under cover of secrecy as under
cover of night. The personal life of every individual is
based on secrecy, and perhaps it is partly for that reason
that civilized man is so nervously anxious that personal
privacy should be respected.

Having taken his daughter to school, Gurov went on
to the Slavyansky Bazar Hotel. He took off his fur coat
in the lobby, went upstairs, and knocked gently at the
door. Anna Sergeyevna, wearing his favorite gray dress,
exhausted by the journey and by waiting, had been ex
pecting him since the previous evening. She was pale,
and looked at him without a smile, and he had hardly
entered when she flung herself on his breast. Their kiss
was a long, lingering one, as though they had not seen
one another for two years.

"Well, darling, how are you getting on there?" he
asked. "What news?"

"Wait; I'll tell you in a moment— I can't speak."

She could not speak; she was crying. She turned
away from him, and pressed her handkerchief to her
eyes.

"Let her have her cry; meanwhile I'll sit down," he
thought, and he seated himself in an armchair.

Then he rang and ordered tea, and while he was
having his tea she remained standing at the window
with her back to him. She was crying out of sheer agitation, in the sorrowful consciousness that their life was

so sad; that they could only see each other in secret and had to hide from people like thieves! Was it not a broken life?

"Come, stop now, dear!" he said.

It was plain to him that this love of theirs would not be over soon, that the end of it was not in sight. Anna Sergeyevna was growing more and more attached to him. She adored him, and it was unthinkable to tell her that their love was bound to come to an end some day; besides, she would not have believed it!

He went up to her and took her by the shoulders, to fondle her and say something diverting, and at that moment he caught sight of himself in the mirror.

His hair was already beginning to turn gray. And it seemed odd to him that he had grown so much older in the last few years, and lost his looks. The shoulders on which his hands rested were warm and heaving. He felt compassion for this life, still so warm and lovely, but probably already about to begin to fade and wither like his own. Why did she love him so much? He always seemed to women different from what he was, and they loved in him not himself, but the man whom their imagination created and whom they had been eagerly seeking all their lives; and afterwards, when they saw their mistake, they loved him nevertheless. And not one of them had been happy with him. In the past he had met women, come together with them, parted from them, but he had never once loved; it was anything you please, but not love. And only now when his head was gray he had fallen in love, really, truly— for the first time in his life.

Anna Sergeyevna and he loved each other as people do who are very close and intimate, like man and wife, like tender friends; it seemed to them that Fate itself had meant them for one another, and they could not understand why he had a wife and she a husband; and it was as though they were a pair of migratory birds, male and female, caught and forced to live in different cages. They forgave each other what they were ashamed of in their past, they forgave everything in the present, and felt that this love of theirs had altered them both.

Formerly in moments of sadness he had soothed himself with whatever logical arguments came into his head, but now he no longer cared for logic; he felt profound compassion, he wanted to be sincere and tender.

"Give it up now, my darling," he said. "You've had your cry; that's enough. Let us have a talk now, we'll think up something."

Then they spent a long time taking counsel together, they talked of how to avoid the necessity for secrecy, for deception, for living in different cities, and not seeing one another for long stretches of time. How could they free themselves from these intolerable fetters?

"How? How?" he asked, clutching his head. "How?"

And it seemed as though in a little while the solution would be found, and then a new and glorious life would begin; and it was clear to both of them that the end was still far off, and that what was to be most complicated and difficult for them was only just beginning.

1899

At Christmas Time

"WHAT'LL I write?" asked Yegor, and dipped his pen in the ink.

Vasilisa had not seen her daughter for four years. After the wedding her daughter Yefimya had gone to Petersburg with her husband, sent two letters home, and then disappeared without leaving a trace. She was neither seen nor heard from. And whether the old woman was milking the cow at dawn, or lighting the stove, or dozing at night, she was always thinking of one thing: how was Yefimya getting on out there, was she alive at all? A letter should have gone off, but the old man did not know how to write, and there was no one to turn to.

But now it was Christmas time, and Vasilisa could bear it no longer, and went to the teahouse to see Yegor, the proprietor's brother-in-law, who had been staying there, doing nothing, ever since he came back from the army; it was said that he could write a fine letter if he were properly paid. At the teahouse Vasilisa had a talk with the cook, then with the proprietress, and then with Yegor himself. Fifteen kopecks was the price agreed on.

And now—this took place in the teahouse kitchen on the second day of the holidays—Yegor was sitting at the table, pen in hand. Vasilisa was standing before him, thoughtful, an expression of care and grief on her face. Pyotr, her husband, a tall, gaunt old man with a brown bald spot, had come with her; he stood staring fixedly ahead of him like a blind man. On the range a piece of pork was being fried in a saucepan; it sizzled and hissed, and seemed actually to be saying: "Flu-flu-flu." It was stifling.

"What'll I write?" Yegor asked again.

"What?" asked Vasilisa, looking at him angrily and suspiciously. "Don't rush me! You're not writing for nothing; you'll get money for it. Well, write: 'To our dear son-in-law, Andrey Hrisanfych, and to our only beloved daughter, Yefimya Petrovna, our love, a low bow, and our parental blessing enduring forever and ever.'"

"Done; keep going."

"'And we also send wishes for a merry Christmas, we are alive and well, hoping you are the same, please God, the Heavenly King.'"

Vasilisa thought for a moment and exchanged glances with the old man.

"'Hoping you are the same, please God, the Heavenly King,'" she repeated, and burst into tears.

She could say nothing further. And yet before, when she had lain awake at night thinking of it, it had seemed to her that she could not get all she had to say into ten letters. Since the time when her daughter had gone away with her husband much water had flowed under the bridges, the old people had lived like orphans, and sighed heavily at night as though they had buried their daughter. And during all that time how many events had occurred in the village, how many weddings and funerals! What long winters! What long nights!

"It's hot," said Yegor, unbuttoning his vest. "Must be a hundred and fifty degrees. What else?" he asked.

The old couple were silent.

"What does your son-in-law do there?" asked Yegor.

"He used to be a soldier, son, you know," the old

man answered in a weak voice. "He came back from the service the same time you did. He used to be a soldier, and now, to be sure, he is in Petersburg at a hyderpathic establishment. The doctor treats sick people with water. So, he works as a doorman, to be sure, at the doctor's."

"It's written down here," said the old woman, taking a letter out of a kerchief. "We got it from Yefimya, goodness knows when. Maybe they're no longer in this world."

Yegor thought a little and then began writing rapidly:

"At the present time," he wrote, "as your fate has of itself assined you to a Militery Carere, we advise you to look into the Statutes on Disiplinery Fines and Criminal Laws of the War Department and you will discover in that Law the Sivelisation of the Officials of the War Department."

He was writing and reading aloud what he had written, while Vasilisa kept thinking that the letter should tell about how needy they had been the previous year, how the flour had not lasted even till Christmas, and they had had to sell the cow. She ought to ask for money, ought to say that the old man was often ailing and would soon no doubt give up his soul to God . . . but how to put it in words? What should be said first and what next?

"Observe," Yegor went on writing, "in volume five of Militery Regulashuns. Soldier is a common name and an honorable one. The Topmost General and the lowest Private is both called soldier . . ."

The old man moved his lips and said quietly:

"To have a look at the grandchildren, that wouldn't be bad."

"What grandchildren?" asked the old woman, and she gave him a cross look; "maybe there ain't any."

"Grandchildren? Maybe there are some. Who knows?"

"And thereby you can judge," Yegor hurried on, "what a Foreign enemy is and what an Internal enemy. Our foremost Internal Enemy is Bacchus."

The pen creaked, forming flourishes on the paper that looked like fish-hooks. Yegor wrote hurriedly, reading every line over several times. He sat on a stool, his feet spread wide apart under the table, a well-fed, lusty fellow, with a coarse snout and a red nape. He was vulgarity itself: coarse, arrogant, invincible, proud of having been born and bred in a teahouse; and Vasilisa knew perfectly well that here was vulgarity but she could not put it into words, and only looked at Yegor angrily and suspiciously. The sound of his voice and the incomprehensible words, the heat and the stuffiness, made her head ache and threw her thoughts into confusion, and she said nothing further, stopped thinking, and simply waited for him to cease scratching away. But the old man looked on with full confidence. He had faith in his old woman, who had brought him there, and in Yegor; and when he had mentioned the hydropathic establishment earlier it was clear from his expression that he had faith in the establishment and in the healing virtues of water.

Having finished writing, Yegor got up, and read the entire letter from the beginning. The old man did not understand it, but he nodded his head trustfully.

"That's all right; it's smooth . . ." he said. "God give you health. That's all right . . ."

They laid three five-kopeck pieces on the table and went out of the teahouse; the old man stared fixedly before him as though he were blind, and his countenance showed perfect trustfulness; but as Vasilisa went out of the teahouse she made an angry pass at the dog, and said crossly:

"Ugh, the pest!"

The old woman, disturbed by her thoughts, did not sleep all night, and at daybreak she got up, said her prayers, and went to the station to send off the letter.

It was some seven miles to the station.

II

Dr. B. O. Moselweiser's hydropathic establishment was open on New Year's Day just as on ordinary days; but the doorman, Andrey Hrisanfych, wore a uniform with new braid, his boots had an extra polish, and he greeted every visitor with a "Happy New Year!"

Andrey Hrisanfych was standing at the door in the morning, reading the newspaper. Precisely at ten o'clock a general arrived, one of the regular patients, and directly after him came the postman; Andrey Hrisanfych helped the general off with his overcoat and said:

"Happy New Year, Your Excellency!"

"Thank you, my good man; the same to you."

And as he walked upstairs the general asked, nodding towards a door (he asked the same question every day and always forgot the answer):

"And what's in that room?"

"That's the massage room, Your Excellency."

When the general's steps had died away, Andrey Hrisanfych looked over the mail and found one letter addressed to himself. He opened it, read several lines, then, glancing at the newspaper, walked unhurriedly to his own quarters, which were on the same floor, at the end of the corridor. His wife Yefimya was sitting on the bed, nursing her baby; another child, the eldest, was standing close by, his curly head resting on her knee; a third was asleep on the bed.

Entering the room, Andrey handed his wife the letter, and said:

"Must be from the village."

Then he walked out again without removing his eyes from the paper, and stopped in the corridor, not far from his door. He could hear Yefimya reading the first lines in a trembling voice. She read them and could read no more; these lines were enough for her. She burst into tears, and hugging and kissing her eldest child, she began to speak—and it was impossible to tell whether she were laughing or crying.

"It's from granny, from grandpa," she said. "From the country. Queen of Heaven, saints and martyrs! The snow is piled up to the roofs there now—the trees are white as white can be. Children are out on tiny little sleds—and darling bald old grandpa is up on the stove —and there is a little yellow puppy— My precious darlings!"

Hearing this, Andrey Hrisanfych recalled that three or four times his wife had given him letters and asked him to send them to the village, but some important business had always intervened; he had not sent the letters and somehow they were mislaid.

"And little hares hop about in the fields," Yefimya continued mournfully, bathed in tears, and kissing her boy. "Grandpa is gentle and good; granny is good, too, and kindhearted. In the village folks are friendly, they fear God—and there is a little church in the village; the peasants sing in the choir. If only the Queen of Heaven, the Mother of God would take us away from here!"

Andrey Hrisanfych returned to his room to have a smoke before another patient arrived, and Yefimya suddenly stopped speaking, grew quiet, and wiped her eyes, and only her lips quivered. She was very much afraid of him—oh, how afraid of him she was! She trembled and was terrorized at the sound of his steps, his look, she dared not say a word in his presence.

Andrey Hrisanfych lit a cigarette, but at that very moment there was a ring from upstairs. He put out his cigarette and, assuming a very grave face, hastened to the front door.

The general was coming downstairs, fresh and rosy from his bath.

"And what's in that room?" he asked, pointing to a door.

Andrey Hrisanfych came to attention, and announced loudly:

"Charcot douche, Your Excellency!"

1900

On Official Business

THE deputy examining magistrate and the county physician were on their way to an autopsy in the village of Syrnya. En route they were caught in a blizzard; they wasted a great deal of time traveling in circles and arrived at their destination not at midday, as they had intended, but in the evening when it was already dark. They put up for the night at the village headquarters.[1] It was here that the dead body happened to be lying, the corpse of the Zemstvo insurance agent Lesnitzky, who had come to Syrnya three days previously and, af-

---

[1] A cottage in which community meetings and sessions of the village elders were held and which was sometimes used as a hostelry.

ter settling in the village headquarters and ordering the samovar, had shot himself, to the complete surprise of everyone; and the fact that he had ended his life under such strange circumstances, with the samovar before him and the food he had brought along laid out on the table, led many to suspect murder; an inquest was in order.

In the entry the doctor and the examining magistrate stamped their feet to shake off the snow, and near by stood an old man who belonged to the lowest order of rural police: Ilya Loshadin; he was holding a little tin lamp in his hands to give them light. There was a strong smell of kerosene.

"Who are you?" asked the doctor.

"The p'liceman," answered Loshadin.

He used to spell it "pleaceman" when he signed the receipts at the post office.

"And where are the inquest witnesses?"

"They must have gone to have tea, your honor."

To the right was the best room, the travelers' or gentry's room; to the left a room for the lower orders with a big stove and a sleeping platform. The doctor and the examining magistrate, followed by the policeman, holding the lamp high above his head, went into the best room. Here, motionless on the floor, close to the table legs, lay a long body, covered with a white sheet. In the dim light of the lamp, in addition to the white cover, a pair of new rubbers could be clearly seen, and everything about the place was weird and sinister: the dark walls, and the silence, and the rubbers, and the immobility of the dead body. On the table stood a samovar, long since cold; and round it packages, probably containing food.

"To shoot oneself in the village headquarters, how tactless!" said the doctor. "If you do want to put a bullet through your brain, you ought to do it at home, in some shed."

He sank onto a bench, just as he was, in his cap, his fur coat, and his felt boots; his companion, the magistrate, sat down opposite him.

"These hysterical and neurasthenic people are great egoists," the doctor went on bitterly. "If a neurasthenic sleeps in the same room with you, he rustles his newspaper; when he dines with you, he has a row with his wife unrestrained by your presence; and when he feels like shooting himself, he shoots himself in village headquarters, so as to give everybody the greatest amount of trouble. Under all circumstances these gentlemen think only of themselves! That's why elderly people so dislike our 'nervous age.'"

"Elderly people dislike so many things," said the magistrate, yawning. "You ought to point out to the old fellows the difference between the suicides of the past and the suicides of the present. Formerly the so-called gentleman shot himself because he had embezzled Government funds, but nowadays it's because he's fed up with life, depressed. Which is better?"

"Fed up with life, depressed; but you must admit that he might have shot himself somewhere else than at the village headquarters."

"Such aggravation!" said the policeman, "such aggravation! It's a regular punishment. Folks are all upset, your honor; they've not slept these three nights. The children are crying. The cows ought to be milked but the women won't go to the barn—they're scared—that they may see the dead gentleman in the dark. Sure they're foolish women, but some of the men is scared, too. As soon as it's dark they won't pass the place alone, but only in a drove. And the witnesses too—"

Dr. Starchenko, a middle-aged, dark-bearded man in

spectacles, and the magistrate Lyzhin, a fair-haired man, still young, who had taken his degree only two years before and looked more like a student than an official, sat in silence, musing. They were annoyed at having been delayed. Now, although it was not yet six o'clock, they had to wait till morning, spending the night here; and they pictured a long evening, a long, dark night, boredom, wretched beds, cockroaches, morning chill; and listening to the storm that howled in the chimney and in the garret, they both thought how unlike all this was the life they would have wished for themselves and of which they had once dreamed, and how far away they both were from their contemporaries, who at that moment were walking about the lighted streets in town without noticing the weather, or getting ready for the theater, or sitting in their studies over a book. Oh, how much they would have given now only to stroll along the Nevsky or along Petrovka in Moscow, to listen to decent singing, to spend an hour or so in a restaurant!

Hoo-oo-oo! sang the storm in the garret, and something outside banged viciously, probably the signboard on the cottage. Hoo-oo-oo!

"You can do as you like, but I don't want to stay here," said Starchenko, getting up. "It's not six yet; it's too early to go to bed; I'll drive somewhere. Von Taunitz lives not far from here, only a couple of miles from Syrnya. I'll drive there and spend the evening with him. Officer, go and tell my coachman not to take the horses out. And what will you do?" he asked Lyzhin.

"I don't know; I'll probably go to sleep."

The doctor wrapped his fur coat round him and went out. He could be heard talking to the coachman and there was the sound of bells shaking on the frozen horses. He drove off.

"It's not right for you, sir, to spend the night in here," said the policeman. "Go into the other room. It's not clean there, but for one night it don't matter. I'll get a samovar from a peasant and heat it directly. I'll pile up some hay for you and then you can go to sleep, and God be with you, your honor."

A little later the magistrate was sitting at a table in the other room, drinking tea, while Loshadin the policeman stood at the door, talking. He was an old man of about sixty, short and very lean, hunched and white-haired, with a naive smile on his face and watery eyes; and he kept smacking his lips as though he were sucking a candy. He was wearing a short sheepskin coat and felt boots, and did not let his stick out of his hands. The magistrate's youth aroused his compassion and that was probably why he addressed him familiarly.

"Fyodor Makarych, the Elder, gave orders that he was to be informed when the police inspector or the examining magistrate came," he said, "so I reckon I must go now. It's nearly three miles to the district office, and the storm's bad, the snowdrifts are a caution—blamed if I'll get there before midnight. Listen to it howl!"

"I don't need the elder," said Lyzhin. "There's nothing for him to do here."

He looked at the old man with curiosity and asked:

"Tell me, grandfather, how many years is it you've been a policeman?"

"Why, about thirty. Five years after the Freedom[1] I got to be policeman, you can figure out for yourself. And I've been on the go every day since. People have holidays, but me, I'm always on the go. When it's Easter and the church bells are ringing and Christ has risen,

---

[1] The emancipation of the serfs, proclaimed in 1861.

I keep on trotting, with my bag. To the treasury, to the post office, to the police inspector's lodgings, to the district magistrate, to the tax collector, to the municipal office, to the gentry, to the peasants, to all Orthodox folk. I carry packages, notices, tax blanks, letters, all kinds of forms, reports, and you know, kind sir, your honor, they've got such forms nowadays to write numbers on —yellow, white, red—and every gentleman or priest or well-to-do peasant must write down a dozen times a year how much he has sown or harvested, how many bushels or poods he has of rye, how many of oats, and of hay, and all about the weather, you know, and insects, too, of all kinds. Of course you can write what you like, it's only a rule, but you must go and hand out the papers and then go and collect 'em again. Here, for instance, there's no call to cut open the gentleman; you know yourself it's all foolishness, you only dirty your hands, but here you've gone to the trouble, your honor, you've come because it's the rule, there's no getting round it. For thirty years I've been walking my legs off according to rule. In summer it's all right, it is warm and dry; but in winter and fall it puts you out. There were times I was drowning and times I was near froze to death; all kinds of things happened to me—wicked people in the woods took my bag away; I've got it in the neck and I've been brought to law."

"What for?"

"Fraud."

"What do you mean, fraud?"

"Why, you see, Khrisanf Grigoryev, the clerk, sold the contractor some boards as didn't belong to him— cheated him, that is. I was mixed up in it. They sent me to the tavern for vodka; well, the clerk didn't go shares with me—didn't even stand me a drink; but seeing as I'm a poor man, and so a no-account person, not to be

relied on—to look at, that is—we were both brought
to trial; he was sent to prison, but, praise God! I was
acquitted on all counts. They read a paper, you know,
in the court, about it. And they were all in uniform—in
the court, I mean. I can tell you, your honor, for anyone
not used to 'em, my duties are a caution, Lord keep you
from them; but me, I don't mind it. Matter of fact,
when I'm not on the go, my feet hurt. And at home it's
worse for me. At home you have to light the stove for
the clerk in the district office, to fetch water for him, to
clean his boots."

"And what's your salary?" Lyzhin asked.

"Eighty-four rubles a year."

"I'll bet there are other little sums coming in. There
are, aren't there?"

"Other little sums? No, indeed! Gentlemen nowadays
don't often give tips. Gentlemen is strict nowadays, they
take offense easy. If you bring him a paper, he's offended, if you take off your cap to him, he's offended.
'You used the wrong entrance,' he says. 'You're a drunkard,' he says. 'You smell of onion; you're a blockhead,'
he says; 'you're the son of a bitch.' There are some as is
decent, of course; but what does it get you? They only
laugh at you and call you names. Take Squire Altuhin,
for instance, he's good-natured; and to look at him, he's
sober and in his right mind, but as soon as he lays eyes
on me he shouts God knows what. The name he calls
me! 'You—' says he."

The policeman pronounced some word but in such a
low voice that it was impossible to make out what he
said.

"What?" asked Lyzhin. "Say it again."

"'Administration,'" the policeman repeated aloud.
"He's been calling me that for a long time, for maybe
six years. 'Hello, Administration!' But I don't mind; let

him, God bless him! A lady will send you a glass of vodka and a piece of pie sometimes, and you drink her health. But it's mostly the peasants that give me something; peasants are more warm-hearted, they fear God: one will give you a piece of bread, another some cabbage soup, and there's some as stand you a glass. The village Elders treat you to tea in the tavern. Here the inquest witnesses have gone to drink tea. 'Loshadin,' they says, 'you stay here and keep watch for us,' and each of 'em gives me a kopeck. They're scared, not being used to it, and yesterday they gave me fifteen kopecks and stood me a glass."

"And you, aren't you scared?"

"I am, sir; but of course it's all in the line of duty, there's no getting round it. Last year I was taking an arrested man into town and he laced into me and took it out of my hide! And all around us—fields, woods— how could I get away from him? And that's how it is here. I remember the gentleman, this Lesnitzky, when he was that high, and I knew his father and his mama. I am from the village of Nedoshchotova, and the Lesnitzkys, they weren't more than two thirds of a mile from us and even less, their land bordered on ours, and the old master, Lesnitzky, he had a sister, a God-fearing, charitable maiden lady. God rest the soul of Thy servant, Yulia, of sainted memory! She never married, and when she was dying she divided up all her property; she left two hundred and fifty acres to the monastery, and five hundred to our village commune for her soul's sake; but her brother, I mean the master, he hid the paper, they say he burnt it in the stove, and took all this land for himself. To be sure, he thought it would be to his benefit; but no, wait, you can't get on in the world by wrongdoing, brother. For twenty years the master didn't go to confession. There was something as kept him from church, you see, and he died without the sacrament. He busted. He was as fat as they come. He busted lengthwise. Then everything was taken away from Seryozha, the young master, I mean, to pay the debts—every last thing. Well, he hadn't got very far with his book learning, he couldn't do anything, and the president of the Zemstvo Board, his uncle, he says to himself: 'I'll take him'—Seryozha, I mean—'to be our agent; let him insure people, that's easy work.' And the gentleman was young and proud, he wanted to live in better style, on a grander scale, and have things his way; to be sure, it hurt his feelings to be jolting about the county in a trashy cart and talking to the peasants; he would walk and keep looking on the ground, looking on the ground and saying nothing; if you called him right in his ear, 'Sergey Sergeyich!' he would look round like this, 'Eh?' and stare at the ground again; and now you see he's laid hands on himself. It don't fit, your honor, it's wrong, this thing, and there's no understanding what goes on in the world, merciful Lord! Say your father was rich and you're poor; it's eating humble pie, no denying it, but there, you've got to put up with it. I used to live well, too, your honor; I had two horses, three cows, I used to keep twenty head of sheep; but that time's past, and here I am with nothing but a bag, and even that's not mine, it's the Government's. And now in our village, if the truth be told, my house is the worst of the lot. Mokey had four footmen to scrape and bow, Mokey is a footman himself now; Petrak had four workmen to dig and delve, and now Petrak is a workman himself."

"And how was it you came down in the world?" asked the magistrate.

"My sons are terrible boozers. They get so soused, so soused there's no saying what it's like, you wouldn't believe me."

Lyzhin listened and thought how he, Lyzhin, would go back to Moscow sooner or later, while this old man would stay here forever and would always be on the go. And how many times in his life he would come across such battered, unkempt, "no-account" old men, whose souls cherished equally the fifteen kopeck piece, the glass of vodka, and the profound belief that you can't get along in this world by wrongdoing.

Then he grew tired of listening, and told the old man to bring him some hay for his bed. In the traveler's room there was an iron bedstead with a pillow and a quilt, and it could have been brought in; but the deceased had been lying beside it for nearly three days (and he may have been sitting on it just before his death), and now it would be disagreeable to sleep on it.

"It's only half past seven," thought Lyzhin, glancing at his watch. "How awful!"

He was not sleepy, but having no means of passing the time, he lay down and covered himself with a plaid. Loshadin went in and out several times, clearing away the dishes; smacking his lips and sighing, he kept stomping about the table; at last he took his little lamp and went out, and looking at his long gray hair and bent body from behind, Lyzhin reflected: "Just like a magician in an opera."

It grew dark. The moon must have been behind the clouds, as the windows and the snow on the window-frames could be seen distinctly.

"Hoo-oo-oo!" sang the storm. "Hoo-oo-oo!"

"He-e-e-lp!" shrieked a woman in the garret, or so it sounded. "He-e-e-lp!"

Thump! something outside banged against the wall. Bang!

The magistrate listened; there was no woman up there, it was the wind wailing. It was chilly, and he put his fur coat over his plaid. As he got warm, he thought how all this—the blizzard, and the cottage, and the old man, and the dead body lying in the next room—how all this was remote from the life he desired for himself, and how alien it all was to him, how petty, uninteresting. If this man had killed himself in Moscow or somewhere near the city, and he had had to hold an inquest on him there, it would have been interesting, important, and perhaps it would have seemed terrible to sleep in the room next to that in which the corpse lay. Here, hundreds of miles from Moscow, all this appeared somehow in a different light; it was not life, not human beings, but something that existed "according to rule," as Loshadin said; it would not leave the faintest trace in the memory and would be forgotten as soon as he, Lyzhin, drove away from Syrnya. The fatherland, the real Russia, was Moscow, Petersburg; but these were the provinces, the colonies. When you dream of playing a part, of becoming known, of being, for instance, examining magistrate in important cases or prosecutor in a circuit court, of being a social lion, you inevitably think of Moscow. If you are to live, then it must be in Moscow; here, nothing matters to you; you get reconciled readily to your insignificant role, and only look for one thing in life—to get away, to get away as quickly as possible. And in his mind Lyzhin hurried through the Moscow streets, called on acquaintances, met relatives, colleagues, and his heart contracted sweetly at the thought that he was only twenty-six, and that if in five or ten years he could break away from here and get to Moscow, even then it would not be too late and he would still have a whole life ahead of him. And as he began to doze off, and as his thoughts became confused, he imagined the long corridors of the Moscow court, himself delivering a speech, his sisters, the orchestra which for some reason kept droning: Hoo-oo-oo! Hoo-oo-oo!

Thump! Bang! sounded again. Thump!

And he suddenly recalled how one day, when he was talking to the bookkeeper at the Zemstvo office, a thin pale gentleman with dark eyes and black hair came up to the counter; he had a disagreeable look in his eyes such as one sees in people who have slept too long after dinner, and it marred his delicate, intelligent profile; and the high boots that he was wearing did not suit him, they looked clumsy. The bookkeeper had introduced him: "This is our Zemstvo agent."

"So that was Lesnitzky—this very man," it now occurred to Lyzhin.

He recalled Lesnitzky's low voice, called to mind his gait, and it seemed to him that someone was walking beside him now with a step like Lesnitzky's.

All at once he was terrified, his head felt cold.

"Who's there?" he asked fearfully.

"The p'liceman!"

"What do you want here?"

"I've come to ask, your honor— You said this evening as the elder wasn't needed, but I'm afraid he'll be angry. He told me to let him know. Shouldn't I go?"

"The deuce, I'm fed up with you," said Lyzhin with vexation, and covered himself up again.

"Maybe he'll be angry. I'll go, your honor. I hope you'll be all right here."

And Loshadin went out. There was coughing and whispering in the entry. The inquest witnesses must have returned.

"We'll let these poor devils get off as early as possible tomorrow—" thought the examining magistrate; "we'll do the autopsy as soon as it's light."

He began to doze off when suddenly he again became conscious of steps, not timid this time, but quick and noisy. A door slammed, voices were heard, the scratching of a match. . . .

"Are you asleep? Are you asleep?" Dr. Starchenko asked hurriedly and crossly as he lit one match after another. He was covered with snow from head to foot and he had brought cold air in with him. "Are you asleep? Get up! Let's go to von Taunitz's. He's sent his horses to fetch you. Let's go. There you will have supper, at least, and sleep decently. You see I've come for you myself. The horses are excellent, we'll get there in twenty minutes."

"What time is it now?"

"Quarter past ten."

Lyzhin, sleepy and out of sorts, put on his felt boots, his fur coat, cap and hood, and went out with the doctor. The frost had abated, but a strong, piercing wind was blowing and chasing down the street clouds of snow that seemed to flee in terror; high drifts had already piled up against fences and on door-steps. The doctor and the magistrate got into the sleigh, and the white coachman bent over them to button up the apron. They were both hot.

"Go ahead!"

They drove through the village. "Cutting a fluffy furrow there," the magistrate quoted the poet to himself, as he listlessly watched the working of the outrunner's legs. There were lights in all the cabins, as though it were the eve of a high holiday: the peasants had stayed up because they were afraid of the dead man. The coachman sullenly held his peace, he must have turned glum while he was waiting at the village headquarters, and now he too was thinking of the deceased.

"When they found out at von Taunitz's," said Starchenko, "that you were spending the night in the village, they all attacked me for not having brought you along with me."

At the turning, as they left the village behind them, the coachman suddenly shouted at the top of his voice: "Get off the road!"

A man flashed by: he was standing in the snow up to his knees, having moved off the road, and was staring at the troika. The magistrate caught sight of a hooked staff, a beard, and a bag slung sideways, and it seemed to him that it was Loshadin, and he even fancied that the man was smiling. He flashed by and vanished.

The road at first skirted the forest, then, broadening, cut through it; old pines and a young birch grove shot past, as well as tall, gnarled young oaks standing singly in the clearings where the wood had recently been cut; but soon everything was lost in clouds of snow; the coachman said that he could see the forest, but the magistrate could see nothing but the outrunner. The wind blew at their backs.

Suddenly the horses stopped.

"Well, what now?" asked Starchenko crossly.

Without a word the coachman climbed down from the box and began to run around the sleigh on his heels; he made larger and larger circles, getting further and further away from the sleigh, and it looked as though he were dancing; finally he returned and began turning off to the right.

"You've lost your way, eh?" asked Starchenko.

"No ma-a-atter—"

They came to a hamlet with not a light in it. Then again, forest and fields. And again they lost their way, and the coachman climbed down from the box and performed his dance. The troika flew along a dark road under overarching trees, flew swiftly, and the hooves of the fiery outrunner knocked against the dashboard.

Here the trees roared fearfully and resonantly, and it was pitch dark, so that those in the sleigh felt as though they were rushing into an abyss. Suddenly bright light from an entrance and windows flashed upon their eyes, and they heard the friendly, steady barking of dogs and the sound of voices. They had arrived.

While they were taking off their fur coats and felt boots downstairs in the entry, *"Un petit verre de Clic-quot"* was being played on the piano upstairs, and the stamping of children's feet was heard. Immediately they were enveloped in the genial warmth and the smell peculiar to an old mansion where, whatever the weather, it is warm and clean and comfortable.

"That's splendid!" said von Taunitz, a fat man with an incredibly broad neck and sidewhiskers, pressing the magistrate's hand. "That's splendid! Glad to see you here, delighted to make your acquaintance. We're by way of being colleagues, you know. At one time I served as assistant prosecutor, but not for long, only two years. I came here to see to the estate, and I have grown old here—in a word, I'm an old fogey. Glad to see you here," he continued, obviously controlling his voice so as not to speak loudly; he and his guests were on their way upstairs. "I have no wife. She died. But here are my daughters, let me introduce you," and turning round, he shouted downstairs in a stentorian voice, "Tell Ignat to have the sleigh ready by eight o'clock tomorrow!"

In the drawing room were his four daughters, young, pretty girls, all in gray dresses and with their hair done in the same style, and their cousin, also young and attractive, with her children. Starchenko, who was already acquainted with them, at once began begging them to sing something, and two of the young ladies kept on declaring that they could not sing and had no music; then the cousin sat down at the piano and with quavering voices they sang a duet from "The Queen of Spades." Again *"Un petit verre de Clicquot"* was played, and the children danced about, stamping their feet in time. And Starchenko pranced about, too. Everybody laughed.

Then the children said good night and went off to bed. The magistrate laughed, danced a quadrille, paid court to the ladies, and kept wondering whether it were not all a dream. The wretched room at the village headquarters, the pile of hay in the corner, the rustle of the cockroaches, the disgusting, poverty-stricken setting, the voices of the inquest witnesses, the wind, the blizzard, the danger of getting lost; and suddenly these magnificent, bright rooms, the sound of the piano, the beautiful girls, the curly-headed children, the gay, happy laughter—such a transformation seemed to him like what happens in a fairy tale, and it seemed incredible that such transformations were possible within a distance of two miles in the course of a single hour. And dismal thoughts prevented him from enjoying himself, and he kept thinking that all about him was not life but scraps of life, fragments, that everything here was accidental, that one could draw no conclusion from it; and he even felt sorry for these girls, who were living and would die here in the wilds, in the provinces, far away from civilization where nothing is accidental, but everything is rational and governed by law, and where, for example, every suicide is intelligible, and it is possible to explain its why and wherefore and its significance in the general scheme of things. It occurred to him that since the life about him here in the wilds was unintelligible to him, and since he did not see it, it meant that it was nonexistent.

At supper the talk was of Lesnitzky.

"He left a wife and child," said Starchenko. "I would forbid marriage to neurasthenics and people with a deranged nervous system, I would deprive them of the right and the capacity to have offspring. To bring neurasthenic children into the world is a crime."

"The unfortunate young man," said von Taunitz, sighing gently and shaking his head. "How much thinking you must do, how much suffering you must go through before you decide to take your own life—a young life! A misfortune like that can happen in any family, and that's terrible. It's hard to bear it, intolerable."

All the girls listened silently, with grave faces, looking at their father. On his part, Lyzhin felt that he ought to say something, but he couldn't think of anything, and merely observed:

"Yes, suicide is an undesirable phenomenon."

He slept in a warm room, in a soft bed, covered with a blanket, under which was a fine clean sheet, but for some reason did not feel comfortable; perhaps it was because the doctor and von Taunitz were talking for a long time in the next room, and overhead, in the attic and in the chimney, the wind was roaring just as it did at the village headquarters and howling as plaintively: Hoo-oo-oo-oo!

Von Taunitz's wife had died two years previously, and he had not yet reconciled himself to the fact, and no matter what he talked about, he always referred to his wife; and there was nothing about him to suggest the public prosecutor any more.

"Is it possible that I may get into such a state some day?" thought Lyzhin, as he was falling asleep and as he listened through the wall to his host's subdued and, as it were, orphaned voice.

The magistrate's sleep was restless. He was hot and uncomfortable, and he dreamed that he was not at von

Taunitz's, not in the soft clean bed, but still at the village headquarters, lying on the hay, and hearing the low voices of the witnesses; he imagined that Lesnitzky was near by, fifteen paces away. In his dream he recalled how the insurance agent, black-haired, pale, wearing high, dusty boots, had approached the bookkeeper's counter. "This is our insurance agent—" Then he dreamed that Lesnitzky and Loshadin the policeman were walking through the open country in the snow, side by side, supporting each other; the blizzard was eddying above them, and the wind was blowing at their backs, but they walked on, chanting, "We go on, go on, go on. . . ."

The old man looked like a magician in an opera, and indeed both of them looked as though they were performing in a theater:

"We go on, go on, go on! You are where it is warm and bright and cozy, but we go on in the cold, in the storm, through deep snow. We know nothing of rest, we know nothing of joy. We carry the whole burden of this life, of ours and yours. Hoo-oo-oo! We go on, go on, go on . . ."

Lyzhin woke and sat up in bed. What a muddled, bad dream! And why did he couple the policeman and the agent in his dream? What nonsense! And now, as Lyzhin sat up in bed, clasping his head in his hands, his heart beating wildly, it seemed that indeed the lives of the policeman and the insurance agent had something in common. Didn't they go through life side by side, holding on to one another? Some tie, invisible yet significant and essential, existed between the two of them, even between them and von Taunitz, and among all, all; in this life, even in these wilds, nothing is accidental, everything is filled with one common idea, everything has one soul, one aim, and to understand it, it is not

enough to think, to reason, perhaps one must also have
the gift of insight into life, a gift which evidently is not
vouchsafed to all. And the unhappy "neurasthenic"—as
the doctor called him—who had broken down and
killed himself, as well as the old peasant who spent his
whole life trotting from one man to another every day,
were accidents, fragments of life, only for him who
thought of his own life as accidental, but were parts of
one marvelous and rational organism for one who regarded his own life as part of that common whole, and
had a penetrating insight into that fact. So Lyzhin
thought, and it was a thought that he had long secretly
harbored and that only now unfolded fully and distinctly in his consciousness.

He lay down and began to drop off; and suddenly
they were again walking along together and chanting:
"We go on, go on, go on. . . . We take from life all
that it holds of what is most bitter and burdensome, and
we leave to you what is easy and joyous; and sitting at
supper, you can discuss coldly and reasonably why we
suffer and perish, and why we are not as healthy and
contented as you."

What they were chanting had occurred to him before,
but this thought crouched somewhere in the background
behind other thoughts and flickered timidly like a distant light in misty weather. And he felt that this suicide
and the peasant's misery lay on his conscience, too; to
be reconciled to the fact that these people, submitting to
their fate, shouldered all that was darkest and most burdensome in life—how terrible that was! To be reconciled to this, and to wish for oneself a bright and active
life among happy, contented people, and constantly to
dream of such a life, that meant dreaming of new suicides of men crushed by toil and care, or of weak, forgotten men of whom people only talk sometimes at

supper with vexation or sneers, but to whom no help is offered. And again:

"We go on, go on, go on. . . ."

As though someone were knocking with a little hammer on his temples.

He woke early in the morning with a headache, roused by a noise; in the next room von Taunitz was saying to the doctor in a loud voice:

"You can't leave now. Look at what's doing outdoors. Don't argue, but just ask the coachman: he won't drive you in such weather if you pay him a million."

"But it's only two miles," the doctor was saying in an imploring voice.

"But even if it were a quarter of a mile. If you can't, you can't. As soon as you drive out of the gates, it will be just hell, you will lose your way in a minute. I won't let you go, no matter what you say."

"By evening it's bound to quiet down," said the peasant who was lighting the stove.

In the next room the doctor began talking of the severe climate that influences the Russian character, of the long winters that, restricting freedom of movement, interfere with the intellectual growth of the people; and Lyzhin heard these pronouncements with vexation, looked out of the window at the drifts that had piled up against the fence, stared at the white dust that filled all visible space, at the trees that bent despairing now to the right, now to the left, listened to the howling and the banging, and thought gloomily:

"Well, what moral can you draw from all this? It's a blizzard, and that's all there is to it . . ."

They lunched at noon, then wandered aimlessly about the house; they stood at the windows.

"And Lesnitzky is lying there," thought Lyzhin, as he watched the snow eddies furiously circling above the

drifts. "Lesnitzky is lying there, and the inquest witnesses are waiting—"

They spoke of the weather, remarking that the snowstorm usually lasted two days and two nights, rarely
longer. At six they dined, then they played cards, sang,
danced; finally they had supper. The day was over, they
went to bed.

In the small hours of the morning everything quieted
down. When they got up and looked out of the windows,
the naked willows with their weakly drooping branches
were standing quite motionless; the sky was overcast
and the air was still, as though nature were now
ashamed of its orgy, its mad nights, and the free rein it
had given its passions. The horses, harnessed tandem,
had been waiting at the steps since five o'clock in the
morning. When it was fully light the doctor and the
magistrate put on their fur coats and felt boots, and taking leave of their host, went out.

At the steps beside the coachman stood our policeman, Ilya Loshadin, hatless, with his old leather bag
slung over his shoulder, covered with snow all over; his
face was red and wet with perspiration. The footman
who had gone out to help the guests into the sleigh and
cover their legs, looked at him severely and said:

"What are you standing here for, you old devil? Go
chase yourself!"

"Your honor, folks are uneasy," said Loshadin, a naive
smile spreading over his face, and evidently glad to see
at last the men he had been waiting for so long. "Folks
are very uneasy, the children are crying. They thought,
your honor, as you had gone back to the town again.
Show us the mercy of heaven, kind gentlemen!"

The doctor and the magistrate said nothing, got into
the sleigh, and drove off to Syrnya.

1899

In the Ravine

THE village of Ukleyevo lay in a ravine, so that only the belfry and the chimneys of the cotton mills could be seen from the highroad and the railway station. When visitors asked what village this was, they were told:

"That's the village where the sexton ate all the caviar at the funeral."

It had happened at a funeral feast in the house of the manufacturer Kostukov that the old sexton saw among the savories some large-grained caviar and began eating it greedily; people nudged him, tugged at his sleeve, but he seemed petrified with enjoyment: felt nothing, and only went on eating. He ate up all the caviar, and there were some four pounds in the jar. And years had passed since then, the sexton had long been dead, but the caviar was still remembered. Whether life was so poor here or people had not been clever enough to notice anything but that unimportant incident that had occurred ten years before, anyway the people had nothing else to tell about the village of Ukleyevo.

The village was never free from fever, and the mud was thick there even in the summer, especially near the fences over which hung old willow-trees that gave deep shade. Here there was always a smell from the factory refuse and the acetic acid which was used in the manufacture of the calico.

The three cotton mills and the tanyard were not in the village itself, but a little way off. They were small plants, and not more than four hundred workmen were employed in all of them. The tanyard often made the water in the little river stink; the refuse contaminated the meadows, the peasants' cattle suffered from anthrax, and the tanyard was ordered closed. It was considered to be closed but went on working in secret with the connivance of the local police officer and the district doctor, each of whom was paid ten rubles a month by the owner. In the whole village there were only two decent houses built of brick with iron roofs; one of them was occupied by the district government office, in the other, a two-storied house just opposite the church, lived Grigory Petrovich Tzybukin, a townsman who hailed from Yepifan.

Grigory kept a grocery, but that was only for the sake of appearances: in reality he sold vodka, cattle, hides, grain, and pigs; he traded in anything that came to hand, and when, for instance, magpies were wanted abroad for ladies' hats, he made thirty kopecks on every pair of birds; he bought timber for felling, lent money at interest, and altogether was a resourceful old man.

He had two sons. The elder, Anisim, served in the police as a detective and was rarely at home. The younger, Stepan, had gone in for trade and helped his father, but no great help was expected from him as he was weak in health and deaf; his wife Aksinya, a handsome woman with a good figure, who wore a hat and carried a parasol on holidays, got up early and went to bed late, and ran about all day long, picking up her skirts and jingling her keys, going from the warehouse to the cellar and from there to the shop, and old Tzybukin looked at her good-humoredly while his eyes glowed, and at such moments he regretted she had not been married to his elder son instead of to the younger one, who was deaf, and obviously no judge of female beauty.

The old man had always had an inclination for family life, and he loved his family more than anything on earth, especially his elder son, the detective, and his daughter-in-law. Aksinya had no sooner married the deaf son than she began to display an extraordinary gift for business, and knew who could be allowed to run up a bill and who could not; she kept the keys and would not trust them even to her husband; she rattled away at the abacus, looked at the horses' teeth like a peasant, and was always laughing or shouting; and whatever she did or said, the old man was simply delighted and muttered:

"Well done, daughter-in-law! Well done, my beauty!"

He had been a widower, but a year after his son's marriage he could not resist getting married himself. A girl was found for him, in a village twenty miles from Ukleyevo, Varvara Nikolaevna by name, no longer young, but good-looking, comely, and coming from a decent family. No sooner had she moved into a little room in the upper story than everything in the house seemed to brighten up as though new glass had been put into all the windows. The lamps gleamed before the icons, the tables were covered with snow-white cloths, plants with red buds made their appearance in the windows and in the front garden, and at dinner, instead of eating from a single bowl, each person had a separate plate set for him. Varvara Nikolaevna had a pleasant, friendly smile, and it seemed as though the whole house were smiling too. Beggars and pilgrims, male and female, began to come into the yard, a thing which had never happened in the past; the plaintive sing-song voices of the Ukleyevo peasant women and the apologetic coughs of weak, seedy-looking men, who had been dismissed from the factory for drunkenness were heard under the windows. Varvara helped them with money, with bread, with old clothes, and afterwards, when she felt more at home, began taking things out of the shop. One day the deaf man saw her take four ounces of tea and that disturbed him.

"Here, mother's taken four ounces of tea," he informed his father afterwards; "where is that to be entered?"

The old man made no reply but stood still and thought a moment, moving his eyebrows, and then went upstairs to his wife.

"Varvarushka, if you want anything out of the shop," he said affectionately, "take it, my dear. Take it and welcome; don't hesitate."

And the next day the deaf man, running across the yard, called to her:

"If there is anything you want, mother dear, help yourself."

There was something new, something gay and light-hearted in her alms-giving, just as there was in the lamps before the icons and in the red flowers. When on the eve of a fast or during the local church festival, which lasted three days, they palmed off on the peasants tainted salt meat, smelling so strong it was hard to stand near the tub of it, and took scythes, caps, and their wives' kerchiefs in pledge from the drunken men; when the factory hands, stupefied with bad vodka, lay rolling in the mud, and sin seemed to hover thick like a fog in the air, then it was a relief to think that up there in the house there was a gentle, neatly dressed woman who had nothing to do with salt meat or vodka; her charity had in those oppressive, murky days the effect of a safety valve in a machine.

The days in Tzybukin's house were busy ones. Before the sun was up Aksinya was snorting as she washed in the outer room, and the samovar was boiling in the kitchen with a hum that boded no good. Old Grigory Petrovich, dressed in a long black jacket, cotton breeches and shiny top boots, looking a dapper little figure, walked about the rooms, tapping with his little heels like the father-in-law in the well-known song. The shop was opened. When it was daylight a racing droshky was brought up to the front door and the old man got jauntily into it, pulling his big cap down to his ears; and, looking at him, no one would have said he was fifty-six. His wife and daughter-in-law saw him off, and at such times when he had on a good, clean coat, and a huge black stallion that had cost three hundred rubles was harnessed to the droshky, the old man did not like the peasants to come up to him with their complaints and petitions; he hated the peasants and disdained them, and if he saw some peasants waiting at the gate, he would shout angrily:

"Why are you standing there? Move on."

Or if it were a beggar, he would cry:

"God will provide!"

He would drive off on business; his wife, in a dark dress and a black apron, tidied the rooms or helped in the kitchen. Aksinya attended to the shop, and from the yard could be heard the clink of bottles and of money, her laughter and loud talk, and the angry voices of customers whom she had offended; and at the same time it could be seen that the illicit sale of vodka was already going on in the shop. The deaf man sat in the shop, too, or walked about the street bareheaded, with his hands in his pockets looking absent-mindedly now at the houses, now at the sky overhead. Six times a day they had tea; four times a day they sat down to meals. And in the evening they counted their takings, put them down, went to bed, and slept soundly.

All the three cotton mills at Ukleyevo were connected by telephone with the houses of their owners—Hrymin Seniors, Hrymin Juniors, and Kostukov. A telephone was installed in the government office, too, but it soon went out of order when it started to swarm with bugs and cockroaches. The district elder was semiliterate and wrote every word in the official documents with a capital. But when the telephone went out of order he said:

"Yes, now we shall be badly off without a telephone."

The Hrymin Seniors were continually at law with the Juniors, and sometimes the Juniors quarreled among themselves and went to law, and their mill did not work for a month or two till they were reconciled again, and this was an entertainment for the people of Ukleyevo, as there was a great deal of talk and gossip on the occasion of each quarrel. On holidays Kostukov and the Juniors would go driving and they would dash about Ukleyevo and run down calves. Aksinya, dressed to kill and rustling her starched petticoats, used to promenade up and down the street near her shop; the Juniors would snatch her up and carry her off as though by force. Then old Tzybukin, too, would drive out to show his new horse and he would take Varvara with him.

In the evening, after these drives, when people were going to bed, an expensive concertina was played in the Juniors' yard and, if the moon was shining, those strains thrilled the heart, and Ukleyevo no longer seemed a wretched hole.

II

The elder son, Anisim, came home very rarely, only on great holidays, but he often sent by a returning villager presents and letters written by someone else in a very beautiful hand, always on a sheet of foolscap that looked like a formal petition. The letters were full of expressions that Anisim never made use of in conversation: "Dear papa and mamma, I send you a pound of orange pekoe tea for the satisfaction of your physical needs."

At the bottom of every letter was scratched, as though with a broken pen: "Anisim Tzybukin," and again in the same excellent hand: "Agent."

The letters were read aloud several times, and the old father, touched, red with emotion, would say:

"Here he did not care to stay at home, he has gone in for a learned profession. Well, let him go his way! Every man to his own trade!"

It happened that just before Carnival there was a heavy rain mixed with sleet; the old man and Varvara went to the window to look at it, and, lo and behold! Anisim drove up in a sledge from the station. He was quite unexpected. He came indoors, looking anxious and troubled about something, and he remained the same for the rest of his stay; there was something jaunty in his manner. He was in no haste to go away, and it looked as though he had been dismissed from the service. Varvara was pleased to see him; she kept looking at him with a sly expression, sighing, and shaking her head.

"How is this, my friends?" she said. "The lad's in his twenty-eighth year, and he is still leading a gay bachelor life; tut, tut, tut. . . ."

From the adjacent room her soft, even speech continued to sound like tut, tut, tut. She began whispering with her husband and Aksinya, and their faces, too, assumed a sly and mysterious expression as though they were conspirators.

It was decided to marry Anisim.

"The younger brother has long been married," said Varvara, "and you are still without a helpmate like a cock at a fair. What is the meaning of it? Tut, tut, you will be married, please God, then as you choose—you can go into the service and your wife will remain here at home to help us. There is no order in your life, young man, and I see you have forgotten how to live properly. Tut, tut, all of you townspeople are sinners."

Since the Tzybukins were rich, the prettiest girls were chosen as brides for them. For Anisim, too, they found a handsome one. He was himself of an uninteresting and inconspicuous appearance; of a weak and sickly constitution and short stature; he had full, puffy cheeks which looked as though he were blowing them out; there was a sharp look in his unblinking eyes; his beard was red and scanty, and when he was thinking he always put it into his mouth and bit it; moreover he drank and that was noticeable from his face and his walk. But when he was informed that they had found a very beautiful bride for him, he said:

"Oh well, I am not a fright myself. All of us Tzybukins are handsome, I must say."

The village of Torguyevo was near the town. Half of it had lately been incorporated into the town, the other half remained a village. In the first half there was a widow living in her own little house; she had a sister living with her who was quite poor and went out to work by the day, and this sister had a daughter called Lipa, a girl who went out to work too. People in Torguyevo were already talking about Lipa's good looks, but her terrible poverty put everyone off; people opined that only some widower or elderly man would marry her in spite of her poverty, or would perhaps take her to himself without marriage, and that her mother would get enough to eat living with her. Varvara heard about Lipa from the matchmakers, and she drove over to Tor-guyevo.

Then a proper visit of inspection was arranged at the house of the girl's aunt, with refreshments and wine, and Lipa wore a new pink dress made on purpose for this occasion, and a crimson ribbon like a flame gleamed in her hair. She was pale, thin, and frail, with soft, delicate features sunburnt from working in the open air; a shy, mournful smile always hovered about her face, and there was a childlike look in her eyes, trustful and curious.

She was young, still a child, her bosom still scarcely perceptible, but she could be married because she had reached the legal age. She really was beautiful, and the only thing that might be thought unattractive was her big masculine hands which hung idle now like two big claws.

"There is no dowry—but we don't mind that," said Tzybukin to the aunt. "We took a wife from a poor family for our son Stepan, too, and now we can't say too much for her. In the house and in the shop alike she has hands of gold."

Lipa stood in the doorway and looked as though she would say: "Do with me as you will, I trust you," while her mother Praskovya the charwoman hid in the kitchen numb with shyness. At one time in her youth a merchant whose floors she was scrubbing stamped at her in a rage; she went chill with terror and there always was a feeling of fear at the bottom of her heart. And that fear made her arms and legs tremble and her cheeks twitch. Sitting in the kitchen she tried to hear what the visitors were saying, and she kept crossing herself, pressing her fingers to her forehead, and gazing at the icons. Anisim, slightly drunk, would open the door into the kitchen and say in a free-and-easy way:

"Why are you sitting in here, precious mamma? We are dull without you."

And Praskovya, overcome with timidity, pressing her hands to her lean, wasted bosom, would say:

"Oh, not at all. . . . It's very kind of you, sir."

After the visit of inspection the wedding day was fixed. Then Anisim walked about the rooms at home whistling, or suddenly thinking of something, would fall to brooding and would look at the floor fixedly, silently, as though he would probe to the depths of the earth. He expressed neither pleasure that he was to be married, married so soon, the week after Easter, nor a desire to see his bride, but simply went on whistling. And it was evident that he was only getting married because his father and stepmother wished him to, and because it was the village custom to marry off the son in order to have a woman to help in the house. When he went away he seemed in no haste, and behaved altogether not as he had done on previous visits; he was unusually jaunty and talked inappropriately.

III

In the village of Shikalova lived two dressmakers, sisters, belonging to the Flagellant sect. The new clothes for the wedding were ordered from them, and they often came to try them on, and stayed a long while drinking tea. They were making for Varvara a brown dress with black lace and bugles on it, and for Aksinya a light green dress with a yellow front, and a train. When the dressmakers had finished their work Tzybukin paid them not in money but in goods from the shop, and they went away depressed, carrying parcels of tallow candles and tins of sardines which they did not in the least need, and when they got out of the village into the open country they sat down on a hillock and cried.

Anisim arrived three days before the wedding, rigged out in new clothes from top to toe. He had dazzling indiarubber galoshes, and instead of a cravat wore a red cord with little balls on it, and over his shoulder he had hung an overcoat, also new, without putting his arms into the sleeves.

After crossing himself sedately before the icon, he greeted his father and gave him ten silver rubles and ten half-rubles; to Varvara he gave as much, and to Aksinya twenty quarter-rubles. The chief charm of the present lay in the fact that all the coins, as though carefully matched, were new and glittered in the sun. Trying to seem grave and sedate he screwed up his face and puffed out his cheeks, and he smelled of spirits: he must have visited the refreshment bar at every station. And again there was something free-and-easy about the man —something superfluous and out of place. Then Anisim had a bite and drank tea with the old man, and Varvara kept turning the new coins over in her hands and inquired about villagers who had gone to live in the town.

"They are all right, thank God, they get on quite well," said Anisim. "Only something has happened to Ivan Yegorov: his old woman, Sofya Nikiforovna, is dead. Of consumption. They ordered the memorial dinner for the peace of her soul from the confectioner's at two and a half rubles a head. And there was wine. There were peasants from our village, and Yegorov paid two and a half rubles for them, too. They didn't eat a thing, though. What does a peasant understand about sauces!"

"Two and a half rubles!" said his father, shaking his head.

"Well, it's not like the country there. You go into a

restaurant to have a snack, you order one thing and another, a crowd collects, you have a drink—and before you know it it is daylight and you've three or four rubles each to pay. And when you are with Samorodov he likes to have coffee with cognac in it after everything, and cognac is sixty kopecks a little glass."

"And he is making it all up," said the old man delightedly; "he is making it all up!"

"I am always with Samorodov now. It's Samorodov who writes my letters to you. He writes splendidly. And if I were to tell you, mamma," Anisim went on gaily, addressing Varvara, "the sort of fellow that Samorodov is, you would not believe me. We call him Muhtar, because he is black like an Armenian. I can see through him, I know all his affairs as well as I know the five fingers of my hand, and he feels that, and he always follows me about, we're as thick as thieves. He seems not to like it in a way, but he can't get on without me. Where I go he goes. I have a true sharp eye, mamma. I see a peasant selling a shirt at the rag fair, 'Stay, that shirt was stolen.' And really it turns out it is so: the shirt was stolen."

"How can you tell?" asked Varvara.

"I just know it, I have just an eye for it. I know nothing about the shirt, only for some reason I seem drawn to it: it's stolen, and that's all I can say. The boys in the department have got a saying: 'Oh, Anisim has gone to shoot snipe!' That means looking for stolen goods. Yes. . . . Anybody can steal, but it is another thing to keep what you've stolen! The earth is wide, but there is no place on it to hide stolen goods."

"A ram and two ewes were carried off from the Guntorevs' last week," said Varvara, and she heaved a sigh, "and there is no one to try and find them. . . . Oh, oh, oh . . ."

"Well, I might have a try. I could do that."

The day of the wedding arrived. It was a cool but bright, cheerful April day. Since early morning people were driving about Ukleyevo in carriages drawn by teams of two or three horses, the bells jingling, and gay ribbons decorating the yokes and manes. The rooks, disturbed by this activity, were cawing noisily in the willows, and the starlings sang their loudest unceasingly as though rejoicing that there was a wedding at the Tzybukins'.

Indoors the tables were already loaded with long fish, smoked hams, stuffed fowls, boxes of sprats, pickled savories of various sorts, and many bottles of vodka and wine; there was a smell of smoked sausage and of sour lobster. Old Tzybukin walked about near the tables, tapping with his heels and sharpening the knives against each other. They kept calling Varvara and asking for things, and she, breathless and distraught, was constantly running in and out of the kitchen, where the man cook from Kostukov's and a woman cook employed by Hrymin Juniors had been at work since early morning. Aksinya, with her hair curled, in her stays without her dress on, in new creaky boots, flew about the yard like a whirlwind showing glimpses of her bare knees and bosom. It was noisy, there was a sound of scolding and oaths; passers-by stopped at the wide-open gates, and in everything there was a feeling that something extraordinary was happening.

"They have gone for the bride!"

The carriage bells jingled and died away far beyond the village. . . . Between two and three o'clock people ran up: again there was a jingling of bells: they were bringing the bride! The church was full, the candelabra were lighted, the choir were singing from music books as old Tzybukin had wished it. The glare of the lights and the bright-colored dresses dazzled Lipa; she felt as though the singers with their loud voices were hitting her on the head with hammers. The stays, which she had put on for the first time in her life, and her shoes pinched her, and her face looked as though she had only just come to herself after fainting; she gazed about without understanding. Anisim, in his black coat with a red cord instead of a tie, stared at the same spot lost in thought, and at every loud burst of singing hurriedly crossed himself. He felt touched and disposed to weep. This church was familiar to him from earliest childhood; at one time his dead mother used to bring him here to take the sacrament; at one time he used to sing in the choir; every icon he remembered so well, every corner. Here he was being married, he had to take a wife for the sake of doing the proper thing, but he was not thinking of that now, he had somehow forgotten his wedding completely. Tears dimmed his eyes so that he could not see the icons, he felt heavy at heart; he prayed and besought God that the misfortunes that threatened him, that were ready to burst upon him tomorrow, if not today, might somehow pass him by as storm-clouds in time of drought pass over a village without yielding one drop of rain. And so many sins were heaped up in the past, so many sins and getting away from them or wiping them out was so beyond hope that it seemed incongruous even to ask forgiveness. But he did ask forgiveness, and even gave a loud sob, but no one took any notice of that, since they supposed he had had a drop too much.

There was the sound of a fretful childish wail:

"Take me away from here, mamma darling!"

"Quiet there!" cried the priest.

When the young couple returned from the church people ran after them; there were crowds, too, round

the shop, round the gates, and in the yard under the
windows. Peasant women came to sing songs in their
honor. The young couple had scarcely crossed the threshold when the choristers, who were already standing in
the outer room with their music books, broke into a
chant at the top of their voices; a band brought expressly
from the town struck up. Sparkling Don wine was
brought in tall glasses, and Yelizarov, a carpenter who
was also a contractor, a tall, gaunt old man with eyebrows so bushy that his eyes could scarcely be seen,
said, addressing the pair:

"Anisim and you, my child, love one another, lead a
godly life, little children, and the Heavenly Mother will
not abandon you."

He fell upon the old father's shoulder and gave a sob.

"Grigory Petrovich, let us weep, let us weep with
joy!" he said in a thin voice, and then at once burst out
laughing and continued in a loud bass. "Ho-ho-ho! This
one, too, is a fine daughter-in-law for you! Everything is
in its place in her; everything runs smoothly, no creaking, the whole mechanism works well, lots of screws in
it."

He was a native of the Yegoryev district, but had
worked in the mills at Ukleyevo and in the neighborhood since his youth, and had made it his home. For
years he had been a familiar figure, as old and gaunt and
lanky as now, and for years he had had the nickname
"Crutch." Perhaps because he had done nothing but
repair work for forty years, he judged everybody and
everything by its soundness, always asking himself if
things were in need of repair. Before sitting down to
table he tried several chairs to see whether they were
solid, and he touched the smoked white-fish, too.

After the Don wine, they all sat down to table. The
visitors talked, moving their chairs. The choristers were

singing in the outer room. The band was playing, and at the same time the peasant women in the yard were singing their songs in unison, and there was an awful, wild medley of sounds which made one giddy.

Crutch fidgeted about on his chair and prodded his neighbors with his elbows, prevented people from talking, and laughed and cried alternately.

"Children, children, children," he muttered rapidly. "Aksinya my dear, Varvara darling, let's all live in peace and harmony, my dear little hatchets . . ."

He drank little and was now drunk from only one glass of English bitters. The revolting bitters, made from nobody knows what, intoxicated everyone who drank it, stunning them as it were. Tongues began to falter.

The local clergy were present, and the clerks from the mills with their wives, tradesmen and tavern-keepers from the other villages. The clerk and the elder of the rural district who had served together for fourteen years, and who had during all that time never signed a single document for anybody or let a single person out of the office without deceiving or insulting him, were sitting now side by side, both fat and replete, and it seemed as though they were so steeped in injustice and falsehood that even the skin of their faces had a peculiar, thievish look. The clerk's wife, a thin woman with a squint, brought all her children with her, and like a bird of prey looked aslant at the plates, snatched everything she could get hold of and put it in her own or her children's pockets.

Lipa sat as though turned to stone, still with the same expression as in church. Anisim had not said a single word to her since he had made her acquaintance, so that he did not yet know the sound of her voice; and now, sitting beside her, he remained mute and went on drink-

ing bitters, and when he got drunk he began talking to
Lipa's aunt sitting opposite:

"I have a friend called Samorodov. A peculiar man.
He is by rank an honorary citizen, and he can talk. But
I know him through and through, auntie, and he knows
it. Pray join me in drinking to Samorodov's health,
auntie!"

Varvara, worn out and distracted, walked round the
table, pressing the guests to eat, and was evidently
pleased that there were so many dishes and that everything was so lavish—no one could disparage them now.
The sun set, but the dinner went on: the guests were
beyond knowing what they were eating or drinking, it
was impossible to distinguish what was said, and only
from time to time when the band subsided some peasant
woman could be heard shouting outside:

"You've sucked the blood out of us, you plunderers; a
plague on you!"

In the evening they danced to the band. The Hrymin
Juniors came, bringing wine of their own, and one of
them, when dancing a quadrille, held a bottle in each
hand and a wineglass in his mouth, and that made everyone laugh. In the middle of the quadrille they suddenly
crooked their knees and danced in a squatting position;
Aksinya in green flew by like a flash, raising a wind with
her train. Someone trod on her flounce and Crutch
shouted:

"Hey, they have torn off the baseboard! Children!"

Aksinya had naive gray eyes which rarely blinked,
and a naive smile played continually on her face. And
in those unblinking eyes, and in that little head on the
long neck, and in her slenderness there was something
snakelike; all in green, with her yellow bosom and the
smile on her lips, she looked like a viper that peers out of

the young rye in the spring at the passers-by, stretching itself and lifting its head. The Hrymins were free in their behavior to her, and it was very noticeable that she had long been on intimate terms with the eldest of them. But her deaf husband saw nothing, he did not look at her; he sat with his legs crossed and ate nuts, cracking them so loudly that it sounded like pistol shots.

But, behold, old Tzybukin himself walked into the middle of the room and waved his handkerchief as a sign that he, too, wanted to dance the Russian dance, and all over the house and from the crowd in the yard rose a hum of approbation:

"It's *himself* has stepped out! *Himself!*"

Varvara danced, but the old man only waved his handkerchief and kicked up his heels, but the people in the yard, propped against one another, peeping in at the windows, were in raptures, and for the moment forgave him everything—his wealth and the wrongs he had done them.

"Well done, Grigory Petrovich!" was heard in the crowd. "Go it! You can still do it! Ha-ha!"

It was kept up till late, till two o'clock in the morning. Anisim, staggering, went to take leave of the singers and musicians, and gave each of them a new half-ruble. His father, who was not staggering but treading more heavily on one leg, saw his guests off, and said to each of them:

"The wedding has cost two thousand."

As the party was breaking up, someone took the Shikalova innkeeper's good coat instead of his own old one, and Anisim suddenly flew into a rage and began shouting:

"Stop, I'll find it at once; I know who stole it! Stop!"

He ran out into the street in pursuit of someone, but he was caught, brought back home, shoved, drunken, red with anger and wet, into the room where the aunt was undressing Lipa, and was locked in.

IV

Five days had passed. Anisim, who was ready to leave, went upstairs to say good-by to Varvara. All the lamps were burning before the icons, there was a smell of incense, while she sat at the window knitting a stocking of red wool.

"You have not stayed with us long," she said. "You're bored, I suppose. Tut, tut, tut. . . . We live comfortably; we have plenty of everything. We celebrated your wedding properly, in good style; your father says it came to two thousand. In fact we live like merchants, only it's dreary here. We treat the people very badly. My heart aches, my dear; how we treat them, my goodness! Whether we barter a horse or buy something or hire a laborer—it's cheating in everything. Cheating and cheating. The hempseed oil in the shop is bitter, rancid, worse than pitch. But surely, tell me pray, couldn't we sell good oil?"

"Every man to his trade, mamma."

"But you know we all have to die? Oh, oh, really you ought to talk to your father . . . !"

"Why, you should talk to him yourself."

"Well, well, I did put in a word, but he said just what you do: 'Every man to his own trade.' Do you suppose in the next world they'll consider what trade you have been put to? God's judgment is just."

"Of course, they won't consider," said Anisim, and he heaved a sigh. "There is no God, anyway, you know, mamma, so what considering can there be?"

Varvara looked at him with surprise, burst out laughing, and struck her hands together. Perhaps because she was so genuinely surprised at his words and looked at him as though he were queer, he was embarrassed.

"Perhaps there is a God, only there is no faith. When I was being married I was not myself. Just as you may take an egg from under a hen and there is a chicken chirping in it, so my conscience suddenly piped up, and while I was being married I thought all the time: 'There is a God!' But when I left the church, it was nothing. And indeed, how can I tell whether there is a God or not? We are not taught right from childhood, and while the babe is still at his mother's breast he is only taught 'every man to his own trade.' Father does not believe in God, either. You were saying that Guntorev had some sheep stolen. . . . I have found them; it was a peasant at Shikalova stole them; he stole them, but father's got the hides . . . so that's all his faith amounts to."

Anisim winked and wagged his head.

"The elder does not believe in God, either," he went on. "Nor the clerk, nor the sexton. And as for their going to church and keeping the fasts, that is simply to prevent people talking ill of them, and in case it really may be true that there will be a Day of Judgment. Nowadays people say that the end of the world has come because people have grown weak, do not honor their parents, and so on. All that is a trifle. My idea, mamma, is that all our trouble is because there is so little conscience in people. I see through things, mamma, and I understand. If a man has a stolen shirt I see it. A man sits in a tavern and you fancy he is drinking tea and no more, but to me the tea is neither here nor there; I see farther, he has no conscience. You can go about the whole day and not meet one man with a conscience. And the whole reason is that they don't know whether there is a God or not. . . . Well, good-by, mamma, keep alive and well, don't remember evil against me."

Anisim bowed down at Varvara's feet.

"I thank you for everything, mamma," he said. "You are a great asset to our family. You are a very decent woman, and I am very pleased with you."

Much moved, Anisim went out, but returned again and said:

"Samorodov has got me mixed up in something: I shall either make my fortune or come to grief. If anything happens, then you must comfort my father, mamma."

"Oh, nonsense, don't you worry, tut, tut, tut . . . God is merciful. And Anisim, you should pet your wife a little, instead you give each other sulky looks; you might smile at least."

"Yes, she is rather a queer one," said Anisim, and he gave a sigh. "She does not understand anything, she never speaks. She is very young, let her grow up."

A tall, sleek white stallion was already standing at the front door, harnessed to the chaise.

Old Tzybukin jumped in, sat down jauntily, and took the reins. Anisim kissed Varvara, Aksinya, and his brother. On the steps Lipa, too, was standing; she was standing motionless, looking away, and it seemed as though she had not come to see him off but just by chance for some unknown reason. Anisim went up to her and just touched her cheeks with his lips.

"Good-by," he said.

And without looking at him she gave a strange smile; her face began to quiver, and everyone for some reason felt sorry for her. Anisim, too, leaped into the chaise with a bound and put his arms jauntily akimbo, for he considered himself a good-looking fellow.

When they drove up out of the ravine Anisim kept looking back towards the village. It was a warm, bright day. The cattle were being driven out for the first time, and the peasant girls and women were walking by the herd in their holiday dresses. The dun-colored bull bellowed, glad to be free, and pawed the ground with his forefeet. On all sides, above and below, the larks were singing. Anisim looked round at the elegant white church—it had only lately been whitewashed—and he thought how he had been praying in it five days before; he looked round at the school with its green roof, at the little river in which he used to bathe and catch fish, and there was a stir of joy in his heart, and he wished that a wall might rise up from the ground and prevent him from going farther, and that he might be left with nothing but the past.

At the station they went to the refreshment room and drank a glass of sherry each. His father felt in his pocket for his purse to pay.

"I will stand treat," said Anisim. The old man, touched and delighted, slapped him on the shoulder, and winked to the waiter as much as to say, "See what a fine son I have got."

"You ought to stay at home in the business, Anisim," he said; "you would be worth any price to me! I would gild you from head to foot, my son."

"It can't be done, papa."

The sherry was sour and smelled of sealing-wax, but they had another glass.

When old Tzybukin returned home from the station, at first he did not recognize his younger daughter-in-law. As soon as her husband had driven out of the yard, Lipa was transformed and suddenly brightened up. Wearing a shabby skirt with her feet bare and her sleeves tucked up to the shoulders, she was scrubbing the stairs in the entry and singing in a silvery little voice, and when she brought out a big tub of slops and looked up at the sun with her childlike smile it seemed as though she, too, were a lark.

An old laborer who was passing by the door shook his head and cleared his throat.

"Yes, indeed, your daughters-in-law, Grigory Petrovich, are a blessing from God," he said. "Not women, but treasures!"

v

On Friday the eighth of July, Yelizarov, nicknamed Crutch, and Lipa were returning from the village of Kazanskoye, where they had been to a service on the occasion of a local church holiday in honor of the Holy Mother of Kazan. A good distance behind them walked Lipa's mother Praskovya, who always fell back, as she was ill and short of breath. It was drawing towards evening.

"A-a-a . . ." said Crutch, wondering as he listened to Lipa. "A-a! . . . We-ell!"

"I am very fond of jam, Ilya Makarych," said Lipa. "I sit down in my little corner and drink tea and eat jam. Or I drink it with Varvara Nikolayevna, and she tells some story full of feeling. She has a lot of jam—four jars. 'Have some, Lipa,' she says, 'eat as much as you like.' "

"A-a-a, four jars!"

"They live very well. We have white bread with our tea; and meat, too, as much as one wants. They live very well, only I am frightened in their presence, Ilya Makarych. Oh, oh, how frightened I am!"

"Why are you frightened, child?" asked Crutch, and he looked back to see how far behind Praskovya was.

"At first, after the wedding, I was afraid of Anisim

Grigorich. Anisim Grigorich did nothing, he didn't ill-treat me, only when he comes near me a cold shiver runs all over me, through all my bones. And I did not sleep one night, I trembled all over and kept praying to God. And now I am afraid of Aksinya, Ilya Makarych. It's not that she does anything, she is always laughing, but sometimes she glances at the window, and her eyes are so angry and there is a greenish gleam in them— like the eyes of the sheep in the pen. The Hrymin Juniors are leading her astray: 'Your old man,' they tell her, 'has a bit of land at Butyokino, a hundred acres,' they say, 'and there is sand and water there, so you, Aksinya,' they say, 'build a brickyard there and we will go shares in it.' Bricks now are twenty rubles the thousand, it's a profitable business. Yesterday at dinner Aksinya said to the old man: 'I want to build a brickyard at Butyokino; I'm going into the business on my own account.' She laughed as she said it. And Grigory Petrovich's face darkened, one could see he did not like it. 'As long as I live,' he said, 'the family must not break up, we must keep together.' She gave a look and gritted her teeth. . . . Fritters were served, she would not eat them."

"A-a-a! . . ." Crutch was surprised.

"And tell me, if you please, when does she sleep?" said Lipa. "She sleeps for half an hour, then jumps up and keeps walking and walking about to see whether the peasants have not set fire to something, have not stolen something. . . . She frightens me, Ilya Makarych. And the Hrymin Juniors did not go to bed after the wedding, but drove to the town to go to law with each other; and folks do say it is all on account of Aksinya. Two of the brothers have promised to build her a brickyard, but the third is offended, and the factory has been at a standstill for a month, and my uncle

Prohor is without work and goes about from house to house getting crusts. 'Hadn't you better go working on the land or sawing up wood, meanwhile, uncle?' I tell him; 'why disgrace yourself?' 'I've got out of the way of it,' he says; 'I don't know how to do any sort of peasant's work now, Lipinka.' . . ."

They stopped to rest and wait for Praskovya near a copse of young aspen-trees. Yelizarov had long been a contractor in a small way, but he kept no horse, going on foot all over the district with nothing but a little bag in which there was bread and onions, and stalking along with big strides, swinging his arms. And it was difficult to walk with him.

At the entrance to the copse stood a milestone. Yelizarov touched it to see if it was firm. Praskovya reached them out of breath. Her wrinkled and always scared-looking face was beaming with happiness; she had been at church today like anyone else, then she had been to the fair and there had drunk pear cider. For her this was unusual, and it even seemed to her now that she had lived for her own pleasure that day for the first time in her life. After resting they all three walked on side by side. The sun had already set, and its beams filtered through the copse, gleaming on the trunks of the trees. There was a faint sound of voices ahead. The Ukleyevo girls had gone on long before but had lingered in the copse, probably gathering mushrooms.

"Hey, wenches!" cried Yelizarov. "Hey, my beauties!"

There was a sound of laughter in response.

"Crutch is coming! Crutch! The old horseradish."

And the echo laughed, too. And then the copse was left behind. The tops of the factory chimneys came into view. The cross on the belfry glittered: this was the village: "the one at which the sexton ate all the caviar at the funeral." Now they were almost home; they only had to go down into the big ravine. Lipa and Praskovya, who had been walking barefoot, sat down on the grass to put on their shoes, Yelizarov sat down with them. If they looked down from above, Ukleyevo looked beautiful and peaceful with its willow-trees, its white church, and its little river, and the only blot on the picture was the roof of the factories, painted for the sake of cheapness a dark sullen color. On the slope on the farther side they could see the rye—some in stacks and sheaves here and there as though strewn about by the storm, and some freshly cut lying in swathes; the oats, too, were ripe and glistened now in the sun like mother-of-pearl. It was harvest-time. Today was a holiday, tomorrow they would harvest the rye and cart the hay, and then Sunday a holiday again; every day there were mutterings of distant thunder. It was muggy and looked like rain, and, gazing now at the fields, everyone thought, God grant we get the harvest in in time; and everyone felt at once gay and joyful and anxious at heart.

"Mowers ask a high price nowadays," said Praskovya. "One ruble and forty kopecks a day."

People kept coming from the fair at Kazanskoye: peasant women, mill hands in new caps, beggars, children. . . . A cart would drive by stirring up the dust and behind it would run an unsold horse, and it seemed glad it had not been sold; then a cow was led along by the horns, resisting stubbornly; then a cart again, and in it drunken peasants swinging their legs. An old woman led a little boy in a big cap and big boots; the boy was tired out with the heat and the heavy boots which prevented him from bending his legs at the knees, but yet he blew a tin trumpet unceasingly with all his might. They had gone down the slope and turned into the street, but the trumpet could still be heard.

"Our mill owners don't seem quite themselves . . ."

said Yelizarov. "It's bad. Kostukov got angry with me. 'Too many battens have been used for the cornices.' 'Too many? As many have been used as were needed, Vassily Danilych; I don't eat them with my porridge.' 'How can you speak to me like that?' said he, 'You good-for-nothing, you blockhead! Don't forget yourself! It was I made you a contractor.' 'That's nothing so wonderful,' said I. 'Even before I got to be a contractor I used to have tea every day.' 'You are all crooks . . .' he said. I held my peace. 'We are crooks in this world,' thought I, 'and you will be the crooks in the next. . . .' Ha-ha-ha! The next day he was softer. 'Don't you bear malice against me for my words, Makarych,' he said. 'If I said too much,' says he, 'what of it? I am a merchant of the first guild, your better—you ought to hold your tongue.' 'You,' said I, 'are a merchant of the first guild and I am a carpenter, that's correct. And Saint Joseph was a carpenter, too. Ours is a righteous and godly calling, and if you are pleased to be my better you are very welcome to it, Vassily Danilych.' And later on, after that conversation I mean, I thought: 'Which was the better man? A merchant of the first guild or a carpenter?' The carpenter must be, children!"

Crutch thought a minute and added:

"Yes, that's how it is, children. He who works, he who is patient is the better man."

By now the sun had set and a thick mist as white as milk was rising over the river, in the church enclosure, and in the open spaces round the mills. Now when darkness was coming on rapidly, when lights were twinkling below, and when it seemed as though the mists were hiding a fathomless abyss, Lipa and her mother who were born in poverty and prepared to live so till the end, giving up to others everything except their frightened, gentle souls, may perhaps have fancied for a minute that in this vast, mysterious world, among the endless series of lives, they too counted for something, and they too were better than someone; they liked sitting up there, they smiled happily and forgot that they must go down below again all the same.

At last they reached home. The mowers were sitting on the ground at the gates near the shop. As a rule the Ukleyevo peasants refused to work for Tzybukin, and he had to hire strangers, and now in the darkness it seemed as though there were men with long black beards sitting there. The shop was open, and through the doorway they could see the deaf man playing checkers with a boy. The mowers were singing softly, almost inaudibly, or were loudly demanding their wages for the previous day, but they were not paid for fear they should go away before tomorrow. Old Tzybukin, with his coat off, was sitting in his waistcoat with Aksinya under the birch-tree, drinking tea; a lighted lamp was on the table.

"I say, grandfather," a mower called from outside the gates, as though taunting him, "pay us half anyway! Hey, grandfather."

And at once there was the sound of laughter, and then again they sang almost inaudibly. . . . Crutch, too, sat down to have some tea.

"We have been to the fair, you know," he began telling them. "We had a fine time, a very fine time, my children, praise the Lord. But an unfortunate thing happened: Sashka the blacksmith bought some tobacco and gave the shopman half a ruble, you know. And the half ruble was a false one"—Crutch went on, and he meant to speak in a whisper, but he spoke in a smothered husky voice which was audible to everyone. "The half-ruble turned out to be a bad one. He was asked where he got it. 'Anisim Tzybukin gave it me,' he said, 'when

I was at his wedding,' he said. They called the police, took the man away. . . . Look out, Grigory Petrovich, that nothing comes of it, no talk. . . ."

"Gra-ndfather!" the same voice called tauntingly outside the gates. "Gra-andfather!"

A silence followed.

"Ah, little children, little children, little children . . ." Crutch muttered rapidly, and he got up. He was overcome with drowsiness. "Well, thank you for the tea, for the sugar, little children. It is time to sleep. I'm broken down, my beams have rotted away. Ho-ho-ho!"

As he walked away he said: "I suppose it's time I was dead," and he gave a sob. Old Tzybukin did not finish his tea but sat on a little, pondering; and his face looked as though he were listening to the footsteps of Crutch, who was far down the street.

"Sashka the blacksmith told a lie, I expect," said Aksinya, guessing his thoughts.

He went into the house and came back a little later with a parcel; he opened it, and there was the gleam of rubles—perfectly new coins. He took one, tried it with his teeth, flung it on the tray; then flung down another.

"The rubles really are false . . ." he said, looking at Aksinya and seeming perplexed. "These are those Anisim brought, his present. Take them, daughter," he whispered, and thrust the parcel into her hands. "Take them and throw them into the well . . . confound them! And mind there is no talk about it. Harm might come of it. . . . Take away the samovar, put out the light."

Lipa and her mother sitting in the barn saw the lights go out one after another; only up in Varvara's room there were blue and red icon lamps gleaming, and a feeling of peace, contentment, and happy ignorance seemed to float down from there. Praskovya could never get used to her daughter's being married to a rich man, and when she came to the house she huddled timidly in the entry with a beseeching smile on her face, and tea and sugar were sent out to her. And Lipa could not get used to it either, and after her husband had gone away she did not sleep in her bed, but lay down anywhere to sleep, in the kitchen or the shed, and every day she scrubbed the floor or washed the clothes, and felt as though she were hired by the day. And now, on coming back from the service at Kazanskoye, they had tea in the kitchen with the cook; then they went into the shed and lay down on the ground between the sledge and the wall. It was dark here and smelled of harness. The lights went out about the house, then they could hear the deaf man shutting up the shop, the mowers settling themselves about the yard to sleep. In the distance at the Hrymin Juniors' they were playing the expensive accordion . . . Praskovya and Lipa began to drop off.

When they were awakened by somebody's steps, the moon was shining brightly; at the entrance to the shed stood Aksinya with her bedding in her arms.

"Maybe it's a bit cooler here," she said; then she came in and lay down almost in the doorway so that the moonlight fell full upon her.

She did not sleep, but breathed heavily, tossing from side to side with the heat, throwing off almost all the bedclothes. And in the magic moonlight what a beautiful, what a proud animal she was! A little time passed, and then steps were heard again: the old father, white all over, appeared in the doorway.

"Aksinya," he called, "are you here?"

"Well?" she responded angrily.

"I told you just now to throw the money into the well, did you do it?"

"What next! Throwing property into the water! I gave it to the mowers . . ."

"Oh my God!" cried the old man, dumfounded and alarmed. "Oh my God! you wicked woman. . . ."

He struck his hands together and went out, and kept talking to himself as he went away. And a little later Aksinya sat up and sighed heavily with annoyance, then rose and, gathering up her bedclothes in her arms, went out.

"Why did you marry me into this family, mother?" said Lipa.

"One has to be married, daughter. It was not us that ordered things so."

And a feeling of inconsolable woe was ready to take possession of them. But it seemed to them that someone was looking down from the height of the heavens, out of the blue, where the stars were, that someone saw everything that was going on in Ukleyevo, and was watching over them. And however powerful evil was, yet the night was calm and beautiful, and yet in God's world there is and will be righteousness as calm and beautiful, and everything on earth is only waiting to be made one with righteousness, even as the moonlight is blended with the night.

And both, huddling close to one another, fell asleep comforted.

VI

News had come long before that Anisim had been put in prison for counterfeiting money and circulating it. Months went by, more than half a year went by, the long winter was over, spring had begun, and everyone in the house and in the village had grown used to the fact that Anisim was in prison. And when anyone passed by the house or the shop at night he would remember that Anisim was in prison; and when they rang at the churchyard for some reason, that, too, reminded people that he was in prison awaiting trial.

It seemed as though a shadow had fallen upon the house. It looked more somber, the roof had become rusty, the green paint on the heavy, iron-bound door into the shop had faded; and old Tzybukin himself seemed to have grown darker. He had given up cutting his hair and beard, and looked shaggy. He no longer sprang jauntily into his chaise, nor shouted to beggars: "God will provide!" His strength was on the wane, and that was evident in everything. People were less afraid of him now, and the police officer drew up a formal charge against him in the shop, though he received his regular bribe as before; and three times the old man was called up to the town to be tried for the illicit sale of spirits, and the case was continually adjourned owing to the nonappearance of witnesses, and old Tzybukin was worn out with worry.

He often went to see his son, hired lawyers, handed in petitions, presented a banner to some church. He presented the warden of the prison in which Anisim was confined with a long spoon and a silver holder for a tea-glass with the inscription: "The soul knows its right measure."

"There is no one to look after things for us," said Varvara. "Tut, tut. . . . You ought to ask someone of the gentry to write to the head officials. . . . At least they might let him out on bail! Why wear the poor fellow out?"

She, too, was grieved, but she nevertheless grew stouter and whiter; she lighted the lamps before the icons as before, and saw that everything in the house was clean, and regaled the guests with jam and apple tarts. The deaf man and Aksinya looked after the shop.

A new project was in progress—a brickyard in Butyo-kino—and Aksinya went there almost every day in the chaise. She drove herself, and when she met acquaintances she stretched out her neck like a snake in the young rye, and smiled naively and enigmatically. Lipa spent her time playing with the baby which had been born to her just before Lent. It was a tiny, thin, pitiful little baby, and it was strange that it should cry and gaze about and be considered a human being, and even be called Nikifor. He lay in his cradle, and Lipa would walk away towards the door and say, bowing to him:

"How do you do, Nikifor Anisimych!"

And she would rush at him and kiss him. Then she would walk away to the door, bow again, and say:

"How do you do, Nikifor Anisimych!"

And he kicked up his little red legs, and his crying was mixed with laughter like the carpenter Yelizarov's.

At last the day of the trial was fixed. Tzybukin went away some five days before. Then the Tzybukins heard that the peasants called as witnesses had been fetched; their old workman who was one of those to receive a notice to appear went too.

The trial was on a Thursday. But Sunday had passed, and Tzybukin was still not back, and there was no news. Towards evening on Tuesday Varvara was sitting at the open window, waiting for her husband to come. In the next room Lipa was playing with her baby. She was tossing him up in her arms and saying ecstatically:

"You will grow ever so big, ever so big. You will be a peasant, we shall go out to work by the day together! We shall go out to work by the day together!"

"Come, come," said Varvara, offended. "Go out to work by the day, what an idea, you silly thing! He will be a merchant . . . !"

Lipa sang softly, but a minute later she forgot and began again:

"You will grow ever so big, ever so big. You will be a peasant, we'll go out to work by the day together."

"There she is at it again!"

Lipa, with Nikifor in her arms, stood still in the doorway and asked:

"Why do I love him so much, maminka? Why do I feel so sorry for him?" she went on in a quivering voice, and her eyes glistened with tears.

"Who is he? What is he like? As light as a little feather, as a little crumb, but I love him, I love him as if he were a real person. Here he can do nothing, he can't talk, and yet I know from his little eyes what he wants."

Varvara pricked up her ears: the sound of the evening train coming into the station reached her. Had her husband come? She did not hear and she did not heed what Lipa was saying, she had no idea how the time passed, but only trembled all over—not with dread, but with intense curiosity. She saw a cart full of peasants roll quickly by with a rattle. It was the witnesses coming back from the station. When the cart passed the shop the old workman jumped out and walked into the yard. She could hear him being greeted in the yard and being asked some questions. . . .

"Loss of rights and all property," he said loudly, "and six years' penal servitude in Siberia."

She could see Aksinya come out of the shop by the back way; she had just been selling kerosene, and in one hand held a bottle and in the other a can, and she had some silver coins in her mouth.

"Where is father?" she asked, lisping.

"At the station," answered the laborer.

" 'When it gets a little darker,' he said, 'then I'll come.' "

And when it became known all through the household that Anisim was sentenced to penal servitude, the cook in the kitchen suddenly broke into a wail as though at a funeral, imagining that this was demanded by the proprieties:

"Who will care for us now you have gone, Anisim Grigorich, our bright falcon. . . ."

The dogs began barking in alarm. Varvara ran to the window, and rushing about in distress, shouted to the cook with all her might, straining her voice:

"Sto-op, Stepanida, sto-op! Don't harrow us, for Christ's sake!"

They forgot to set the samovar, they could think of nothing. Only Lipa could not make out what it was all about and went on playing with her baby.

When the old father arrived from the station they asked him no questions. He greeted them and walked through all the rooms in silence; he had no supper.

"There was no one to see about things . . ." Varvara began when they were alone. "I said you should have asked some of the gentry, you would not listen to me at the time. . . . A petition would . . ."

"I saw to things," said her husband with a wave of his hand. "When Anisim was condemned I went to the gentleman who was defending him. 'It's no use now,' he said, 'it's too late'; and Anisim said the same; it's too late. But all the same as I came out of court I engaged a lawyer and gave him an advance. I'll wait a week and then I'll go again. It is as God wills."

Again the old man walked through all the rooms, and when he went back to Varvara he said:

"I must be ill. My head's in a sort of . . . fog. My thoughts are mixed up."

He closed the door that Lipa might not hear, and went on softly:

"I am worried about the money. Do you remember before his wedding Anisim's bringing me some new rubles and half-rubles? One parcel I put away at the time, but the others I mixed with my own money. When my uncle Dmitri Filatych—the kingdom of Heaven be his—was alive, he used to go to Moscow and to the Crimea to buy goods. He had a wife, and this same wife, when he was away buying goods, used to take up with other men. They had half a dozen children. And when uncle was in his cups he would laugh and say: 'I never can make out,' he used to say, 'which are my children and which are other people's.' An easy-going disposition, to be sure; and so now I can't tell which are genuine rubles and which are false ones. And they all seem false to me."

"Nonsense, God bless you."

"I buy a ticket at the station, I give the man three rubles, and I keep fancying they are counterfeit. And I am frightened. I must be ill."

"There's no denying it, we are all in God's hands. . . . Oh dear, dear . . ." said Varvara, and she shook her head. "You ought to think about this, Grigory Petrovich: you never know, anything may happen, you are not a young man. See they don't wrong your grandchild when you are dead and gone. Oh, I am afraid they will be unfair to Nikifor! He is as good as fatherless, his mother's young and foolish . . . You ought to settle something on the poor little boy, at least the land, Butyokino, Grigory Petrovich, really! Think it over!" Varvara went on persuading him. "He's such a pretty boy, it's a pity! You go tomorrow and make out a deed; why put it off?"

"I'd forgotten my grandson," said Tzybukin. "I must

go and have a look at him. So you say the boy is all right? Well, let him grow up, please God."

He opened the door and, crooking his finger, beckoned to Lipa. She went up to him with the baby in her arms.

"If there is anything you want, Lipynka, you ask for it," he said. "And eat anything you like, we don't grudge it, so long as it does you good. . . ." He made the sign of the cross over the baby. "And take care of my grandchild. My son is gone, but my grandson is left."

Tears rolled down his cheeks; he gave a sob and went away. Soon afterwards he went to bed and slept soundly after seven sleepless nights.

VII

Old Tzybukin went to the town for a short visit. Someone told Aksinya that he had gone to the notary to make his will and that he was leaving Butyokino, the very place where she had set up a brickyard, to Nikifor, his grandson. She was informed of this in the morning when old Tzybukin and Varvara were sitting near the steps under the birch-tree, having their tea. She closed the shop in the front and at the back, gathered together all the keys she had, and flung them at her father-in-law's feet.

"I am not going on working for you," she began in a loud voice, and suddenly broke into sobs. "It seems I am not your daughter-in-law, but a servant! Everybody's jeering and saying, 'See what a servant the Tzybukins have got hold of!' I did not hire myself out to you! I am not a beggar, I am not a homeless wench, I have a father and mother."

She did not wipe away her tears; she fixed upon her father-in-law eyes full of tears, vindictive, squinting with anger; her face and neck were red and tense, and she was shouting at the top of her voice.

"I don't mean to go on slaving for you!" she continued. "I am worn out. When it is work, when it is sitting in the shop day in and day out, sneaking out at night for vodka—then it is my share, but when it is giving away the land then it is for that convict's wife and her imp. She is mistress here, and I am her servant. Give her everything, the convict's wife, and may it choke her! I am going home! Find yourselves some other fool, you damned bloodsuckers!"

The old man had never in his life scolded or punished his children, and had never dreamed that one of his family could speak to him rudely or behave disrespectfully; and now he was very much frightened; he ran into the house and hid behind the cupboard. And Varvara was so much flustered that she could not get up from her seat, and only waved her hands before her as though she were warding off a bee.

"Oh, Holy Saints! What's the meaning of it?" she muttered in horror. "What is she shouting? Oh, dear, dear! . . . People will hear! Hush. Oh, hush!"

"You have given Butyokino to the convict's wife," Aksinya went on bawling. "Give her everything now, I don't want anything from you! Go to hell! You are all a gang of thieves here! I have seen enough, I have had my fill of it! You have robbed people coming and going; you have robbed old and young alike, you brigands! And who has been selling vodka without a license? And false money? You've stuffed your coffers full of false coins, and now I am no more use!"

By now a crowd had collected at the open gate and was staring into the yard.

"Let the people look," bawled Aksinya. "I'll put you

all to shame! You shall burn up with shame! You'll grovel at my feet. Hey! Stepan," she called to the deaf man, "let us go home this minute! Let us go to my father and mother; I don't want to live with convicts. Get ready!"

Clothes were hanging on lines stretched across the yard; she snatched off her petticoats and blouses still wet and flung them into the deaf man's arms. Then in her fury she dashed about the yard where the linen hung, tore down all of it, and what was not hers she threw on the ground and trampled upon.

"Holy Saints, stop her," moaned Varvara.

"What a woman! Give her Butyokino! Give it to her, for Christ's sake!"

"Well! Wha-at a woman!" people were saying at the gate. "She's a wo-oman! She's going it—something like!"

Aksinya ran into the kitchen where laundering was being done. Lipa was washing alone, the cook had gone to the river to rinse the clothes. Steam was rising from the trough and from the caldron near the stove, and the air in the kitchen was close and thick with vapor. On the floor was a heap of unwashed clothes, and Nikifor, kicking up his little red legs, lay on a bench near them, so that if he fell he should not hurt himself. Just as Aksinya went in Lipa took the former's chemise out of the heap and put it in the trough, and was just stretching out her hand to a big pitcher of boiling water which was standing on the table.

"Give it here," said Aksinya, looking at her with hatred, and snatching the chemise out of the trough; "it is not your business to touch my linen! You are a convict's wife, and ought to know your place and who you are!"

Lipa gazed at her, taken aback, and did not understand, but suddenly she caught the look Aksinya turned upon the child, and at once she understood and went numb all over.

"You've taken my land, so here you are!" Saying this Aksinya snatched up the pitcher with the boiling water and flung it over Nikifor.

After this there was heard a scream such as had never been heard before in Ukleyevo, and no one would have believed that a little weak creature like Lipa could scream like that. And it was suddenly quiet in the yard. Askinya walked into the house in silence with the old naive smile on her lips. . . . The deaf man kept moving about the yard with his arms full of linen, then he began hanging it up again, silently, without haste. And until the cook came back from the river no one ventured to go into the kitchen to see what had happened there.

VIII

Nikifor was taken to the district hospital, and towards evening he died there. Lipa did not wait to be fetched, but wrapped the dead baby in its little quilt and carried it home.

The hospital, a new one recently built, with big windows, stood high up on a hill; it was glittering in the setting sun and looked as though it were on fire from inside. There was a little village below. Lipa went down the road, and before reaching the village sat down by a pond. A woman brought a horse to water but the horse would not drink.

"What more do you want?" the woman said to it softly, in perplexity. "What more do you want?"

A boy in a red shirt, sitting at the water's edge, was washing his father's boots. And not another soul was in sight either in the village or on the hill.

"It's not drinking," said Lipa, looking at the horse.

Then the woman with the horse and the boy with the boots walked away, and there was no one left at all. The sun went to sleep, covering itself with cloth of gold and purple, and long clouds, red and lilac, stretched across the sky, guarded its rest. Somewhere far away a bittern cried, a hollow, melancholy sound as of a cow shut up in a barn. The cry of that mysterious bird was heard every spring, but no one knew what it was like or where it lived. At the top of the hill by the hospital, in the bushes close to the pond, and in the fields, the nightingales were trilling. The cuckoo kept reckoning someone's years and losing count and beginning again. In the pond the frogs called angrily to one another, straining themselves to bursting, and one could even make out the words: "That's what you are! That's what you are!" What a noise there was! It seemed as though all these creatures were singing and shouting so that no one might sleep on that spring night, so that all, even the angry frogs, might appreciate and enjoy every minute: life is given only once.

A silver half-moon was shining in the sky; there were many stars. Lipa had no idea how long she sat by the pond, but when she got up and walked on everybody was asleep in the little village, and there was not a single light. It was probably about eight miles' walk home, but neither body nor mind seemed equal to it. The moon gleamed now in front, now on the right, and the same cuckoo kept calling in a voice grown husky, with a chuckle as though gibing at her: "Hey, look out, you'll lose your way!" Lipa walked rapidly; she lost her kerchief . . . she looked at the sky and wondered where her baby's soul was now: was it following her, or floating aloft yonder among the stars and not thinking of her, the mother, any more? Oh, how lonely it is in the open country at night, in the midst of that singing when you yourself cannot sing; in the midst of the incessant cries of joy when you yourself cannot be joyful, when the moon, which cares not whether it is spring or winter, whether men are alive or dead, looks down, lonely, too. . . . When there is grief in the heart it is hard to be without people. If only her mother, Praskovya, had been with her, or Crutch, or the cook, or some peasant!

"Boo-oo!" cried the bittern. "Boo-oo!"

And suddenly the sound of human speech became clearly audible:

"Hitch up the horses, Vavila!"

Ahead of her, by the wayside a camp fire was burning: the flames had died down, there were only red embers. She could hear the horses munching. In the darkness she could see the outlines of two carts, one with a barrel, the other, a lower one, with sacks in it, and the figures of two men; one was leading a horse to put it into the shafts, the other was standing motionless by the fire with his hands behind his back. A dog growled near the carts. The one who was leading the horse stopped and said:

"Someone seems to be coming along the road."

"Sharik, be quiet!" the other man called to the dog.

And from the voice one could tell that he was an old man. Lipa stopped and said:

"God aid you."

The old man went up to her and said after a pause: "Good evening!"

"Your dog does not bite, grandfather?"

"No, come along, he won't touch you."

"I have been at the hospital," said Lipa after a pause. "My little son died there. Here I am carrying him home."

It must have been unpleasant for the old man to hear this, for he moved away and said hurriedly:

"No matter, my dear. It's God's will. You are daw-dling, lad," he added, addressing his companion; "look alive!"

"Your yoke isn't there," said the young man; "I don't see it."

"That's just like Vavila!"

The old man picked up an ember, blew on it—only his eyes and nose were lighted up—then, when they had found the yoke, he went over to Lipa with the light and looked at her, and his look expressed compassion and tenderness.

"You are a mother," he said; "every mother grieves for her child."

And he sighed and shook his head as he said it. Vavila threw something on the fire, stamped it out—and at once it was very dark; the immediate scene vanished, and as before there were only the fields, the sky with the stars, and the noise of the birds keeping each other from sleep. And the landrail called, it seemed, in the very place where the fire had been.

But a minute passed, and the two carts and the old man and lanky Vavila became visible again. The carts creaked as they rolled out on the road.

"Are you holy men?" Lipa asked the old man.

"No. We are from Firsanovo."

"You looked at me just now and my heart was soft-ened. And the lad is so gentle. I thought you must be holy men."

"Have you far to go?"

"To Ukleyevo."

"Get in, we will give you a lift as far as Kuzmenki, then you go straight on and we turn off to the left."

Vavila got into the cart with the barrel and the old man and Lipa got into the other. They moved at a walk-ing pace, Vavila in front.

"My baby was in torment all day," said Lipa. "He looked at me with his little eyes and said nothing; he wanted to speak and could not. Lord God! Queen of Heaven! In my grief I kept falling down on the floor. I would be standing there and then I would fall down by the bedside. And tell me, grandfather, why should a little one be tormented before his death? When a grown-up person, a man or woman, is in torment, his sins are forgiven, but why a little one, when he has no sins? Why?"

"Who can tell?" answered the old man.

They drove on for half an hour in silence.

"We can't know everything, how and why," said the old man. "A bird is given not four wings but two because it is able to fly with two; and so man is not permitted to know everything but only a half or a quarter. As much as he needs to know in order to live, so much he knows."

"It is better for me to go on foot, grandfather. Now my heart is all of a tremble."

"Never mind, sit still."

The old man yawned and made the sign of the cross over his mouth.

"Never mind," he repeated. "Yours is not the worst of sorrows. Life is long, there is good and bad yet to come, there is everything yet to come. Great is mother Russia," he said, and looked round on either side of him. "I have been all over Russia, and I have seen everything in her, and you may believe my words, my dear. There will be good and there will be bad. I went as a delegate from my village to Siberia, and I have been to the Amur River and the Altai Mountains and I lived in Siberia; I worked the land there, then I got homesick for mother Russia and I came back to my native village. We went back to Russia on foot; and I remember we went on a ferry, and I was thin as thin, all in rags, bare-foot, freezing with cold, and gnawing a crust, and a gentleman who was on the ferry—the kingdom of Heaven be his if he is dead—looked at me pitifully, and tears came into his eyes. 'Ah,' he said, 'your bread is black, your days are black. . . .' And when I got home, as the saying is, there was neither stick nor stone; I had a wife, but I left her behind in Siberia, she was buried there. So I am a hired man now. And I tell you: since then I have had it good as well as bad. Here I do not want to die, my dear, I would be glad to live another twenty years; so there has been more of the good. And great is our mother Russia!" and again he gazed on either side and looked round.

"Grandfather," Lipa asked, "when anyone dies, how many days does his soul walk the earth?"

"Who can tell! Ask Vavila here, he has been to school. Now they teach them everything. Vavila!" the old man called to him.

"Yes!"

"Vavila, when anyone dies how long does his soul walk the earth?"

Vavila stopped the horse and only then answered:

"Nine days. After my uncle Kirilla died, his soul lived in our cottage thirteen days."

"How do you know?"

"For thirteen days there was a knocking in the stove."

"Well, all right. Go on," said the old man, and it could be seen that he did not believe a word of all that.

Near Kuzmenki the cart turned into the highroad while Lipa walked straight on. By now it was getting light. As she went down into the ravine the Ukleyevo houses and the church were hidden in fog. It was cold, and it seemed to her that the same cuckoo was calling still.

When Lipa reached home the cattle had not yet been driven out; everyone was asleep. She sat down on the steps and waited. The old man was the first to come out; he understood what had happened from the first glance at her, and for a long time he could not utter a word, but only smacked his lips.

"Oh, Lipa," he said, "you did not take care of my grandchild. . . ."

Varvara was awakened. She struck her hands together and broke into sobs, and immediately began laying out the baby.

"And he was a pretty child . . ." she said. "Oh, dear, dear. . . . You had the one child, and you did not take enough care of him, you silly thing. . . ."

There was a requiem service in the morning and again in the evening. The funeral took place the next day, and after it the guests and the priests ate a great deal, and with such greed that one might have thought that they had not tasted food for a long time. Lipa waited at table, and the priest, lifting his fork on which there was a salted mushroom, said to her:

"Don't grieve for the babe. For of such is the kingdom of Heaven."

And only when they had all left Lipa realized fully that there was no Nikifor and never would be, she realized it and broke into sobs. And she did not know what room to go into to sob, for she felt that now that her child was dead there was no place for her in the house, that she had no reason to be there, that she was in the way; and the others felt it, too.

"Now what are you bellowing for?" Aksinya shouted, suddenly appearing in the doorway; because of the funeral she was dressed all in new clothes and had powdered her face. "Shut up!"

Lipa tried to stop but could not, and sobbed louder than ever.

"Do you hear?" shouted Aksinya, and stamped her foot in violent anger. "Who is it I am speaking to? Get out of the house and don't set foot here again, you convict's wife. Get out."

"There, there, there," the old man put in fussily. "Aksinya, don't make such an outcry, my dear. . . . She is crying, it is only natural . . . her child is dead. . . ."

" 'It's only natural,' " Aksinya mimicked him. "Let her stay the night here, and don't let me see a trace of her here tomorrow! 'It's only natural!' . . ." she mimicked him again, and, laughing, went into the shop.

Early the next morning Lipa went off to her mother at Torguyevo.

IX

The roof and the front door of the shop have now been repainted and are as bright as though they were new, there are gay geraniums in the windows as of old, and what happened in Tzybukin's house and yard three years ago is almost forgotten.

Grigory Petrovich is still looked upon as the master, but in reality everything has passed into Aksinya's hands; she buys and sells, and nothing can be done without her consent. The brickyard is working well; and as bricks are wanted for the railway the price has gone up to twenty-four rubles a thousand; peasant women and girls cart the bricks to the station and load them up in cars and earn a quarter-ruble a day for the work.

Aksinya has gone into partnership with the Hrymin Juniors, and their mill is now called Hrymin Juniors and Co. They have opened a tavern near the station, and now the expensive accordion is played not at the mill but at the tavern, and the postmaster, who is engaged in some sort of business, too, often goes there, and so does the stationmaster. Hrymin Juniors have presented the deaf man with a gold watch, and he is constantly taking it out of his pocket and putting it to his ear.

People say of Aksinya that she has become a person of power; and it is true that when she drives to her brick-yard in the morning, handsome and happy, with the naive smile on her face, and afterwards when she gives orders there, one is aware of her great power. Everyone is afraid of her in the house and in the village and in the brickyard. When she goes to the post the postmaster jumps up and says to her:

"I humbly beg you to be seated, Aksinya Abramovna!"

A certain landowner, middle-aged but foppish, in a tunic of fine cloth and high patent leather boots, sold her a horse, and was so carried away by talking to her that he knocked down the price to meet her wishes. He held her hand a long time and, looking into her merry, sly, naive eyes, said:

"For a woman like you, Aksinya Abramovna, I should be ready to do anything you please. Only say when we can meet where no one will interfere with us."

"Why, whenever you like."

And since then the elderly fop has been driving up to the shop almost every day to drink beer. And the beer is horrid, bitter as wormwood. The landowner wags his head, but drinks it.

Old Tzybukin does not have anything at all to do with the business now. He does not keep any money because he cannot tell good from counterfeit coins, but he is silent, he says nothing of this weakness. He has become forgetful, and if they don't give him food he does not ask for it. They have grown used to having dinner without him, and Varvara often says:

"He went to bed again yesterday without eating anything."

And she says it unconcernedly because she is used to it. For some reason, summer and winter alike, he wears a fur coat, and only in very hot weather he does not go out but sits at home. As a rule he puts on his fur coat, wraps it round him, turns up his collar, and walks about the village, along the road to the station, or sits from morning till night on the seat near the church gates. He sits there without stirring. Passers-by bow to him, but he does not respond, for as of old he dislikes the peasants. If he is asked a question he answers quite rationally and politely, but briefly.

There is a rumor going about in the village that his daughter-in-law has turned him out of the house and gives him nothing to eat, and that he is fed by charitable folk; some are glad, others are sorry for him.

Varvara has grown even fatter and her skin whiter, and as before she is active in good works, and Aksinya does not interfere with her.

There is so much jam now that they have not time to eat it before the fresh fruit comes in; it goes sugary, and Varvara almost sheds tears, not knowing what to do with it.

They have begun to forget about Anisim. Some time ago there came a letter from him written in verse on a big sheet of paper as though it were a petition, all in the same splendid handwriting. Evidently his friend Samorodov was doing time with him. Under the verses in an ugly, scarcely legible handwriting there was a single line: "I am ill here all the time; I am wretched, for Christ's sake help me!"

One fine autumn day towards evening old Tzybukin was sitting near the church gates, with the collar of his fur coat turned up and nothing of him could be seen but his nose and the peak of his cap. At the other end of the long bench sat Yelizarov the contractor, and beside him Yakov the school watchman, a toothless old man of seventy. Crutch and the watchman were talking.

"Children ought to give food and drink to the old. . . . Honor thy father and mother . . ." Yakov was saying with irritation, "while she, this woman, has turned her father-in-law out of his own house; the old man has neither food nor drink, where is he to go? He has not had a morsel these three days."

"Three days!" said Crutch, amazed.

"Here he sits and does not say a word. He has grown feeble. And why be silent? He ought to prosecute her, they wouldn't pat her on the back in court."

"Wouldn't pat whom on the back?" asked Crutch, not hearing.

"What?"

"The woman's all right, she does her best. In their line of business they can't get on without that . . . without sin, I mean. . . ."

"From his own house," Yakov went on with irritation. "Save up and buy your own house, then turn people out of it! She is a nice one, to be sure! A pla-ague!"

Tzybukin listened and did not stir.

"Whether it is your own house or others' it makes no difference so long as it is warm and the women don't scold . . ." said Crutch, and he laughed. "When I was young I was very fond of my Nastasya. She was a quiet woman. And she used to be always at it: 'Buy a house, Makarych! Buy a house, Makarych! Buy a horse, Makarych!' She was dying and yet she kept on saying, 'Buy yourself a racing droshky, Makarych, so that you don't have to walk.' And I bought her nothing but ginger-bread."

"Her husband's deaf and stupid," Yakov went on, not listening to Crutch; "a regular fool, just like a goose. He can't understand anything. Hit a goose on the head with a stick and even then it does not understand."

Crutch got up to go home. Yakov also got up, and both of them went off together, still talking. When they had gone fifty paces old Tzybukin got up, too, and walked after them, stepping uncertainly as though on slippery ice.

The village was already plunged in the dusk of evening and the sun only gleamed on the upper part of the road which ran wriggling like a snake up the slope. Old women were coming back from the woods and children with them; they were bringing baskets of mushrooms. Peasant women and girls came in a crowd from the station where they had been loading the cars with bricks, and their noses and the skin under their eyes were covered with red brick-dust. They were singing. Ahead of them all was Lipa, with her eyes turned towards the sky, she was singing in a high voice, breaking into trills as though exulting in the fact that at last the day was over and the time for rest had come. In the crowd walking with a bundle in her arms, breathless as usual, was her mother, Praskovya, who still went out to work by the day.

"Good evening, Makarych!" cried Lipa, seeing Crutch. "Good evening, dear!"

"Good evening, Lipinka," cried Crutch delighted. "Girls, women, love the rich carpenter! Ho-ho! My little children, my little children. (Crutch gave a sob.) My dear little hatchets!"

Crutch and Yakov went on farther and could still be heard talking. Then after them came old Tzybukin and there was a sudden hush in the crowd. Lipa and Praskovya had dropped a little behind, and when the old man was abreast of them Lipa bowed down low and said:

"Good evening, Grigory Petrovich."

Her mother, too, bowed. The old man stopped and, saying nothing, looked at the two; his lips were quivering and his eyes full of tears. Lipa took out of her mother's bundle a piece of pie stuffed with buckwheat and gave it to him. He took it and began eating.

The sun had set by now: its glow died away on the upper part of the road too. It was getting dark and cool. Lipa and Praskovya walked on and for some time kept crossing themselves.

1900

PLAYS

The Boor

A JEST IN ONE ACT

YELENA IVANOVNA POPOVA, a little widow with dimpled cheeks, a landowner.

GRIGORY STEPANOVICH SMIRNOV, a middle-aged gentleman farmer.

LUKA, Mme. Popova's footman, an old man.

THE drawing room in Mme. Popova's manor house. Mme. Popova, in deep mourning, her eyes fixed on a photograph, and Luka.

LUKA: It isn't right, madam. You're just killing yourself. The maid and the cook have gone berrying, every living thing rejoices, even the cat knows how to enjoy life and wanders through the courtyard catching birds, but you stay in the house as if it were a convent and take no pleasure at all. Yes, really! It's a whole year now, I figure, that you haven't left the house!

MME. POPOVA: And I never will leave it . . . What for? My life is over. He lies in his grave, and I have buried myself within these four walls. We are both dead.

LUKA: There you go again! I oughtn't to listen to you, really. Nikolay Mihailovich is dead, well, there is nothing to do about it, it's the will of God; may the kingdom of Heaven be his. You have grieved over it, and that's enough; there's a limit to everything. One can't cry and wear mourning forever. The time came when my old woman, too, died. Well? I grieved over it, I cried for a month, and that was enough for her, but to go on wailing all my life, why, the old woman isn't worth it. *Sighs.* You've forgotten all your neighbors. You don't go out and you won't receive anyone. We live, excuse me, like spiders—we never see the light of day. The mice have eaten the livery. And it isn't as if there were no nice people around—the county is full of gentlemen. A regiment is quartered at Ryblov and every officer is a good-looker, you can't take your eyes off them. And every Friday there's a ball at the camp, and 'most every day the military band is playing. Eh, my dear lady, you're young and pretty, just peaches and cream, and you could lead a life of pleasure. Beauty doesn't last forever, you know. In ten years' time you'll find yourself wanting to strut like a pea-hen and dazzle the officers, but it will be too late.

MME. POPOVA, *resolutely:* I beg you never to mention this to me again! You know that since Nikolay Mihailovich died, life has been worth nothing to me. You think that I am alive, but it only seems so to you! I vowed to myself that never to the day of my death would I take off my mourning or see the light. Do you hear me? Let his shade see how I love him! Yes, I know, it is no secret to you that he was often unjust to me, cruel, and . . . even unfaithful, but I shall be true to the end, and prove to him how I can love. There, in the other world, he will find me just the same as I was before he died . . .

LUKA: Instead of talking like that, you ought to go and take a walk in the garden, or have Toby or Giant put in the shafts and drive out to pay calls on the neighbors.

MME. POPOVA: Oh! *Weeps.*

LUKA: Madam! Dear madam! What's wrong? Bless you!

MME. POPOVA: He was so fond of Toby! When he drove out to the Korchagins and the Vlasovs it was always with Toby. What a wonderful driver he was! How graceful he was, when he pulled at the reins with all his might! Do you remember? Toby, Toby! Tell them to give him an extra measure of oats today.

LUKA: Very well, madam. *The doorbell rings sharply.*

MME. POPOVA, *startled:* Who is it? Say that I am at home to no one.

LUKA: Very good, madam. *Exits.*

MME. POPOVA, *looking at the photograph:* You shall see, *Nicolas,* how I can love and forgive. My love will die only with me, when my poor heart stops beating. *Laughs through her tears.* And aren't you ashamed? I am a good, faithful little wife, I've locked myself in and shall remain true to you to the grave, and you . . . aren't you ashamed, you naughty boy? You were unfaithful to me, you made scenes, you left me alone for weeks . . . LUKA *enters.*

LUKA, *disturbed:* Madam, someone is asking for you, wants to see you . . .

MME. POPOVA: But you told him, didn't you, that since my husband's death I receive no one?

LUKA: Yes, I did, but he wouldn't listen to me, he says it's a very urgent matter.

MME. POPOVA: I do not re-ceive anyone!

LUKA: I told him, but . . . he's a perfect devil . . . he curses and barges right in . . . he's in the dining-room now.

MME. POPOVA, *annoyed:* Very well, ask him in . . . What rude people! *Exit* LUKA. How irritating! What do they want of me? Why do they have to intrude on my solitude? *Sighs.* No, I see I shall really have to enter a convent. *Pensively:* Yes, a convent . . . *Enter* SMIRNOV *and* LUKA.

SMIRNOV, *to* LUKA: Blockhead, you talk too much. You jackass! *Seeing* MME. POPOVA, *with dignity.* Madam, I have the honor to introduce myself: Landowner Grigory Stepanovich Smirnov, lieutenant of the artillery, retired. I am compelled to disturb you in connection with a very weighty matter.

MME. POPOVA, *without offering her hand:* What do you wish?

SMIRNOV: At his death your late husband, with whom I had the honor of being acquainted, was in my debt to the amount of 1200 rubles, for which I hold two notes. As I have to pay interest on a loan to the Land Bank tomorrow, I must request you, madam, to pay me the money today.

MME. POPOVA: Twelve hundred. . . . And for what did my husband owe you the money?

SMIRNOV: He used to buy oats from me.

MME. POPOVA, *sighing, to* LUKA: So don't forget, Luka, to tell them to give Toby an extra measure of oats. *Exit* LUKA. *To* SMIRNOV. If Nikolay Mihailovich owed you money, I shall pay you, of course; but you must excuse me, I haven't any ready cash today. The day after tomorrow my steward will be back from town and I will see that he pays you what is owing to you, but just now I cannot comply with your request. Besides, today is exactly seven months since my husband's death and I am in no mood to occupy myself with money matters.

SMIRNOV: And I am in the mood to be carried out feet foremost if I don't pay the interest tomorrow. They'll seize my estate!

MME. POPOVA: The day after tomorrow you will receive your money.

SMIRNOV: I need the money today, not the day after tomorrow.

MME. POPOVA: I am sorry, but I cannot pay you today.

SMIRNOV: And I can't wait till the day after tomorrow.

MME. POPOVA: But what can I do if I don't have the money now!

SMIRNOV: So you can't pay me?

MME. POPOVA: No, I can't.

SMIRNOV: H'm . . . So that's your last word?

MME. POPOVA: My last word.

SMIRNOV: Your last word? Positively?

MME. POPOVA: Positively.

SMIRNOV: Many thanks. I'll make a note of it. *Shrugs his shoulders.* And they want me to keep cool! I meet the tax commissioner on the road, and he asks me: "Why are you always in a bad humor, Grigory Stepanovich?" But in heaven's name, how can I help being in a bad humor? I'm in desperate need of money. I left home yesterday morning at dawn and called on all my debtors and not one of them paid up! I wore myself out, slept the devil knows where, in some Jewish inn next to a barrel of vodka . . . Finally I come here, fifty miles from home, hoping to get something, and I'm confronted with a "mood." How can I help getting in a temper?

MME. POPOVA: I thought I made it clear to you that you will get your money as soon as my steward returns from town.

SMIRNOV: I didn't come to your steward, but to you! What the devil—pardon the expression—do I care for your steward!

MME. POPOVA: Excuse me, sir, I am not accustomed to such language or to such a tone. I won't listen to you any more. *Exits rapidly.*

SMIRNOV: That's a nice thing! Not in the mood . . .

husband died seven months ago! What about me? Do I
have to pay the interest or don't I? I'm asking you: do
I have to pay the interest or don't I? Well, your husband
died, you're not in the mood, and all that . . . and
your steward, devil take him, has gone off somewhere,
but what do you want me to do? Am I to escape my
creditors in a balloon, eh? Or take a running start and
dash my head against a wall? I call on Gruzdev, he's
not at home, Yaroshevich is hiding, I had an awful row
with Kuritzyn and nearly threw him out of the window;
Mazutov has an upset stomach, and this one isn't in the
mood! Not one scoundrel will pay up! And it's all because I've spoiled them, because I'm a milksop, a softy,
a weak sister. I'm too gentle with them altogether! But
wait! You'll find out what I'm like! I won't let you make
a fool of me, devil take it! I'll stay right here till she
pays up! Ugh! I'm in a perfect rage today, in a rage!
Every one of my nerves is trembling with fury, I can
hardly breathe. Ouf! Good Lord, I even feel sick!
Shouts. You there! *Enter* LUKA.

LUKA: What do you wish?

SMIRNOV: Give me some *kvass* or a drink of water!
Exit LUKA. No, but the logic of it! A fellow is in desperate need of cash, is on the point of hanging himself, but
she won't pay up, because, you see, she isn't in the
mood to occupy herself with money matters! Real petti-
coat logic! That's why I've never liked to talk to women,
and I don't now. I'd rather sit on a powder-keg than
talk to a woman. Brr! I'm getting gooseflesh—that skirt
made me so furious! I just have to see one of these
poetic creatures from a distance and my very calves
begin to twitch with rage. It's enough to make me yell
for help. *Enter* LUKA.

LUKA, *handing* SMIRNOV *a glass of water:* Madam is ill
and will see no one.

SMIRNOV: Get out! *Exit* LUKA. Ill and will see no one! All right, don't see me. I'll sit here until you pay up. If you're sick for a week, I'll stay a week; if you're sick a year, I'll stay a year. I'll get my own back, my good woman. You won't get round me with your widow's weeds and your dimples . . . We know those dimples! *Shouts through the window.* Semyon, take out the horses! We're not leaving so soon! I'm staying on! Tell them at the stables to give the horses oats. You block-head, you've let the left outrider's leg get caught in the reins again! *Mimicking the coachman.* "It don't matter" . . . I'll show you "don't matter." *Walks away from the window.* It's horrible . . . the heat is terrific, nobody has paid up, I slept badly, and here's this skirt in mourning, with her moods! I have a headache. Shall I have some vodka? Yes, I think I will. *Shouts.* You there! *Enter* LUKA.

LUKA: What do you wish?

SMIRNOV: Give me a glass of vodka. *Exit* LUKA. Ouf! *Sits down and looks himself over.* I cut a fine figure, I must say! All dusty, boots dirty, unwashed, uncombed, straw on my vest. The little lady must have taken me for a highwayman. *Yawns.* It's a bit uncivil to barge into a drawing-room in such shape, but never mind . . . I'm no caller, just a creditor, and there are no rules as to what the creditor should wear. *Enter* LUKA.

LUKA, *handing* SMIRNOV *the vodka:* You allow yourself too many liberties, sir . . .

SMIRNOV, *crossly:* What?

LUKA: I . . . nothing . . . I just meant . . .

SMIRNOV: To whom do you think you're talking? Shut up!

LUKA, *aside:* There's a demon in the house . . . The Evil Spirit must have brought him . . . *Exit* LUKA.

SMIRNOV: Oh, what a rage I'm in! I'm mad enough to

grind the whole world to powder. I feel sick. *Shouts.*
You there! *Enter* MME. POPOVA.

MME. POPOVA, *with downcast eyes:* Sir, in my solitude
I've long since grown unaccustomed to the human voice,
and I cannot bear shouting. I beg you not to disturb my
peace!

SMIRNOV: Pay me my money and I'll drive off.

MME. POPOVA: I told you in plain language, I have no
ready cash now. Wait till the day after tomorrow.

SMIRNOV: And I had the honor of telling you in plain
language that I need the money today, not the day after
tomorrow. If you don't pay me today, I'll have to hang
myself tomorrow.

MME. POPOVA: But what shall I do if I have no money?
How odd!

SMIRNOV: So you won't pay me now, eh?

MME. POPOVA: I can't.

SMIRNOV: In that case I stay and I'll sit here till I get
the money. *Sits down.* You'll pay me the day after tomorrow? Excellent. I'll sit here till the day after tomorrow. *Jumps up.* I ask you: Do I have to pay the interest
tomorrow or don't I? Or do you think I'm joking?

MME. POPOVA: Sir, I beg you not to shout. This is no
stable.

SMIRNOV: Never mind the stable, I'm asking you: Do
I have to pay the interest tomorrow or not?

MME. POPOVA: You don't know how to behave in the
presence of ladies!

SMIRNOV: No, madam, I do know how to behave in
the presence of ladies!

MME. POPOVA: No, you do not! You are a rude, ill-
bred man! Decent people don't talk to women that way!

SMIRNOV: Admirable! How would you like me to talk
to you? In French, eh? *Rages, and lisps: Madame, je
vous prie,* I am delighted that you do not pay me my

money . . . Ah, *pardonnez-moi* if I have discommoded you! It's such delightful weather today! And how your mourning becomes you! *Scrapes his foot.*

MME. POPOVA: That's rude and silly.

SMIRNOV, *mimicking her:* Rude and silly! I don't know how to behave in the presence of ladies! Madam, I've seen more ladies than you've seen sparrows! I've fought three duels on account of women, I've jilted twelve women and been jilted by nine! Yes, madam! Time was when I played the fool, sentimentalized, used honeyed words, went out of my way to please, bowed and scraped . . . I used to love, pine, sigh at the moon, feel blue, melt, freeze . . . I loved passionately, madly, all sorts of ways, devil take me; I chattered like a magpie about the emancipation of women, I wasted half my fortune on affairs of the heart, but now, please excuse me! Now you won't bamboozle me! Enough! Dark eyes, burning eyes, ruby lips, dimpled cheeks, the moon, whispers, timid breathing . . . I wouldn't give a brass farthing for all this now, madam. Present company excepted, all women, young or old, put on airs, pose, gossip, are liars to the marrow of their bones, are malicious, vain, petty, cruel, revoltingly unreasonable, and as for this (*taps his forehead*), pardon my frankness, a sparrow can give ten points to any philosopher in skirts! You look at one of these poetic creatures: She's all muslin and fluff, an airy demi-goddess, a million transports, but look into her soul and what do you see but a common crocodile! *Grips the back of his chair so that it cracks and breaks.* But what is most revolting, this crocodile for some reason imagines that the tender feelings are her special province, her privilege, her monopoly! Why, devil take it, hang me by my feet on that nail, but can a woman love anything except a lap-dog? When she's in love all she can do is whimper and turn on the waterworks! While a man suffers and makes sacrifices, her love finds expression only in swishing her train and trying to get a firmer grip on your nose. You, madam, have the misfortune of being a woman, so you know the nature of women down to the ground. Tell me honestly, then, did you ever see a woman who was sincere, faithful, and constant? You never did! Only old women and frights are faithful and constant. You'll sooner come across a horned cat or a white woodcock than a constant woman!

MME. POPOVA: Allow me to ask, then, who, in your opinion, is faithful and constant in love? Not man?

SMIRNOV: Yes, madam, man!

MME. POPOVA: Man! *With bitter laughter.* Man is faithful and constant in love! That's news! *Hotly.* What earthly right do you have to say that? Men faithful and constant! If such is the case, let me tell you that of all the men I have ever known my late husband was the best. I loved him passionately, with my whole soul, as only a young, deep-natured woman can love. I gave him my youth, my happiness, my life, my fortune; I lived and breathed by him; I worshiped him like a heathen, and . . . and what happened? This best of men deceived me shamelessly at every step! After his death I found a whole drawerful of love letters in his desk, and while he was alive—I can't bear to recall it!—he would leave me alone for weeks on end; he made love to other women before my very eyes, and he was unfaithful to me; he squandered my money and mocked my feelings. And in spite of it all, I loved him and was faithful to him. More than that, he died, and I am still faithful to him, still constant. I have buried myself forever within these four walls, and I will not take off my mourning till I go to my grave.

SMIRNOV, *laughing scornfully:* Mourning! I wonder

who you take me for! As if I didn't know why you are masquerading in black like this and why you've buried yourself within four walls! Of course I do! It's so mysterious, so poetic! Some cadet or some puny versifier will ride past the house, glance at the windows, and say to himself: "Here lives the mysterious Tamara who, for love of her husband, has buried herself within four walls." We know those tricks!

MME. POPOVA, *flaring up:* What! How dare you say this to me!

SMIRNOV: You've buried yourself alive, but you haven't forgotten to powder your nose.

MME. POPOVA: How dare you talk to me like that!

SMIRNOV: Please don't scream, I'm not your steward! Allow me to call a spade a spade. I'm no woman and I'm used to talking straight from the shoulder! So please don't shout!

MME. POPOVA: I'm not shouting, you are shouting! Please leave me alone!

SMIRNOV: Pay me my money, and I'll go.

MME. POPOVA: I won't give you any money.

SMIRNOV: No, madam, you will!

MME. POPOVA: Just to spite you, I won't give you a penny. Only leave me alone!

SMIRNOV: I haven't the pleasure of being either your husband or your fiancé, so kindly, no scenes. *Sits down.* I don't like them.

MME. POPOVA, *choking with rage:* You've sat down?

SMIRNOV: I've sat down.

MME. POPOVA: I ask you to leave.

SMIRNOV: Give me my money . . . *aside.* Oh, what a rage I'm in, what a rage!

MME. POPOVA: Such impudence! I don't want to talk to you. Please get out. *Pause.* Are you going? No?

SMIRNOV: No.

Mme. Popova: No?

Smirnov: No!

Mme. Popova: Very well, then. *Enter* Luka.

Mme. Popova: Luka, show this gentleman out!

Luka, *approaching* Smirnov: Sir, be good enough to leave when you are asked to. Don't be—

Smirnov, *jumping to his feet:* Shut up! Who do you think you're talking to! I'll make hash of you!

Luka, *clutching at his heart:* Mercy on us! Holy saints! *Drops into an armchair.* Oh, I'm sick, I'm sick! I can't get my breath!

Mme. Popova: But where is Dasha? Dasha? *Shouts.* Dasha! Pelageya! Dasha! *Rings.*

Luka: Oh, they've all gone berrying . . . There's no one here . . . I'm sick, water!

Mme. Popova, *to* Smirnov: Please, get out!

Smirnov: Can't you be a little more civil?

Mme. Popova, *clenching her fists and stamping her feet:* You're a boor! A brute, a bully, a monster!

Smirnov: What! What did you say?

Mme. Popova: I said that you were a brute, a monster.

Smirnov, *advancing upon her:* Excuse me, but what right have you to insult me?

Mme. Popova: Yes, I insulted you. What of it? Do you think I'm afraid of you?

Smirnov: And you think, just because you're a poetic creature, you can insult people with impunity, eh? I challenge you!

Luka: Mercy on us! Holy saints! Water!

Smirnov: We'll shoot it out!

Mme. Popova: Just because you have big fists and bellow like a bull, you think I'm afraid of you, eh? Bully!

Smirnov: I challenge you! I won't allow anybody to insult me, and it makes no difference to me that you're a woman, a member of the weaker sex.

Mme. Popova, *trying to outshout him:* Brute, brute, brute!

Smirnov: It's high time to abandon the prejudice that men alone must pay for insults. Equal rights are equal rights, devil take it! I challenge you!

Mme. Popova: You want to shoot it out? Well and good.

Smirnov: This very minute.

Mme. Popova: This very minute. I have my husband's pistols. I'll bring them directly. *Walks rapidly away and turns back.* What pleasure it will give me to put a bullet into your brazen head! Devil take you! *Exits.*

Smirnov: I'll bring her down like a duck. I'm no boy, no sentimental puppy. There's no weaker sex as far as I'm concerned.

Luka, *to* Smirnov: Master, kind sir! *Going down on his knees.* Have pity on an old man, do me a favor—go away from here! You've frightened me to death, and now you want to fight a duel!

Smirnov, *not listening to him:* A duel! That's equal rights, that's emancipation! That's equality of the sexes for you! I'll bring her down as a matter of principle. But what a woman! *Mimics her.* "Devil take you . . . I'll put a bullet into your brazen head." What a woman! She flushed and her eyes shone! She accepted the challenge! Word of honor, it's the first time in my life that I've seen one of that stripe.

Luka: Kind master, please go away, and I will pray for you always.

Smirnov: That's a woman! That's the kind I understand! A real woman! Not a sour-faced, spineless crybaby, but a creature all fire and gunpowder, a cannonball! It's a pity I have to kill her!

Luka, *crying:* Sir, kind sir, please go away!

Smirnov: I positively like her! Positively! Even though

she has dimples in her cheeks, I like her! I am even ready to forgive her the debt . . . And I'm not angry any more. A remarkable woman! *Enter* MME. POPOVA *with the pistols.*

MME. POPOVA: Here are the pistols. But before we fight, please show me how to shoot. I never held a pistol in my hands before.

LUKA: Lord, have mercy on us! I'll go and look for the gardener and the coachman. Why has this calamity befallen us? *Exits.*

SMIRNOV, *examining the pistols:* You see, there are several makes of pistols. There are Mortimers, specially made for duelling, they are fired with the percussion cap. What you have here are Smith and Wesson triple-action, central-fire revolvers with extractors. Excellent pistols! Worth ninety rubles a pair at least. You hold the revolver like this . . . *Aside.* The eyes, the eyes! A woman to set you on fire!

MME. POPOVA: Like this?

SMIRNOV: Yes, like this. Then you cock the trigger . . . and you take aim like this . . . throw your head back a little! Stretch your arm out properly . . . Like this . . . Then you press this gadget with this finger, and that's all there is to it. . . . The main thing is: Keep cool and take aim slowly. . . . And try not to jerk your arm.

MME. POPOVA: Very well. It's inconvenient to shoot indoors, let's go into the garden.

SMIRNOV: All right. Only I warn you, I'll fire into the air.

MME. POPOVA: That's all that was wanting. Why?

SMIRNOV: Because . . . because . . . It's my business why.

MME. POPOVA: You're scared, eh? Ah, ah, ah! No, sir, don't try to get out of it! Be so good as to follow me.

I shan't rest until I've drilled a hole in your forehead
. . . this forehead that I hate so! Scared?

SMIRNOV: Yes, I am scared.

MME. POPOVA: You're lying! Why do you refuse to
fight?

SMIRNOV: Because . . . because I . . . like you.

MME. POPOVA *laughing bitterly:* He likes me! He dares
to say that he likes me! *Shows him the door.* You may
go.

SMIRNOV, *silently puts down the revolver, takes his
cap and walks to the door; there he stops and for half
a minute the pair look at each other without a word;
then he says, hesitatingly approaching* MME. POPOVA:
Listen . . . Are you still angry? I'm in a devil of a
temper myself, but you see . . . how shall I put it?
. . . the thing is . . . you see . . . it's this way . . .
in fact . . . *Shouts.* Well, am I to blame if I like **you**?
Clutches the back of his chair; it cracks and breaks. **The**
devil! What fragile furniture you have! I like you. You
understand. I've almost fallen in love.

MME. POPOVA: Go away from me. I hate you.

SMIRNOV: God, what a woman! Never in my life have I
seen anything like her! I'm lost. I'm done for. I'm
trapped like a mouse.

MME. POPOVA: Go away, or I'll shoot.

SMIRNOV: Shoot! You can't understand what happiness
it would be to die before those enchanting eyes . . . to
die of a revolver shot fired by this little velvet hand! I've
lost my mind. Think a moment and decide right now,
because if I leave this house, we'll never see each other
again. Decide. I'm a landed gentleman, a decent fellow,
with an income of ten thousand a year; I can put a
bullet through a penny thrown into the air; I have a
good stable. Will you be my wife?

MME. POPOVA, *indignant, brandishing the revolver:*
We'll shoot it out! Come along! Get your pistol.

SMIRNOV: I've lost my mind. I don't understand anything. *Shouts.* You there! Some water!

MME. POPOVA *shouts:* Come! Let's shoot it out!

SMIRNOV: I've lost my mind. I've fallen in love like a
boy, like a fool. *Seizes her by the hand; she cries out
with pain.* I love you. *Goes down on his knees.* I love
you as I've never loved before. I jilted twelve women
and was jilted by nine. But I didn't love one of them as
I do you. I've gotten sentimental. I'm melting. I'm weak
as water. Here I am on my knees like a fool, and I offer
you my hand. It's a shame, a disgrace! For five years I've
not been in love. I took a vow. And suddenly I'm
bowled over, swept off my feet. I offer you my hand—
yes or no? You won't? Then don't! *Rises and walks
rapidly to the door.*

MME. POPOVA: Wait a minute.

SMIRNOV *stops:* Well?

MME. POPOVA: Never mind. Go . . . But no, wait a
minute . . . No, go, go! I detest you! Or no . . . don't
go! Oh, if you knew how furious I am, how furious!
Throws the revolver on the table. My fingers are
cramped from holding this vile thing. *Tears her handkerchief in a fit of temper.* What are you standing there
for? Get out!

SMIRNOV: Good-by.

MME. POPOVA: Yes, yes, go! *Shouts.* Where are you going? Wait a minute . . . But no, go away . . . Oh,
how furious I am! Don't come near me, don't come near
me!

SMIRNOV, *approaching her:* I'm disgusted with myself!
Falling in love like a moon-calf, going down on my
knees. It gives me gooseflesh. *Rudely.* I love you. What

on earth made me fall in love with you? Tomorrow I have to pay the interest. And we've started mowing. And here are you! . . . *Puts his arm around her waist.* I shall never forgive myself for this.

MME. POPOVA: Get away from me! Hands off! I hate you! Let's shoot it out!

A prolonged kiss. Enter LUKA *with an ax, the gardener with a rake, the coachman with a pitchfork, and hired men with sticks.*

LUKA, *catching sight of the pair kissing:* Mercy on us! Holy saints! *Pauses.*

MME. POPOVA, *dropping her eyes:* Luka, tell them at the stables that Toby isn't to have any oats at all today.

1888

The Cherry Orchard

A COMEDY IN FOUR ACTS

Lubov Andreyevna Ranevskaya, a landowner.

Anya, her seventeen-year-old daughter.

Varya, her adopted daughter, twenty-two years old.

Leonid Andreyevich Gayev, Mme. Ranevskaya's brother.

Yermolay Alexeyevich Lopahin, a merchant.

Pyotr Sergeyevich Trofimov, a student.

Simeonov-Pishchik, a landowner.

Charlotta Ivanovna, a governess.

Semyon Yepihodov, a clerk.

Dunyasha, a maid.

Firs [pronounced *fierce*], a man-servant, aged eighty-seven.

Yasha, a young valet.

A Tramp.

Stationmaster, Post Office Clerk, Guests, Servants.

The action takes place on Mme. Ranevskaya's estate.

Act I

A ROOM *that is still called the nursery. One of the
doors leads into Anya's room. Dawn, the sun will
soon rise. It is May, the cherry trees are in blossom, but
it is cold in the orchard; there is a morning frost. The
windows are shut. Enter* DUNYASHA *with a candle, and*
LOPAHIN *with a book in his hand.*

LOPAHIN: The train is in, thank God. What time is it?

DUNYASHA: Nearly two. *Puts out the candle.* It's light
already.

LOPAHIN: How late is the train, anyway? Two hours
at least. *Yawns and stretches.* I'm a fine one! What a fool
I've made of myself! I came here on purpose to meet
them at the station, and then I went and overslept. I fell
asleep in my chair. How annoying! You might have
waked me . . .

DUNYASHA: I thought you'd left. *Listens.* I think
they're coming!

LOPAHIN, *listens:* No, they've got to get the luggage,
and one thing and another . . . *Pause.* Lubov Andreyevna spent five years abroad, I don't know what
she's like now . . . She's a fine person—lighthearted,
simple. I remember when I was a boy of fifteen, my poor
father—he had a shop here in the village then—
punched me in the face with his fist and made my nose
bleed. We'd come into the yard, I don't know what for,
and he'd had a drop too much. Lubov Andreyevna, I
remember her as if it were yesterday—she was still
young and so slim—led me to the wash-basin, in this
very room . . . in the nursery. "Don't cry, little peasant," she said, "it'll heal in time for your wedding. . . ."

Pause. Little peasant . . . my father was a peasant, it's true, and here I am in a white waistcoat and yellow shoes. A pig in a pastry shop, you might say. It's true I'm rich, I've got a lot of money. . . . But when you look at it closely, I'm a peasant through and through. *Pages the book.* Here I've been reading this book and I didn't understand a word of it. . . . I was reading it and fell asleep. . . . *Pause.*

DUNYASHA: And the dogs were awake all night, they feel that their masters are coming.

LOPAHIN: Dunyasha, why are you so—

DUNYASHA: My hands are trembling. I'm going to faint.

LOPAHIN: You're too soft, Dunyasha. You dress like a lady, and look at the way you do your hair. That's not right. One should remember one's place.

Enter YEPIHODOV *with a bouquet; he wears a jacket and highly polished boots that squeak badly. He drops the bouquet as he comes in.*

YEPIHODOV, *picking up the bouquet:* Here, the gardener sent these, said you're to put them in the dining room. *Hands the bouquet to* DUNYASHA.

LOPAHIN: And bring me some *kvass.*

DUNYASHA: Yes, sir. *Exits.*

YEPIHODOV: There's a frost this morning—three degrees below—and yet the cherries are all in blossom. I cannot approve of our climate. *Sighs.* I cannot. Our climate does not activate properly. And, Yermolay Alexeyevich, allow me to make a further remark. The other day I bought myself a pair of boots, and I make bold to assure you, they squeak so that it is really intolerable. What should I grease them with?

LOPAHIN: Oh, get out! I'm fed up with you.

YEPIHODOV: Every day I meet with misfortune. And I don't complain, I've got used to it, I even smile.

DUNYASHA *enters, hands* LOPAHIN *the kvass.*

YEPIHODOV: I am leaving. *Stumbles against a chair, which falls over.* There! *Triumphantly, as it were.* There again, you see what sort of circumstance, pardon the expression. . . . It is absolutely phenomenal! *Exits.*

DUNYASHA: You know, Yermolay Alexeyevich, I must tell you, Yepihodov has proposed to me.

LOPAHIN: Ah!

DUNYASHA: I simply don't know . . . he's a quiet man, but sometimes when he starts talking, you can't make out what he means. He speaks nicely—and it's touching—but you can't understand it. I sort of like him though, and he is crazy about me. He's an unlucky man . . . every day something happens to him. They tease him about it here . . . they call him, Two-and-Twenty Troubles.

LOPAHIN, *listening:* There! I think they're coming.

DUNYASHA: They *are* coming! What's the matter with me? I feel cold all over.

LOPAHIN: They really are coming. Let's go and meet them. Will she recognize me? We haven't seen each other for five years.

DUNYASHA, *in a flutter:* I'm going to faint this minute. . . . Oh, I'm going to faint!

Two carriages are heard driving up to the house. LOPAHIN *and* DUNYASHA *go out quickly. The stage is left empty. There is a noise in the adjoining rooms.* FIRS, *who had driven to the station to meet* LUBOV ANDRE-YEVNA RANEVSKAYA, *crosses the stage hurriedly, leaning on a stick. He is wearing an old-fashioned livery and a tall hat. He mutters to himself indistinctly. The hubbub off-stage increases.* A VOICE: "Come, let's go this way." *Enter* LUBOV ANDREYEVNA, ANYA *and* CHARLOTTA IVA-NOVNA, *with a pet dog on a leash, all in traveling dresses;* VARYA, *wearing a coat and kerchief;* GAYEV, SIMEONOV-

PISHCHIK, LOPAHIN, DUNYASHA *with a bag and an umbrella, servants with luggage. All walk across the room.*

ANYA: Let's go this way. Do you remember what room this is, mamma?

MME. RANEVSKAYA, *joyfully, through her tears:* The nursery!

VARYA: How cold it is! My hands are numb. *To* MME. RANEVSKAYA. Your rooms are just the same as they were mamma, the white one and the violet.

MME. RANEVSKAYA: The nursery! My darling, lovely room! I slept here when I was a child . . . *Cries.* And here I am, like a child again! *Kisses her brother and* VARYA, *and then her brother again.* Varya's just the same as ever, like a nun. And I recognized Dunyasha. *Kisses* DUNYASHA.

GAYEV: The train was two hours late. What do you think of that? What a way to manage things!

CHARLOTTA, *to* PISHCHIK: My dog eats nuts, too.

PISHCHIK, *in amazement:* You don't say so!

All go out, except ANYA *and* DUNYASHA.

DUNYASHA: We've been waiting for you for hours. *Takes* ANYA's *hat and coat.*

ANYA: I didn't sleep on the train for four nights and now I'm frozen . . .

DUNYASHA: It was Lent when you left; there was snow and frost, and now . . . My darling! *Laughs and kisses her.* I have been waiting for you, my sweet, my darling! But I must tell you something . . . I can't put it off another minute . . .

ANYA, *listlessly:* What now?

DUNYASHA: The clerk, Yepihodov, proposed to me, just after Easter.

ANYA: There you are, at it again . . . *Straightening her hair.* I've lost all my hairpins . . . *She is staggering with exhaustion.*

DUNYASHA: Really, I don't know what to think. He loves me—he loves me so!

ANYA, *looking towards the door of her room, tenderly:* My own room, my windows, just as though I'd never been away. I'm home! Tomorrow morning I'll get up and run into the orchard. Oh, if I could only get some sleep. I didn't close my eyes during the whole journey— I was so anxious.

DUNYASHA: Pyotr Sergeyevich came the day before yesterday.

ANYA, *joyfully:* Petya!

DUNYASHA: He's asleep in the bath-house. He has settled there. He said he was afraid of being in the way. *Looks at her watch.* I should wake him, but Miss Varya told me not to. "Don't you wake him," she said.

Enter VARYA *with a bunch of keys at her belt.*

VARYA: Dunyasha, coffee, and be quick . . . Mamma's asking for coffee.

DUNYASHA: In a minute. *Exits.*

VARYA: Well, thank God, you've come. You're home again. *Fondling* ANYA. My darling is here again. My pretty one is back.

ANYA: Oh, what I've been through!

VARYA: I can imagine.

ANYA: When we left, it was Holy Week, it was cold then, and all the way Charlotta chattered and did her tricks. Why did you have to saddle me with Charlotta?

VARYA: You couldn't have traveled all alone, darling —at seventeen!

ANYA: We got to Paris, it was cold there, snowing. My French is dreadful. Mamma lived on the fifth floor; I went up there, and found all kinds of Frenchmen, ladies, an old priest with a book. The place was full of tobacco smoke, and so bleak. Suddenly I felt sorry for mamma, so sorry, I took her head in my arms and hugged her and couldn't let go of her. Afterwards mamma kept fondling me and crying . . .

VARYA, *through tears:* Don't speak of it . . . don't.

ANYA: She had already sold her villa at Mentone, she had nothing left, nothing. I hadn't a kopeck left either, we had only just enough to get home. And mamma wouldn't understand! When we had dinner at the stations, she always ordered the most expensive dishes, and tipped the waiters a whole ruble. Charlotta, too. And Yasha kept ordering, too—it was simply awful. You know Yasha's mamma's footman now, we brought him here with us.

VARYA: Yes, I've seen the blackguard.

ANYA: Well, tell me—have you paid the interest?

VARYA: How could we?

ANYA: Good heavens, good heavens!

VARYA: In August the estate will be put up for sale.

ANYA: My God!

LOPAHIN *peeps in at the door and bleats.*

LOPAHIN: Meh-h-h. *Disappears.*

VARYA, *through tears:* What I couldn't do to him! *Shakes her fist threateningly.*

ANYA, *embracing* VARYA, *gently:* Varya, has he proposed to you? VARYA *shakes her head.* But he loves you. Why don't you come to an understanding? What are you waiting for?

VARYA: Oh, I don't think anything will ever come of it. He's too busy, he has no time for me . . . pays no attention to me. I've washed my hands of him—I can't bear the sight of him. They all talk about our getting married, they all congratulate me—and all the time there's really nothing to it—it's all like a dream. *In another tone.* You have a new brooch—like a bee.

ANYA, *sadly:* Mamma bought it. *She goes into her own room and speaks gaily like a child.* And you know, in Paris I went up in a balloon.

VARYA: My darling's home, my pretty one is back! DUNYASHA *returns with the coffee-pot and prepares coffee.* VARYA *stands at the door of* ANYA's *room.* All day long, darling, as I go about the house, I keep dreaming. If only we could marry you off to a rich man, I should feel at ease. Then I would go into a convent, and afterwards to Kiev, to Moscow . . . I would spend my life going from one holy place to another . . . I'd go on and on . . . What a blessing that would be!

ANYA: The birds are singing in the orchard. What time is it?

VARYA: It must be after two. Time you were asleep, darling. *Goes into* ANYA's *room.* What a blessing that would be!

YASHA *enters with a plaid and a traveling bag, crosses the stage.*

YASHA, *finically:* May I pass this way, please?

DUNYASHA: A person could hardly recognize you, Yasha. Your stay abroad has certainly done wonders for you.

YASHA: Hm-m . . . and who are you?

DUNYASHA: When you went away I was that high—*Indicating with her hand.* I'm Dunyasha—Fyodor Kozoyedev's daughter. Don't you remember?

YASHA: Hm! What a peach! *He looks round and embraces her. She cries out and drops a saucer.* YASHA *leaves quickly.*

VARYA, *in the doorway, in a tone of annoyance:* What's going on here?

DUNYASHA, *through tears:* I've broken a saucer.

VARYA: Well, that's good luck.

ANYA, *coming out of her room:* We ought to warn mamma that Petya's here.

VARYA: I left orders not to wake him.

ANYA, *musingly:* Six years ago father died. A month later brother Grisha was drowned in the river. . . . Such a pretty little boy he was—only seven. It was more than mamma could bear, so she went away, went away without looking back . . . *Shudders.* How well I understand her, if she only knew! *Pauses.* And Petya Trofimov was Grisha's tutor, he may remind her of it all . . .

Enter FIRS, *wearing a jacket and a white waistcoat. He goes up to the coffee-pot.*

FIRS, *anxiously:* The mistress will have her coffee here. *Puts on white gloves.* Is the coffee ready? *Sternly, to* DUNYASHA. Here, you! And where's the cream?

DUNYASHA: Oh, my God! *Exits quickly.*

FIRS, *fussing over the coffee-pot:* Hah! the addlehead! *Mutters to himself.* Home from Paris. And the old master used to go to Paris too . . . by carriage. *Laughs.*

VARYA: What is it, Firs?

FIRS: What is your pleasure, Miss? *Joyfully.* My mistress has come home, and I've seen her at last! Now I can die. *Weeps with joy.*

Enter MME. RANEVSKAYA, GAYEV, *and* SIMEONOV-PISHCHIK. *The latter is wearing a tight-waisted, pleated coat of fine cloth, and full trousers.* GAYEV, *as he comes in, goes through the motions of a billiard player with his arms and body.*

MME. RANEVSKAYA: Let's see, how does it go? Yellow ball in the corner! Bank shot in the side pocket!

GAYEV: I'll tip it in the corner! There was a time, sister, when you and I used to sleep in this very room, and now I'm fifty-one, strange as it may seem.

LOPAHIN: Yes, time flies.

GAYEV: Who?

LOPAHIN: I say, time flies.

GAYEV: It smells of patchouli here.

ANYA: I'm going to bed. Good night, mamma. *Kisses her mother.*

MME. RANEVSKAYA: My darling child! *Kisses her hands.* Are you happy to be home? I can't come to my senses.

ANYA: Good night, uncle.

GAYEV, *kissing her face and hands:* God bless you, how like your mother you are! *To his sister.* At her age, Luba, you were just like her.

ANYA *shakes hands with* LOPAHIN *and* PISHCHIK, *then goes out, shutting the door behind her.*

MME. RANEVSKAYA: She's very tired.

PISHCHIK: Well, it was a long journey.

VARYA, *to* LOPAHIN *and* PISHCHIK: How about it, gentlemen? It's past two o'clock—isn't it time for you to go?

MME. RANEVSKAYA, *laughs:* You're just the same as ever, Varya. *Draws her close and kisses her.* I'll have my coffee and then we'll all go. FIRS *puts a small cushion under her feet.* Thank you, my dear. I've got used to coffee. I drink it day and night. Thanks, my dear old man. *Kisses him.*

VARYA: I'd better see if all the luggage has been brought in. *Exits.*

MME. RANEVSKAYA: Can it really be I sitting here? *Laughs.* I feel like dancing, waving my arms about. *Covers her face with her hands.* But maybe I am dreaming! God knows I love my country, I love it tenderly; I couldn't look out of the window in the train, I kept crying so. *Through tears.* But I must have my coffee. Thank you, Firs, thank you, dear old man. I'm so happy that you're still alive.

FIRS: Day before yesterday.

GAYEV: He's hard of hearing.

LOPAHIN: I must go soon, I'm leaving for Kharkov about five o'clock. How annoying! I'd like to have a good look at you, talk to you . . . You're just as splendid as ever.

PISHCHIK, *breathing heavily:* She's even better-looking. . . . Dressed in the latest Paris fashion. . . . Perish my carriage and all its four wheels. . . .

LOPAHIN: Your brother, Leonid Andreyevich, says I'm a vulgarian and an exploiter. But it's all the same to me—let him talk. I only want you to trust me as you used to. I want you to look at me with your touching, wonderful eyes, as you used to. Dear God! My father was a serf of your father's and grandfather's, but you, you yourself, did so much for me once . . . so much . . . that I've forgotten all about that; I love you as though you were my sister—even more.

MME. RANEVSKAYA: I can't sit still, I simply can't. *Jumps up and walks about in violent agitation.* This joy is too much for me. . . . Laugh at me, I'm silly! My own darling bookcase! My darling table! *Kisses it.*

GAYEV: While you were away, nurse died.

MME. RANEVSKAYA, *sits down and takes her coffee:* Yes, God rest her soul; they wrote me about it.

GAYEV: And Anastasy is dead. Petrushka Kossoy has left me and has gone into town to work for the police inspector. *Takes a box of sweets out of his pocket and begins to suck one.*

PISHCHIK: My daughter Dashenka sends her regards.

LOPAHIN: I'd like to tell you something very pleasant —cheering. *Glancing at his watch.* I am leaving directly. There isn't much time to talk. But I will put it in a few words. As you know, your cherry orchard is to be sold to pay your debts. The sale is to be on the twenty-second of August; but don't you worry, my dear, you may sleep in peace; there is a way out. Here is my plan. Give me your attention! Your estate is only fifteen miles from the town; the railway runs close by it; and if the cherry orchard and the land along the river bank were cut up into lots and these leased for summer cottages, you would have an income of at least 25,000 rubles a year out of it.

GAYEV: Excuse me. . . . What nonsense.

MME. RANEVSKAYA: I don't quite understand you, Yermolay Alexeyevich.

LOPAHIN: You will get an annual rent of at least ten rubles per acre, and if you advertise at once, I'll give you any guarantee you like that you won't have a square foot of ground left by autumn, all the lots will be snapped up. In short, congratulations, you're saved. The location is splendid—by that deep river. . . . Only, of course, the ground must be cleared . . . all the old buildings, for instance, must be torn down, and this house, too, which is useless, and, of course, the old cherry orchard must be cut down.

MME. RANEVSKAYA: Cut down? My dear, forgive me, but you don't know what you're talking about. If there's one thing that's interesting—indeed, remarkable—in the whole province, it's precisely our cherry orchard.

LOPAHIN: The only remarkable thing about this orchard is that it's a very large one. There's a crop of cherries every other year, and you can't do anything with them; no one buys them.

GAYEV: This orchard is even mentioned in the Encyclopedia.

LOPAHIN, *glancing at his watch:* If we can't think of a way out, if we don't come to a decision, on the twenty-second of August the cherry orchard and the whole estate will be sold at auction. Make up your minds! There's no other way out—I swear. None, none.

FIRS: In the old days, forty or fifty years ago, the cherries were dried, soaked, pickled, and made into jam, and we used to—

GAYEV: Keep still, Firs.

FIRS: And the dried cherries would be shipped by the cartload. It meant a lot of money! And in those days the dried cherries were soft and juicy, sweet, fragrant. . . . They knew the way to do it, then.

MME. RANEVSKAYA: And why don't they do it that way now?

FIRS: They've forgotten. Nobody remembers it.

PISHCHIK, *to* MME. RANEVSKAYA: What's doing in Paris? Eh? Did you eat frogs there?

MME. RANEVSKAYA: I ate crocodiles.

PISHCHIK: Just imagine!

LOPAHIN: There used to be only landowners and peasants in the country, but now these summer people have appeared on the scene. . . . All the towns, even the small ones, are surrounded by these summer cottages; and in another twenty years, no doubt, the summer population will have grown enormously. Now the summer resident only drinks tea on his porch, but maybe he'll take to working his acre, too, and then your cherry orchard will be a rich, happy, luxuriant place.

GAYEV, *indignantly:* Poppycock!

Enter VARYA *and* YASHA.

VARYA: There are two telegrams for you, mamma dear. *Picks a key from the bunch at her belt and noisily opens an old-fashioned bookcase.* Here they are.

MME. RANEVSKAYA: They're from Paris. *Tears them up without reading them.* I'm through with Paris.

GAYEV: Do you know, Luba, how old this bookcase

is? Last week I pulled out the bottom drawer and there
I found the date burnt in it. It was made exactly a hundred years ago. Think of that! We could celebrate its
centenary. True, it's an inanimate object, but nevertheless, a bookcase . . .

PISHCHIK, *amazed:* A hundred years! Just imagine!

GAYEV: Yes. *Tapping it.* That's something. . . . Dear,
honored bookcase, hail to you who for more than a century have served the glorious ideals of goodness and
justice! Your silent summons to fruitful toil has never
weakened in all those hundred years (*through tears*),
sustaining, through successive generations of our family,
courage and faith in a better future, and fostering in
us ideals of goodness and social consciousness. . . .
Pauses.

LOPAHIN: Yes . . .

MME. RANEVSKAYA: You haven't changed a bit,
Leonid.

GAYEV, *somewhat embarrassed:* I'll play it off the red
in the corner! Tip it in the side pocket!

LOPAHIN, *looking at his watch:* Well, it's time for me
to go . . .

YASHA, *handing a pill box to* MME. RANEVSKAYA: Perhaps you'll take your pills now.

PISHCHIK: One shouldn't take medicines, dearest lady,
they do neither harm nor good. . . . Give them here,
my valued friend. *Takes the pill box, pours the pills into
his palm, blows on them, puts them in his mouth, and
washes them down with some kvass.* There!

MME. RANEVSKAYA, *frightened:* You must be mad!

PISHCHIK: I've taken all the pills.

LOPAHIN: What a glutton!

All laugh.

FIRS: The gentleman visited us in Easter week, ate
half a bucket of pickles, he did . . . *Mumbles.*

MME. RANEVSKAYA: What's he saying?

VARYA: He's been mumbling like that for the last three years—we're used to it.

YASHA: His declining years!

CHARLOTTA IVANOVNA, *very thin, tightly laced, dressed in white, a lorgnette at her waist, crosses the stage.*

LOPAHIN: Forgive me, Charlotta Ivanovna, I've not had time to greet you. *Tries to kiss her hand.*

CHARLOTTA, *pulling away her hand:* If I let you kiss my hand, you'll be wanting to kiss my elbow next, and then my shoulder.

LOPAHIN: I've no luck today. *All laugh.* Charlotta Ivanovna, show us a trick.

MME. RANEVSKAYA: Yes, Charlotta, do a trick for us.

CHARLOTTA: I don't see the need. I want to sleep. *Exits.*

LOPAHIN: In three weeks we'll meet again. *Kisses* MME. RANEVSKAYA's *hand.* Good-by till then. Time's up. *To* GAYEV: Bye-bye. *Kisses* PISHCHIK. Bye-bye. *Shakes hands with* VARYA, *then with* FIRS *and* YASHA. I hate to leave. *To* MME. RANEVSKAYA: If you make up your mind about the cottages, let me know; I'll get you a loan of 50,000 rubles. Think it over seriously.

VARYA, *crossly:* Will you never go!

LOPAHIN: I'm going, I'm going. *Exits.*

GAYEV: The vulgarian. But, excuse me . . . Varya's going to marry him, he's Varya's fiancé.

VARYA: You talk too much, uncle dear.

MME. RANEVSKAYA: Well, Varya, it would make me happy. He's a good man.

PISHCHIK: Yes, one must admit, he's a most estimable man. And my Dashenka . . . she too says that . . . she says . . . lots of things. *Snores; but wakes up at once.* All the same, my valued friend, could you oblige

me . . . with a loan of 240 rubles? I must pay the interest on the mortgage tomorrow.

VARYA, *alarmed:* We can't, we can't!

MME. RANEVSKAYA: I really haven't any money.

PISHCHIK: It'll turn up. *Laughs.* I never lose hope, I
thought everything was lost, that I was done for, when
lo and behold, the railway ran through my land . . .
and I was paid for it. . . . And something else will
turn up again, if not today, then tomorrow . . . Dashenka will win two hundred thousand . . . she's got a
lottery ticket.

MME. RANEVSKAYA: I've had my coffee, now let's go
to bed.

FIRS, *brushes off* GAYEV; *admonishingly:* You've got
the wrong trousers on again. What am I to do with you?

VARYA, *softly:* Anya's asleep. *Gently opens the window.* The sun's up now, it's not a bit cold. Look, mamma
dear, what wonderful trees. And heavens, what air! The
starlings are singing!

GAYEV, *opens the other window:* The orchard is all
white. You've not forgotten it? Luba? That's the long
alley that runs straight, straight as an arrow; how it
shines on moonlight nights, do you remember? You've
not forgotten?

MME. RANEVSKAYA, *looking out of the window into
the orchard:* Oh, my childhood, my innocent childhood.
I used to sleep in this nursery—I used to look out into
the orchard, happiness waked with me every morning,
the orchard was just the same then . . . nothing has
changed. *Laughs with joy.* All, all white! Oh, my orchard! After the dark, rainy autumn and the cold winter, you are young again, and full of happiness, the
heavenly angels have not left you . . . If I could free
my chest and my shoulders from this rock that weighs
on me, if I could only forget the past!

GAYEV: Yes, and the orchard will be sold to pay our debts, strange as it may seem. . . .

MME. RANEVSKAYA: Look! There is our poor mother walking in the orchard . . . all in white . . . *Laughs with joy.* It is she!

GAYEV: Where?

VARYA: What are you saying, mamma dear!

MME. RANEVSKAYA: There's no one there, I just imagined it. To the right, where the path turns towards the arbor, there's a little white tree, leaning over, that looks like a woman . . .

TROFIMOV *enters, wearing a shabby student's uniform and spectacles.*

MME. RANEVSKAYA: What an amazing orchard! White masses of blossom, the blue sky . . .

TROFIMOV: Lubov Andreyevna! *She looks round at him.* I just want to pay my respects to you, then I'll leave at once. *Kisses her hand ardently.* I was told to wait until morning, but I hadn't the patience . . . MME. RANEVSKAYA *looks at him, perplexed.*

VARYA, *through tears:* This is Petya Trofimov.

TROFIMOV: Petya Trofimov, formerly your Grisha's tutor. . . . Can I have changed so much? MME. RANEVSKAYA *embraces him and weeps quietly.*

GAYEV, *embarrassed:* Don't, don't, Luba.

VARYA, *crying:* I told you, Petya, to wait until tomorrow.

MME. RANEVSKAYA: My Grisha . . . my little boy . . . Grisha . . . my son.

VARYA: What can one do, mamma dear, it's God's will.

TROFIMOV, *softly, through tears:* There . . . there.

MME. RANEVSKAYA, *weeping quietly:* My little boy was lost . . . drowned. Why? Why, my friend? *More quietly.* Anya's asleep in there, and here I am talking so loudly . . . making all this noise. . . . But tell me, Petya, why do you look so badly? Why have you aged so?

TROFIMOV: A mangy master, a peasant woman in the train called me.

MME. RANEVSKAYA: You were just a boy then, a dear little student, and now your hair's thin—and you're wearing glasses! Is it possible you're still a student? *Goes towards the door.*

TROFIMOV: I suppose I'm a perpetual student.

MME. RANEVSKAYA, *kisses her brother, then* VARYA: Now, go to bed . . . You have aged, too, Leonid.

PISHCHIK, *follows her:* So now we turn in. Oh, my gout! I'm staying the night here . . . Lubov Andreyevna, my angel, tomorrow morning. . . . I do need 240 rubles.

GAYEV: He keeps at it.

PISHCHIK: I'll pay it back, dear . . . it's a trifling sum.

MME. RANEVSKAYA: All right, Leonid will give it to you. Give it to him, Leonid.

GAYEV: Me give it to him! That's a good one!

MME. RANEVSKAYA: It can't be helped. Give it to him! He needs it. He'll pay it back.

MME. RANEVSKAYA, TROFIMOV, PISHCHIK, *and* FIRS *go out;* GAYEV, VARYA, *and* YASHA *remain.*

GAYEV: Sister hasn't got out of the habit of throwing money around. *To* YASHA. Go away, my good fellow, you smell of the barnyard.

YASHA, *with a grin:* And you, Leonid Andreyevich, are just the same as ever.

GAYEV: Who? *To* VARYA: What did he say?

VARYA, *to* YASHA: Your mother's come from the village; she's been sitting in the servants' room since yesterday, waiting to see you.

YASHA: Botheration!

VARYA: You should be ashamed of yourself!

YASHA: She's all I needed! She could have come to-morrow. *Exits.*

VARYA: Mamma is just the same as ever; she hasn't changed a bit. If she had her own way, she'd keep nothing for herself.

GAYEV: Yes . . . *Pauses.* If a great many remedies are offered for some disease, it means it is incurable; I keep thinking and racking my brains; I have many remedies, ever so many, and that really means none. It would be fine if we came in for a legacy; it would be fine if we married off our Anya to a very rich man; or we might go to Yaroslavl and try our luck with our aunt, the Countess. She's very, very rich, you know . . .

VARYA, *weeping:* If only God would help us!

GAYEV: Stop bawling. Aunt's very rich, but she doesn't like us. In the first place, sister married a lawyer who was no nobleman . . . ANYA *appears in the doorway.* She married beneath her, and it can't be said that her behavior has been very exemplary. She's good, kind, sweet, and I love her, but no matter what extenuating circumstances you may adduce, there's no denying that she has no morals. You sense it in her least gesture.

VARYA, *in a whisper:* Anya's in the doorway.

GAYEV: Who? *Pauses.* It's queer, something got into my right eye—my eyes are going back on me. . . . And on Thursday, when I was in the circuit court—

Enter ANYA.

VARYA: Why aren't you asleep, Anya?

ANYA: I can't get to sleep, I just can't.

GAYEV: My little pet! *Kisses* ANYA's *face and hands.* My child! *Weeps.* You are not my niece, you're my angel! You're everything to me. Believe me, believe—

ANYA: I believe you, uncle. Everyone loves you and

respects you . . . but, uncle dear, you must keep still.
. . . You must. What were you saying just now about
my mother? Your own sister? What made you say that?

GAYEV: Yes, yes . . . *Covers his face with her hand.*
Really, that was awful! Good God! Heaven help me!
Just now I made a speech to the bookcase . . . so stupid!
And only after I was through, I saw how stupid it was.

VARYA: It's true, uncle dear, you ought to keep still.
Just don't talk, that's all.

ANYA: If you could only keep still, it would make
things easier for you too.

GAYEV: I'll keep still. *Kisses* ANYA's *and* VARYA's
hands. I will. But now about business. On Thursday
I was in court; well, there were a number of us there,
and we began talking of one thing and another, and this
and that, and do you know, I believe it will be possible
to raise a loan on a promissory note, to pay the interest
at the bank.

VARYA: If only God would help us!

GAYEV: On Tuesday I'll go and see about it again. *To*
VARYA. Stop bawling. *To* ANYA. Your mamma will talk
to Lopahin, and he, of course, will not refuse her . . .
and as soon as you're rested, you'll go to Yaroslavl to the
Countess, your great-aunt. So we'll be working in three
directions at once, and the thing is in the bag. We'll pay
the interest—I'm sure of it. *Puts a candy in his mouth.*
I swear on my honor, I swear by anything you like, the
estate shan't be sold. *Excitedly.* I swear by my own happiness! Here's my hand on it, you can call me a swin-
dler and a scoundrel if I let it come to an auction! I
swear by my whole being.

ANYA, *relieved and quite happy again:* How good
you are, uncle, and how clever! *Embraces him.* Now I'm
at peace, quite at peace, I'm happy.

Enter Firs.

Firs, *reproachfully:* Leonid Andreyevich, have you no fear of God? When are you going to bed?

Gayev: Directly, directly. Go away, Firs, I'll . . . yes, I will undress myself. Now, children, 'nightie-'nightie. We'll consider details tomorrow, but now go to sleep. *Kisses* Anya *and* Varya. I am a man of the 'Eighties; they have nothing good to say of that period nowadays. Nevertheless, in the course of my life I have suffered not a little for my convictions. It's not for nothing that the peasant loves me; one should know the peasant; one should know from which—

Anya: There you go again, uncle.

Varya: Uncle dear, be quiet.

Firs, *angrily:* Leonid Andreyevich!

Gayev: I'm coming, I'm coming! Go to bed! Double bank shot in the side pocket! Here goes a clean shot . . .

Exits, Firs *hobbling after him.*

Anya: I am at peace now. I don't want to go to Yaroslavl—I don't like my great-aunt, but still, I am at peace, thanks to uncle. *Sits down.*

Varya: We must get some sleep. I'm going now. While you were away something unpleasant happened. In the old servants' quarters there are only the old people, as you know; Yefim, Polya, Yevstigney, and Karp, too. They began letting all sorts of rascals in to spend the night. . . . I didn't say anything. Then I heard they'd been spreading a report that I gave them nothing but dried peas to eat—out of stinginess, you know . . . and it was all Yevstigney's doing. . . . All right, I thought, if that's how it is, I thought, just wait. I sent for Yevstigney. . . . *Yawns.* He comes. . . . "How's this, Yevstigney?" I say, "You fool . . ." *Looking at* Anya. Anichka! *Pauses.* She's asleep. *Puts her arm around*

ANYA. Come to your little bed. . . . Come . . . *Leads her.* My darling has fallen asleep. . . . Come.

They go out. Far away beyond the orchard a shepherd is piping. TROFIMOV *crosses the stage and, seeing* VARYA *and* ANYA, *stands still.*

VARYA: Sh! She's asleep . . . asleep . . . Come, darling.

ANYA, *softly, half-asleep:* I'm so tired. Those bells . . . uncle . . . dear. . . . Mamma and uncle . . .

VARYA: Come, my precious, come along. *They go into* ANYA'S *room.*

TROFIMOV, *with emotion:* My sunshine, my spring!

Act II

A MEADOW. *An old, long-abandoned, lopsided little chapel; near it, a well, large slabs, which had apparently once served as tombstones, and an old bench. In the background, the road to the Gayev estate. To one side poplars loom darkly, where the cherry orchard begins. In the distance a row of telegraph poles, and far off, on the horizon, the faint outline of a large city which is seen only in fine, clear weather. The sun will soon be setting.* CHARLOTTA, YASHA, *and* DUNYASHA *are seated on the bench.* YEPIHODOV *stands near and plays a guitar. All are pensive.* CHARLOTTA *wears an old peaked cap. She has taken a gun from her shoulder and is straightening the buckle on the strap.*

CHARLOTTA, *musingly:* I haven't a real passport, I don't know how old I am, and I always feel that I am very young. When I was a little girl, my father and mother used to go from fair to fair and give performances, very good ones. And I used to do the *salto mortale,* and all sorts of other tricks. And when papa and mamma died, a German lady adopted me and began to educate me. Very good. I grew up and became a governess. But where I come from and who I am, I don't know. . . . Who were my parents? Perhaps they weren't even married. . . . I don't know. . . . *Takes a cucumber out of her pocket and eats it.* I don't know a thing. *Pause.* One wants so much to talk, and there isn't anyone to talk to. . . . I haven't anybody.

YEPIHODOV, *plays the guitar and sings:* "What care I for the jarring world? What's friend or foe to me? . . ." How agreeable it is to play the mandolin.

DUNYASHA: That's a guitar, not a mandolin. *Looks in a hand mirror and powders her face.*

YEPIHODOV: To a madman in love it's a mandolin. *Sings:* "Would that the heart were warmed by the fire of mutual love!" YASHA *joins in.*

CHARLOTTA: How abominably these people sing. Pfui! Like jackals!

DUNYASHA, *to* YASHA: How wonderful it must be though to have stayed abroad!

YASHA: Ah, yes, of course, I cannot but agree with you there. *Yawns and lights a cigar.*

YEPIHODOV: Naturally. Abroad, everything has long since achieved full perplexion.

YASHA: That goes without saying.

YEPIHODOV: I'm a cultivated man, I read all kinds of remarkable books. And yet I can never make out what direction I should take, what is it that I want, properly speaking. Should I live, or should I shoot myself, properly speaking? Nevertheless, I always carry a revolver about me. . . . Here it is . . . *Shows revolver.*

CHARLOTTA: I've finished. I'm going. *Puts the gun over her shoulder.* You are a very clever man, Yepihodov, and a very terrible one; women must be crazy about you. Br-r-r! *Starts to go.* These clever men are all so stupid; there's no one for me to talk to . . . always alone, alone, I haven't a soul . . . and who I am, and why I am, nobody knows. *Exits unhurriedly.*

YEPIHODOV: Properly speaking and letting other subjects alone, I must say regarding myself, among other things, that fate treats me mercilessly, like a storm treats a small boat. If I am mistaken, let us say, why then do I wake up this morning, and there on my chest is a spider of enormous dimensions . . . like this . . . *indicates with both hands.* Again, I take up a pitcher of kvass to have a drink, and in it there is something unseemly to the highest degree, something like a cockroach. *Pause.* Have you read Buckle? *Pause.* I wish to have a word with you, Avdotya Fyodorovna, if I may trouble you.

DUNYASHA: Well, go ahead.

YEPIHODOV: I wish to speak with you alone. *Sighs.*

DUNYASHA, *embarrassed:* Very well. Only first bring me my little cape. You'll find it near the wardrobe. It's rather damp here.

YEPIHODOV: Certainly, ma'am; I will fetch it, ma'am. Now I know what to do with my revolver. *Takes the guitar and goes off playing it.*

YASHA: Two-and-Twenty Troubles! An awful fool, between you and me. *Yawns.*

DUNYASHA: I hope to God he doesn't shoot himself! *Pause.* I've become so nervous, I'm always fretting. I was still a little girl when I was taken into the big house, I am quite unused to the simple life now, and my hands are white, as white as a lady's. I've become so soft, so delicate, so refined, I'm afraid of everything. It's so terrifying; and if you deceive me, Yasha, I don't know what will happen to my nerves. YASHA *kisses her.*

YASHA: You're a peach! Of course, a girl should never forget herself; and what I dislike more than anything is when a girl don't behave properly.

DUNYASHA: I've fallen passionately in love with you; you're educated—you have something to say about everything. *Pause.*

YASHA, *yawns:* Yes, ma'am. Now the way I look at it, if a girl loves someone, it means she is immoral. *Pause.* It's agreeable smoking a cigar in the fresh air. *Listens.* Someone's coming this way . . . It's our madam and the others. DUNYASHA *embraces him impulsively.* You go home, as though you'd been to the river to bathe; go by the little path, or else they'll run into you and suspect me of having arranged to meet you here. I can't stand that sort of thing.

DUNYASHA, *coughing softly:* Your cigar's made my head ache. *Exits.* YASHA *remains standing near the chapel. Enter* MME. RANEVSKAYA, GAYEV, *and* LOPAHIN.

LOPAHIN: You must make up your mind once and for all—there's no time to lose. It's quite a simple question, you know. Do you agree to lease your land for summer cottages or not? Answer in one word, yes or no; only one word!

MME. RANEVSKAYA: Who's been smoking such abominable cigars here? *Sits down.*

GAYEV: Now that the railway line is so near, it's made things very convenient. *Sits down.* Here we've been able to have lunch in town. Yellow ball in the side pocket! I feel like going into the house and playing just one game.

MME. RANEVSKAYA: You can do that later.

LOPAHIN: Only one word! *Imploringly.* Do give me an answer!

GAYEV, *yawning:* Who?

MME. RANEVSKAYA, *looks into her purse:* Yesterday

I had a lot of money and now my purse is almost empty. My poor Varya tries to economize by feeding us just milk soup; in the kitchen the old people get nothing but dried peas to eat, while I squander money thoughtlessly. *Drops the purse, scattering gold pieces.* You see there they go . . . *Shows vexation.*

YASHA: Allow me—I'll pick them up. *Picks up the money.*

MME. RANEVSKAYA: Be so kind, Yasha. And why did I go to lunch in town? That nasty restaurant, with its music and the tablecloth smelling of soap . . . Why drink so much, Leonid? Why eat so much? Why talk so much? Today again you talked a lot, and all so inappropriately about the 'Seventies, about the decadents. And to whom? Talking to waiters about decadents!

LOPAHIN: Yes.

GAYEV, *waving his hand:* I'm incorrigible; that's obvious. *Irritably, to* YASHA. Why do you keep dancing about in front of me?

YASHA, *laughs:* I can't hear your voice without laughing—

GAYEV: Either he or I—

MME. RANEVSKAYA: Go away, Yasha; run along.

YASHA, *handing* MME. RANEVSKAYA *her purse:* I'm going, at once. *Hardly able to suppress his laughter.* This minute. *Exits.*

LOPAHIN: That rich man, Deriganov, wants to buy your estate. They say he's coming to the auction himself.

MME. RANEVSKAYA: Where did you hear that?

LOPAHIN: That's what they are saying in town.

GAYEV: Our aunt in Yaroslavl has promised to help; but when she will send the money, and how much, no one knows.

LOPAHIN: How much will she send? A hundred thousand? Two hundred?

MME. RANEVSKAYA: Oh, well, ten or fifteen thousand; and we'll have to be grateful for that.

LOPAHIN: Forgive me, but such frivolous people as you are, so queer and unbusinesslike—I never met in my life. One tells you in plain language that your estate is up for sale, and you don't seem to take it in.

MME. RANEVSKAYA: What are we to do? Tell us what to do.

LOPAHIN: I do tell you, every day; every day I say the same thing! You must lease the cherry orchard and the land for summer cottages, you must do it and as soon as possible—right away. The auction is close at hand. Please understand! Once you've decided to have the cottages, you can raise as much money as you like, and you're saved.

MME. RANEVSKAYA: Cottages—summer people—forgive me, but it's all so vulgar.

GAYEV: I agree with you absolutely.

LOPAHIN: I shall either burst into tears or scream or faint! I can't stand it! You've worn me out! *To* GAYEV. You're an old woman!

GAYEV: Who?

LOPAHIN: An old woman! *Gets up to go.*

MME. RANEVSKAYA, *alarmed:* No, don't go! Please stay, I beg you, my dear. Perhaps we shall think of something.

LOPAHIN: What is there to think of?

MME. RANEVSKAYA: Don't go, I beg you. With you here it's more cheerful anyway. *Pause.* I keep expecting something to happen, it's as though the house were going to crash about our ears.

GAYEV, *in deep thought:* Bank shot in the corner. . . , Three cushions in the side pocket. . . .

MME. RANEVSKAYA: We have been great sinners . . ,

LOPAHIN: What sins could you have committed?

GAYEV, *putting a candy in his mouth:* They say I've eaten up my fortune in candy! *Laughs.*

MME. RANEVSKAYA: Oh, my sins! I've squandered money away recklessly, like a lunatic, and I married a man who made nothing but debts. My husband drank himself to death on champagne, he was a terrific drinker. And then, to my sorrow, I fell in love with another man, and I lived with him. And just then—that was my first punishment—a blow on the head: my little boy was drowned here in the river. And I went abroad, went away forever . . . never to come back, never to see this river again . . . I closed my eyes and ran, out of my mind. . . . But he followed me, pitiless, brutal. I bought a villa near Mentone, because he fell ill there; and for three years, day and night, I knew no peace, no rest. The sick man wore me out, he sucked my soul dry. Then last year, when the villa was sold to pay my debts, I went to Paris, and there he robbed me, abandoned me, took up with another woman, I tried to poison myself—it was stupid, so shameful—and then suddenly I felt drawn back to Russia, back to my own country, to my little girl. *Wipes her tears away.* Lord, Lord! Be merciful, forgive me my sins—don't punish me any more! *Takes a telegram out of her pocket.* This came today from Paris—he begs me to forgive him, implores me to go back . . . *Tears up the telegram.* Do I hear music? *Listens.*

GAYEV: That's our famous Jewish band, you remember? Four violins, a flute, and a double bass.

MME. RANEVSKAYA: Does it still exist? We ought to send for them some evening and have a party.

LOPAHIN, *listens:* I don't hear anything. *Hums softly:* "The Germans for a fee will Frenchify a Russian." *Laughs.* I saw a play at the theater yesterday—awfully funny.

MME. RANEVSKAYA: There was probably nothing funny about it. You shouldn't go to see plays, you should look at yourselves more often. How drab your lives are—how full of unnecessary talk.

LOPAHIN: That's true; come to think of it, we do live like fools. *Pause.* My pop was a peasant, an idiot; he understood nothing, never taught me anything, all he did was beat me when he was drunk, and always with a stick. Fundamentally, I'm just the same kind of blockhead and idiot. I was never taught anything—I have a terrible handwriting, I write so that I feel ashamed before people, like a pig.

MME. RANEVSKAYA: You should get married, my friend.

LOPAHIN: Yes . . . that's true.

MME. RANEVSKAYA: To our Varya, she's a good girl.

LOPAHIN: Yes.

MME. RANEVSKAYA: She's a girl who comes of simple people, she works all day long; and above all, she loves you. Besides, you've liked her for a long time now.

LOPAHIN: Well, I've nothing against it. She's a good girl. *Pause.*

GAYEV: I've been offered a place in the bank—6,000 a year. Have you heard?

MME. RANEVSKAYA: You're not up to it. Stay where you are.

FIRS *enters, carrying an overcoat.*

FIRS, *to* GAYEV: Please put this on, sir, it's damp.

GAYEV, *putting it on:* I'm fed up with you, brother.

FIRS: Never mind. This morning you drove off without saying a word. *Looks him over.*

MME. RANEVSKAYA: How you've aged, Firs.

FIRS: I beg your pardon?

LOPAHIN: The lady says you've aged.

FIRS: I've lived a long time; they were arranging my

wedding and your papa wasn't born yet. *Laughs.* When freedom came I was already head footman. I wouldn't consent to be set free then; I stayed on with the master . . . *Pause.* I remember they were all very happy, but why they were happy, they didn't know themselves.

LOPAHIN: It was fine in the old days! At least there was flogging!

FIRS, *not hearing:* Of course. The peasants kept to the masters, the masters kept to the peasants; but now they've all gone their own ways, and there's no making out anything.

GAYEV: Be quiet, Firs. I must go to town tomorrow. They've promised to introduce me to a general who might let us have a loan.

LOPAHIN: Nothing will come of that. You won't even be able to pay the interest, you can be certain of that.

MME. RANEVSKAYA: He's raving, there isn't any general. *Enter* TROFIMOV, ANYA, *and* VARYA.

GAYEV: Here come our young people.

ANYA: There's mamma, on the bench.

MME. RANEVSKAYA, *tenderly:* Come here, come along, my darlings. *Embraces* ANYA *and* VARYA. If you only knew how I love you both! Sit beside me—there, like that. *All sit down.*

LOPAHIN: Our perpetual student is always with the young ladies.

TROFIMOV: That's not any of your business.

LOPAHIN: He'll soon be fifty, and he's still a student!

TROFIMOV: Stop your silly jokes.

LOPAHIN: What are you so cross about, you queer bird?

TROFIMOV: Oh, leave me alone.

LOPAHIN, *laughs:* Allow me to ask you, what do you think of me?

TROFIMOV: What I think of you, Yermolay Alexeyevich, is this: you are a rich man who will soon be a millionaire. Well, just as a beast of prey, which devours everything that comes in its way, is necessary for the process of metabolism to go on, so you too are necessary. *All laugh.*

VARYA: Better tell us something about the planets, Petya.

MME. RANEVSKAYA: No, let's go on with yesterday's conversation.

TROFIMOV: What was it about?

GAYEV: About man's pride.

TROFIMOV: Yesterday we talked a long time, but we came to no conclusion. There is something mystical about man's pride in your sense of the word. Perhaps you're right, from your own point of view. But if you reason simply, without going into subtleties, then what call is there for pride? Is there any sense in it, if man is so poor a thing physiologically, and if, in the great majority of cases, he is coarse, stupid, and profoundly unhappy? We should stop admiring 'ourselves. We should work, and that's all.

GAYEV: You die, anyway.

TROFIMOV: Who knows? And what does it mean— to die? Perhaps man has a hundred senses, and at his death only the five we know perish, while the other ninety-five remain alive.

MME. RANEVSKAYA: How clever you are, Petya!

LOPAHIN, *ironically:* Awfully clever!

TROFIMOV: Mankind goes forward, developing its powers. Everything that is now unattainable for it will one day come within man's reach and be clear to him; only we must work, helping with all our might those who seek the truth. Here among us in Russia only the very few work as yet. The great majority of the intelligentsia, as far as I can see, seek nothing, do nothing, are totally unfit for work of any kind. They call themselves the intelligentsia, yet they are uncivil to their servants, treat the peasants like animals, are poor students, never read anything serious, do absolutely nothing at all, only talk about science, and have little appreciation of the arts. They are all solemn, have grim faces, they all philosophize and talk of weighty matters. And meanwhile the vast majority of us, ninety-nine out of a hundred, live like savages. At the least provocation—a punch in the jaw, and curses. They eat disgustingly, sleep in filth and stuffiness, bedbugs everywhere, stench and damp and moral slovenliness. And obviously, the only purpose of all our fine talk is to hoodwink ourselves and others. Show me where the public nurseries are that we've heard so much about, and the libraries. We read about them in novels, but in reality they don't exist, there is nothing but dirt, vulgarity, and Asiatic backwardness. I don't like very solemn faces, I'm afraid of them, I'm afraid of serious conversations. We'd do better to keep quiet for a while.

Lopahin: Do you know, I get up at five o'clock in the morning, and I work from morning till night; and I'm always handling money, my own and other people's, and I see what people around me are really like. You've only to start doing anything to see how few honest, decent people there are. Sometimes when I lie awake at night, I think: "Oh, Lord, thou hast given us immense forests, boundless fields, the widest horizons, and living in their midst, we ourselves ought really to be giants."

Mme. Ranevskaya: Now you want giants! They're only good in fairy tales; otherwise they're frightening.

Ypihodov *crosses the stage at the rear, playing the guitar.*

Mme. Ranevskaya, *pensively:* There goes Yepihodov.

Anya, *pensively:* There goes Yepihodov.

GAYEV: Ladies and gentlemen, the sun has set.

TROFIMOV: Yes.

GAYEV, *in a low voice, declaiming as it were:* Oh, Nature, wondrous Nature, you shine with eternal radiance, beautiful and indifferent! You, whom we call our mother, unite within yourself life and death! You animate and destroy!

VARYA, *pleadingly:* Uncle dear!

ANYA: Uncle, again!

TROFIMOV: You'd better bank the yellow ball in the side pocket.

GAYEV: I'm silent, I'm silent . . .

All sit plunged in thought. Stillness reigns. Only FIRS's *muttering is audible. Suddenly a distant sound is heard, coming from the sky as it were, the sound of a snapping string, mournfully dying away.*

MME. RANEVSKAYA: What was that?

LOPAHIN: I don't know. Somewhere far away, in the pits, a bucket's broken loose; but somewhere very far away.

GAYEV: Or it might be some sort of bird, perhaps a heron.

TROFIMOV: Or an owl . . .

MME. RANEVSKAYA, *shudders:* It's weird, somehow. *Pause.*

FIRS: Before the calamity the same thing happened—the owl screeched, and the samovar hummed all the time.

GAYEV: Before what calamity?

FIRS: Before the Freedom.[1] *Pause.*

MME. RANEVSKAYA: Come, my friends, let's be going. It's getting dark. *To* ANYA. You have tears in your eyes. What is it, my little one? *Embraces her.*

ANYA: I don't know, mamma; it's nothing.

---

[1] The emancipation of the serfs, proclaimed in 1861.

TROFIMOV: Somebody's coming.

A TRAMP *appears, wearing a shabby white cap and an overcoat. He is slightly drunk.*

TRAMP: Allow me to inquire, will this short-cut take me to the station?

GAYEV: It will. Just follow that road.

TRAMP: My heartfelt thanks. *Coughing.* The weather is glorious. *Recites,* "My brother, my suffering brother . . . Go down to the Volga! Whose groans . . . ?" *To* VARYA. Mademoiselle, won't you spare 30 kopecks for a hungry Russian?

VARYA, *frightened, cries out.*

LOPAHIN, *angrily:* Even panhandling has its pro- prieties.

MME. RANEVSKAYA, *scared:* Here, take this. *Fumbles in her purse.* I haven't any silver . . . never mind, here's a gold piece.

TRAMP: My heartfelt thanks. *Exits. Laughter.*

VARYA, *frightened:* I'm leaving, I'm leaving . . . Oh, mamma dear, at home the servants have nothing to eat, and you gave him a gold piece!

MME. RANEVSKAYA: What are you going to do with me? I'm such a fool. When we get home, I'll give you everything I have. Yermolay Alexeyevich, you'll lend me some more . . .

LOPAHIN: Yes, ma'am.

MME. RANEVSKAYA: Come, ladies and gentlemen, it's time to be going. Oh! Varya, we've settled all about your marriage. Congratulations!

VARYA, *through tears:* Really, mamma, that's not a joking matter.

LOPAHIN: "Aurelia, get thee to a nunnery, go . . ."

GAYEV: And do you know, my hands are trembling: I haven't played billiards in a long time.

Lopahin: "Aurelia, nymph, in your orisons, remember me!"

Mme. Ranevskaya: Let's go, it's almost suppertime.

Varya: He frightened me! My heart's pounding.

Lopahin: Let me remind you, ladies and gentlemen, on the 22nd of August the cherry orchard will be up for sale. Think about that! Think!

All except Trofimov *and* Anya *go out.*

Anya, *laughs:* I'm grateful to that tramp, he frightened Varya and so we're alone.

Trofimov: Varya's afraid we'll fall in love with each other all of a sudden. She hasn't left us alone for days. Her narrow mind can't grasp that we're above love. To avoid the petty and illusory, everything that prevents us from being free and happy—that is the goal and meaning of our life. Forward! Do not fall behind, friends!

Anya, *strikes her hands together:* How well you speak! *Pause.* It's wonderful here today.

Trofimov: Yes, the weather's glorious.

Anya: What have you done to me, Petya? Why don't I love the cherry orchard as I used to? I loved it so tenderly. It seemed to me there was no spot on earth lovelier than our orchard.

Trofimov: All Russia is our orchard. Our land is vast and beautiful, there are many wonderful places in it. *Pause.* Think of it, Anya, your grandfather, your great-grandfather and all your ancestors were serf-owners, owners of living souls, and aren't human beings looking at you from every tree in the orchard, from every leaf, from every trunk? Don't you hear voices? Oh, it's terrifying! Your orchard is a fearful place, and when you pass through it in the evening or at night, the old bark on the trees gleams faintly, and the cherry trees seem to be dreaming of things that happened a hundred, two hundred years ago and to be tormented by painful visions. What is there to say? We're at least two hundred years behind, we've really achieved nothing yet, we have no definite attitude to the past, we only philosophize, complain of the blues, or drink vodka. It's all so clear: in order to live in the present, we should first redeem our past, finish with it, and we can expiate it only by suffering, only by extraordinary, unceasing labor. Realize that, Anya.

ANYA: The house in which we live has long ceased to be our own, and I will leave it, I give you my word.

TROFIMOV: If you have the keys, fling them into the well and go away. Be free as the wind.

ANYA, *in ecstasy:* How well you put that!

TROFIMOV: Believe me, Anya, believe me! I'm not yet thirty, I'm young, I'm still a student—but I've already suffered so much. In winter I'm hungry, sick, harassed, poor as a beggar, and where hasn't Fate driven me? Where haven't I been? And yet always, every moment of the day and night, my soul is filled with inexplicable premonitions. . . . I have a premonition of happiness, Anya. . . . I see it already!

ANYA, *pensively:* The moon is rising.

YEPIHODOV *is heard playing the same mournful tune on the guitar. The moon rises. Somewhere near the poplars* VARYA *is looking for* ANYA *and calling* "Anya, where are you?"

TROFIMOV: Yes, the moon is rising. *Pause.* There it is, happiness, it's approaching, it's coming nearer and nearer, I can already hear its footsteps. And if we don't see it, if we don't know it, what does it matter? Others will!

VARYA's *voice:* "Anya! Where are you?"

TROFIMOV: That Varya again! *Angrily.* It's revolting!

ANYA: Never mind, let's go down to the river. It's lovely there.

TROFIMOV: Come on. *They go.*

VARYA's *voice:* "Anya! Anya!"

Act III

A DRAWING-ROOM *separated by an arch from a ballroom. Evening. Chandelier burning. The Jewish band is heard playing in the anteroom. In the ballroom they are dancing the* Grand Rond. PISHCHIK *is heard calling,* "Promenade à une paire." PISHCHIK *and* CHARLOTTA, TROFIMOV *and* MME. RANEVSKAYA, ANYA *and the* POST OFFICE CLERK, VARYA *and the* STATIONMASTER, *and others, enter the drawing-room in couples.* DUNYASHA *is in the last couple.* VARYA *weeps quietly, wiping her tears as she dances. All parade through drawing-room.* PISHCHIK *calling* "Grand rond, balancez!" *and* "Les cavaliers à genoux et remerciez vos dames!" FIRS *wearing a dress-coat, brings in soda-water on a tray.* PISHCHIK *and* TROFIMOV *enter the drawing-room.*

PISHCHIK: I'm a full-blooded man; I've already had two strokes. Dancing's hard work for me; but as they say, "If you run with the pack, you can bark or not, but at least wag your tail." Still, I'm as strong as a horse. My late lamented father, who would have his joke, God rest his soul, used to say, talking about our origin, that the ancient line of the Simeonov-Pishchiks was descended from the very horse that Caligula had made a senator. *Sits down.* But the trouble is, I have no money. A hungry dog believes in nothing but meat. *Snores and wakes up at once.* It's the same with me—I can think of nothing but money.

TROFIMOV: You know, there *is* something equine about your figure.

PISHCHIK: Well, a horse is a fine animal—one can sell a horse.

Sound of billiards being played in an adjoining room. VARYA *appears in the archway.*

TROFIMOV, *teasing her:* Madam Lopahina! Madam Lopahina!

VARYA, *angrily:* Mangy master!

TROFIMOV: Yes, I am a mangy master and I'm proud of it.

VARYA, *reflecting bitterly:* Here we've hired musicians, and what shall we pay them with? *Exits.*

TROFIMOV, *to* PISHCHIK: If the energy you have spent during your lifetime looking for money to pay interest had gone into something else, in the end you could have turned the world upside down.

PISHCHIK: Nietzsche, the philosopher, the greatest, most famous of men, that colossal intellect, says in his works, that it is permissible to forge banknotes.

TROFIMOV: Have you read Nietzsche?

PISHCHIK: Well . . . Dashenka told me . . . And now I've got to the point where forging banknotes is about the only way out for me. . . . The day after to-morrow I have to pay 310 rubles—I already have 130 . . . *Feels in his pockets. In alarm.* The money's gone! I've lost my money! *Through tears.* Where's my money? *Joyfully.* Here it is! Inside the lining . . . I'm all in a sweat . . .

Enter MME. RANEVSKAYA *and* CHARLOTTA.

MME. RANEVSKAYA, *hums the "Lezginka":* Why isn't Leonid back yet? What is he doing in town? *To* DUN-YASHA. Dunyasha, offer the musicians tea.

TROFIMOV: The auction hasn't taken place, most likely.

MME. RANEVSKAYA: It's the wrong time to have the band, and the wrong time to give a dance. Well, never mind. *Sits down and hums softly.*

CHARLOTTA, *hands* PISHCHIK *a pack of cards:* Here is a pack of cards. Think of any card you like.

PISHCHIK: I've thought of one.

CHARLOTTA: Shuffle the pack now. That's right. Give it here, my dear Mr. Pishchik. *Ein, zwei, drei!* Now look for it—it's in your side pocket.

PISHCHIK, *taking the card out of his pocket:* The eight of spades! Perfectly right! Just imagine!

CHARLOTTA, *holding pack of cards in her hands. To* TROFIMOV: Quickly, name the top card.

TROFIMOV: Well, let's see—the queen of spades.

CHARLOTTA: Right! *To* PISHCHIK. Now name the top card.

PISHCHIK: The ace of hearts.

CHARLOTTA: Right! *Claps her hands and the pack of cards disappears.* Ah, what lovely weather it is today! *A mysterious feminine voice which seems to come from under the floor, answers her:* "Oh, yes, it's magnificent weather, madam."

CHARLOTTA: You are my best ideal.

VOICE: "And I find you pleasing too, madam."

STATIONMASTER, *applauding:* The lady ventriloquist, bravo!

PISHCHIK, *amazed:* Just imagine! Enchanting Charlotta Ivanovna, I'm simply in love with you.

CHARLOTTA: In love? *Shrugs her shoulders.* Are you capable of love? *Guter Mensch, aber schlechter Musikant!*

TROFIMOV, *claps* PISHCHIK *on the shoulder:* You old horse, you!

CHARLOTTA: Attention please! One more trick! *Takes*

a plaid from a chair. Here is a very good plaid; I want to sell it. *Shaking it out.* Does anyone want to buy it?

PISHCHIK, *in amazement:* Just imagine!

CHARLOTTA: *Ein, zwei, drei! Raises the plaid quickly, behind it stands* ANYA. *She curtsies, runs to her mother, embraces her, and runs back into the ballroom, amidst general enthusiasm.*

MME. RANEVSKAYA, *applauds:* Bravo! Bravo!

CHARLOTTA: Now again! *Ein, zwei, drei! Lifts the plaid; behind it stands* VARYA *bowing.*

PISHCHIK, *running after her:* The rascal! What a woman, what a woman! *Exits.*

MME. RANEVSKAYA: And Leonid still isn't here. What is he doing in town so long? I don't understand. It must be all over by now. Either the estate has been sold, or the auction hasn't taken place. Why keep us in suspense so long?

VARYA, *trying to console her:* Uncle's bought it, I feel sure of that.

TROFIMOV, *mockingly:* Oh, yes!

VARYA: Great-aunt sent him an authorization to buy it in her name, and to transfer the debt. She's doing it for Anya's sake. And I'm sure that God will help us, and uncle will buy it.

MME. RANEVSKAYA: Great-aunt sent fifteen thousand to buy the estate in her name, she doesn't trust us, but that's not even enough to pay the interest. *Covers her face with her hands.* Today my fate will be decided, my fate—

TROFIMOV, *teasing* VARYA: Madam Lopahina!

VARYA, *angrily:* Perpetual student! Twice already you've been expelled from the university.

MME. RANEVSKAYA: Why are you so cross, Varya? He's teasing you about Lopahin. Well, what of it? If you want to marry Lopahin, go ahead. He's a good man, and interesting; if you don't want to, don't. No-body's compelling you, my pet!

VARYA: Frankly, mamma dear, I take this thing seri-ously; he's a good man and I like him.

MME. RANEVSKAYA: All right then, marry him. I don't know what you're waiting for.

VARYA: But, mamma, I can't propose to him myself. For the last two years everyone's been talking to me about him—talking. But he either keeps silent, or else cracks jokes. I understand; he's growing rich, he's ab-sorbed in business—he has no time for me. If I had money, even a little, say, 100 rubles, I'd throw every-thing up and go far away—I'd go into a nunnery.

TROFIMOV: What a blessing . . .

VARYA: A student ought to be intelligent. *Softly, with tears in her voice.* How homely you've grown, Petya! How old you look! *To* MME. RANEVSKAYA, *with dry eyes.* But I can't live without work, mamma dear; I must keep busy every minute.

Enter YASHA.

YASHA, *hardly restraining his laughter:* Yepihodov has broken a billiard cue! *Exits.*

VARYA: Why is Yepihodov here? Who allowed him to play billiards? I don't understand these people! *Exits.*

MME. RANEVSKAYA: Don't tease her, Petya. She's un-happy enough without that.

TROFIMOV: She bustles so—and meddles in other people's business. All summer long she's given Anya and me no peace. She's afraid of a love-affair between us. What business is it of hers? Besides, I've given no grounds for it, and I'm far from such vulgarity. We are above love.

MME. RANEVSKAYA: And I suppose I'm beneath love? *Anxiously.* What can be keeping Leonid? If I only knew whether the estate has been sold or not. Such a calamity seems so incredible to me that I don't know what to think—I feel lost. . . . I could scream. . . . I could do something stupid. . . . Save me, Petya, tell me something, talk to me!

TROFIMOV: Whether the estate is sold today or not, isn't it all one? That's all done with long ago—there's no turning back, the path is overgrown. Calm yourself, my dear. You mustn't deceive yourself. For once in your life you must face the truth.

MME. RANEVSKAYA: What truth? You can see the truth, you can tell it from falsehood, but I seem to have lost my eyesight, I see nothing. You settle every great problem so boldly, but tell me, my dear boy, isn't it because you're young, because you don't yet know what one of your problems means in terms of suffering? You look ahead fearlessly, but isn't it because you don't see and don't expect anything dreadful, because life is still hidden from your young eyes? You're bolder, more honest, more profound than we are, but think hard, show just a bit of magnanimity, spare me. After all, I was born here, my father and mother lived here, and my grandfather; I love this house. Without the cherry orchard, my life has no meaning for me, and if it really must be sold, then sell me with the orchard. *Embraces* TROFIMOV, *kisses him on the forehead.* My son was drowned here. *Weeps.* Pity me, you good, kind fellow!

TROFIMOV: You know, I feel for you with all my heart.

MME. RANEVSKAYA: But that should have been said differently, so differently! *Takes out her handkerchief— a telegram falls on the floor.* My heart is so heavy today —you can't imagine! The noise here upsets me—my inmost being trembles at every sound—I'm shaking all over. But I can't go into my own room; I'm afraid to be alone. Don't condemn me, Petya. . . . I love you as though you were one of us, I would gladly let you marry Anya—I swear I would—only, my dear boy, you must study—you must take your degree—you do nothing, you let yourself be tossed by Fate from place to place—it's so strange. It's true, isn't it? And you should do something about your beard, to make it grow somehow! *Laughs.* You're so funny!

TROFIMOV, *picks up the telegram:* I've no wish to be a dandy.

MME. RANEVSKAYA: That's a telegram from Paris. I get one every day. One yesterday and one today. That savage is ill again—he's in trouble again. He begs forgiveness, implores me to go to him, and really I ought to go to Paris to be near him. Your face is stern, Petya; but what is there to do, my dear boy? What am I to do? He's ill, he's alone and unhappy, and who is to look after him, who is to keep him from doing the wrong thing, who is to give him his medicine on time? And why hide it or keep still about it—I love him! That's clear. I love him, love him! He's a millstone round my neck, he'll drag me to the bottom, but I love that stone, I can't live without it. *Presses* TROFIMOV's *hand.* Don't think badly of me, Petya, and don't say anything, don't say . . .

TROFIMOV, *through tears:* Forgive me my frankness in heaven's name; but, you know, he robbed you!

MME. RANEVSKAYA: No, no, no, you mustn't say such things! *Covers her ears.*

TROFIMOV: But he's a scoundrel! You're the only one who doesn't know it. He's a petty scoundrel—a nonentity!

MME. RANEVSKAYA, *controlling her anger:* You are twenty-six or twenty-seven years old, but you're still a schoolboy.

TROFIMOV: That may be.

MME. RANEVSKAYA: You should be a man at your age. You should understand people who love—and ought to be in love yourself. You ought to fall in love! *Angrily.* Yes, yes! And it's not purity in you, it's prudishness, you're simply a queer fish, a comical freak!

TROFIMOV, *horrified:* What is she saying?

MME. RANEVSKAYA: "I am above love!" You're not above love, but simply, as our Firs says, you're an addlehead. At your age not to have a mistress!

TROFIMOV, *horrified:* This is frightful! What is she saying! *Goes rapidly into the ballroom, clutching his head.* It's frightful—I can't stand it, I won't stay! *Exits, but returns at once.* All is over between us! *Exits into anteroom.*

MME. RANEVSKAYA, *shouts after him:* Petya! Wait! You absurd fellow, I was joking. Petya!

Sound of somebody running quickly downstairs and suddenly falling down with a crash. ANYA *and* VARYA *scream. Sound of laughter a moment later.*

MME. RANEVSKAYA: What's happened?

ANYA *runs in.*

ANYA, *laughing:* Petya's fallen downstairs! *Runs out.*

MME. RANEVSKAYA: What a queer bird that Petya is!

STATIONMASTER, *standing in the middle of the ballroom, recites Alexey Tolstoy's "Magdalene," to which all listen, but after a few lines, the sound of a waltz is heard from the anteroom and the reading breaks off. All dance.* TROFIMOV, ANYA, VARYA, *and* MME. RANEVSKAYA *enter from the anteroom.*

MME. RANEVSKAYA: Petya, you pure soul, please forgive me. . . . Let's dance.

Dances with PETYA. ANYA *and* VARYA *dance.* FIRS *enters, puts his stick down by the side door.* YASHA *enters from the drawing-room and watches the dancers.*

YASHA: Well, grandfather?

FIRS: I'm not feeling well. In the old days it was generals, barons, and admirals that were dancing at our balls, and now we have to send for the Post Office clerk and the Stationmaster, and even they aren't too glad to come. I feel kind of shaky. The old master that's gone, their grandfather, dosed everyone with sealing-wax, whatever ailed 'em. I've been taking sealing-wax every day for twenty years or more. Perhaps that's what's kept me alive.

YASHA: I'm fed up with you, grandpop. *Yawns.* It's time you croaked.

FIRS: Oh, you addlehead! *Mumbles.*

TROFIMOV *and* MME. RANEVSKAYA *dance from the ballroom into the drawing-room.*

MME. RANEVSKAYA: *Merci.* I'll sit down a while. *Sits down.* I'm tired.

Enter ANYA.

ANYA, *excitedly:* There was a man in the kitchen just now who said the cherry orchard was sold today.

MME. RANEVSKAYA: Sold to whom?

ANYA: He didn't say. He's gone. *Dances off with* TROFIMOV.

YASHA: It was some old man gabbing, a stranger.

FIRS: And Leonid Andreyevich isn't back yet, he hasn't come. And he's wearing his lightweight between-season overcoat; like enough, he'll catch cold. Ah, when they're young they're green.

MME. RANEVSKAYA: This is killing me. Go, Yasha, find out to whom it has been sold.

YASHA: But the old man left long ago. *Laughs.*

MME. RANEVSKAYA: What are you laughing at? What are you pleased about?

YASHA: That Yepihodov is such a funny one. A funny fellow, Two-and-Twenty Troubles!

MME. RANEVSKAYA: Firs, if the estate is sold, where will you go?

FIRS: I'll go where you tell me.

MME. RANEVSKAYA: Why do you look like that? Are you ill? You ought to go to bed.

FIRS: Yes! *With a snigger.* Me go to bed, and who's to hand things round? Who's to see to things? I'm the only one in the whole house.

YASHA, *to* MME. RANEVSKAYA: Lubov Andreyevna, allow me to ask a favor of you, be so kind! If you go back to Paris, take me with you, I beg you. It's positively impossible for me to stay here. *Looking around; sotto voce.* What's the use of talking? You see for yourself, it's an uncivilized country, the people have no morals, and then the boredom! The food in the kitchen's revolting, and besides there's this Firs wanders about mumbling all sorts of inappropriate words. Take me with you, be so kind!

Enter PISHCHIK.

PISHCHIK: May I have the pleasure of a waltz with you, charming lady? MME. RANEVSKAYA *accepts.* All the same, enchanting lady, you must let me have 180 rubles. . . . You must let me have (*dancing*) just one hundred and eighty rubles. *They pass into the ballroom.*

YASHA, *hums softly:* "Oh, wilt thou understand the tumult in my soul?"

In the ballroom a figure in a gray top hat and checked trousers is jumping about and waving its arms; shouts: "Bravo, Charlotta Ivanovna!"

DUNYASHA, *stopping to powder her face; to* FIRS: The young miss has ordered me to dance. There are so many gentlemen and not enough ladies. But dancing makes me dizzy, my heart begins to beat fast, Firs Nikolayevich. The Post Office clerk said something to me just now that quite took my breath away. *Music stops.*

Firs: What did he say?

Dunyasha: "You're like a flower," he said.

Yasha, *yawns:* What ignorance. *Exits.*

Dunyasha: "Like a flower!" I'm such a delicate girl. I simply adore pretty speeches.

Firs: You'll come to a bad end.

Enter Yepihodov.

Yepihodov, *to* Dunyasha: You have no wish to see me, Avdotya Fyodorovna . . . as though I was some sort of insect. *Sighs.* Ah, life!

Dunyasha: What is it you want?

Yepihodov: Indubitably you may be right. *Sighs.* But of course, if one looks at it from the point of view, if I may be allowed to say so, and apologizing for my frankness, you have completely reduced me to a state of mind. I know my fate. Every day some calamity befalls me, and I grew used to it long ago, so that I look upon my fate with a smile. You gave me your word, and though I—

Dunyasha: Let's talk about it later, please. But just now leave me alone, I am daydreaming. *Plays with a fan.*

Yepihodov: A misfortune befalls me every day; and if I may be allowed to say so, I merely smile, I even laugh.

Enter Varya.

Varya, *to* Yepihodov: Are you still here? What an impertinent fellow you are really! Run along, Dunyasha. *To* Yepihodov. Either you're playing billiards and breaking a cue, or you're wandering about the drawing-room as though you were a guest.

Yepihodov: You cannot, permit me to remark, penalize me.

Varya: I'm not penalizing you; I'm just telling you. You merely wander from place to place, and don't do your work. We keep you as a clerk, but Heaven knows what for.

YEPIHODOV, *offended:* Whether I work or whether I walk, whether I eat or whether I play billiards, is a matter to be discussed only by persons of understanding and of mature years.

VARYA, *enraged:* You dare say that to me—you dare? You mean to say I've no understanding? Get out of here at once! This minute!

YEPIHODOV, *scared:* I beg you to express yourself delicately.

VARYA, *beside herself:* Clear out this minute! Out with you!

YEPIHODOV *goes towards the door,* VARYA *following.*

VARYA: Two-and-Twenty Troubles! Get out—don't let me set eyes on you!

Exit YEPIHODOV. *His voice is heard behind the door:* "I shall lodge a complaint against you!"

VARYA: Oh, you're coming back? *She seizes the stick left near door by* FIRS. Well, come then . . . come . . . I'll show you . . . Ah, you're coming? You're coming? . . . Come . . . *Swings the stick just as* LO-PAHIN *enters.*

LOPAHIN: Thank you kindly.

VARYA, *angrily and mockingly:* I'm sorry.

LOPAHIN: It's nothing. Thank you kindly for your charming reception.

VARYA: Don't mention it. *Walks away, looks back and asks softly.* I didn't hurt you, did I?

LOPAHIN: Oh, no, not at all. I shall have a large bump, though.

Voices from the ballroom: "Lopahin is here! Lopa-hin!"

Enter PISHCHIK.

PISHCHIK: My eyes do see, my ears do hear! *Kisses* LOPAHIN.

LOPAHIN: You smell of cognac, my dear friends. And we've been celebrating here, too.

Enter MME. RANEVSKAYA.

MME. RANEVSKAYA: Is that you, Yermolay Alexeyevich? What kept you so long? Where's Leonid?

LOPAHIN: Leonid Andreyevich arrived with me. He's coming.

MME. RANEVSKAYA: Well, what happened? Did the sale take place? Speak!

LOPAHIN, *embarrassed, fearful of revealing his joy:* The sale was over at four o'clock. We missed the train— had to wait till half past nine. *Sighing heavily.* Ugh. I'm a little dizzy.

Enter GAYEV. *In his right hand he holds parcels, with his left he is wiping away his tears.*

MME. RANEVSKAYA: Well, Leonid? What news? *Impatiently, through tears.* Be quick, for God's sake!

GAYEV, *not answering, simply waves his hand. Weeping, to* FIRS: Here, take these; anchovies, Kerch herrings . . . I haven't eaten all day. What I've been through! *The click of billiard balls comes through the open door of the billiard room and* YASHA's *voice is heard:* "Seven and eighteen!" GAYEV's *expression changes, he no longer weeps.* I'm terribly tired. Firs, help me change. *Exits, followed by* FIRS.

PISHCHIK: How about the sale? Tell us what happened.

MME. RANEVSKAYA: Is the cherry orchard sold?

LOPAHIN: Sold.

MME. RANEVSKAYA: Who bought it?

LOPAHIN: I bought it.

Pause. MME. RANEVSKAYA *is overcome. She would*

fall to the floor, were it not for the chair and table near which she stands. VARYA *takes the keys from her belt, flings them on the floor in the middle of the drawing-room and goes out.*

LOPAHIN: I bought it. Wait a bit, ladies and gentlemen, please, my head is swimming, I can't talk. *Laughs.* We got to the auction and Deriganov was there already. Leonid Andreyevich had only 15,000 and straight off Deriganov bid 30,000 over and above the mortgage. I saw how the land lay, got into the fight, bid 40,000. He bid 45,000. I bid fifty-five. He kept adding five thousands, I ten. Well . . . it came to an end. I bid ninety above the mortgage and the estate was knocked down to me. Now the cherry orchard's mine! Mine! *Laughs uproariously.* Lord! God in Heaven! The cherry orchard's mine! Tell me that I'm drunk—out of my mind—that it's all a dream. *Stamps his feet.* Don't laugh at me! If my father and my grandfather could rise from their graves and see all that has happened—how their Yermolay, who used to be flogged, their half-literate Yermolay, who used to run about barefoot in winter, how that very Yermolay has bought the most magnificent estate in the world. I bought the estate where my father and grandfather were slaves, where they weren't even allowed to enter the kitchen. I'm asleep—it's only a dream—I only imagine it. . . . It's the fruit of your imagination, wrapped in the darkness of the unknown! *Picks up the keys, smiling genially.* She threw down the keys, wants to show she's no longer mistress here. *Jingles keys.* Well, no matter. *The band is heard tuning up.* Hey, musicians! Strike up! I want to hear you! Come, everybody, and see how Yermolay Lopahin will lay the ax to the cherry orchard and how the trees will fall to the ground. We will build summer cottages there, and our grandsons and great-grandsons will see a new life here. Music! Strike up!

The band starts to play. Mme. Ranevskaya *has sunk into a chair and is weeping bitterly.*

Lopahin, *reproachfully:* Why, why didn't you listen to me? My dear friend, my poor friend, you can't bring it back now. *Tearfully.* Oh, if only this were over quickly! Oh, if only our wretched, disordered life were changed!

Pishchik, *takes him by the arm; sotto voce:* She's crying. Let's go into the ballroom. Let her be alone. Come. *Takes his arm and leads him into the ballroom.*

Lopahin: What's the matter? Musicians, play so I can hear you! Let me have things the way I want them. *Ironically.* Here comes the new master, the owner of the cherry orchard. *Accidentally he trips over a little table, almost upsetting the candelabra.* I can pay for everything. *Exits with* Pishchik. Mme. Ranevskaya, *alone, sits huddled up, weeping bitterly. Music plays softly. Enter* Anya *and* Trofimov *quickly.* Anya *goes to her mother and falls on her knees before her.* Trofimov *stands in the doorway.*

Anya: Mamma, mamma, you're crying! Dear, kind, good mamma, my precious, I love you, I bless you! The cherry orchard is sold, it's gone, that's true, quite true. But don't cry, mamma, life is still before you, you still have your kind, pure heart. Let us go, let us go away from here, darling. We will plant a new orchard, even more luxuriant than this one. You will see it, you will understand, and like the sun at evening, joy—deep, tranquil joy—will sink into your soul, and you will smile, mamma. Come, darling, let us go.

Act IV

*S*CENE *as in Act I. No window curtains or pictures,
only a little furniture, piled up in a corner, as if
for sale. A sense of emptiness. Near the outer door and
at the back, suitcases, bundles, etc., are piled up. A
door open on the left and the voices of* VARYA *and*
ANYA *are heard.* LOPAHIN *stands waiting.* YASHA *holds
a tray with glasses full of champagne.* YEPIHODOV *in
the anteroom is tying up a box. Behind the scene a hum
of voices: peasants have come to say good-by. Voice of*
GAYEV: "*Thanks, brothers, thank you.*"

YASHA: The country folk have come to say good-by.
In my opinion, Yermolay Alexeyevich, they are kindly
souls, but there's nothing in their heads. *The hum dies
away. Enter* MME. RANEVSKAYA *and* GAYEV. *She is not
crying, but is pale, her face twitches and she cannot
speak.*

GAYEV: You gave them your purse, Luba. That won't
do! That won't do!

MME. RANEVSKAYA: I couldn't help it! I couldn't!
They go out.

LOPAHIN, *calls after them:* Please, I beg you, have a
glass at parting. I didn't think of bringing any champagne from town and at the station I could find only
one bottle. Please, won't you? *Pause.* What's the matter,
ladies and gentlemen, don't you want any? *Moves away
from the door.* If I'd known, I wouldn't have bought it.
Well, then I won't drink any, either. YASHA *carefully
sets the tray down on a chair.* At least you have a glass,
Yasha.

YASHA: Here's to the travelers! And good luck to

those that stay! *Drinks.* This champagne isn't the real stuff, I can assure you.

LOPAHIN: Eight rubles a bottle. *Pause.* It's devilishly cold here.

YASHA: They didn't light the stoves today—it wasn't worth it, since we're leaving. *Laughs.*

LOPAHIN: Why are you laughing?

YASHA: It's just that I'm pleased.

LOPAHIN: It's October, yet it's as still and sunny as though it were summer. Good weather for building. *Looks at his watch, and speaks off.* Bear in mind, ladies and gentlemen, the train goes in forty-seven minutes, so you ought to start for the station in twenty minutes. Better hurry up!

Enter TROFIMOV *wearing an overcoat.*

TROFIMOV: I think it's time to start. The carriages are at the door. The devil only knows what's become of my rubbers; they've disappeared. *Calling off.* Anya! My rubbers are gone. I can't find them.

LOPAHIN: I've got to go to Kharkov. I'll take the same train you do. I'll spend the winter in Kharkov. I've been hanging round here with you, till I'm worn out with loafing. I can't live without work—I don't know what to do with my hands, they dangle as if they didn't belong to me.

TROFIMOV: Well, we'll soon be gone, then you can go on with your useful labors again.

LOPAHIN: Have a glass.

TROFIMOV: No, I won't.

LOPAHIN: So you're going to Moscow now?

TROFIMOV: Yes. I'll see them into town, and tomorrow I'll go on to Moscow.

LOPAHIN: Well, I'll wager the professors aren't giving any lectures, they're waiting for you to come.

TROFIMOV: That's none of your business.

LOPAHIN: Just how many years have you been at the university?

TROFIMOV: Can't you think of something new? Your joke's stale and flat. *Looking for his rubbers.* We'll probably never see each other again, so allow me to give you a piece of advice at parting: don't wave your hands about! Get out of the habit. And another thing: building bungalows, figuring that summer residents will eventually become small farmers, figuring like that is just another form of waving your hands about. . . . Never mind, I love you anyway; you have fine, delicate fingers, like an artist; you have a fine, delicate soul.

LOPAHIN, *embracing him:* Good-by, my dear fellow. Thank you for everything. Let me give you some money for the journey, if you need it.

TROFIMOV: What for? I don't need it.

LOPAHIN: But you haven't any.

TROFIMOV: Yes, I have, thank you. I got some money for a translation—here it is in my pocket. *Anxiously.* But where are my rubbers?

VARYA, *from the next room:* Here! Take the nasty things. *Flings a pair of rubbers onto the stage.*

TROFIMOV: What are you so cross about, Varya? Hm . . . and these are not my rubbers.

LOPAHIN: I sowed three thousand acres of poppies in the spring, and now I've made 40,000 on them, clear profit; and when my poppies were in bloom, what a picture it was! So, as I say, I made 40,000; and I am offering you a loan because I can afford it. Why turn up your nose at it? I'm a peasant—I speak bluntly.

TROFIMOV: Your father was a peasant, mine was a druggist—that proves absolutely nothing whatever. LOPAHIN *takes out his wallet.* Don't, put that away! If you were to offer me two hundred thousand I wouldn't take it. I'm a free man. And everything that all of you, rich and poor alike, value so highly and hold so dear, hasn't the slightest power over me. It's like so much fluff floating in the air. I can get on without you, I can pass you by, I'm strong and proud. Mankind is moving towards the highest truth, towards the highest happiness possible on earth, and I am in the front ranks.

LOPAHIN: Will you get there?

TROFIMOV: I will. *Pause.* I will get there, or I will show others the way to get there.

The sound of axes chopping down trees is heard in the distance.

LOPAHIN: Well, good-by, my dear fellow. It's time to leave. We turn up our noses at one another, but life goes on just the same. When I'm working hard, without resting, my mind is easier, and it seems to me that I too know why I exist. But how many people are there in Russia, brother, who exist nobody knows why? Well, it doesn't matter. That's not what makes the wheels go round. They say Leonid Andreyevich has taken a position in the bank, 6,000 rubles a year. Only, of course, he won't stick to it, he's too lazy. . . .

ANYA, *in the doorway:* Mamma begs you not to start cutting down the cherry-trees until she's gone.

TROFIMOV: Really, you should have more tact! *Exits.*

LOPAHIN: Right away—right away! Those men . . . *Exits.*

ANYA: Has Firs been taken to the hospital?

YASHA: I told them this morning. They must have taken him.

ANYA, *to* YEPIHODOV *who crosses the room:* Yepihodov, please find out if Firs has been taken to the hospital.

YASHA, *offended:* I told Yegor this morning. Why ask a dozen times?

YEPIHODOV: The aged Firs, in my definitive opinion,

is beyond mending. It's time he was gathered to his fathers. And I can only envy him. *Puts a suitcase down on a hat-box and crushes it.* There now, of course. I knew it! *Exits.*

YASHA, *mockingly:* Two-and-Twenty Troubles!

VARYA, *through the door:* Has Firs been taken to the hospital?

ANYA: Yes.

VARYA: Then why wasn't the note for the doctor taken too?

ANYA: Oh! Then someone must take it to him. *Exits.*

VARYA, *from adjoining room:* Where's Yasha? Tell him his mother's come and wants to say good-by.

YASHA, *waves his hand:* She tries my patience.

DUNYASHA *has been occupied with the luggage. Seeing YASHA alone, she goes up to him.*

DUNYASHA: You might just give me one little look, Yasha. You're going away. . . . You're leaving me . . . *Weeps and throws herself on his neck.*

YASHA: What's there to cry about? *Drinks champagne.* In six days I shall be in Paris again. Tomorrow we get into an express train and off we go, that's the last you'll see of us. . . . I can scarcely believe it. *Vive la France!* It don't suit me here, I just can't live here. That's all there is to it. I'm fed up with the ignorance here, I've had enough of it. *Drinks champagne.* What's there to cry about? Behave yourself properly, and you'll have no cause to cry.

DUNYASHA, *powders her face, looking in pocket mirror:* Do send me a letter from Paris. You know I loved you, Yasha, how I loved you! I'm a delicate creature, Yasha.

YASHA: Somebody's coming! *Busies himself with the luggage; hums softly.*

Enter Mme. Ranevskaya, Gayev, Anya, *and* Charlotta.

Gayev: We ought to be leaving. We haven't much time. *Looks at* Yasha. Who smells of herring?

Mme. Ranevskaya: In about ten minutes we should be getting into the carriages. *Looks around the room.* Good-by, dear old home, good-by, grandfather. Winter will pass, spring will come, you will no longer be here, they will have torn you down. How much these walls have seen! *Kisses* Anya *warmly.* My treasure, how radiant you look! Your eyes are sparkling like diamonds. Are you glad? Very?

Anya, *gaily:* Very glad. A new life is beginning, mamma.

Gayev: Well, really, everything is all right now. Before the cherry orchard was sold, we all fretted and suffered; but afterwards, when the question was settled finally and irrevocably, we all calmed down, and even felt quite cheerful. I'm a bank employee now, a financier. The yellow ball in the side pocket! And anyhow, you are looking better Luba, there's no doubt of that.

Mme. Ranevskaya: Yes, my nerves are better, that's true. *She is handed her hat and coat.* I sleep well. Carry out my things, Yasha. It's time. *To* Anya. We shall soon see each other again, my little girl. I'm going to Paris, I'll live there on the money your great-aunt sent us to buy the estate with—long live Auntie! But that money won't last long.

Anya: You'll come back soon, soon, mamma, won't you? Meanwhile I'll study, I'll pass my high school examination, and then I'll go to work and help you. We'll read all kinds of books together, mamma, won't we? *Kisses her mother's hands.* We'll read in the autumn evenings, we'll read lots of books, and a new wonderful world will open up before us. *Falls into a revery.* Mamma, do come back.

MME. RANEVSKAYA: I will come back, my precious. *Embraces her daughter. Enter* LOPAHIN *and* CHARLOTTA *who is humming softly.*

GAYEV: Charlotta's happy: she's singing.

CHARLOTTA, *picks up a bundle and holds it like a baby in swaddling-clothes:* Bye, baby, bye. *A baby is heard crying* "Wah! Wah!" Hush, hush, my pet, my little one. "Wah! Wah!" I'm so sorry for you! *Throws the bundle down.* You will find me a position, won't you? I can't go on like this.

LOPAHIN: We'll find one for you, Charlotta Ivanovna, don't worry.

GAYEV: Everyone's leaving us. Varya's going away. We've suddenly become of no use.

CHARLOTTA: There's no place for me to live in town, I must go away. *Hums.*

Enter PISHCHIK.

LOPAHIN: There's nature's masterpiece!

PISHCHIK, *gasping:* Oh . . . let me get my breath . . . I'm in agony. . . . Esteemed friends . . . Give me a drink of water. . . .

GAYEV: Wants some money, I suppose. No, thank you . . . I'll keep out of harm's way. *Exits.*

PISHCHIK: It's a long while since I've been to see you, most charming lady. *To* LOPAHIN. So you are here . . . glad to see you, you intellectual giant . . . There . . . *Gives* LOPAHIN *money.* Here's 400 rubles, and I still owe you 840.

LOPAHIN, *shrugging his shoulders in bewilderment:* I must be dreaming . . . Where did you get it?

PISHCHIK: Wait a minute . . . It's hot . . . A most extraordinary event! Some Englishmen came to my place and found some sort of white clay on my land . . .

To Mme. Ranevskaya. And 400 for you . . . most lovely . . . most wonderful . . . *Hands her the money.* The rest later. *Drinks water.* A young man in the train was telling me just now that a great philosopher recommends jumping off roofs. "Jump!" says he; "that's the long and the short of it!" *In amazement.* Just imagine! Some more water!

Lopahin: What Englishmen?

Pishchik: I leased them the tract with the clay on it for twenty-four years. . . . And now, forgive me, I can't stay. . . . I must be dashing on. . . . I'm going over to Znoikov . . . to Kardamanov . . . I owe them all money . . . *Drinks water.* Good-by, everybody . . . I'll look in on Thursday . . .

Mme. Ranevskaya: We're just moving into town; and tomorrow I go abroad.

Pishchik, *upset:* What? Why into town? That's why the furniture is like that . . . and the suitcases . . . Well, never mind! *Through tears.* Never mind . . . Men of colossal intellect, these Englishmen . . . Never mind . . . Be happy. God will come to your help . . . Never mind . . . Everything in this world comes to an end. *Kisses* Mme. Ranevskaya's *hand.* If the rumor reaches you that it's all up with me, remember this old . . . horse, and say: Once there lived a certain . . . Simeonov-Pishchik . . . the kingdom of Heaven be his . . . Glorious weather! . . . Yes . . . *Exits, in great confusion, but at once returns and says in the doorway:* My daughter Dashenka sends her regards. *Exit.*

Mme. Ranevskaya: Now we can go. I leave with two cares weighing on me. The first is poor old Firs. *Glancing at her watch.* We still have about five minutes.

Anya: Mamma, Firs has already been taken to the hospital. Yasha sent him there this morning.

MME. RANEVSKAYA: My other worry is Varya. She's used to getting up early and working; and now, with no work to do, she is like a fish out of water. She has grown thin and pale, and keeps crying, poor soul. *Pause.* You know this very well, Yermolay Alexeyevich; I dreamed of seeing her married to you, and it looked as though that's how it would be. *Whispers to* ANYA, *who nods to* CHARLOTTA *and both go out.* She loves you. You find her attractive. I don't know, I don't know why it is you seem to avoid each other; I can't understand it.

LOPAHIN: To tell you the truth, I don't understand it myself. It's all a puzzle. If there's still time, I'm ready now, at once. Let's settle it straight off, and have done with it! Without you, I feel I'll never be able to propose.

MME. RANEVSKAYA: That's splendid. After all, it will only take a minute. I'll call her at once. . . .

LOPAHIN: And luckily, here's champagne too. *Looks at the glasses.* Empty! Somebody's drunk it all. YASHA *coughs.* That's what you might call guzzling . . .

MME. RANEVSKAYA, *animatedly:* Excellent! We'll go and leave you alone. Yasha, *allez!* I'll call her. *At the door.* Varya, leave everything and come here. Come! *Exits with* YASHA.

LOPAHIN, *looking at his watch:* Yes . . . *Pause behind the door, smothered laughter and whispering; at last, enter* VARYA.

VARYA, *looking over the luggage in leisurely fashion:* Strange, I can't find it . . .

LOPAHIN: What are you looking for?

VARYA: Packed it myself, and I don't remember . . . *Pause.*

LOPAHIN: Where are you going now, Varya?

VARYA: I? To the Ragulins'. I've arranged to take charge there—as housekeeper, if you like.

LOPAHIN: At Yashnevo? About fifty miles from here. *Pause.* Well, life in this house is ended!

VARYA, *examining luggage:* Where is it? Perhaps I put it in the chest. Yes, life in this house is ended . . . There will be no more of it.

LOPAHIN: And I'm just off to Kharkov—by this next train. I've a lot to do there. I'm leaving Yepihodov here . . . I've taken him on.

VARYA: Oh!

LOPAHIN: Last year at this time it was snowing, if you remember, but now it's sunny and there's no wind. It's cold, though . . . It must be three below.

VARYA: I didn't look. *Pause.* And besides, our thermometer's broken. *Pause. Voice from the yard:* "Yermolay Alexeyevich!"

LOPAHIN, *as if he had been waiting for the call:* This minute! *Exit quickly.* VARYA *sits on the floor and sobs quietly, her head on a bundle of clothes. Enter* MME. RANEVSKAYA *cautiously.*

MME. RANEVSKAYA: Well? *Pause.* We must be going.

VARYA, *wiping her eyes:* Yes, it's time, mamma dear. I'll be able to get to the Ragulins' today, if only we don't miss the train.

MME. RANEVSKAYA, *at the door:* Anya, put your things on. *Enter* ANYA, GAYEV, CHARLOTTA. GAYEV *wears a heavy overcoat with a hood. Enter servants and coachmen.* YEPIHODOV *bustles about the luggage.*

MME. RANEVSKAYA: Now we can start on our journey.

ANYA, *joyfully:* On our journey!

GAYEV: My friends, my dear, cherished friends, leaving this house forever, can I be silent? Can I at leave-taking refrain from giving utterance to those emotions that now fill my being?

ANYA, *imploringly:* Uncle!

VARYA: Uncle, uncle dear, don't.

GAYEV, *forlornly:* I'll bank the yellow in the side pocket . . . I'll be silent . . .

Enter TROFIMOV, *then* LOPAHIN.

TROFIMOV: Well, ladies and gentlemen, it's time to leave.

LOPAHIN: Yepihodov, my coat.

MME. RANEVSKAYA: I'll sit down just a minute. It seems as though I'd never before seen what the walls of this house were like, the ceilings, and now I look at them hungrily, with such tender affection.

GAYEV: I remember when I was six years old sitting on that window sill on Whitsunday, watching my father going to church.

MME. RANEVSKAYA: Has everything been taken?

LOPAHIN: I think so. *Putting on his overcoat.* Yepihodov, see that everything's in order.

YEPIHODOV, *in a husky voice:* You needn't worry, Yermolay Alexeyevich.

LOPAHIN: What's the matter with your voice?

YEPIHODOV: I just had a drink of water. I must have swallowed something.

YASHA, *contemptuously:* What ignorance!

MME. RANEVSKAYA: When we're gone, not a soul will be left here.

LOPAHIN: Until the spring.

VARYA *pulls an umbrella out of a bundle, as though about to hit someone with it.* LOPAHIN *pretends to be frightened.*

VARYA: Come, come, I had no such idea!

TROFIMOV: Ladies and gentlemen, let's get into the carriages—it's time. The train will be in directly.

VARYA: Petya, there they are, your rubbers, by that trunk. *Tearfully:* And what dirty old things they are!

TROFIMOV, *puts on rubbers:* Let's go, ladies and gentlemen.

GAYEV, *greatly upset, afraid of breaking down:* The train . . . the station . . . Three cushions in the side pocket, I'll bank this one in the corner . . .

MME. RANEVSKAYA: Let's go.

LOPAHIN: Are we all here? No one in there? *Locks the side door on the left.* There are some things stored here, better lock up. Let us go!

ANYA: Good-by, old house! Good-by, old life!

TROFIMOV: Hail to you, new life!

Exit with ANYA. VARYA *looks round the room and goes out slowly.* YASHA *and* CHARLOTTA *with her dog go out.*

LOPAHIN: And so, until the spring. Go along, friends . . . 'Bye-'bye! *Exits.*

MME. RANEVSKAYA *and* GAYEV *remain alone. As though they had been waiting for this, they throw themselves on each other's necks, and break into subdued, restrained sobs, afraid of being overheard.*

GAYEV, *in despair:* My sister! My sister!

MME. RANEVSKAYA: Oh, my orchard—my dear, sweet, beautiful orchard! My life, my youth, my happiness—good-by! Good-by! *Voice of* ANYA, *gay and summoning:* "Mamma!" *Voice of* TROFIMOV, *gay and excited:* "Halloo!"

MME. RANEVSKAYA: One last look at the walls, at the windows . . . Our poor mother loved to walk about this room . . .

GAYEV: My sister, my sister! *Voice of* ANYA: "Mamma!" *Voice of* TROFIMOV: "Halloo!"

MME. RANEVSKAYA: We're coming.

They go out. The stage is empty. The sound of doors being locked, of carriages driving away. Then silence.

In the stillness is heard the muffled sound of the ax striking a tree, a mournful, lonely sound.

Footsteps are heard. FIRS *appears in the doorway on the right. He is dressed as usual in a jacket and white waistcoat and wears slippers. He is ill.*

FIRS, *goes to the door, tries the handle:* Locked! They've gone . . . *Sits down on the sofa.* They've forgotten me . . . Never mind . . . I'll sit here a bit . . . I'll wager Leonid Andreyevich hasn't put his fur coat on, he's gone off in his light overcoat . . . *Sighs anxiously.* I didn't keep an eye on him . . . Ah, when they're young, they're green . . . *Mumbles something indistinguishable.* Life has gone by as if I had never lived. *Lies down.* I'll lie down a while . . . There's no strength left in you, old fellow; nothing is left, nothing. Ah, you addlehead! *Lies motionless. A distant sound is heard coming from the sky as it were, the sound of a snapping string mournfully dying away. All is still again, and nothing is heard but the strokes of the ax against a tree far away in the orchard.*

LETTERS

Letters

(The elderly novelist to whom this letter is addressed won his reputation in the middle of the century and was thus a survivor of the Golden Age of Russian literature. He had written to young Chekhov, with whom he was not acquainted, hailing him as the outstanding writer of his generation and urging him to undertake a serious piece of work that would demand time and thought, even if it meant going hungry.)

Moscow, March 28, 1886

Your letter, my kind, ardently beloved bringer of good tidings, struck me like a thunderbolt. I nearly cried, I got all excited, and now I feel that your message has left a deep mark on my soul. As you have been kind to my youth, so may God succor your old age. For my part, I can find neither words nor deeds with which to thank you. You know with what eyes ordinary people regard the elect such as you, and so you can imagine how your letter has affected my self-esteem. It is better than any diploma, and for a fledgeling writer it is bounty now and in time to come. I am almost in a daze. It is not within my power to judge whether I merit this high reward. I can only repeat that it has overwhelmed me.

If I have a gift that should be respected, I confess before the purity of your heart that hitherto I have not respected it. I felt that I did have talent, but I had got used to thinking it insignificant. Purely external causes are enough to make one unjust to oneself, suspicious, and diffident. And, as I think of it now, there have been plenty of such causes in my case. All those who are near to me have always treated my writing with condescension and have never stopped advising me in a friendly manner not to give up real work for scribbling. I have hundreds of acquaintances in Moscow, among them a score or so of people who write, and I cannot recall a single one who would read me or regard me as an artist. In Moscow there is a Literary Circle, so-called: gifted writers and mediocrities of all ages and complexions meet once a week in a restaurant and give their tongues free rein. If I were to go there and read them even a fragment of your letter, they would laugh in my face. In the five years that I have been knocking about newspaper offices I have come to accept this general view of my literary insignificance; before long I got used to taking an indulgent view of my labors, and so the fat was in the fire. That's the first cause. The second is that I am a physician and am up to my ears in medical work, so that the saw about chasing two hares[1] has robbed no one of more sleep than me.

I am writing all this for the sole purpose of exonerating myself to at least some degree in your eyes. Up till now my attitude towards my literary work has been extremely frivolous, casual, thoughtless. I cannot think of a *single* story at which I worked for more than a day, and "The Huntsman," which you liked, I wrote in a bathing-cabin. I wrote my stories the way reporters write notices of fires: mechanically, half-consciously, without caring a pin either about the reader or myself . . . I wrote and tried my best not to use up on a story the

---

[1] The allusion is to the Russian proverb: chase two hares, and you catch neither.

images and scenes which are dear to me and which, God knows why, I treasured and carefully concealed.

What first impelled me to self-criticism was a very friendly and, I believe, sincere letter from Suvorin.[1] I began to plan writing something decent, but I still lacked faith in my ability to produce anything worth while.

And then like a bolt from the blue came your letter. Excuse the comparison, but it had the effect on me of a Governor's order to leave town within twenty-four hours: I suddenly felt the urgent need to hurry and get out of the hole in which I was stuck . . .

I will stop—but not soon—doing work that has to be delivered on schedule. It is impossible to get out of the rut I am in all at once. I don't object to going hungry, as I went hungry in the past, but it is not a question of myself . . . To writing I give my leisure: two or three hours during the day and a fraction of the night, that is, an amount of time that is good only for short pieces. In the summer when I have more spare time and fewer expenses I shall undertake some serious piece of work . . .

All my hope is pinned to the future. I am only twenty-six. Perhaps I shall succeed in achieving something, though time flies fast.

Forgive this long letter and do not hold it against a man who for the first time in his life has made bold to indulge in the pleasure of writing to Grigorovich.

If possible, send me your photograph. I am so overcome by your kindness that I feel like writing you not a sheet, but a whole ream. May God grant you happiness and health, and believe the sincerity of your deeply respectful and grateful

A. CHEKHOV

---

[1] The editor—see letters to him.

TO HIS BROTHER NIKOLAY

(Nikolay was something of a painter; he designed the cover of Anton's first volume of short stories. The shiftless fellow was to die of consumption two years after this letter was written.)

Moscow, [end of] 1886

You have often complained to me that people didn't "understand" you! Goethe and Newton didn't complain of that . . . Christ alone did, but He was speaking not of His ego, but of His teaching. You are perfectly well understood. And if you don't understand yourself, it is not the fault of others.

I assure you that as a brother and a friend I understand you and sympathize with you heartily. I know all your good qualities as I know my five fingers; I value and deeply respect them. I can enumerate those qualities if you like, to prove that I understand you. I think you are kind to the point of spinelessness, sincere, magnanimous, unselfish, ready to share your last copper; you are free from envy and hatred; you are simple-hearted, you pity men and beasts; you are trustful, not spiteful, and do not remember evil. You have a gift from Heaven such as others do not possess: you have talent. This talent places you above millions of people, for only one out of two million on earth is an artist. Your talent sets you apart: even if you were a toad or a tarantula, you would be respected, for to talent everything is forgiven.

You have only one fault. Your false position, your unhappiness, your intestinal catarrh are all due to it. It is your utter lack of culture. Please forgive me, but *veritas magis amicitiae* . . . You see, life sets its terms. To feel at ease among cultivated people, to be at home and comfortable with them, one must have a certain amount of culture. Talent has brought you into that circle, you belong to it, but—you are drawn away from it, and you waver between cultured people and the tenants opposite.

Cultured people must, in my opinion, meet the following conditions:

1. They respect human personality, and for this reason they are always affable, gentle, civil, and ready to give in to others. They do not raise a rumpus over a hammer or a lost eraser; when they live with you they do not make you feel that they are doing you a favor, and on leaving they do not say: "Impossible to live with you!" They overlook noise, cold, overdone meat, jokes, the presence of strangers in their rooms.

2. They are sorry not only for beggars and cats. Their hearts ache over what the naked eye does not see . . . They sit up nights in order to help P——, to keep their brothers at the university, and to buy clothes for their mother.

3. They respect the property of others and therefore pay their debts.

4. They are candid, and dread lying as they dread fire. They do not lie even about trifles. A lie insults the listener and debases him in the eyes of the speaker. They do not pose; they behave in the street as they do at home; they do not show off before their inferiors. They do not chatter and do not force uninvited confidences on others. Out of respect for the ears of other people they often keep silent.

5. They do not belittle themselves to arouse compassion in others. They do not play on other people's heart-strings so as to elicit sighs and be fussed over. They do not say: "People don't understand me" or "I

have frittered away my talent," because all that is striving after cheap effect; it is vulgar, stale, false.

6. They are not vain. They do not care for such paste
diamonds as familiarity with celebrities, the handclasp
of the drunken P——, the raptures of a stray spectator
in a picture gallery, popularity in beer-halls . . . When
they have done a kopeck's worth of work they do not
strut about as though they had done a hundred rubles'
worth, and they do not brag of having the entrée where
others are not admitted. The truly talented always keep
in the shade, among the crowd, far from the show. Even
Krylov said that an empty barrel is noisier than a full
one.

7. If they possess talent they respect it. They sacrifice peace, women, wine, vanity to it. They are proud of
their talent; they are aware that their calling is not just
to live with people but to have an educative influence
on them. Besides they are fastidious.

8. They develop their esthetic sense. They cannot
fall asleep in their clothes, see the cracks in the wall full
of insects, breathe foul air, walk on a spittle-covered
floor, eat from a pot off a kerosene stove. They seek as
far as possible to tame and ennoble the sexual instinct.
What they want from a woman is not a bed-fellow, not
equine sweat, not a cleverness that shows itself in the
ability to —— and to lie incessantly. What they need,
especially if they are artists, is freshness, elegance, humanity, the capacity for being not a —— but a mother.
They do not swill vodka at all hours. They do not sniff
about cupboards, for they are not pigs. They drink only
when they are free, on occasion. For they want *mens
sana in corpore sano*. . . .

And so on. That is what cultivated people are like. In
order to educate yourself and not be below the level of

your surroundings it is not enough to have read *Pick-wick Papers* and memorized a monologue from *Faust*. It is not enough to come to Yakimanka [where the family lived], only to leave a week later.

What is needed is continuous work, day and night, constant reading, study, will-power . . . Every hour counts.

Trips to Yakimanka and back will not help. You must make a clean break. Come to us; smash the vodka bottle; lie down and read—Turgenev, if you like, whom you have not read. Give up your conceit, you are not a child. You will soon be thirty. It is time!

I am waiting . . . We are all waiting . . .

Yours,

A. CHEKHOV

TO HIS SISTER MARIA

(This, Chekhov's only sister, a schoolteacher, was the member of his family closest to him. After his death she edited a six-volume collection of his letters and as recently as 1934 was in charge of the Chekhov Museum at Yalta. In the spring of 1887 Chekhov revisited his birthplace, Taganrog, and a few neighboring towns. This letter is written from one of them.)

[Novocherkassk,] April 25, [1887]

I am now on my way from Novocherkassk to Zverevo. There was a wedding yesterday that had been going on since the day before, a real Cossack wedding, with music, women caterwauling, and a loathsome drinking bout. I got so many discordant impressions that it is impossible to set them down on paper, and I must put it off till I return to Moscow. The bride is sixteen. The wedding took place in the local cathedral. I acted as best man, in a borrowed frock-coat, wide pantaloons and without a single stud—in Moscow such a best man would get it in the neck, but here I was the greatest swell.

I saw a lot of wealthy marriageable girls. There was an enormous selection, but I was so drunk the whole time that I took bottles for girls and girls for bottles. Apparently, thanks to my drunken condition, the local maidens decided that I was witty and "a wag." The girls here are a flock of sheep: if one gets up and leaves the ballroom, all the others file after her. One of them, the smartest and the most daring, wishing to show that she knew something about fine manners and diplomacy, kept striking me on the hand with her fan and saying, "Oh, you naughty man!" But all the time her face wore an expression of fear. I taught her to say to her swains, "How naive you are!"

Apparently in obedience to a local custom, the newly-weds kissed every minute, kissed so vehemently that every time their lips made an explosive noise, and I had a taste of oversweet raisins in my mouth, and got a spasm in my left calf. Their kisses did the varicose vein in my left leg no good.

I can't tell you how much fresh caviar I ate and how much local red wine I drank. It's a wonder I didn't burst! * * *

At Zverevo I'll have to wait for the train from nine in the evening till five in the morning. Last time I had to sleep in a second-class car on a spur. At night I went out of the car to relieve myself and it was miraculous out there: the moon, the boundless steppe—a desert with ancient grave-mounds—the silence of the tomb, and the cars and rails standing out boldly against the dim sky— a dead world. It was an unforgettable picture. It is a pity Mishka [his brother Mikhail] couldn't come with me. He would have gone mad with all these impressions. * * *

Good-by. I hope everybody is weil.

A. Chekhov

(In the course of his trip to Taganrog Chekhov visited a monastery on the Donetz river.)

Taganrog, May 11, [1887]

The monks, very pleasant people, gave me a very unpleasant room with a mattress like a pancake. I spent two nights at the monastery and got no end of impressions. On aocount of St. Nicholas's Feast, 15,000 pilgrims flocked to the place, 8/9 of them old women. I didn't know that there were so many old women in the world, or I should have shot myself a long time ago . . . The services are endless: at midnight they ring the bells for matins, at 5 A.M. for early Mass, at 9 for late Mass, at 3 for nones, at 5 for vespers, at 6 for compline. Before each service you hear the weeping sound of a bell in the corridors, and a monk runs along crying in the voice of a creditor who implores his debtor to pay at least five kopecks on the ruble, "Lord Jesus Christ, have mercy on us! Pray come to matins!"

It is awkward to remain in your room, so you get up and go . . . I found a nice spot for myself on the bank of the Donetz and stayed there all the time that the services were going on.

I've bought an icon for Aunt F. Y.

All of the 15,000 pilgrims get monastic grub free: *shchi*[1] with dried gudgeon and gruel. Both are delicious and so is the rye bread.

The bell-ringing is remarkable. The singers are poor. I took part in a church procession carried by rowboats.

---

[1] A vegetable soup of which cabbage is often the main ingredient.

TO ALEXEY N. PLESHCHEYEV

(The recipient of this letter, an elderly poet whom Chekhov called his literary godfather, was fiction editor of the monthly which was the first to publish his work. Osip Notovich and Grigory Gradovsky were liberal journalists.)

Moscow, October, 1889

I am afraid of those who look for a tendency between the lines and who insist on seeing me as necessarily either a liberal or a conservative. I am not a liberal, not a conservative, not a gradualist, not a monk, not an indifferentist. I should like to be a free artist and nothing more, and I regret that God has not given me the power to be one. I hate lying and violence, whatever form they take, and I am equally repelled by secretaries of consistories and by Notovich and Gradovsky. Pharisaism, stupidity, and tyranny reign not in shopkeepers' homes and in lock-ups alone; I see them in science, in literature, in the younger generation . . . That is why I have no partiality either for gendarmes, or butchers, or scholars, or writers, or young people. I regard trade-marks and labels as a kind of prejudice. My holy of holies is the human body, health, intelligence, talent, inspiration, love, and absolute freedom—freedom from violence and falsehood, no matter how the last two manifest themselves. This is the program I would follow if I were a great artist.

TO ALEXEY S. SUVORIN

(The addressee was a playwright as well as an influential conservative journalist and editor, who achieved wealth as a publisher and bookseller. He was Chekhov's close friend and his chief correspondent, the recipient of some 300 letters from him. The letter below and five subsequent ones have to do with Chekhov's trip to the penal colony on the island of Sakhalin, where he spent a little over three months, beginning July 11, 1890. At the invitation of the Russian government, Alexander von Humboldt, the naturalist, explored Asiatic Russia in 1829; in the 1880's George Kennan made a thorough study of the Siberian penal system.)

Moscow, March 9 [1890]
(The feast of Forty Mar-
tyrs and of 10,000 Larks)

Both of us are mistaken about Sakhalin, but you probably more than I. I am going there fully convinced that my trip will not result in any valuable contribution either to literature or science: I lack the knowledge, the time, and the ambition for that. My plans are not those of a Humboldt or a Kennan. I want to write 100 to 200 pages and thereby pay off some of my debt to medicine, towards which, as you know, I have behaved like a pig. Possibly I shall not be able to write anything, nevertheless the journey does not lose its charm for me: by reading, looking around and listening, I shall get to know and to learn a great deal. I haven't left yet, but thanks to the books that I have been obliged to read, I have learned much of what everyone should know under penalty of forty lashes, and of which I was formerly ignorant. Besides, I believe that the trip will mean six months of incessant work, physical and mental, and this I need, for I am a Ukrainian[1] and have already begun to be lazy. One must keep in training. My trip may be a trifle, the result of obstinacy, a whim, but consider and tell me what I lose by going. Time? Money? Comfort? My time is worth nothing, money I never have anyway,

---

[1] Having been born at Taganrog, which lies on the border of Ukrainian territory, Chekhov sometimes described himself as a *hohol* (Ukrainian) to account for his laziness, allegedly a characteristic of the Southerners. As a matter of fact, both his parents were of Great Russian stock.

as for privations, I shall travel by carriage not more than
25 to 30 days—and all the rest of the time I shall be
sitting on the deck of a steamer or in a room and constantly bombard you with letters.

Suppose the trip gives me absolutely nothing, still
won't the whole journey yield at least two or three days
that I shall remember all my life, with rapture or with
bitterness? And so on, and so on. That's how it is, sir.
All this is unconvincing, but neither do your arguments
convince me. You say, for instance, that Sakhalin is of
no use and no interest to anybody. But is that so? Sakhalin could be of no use or interest only to a country
that did not exile thousands of people there and did not
spend millions on it. After Australia in the past and
Cayenne, Sakhalin is the only place where you can
study colonization by convicts. All Europe is interested
in it, and it is of no use to us? No longer ago than 25 or
30 years, our own compatriots in exploring Sakhalin performed amazing feats that make man worthy of deifica-
tion, and yet that's of no use to us, we know nothing
about those men, we sit within four walls and complain
that God made a botch of man. Sakhalin is a place of
unbearable sufferings, such as only human beings, free
or bond, can endure. The men directly or indirectly
connected with it solved terrible, grave problems and
are still solving them. If I were sentimental—I am sorry
I am not—I would say that to places like Sakhalin we
should make pilgrimages, like the Turks who travel to
Mecca, and navy men and criminologists in particular
should regard Sakhalin as military men do Sevastopol.
From the books I have been reading it is clear that we
have let *millions* of people rot in prison, destroying them
carelessly, thoughtlessly, barbarously; we drove people
in chains through the cold across thousands of miles,
infected them with syphilis, depraved them, multiplied

criminals, and placed the blame for all this on red-nosed prison wardens. All civilized Europe knows now that it is not the wardens who are to blame, but all of us, yet this is no concern of ours, we are not interested. The vaunted Sixties did *nothing* for the sick and the prisoners, thus violating the basic commandment of Christian civilization. In our time something is being done for the sick, but for prisoners nothing; prison problems don't interest our jurists at all. No, I assure you, we need Sakhalin and it is important to us, and the only thing to be regretted is that I am the one to go there and not someone else who is better equipped for the task and is more capable of arousing public interest * * *

Your A. CHEKHOV

TO HIS SISTER MARIA

(The Tunguses are natives of eastern Siberia; the reference may have been a family joke. The Pechenegs were a nomad tribe that roamed the steppes in ancient times. Chekhov liked to use the name as a synonym for a benighted savage.)

April 29, 1890

My Tung_s friends!

The Kama is a very tedious river. To appreciate its beauties one must be a Pecheneg, sit motionless on a barge near a barrel of petroleum or a sack of dried Caspian roach, continually swilling rotgut. The banks are bare, the trees are bare, the ground is barren, with strips of snow, and the devil himself couldn't raise a sharper and more disgusting wind. When a cold wind blows and ruffles the water, which after the floods is the color of coffee slops, one is chilled and bored and wretched. The strains of accordions coming from the banks sound dismal. and the figures in ragged sheepskin coats standing stock-still on the barges that we pass seem petrified by some endless sorrow. The towns on the Kama are gray; the only occupation of their inhabitants, it seems, is the manufacture of clouds, boredom, wet fences, and mud in the streets. The landing-places are crowded with the *intelligentsia*, for whom the arrival of a steamer is an event . . . Everything about these gentry suggests "the second fiddle"; apparently not one of them earns more than 35 rubles and they are probably all dosing themselves for some ailment or other * * *

I was two and a half years sailing to Perm—or so it seemed to me. We landed there at 2 A.M. The train was scheduled to leave at 6 P.M. It was raining. Rain, cold, mud—brrr! * * *

Waking up yesterday morning on board a train and looking out of the window, I felt disgusted with Nature: the ground was white, the trees were covered with hoarfrost and a regular blizzard was chasing the train. Now isn't that revolting? The sons of bitches . . . I have no rubbers, I pulled on my big boots and walking to the buffet for coffee I perfumed the whole Ural province with their tarry smell . . . When we got to Yekaterinburg [now Sverdlovsk], there was rain, sleet, snow * * *

In Russia all the towns are alike. Yekaterinburg is exactly like Perm or Tula, or like Sumy and Gadyach. The ringing of the bells is magnificent, velvety. I stopped at the American Hotel (not at all bad) and immediately wrote to A. M. S. [a relative] to say that I meant to stay in my hotel room two days and take Hunyádi [a laxative] which, let me say not without pride, I drink with signal success.

The people here inspire the new arrival with a feeling akin to horror. They have prominent cheekbones, big brows, broad shoulders, tiny eyes, and huge fists. They are born in the local cast-iron foundries and are brought into the world not by an accoucheur, but by a machinist. A fellow like that comes into your room with a samovar or a decanter and you expect him to murder you. I move aside. This morning just such an individual came in— high-cheekboned, big-browed, sullen, towering to the ceiling, several feet across the shoulders, and wearing a fur coat besides. Well, I thought, this one is sure to murder me. It turned out that it was A. M. S. We talked. He is a member of the Zemstvo Board, manages his cousin's mill where they have electric light, edits *The Yekaterinburg Week* which is censored by the Chief of Police, Baron Taube, is married, has two children, is growing rich, gaining weight, getting old, and lives "substantially." He says he has no time to be bored. Advised me to visit the museum, the plants, the mines; I thanked him for the advice. He invited me to tea, I invited him to have dinner with me. He did not invite me to dinner, and generally did not insist on my coming to see him. From this mamma may conclude that the relatives' heart has not softened, and that S. and I are not essential to one another . . . Relatives are a tribe I am indifferent to * * *

Your Homo Sachaliensis,

A. CHEKHOV

TO MME. MARIA V. KISELEVA

(The addressee, a cultivated woman who wrote stories, was the daughter of the Director of the Imperial Theatres in Moscow and the wife of a landowner, from whom the Chekhovs had rented a summer cottage for several seasons.)

On the shores of the Irtysh, May 7, 1890

Greetings, truly esteemed Maria Vladimirovna!

I wanted to write you a farewell letter from Moscow, but had not time and had to put it off indefinitely. I am writing you now in a hut on the bank of the Irtysh. It is night.

This is how I came to be here. I drove across Siberia in my own carriage. I have already covered some 475 miles. I have become a martyr from head to foot. Since morning a sharp cold wind has been blowing and a most disgusting rain has been coming down. Observe that spring hasn't reached Siberia yet: the earth is brown, the trees bare, and wherever you look you see white strips of snow. I wear my fur coat and felt boots day and night. Well, so it began blowing this morning. Heavy leaden clouds, brown earth, mud, rain, wind . . . brrr! I drive and drive . . . I drive on endlessly, and the weather gets no better. Towards evening they tell me at the station that there is no going any farther, as the roads are flooded and the bridges washed away. Knowing how fond these private drivers are of scaring one with the elements so as to keep the traveler overnight (it is profitable), I did not believe them and ordered a team of three horses hitched up. Well? Woe is me, I had hardly driven more than three miles when I discovered that great lakes covered the bank of the Irtysh; the road was under water and the bridges indeed either were washed away or had broken down. What prevented me from turning back was partly stubbornness, partly the desire to leave these dreary parts as quickly as possible.

We began making our way across the lakes. Heavens, I never went through anything like that in my life! Biting wind, cold, disgusting rain, and with it all, climb out of the coach (an open one) if you please, and hold the horses: over each little bridge one could only lead the horses one at a time. Where had I landed? Where was I? Wastes and desolation all around; the shores of the Irtysh are bare and sullen.

We drive into the largest lake. Now I would gladly turn back, but that's difficult. We drive over a long, narrow tongue of land. It comes to an abrupt end and we go plop! Then there is another strip of land and again— plop! My hands grow numb with cold, and the wild ducks seem to mock us and hover overhead in huge flocks. It grows dark. The driver is silent—he has lost his head. But at last we reach the final tongue of land which separates the lake from the Irtysh. The river's sloping bank rises no more than two feet above the level of the water; it is clayey, bare, gullied, and looks slippery. The water is muddy. White waves beat against the clay, but the river itself does not roar or boom, but emits a queer sound as though someone were knocking on coffins under water . . . The opposite bank is an unbroken, desolate plain. . . .

But here is the ferry. We must cross to the other side. A peasant emerges from a hut and, shrinking from the rain, says that the ferry cannot make the trip as it is too windy (the ferries hereabouts are worked by oars). He advises us to wait for calm weather.

So here I am at night in a hut standing in the middle of a lake on the very shore of the Irtysh. The penetrating humidity is in my bones and loneliness is in my soul; I listen to my Irtysh knocking on the coffins and to the wind howling and I ask myself: "Where am I? What am I here for?"

In the next room the ferrymen and my driver are asleep. They are decent men. If they were bad, they could very well rob me and then drown me in the Irtysh. The hut stands solo on the shore, there are no witnesses.

The road to Tomsk is absolutely safe as far as brigandage is concerned. It is bad form to so much as talk of robberies. They don't even steal from travelers. When you go into a hut, you can leave your belongings in the yard and everything will be safe.

Just the same, I did almost get killed. Imagine the hour before dawn. I am driving along in my carriage and thinking, thinking . . . Suddenly I see a troika head-'ng for us at full speed; my driver turns right in the very 'ick of time and the troika dashes past us . . . It is fol-owed by another coach also going at full speed. We turn to the right, it turns to the left. "We'll collide!" flashes through my mind. Another instant, and there is a crash, the horses tangle in a black mass, my carriage rears up and I am on the ground with all my bags and bundles on top of me. I jump up and see: a third troika bearing down on us!

My mother must have prayed for me the night before. If I had been asleep or if the third carriage had followed hard upon the second, I should have been killed or crip-pled. It appears that the first driver had whipped up his horses and the drivers in the second and third troikas were asleep and didn't see us. After the crash there was complete stupefaction on both sides, followed by fero-cious cursing. The harness was torn, the shafts broken, the yokes lay about on the road. And how drivers swear! At night, in the midst of the cursing, frenzied horde I was overcome by a sense of utter loneliness such as I have never known before.

But my paper is giving out . . . The rain is pelting the windows. May all the saints bless you! I'll write again. My address is: Aleksandrovsk, Island of Sakhalin.

Yours,

A. CHEKHOV

TO HIS SISTER MARIA

Tomsk, May 16, 1890

In the morning they would not ferry me across: it was too windy. We had to take a rowboat. As I cross the river the rain lashes, the wind blows, the baggage gets soaked, the felt boots, which had been drying overnight on the stove, are again turning into jelly. Oh, my beloved leather coat! If I didn't catch cold, I owe that to it alone. When I come back, rub it down with lard or castor oil, as a reward. I sat on the bank for a whole hour on a suitcase, waiting for horses to arrive from the village. I remember how slippery it was climbing up that bank. In the village I warmed up and had tea. Deportees came begging for alms. Every family bakes a *pood* [36 pounds] of white bread for them every day. A sort of tax, this.

The deportees take the bread and trade it for drink at some pothouse. One of the deportees, a raggedy, clean-shaven old man, whose eyes had been *knocked out* for him by his fellow convicts in a tavern, having heard that a chance traveler was in the house and taking me for a merchant, began reciting prayers and chanting. He chanted a prayer for health and another for the repose of the dead, and Easter canticles . . . What didn't he sing! Then he began telling lies about his having come of a merchant family of Moscow. I noticed the contempt in which this boozer held the peasants on whom he sponged!

On the 11th I hired a post chaise and started off. Out of boredom I took to reading the complaint books at the stations. I made a discovery which astonished me and which, in raw or rainy weather, is invaluable: these stations have privies in their entries. Oh, you can't appreciate this!

On the 12th of May they would not let me have any horses, saying that travel was out of the question, since the Ob had overflowed its banks and inundated all the meadowlands. "You turn off the post road and go as far as Krasnyi Yar; from there you will go about eight miles by boat to Dubrovino, and at Dubrovino they'll let you have post horses." I started for Kr. Yar with horses hired from a private person. Arrived there in the morning. I was told that they did have a boat, but that I'd have to wait awhile, since grandfather had sent a workman off to row the assessor's clerk to Dubrovino. Very well, we'll wait. One hour passes, then another, and a third. Noon comes, then evening. *Allah kerim* (Allah is generous), all the tea I drank, all the bread I ate, all the thoughts I thought! And how I slept! Night came, and still no boat. Morning came. Finally, at nine o'clock the workman was back. Thank heavens, we're off! And how smoothly we row! The air is calm, the boatmen are skilled, the islands are beautiful . . . The flood had caught men and cattle off guard, and I see peasant women going out in boats to the islands to milk the cows. These cows are lean, despondent; because of the cold there is no feed at all to be had.

We covered eight miles. At the Dubrovino posthouse I had tea and with it I was served—just imagine!—waffles. The woman who runs the place must be a deportee or the wife of one. At the next station the clerk, an old Pole, to whom I gave antipyrin to relieve his headache, complained of his poverty and told me that Count Sapieha, Chamberlain of the Court of Austria and a Pole, who helped Poles, had recently passed through Siberia. "He stopped near this station," the clerk told me, "but I never knew it! Holy Mother of God! He would have helped me. I wrote to him in Vienna, but got no reply—" and so on. Why am I not Sapieha? I would send this poor fellow back to his native land.

On the 14th of May I was again refused horses. The Tom was in flood. What a nuisance! Not a nuisance, but a calamity! Tomsk thirty-five miles away, and then this, so unexpectedly. In my place a woman would have burst into sobs. Some kind folks found a way out for me: "You go as far as the Tom, your Honor—it's only four miles from here; there they'll row you across to Yar, and from there Ilya Markovich will take you by horse to Tomsk." I hire a private coach and go to the Tom, to the spot where the boat ought to be. I drive up: no boat. It has just gone off with the mail and isn't likely to come back soon, since there's a gale blowing. I begin my wait. The ground is covered with snow, the rain is sleety, and then there's the wind . . . An hour passes, then another, no boat. Fate is mocking me! I go back to the station. Here three troikas and a postman are getting ready to set out in the direction of the Tom. I tell them there is no boat. They remain. Fate rewards me: the clerk, in answer to my hesitant query as to the chances of getting a bite of something, tells me that the proprietress has cabbage soup. Oh, rapture! Oh, most radiant day! And the proprietress' daughter actually brings me excellent cabbage soup, with wonderful meat, roast potatoes, and cucumbers. . . . After the potatoes I let myself go completely and make me some coffee. A spree!

At dusk, the postman, an elderly man who had been through a great deal and who did not dare sit down in my presence, started getting ready for the trip to the Tom. So did I. We started off. As soon as we reached the river, a boat appeared, a longer boat than I had ever dreamed of. While the mail was being loaded onto the boat I witnessed a strange phenomenon: there was a peal of thunder, and that with snow on the ground and a cold wind blowing. The boat took on its load and cast off. Forgive me, Misha [his brother Mikhail], but I was glad I had not taken you along. How clever I had been in not taking anybody along on this trip! At first our boat floated over a flooded meadow, close to a clump of willow shrubs . . . As usually happens before a storm, a strong wind suddenly swept over the water, raising waves. The boatman seated at the helm was of the opinion that we should weather the storm among the willow shrubs. The others countered that if the weather worsened we might have to stay among the willows until nightfall, and be drowned anyway. We put the matter to a vote, and it was decided to go on. My bad luck, how it mocks me! Why all those pranks? We rowed on silently, concentrating on the task before us . . . I remember the figure of the postman who had been through the mill. I remember a little soldier, who suddenly turned as crimson as cherry juice. Should the boat capsize, I thought, I would throw off my furlined jacket and my leather coat, then the felt boots, then, and so on. But now the bank was coming nearer and nearer . . . Lighter, lighter grew my soul, my heart contracted with joy; for some reason I sighed deeply, as though I were suddenly at rest, and then jumped onto the wet, slippery bank . . . Thank God!

At Ilya Markovich's, the convert's, we are told that we can't start out at night—the going is bad, we'll have to stay overnight. Well and good; I stay over. After dinner I sit down to write you this letter, which is interrupted by the arrival of the assessor. This assessor is a thick mixture of Nozdryov [the bully in Gogol's *Dead Souls*], Hlestakov [the braggart in Gogol's *Inspector*

General], and plain dog. A drunkard, a lecher, a liar, a singer, a raconteur, and, with all that, a kindhearted man. He has brought with him a large chest full of official papers, a bed and mattress, a gun, and a clerk. The clerk is a splendid, cultivated fellow, an outspoken liberal who had studied in Petersburg. Though a free man, he finds himself for some reason in Siberia, is infected to the marrow of his bones with every disease, and is drinking himself to death thanks to his superior, who calls him familiarly Kolya. The representative of the law sends for some cordial. "Doctor," he vociferates, "drink one more glass, and I'll bow down to your very feet!" I drink, of course. The representative of the law drinks mightily, lies like a trooper, and swears foully. We go to bed. In the morning cordial is again sent for. They swill it until ten, and at last start out. Ilya Markovich, the convert, whom the peasants hereabouts worship, I was told, gives me horses to take me as far as Tomsk.

TO NIKOLAY A. LEIKIN

(This correspondent was the editor of a Petersburg comic weekly for which Chekhov wrote in his youth.)

Irkutsk, June 5, 1890

Greetings, my most kind Nikolay Alexandrovich! I send you the warmest regards from Irkutsk, from the depths of Siberia. I arrived in Irkutsk last night, and am very glad I did, since the journey knocked me out completely, and I was missing my relatives and friends, to whom I have not written for a long time. And now, what is there of interest to write you about? I'll begin by saying that the trip is unusually long. I have covered some two thousand miles by carriage from Tyumen to Irkutsk. From Tyumen to Irkutsk I waged war against

cold and rivers in flood; the frosts were terrible; on the
Feast of Ascension there was a frost and a snowfall, so
that I didn't get a chance to take off my sheepskin coat
and felt boots until I got to the hotel at Tomsk. As for
the rivers in flood, they are a plague of Egypt. The rivers
overflowed their banks and inundated the meadowlands
for miles around, and the roads with them; it was constantly necessary to exchange my carriage for a boat—
and as for boats, they weren't to be had for nothing;
for a good boat one had to pay with one's heart's blood,
since it was necessary to sit for days and nights on end
in the rain and the cold wind, and wait and wait . . .
From Tomsk to Krasnoyarsk there was a desperate war
against insuperable mud. My God, it's fearful even to
recall it! How many times I had to have my carriage re-
paired, to trudge beside it, to curse, to crawl out of it
and climb back into it again, and so on. There were
times when the ride from one station to the next took six
to ten hours, and from ten to sixteen hours were needed
to repair the vehicle. The heat and dust during the trip
from Krasnoyarsk to Irkutsk were dreadful. Add to this
hunger, dust in your nose, eyes glued together for want
of sleep, eternal fear that something may break in the
carriage (which was my own), and boredom . . . But
just the same I am content and thank God for having
given me the strength and opportunity to make this
journey. I have seen and lived through a great deal, and
everything is exceedingly interesting and new to me, not
as a man of letters but simply as a human being. The
Yenisey river, the *taiga* [forest], the stations, the drivers,
untamed Nature, the wild life, the physical agonies
caused by the hardships of travel, the delights of resting
—altogether everything is so wonderful that I can't
even describe it. For one thing, during more than a
month I have been out in the fresh air day and night,

which is interesting and wholesome; for a whole month I have seen the sunrise from beginning to end.

From here I am going to Baikal, then to Chita, and on to Sretensk, where I exchange my horses for a steamer and sail down the Amur to my journey's end. I am in no hurry, since I have no wish to be in Sakhalin before the first of July.

Your Homo Sachaliensis
A. CHEKHOV

TO ALEXEY S. SUVORIN

Moscow, December 9, 1890

Greetings, my precious friend! Hurrah! There, I am at home at last sitting at my desk, praying to my moulting penates and writing to you. I have a pleasant feeling, as if I had never left home. I'm well, and serene to the marrow of my bones. Here is a report, of the briefest sort, for you. It wasn't two months I spent on Sakhalin, as you have it in your paper, but three, plus two days. My work was intensive; I took a full and detailed census of the entire population of the island and saw *everything*, except an execution. When we meet, I will show you a whole trunkful of odds and ends about the convicts, raw material that cost me plenty. I know a great deal now, but I came back with a wretched feeling. As long as I was staying in Sakhalin, I only felt a certain bitterness in my innards, as if from rancid butter; but now, in retrospect, the island seems to me a perfect hell. For two months I worked hard, without sparing myself in any way, while during the third month I began to feel the strain of the bitterness I spoke of, the tedium, and the thought that cholera was heading from Vladivostok to Sakhalin and that I was running the risk of having to winter in the penal colony. But, thank Heaven, the cholera let up, and on October 13th the steamer bore me away from Sakhalin.

I stopped at Vladivostok. About our Maritime Region and our east coast, with its fleet, its problems, its dreams of the Pacific I shall say but one thing: it's all appalling poverty! Poverty, ignorance, and paltriness, such as can drive one to despair. One honest man to ninety-nine thieves, who desecrate the name of Russia . . . We by-passed Japan, since there was cholera there. For that reason I did not buy any Japanese articles for you, and the 500 rubles you gave me for such purchases I spent upon my own needs, which, according to law, gives you the right to have me deported to Siberia. The first foreign port we touched was Hong Kong. The bay is wonderful; the sea traffic is such as I haven't seen the like of even in pictures; there are splendid roads, horse-drawn streetcars, a railway going up the mountain, museums, botanical gardens; no matter where you look you see the Englishmen's tender solicitude for the men in their service; there is even a club for sailors. I rode in jinrickshas, which is to say, in a vehicle drawn by a man; bought all sorts of rubbish from the Chinese, and waxed indignant as I listened to my Russian fellow-travelers upbraiding the English for their exploitation of the natives. Yes, thought I, the Englishman exploits Chinese, sepoys, Hindus, but then he gives them roads, aqueducts, museums, Christianity; you too exploit, but what do you give?

When we left Hong Kong the steamer began to roll. It had no cargo and it swung through an angle of 38 degrees, so that we were afraid it would capsize. I am not subject to seasickness; this discovery was a pleasant surprise. On the way to Singapore we threw two corpses into the ocean. When you see a dead man, wrapped in canvas, go flying head over heels into the water, and when you recall that there are several miles to the bottom, a fear comes over you, and for some reason you imagine that you yourself will die and be cast into the sea. The horned cattle we were carrying sickened. Dr. Shcherbak and your humble servant having passed sentence upon them, they were slaughtered and thrown into the ocean.

Singapore I remember poorly because while I was touring it I felt sad for some reason and all but wept. Ceylon came next—the site of Paradise. Here I covered some 70 miles by rail and had my fill of palm groves and bronze-skinned women. When I have children, I'll say to them, not without pride: "You sons of bitches, in my time I had dalliance with a dark-eyed Hindu—and where? In a coconut grove, on a moonlit night!" From Ceylon we sailed for thirteen days and nights without a single stop and grew dazed with boredom. I can stand heat well. The Red Sea is dismal. As I gazed on Mount Sinai I was deeply moved.

God's world is good. Only one thing isn't good: ourselves. How little there is in us of justice and humility, how poor is our conception of patriotism! The drunken, bedraggled, good-for-nothing of a husband loves his wife and child, but what's the good of that love? We, so the newspapers say, love our great country, but how is that love expressed? Instead of knowledge—inordinate brazenness and conceit, instead of hard work—laziness and swinishness; there is no justice; the concept of honor does not go beyond "the honor of the uniform," the uniform which is the everyday adornment of the prisoners' dock. What is needed is work; everything else can go to the devil. The main thing is to be just—the rest will be added unto us. * * *

May Heaven protect you.

Your A. CHEKHOV

TO MME. MARIA V. KISELEVA

Rome, April 1, [1891]

The Pope has charged me to offer you birthday greetings and wish you as much money as he has room. And he has 11,000 rooms! Wandering through the Vatican, I wilted with exhaustion, and when I returned home, my feet felt as if they were made of cotton.

I eat at the table d'hôte. Fancy, opposite me sit two Dutch girls, one resembles Pushkin's Tatyana, the other, her sister Olga. I look at both all through dinner and picture to myself a spotless little white cottage with a turret, excellent butter, superb Dutch cheese, Dutch herring, a venerable-looking pastor, a sedate schoolmaster—and I want to marry a Dutch girl and be painted with her beside the spotless little cottage on a tray.

I have seen everything, trotted everywhere, sniffed at everything I was told to. But so far I feel simply fatigue and a desire for cabbage soup with buckwheat porridge. Venice fascinated me and turned my head, but since I bade it good-by, it has been just Baedecker and bad weather * * *

Ties are wonderfully cheap here. So cheap that maybe I'll try eating them. Two for a franc.

Tomorrow I go to Naples. Pray that I meet a beautiful Russian lady there, preferably a widow or a divorcée. The guidebooks say that a love affair is indispensable to an Italian tour. Well, devil take it, if a love affair, then a love affair! Don't forget your sinful but respectful and sincerely devoted,

A. CHEKHOV

Greetings to Messieurs the starlings.

TO ALEXEY S. SUVORIN

Melihovo, April 8, 1892

Levitan, the artist, is staying with me. Last evening we were out shooting. He shot at a snipe, and the bird, hit in the wing, fell into a puddle. I picked it up: a long beak, big black eyes, and beautiful plumage. It looked astonished. What were we to do with it? Levitan frowned, shut his eyes, and begged me with a tremor in his voice, "My dear fellow, hit his head against the gun-stock." I said, "I can't." He went on nervously shrugging his shoulders, twitching his head, and begging me; and the snipe went on looking at us in astonishment. I had to obey Levitan and kill it. One more beautiful enam-ored creature gone, while two fools went home and sat down to supper.

(The writer begins this letter by pointing out that the artists of his generation, whether writers or painters, have produced nothing but "lemonade," nothing capable of going to a man's head.)

Melihovo, Nov. 25, 1892

Science and technology are passing through a great period now, but for our writing fraternity it is a flabby, sour, dull time; we ourselves are sour and dull, and can only beget rubber boys, and the only one who does not see it is Stasov [an art critic] whom Nature has endowed with the rare ability to get drunk even on slops. The cause of this is not our stupidity, or our lack of talent, or our insolence * * * but a disease which for an artist is worse than syphilis and impotence. We lack "something" —that is true, and it means that if you lift the skirt of our Muse, you will find the spot level. Remember that the writers whom we call eternal or simply good and who in-

toxicate us have one very important characteristic in common: they move in a certain direction and they summon
you there too, and you feel, not with your mind alone, but
with your whole being, that they have a goal, like the
ghost of Hamlet's father who does not come and trouble
the imagination for nothing. Some, depending on their
caliber, have immediate objects: abolition of serfdom,
liberation of their country, politics, beauty, or, like Denis
Davydov [author of drinking songs], simply vodka; others
have remote objectives: God, immortality, the happiness
of mankind, and so forth. The best of them are realistic,
and paint life as it is, but because every line is permeated,
as with sap, by the consciousness of a purpose, you are
aware not only of life as it is, but of life as it ought to be,
and that captivates you. And we? We! We paint life as it
is, and beyond that neither whoa! nor giddap! Whip us
and we cannot go a step farther. We have neither immediate nor distant aims and our souls are a yawning
void. We have no politics, we don't believe in revolution,
we have no God, we are not afraid of ghosts, and I personally am not afraid even of death and blindness. One
who desires nothing, hopes for nothing, and fears nothing
cannot be an artist. Whether it is a disease or not—that
is a question of name and doesn't matter, but it must be
admitted that our situation is unenviable . . .

(Here Chekhov resumes the discussion of purposiveness
in art begun in the previous letter.)

Melihovo, Dec. 3, 1892

That the writers and artists of the latest generation
lack an aim in their work is a curious phenomenon that
is entirely legitimate and logical, and if Mme. S——,
for no reason at all, got scared by a bogey, that doesn't
mean that my letter was wily and disingenuous. You
yourself discovered it to be insincere only after she had

written you, or you would not have sent her my letter in the first place. In my letters to you I am often unjust and naive, but I never write about what I don't have at heart.

If you are looking for insincerity, you will find tons of it in her letter. "The greatest miracle is man himself and we shall never tire of studying him." Or: "The aim of life is life itself." Or: "I believe in life, in its bright moments, for the sake of which one can, indeed one must, live; I believe in man, in that part of his soul which is good . . ." Can all this be sincere, and does it mean anything? This isn't an outlook, it's caramels. She underscores "can" and "must" because she is afraid to speak of what is and what has to be reckoned with. Let her first say what is, and only then I will listen to what one can and must do. She believes in "life," and that means that if she is intelligent, she believes in nothing, and if she is a country wife, she believes in a peasant God and crosses herself in the dark.

Under the influence of her letter you write me about "life for life's sake." Thank you very much. You've got to admit that her letter with its paean to life is a thousand times more funereal than mine. I write that we are without aims, and you realize that I consider aims necessary and would gladly go looking for them, but Mme. S—— writes that one must not delude man with all manner of good things that he will never get: "prize that which is," and in her opinion all our trouble comes from the fact that we keep pursuing lofty and distant aims. If this isn't a country wife's logic, it's the philosophy of despair. He who sincerely believes that man needs lofty and distant aims as little as a cow does, that "all our trouble" comes from pursuing these aims—has nothing left him but to eat, drink, sleep, or if he is fed up with that, he can take a running start and dash his head against the corner of a chest.

I'm not scolding the lady, I'm only saying that she is far from being a very jolly person. She is apparently nice enough, but all the same you shouldn't have shown her my letter. She is a stranger to me and I feel awkward about it now.

Hereabouts people are already riding tandem [on narrow winter roads] and cooking cabbage soup with smelts. We have already had two snowstorms that ruined the roads, but now the weather is calm and it smells of Christmas.

(Chekhov begins by expressing strong doubt of Dreyfus's guilt and speaking in glowing terms of Zola, who was then being tried for libel because he had denounced the French General Staff as having falsely convicted the Jewish officer.)

Nice, Feb. 6, 1898

I acquainted myself with the case by reading the stenographic reports, which are quite different from what you find in the papers, and Zola's stand is clear to me. The main thing is that he is sincere, i.e., he bases his judgments only on what he sees, and not, like others, on phantoms. Of course, sincere people too may be mistaken, but such mistakes are less harmful than reasoned insincerity, prejudice, or political considerations. Suppose Dreyfus is guilty—still Zola is right, for the writer's duty is not to accuse, not to persecute, but to intercede on behalf even of the guilty, once they are condemned and bear punishment. It will be asked: "But what about politics? And the interests of the State?" But big writers and artists must occupy themselves with politics only insofar as it *is* necessary to put up a defense against politics. There are enough accusers, prosecutors, and gendarmes even without them, and in any event, the role of Paul suits them better than the role of Saul. Whatever the verdict may be, after the trial Zola will nevertheless know a living joy, he will have a splendid old age, and he will die with his conscience at peace, or, to say the least, at ease.

TO OLGA L. KNIPPER

(This was written from Yalta shortly before Chekhov's marriage to his correspondent, an actress connected with the Moscow Art Theatre. The two ladies mentioned were both writers. Pchelnikov had been appointed dramatic censor.)

March 16 [1901]

Greetings, my little dear! I am certainly coming to Moscow, but I don't know whether I'll go to Sweden this year. I am fed up with gadding about, and besides it seems as if I were getting to be quite an old man as far as health is concerned, so that, by the way, you will acquire in my person not a husband but a grandfather. I dig in my garden now for whole days together, the weather is warm, exquisite, everything's in flower, the birds are singing, there are no visitors, it is simply not life but peaches and cream. I have quite given up literature, and when I marry you, I'll order you to give up the stage and we'll live together like planters. You don't want to? Very well then, go on acting another five years and then we shall see.

Today, out of the blue, I received *The Russian Veteran,* a special army newspaper, and in it I found a notice of *Three Sisters.* It is No. 56, March 11th. It's all right, it's laudatory, and finds no fault with the military side.

Write to me, my good darling, your letters give me

joy. You are unfaithful to me because, as you write, you are a human being and a woman; oh, very well, be unfaithful, only be the good, splendid person that you are. I am an old geezer, it is impossible to keep from being unfaithful to me, I understand that very well, and if I happen to be unfaithful to you, you will excuse it, because you realize that though the beard turns gray, the devil's at play. Isn't that so?

Do you see Madam Avilova? Have you made friends with Madam Chyumina? I suspect you've already begun writing stories and novels in secret. If I catch you, then good-by, I'll divorce you.

I read about Pchelnikov's appointment in the papers, and I was astonished, astonished that Pchelnikov was not above accepting such a queer position. But they'll hardly take *Dr. Stockman* off your repertory, it's a conservative play, you know.

Though I have given up literature, still I write something now and then, out of habit. Just now I am writing a story called "The Bishop," on a subject that has been in my head for fifteen years.

I embrace you, traitress, a hundred times, I kiss you hard. Write, write, my joy, or else when we are married, I'll beat you.

Your Elder Ant—

(The Nemirovich mentioned here is Vladimir Nemirovich-Danchenko, co-founder with Stanislavsky of the Moscow Art Theatre. Kuprin is the late novelist. Gorky and Vladimir Posse, a radical journalist, were implicated in the public demonstrations and student riots then current.)

Thursday [*Yalta, April 19, 1901*]

Dog Olka! I shall come early in May. As soon as you get my telegram, go immediately to the Dresden Hotel and inquire if Room 45 is free, in other words, reserve a cheap room.

I often see Nemirovich, he is very nice . . . I am coming to Moscow chiefly to gallivant and gorge myself. We'll go to Petrovskoe-Razumovskoe [a suburb of Moscow] and to Zvenigorod [a near-by town], we'll go everywhere, if the weather is good. If you consent to go down the Volga with me, we'll eat sturgeon.

Kuprin is apparently in love—under an enchantment. He fell in love with a huge, husky woman whom you know and whom you advised me to marry.

If you give me the word that not a soul in Moscow will know about our wedding until it has taken place, I am ready to marry you on the very day of my arrival. For some reason I am terribly afraid of the wedding ceremony and congratulations and the champagne that you must hold in your hand while you smile vaguely. I wish we could go straight from church to Zvenigorod. Or perhaps we could get married at Zvenigorod. Think, think, darling! You are clever, they say.

The weather at Yalta is pretty rotten. A fierce wind. The roses are blooming, but not fully; they will, though. The irises are magnificent.

Everything is all right with me, except for one trifle: my health.

Gorky has not been deported, but arrested; he is held in Nizhny. Posse too has been arrested.

I embrace you, Olka.

Your Antoine.

(Chekhov's wedding took place in all privacy on May 25 in the presence of four witnesses, none of them members of his family. After the ceremony the couple called on the bride's mother and then took a train to Nizhny-Novgorod [now Gorky], where they boarded a Volga steamer.)

Yalta, Jan. 13, 1903

My dear Olya,

On the morning of the 11th, after Masha [his sister] had left town, I didn't feel quite right; I had a pain in my chest, I felt sick to my stomach, a temperature of 100°, and yesterday it was the same thing. I slept well, though I was disturbed by pain. Altschuler [his physician] looked in. I had to put on a compress again (it is an immense one). This morning my temperature was almost normal, I feel weak, and shall put on a plaster directly, but still I had a right to wire you today that all is well. Now everything is all right. I am getting better, tomorrow I shall be quite well again. I hide nothing from you, do understand that, and don't upset yourself telegraphing. If anything serious, or even resembling anything serious, should happen, you would be the first I should tell.

You are out of sorts? Chuck it, darling. It will all come out in the wash.

Today the earth is covered with snow, it is foggy, cheerless. It saddens me to think that so much time has passed without my doing any work, and that apparently I am no longer a worker. To sit in an armchair with a compress on and mope is not very jolly. Will you stop loving me, darling? In your letter of yesterday you wrote that you had lost your looks. As though it mattered! If you were to grow a nose like a crane's, even then I should love you.

I embrace my own, my good dachshund. I kiss and embrace you again. Write!!

Your A.

Works about Chekhov

Both the author's private history and his contribution to fiction and drama are dealt with from contrasting standpoints by Ronald Hingley in *Chekhov, a Biographical and Critical Study* (London, 1957) and by Vladimir V. Ermilov (Yermilov) in *Anton Chekhov,* originally published in Moscow and translated from the Russian by Ivy Litvinov (London, 1957). Hingley and Yermilov hold to the diverse views of literature prevailing respectively in the West and in the Communist world.

The biographical aspect is stressed in *The Life and Letters of Anton Tchekhov,* translated and edited by S. S. Koteliansky and Philip Tomlinson (London, New York, 1925); Irène Némirovsky, *Life of Chekhov,* translated by Eric de Mauny (London, 1950); David Magarshack, *Chekhov, a Life* (London, 1953); Nina Toumanova, *Anton Chekhov, the Voice of Twilight Russia* (New York, 1960); Ernest J. Simmons, *Chekhov, a Biography* (Boston, 1962). There are, too, Walter H. Bruford, *Chekhov and His Russia, a Sociological Study* (London, 1948) and his *Anton Chekhov* (New Haven, 1957).

Reminiscences of Chekhov set down by his contemporaries are, of course, an important biographical source. These are: *Reminiscences of Anton Chekhov* by Maxim Gorky, Alexander Kuprin, and I. A. Bunin, translated by S. S. Koteliansky and Leonard Woolf (New York, 1921); S. S. Koteliansky, editor, *Anton Chekhov: Literary and Theatrical Reminiscences* (London, 1927); Korney I. Chukovsky, *Chekhov the Man,* translated from the Russian by Pauline Rose (London, New York, 1945); Maxim Gorky, *Reminiscences,* which contains the Gorky-Chekhov correspondence and "Chekhov in Gorky's Diary" (New York, 1946); Lydia A. Avilova, *Chekhov in My Life, a Love Story,* translated by David

Magarshack (London, 1950). "50th Anniversary of Chekhov's Death" (*Voks bulletin,* Moscow, no. 86, May–June,
1954) includes reminiscences by Chekhov's widow and a
number of papers on Chekhov's influence abroad, including
one on Chekhov in Iran. Entire text in English.

Of the studies devoted largely to the story, the following
may be singled out: Edward Garnett, *Friday Nights: Literary Criticisms and Appreciations,* first series (New York,
1922) [contains "Chekhov and His Art"]; William A. Ger-
hardi, *Anton Chekhov, a Critical Study* (New York, 1923);
Dorothy Brewster and Angus Burrell, *Dead Reckonings in
Fiction* (Toronto, 1924); Janko Lavrin, *Studies in European Literature* (London, 1926) [contains "Chekhov and
Maupassant"]; Oliver Elton, *Chekhov* (Oxford, 1929), reprinted in his *Essays and Addresses* (London, 1939); Ed-
mund Wilson, "Seeing Chekhov Plain" (*The New Yorker,*
Nov. 22, 1952); Ilya Ehrenburg, *Chekhov, Stendhal and
Other Essays* (New York, 1963); Thomas G. Winner, *Chek-
hov and His Prose* (New York, 1966); Lev Shestov, *Chek-
hov and Other Essays,* with a new introduction by Sidney
Monas (Ann Arbor, 1966)—this work by the highly original
Russian thinker is a reprint of a volume issued under a
Dublin and London imprint in 1916.

The plays are one of the subjects discussed in the pub-
lications noted below: Ashley Dukes, *Modern Dramatists*
(London, 1911); Oliver M. Sayler, *The Russian Theatre*
(New York, 1922); Ronald Peacock, *The Poet in the
Theatre* (New York, 1946); Eric Bentley, *The Playwright
as Thinker, a Study of Drama in Modern Times* (New York,
1946) and his "Chekhov as Playwright" (*Kenyon Review,*
1949, vol. 11); David Magarshack, *Chekhov the Dramatist*
(New York, 1952); Frank L. Lucas, *The Drama of Chekhov,
Synge, Yeats and Pirandello* (London, 1963); Maurice
Valency, *The Breaking String, the Plays of Anton Chekhov*
(New York, 1966). *English and American Criticism of
Chekhov* (Chicago, 1948), a University of Chicago thesis by
Charles W. Meister, contains, *inter alia,* lists of the plays
(with reviews). At this point it is appropriate to note the
autobiographies of two eminent theatrical figures with
whom Chekhov was associated: Konstantin S. Stanislavsky,
My Life in Art, translated from the Russian by J. J. Robbins
(Boston, 1924), and Vladimir I. Nemorovich-Danchenko,

My Life in the Russian Theatre, translated by John Cournos (Boston, 1936).

A catalogue of Chekhov literature in English is available in the form of a bibliography of 480 entries produced by the New York Public Library. It consists of lists of works by and about the author, compiled by Anna Heifetz and published in 1949, and a supplement assembled by Rissa Yachnin and issued in 1960 on the occasion of the centennial of Chekhov's birth. Here are references to translations of his writings, to studies, memoirs, essays, articles, no matter how brief, in periodicals, including a note on Russian literary trends in the London *Atheneum,* July 6, 1889, which has the distinction of containing what seems to be the earliest mention of Chekhov in the English press. The author of the piece was Paul Miliukov, who after the Czar's abdication became Minister of Foreign Affairs and died in exile.